THE GARDENER'S
ILLUSTRATED ENCYCLOPEDIA
OF
CLIMBERS
—— & ——
WALL SHRUBS

To my wife Lin
with my continuing love and affection.

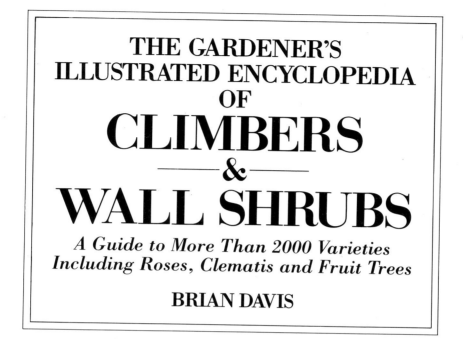

THE GARDENER'S
ILLUSTRATED ENCYCLOPEDIA
OF
CLIMBERS
—&—
WALL SHRUBS

A Guide to More Than 2000 Varieties
Including Roses, Clematis and Fruit Trees

BRIAN DAVIS

VIKING

VIKING
Penguin Books Ltd, Harmondsworth,
Middlesex, England
Viking Penguin Inc., 40 West 23rd Street,
New York, New York 10010, USA
Penguin Books Australia Ltd, Ringwood,
Victoria, Australia
Penguin Books Canada Ltd,
2801 John Street, Markham, Ontario,
Canada L3R 1B4
Penguin Books (NZ) Ltd 182–190 Wairau
Road, Auckland 10, New Zealand

First published in Great Britain by Viking
1990

Illustrations on p.41 *Clematis Rehderiana*,
p.94 *Magnolia × Watsonii*, p.120 *Pyrus
Salicifolia*, p.155 *Viburnum Lantana*
courtesy of Harry Smith Horticultural
Photographic Collection

Designed and produced by
Breslich & Foss,
Golden House,
28–31 Great Pulteney Street,
London W1R 3DD

Project Editor: Tessa Rose
Editorial: Diana Vowles
Illustrator: Susan Kinsey
Design Styling: Roger Daniels
Typesetting: Chapterhouse, Formby,
Merseyside
Printed in Hong Kong

A CIP catalogue record for this book is
available from the British Library

ISBN 0-670-82929-3

Front Cover Picture
Clematis 'Perle d'Azure'

Back Cover Pictures
Top Left: *Rosa* 'Fred Loads'
Top Right: *Clematis* 'Nellie Moser'
Below Left: *Malus pumila* 'Laxton's
Superb'
Below Right: *Kolkwitzia Amabilis*

I wish to thank Gill Connell and Anne
Preston for their patience with the text, the
staff at Breslich & Foss for the production
of this book, and all those who have
allowed me to experiment with planting
climbers and wall shrubs in national, private
and botanical gardens.

CONTENTS

INTRODUCTION

With the increasingly limited size of modern gardens, climbers and wall shrubs are a boon in that they offer an excellent way of providing a good display of flowers and foliage without encroaching too far on the main area of the plot.

The range of true climbers such as clematis, ivy, honeysuckle and roses is vast and this book covers the majority that are available in commercial production. However, many gardeners fail to take into account the large numbers of trees, shrubs, perennials and annuals that can adapt well to wall-training.

This book describes over 2,000 species and varieties from which the reader will be able to choose the most suitable plants for his or her garden, taking into account the soil, climate and, perhaps most importantly, the amount of space available; the commonest error when growing climbers and wall shrubs is that of underestimating their growth potential in height, width and forward projection from the supporting wall or fence.

The photographs have been chosen to depict each plant's principal attraction and I hope that, together with the text, they will give pleasure to the casual browser as well as to those who wish to add to the delights of their gardens.

BRIAN DAVIS

How To Use This Book

Botanical name
The name for each entry consists of the botanical name of an individual plant or genus. The name used is that accepted as current at the time of publication. Synonyms in current use are bracketed following the main heading.

Common name
There are numerous common names in use, often more than one for a single plant, and these may vary from region to region. Many are descriptive and may help the gardener to identify a plant, but they should not be relied upon when ordering from a nursery; only the botanical name guarantees accurate identification.

Family name
This is not usually of practical importance to the gardener, but it indicates a family relationship between plants often of very different appearance and helps to identify the cultural requirements of a plant and some aspects of its performance.

Classification
A very wide range of plants can be considered for use as climbers and wall shrubs and this entry records the classification under which the plant is normally found.

Deciduous, evergreen or semi-evergreen
An evergreen retains some leaves throughout the year; a deciduous plant sheds its leaves in autumn and winter. A tree or shrub is described as semi-evergreen if it loses some but not all of its leaves during the colder months. Foliage retention depends on climate and conditions; in a mild winter, for example, a deciduous shrub may retain some foliage, and in particularly harsh conditions an evergreen may shed a larger number of leaves than accounted for by normal ageing and replacement of foliage. Details of all such variations are given as appropriate.

Special features
Entries begin with a reference to attractive features of the plant, seasonal displays and special requirements.

Origin
Knowledge of the native environment of a plant can help to explain the conditions required for successful cultivation. This section gives the country or region of natural origin or indicates that the plant has been bred in a garden or nursery.

Use
Information relevant to selection and planting is given here; details of shape, size, location and special uses such as ground cover or suitability for growing through shrubs or trees.

Description
The following details are given under separate sub-headings:
Flower Shape, size, colour and fragrance. The flowering season given should be considered in relation to local conditions, for example, an early spring-flowering climber or wall shrub will come into bloom sooner in a mild location than in an area subject to relatively harsh, extended winters.
Foliage Shape and arrangement on the stem, size, colour and texture, including seasonal

variations such as a distinct change of colour in autumn. The Botanical Glossary on page 172 includes illustrations of leaf shapes referred to within the dictionary entries.
Stem Colour, texture and growth habit, including special features such as thorns or an attractive bark. The growth rate of the plant is given in general terms of very fast, fast, medium or slow: slow indicates an increase of no more than 6–8 in (15–20 cm) each year; medium an average of 18–24 in (45–60 cm) annually; fast 3 ft (91 cm) or more annually. A very fast growth rate can be up to 6 ft (1.8 m) of growth in one year. Individual rates of growth and annual increase cannot be precisely predicted as performance depends on the location, type of soil, climatic conditions and cultivation methods.
Fruit Shape, size, colour and specific uses, if any, including fleshy fruits, nuts, seedheads and seed pods.

Hardiness
Described in terms of the lowest temperature the plant will tolerate. Hardiness is also affected by soil type and moisture content, altitude, aspect and cultivation methods, and experience has shown that climbers and wall shrubs can prove themselves hardy in temperatures at which they might have been expected to fail, or vice versa. The stated temperature is the best guideline for choosing a plant suited to your local climate, and details are given of susceptibility to other factors such as wind chill, and unexpected late frosts. Walls and fences can often extend the range of hardiness by creating a microclimate and this has been accounted for in the minimum temperature suggested.

Soil requirements
Some climbers and wall shrubs can grow happily on any soil type, but for others the requirement for acid or alkaline soil is a vital factor in successful cultivation. Acid loving plants cannot succeed on alkaline soil as they are unable to obtain the necessary nutrients iron, magnesium and nitrogen; lack of these elements causes a condition called chlorosis, signified by yellowing of the leaves, which can become terminal. Plants preferring alkaline soil are generally more tolerant of acid types. Apart from these preferences, the plant's tolerance of other soil conditions is also described.

Sun/Shade aspect
Too much or too little shade may cause damage to a climber or wall shrub; the colour of foliage or the rate or habit of growth may also be affected. Shade conditions are indicated in terms of light, medium or deep shade. Light shade refers to permanent but broken shade, when some light is available for about two-thirds of the day. Medium shade refers to a deeper degree of shade, but with some full light available during the day. Deep shade is that found under a heavy canopy of trees or in the shadow of a tall building with no direct sunlight. Some climbers and wall shrubs prefer a position in full sun, while others are likely to suffer sun scorch damage.

Information is also given in this section as to the relationship between the planting position, movement of the sun and exposure to atmospheric conditions, indicating whether the tree or shrub needs a warm, sunny, protected site or will tolerate one that is more cool and exposed.

Pruning
Advice is given on the most suitable method of pruning, the appropriate time of year, and the best way of training to shape and control overall growth.

Training
A number of shrubs and climbers can or must be trained against walls, trellises or other supports. This section outlines the various methods, techniques and materials required for the specific plant.

Propagation and nursery production
This section describes the main propagation methods in nursery production, the form in which the plant is found on sale, its general availability and the best planting height. The majority of the climbers and wall shrubs listed can be obtained through local garden centres and nurseries: where specialist sources are recommended, seek advice from a horticultural association, a garden society, or a specialist gardening publication. Many suppliers offer a mail-order facility which may be useful for obtaining less common varieties. Recommendation is given on whether to purchase plants bare-rooted, root-balled (balled-and-burlapped) or container-grown. These terms are fully explained in the Practical Glossary on page 170 and details of planting methods are shown on page 168. The recommended planting heights are those which will encourage establishment and healthy growth, larger or smaller stock may be less successful.

Problems
Susceptibility to disease or damage and known problems of cultivation are described in this section, underlining any potential problems mentioned elsewhere in the text. Any special points to note on purchase, planting and cultivation are highlighted.

Forms of interest
Related species, varieties, cultivars and hybrids that are similar to the main entry are listed under this heading, with information given on the characteristics and appearance of each form and on any variations in the details of soil and cultivation requirements provided in the main entry. Related forms that are significantly different in appearance or characteristics are given a separate main entry.

Average height and spread
The heights and spreads given over five, ten and twenty years are a general guideline to the size of the plant and the area it should be allowed. The actual size of the climber or wall shrub will be influenced by local climate, soil conditions and methods of cultivation. The support of a wall or fence will increase the overall height and spread of any shrub from the dimensions it would reach if freestanding. The protrusion from the wall or fence that may be expected at the height of the year's growth is as important as the height and spread.

Illustration
Every entry is illustrated with one or more colour photographs showing the best feature of a particular species or variety, and with a line drawing showing the overall shape of the mature plant. Note that line illustrations are not scaled in proportion to each other and should be considered individually in relation to the average heights and spreads given.

Botanical name
A single subject or a group of related forms
and varieties.

Family name
The main category of botanical classification.

Special features
Main attractions and cultivation details
highlighted for quick reference.

Origin
The native environment of the plant or its
origin in cultivation.

Description
Colour, size, shape, seasonal changes and
special features of flowers, foliage, stems
and fruits.

ERYTHRINA
CRISTA-GALLI

CORAL TREE, COXCOMB

Leguminosae   *Wall Shrub*
Deciduous

An interesting shrub for a sun-facing wall.

Origin From Brazil.
Use As a medium-sized, summer-flowering
sub-shrub for sunny walls and fences.
Description *Flower* Racemes of deep scarlet
florets, waxy-textured, borne in large clusters
at ends of shoots, mid to late summer. *Foliage*
Leaves medium-sized, trifoliate, 4–5 in
(10–12 cm) long, leaflets ovate. Grey/green,
giving some yellow autumn colour. *Stem*
Strong, upright, becoming arching with
weight of flowers, grey to grey/green. Small
sharp spines at each leaf axil. Dies to ground
level each winter, regenerating following
spring. Fast-growing, annually produced
stems. *Fruit* Insignificant.

Erythrina crista-galli **in flower**

Hardiness Tolerates a minimum winter temperature of 23°F (–5°C).
Soil requirements Good, light, open soil.
Sun/Shade aspect Plant facing full sun, in a
protected position against a wall or fence.
Pruning None required, but in early spring
remove any old shoots retained through
winter.
Training Requires no training, freestanding.
Propagation and nursery production Produced by root division and from seed. Purchase container-grown without stems while
dormant, if available, or as plants up to
12–18 in (30–45 cm). Extremely scarce, should
be sought from specialist nurseries.
Problems Difficult to establish, taking some
years to flower.
Similar forms of interest None.
Average height and spread
Five years
5 × 5 ft (1.5 × 1.5 m)
Ten years
6 × 8 ft (1.8 × 2.4 m)
Twenty years
6 × 10 ft (1.8 × 3 m)
Protrudes up to 3 ft (91 cm) from wall or
fence.

Common name
All variations in common usage are included.

Type
Evergreen, semi-evergreen or deciduous.
(Leaves retained all year round,
shed partially or fully.)

Classification
Denotes the botanical group in which the
plant is placed.

Use
Details of size, shape, seasonal effect,
suitable location and special uses such as
hedge-planting or screening.

Colour photograph
For every entry, shows the seasonal feature of
primary attraction in a selected named form.

Soil requirements
Particular preferences or dislikes in soil types
and conditions.

Pruning
Seasonal pruning requirements and advice on
shaping and control.

Propagation and nursery production
Details of the way the plant is grown and
presented at purchase; availability;
best planting heights.

Forms of interest
Alphabetical listing of species, cultivars and
related forms with description and
cultivation notes.

Line drawing
For every entry, shows the growth pattern of
branches and twigs making the overall shape
of the climber or wall shrub.

Hardiness
Tolerance of outdoor temperature and
winter conditions.

Sun/Shade aspect
Light requirements or shade protection
according to a given scale from full sun to
deep shade.

Training
Methods of training plants, along with
equipment and materials required.

Problems
Special cultivation requirements, susceptibility
to disease or damage etc.

Average height and spread
The proportions of the climber or wall shrub
at five, ten and twenty years after planting.
The protrusion that might be expected is
also indicated.

ABELIA × GRANDIFLORA

ABELIA, GLASSY ABELIA
Caprifoliaceae   *Wall Shrub*
Semi-evergreen

An attractive range of varieties, suited to
most temperate areas. Makes a good effect
when fan-trained against a sheltered,
sunny wall.

Abelia × grandiflora in flower

Origin Unknown. The parent plant was
named after Dr Clarke Abel (1780–1826).
Use As a semi-evergreen flowering, fan-
trained wall shrub.
Description *Flower* Pink and white, small to
medium-sized, hanging, bell-shaped flowers
borne in small clusters on wood 2–3 years old
or more, from late summer to early autumn.
Foliage Leaves 1–2½ in (2.5–6 cm) long, ovate,
pointed, olive-green with red shading. May
fall from late autumn or be retained into early
spring following mild winter. *Stem* Light
green with brown shading. Upright when
young, becoming more branching in second
and third year and darker brown. New shoots
grow from base up through the older framework. By pruning and tying-in a fan-shaped
effect can be achieved. Medium rate of
growth. *Fruit* Small, translucent seeds in
clusters.

Abelia chinensis in flower

Hardiness Tolerates a minimum winter temperature of 14°F (−10°C).
Soil requirements Any soil, but new growth
less vigorous on dry soils. On extremely
alkaline soils, chlorosis may occur.
Sun/Shade aspect Sunny warm aspect.
Prefers full sun, tolerates light shade.
Pruning On established shrubs, remove one
third of the oldest shoots each year in early
spring to encourage new flowering shoots.
Training Requires wires or individual anchor
points to secure and encourage the fan-
trained shape.
Propagation and nursery production From
semi-ripe cuttings taken in late summer.
Always purchase container grown; found in
garden centres and general nurseries. Best
planting height 15–30 in (38–76 cm).
Problems May appear weak when purchased
but once planted grows quickly. Wood can be
extremely brittle so needs careful handling.
Similar forms of interest *A. chinensis* Taller
growing with fragrant, rose-tinted flowers,
early to midsummer. A more tender variety
from China. *A.* × **'Edward Goucher'** Produces purple/pink trumpet flowers freely.
Foliage grey/green. *A. floribunda* Cherry-red
flowers 2 in (5 cm) long, borne in early summer. Slightly tender in most areas so fan-train
on a sun-facing wall. Of Mexican origin. *A.*
× *grandiflora* **'Francis Mason'** Golden variegated leaf form, a shorter shrub and more

tender than its parent. Bears pale pink to
white flowers throughout late summer and
early autumn. *A. schumannii* A less vigorous
and more tender form, bearing lilac/pink
flowers throughout summer. *A. triflora*
Scented pink-tinged white flowers borne in
threes. Minimum winter temperature 23°F
(−5°C).
Average height and spread
Five years
5 × 5 ft (1.5 × 1.5 m)
Ten years
7 × 7 ft (2.1 × 2.1 m)
Twenty years
9 × 9 ft (2.7 × 2.7 m)
Protrudes up to 3 ft (1 m)
from support.

ABELIOPHYLLUM
DISTICHUM

KOREAN ABELIALEAF, WHITE FORSYTHIA
Oleaceae   *Wall Shrub*
Deciduous

A much overlooked, undemanding
flowering shrub.

Origin From Korea.
Use As a small, fragrant, early spring
flowering wall shrub.
Description *Flower* Tiny white, sweetly
scented flowers with mauve-tinged basal
shading when in bud, borne late winter to
early spring. *Foliage* Leaves ovate, 1–3 in
(2.5–7.5 cm) long, light green, often sparsely
presented. *Stem* Shoots lend well to fan-
training, using wires or individual anchor
points. Slow to medium growth. *Fruit* Insignificant.

Abeliophyllum distichum in late
winter/early spring

Hardiness Tolerates a minimum winter temperature of 4°F (−15°C).
Soil requirements Does well on all soils,
except very alkaline.
Sun/Shade aspect Sheltered aspect. Full sun
or light shade.
Pruning None required.
Training Requires wires or individual anchor
points to secure and encourage a fan-trained
shape.
Propagation and nursery production From
semi-ripe cuttings taken in late summer. Purchase container grown; may be difficult to
find. Best planting height 8–18 in (20–45 cm).
Problems Looks weak and uninteresting in a
container – hence its limited planting.
Similar forms of interest None.
Average height and spread
Five years
4 × 4 ft (1.2 × 1.2 m)
Ten years
5 × 5 ft (1.5 × 1.5 m)
Twenty years
5 × 5 ft (1.5 × 1.5 m)
Protrudes up to 2½ ft (76 cm)
from support.

Abelia × grandiflora 'Francis Mason'

ABUTILON MEGAPOTAMICUM

KNOWN BY BOTANICAL NAME

Malvaceae   *Wall Shrub*
Deciduous

An interesting tender flowering shrub for use in mild areas.

Origin From Brazil.
Use As a wall shrub in warmer regions or for growing in conservatories.
Description *Flower* Medium-sized, hanging, bell-shaped flowers with yellow petals, red calyx and purple anthers, born in late summer and early autumn. *Foliage* Leaves ovate, 2–4 in (5–10 cm) long, with toothed edges. Olive-green with purple/red shading and veins. *Stem* Light to mid brown, upright, slightly arching. Medium rate of growth. *Fruit* Insignificant.

Abutilon megapotamicum in flower

Hardiness Tolerates a minimum temperature of 23°F (−5°C). May die back in winter but normally renews from ground level in early spring.
Soil requirements Any soil but does best on moist, rich types.
Sun/Shade aspect Sheltered aspect. Full sun to light shade.
Pruning Remove one third of old flowering wood on established shrubs in early to mid spring.
Training Requires wires or individual anchor points to achieve a fan-trained shape.
Propagation and nursery production From softwood cuttings taken in early summer. Best planting height 2–3 ft (60–91 cm). Always purchase container grown. Available from specialist nurseries and garden centres.
Problems A shrub of weak constitution and not fully hardy.
Similar forms of interest *A.m.* 'Variegatum' Golden variegated foliage, tender, tolerates no frost. Yellow flowers with red calyx and purple anthers.
Average height and spread
Five years
6 × 6 ft (1.8 × 1.8 m)
Ten years
7 × 7 ft (2.1 × 2.1 m)
Twenty years
9 × 9 ft (2.7 × 2.7 m)
Protrudes up to 3 ft (91 cm) from support.

ABUTILON MEGAPOTAMICUM (Large-leaved and Flowering Forms)

KNOWN BY BOTANICAL NAME

Malvaceae   *Wall Shrub*
Deciduous

An attractive, interesting flowering wall shrub, but requiring protection or favourable areas.

Origin Of garden origin.
Use As a fan-trained wall shrub for walls and fences, or for growing in conservatories, both as a fan-shaped wall shrub or as a pillar.
Description *Flower* Hanging, large, bell-shaped flowers up to 1½ in (4 cm) long and 1½ in (4 cm) wide. Wide range of colours including red, pink, yellow and apricot, produced from mid summer to early autumn. *Foliage* Leaves oval, up to 5 in (12 cm) long with toothed edges. Mid to olive-green in colour. Some yellow tints. Some variegated forms. *Stem* Upright, becoming spreading. Vigorous, up to 5 ft (1.5 m) of growth per year. *Fruit* Insignificant.
Hardiness Tolerates a minimum winter temperature of 23°F (−5°C) but any excessive cold winds will cause severe stem damage and may be fatal.
Soil requirements Moderately alkaline to acid, with adequate moisture and food content for rapid growth.
Sun/Shade aspect Very sheltered aspect in full sun to light shade.
Pruning Remove one third of old flowering wood on established shrubs to ground level in early to mid spring. Can be severely cut back to a stool in early spring if required and will quickly rejuvenate.
Training Requires wires or individual anchor points to secure and encourage a fan-trained shape.
Propagation and nursery production From softwood cuttings taken in early summer. Best planting height 2–3 ft (60–91 cm). Always purchase container grown. Available from specialist nurseries.
Problems Always susceptible to damage by severe cold.
Similar forms of interest *A.* × *milleri* Orange petals and crimson stamens. Very large dark green leaves. *Abutilon* × *milleri* 'Variegatum' Orange petals, crimson stamens. Foliage splashed gold. Very tender. *A.* 'Ashford Red' Foliage apple green. Flowers deep red/pink. Tender. *A.* 'Canary Yellow' Bright yellow. Less hardy. *A.* 'Cerise Queen' Cerise flowers. Less hardy. *A.* × 'Cynthia Pink' Apricot and red flowers. *A.* 'Hinton Seedling' Vermillion flowers. *A.* 'Louise Marignac' Good pink flowers. Less hardy. *A.* 'Nabob' Crimson-red flowers. Less hardy. *A.* 'Souvenir' Orange flowers. Golden variegated foliage.
Average height and spread
Five years
6 × 6 ft (1.8 × 1.8 m)
Ten years
7 × 7 ft (2.1 × 2.1 m)
Twenty years
9 × 9 ft (2.7 × 2.7 m)
Protrudes up to 3 ft (91 cm) from support.

ACACIA (Hardy Forms)

WATTLE

Leguminosae   *Tender Tree*
Evergreen

Useful trees for making fan-trained or upright specimens against very sheltered walls where they gain from the protection.

Origin From Australia.
Use As a freestanding, upright or fan-trained tree for large walls.
Description *Flower* Yellow flowers in clusters or racemes, produced late winter and through spring. Normally fragrant, depending on variety. *Foliage* Attractive grey/green, cut-leaved foliage 6–10 in (15–25 cm) long and 6–8 in (15–20 cm) wide. *Stem* Blue tinged grey/green, fast growing. Adapts to training. *Fruit* Insignificant.
Hardiness Tolerates a minimum winter temperature of 23°F (−5°C) but some terminal stem damage may be caused in severe wind chill conditions.
Soil requirements Does best in light, well-drained soil. Severe alkaline conditions will cause chlorosis.
Sun/Shade aspect Requires a very sheltered aspect. Best in full sun; tolerates light shade.
Pruning None except for training in a fan or upright shape.
Training Will require fixing to wires or individual anchor points.
Propagation and nursery production From seed or from semi-ripe cuttings taken in early spring. Purchase container grown; relatively easy to find in favourable locations. Small plants establish and train better than mature

Abutilon megapotamicum 'Kentish Belle' in flower

specimens; best planting height 3–6 ft (91 cm–1.8 m).
Problems May rarely survive outside the mildest areas.
Forms of interest *A. armata* (Kangaroo thorn) Profuse yellow flowers over the entire branch area in mid spring. Small prickles and small dissected leaves. Large, bushy habit, reaching tree proportions in very favourable areas. *A. baileyana* (Cootamundra wattle) Glaucous, cut-leaved foliage and bright yellow racemes of flowers in later winter, early spring. Two thirds average height and spread. *A. dealbata* (Silver wattle, mimosa) Fern-like, silver-green foliage, masses of yellow flowers. One of the hardiest forms.

Acacia dealbata **in flower**

Average height and spread
Five years
7 × 7 ft (2.1 × 2.1 m) freestanding
12 × 12 ft (3.7 × 3.7 m) fan-trained
Ten years
11 × 11 ft (3.4 × 3.4 m) freestanding
18 × 18 ft (5.5 × 5.5 m) fan-trained
Twenty years
14 × 14 ft (4.3 × 4.3 m)
freestanding
24 × 24 ft (7.3 × 7.3 m)
fan-trained
Protrudes up to 3 ft
(91 cm) from support
if fan-trained,
13 ft (4 m) untrained.

ACER NEGUNDO

BOX MAPLE, ASH-LEAVED MAPLE, BOX ELDER
Aceraceae   *Hardy Tree*
Deciduous
The ability of this attractive foliage maple to regenerate new growth following hard pruning makes it an ideal subject for fan-training.

Origin From North America.
Use As a fan-trained tree for large walls.
Description *Flower* Pendent, 2–4 in (5–10 cm) long sulphur-yellow, fluffy flowers in early spring. *Foliage* Light green pinnate leaves, 6–8 in (15–20 cm) wide and long, with three to five and sometimes up to nine leaflets. Some varieties with pink, gold or white variegation. Soft texture; slightly pendulous habit. Good yellow autumn colour. *Stem* Light to mid green, grey/green with downy texture when young. Upright at first, becoming more branching with age. Medium to fast rate of growth. *Fruit* Pendent, 3 in (7.5 cm) long winged fruits, grey/green when young, ageing to light yellow-brown. On mature trees seed can be plentiful.
Hardiness Tolerates a minimum winter temperature of 0°F (−18°C).

Acer negundo **'Flamingo' in leaf**

Soil requirements Does well on all soil types, except very dry where it may survive but may not thrive. Severely alkaline soils may cause chlorosis.
Sun/Shade aspect Tolerates a moderately exposed aspect in full sun or light to mid shade.
Pruning Cut young trees hard back to within 18 in (45 cm) of their base in spring following planting. Select resulting five to seven shoots and tie into a fan-trained shape. In subsequent years remove all side and forward growths back to 2 in (5 cm) from their origin but maintain and encourage main branches in fan shape.
Training Will require tying to wires or individual anchor points.
Propagation and nursery production *A. negundo* from seed, layering or root-stooling, but variegated forms grafted or budded except for a few found propagated by cuttings on their own roots. Can be purchased bare-rooted, container grown or root-balled (balled-and-burlapped). Always choose one- to two-year-old bush trees and ensure that they are bottom grafted or budded. Best planting height 3–5 ft (91 cm–1.5 m).
Similar forms of interest *A. n.* **'Auratum'** Golden-yellow foliage from spring through summer. Slightly smaller than average. *A. n. californicum* A green-leaved form with pink, pendulous fruits. Less hardy than most. *A. n.* **'Elegans'** (syn. *A. n.* **'Elegantissimum'**) Variegated foliage with yellow edges. Slightly less than average height and spread. *A. n.* **'Flamingo'** Pale to rosy pink variegated leaves at tips of all new growths from late spring, through early summer and often into autumn. Mature leaves variegated white. *A.*

Acer negundo **'Elegans' in leaf**

n. **'Variegatum'** (syn. *A. n.* **'Argenteovariegatum'**) Broad, white leaf margins but likely to revert to green. *A. n. violaceum* Young shoots purple to violet and covered with white bloom. Long, pendent pink flower tassels in spring. Good autumn colours. Slightly less hardy. May have to be sought from specialist nurseries.
Average height and spread
Five years
10 × 10 ft (3 × 3 m)
Ten years
20 × 20 ft (6 × 6 m)
Twenty years
25 × 25 ft (7.6 × 7.6 m)
Protrudes up to 3 ft (91 cm)
from support.

ACTINIDIA ARGUTA
(*A. polygama*)

KNOWN BY BOTANICAL NAME
Actinidiaceae   *Woody Climber*
Deciduous
An attractive foliaged climber, at its best when showing its autumn colour.

Origin From Japan and Korea.
Use As a free-growing climbing plant for covering large areas. Produces fruit in favourable areas. Good on walls, fences, pergolas or over buildings; can be allowed to ramble through large shrubs and trees to provide interest.
Description *Flower* ¾ in (19 mm) across, white with dark purple anthers, fragrant; borne in pairs. Normally only produced in warm climates. *Foliage* Oval, pointed, with toothed edges, up to 5 in (12 cm) long and 2 in (5 cm) wide. Light green turning a good yellow in autumn. *Stem* Grey-green when young, becoming light brown; slightly downy texture. Twining and twisting. Attractive in winter. Medium to fast growing. *Fruit* Oblong, green-yellow, edible. Only produced in warm climates.
Hardiness Tolerates a minimum winter temperature of 13°F (−10°C).
Soil requirements Requires a moist, rich soil, tolerating acid, neutral and moderately alkaline types.
Sun/Shade aspect All but the most exposed aspect. Light shade to full sun.
Pruning Not normally required but can be contained by removal of any offending lateral shoots. It quickly rejuvenates itself with vigorous new growth.
Training Allow to ramble through trees or large shrubs. Provide wires or other large-scale support systems. It twines and does not normally require tying in.

Propagation and nursery production From seed or semi-ripe cuttings. Requires some heat to encourage rooting. Always purchase container grown, in early autumn to early summer, from specialist nurseries. Best planting height 18 in (45 cm) up to 4 ft (1.2 cm).
Problems Can be shy to flower and therefore shy to fruit in all but the warmest areas, although it is worth growing for the autumn foliage effect.

Actinidia arguta in leaf

Similar forms of interest *A. a.* 'Cordifolia' Narrow foliage, scarce. *A. a.* 'Aureo-Variegata' Golden-variegated foliage. Scarce.
Average height and spread
Five years
12 × 12 ft (3.7 × 3.7 m)
Ten years
20 × 20 ft (6 × 6 m)
Twenty years
30 × 30 ft + (9 × 9 m +)
Protrudes up to 2 ft (60 cm) from support.

ACTINIDIA CHINENSIS

CHINESE GOOSEBERRY, KIWI FRUIT
Actinidiaceae   *Woody Fruiting Climber*
Deciduous
Extremely ornamental foliage adorning a vigorous grower which can produce edible fruit in hot summers.

Origin From China.
Use As a fast-growing climber for walls, fences, or through trees and large shrubs.
Description *Flower* Creamy white becoming buff yellow, 1½ in (4 cm) wide, five-petalled, incurving cup shaped, in early to mid summer. Male or female on different plants both needed for pollination. *Foliage* Large, almost round, heavily-veined, 5–8 in (12–20 cm) across. Downy undersides. Light green when young becoming more brown/green with age, good yellow/light orange autumn colour. *Stem* Mid green when young becoming light brown. Vigorous, twisting yet not clinging, wide ranging habit. Medium to fast growing. *Fruit* Small, hairy, oblong, round-ended. Up to 2 in (5 cm) long with gooseberry flavour, not always reliable in all but hottest areas.
Hardiness Tolerates a minimum winter temperature of 14°F (−10°C). Some damage to tips of growth may be caused in spring by frost but normally to no great harm.
Soil requirements A deep, well-fed, light soil for best results although it is tolerant to a wide range except extremely waterlogged.
Sun/Shade aspect All but the most exposed aspects. Full sun to very light shade.
Pruning Train shoots to cover required area, prune back all surplus shoots either after fruiting or in late summer to two buds from the point of origin.

Actinidia chinensis in fruit

Training Tie young shoots of newly planted plants to wires on walls and fences; they normally become self-twining and supporting. In trees and large shrubs, clings by twining.
Propagation and nursery production From semi-ripe cuttings taken in summer. Purchase container grown from good garden centres and specialist nurseries. Best planting height 1½–3 ft (45–91 cm).
Problems Often planted in areas too small to accommodate it. Can be shy to fruit. Male and female plants may be difficult to find.
Similar forms of interest The following commercial varieties may be available: *A. c.* 'Atlas' A good male form for pollinating other varieties; free flowering. *A. c.* 'Heywood' Good female form, heavy cropping on warm south walls, will require a male variety for pollination. *A. c.* 'Tomurii' Male, free flowering, disease resistant.
Average height and spread
Five years
10 × 10 ft (3 × 3 m)
Ten years
20 × 20 ft (6 × 6 m)
Twenty years
39 × 39 ft (12 × 12 m)
Protrudes up to 3 ft (91 cm) from support.

ACTINIDIA KOLOMIKTA

KNOWN BY BOTANICAL NAME
Actinidiaceae   *Woody Climber*
Deciduous
One of the most attractive of all foliage climbers but does require a warm situation.

Origin From China and Japan.
Use As an attractive foliaged climber for sunny positions both on walls and fences.
Description *Flower* Unattractive white fragrant flowers with yellow anthers ⅓ in (1 cm) wide; borne in groups of one to three in early summer. *Foliage* 3–6 in (7.5–15 cm) long 2–4 in (5–10 cm) wide oblong ovate leaves with pronounced veins and toothed edges; tips start white and age to pink, contrasting with dark green remainder, some yellow autumn colour. *Stem* Slender, deep mahogany brown. Not normally self clinging. Medium to fast growing. *Fruit* Oval, yellow, 1 in (2.5 cm) long; sweet and edible but not normally used for culinary or dessert purposes.
Hardiness Tolerates a minimum winter temperature of 14°F (−10°C).
Soil requirements Tolerates both alkaline and acid conditions but may produce more growth on neutral to acid types. Well drained and well fed soil is advised.
Sun/Shade aspect Requires some shelter from exposed aspects. Tolerates light shade but prefers full sun.
Pruning Normally requires none other than cutting in early spring to keep within bounds.
Training Tie main vines to wires against walls and fences as required.
Propagation and nursery production From semi-ripe cuttings. Always purchase container grown. Best planting height 1½–3 ft (45–91 cm). Generally only found in good garden centres and specialist nurseries.
Problems Can, on very dry soils, lose its leaves prematurely in late summer. Attractive to cats which claw the vines, causing damage.
Similar forms of interest None.
Average height and spread
Five years
5 × 5 ft (1.5 × 1.5 m)
Ten years
13 × 13 ft (4 × 4 m)
Twenty years
20 × 20 ft (6 × 6 m)
Protrudes up to 3 ft (91 cm) from support.

Actinidia kolomikta in leaf

13

AKEBIA QUINATA

KNOWN BY BOTANICAL NAME
Lardizabalaceae *Woody Climber*
Deciduous to evergreen
An attractive climbing shrub which if allowed to ramble gives an interesting display of unusual shaped fruit.

Origin From China, Japan and Korea.
Use For growing up through other shrubs or small trees or against walls and fences.
Description *Flower* Pendent racemes 3–5 in (7.5–10 cm) long of male flowers up to ¼ in (5 mm) wide, pale purple in colour. Fragrant. Chocolate-purple female flowers, usually in pairs and 1–1¼ in (2.5–3 cm) wide, are produced in April. *Foliage* Five leaflets carried on a single stalk up to 3–5 in (7.5–12 cm) long; each leaflet oblong to oval in shape, 1½–3 in (4–7.5 cm) long with short 1½ in (4 cm) stalk; light to mid green giving good yellow autumn colour. *Stem* Light green to grey green, loosely twining, wiry in nature. Medium to fast growing. *Fruit* Attractive sausage-shaped grey/violet fruit, 2½–3½ in (6–9 cm) long, splitting lengthwise when ripe. Produced in early autumn.
Hardiness Tolerates a minimum winter temperature of 4°F (−15°C).
Soil requirements Tolerates most soil conditions except waterlogged. Good on alkaline types.
Sun/Shade aspect Needs some protection in exposed aspects. From light shade to full sun, but needs protection from strong, midday summer sun.
Pruning Allow to grow free; every five to six years lightly trim in early spring with hedging shears.
Training Leave to ramble over wires on walls and fences, or over shrubs and trees.
Propagation and nursery production From

Akebia quinata **in flower**

semi-ripe cuttings requiring basal heat to root in midsummer or by layering shoots. Always purchase container grown. Best planting height 1½–3 ft (45–91 cm). Not always readily available – may need searching for from specialist nurseries.
Problems A little unruly in its habit. Flowers and fruit may be hidden both by its own foliage and that of the host it is climbing in.
Similar forms of interest *A. lobata* (syn. *A. trifoliata*) Very scarce in production, flowers smaller, fruits possibly larger and pale violet in colour.
Average height and spread
Five years
6 × 6 ft (1.8 × 1.8 m)
Ten years
18 × 18 ft (5.5 × 5.5 m)
Twenty years
20 × 30 ft (6 × 9 m)
Protrudes up to 2 ft (60 cm) from support.

ALBIZIA JULIBRISSIN

PINK MIMOSA, PINK SIRIS, SILK TREE
Leguminosae *Tender Tree*
Deciduous
Very tender, but included here both for mild areas for fan-training in the open or for use in conservatories.

Origin From Iran to China and Taiwan.
Use As a small fan-trained tree for large walls or for fan-training on conservatory walls.
Description *Flower* Terminal clusters of flowerheads on long stalks, producing a mop-like cluster of pink stamens up to 1 in (2.5 cm) across in mid to late summer. Dense all-over flowering makes a spectacular effect. *Foliage* Bipinnate leaves, 9–18 in (23–45 cm) long. Each of the 6–12 branches of the pinnate leaf carries 20–30 pairs of small, oblong, grey/green leaflets. *Stem* Grey/green, upright when young, quickly spreading. Medium rate of growth, slower in container. *Fruit* Insignificant.
Hardiness Can only flourish in frost-free areas.
Soil requirements Any soil types except very dry.
Sun/Shade aspect Requires a very sheltered aspect. Full sun to very light shade.
Pruning Prune young trees hard in the spring following planting. Tie resulting five to seven shoots into a fan-trained shape. In subsequent year, remove all side growths back to two points from their origin and maintain original main branches in fan shape.
Training Will require fixing to wires or individual anchor points.
Propagation and nursery production From seed. Always purchase container grown; normally supplied 2–5 ft (60 cm–1.5 m) in height. For fan-training always use trees of not more than 2 years old. Available from specialist nurseries.
Problems Often chosen because seen growing well in warm climates, but not adaptable to harsher conditions.
Similar forms of interest *A. j.* 'Rosea' A smaller variety with bright pink flowers, reaching two-thirds average height and spread.
Average height and spread
Five years
8 × 8 ft (2.4 × 2.4 m)
Ten years
16 × 16 ft (4.9 × 4.9 m)
Twenty years
24 × 24 ft (7.3 × 7.3 m)
Protrudes up to 3 ft (91 cm) from support.

Albizia julibrissin **in flower**

AMPELOPSIS BREVIPENDUNCULATA

KNOWN BY BOTANICAL NAME
Vitaceae *Woody Climber*
Deciduous
An interesting vine with good autumn foliage colour.

Origin From North East Asia.
Use Attractive autumn foliage climber to cover walls, fences and pergolas; when used on the latter makes a good shade cover.

Ampelopsis brevipendunculata **in fruit**

Description *Flower* Small, light green, uninteresting. *Foliage* Three- or five-lobed broadly ovate leaves, up to 6 in (12 cm) long. Coarse texture. Downy undersides with pronounced veins often purple red in colour. Good yellow/orange autumn colour. *Stem* Light to green/brown, becoming darker, twining in habit, may be self clinging on old brick walls. Medium to fast growing. *Fruit* Bright blue, grape-like in shape, ¼–½ in (5 mm–1 cm) wide. May require warm summers to fruit well.

Hardiness Tolerates a minimum winter temperature of 14°F (−10°C).

Soil requirements Dislikes extremely wet, dry or poor conditions. Does well on both acid or alkaline soil types.

Sun/Shade aspect Does well in all aspects. Light shade to full sun.

Pruning Not normally required other than that needed for shaping, although in confined spaces can be cut hard back in spring without ill effect.

Training Tie young shoots to wires or wall fixings; normally becomes self-entwining and clinging on walls and fences or over pergolas.

Propagation and nursery production From semi-ripe cuttings. Always purchase container grown. Best planting height 1½–3 ft (45–91 cm). Will need searching for from specialist nurseries.

Problems Can become invasive in good conditions. In too deep shade can become open and lax in habit. In wet autumns may fail to produce good autumn colour.

Forms of interest See further entry.

Average height and spread

Five years
5 × 5 ft (1.5 × 1.5 m)
Ten years
13 × 13 ft (4 × 4 m)
Twenty years
20 × 20 ft (6 × 6 m)
Protrudes up to 2 ft (60 cm) from support.

AMPELOPSIS BREVIPENDUNCULATA 'ELEGANS'
(*A. heterophylla* 'Elegans')

KNOWN BY BOTANICAL NAME

Vitaceae   *Woody Climber*
Deciduous

Although requiring more attention than many climbers the display of pink shoots and foliage makes it worth the effort.

Origin From North East Asia.

Use As an attractive coloured foliage climber for sheltered walls and fences or under protection in greenhouses or conservatories.

Ampelopsis brevipendunculata 'Elegans' in leaf

Description *Flower* Small clusters of creamy white inconspicuous flowers in mid to late spring. May in hot summers produce ⅛ in (2 mm) wide clear blue flowers with black spots. *Foliage* Hand-shaped leaves with some lobed indentations on outer edges varying in size from 2–4 in (5–10 cm) long; some with toothed edges. Grey/green undersides, upper surface white to pink with green variegation. *Stem* Attractive, pink to red when young becoming green to green/brown with age, not

Arbutus unedo in fruit

self-clinging but twining, interlacing itself around a support. Slow to medium growth rate. *Fruit* None of interest.

Hardiness Tolerates a minimum winter temperature of 23°F (−5°C).

Soil requirements Moderately alkaline to acid, requiring a high degree of organic content with good moisture retaining qualities.

Sun/Shade aspect Requires a sheltered aspect. Light shade for preference, will tolerate full sun if adequate moisture is available; if not, scorching may be a problem.

Pruning Prune back all side shoots produced last year to within two buds of origin except shoots which are required for training the main framework, so encouraging a high production of good new pink foliage.

Training Allow to ramble over wires and secure as required, or allow to scramble through an uninteresting shrub both in the open or under protection.

Propagation and nursery production From semi-ripe cuttings taken in early to mid summer. Always purchase container grown. Not readily available and may have to be searched for. Best planting height 1–2 ft (30–60 cm).

Problems Foliage scorching may be caused by late frosts and strong midday summer sun. Can be attacked by mildew in mid to late summer.

Similar forms of interest None.

Average height and spread

Five years
5 × 5 ft (1.5 × 1.5 m)
Ten years
10 × 10 ft (3 × 3 m)
Twenty years
15 × 12 ft (4.6 × 3.7 m)
Protrudes up to 2 ft (60 cm) from support.

ARBUTUS

STRAWBERRY TREE

Ericaceae   *Hardy Tree*
Evergreen

Arbutus varieties do not truly reach tree proportions for a great number of years, but are worth waiting for. When grown against walls added protection is afforded.

Origin From south-eastern Europe and Asia Minor.

Use As a freestanding specimen shrub and eventually a small tree, given protection by its proximity to large walls.

Description *Flower* Medium-sized, cup-shaped flowers, pure white or tinged pink, hanging in small arching panicles up to 3 in (7.5 cm) long, produced throughout spring and early summer. *Foliage* Leaves leathery, ovate to oval, 2–4 in (5–10 cm) long, dark green with paler undersides. Purple shading and purple veining. *Stem* Dark orange to orange/purple. Some varieties look striking in winter. Shrub-forming for the first ten years of its existence, slowly evolving tree-like habit. Upright when young, spreading with age. *Fruit* Globe-shaped to round, strawberry-like fruits, ¼–½ in (5 mm–1 cm) across, produced in autumn and maintained through winter, ripening in spring and often still showing with the next season's flowers.

Hardiness Tolerates a minimum winter temperature of 4°F (−15°C). Defoliation may occur in severe frost conditions, although the plant is rarely destroyed completely.

Soil requirements Does well on all soil types except extremely alkaline. Makes more growth when leafmould or peat is added to soil. Young plants respond well to an annual mulch of organic matter 2–4 in (5–10 cm) deep and at least 3 ft (91 cm) wide around the base.

Sun/Shade aspect Requires a sheltered aspect. Full sun to light shade, with light shade for preference.

Pruning None required.

Training Requires tying to individual anchor points to prevent damage from heavy snowfalls.

Propagation and nursery production From seed or semi-ripe cuttings taken in early summer. Always purchase container grown; some varieties quite hard to obtain and must be sought from specialist nurseries. Usually can only be purchased from 1–1½ ft (30–45 cm) in height.

Problems Slowness of growth is frequently underestimated.

Forms of interest *A. andrachne* (Grecian strawberry tree) Dark red to cinnamon-coloured peeling bark, its main attraction in winter. Often difficult to find in commercial production. From south-eastern Europe and Asia Minor. *A. × andrachnoides* (Killarney strawberry tree) Attractive cinnamon-red winter branches. More lime-tolerant than most. Should be considered normally hardy. Winter and autumn flowering with fruits produced in spring. A cross between *A. andrachne* for its winter stems and *A. unedo* for its fruit. *A. menziessi* (Madroña of California) Peeling, smooth bark, revealing light red to terracotta underbark. Foliage oval, up to 6 in (15 cm) long and 2½ in (6 cm) wide. Fruits orange/red, globe-shaped and of good size, following large terminal pyramid panicles of white flowers in spring. Should be considered slightly tender in most areas with winter frost. *A. unedo* (Killarney strawberry tree) Abundant flowers produced in terminal panicles, white or pink shaded, late autumn to early winter, followed by bright red, granular-surfaced, globe-shaped, edible fruit. Fruits often used for the production of liqueur, especially in Portugal. Slow-growing for the first 15 years of its life. Normally considered as a large shrub. Hardy but with some winter damage to foliage possible in severe wind-chill conditions. From southern Europe, south-western Ireland and Asia Minor. A popular and widely available variety. *A. u.* **'Quercifolia'** Foliage dark green with purple undershading to veins, dissected, similar to leaves of the common oak. Flowers and fruits identical to parent. Scarce in production. *A. u.* **'Rubra'** Dark, rich pink flowers and attractive fruit in hot summers. Slightly less vigorous and less hardy than parent. Difficult to find. Two thirds average height and spread.

Average height and spread
Five years
5 × 5 ft (1.5 × 1.5 m)
Ten years
10 × 10 ft (3 × 3 m)
Twenty years
20 × 20 ft (6 × 6 m)
Protrudes up to 12 ft (3.5 m) from wall or fence.

ARISTOLOCHIA MACROPHYLLA
(*A. sipho*, *A. durior*)

DUTCHMAN'S PIPE

Aristolochiaceae   *Woody Climber*
Deciduous
Of all climbing plants this has the most interesting foliage and flowers, given the right conditions.

Origin From Eastern North America.
Use As a climber for sheltered walls, fences, and pillars.

Aristolochia macrophylla in leaf

Description *Flower* 1–1½ in (2.5–4 cm) long yellow/green siphon-shaped flowers with open mouth effect at top, coloured purple/brown around edges; produced in pairs at leaf axles and carried on tall shoots in early summer. *Foliage* Large, kidney- or heart-shaped, sometimes blunt, sometimes pointed; 4–10 in (10–25 cm) long and wide with downy undersides, light green upper surface; presented on stalks 1–3 in (2.5–7.5 cm) long, yellow autumn colour. Very attractive for shape and size. *Stems* Long, light grey/green turning green/brown twining stems, not self supporting. Medium to fast rate of growth. *Fruit* None of interest.
Hardiness Tolerates a minimum winter temperature of 4°F (−15°C).
Soil requirements Moderately alkaline to acid, requires a good rich organic content to maintain adequate moisture to support the large leaf structure.

Sun/Shade aspect Requires a sheltered aspect. Best in very light shade but will tolerate degrees either side.
Pruning Shorten back previous season's growth in early spring to encourage good production of new foliage and flowers.
Training Tie to wires in a fan shape to show foliage off to best effect.
Propagation and nursery production Soft semi-ripe cuttings taken in late spring/early summer; requires some additional bottom heat to assist rooting. Purchase container grown or root-balled (balled-and-burlapped) from specialist nurseries or better garden centres. Best planting height 1–3 ft (30–91 cm).
Problems May be difficult to find. Can take two years to establish before really good new growth is seen, in which time foliage will be small.
Similar forms of interest None.

Average height and spread
Five years
6 × 4 ft (1.8 × 1.2 m)
Ten years
10 × 10 ft (3 × 3 m)
Twenty years
20 × 20 ft (6 × 6 m)
Protrudes up to 2 ft (60 cm) from support.

AUCUBA JAPONICA

JAPANESE AUCUBA, SPOTTED LAUREL, HIMALAYAN LAUREL, JAPANESE LAUREL

Cornaceae   *Wall Shrub*
Evergreen
A good evergreen shrub that responds well to use against a wall, particularly in shady areas where other plants may be less accommodating.

Origin From Japan.
Use As a freestanding or fan-trained shrub for large walls and fences in shady positions.
Description *Flower* Sulphur-yellow panicles produced in late spring. Each variety carries either male or female flowers, which are similar in appearance; for fruiting, plants of both sexes are needed. *Foliage* Lanceolate, dark, glossy green leaves 3–8 in (7.5–20 cm) long and 1–3 in (2.5–7.5 cm) wide. *Stem* Bright green and glossy. Strong, upright and branching, forming a round-topped shrub. Medium growth rate. *Fruit* On female plants clusters of bright red round fruits appear in autumn and remain through winter and possibly into spring. Produced only if male plant grows nearby.
Hardiness Tolerates a minimum winter temperature of 4°F (−15°C), although some foliage damage may be caused by severe wind chill or late spring frosts.

Soil requirements Tolerates almost any soil, including dry and alkaline.
Sun/Shade aspect Tolerates all aspects. Dislikes full sun, tolerates very deep shade.
Pruning None required but may be cut back hard in spring to control size.
Training Allow to grow freestanding or fan-trained to wires or individual anchor points.
Propagation and nursery production From softwood cuttings taken in mid to late summer. Purchase container grown. Easy to find; many new variegated forms becoming available. Best planting height 6–24 in (15–60 cm).
Problems None, apart from wind chill hazard. The process of fan-training may be a slow operation.
Varieties of interest *A. j.* **'Crotonifolia'** A slightly less vigorous variety with spotted and blotched golden leaves. Male. *A. j.* **'Golden Spangles'** Bright golden variegation. Female. *A. j.* **'Mr Goldstrike'** A new golden variegated variety with red berries. Female. *A. j.* **'Picturata'** Dark green leaves boldly splashed chrome yellow, slightly less vigorous than *A. japonica*. Male. *A. j.* **'Salicifolia'** A green-leaved form with very narrow, tooth-edged dark green foliage. Freely fruiting but not easy to find. Female. *A. j.* **'Variegata'** Leaves liberally splashed golden and yellow. One of the most variegated forms. Female. *A. j.* **'Variegata Gold Dust'** A very good form with golden variegated foliage and red berries in autumn. Female.

Average height and spread
Five years
5 × 5 ft (1.5 × 1.5 m)
Ten years
7 × 7 ft (2.1 × 2.1 m)
Twenty years
15 × 15 ft (4.6 × 4.6 m)
Protrudes up to 3 ft (91 cm) from support if fan-trained, 6 ft (1.8 m) untrained.

AZARA DENTATA

KNOWN BY BOTANICAL NAME

Flacourtiaceae   *Wall Shrub*
Evergreen
These scented flowering evergreens are on the tender side, requiring the protection of a wall in winter.

Origin From Chile.
Use As a fan-trained shrub for walls and fences in sheltered areas or in conservatories and greenhouses.
Description *Flower* Clusters of fragrant yellow flowers in spring, borne in profusion. *Foliage* Leaves ovate or oblong, 1–1½ in (2.5–4 cm) long, bright green to glossy dark green with felted undersides. *Stem* Light

Aucuba japonica **'Variegata'**

Azara dentata **in flower**

green to mid green. Upright when young, becoming more twiggy and spreading with age. Moderate rate of growth. *Fruit* Insignificant.
Hardiness Tolerates a minimum winter temperature of 23°F (−5°C).
Soil requirements Does well on most soils but dislikes excessive alkalinity and waterlogging.
Sun/Shade aspect Very sheltered aspect. Tolerates full sun to mid shade.
Pruning None required.
Training Requires wires or individual anchor points to secure and encourage the fan-trained shape.
Propagation and nursery production From softwood cuttings taken in mid summer. Best planting height 2–3 ft (60–91 cm). Always purchase container grown. Obtainable from specialist nurseries.
Problems None, apart from its lack of hardiness.
Similar forms of interest *A. lanceolata* Narrow, lanceolate leaves and mustard yellow flowers in early summer which are as fragrant as those of *A. dentata*. *A. serrata* Often confused with *A. dentata*, producing similar scented flowers under the edges of each leaf. Leaves more serrated. In hot climates, or in hot summers, small white berries may be produced. One of the hardier forms.
Average height and spread
Five years
5 × 5 ft (1.5 × 1.5 m)
Ten years
8 × 8 ft (2.4 × 2.4 m)
Twenty years
12 × 12 ft (3.7 × 3.7 m)
Protrudes up to 4 ft (1.2 m) from support.

AZARA MICROPHYLLA

KNOWN BY BOTANICAL NAME
Flacourtiaceae　　　　*Wall Shrub*
Evergreen
A shrub offering attractive evergreen foliage and formation in a sheltered position.

Origin From Chile.
Use As a freestanding or fan-trained shrub for large walls and fences.
Description *Flower* Numerous very small, vanilla-scented, yellow to yellow/green flowers carried in clusters at leaf joints between late winter and early spring. Flowering can be very variable in performance. *Foliage* Very attractive small oval leaflets, 1 in (2.5 cm) long, round-ended, toothed edges, dark shiny green, carried uniformly along branches in interesting formation. *Stem* Light green to dark green, becoming grey/green. Upright, slow to

medium growth rate. Responds well to fan-training. *Fruit* None of interest.
Hardiness Tolerates a minimum winter temperature of 14°F (−10°C). Late spring frost may damage new growth.
Soil requirements Tolerates a wide range of soil conditions, only disliking extremely wet or dry types.
Sun/Shade aspect Best in light to medium shade but will tolerate full sun if required as long as adequate moisture is available.
Pruning Not normally required but can have individual limbs removed in spring if necessary for training.
Training Tie to wires or individual anchor points in a fan shape or allow to grow free-standing.
Propagation and nursery production From semi-ripe cuttings taken in early summer. Should always be purchased container grown; may have to be sought from specialist nurseries. Best planting height 6 in–3 ft (15–91 cm).
Problems Can reach the dimensions of a small tree given time and this should be allowed for in initial planting.
Similar forms of interest *A. m.* 'Variegata' Edges of leaves creamy yellow. An interesting plant less hardy than its parent.
Average height and spread
Five years
5 × 3 ft (1.5 × 91 cm)
Ten years
8 × 5 ft (2.4 × 1.5 m)
Twenty years
16 × 10 ft (4.9 × 3 m)
Protrudes up to 3 ft (91 cm) from support if fan-trained, 7 ft (2.1 m) untrained.

Azara microphylla

BERBERIDOPSIS CORALLINA

KNOWN BY BOTANICAL NAME
Flacourtiaceae　　　　*Wall Shrub*
Evergreen
Technically a low, sprawling shrub but when used as a climber shows off its flowers to the best advantage.

Origin From Chile.
Use As a small climbing shrub for sheltered walls and fences.
Description *Flower* Crimson, ¼ in (4 mm) long, globe-shaped, hanging in racemes and contrasting well with foliage. Mid to late summer. *Foliage* Evergreen, oblong, up to 3 in (7.5 cm) in length, 1½ in (4 cm) wide. Tooth-edged, mid green with some orange/red shading towards autumn. *Stem* Not self-clinging. Light green to green/brown, sprawling and spreading. Slow to medium rate of growth. *Fruit* May produce ¼ in (5 mm) round, red berries following hot summers, in late summer/early autumn.
Hardiness Tolerates a minimum winter temperature of 23°F (−5°C) but requires protection from cold winter winds.
Soil requirements Neutral to acid, may tolerate very limited amounts of alkalinity. High degree of organic material required in soil to retain moisture for good growth.

Berberidopsis corallina **in flower**

Sun/Shade aspect Very sheltered aspect. Best in light shade but will tolerate degrees either side. Does well under the protection of greenhouses or conservatories.
Pruning Not normally required.
Training Allow to ramble through wires or other support. Individual branches may be supported and tied.
Propagation and nursery production Sow seed in mid to late spring. Take semi-ripe cuttings in mid summer or layer plants in autumn. Always purchase container grown, best size 6–24 in (15–60 cm). May be difficult to find, only available from specialist nurseries.
Problems Its hardiness is suspect and it may be difficult to obtain but it is worth the effort.
Similar forms of interest None.
Average height and spread
Five years
5 × 3 ft (1.5 m × 91 cm)
Ten years
10 × 6 ft (3 × 1.8 m)
Twenty years
15 × 9 ft (4.6 × 2.7 m)
Protrudes up to 12 in (30 cm) from support.

BIGNONIA CAPREOLATA
(*Doxantha capreolata*)

KNOWN BY BOTANICAL NAME

Bignoniaceae   *Tender Woody Climber*
Evergreen

An extremely spectacular flowering climber but requiring greenhouse or conservatory protection in all but the warmest of locations.

Origin From the southern states of the USA.
Use As a spreading climbing plant for very sheltered walls or fences in the open or for scrambling over wires or greenhouse or conservatory roofs.
Description *Flower* Long tubular flowers up to 2 in (5 cm) long, yellow/red in colour, produced on stalks in clusters of two to five in mid spring through to late summer, depending on planting location. *Foliage* Oblong leaflets make up a branching leaf presented at the end of long stalks, light green in colour. Yellow autumn colour. *Stem* Light green long tendrils, twisting but not self clinging. Medium to fast growing. *Fruit* Narrow capsules with leathery appearance, light grey/green in colour.
Hardiness Tolerates a minimum winter temperature of 32°F (0°C).
Soil requirements Light sandy soil although must have moisture retention. Neutral to acid.
Sun/Shade aspect Very sheltered aspect or under protection of greenhouse or conservatory. Light shade to full sun. Will tolerate deeper degree of shade but may be shy to flower.

Bignonia capreolata in flower

Pruning Trim in spring to keep in desired area.
Training Tie when young then allow to ramble over wires or other framework.
Propagation and nursery production Short cuttings taken early to mid summer and inserted in a sand rooting medium with some bottom heat. Take care not to overwater in early stages. Should always be purchased container grown; best planting height 1–3 ft (30–91 cm). Not readily available – will have to be sought from specialist nurseries.
Problems Its hardiness is often overstated and availability may be difficult.
Similar forms of interest None.
Average height and spread
Five years
6 × 6 ft (1.8 × 1.8 m)
Ten years
12 × 12 ft (3.7 × 3.7 m)
Twenty years
24 × 18 ft (7.3 × 5.5 m)
Protrudes up to 3 ft (91 cm) from support.

BILLARDIER'A
LONGIFLORA

KNOWN BY BOTANICAL NAME

Pittosporaceae   *Tender Woody Climber*
Evergreen

An attractive evergreen climber requiring a protected situation to withstand winters.

Origin From Tasmania.
Use As a climber for sheltered walls and fences outside or for use under protection in greenhouse or conservatory in exposed, cold areas.

Billardier'a longiflora in flower

Description *Flower* Yellow/green turning purple, borne singly over the total area of climber in mid summer. *Stem* Light green turning finally to green/brown, twining not self clinging. Medium rate of growth. *Fruit* Attractive and interesting oval-shaped, blue, 1 in (2.5 cm) long fruits in mid autumn. *Foliage* Hanging, narrow, lance-shaped light green leaves, 1¾ in (4.5 cm) long and ½ in (1 cm) wide, leathery texture; may be sparsely presented.
Hardiness Tolerates a minimum winter temperature of 32°F (0°C).

Soil requirements Neutral to acid although may tolerate small degrees of alkalinity. Requires a high organic content for best results.
Sun/Shade aspect Requires a very sheltered aspect. Prefers light shade but will tolerate degrees either side.
Pruning Trim lightly in spring.
Training Allow to grow over wires or up some type of framework.
Propagation and nursery production Semi-ripe cuttings taken in mid summer inserted into a sand/peat mixture with some heat to roots, or raise from seed. Should always be purchased container grown, will need some searching for from specialist nurseries; best planting height 1–2 ft (30–60 cm).
Problems Not fully hardy.
Similar forms of interest None.
Average height and spread
Five years
5 × 5 ft (1.5 × 1.5 m)
Ten years
10 × 10 ft (3 × 3 m)
Twenty years
15 × 15 ft (4.6 × 4.6 m)
Protrudes up to 18 in (45 cm) from support.

BOUGAINVILLEA
SPECTABILIS

KNOWN BY BOTANICAL NAME

Nyctaginaceae   *Tender Greenhouse Climber*

Deciduous

Although tender in all but the mildest of areas, bougainvillea is included in this publication for its use as a climber for conservatories and large greenhouses.

Origin From Brazil.
Use As a climber for conservatories and greenhouses, planted in large containers or in greenhouse borders.
Description *Flower* Tubular flowers surrounded by large magenta bracts, up to 1½ in (4 cm) wide and long, carried in panicles 9–12 in (23–30 cm) long. *Foliage* Pointed, oval, grey/green to dull green, 1½ in (4 cm) long by ¾ in (2 cm) wide. Normally leathery in texture. *Stem* Angular, branching, grey/green, stiff, vigorous. Medium to fast growth rate. *Fruit* Of no interest.
Hardiness Tolerates a minimum winter temperature of 50°F (10°C).
Soil requirements If grown in large containers a good quality potting compost should be used. If grown in soil, the latter should be lightened with the addition of 25 per cent sand and 25 per cent sedge peat.

Bougainvillea spectabilis in flower

Sun/Shade aspect Must be in a fully protected aspect. Best in full sun but will tolerate light shade.

Pruning Prune all previous season's shoots, other than those needed to form a structure, back to 1 in (2.5 cm) from the base annually in early spring.

Training Tie to wires or individual anchor points.

Propagation and nursery production From soft to semi-ripe cuttings up to 3 in (7.5 cm) long, taken in spring, preferably with a small portion of old wood attached. Root in a pot containing very sandy soil in a protected frame with bottom heat. May be grown from seed but not easy. Always purchase container grown; will have to be sought from specialist growers, florists and houseplant suppliers. Best planting height 6 in–2 ft (15–60 cm).

Problems Foliage may be attacked by insects such as red spider or whitefly. Roots often attacked by mealy bug. Proprietary controls should be used. Keep ventilation as open as possible, particularly in winter, but do not allow temperature to drop below 50°F (10°C).

Similar forms of interest *B. s.* 'Lady Wilson' Cerise flowers. *B. s. lateritia* Brick-red bracts. *B. s. lindleyana* 'Mrs Louise Wathen' (syn. *B. s. l.* 'Orange King') Cinnamon-coloured bracts. *B. s.* 'Mrs Butt' Bright rose bracts. All varieties are difficult to obtain outside very temperate areas.

Average height and spread
Five years
6 × 6 ft (1.8 × 1.8 m)
Ten years
12 × 12 ft (3.7 × 3.7 m)
Twenty years
24 × 24 ft (7.3 × 7.3 m)
Protrudes up to 3 ft (91 cm) from support.

BUDDLEIA ALTERNIFOLIA

FOUNTAIN BUDDLEIA, ALTERNATE-LEAF BUTTERFLY BUSH
Loganiaceae   *Wall Shrub*
Deciduous
A truly beautiful wall shrub, given enough space.

Origin From China.

Use As a large late summer to early autumn flowering, graceful, arching wall shrub. Wall use is particularly suitable for the variety *B. a.* 'Argentea'.

Description *Flower* Small bunches of very fragrant, lilac-coloured, small, trumpet-shaped flowers borne along graceful, arching branches in early summer. *Foliage* Leaves grey/green, lanceolate, 1½–4 in (4–10 cm) long, giving yellow autumn colour. *Stem* Grey-green to mid green, vigorous, long, upright, becoming arching. Fast growing. *Fruit* Brown to grey/brown seedheads in autumn and winter.

Hardiness Tolerates a minimum winter temperature of 4°F (−15°C).

Soil requirements Prefers good, rich, deep soil, although tolerates other soil types.

Sun/Shade aspect Tolerates all but the most severe of aspects. Best in full sun, tolerates slight dappled shade.

Pruning Thin out one third of growth after flowering on established shrubs.

Training Requires wires or individual anchor points to secure and encourage the fan-trained shape.

Propagation and nursery production From softwood cuttings in summer or hardwood cuttings in winter. Always purchase container grown; best planting height 15–36 in (39–91 cm). Available in garden centres and nurseries.

Problems When offered for sale it resembles an old, woody shrub. Once planted out, however, it grows quickly and often fills a larger space than anticipated.

Buddleia alternifolia **in flower**

Similar forms of interest *B. a.* 'Argentea' Slightly more tender and lower growing, with attractive silver foliage and slightly paler blue flowers. Not always easy to find but worth searching out for a sheltered site. Best protected by a sunny, sheltered wall.

Average height and spread
Five years
8 × 8 ft (2.4 × 2.4 m)
Ten years
12 × 12 ft (3.7 × 3.7 m)
Twenty years
15 × 15 ft (4.6 × 4.6 m)
Protrudes up to 6 ft (1.8 m) from support.

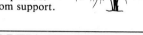

BUDDLEIA (Tender Forms)

KNOWN BY BOTANICAL NAME
Loganiaceae   *Wall Shrub*
Deciduous or evergreen
There are a number of varieties of buddleia that can only be grown in favourable areas with the protection of a wall or fence.

Origin Various.

Use As large fan-trained or freestanding shrubs for walls and fences.

Description *Flower* Racemes 3–12 in (7.5–30 cm) long in a range of colours through white, pink, blue and orange in mid summer to late autumn. *Foliage* Lanceolate, 4–8 in (10–20 cm) long, 1–3 in (2.5–7.5 cm) wide, light green or grey/green, often downy depending on variety. *Stem* Grey/green, often downy when young, becoming grey/brown. Upright. Fast rate of growth. *Fruit* Most forms produce small brown seedheads which have some limited winter attraction.

Hardiness Tolerates a minimum winter temperature of 14°F (−10°C) but only with the protection of a large wall or fence.

Soil requirements Tolerates a wide soil range, only disliking extremely dry conditions. Requires a high degree of organic material and plant nutrient for best results.

Sun/Shade aspect Very sheltered aspect. Full sun for preference but tolerates light shade.

Pruning Prune back all previous season's growth, other than that required for training the main framework, to within 2 in (5 cm) of its origin in early to mid spring.

Training Tie to wires or individual anchor points in a fan shape or allow to grow freestanding.

Propagation and nursery production From semi-ripe cuttings taken in early to mid summer or hardwood cuttings taken in winter. Always purchase container grown; most varieties will have to be sought from specialist nurseries. Best planting height 6 in–3 ft (15–91 cm).

Problems Often exceeds the allotted area. May suffer some winter die-back but normally regenerates.

Forms of interest *B. auriculata* Lax growth carries fragrant creamy white flowers with yellow throats in panicles up to 2 in (5 cm) across and 8 in (20 cm) long. Lanceolate foliage 4 in (10 cm) long, 1 in (2.5 cm) wide, white felted underside, grey/green upper side in late summer to late autumn. From South Africa. *B. caryopteridifolia* Leaves oval to lanceolate, tooth-edged, up to 6 in (15 cm) long, 1 in (2.5 cm) wide. Attractive grey/green. Stems covered with white woolly down. Fragrant lavender-blue flowers in panicles up to 3 in (7.5 cm) long in late spring/early summer. From China. *B. colvillei* Long racemes of deep rose, tubular flowers, borne at the ends of the branches. Foliage ovate, grey/green with some yellow autumn colour. Difficult to find and must be sought from specialist nurseries. *B. c.* 'Kewensis' An attractive form with dark red flowers. Difficult to find. *B. crispa* Fragrant, tubular lilac flowers, grey/green foliage. *B. fallowiana* 'Alba' Panicles of pure white flowers up to 15 in (38 cm) long in early to mid

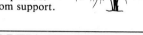
Buddleia fallowiana 'Alba' **in flower**

summer. Attractive grey/green foliage, 10 in (25 cm) long and up to 4 in (10 cm) wide. From China. *B. madagascariensis* Bold orange flowers, very prolific. Tender even in mild areas against walls but if circumstances suit, well worth the effort. *B. salvifolia* Semi-evergreen lanceolate foliage up to 4 in (10 cm) long and 2 in (5 cm) wide, grey/green. Panicles of white to pale lilac flowers with orange markings in each tubular floret in mid to late summer. From South Africa.

Average height and spread
Five years
6 × 6 ft (1.8 × 1.8 m)
Ten years
12 × 12 ft (3.7 × 3.7 m)
Twenty years
18 × 18 ft (5.5 × 5.5 m)
Protrudes up to 4 ft (1.2 m) from support if fan-trained, 8 ft (2.4 m) untrained.

BUPLEURUM FRUTICOSUM

KNOWN BY BOTANICAL NAME

Umbelliferae **Wall Shrub**
Evergreen

Distinctively coloured flowers on an evergreen shrub.

Origin From southern Europe.
Use As a medium sized, evergreen wall shrub for shady walls.
Description *Flower* Ball-shaped clusters of green/cream to yellow/green flowers from mid summer to early autumn. *Foliage* Elliptic, ½–2 in (1–5 cm) long, dark, glossy, grey/green with silver undersides. *Stem* Light green to dark olive-green, forming a rounded shrub, somewhat loose in habit. Medium to slow growth rate. *Fruit* Brown seedheads, interesting in winter.
Hardiness Established shrubs withstand winter temperatures down to 4°F (−15°C), but young plants are less hardy. Good in exposed coastal sites.
Soil requirements Any soil conditions.
Sun/Shade aspect All but the most exposed walls. Best in full sun. Tolerates light shade but becomes looser in habit in deep shade.
Pruning None required. May be trimmed or cut back to maintain shape.
Training Requires wires or individual anchor points to secure and encourage the fan-trained shape.

Bupleurum fruticosum in flower

Propagation and nursery production From seed or from softwood cuttings taken in summer. Best planting height 8–18 in (20–45 cm). Should always be purchased container grown.
Problems Not easy to find.
Similar forms of interest. None.
Average height and spread
Five years
3 × 3 ft (91 × 91 m)
Ten years
6 × 6 ft (1.8 × 1.8 m)
Twenty years
8 × 8 ft (2.4 × 2.4 m)
Protrudes up to 3 ft (91 cm) from support.

CALLISTEMON CITRINUS

AUSTRALIAN BOTTLE BRUSH

Myrtaceae **Wall Shrub**
Evergreen

If the right conditions can be offered, an extremely useful, attractive shrub.

Origin From Australia and Tasmania.
Use As a large, summer flowering wall shrub for mild districts. Ideal in large conservatories and greenhouses.

Callistemon citrinus in flower

Description *Flower* Tufted, brush-like spikes of red flowers, very dense in formation, mid to late summer. *Foliage* Narrow, lanceolate leaves, 1–1½ in (2.5–4 cm) long, light green, often with red/orange shading or pronounced coloured veins. They release an aromatic lemon scent when bruised. *Stem* Light green to grey/green, ageing to grey/brown. Upright when young, becoming more spreading with age. Medium rate of growth, slowing with age. *Fruit* May produce interesting, tufted, light brown seedheads.
Hardiness Tolerates a minimum winter temperature of 23°F (−5°C).
Soil requirements Good, rich, acid soil. Dislikes any alkalinity. If planted in a container in conservatories and greenhouses, the diameter of the container must be at least 21 in (55 cm) and a lime-free potting compost must be used.
Sun/Shade aspect Requires a very protected aspect in full sun. Does not tolerate any shade.
Pruning None required. Remove an old shoot occasionally to rejuvenate from the base.
Training Requires wires or individual anchor points to secure and encourage the fan-trained shape.
Propagation and nursery production From seed or softwood cuttings taken in late spring or early summer. Best planting height 15–30 in (38–76 cm). Purchase container grown. Not always easy to find.
Problems Not to be grown in alkaline soils or in locations with winter conditions well below freezing.

Similar forms of interest *C. c.* 'Splendens' More brilliant flowers. Slightly less height but possibly more hardy.
Average height and spread
Five years
6 × 6 ft (1.8 × 1.8 m)
Ten years
10 × 10 ft (3 × 3 m)
Twenty years
12 × 12 ft (3.7 × 3.7 m)
Protrudes up to 3 ft (91 cm) from support.

CAMELLIA JAPONICA

KNOWN BY BOTANICAL NAME

Theaceae **Wall Shrub**
Evergreen

Although not normally considered as a wall shrub, in the right conditions can become an extremely attractive fan-trained specimen.

Origin From China, Korea and Japan.
Use As a fan-trained shrub for shady, protected walls and fences. Can be used to good effect in a large conservatory as a wall specimen.
Description *Flower* Large, cup-shaped flowers in a wide range of colours, may be single, semi-double, anemone or peony-shaped, loose double or tight double, depending on variety. Size ranges from small to very large. *Foliage* Dark, glossy-green upper surfaces, with grey/green undersides. Ovate to oblong, 3–4 in (7.5–10 cm) long and 1½ in (4 cm) wide. *Stem* Bright to dark green. Upright. Forming a stiff, solid shrub that can be fan-trained. A few varieties are more laxly presented. Slow to medium rate of growth. *Fruit* Insignificant.
Hardiness Tolerates a minimum winter temperature of 14°F (−10°C), but may shed leaves in harsh conditions, occasionally causing plant to fail.
Soil requirements Must have an acid soil: dislikes any alkalinity. If in a conservatory or greenhouse a container of not less than 21 (55 cm) must be used, with a lime-free compost.
Sun/Shade aspect A sheltered sunless aspect. Prefers light to mid shade, dislikes full sun.
Pruning None required. May be cut back to keep within bounds. Young plants may be improved by removing one third of previous season's growth, after flowering, for first 2–3 years.
Training Requires wires or individual anchor points to secure and encourage the fan-trained shape.

Camellia japonica 'Adolphe Audusson' in flower

Propagation and nursery production From cuttings in early to mid summer. Best planting height 1½–6 ft (45 cm–1.8 m), ideally 2–2½ ft (60–76 cm). Purchase container grown. A limited number of varieties can be found in garden centres, less common varieties must be sought from specialist nurseries.

Problems Often planted on alkaline soils, where it fails, or in full sun, which it dislikes. Flowers can be damaged by frost in exposed areas.

Similar forms of interest *C. j.* 'Cornish Snow' Single, small white flowers, a very attractive small-leaved variety. *C. j.* 'Adolphe Audusson' Semi-double, blood-red flowers. *C. j.* 'Apollo' Semi-double rose-red flowers, sometimes with white blotches. *C. j.* 'Arejishi' Rose-red, peony-shaped flowers. *C. j.* 'Betty Sheffield Supreme' Semi-double, white, peony-shaped flowers with rose pink or red edges to each petal. *C. j.* 'Contessa Lavinia Maggi' Double white or pale pink flowers

Camellia japonica 'Elegans'

with cerise stripes. *C. j.* 'Elegans' Peach pink, large flowers. Anemone flower formation. *C. j.* 'Madame Victor de Bisschop' Semi-double, white flowers. *C. j.* 'Mars' Red, semi-double flowers. *C. j.* 'Mathotiana Alba' Double white flowers of great beauty. *C. j.* 'Mathotiana Rosea' A double pink form. *C. j.* 'Mercury' Deep crimson flowers, semi-double in form. *C. j.* 'Nagasaki' Semi-double, rose pink flowers with white stripes. *C. j.* 'Tricolor' Semi-double white flowers with carmine or pink stripe. *C.* × 'Mary Christian' Single, clear pink flowers. Tall growing. *C.* × *williamsii* 'Donation' Clear pink, semi-double flowers. Possibly the best known camellia. Height 8 ft (2.5 m).

The above are just a selected few of the many hundreds of varieties available.

Average height and spread
Five years
3 × 3 ft (91 × 91 cm)
Ten years
6 × 6 ft (1.8 × 1.8 m)
Twenty years
10 × 10 ft (3 × 3 m)
Protrudes up to 3 ft (91 cm) from support.

CAMPSIS GRANDIFLORA
(C. chinesis, Bignonia grandiflora, Tecoma grandiflora)

TRUMPET CREEPER

Bignoniaceae   *Woody Climber*
Deciduous

A spectacular flowering climber but requiring considerable space and a warm wall location for maximum flower production.

Origin From Eastern Asia, China and Japan.
Use As a large rambling climbing vine for sunny locations on walls and fences. Also good for covering large pergolas, gazebos etc. and for climbing large, high-canopied trees where adequate sunshine is available.

Campsis grandiflora **in flower**

Description *Flower* Panicles of six to 12 deep orange/red, wide mouthed, trumpet-shaped flowers up to 3 in (7.5 cm) long. The mouth of each flower is attractively divided into five segments, resembling five lips. Late summer/early autumn. *Foliage* Seven to nine light green oval leaflets up to 3 in (7.5 cm) long with coarse-toothed edges make up a pinnate shaped leaf. Good yellow autumn colour. *Stem* Light green when young, becoming yellow/brown, finally brown, twining, not self-clinging. Fast rate of growth. *Fruit* None of interest.

Hardiness Tolerates a minimum winter temperature of 14°F (−10°C).

Soil requirements Moderately alkaline to acid. Requires a deep, well fed, well drained soil with a high organic content for best results.

Sun/Shade aspect Sheltered aspect. Must be in full sun to ripen previous season's growth and encourage production of subsequent flowers.

Pruning Long, unwanted shoots produced in late spring and summer can be cut hard back after leaf fall in autumn, except those which are required for further training for the vine shape.

Training Tie to wires or trellis on walls and fences. When grown up trees, will require some early support by tying in.

Propagation and nursery production By use

of root cuttings, removal of self-rooted suckers, hardwood cuttings taken in winter and seed collected following a hot summer. Best size to purchase 18 in–4 ft (45 cm–1.2 m). Should always be container grown. Will have to be sought from good general nurseries or specialist growers.

Problems Not quick to cover a required area. Can be shy to come into flower and may require several years before it produces any type of good display. Late to break leaf in spring – often as late as the end of early summer – especially in the year following planting.

Forms of interest See further entry.

Average height and spread
Five years
8 × 8 ft (2.4 × 2.4 m)
Ten years
16 × 16 ft (5 × 5 m)
Twenty years
32 × 32 ft (9.7 × 9.7 m)
Protrudes up to 3 ft (91 cm) from support.

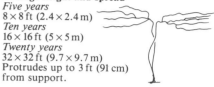

CAMPSIS RADICANS

TRUMPET CREEPER

Bignoniaceae   *Woody Climber*
Deciduous

This group of campis can be more relied upon to flower than *C. grandiflora* but still may take some time to settle and become established.

Origin From south-eastern USA and of garden origin.
Use For sunny walls and fences, for covering large pergolas, gazebos or other similar structures and for climbing large, high-canopied trees where adequate sunshine is available.
Description *Flowers* Four to twelve trumpet-shaped flowers 2–3 in (5–7.5 cm) long and up to 1½ in (4 cm) wide at the mouth presented in clusters at the ends of shoots in late summer to early autumn. The mouth of the flower has an interesting five-lobed effect, giving a lip-like appearance. Orange/red in colour, some red and yellow varieties. *Foliage* Up to 11 almost oval leaflets up to 4 in (10 cm) long with toothed edges form pinnate leaves 8–12 in (20–30 cm) long, light to mid green in colour. Good yellow autumn colour. *Stem*

Campsis × *tagliabuana* 'Madam Gallen' **in flower**

Campsis radicans in flower

Light grey/green when young ageing to creamy brown. Twining with retaining tendrils at leaf joints. Fast rate of growth. *Fruit* None of interest.
Hardiness Tolerates a minimum winter temperature of 4°F (−15°C).
Soil requirements Moderately alkaline to acid; requires a deep, well fed, well drained soil with a high organic content for best results.
Sun/Shade aspect Must be in full sun to ripen previous season's growth and encourage production of subsequent flowers.
Pruning Long, unwanted shoots produced in late spring and summer can be cut hard back after leaf fall in autumn except those that are required for further training.
Training Support with trellis, individual anchor points or wires; there is a certain amount of self-clinging by tendrils, but the weight of branches normally calls for secondary securing.
Propagation and nursery production By use of root cuttings, removal of self-rooted suckers, hardwood cuttings taken in winter or seed collected following a hot summer. Best size to purchase 1½–4 ft (45 cm–1.2 m). Should always be purchased container grown. Available from good garden centres, nurseries and specialist growers.
Problems Can be slow to come into flower and sometimes late to break leaf in spring, often as late as early summer. Often planted in areas where it is unable to fulfil its full potential because of lack of space or an unsuitable aspect.
Similar forms of interest *C. r.* 'Flava' A variety with all yellow flowers. *C. r.* 'Atropurpurea' Deep scarlet flowers; not readily available. *C. r.* 'Yellow Trumpet' Good bold yellow flowers. *C. × tagliabuana* 'Madam Gallen' A good free flowering variety with large salmon red flowers and good foliage.
Average height and spread
Five years
10 × 10 ft (3 × 3 m)
Ten years
20 × 20 ft (6 × 6 m)
Twenty years
30 × 30 ft (9 × 9 m)
Protrudes up to 3 ft (91 cm) from support.

CARAGANA ARBORESCENS 'LORBERGII'

SALT TREE
Leguminosae　　　　　　　　**Hardy Tree**
Deciduous
The attractive feathery foliage is shown off well when fan-trained.

Origin From Siberia and Manchuria.
Use As a small fan-trained tree or shrub for large walls.
Description *Flower* Small, yellow, pea-shaped ¼ in (5 mm) long flowers borne in clusters of up to four on thin stalks, mid to late spring. *Foliage* Very thin, wispy, feathery, light grey/green leaves up to 2 in (5 cm) long. Yellow autumn colour. *Stem* Grey/green with

attractive pronounced buds on branches. Moderately fast growing, slowing with age. *Fruit* Small pods, 1½–2 in (4–5 cm) long, containing four to six seeds, produced in autumn.
Hardiness Tolerates a minimum winter temperature of 0°F (−18°C).
Soil requirements Any soil conditions; tolerates high alkalinity.
Sun/Shade aspect Tolerates all aspects; very wind resistant. Best in full sun, but tolerates light shade.
Pruning Prune young bush trees hard in spring following planting. Select and train resulting five to seven shoots and tie into a fan-trained shape. In subsequent years, remove all side growths back to 2 in (5 cm) from their origin after flowering and maintain main branches in fan shape.
Training Requires tying to wires or individual anchor points.
Propagation and nursery production From grafting on to understock of *C. arborescens*. Ensure that purchased plants are bush and grafted or budded at ground level. Plant bare-rooted, root-balled (balled-and-burlapped) or container grown; best planting height 3 ft (91 cm).

Caragana arborescens 'Lorbergii' in flower

Problems May be late to break leaf in spring and can appear to be dead, but grows quickly once established.
Similar forms of interest None.
Average height and spread
Five years
6 × 6 ft (1.8 × 1.8 m)
Ten years
13 × 13 ft (4 × 4 m)
Twenty years
18 × 18 ft (5.5 × 5.5 m)
Protrudes up to 3 ft (91 cm) from support.

CARPENTERIA CALIFORNICA

KNOWN BY BOTANICAL NAME
Philadelphiaceae　　　　　　*Wall Shrub*
Evergreen
A magnificent flowering shrub, well worth the trouble of finding a favourable wall planting site.

Origin From California.
Use As an evergreen, summer-flowering shrub for mild areas. Ideal for fan-training on a sunny wall, particularly in mild regions.
Description *Flower* 2–3 in (5–7.5 cm) wide, pure white, saucer-shaped flowers with yellow anthers, borne in mid summer on mature wood. *Foliage* Leaves light to bright green, broad, lanceolate, 2–4 in (5–10 cm) long. *Stem* Light to dark green, upright at first, slightly spreading with age, forming a good fan-shape with training. Medium rate of growth. *Fruit* Small brown seedheads give limited winter attraction.
Hardiness Reacts badly to temperatures below 23°F (−5°C) but normally rejuvenates from ground level.
Soil requirements Deep, rich soil. Tolerates both acidity and alkalinity.
Sun/Shade aspect A sheltered aspect in full sun.
Pruning Remove one third of oldest wood each spring to maintain health. May be cut back hard and will rejuvenate, but can take up to two years to flower again.
Training Requires wires or individual anchor points to secure and encourage the fan-trained shape.
Propagation and nursery production From seed or from softwood cuttings taken in mid to late summer. Best planting height 8–24 in (20–60 cm). Purchase container grown. May be difficult to find and should be sought from specialist nurseries.
Problems When young the shrub appears weak, but it develops well after planting.
Similar forms of interest *C. c.* 'Ladham's Variety' Said to be more free-flowering than the parent, with larger flowers. Difficult to find.
Average height and spread
Five years
5 × 5 ft (1.5 × 1.5 m)
Ten years
7 × 7 ft (2.1 × 2.1 m)
Twenty years
9 × 9 ft (2.7 × 2.7 m)
Protrudes up to 4 ft (1.2 m) from support.

Carpenteria californica in flower

Catalpa bignonioides in flower

CATALPA BIGNONIOIDES

INDIAN BEAN TREE, SOUTHERN CATALPA

Bignoniaceae   *Hardy Tree*
Deciduous

An attractive, large-leaved tree that can be adapted for fan-training against a wall, where it can gain some additional protection.

Origin From south-eastern USA.
Use As a large, fan-trained tree for walls.
Description *Flower* Upright panicles 8–10 in (20–25 cm) long of white, bell-shaped flowers with frilled edges, yellow markings and purple spotted throats, produced mid summer. *Foliage* Broadly ovate leaves, 6–10 in (15–25 cm) long and 3–8 in (7.5–20 cm) wide, presented on long stalks. Good yellow autumn colour. Foliage smells unpleasant

Catalpa bignonioides 'Aurea' in leaf

when crushed. *Stem* Light grey/green, becoming green/brown. Strong and upright. Pruning increases branching. Medium to fast growth rate, becoming slower and more spreading after the first five years. *Fruit* Long, narrow, green, ageing to black, slender pods, 8–15 in (20–38 cm) long, produced in early autumn and retained into early winter.
Hardiness Tolerates a minimum winter temperature of 4°F (−15°C), but stem damage can be caused by winter frosts, especially in the golden-leaved varieties; however, this may in fact be an advantage in encouraging the plant to branch.

Soil requirements Requires a deep, rich soil to do well. Shows signs of chlorosis on extremely thin alkaline soils.
Sun/Shade aspect Requires a moderately sheltered aspect. Golden-leaved varieties scorch in full sun.
Pruning Prune young trees hard in spring following planting. Select and train resulting five to seven shoots and tie into a fan-trained shape. In subsequent years, remove all side growths back to two points from their origin and maintain main branches in fan shape.
Training Will require tying to wires or individual anchor points.
Propagation and nursery production From seed or layers for green-leaved varieties. Purple and golden-leaved varieties normally grafted onto understock of *C. bignonioides* or layered. Purchase bare-rooted or container grown; best planting height 3–6 ft (91 cm–1.8 m). Select only young trees that have not formed any main branches. For *C. b.* 'Aurea', buy trees that have been grafted or budded at ground level.
Problems Flowering may be decreased by fan-training but leaves will increase in size, particularly on golden-leaved varieties. May be damaged by high winds or heavy snow; consider location when planting. Young trees rarely look attractive, especially while in nursery production.
Similar forms of interest *C. b.* 'Aurea' Attractive, broad, large, golden-yellow leaves. A less hardy form, even slightly tender. One-third average height and spread, but may reach more in ideal conditions. *C. b.* 'Variegata' Attractive large-leaved foliage, grey/green leaves margined with gold. Limited in commercial production but not impossible to find. *C.* × *hybrida* 'Purpurea'

Catalpa × hybrida 'Purpurea' in leaf

New growth purple to purple/green, ageing to dark green. White flowers. Two-thirds average height and spread. From central USA.
Average height and spread
Five years
16 × 16 ft (4.9 × 4.9 m)
Ten years
30 × 30 ft (9 × 9 m)
Twenty years
39 × 39 ft (12 × 12 m)
Protrudes up to 5 ft (1.5 m) from support.

CEANOTHUS
(Evergreen Forms)

CALIFORNIA LILAC

Rhamnaceae   *Wall Shrub*
Evergreen

If grown in a mild area or protected from winter winds and cold, can give a very spectacular effect in spring and summer when grown as a fan-trained wall shrub.

Origin From southern states of the USA. Many varieties of garden origin.
Use As a fan-trained wall shrub for walls and fences.
Description *Flower* Various shades of blue flowers, some tufted, borne in panicles or umbels in mid to late spring, some varieties early or late summer and even autumn. *Foliage* Leaves mostly ovate, ½–1½ in (1–4 cm) long, light to dark green, in a few varieties broad to narrow lanceolate. All with shiny upper surfaces and dull grey undersides. In some varieties leaves have pronounced tooth edge, others convex, inturned shapes. *Stem* Light green to grey/green. Upright when young, becoming very twiggy. Medium rate of growth. *Fruit* Insignificant.

Ceanothus arboreus 'Trewithen Blue' in flower

Hardiness Tolerates a minimum winter temperature of 14°F (−10°C). Foliage very susceptible to scorch by cold winter winds.
Soil requirements Good, deep, rich soil. Tolerates both acidity and mild alkalinity. Thin chalk or limestone soils will induce severe chlorosis.
Sun/Shade aspect Requires a sheltered aspect; prefers full sun, tolerates light to medium shade.
Pruning Prune shoots by one third on 3–4 year old shrubs, annually after flowering. This will encourage new growth. Treat severe winter damage by cutting back into non-damaged wood.
Training Requires wires or individual anchor points to secure and encourage the fan-trained shape.
Propagation and nursery production From semi-ripe cuttings taken in mid summer. Always purchase container grown. Garden centres and nurseries generally stock a representative range of varieties; specific varieties may be sought from specialist nurseries.

Problems Leaves liable to scorching by cold winds. Will not attain full height and spread in unsuitable areas and likely to experience chlorosis on unsuitable soils.
Forms of interest *C. americanus* (New Jersey Tea) Panicles of white flowers in early to mid summer; dark green ovate leaves. A slightly tender variety reaching two thirds average height and spread. From eastern and central USA. *C. arboreus* (Tree Ceanothus) Deep, vivid blue flowers in panicles borne in spring. Large, ovate, dark green leaves. Slightly more tender than the average and attains one third more height and spread. *C. a.* **'Trewithen Blue'** Flowers slightly scented and deeper blue than *C. arboreus*. *C.* **'A. T. Johnson'** Mid to pale blue panicles of flowers, late spring, some early autumn flowering. A light green, large-leaved variety. Very vigorous in habit, in some situations exceeding average height and spread. *C.* **'Autumnal Blue'** Good-sized panicles of dark blue flowers, late summer and autumn. One of the hardiest varieties. *C.* **'Blue Cushion'** Very deep blue flowers, spreading but close-growing. *C.* **'Burkwoodii'** Rich blue flowers borne mainly late spring and early summer, with good displays intermittently until autumn. Slightly more tender and slightly less height and spread than the average. *C.* **'Cascade'** Powder blue

Ceanothus **'Cascade'** in flower

flowers in open panicles in spring. Foliage light green and more lanceolate than normal. Branches more lax and open, forming attractive, almost pendulous habit. *C.* **'Concha'** Bright blue summer flowers. Scarce. *C.* **'Delight'** Deep blue flowers, produced in panicles 3–4 in (7.5–10 cm) long in mid to late spring. Leaves broad, lanceolate and green. Said to be one of the hardiest varieties. *C. dentatus* (Santa Barbara Ceanothus) Bright blue flowers in late spring, small, tooth-edged dark green leaves. *C.* **'Dignity'** Dark blue flower panicles and dark green foliage. Normally flowers in spring, sometimes intermittently in autumn. *C. divergens* Deep blue flowers, spreading habit. *C.* **'Edinburgh'** (syn. *C.* **'Edinensis'**) Mid blue panicles of flowers in spring. Broad, olive-green leaves. Less than average hardiness. *C.* **'Emily Brown'** Fluffy violet/blue flowers in early summer. Low-growing. May be more tender. *C.* **'Floribundus'** Large clusters of mid blue flowers in late spring. *C.* **'Hurricane Point'** Cornflower-blue flowers late spring/early summer. Good foliage. Low growing. *C. impressus* Deep blue flowers, small, but borne in great profusion. Distinctive foliage effect, with small, curled, dark green leaves, veins being very deeply impressed within the surface. New shoots red to purple/red in colour. One of the hardiest of the ceanothus varieties. *C. i.* **'Puget Blue'** Deeper blue flowers and larger foliage. Possibly less hardy

Ceanothus dentatus in flower

than its parent. *C.* **'Indigo'** Indigo blue flowers in early summer. *C.* **'Italian Skies'** Mid to soft sky-blue panicles of flowers, borne in trusses on branching stems in spring. Medium-sized, round to ovate light green leaves. Less hardy than average. *C.* **'Joyce Coulter'** Deep blue flowers. May be scarce; obtain from specialist nursery. *C.* **'Julia Phelps'** Deep cobalt-blue flowers and deep green leaves. *C.* × *lobbianus* **'Russellianus'** Bright blue flowers, freely borne in mid to late spring. Less hardy than average. *C. pappillosus roweanus* Dark blue flowers in late spring; sticky leaves. Tender. *C. prostratus* (Squaw Carpet) Bright blue flowers borne freely in spring on this creeping, spreading plant with small, dark green to light green, broad to lanceolate leaves. *C.* **'Ray Hartman'** Large deep blue flowers in mid spring to late summer. Hardy. *C. rigidus* Very dark blue flowers in small, short tufted panicles profusely borne mid to late spring. Interesting foliage, very dark olive green, small and crinkled. Hard to find. *C.* **'Snow Flurries'** Snow-white flowers. Less hardy than average. *C.* **'Southmead'** Sky blue flowers in late spring and early summer. A very dense-growing shrub, with light green, broad, lanceolate leaves. Slightly less hardy than average. *C. thyrsiflorus* An abundance of medium-sized, well-spaced, mid blue flower panicles in spring and early summer. Dark green leaves. One of the hardiest varieties. *C. t.* **'Blue Mound'** Covered in short panicles of deep blue flowers, late spring and early summer. Dark green leaves. *C. t.* **'Repens'** (Creeping Blue Blossom) Rich blue flowers in abun-

Ceanothus **'Topaz'** in flower

dance in mid spring. Good-sized, dark green, tooth-edged foliage. *C. t. repens* **'Gnome'** Light blue flowers in spring, deep green leaves. Low habit. *C.* **'Topaz'** Large, well-spaced panicles of indigo blue flowers, mid to late summer. Large, round or ovate, mid green leaves. In cold climates should be considered semi-evergreen or even deciduous. *C.* × *veitchianus* Deep blue flowers, late spring and early summer. Medium-sized, dark green, broadly lanceolate leaves. Taller than average varieties and said to be one of the hardiest. *C.* **'Yankee Point'** Panicles of light blue flowers in mid spring. Light to mid green, medium-sized, narrow, ovate leaves. Compact habit.
Average height and spread
Five years
8 × 8 ft (2.5 × 2.5 m)
Ten years
12 × 12 ft (3.5 × 3.5 m)
Twenty years
18 × 18 ft (5.5 × 5.5 m)
Protrudes up to 5 ft (1.5 m) from support.

CEANOTHUS (Deciduous Forms)

CALIFORNIA LILAC
Rhamnaceae   Wall Shrub
Deciduous
A very attractive range of late summer/early autumn shrubs, ideal for fan-training on walls.

Origin From California but many varieties of garden origin.
Use As a fan-trained wall shrub for walls and fences.
Description *Flower* Flowers in panicles up to 3–4 in (7.5–10 cm) long, various shades of blue, pink or white, in late summer and in some varieties held into early autumn. *Foliage* Leaves medium to large, ovate, 3–5 in (7.5–12 cm) long, tooth-edged, light green to olive-green, some varieties having pink to pink/red leaf stalks. Some yellow autumn colour. *Stem* Upright, strong new growth produced each spring with flowers borne at the tips. Light to mid-green, ageing to dark brown in autumn. Fast to medium rate of growth.
Hardiness Tolerates a minimum winter temperature of 14°F (−10°C).
Soil requirements Good, rich, deep soil, tolerates poorer types if given adequate feeding but liable to chlorosis when severe alkalinity is present.
Sun/Shade aspect Tolerates all but the most exposed of aspects. Best in full sun to very light shade.

Pruning Prune back hard in spring all previous season's growth to 4 in (10 cm) from point of origin except shoots needed to form a fan shape.
Training Requires wires or individual anchor points to secure and encourage the fan-trained shape.
Propagation and nursery production From softwood cuttings in summer or by hardwood cuttings in late autumn to early winter. Best planting height 15 in–3 ft (38–91 cm). Purchase container grown. Most varieties easy to find, especially at flowering time.
Problems If insufficiently pruned becomes weak and performs insipidly. Shoots can occasionally be broken by strong winds.
Forms of interest *C.* 'Gloire de Versailles' A popular variety with large panicles of well-spaced, powder blue flowers, mid to late summer. *C.* 'Henri Defosse' Beautiful large panicles of deepest blue to purple/blue flowers, late summer. Dark green, medium

Ceanothus 'Gloire de Versailles' in flower

sized, elliptic leaves. *C.* 'Marie Simon' Pale pink flowers borne in good-sized panicles, mid to late summer. Mid green oblong leaves with purple/red main veins and leaf stalks. Possibly more tender than average. *C.* 'Perle Rose' Flowers carmine, borne in good-sized panicles, mid to late summer. Foliage smaller than average and with red to purple/red veins. May suffer die-back in winter. May be slower to establish than other varieties.
Average height and spread
Five years
5 × 5 ft (1.5 × 1.5 m)
Ten years
6 × 6 ft (1.8 × 1.8 m)
Twenty years
8 × 8 ft (2.4 × 2.4 m)
Protrudes up to 5 ft (1.5 m) from support.

Ceanothus 'Marie Simon' in flower

CELASTRUS ORBICULATUS

STAFF VINE, CLIMBING BITTERSWEET
Celastraceae　　　　　*Woody Climber*
Deciduous
A large vigorous vine requiring careful space location to produce best fruiting results.

Origin From North East Asia.
Use For growing over large buildings such as garages and sheds, through large established trees and shrubs or over large constructions such as pergolas.
Description *Flower* Small green flowers carried in clusters of up to four in early summer, of little interest. Flowers may be of single sex. *Foliage* Oval, up to 5 in (12 cm) long, with points; carried on short stalks up to 1 in (2.5 cm) long; light to mid green, very good yellow autumn colouring. *Stem* Twisting, twining, not self-clinging; light grey/green when young becoming light creamy brown with age. Some limited winter attraction in good light. Very fast growing. *Fruit* The main attraction. Capsules, bright yellow in colour when ripe, open to reveal a scarlet-coated seed within. Carried in large numbers on mature climbers. The hermaphrodite-flowered form is self fertile and bears fruit without a pollinator; otherwise male and female plants will be necessary.
Hardiness Tolerates a minimum winter temperature of 4°F (−15°C.)

Celastrus orbiculatus in fruit

Soil requirements Does well on all soil types, both alkaline and acid, with no particular preference except for adequate root run.
Sun/Shade aspect Full sun to medium shade with no particular preference.
Pruning Not normally considered practical as it covers an extremely large area but can be reduced in size if required after fruiting.
Training Leave to ramble through whatever type of construction or tree it is to cover. Self supporting by twining effect but not self-clinging.
Propagation and nursery production From seed collected in autumn and sown directly or layer lower shoots. Best planting height 18 in–4 ft (45 cm–1.2 m). Purchase container grown; available from good garden centres and general nurseries.
Problems Its overall size is often underestimated and it must be allowed to achieve this size to produce good displays of fruit. Some all male forms may exist when propagated from seed, but most plants produced in commercial horticulture are of the hermaphrodite form so the problem of also finding space for a female plant normally does not arise.
Similar forms of interest None.
Average height and spread
Five years
10 × 10 ft (3 × 3 m)
Ten years
20 × 20 ft (6 × 6 m)
Twenty years
30 × 30 ft (9 × 9 cm)
Protrudes up to 4 ft (1.2 m) from support.

CERCIS SILIQUASTRUM

JUDAS TREE
Leguminosae　　　　　*Wall Shrub*
Deciduous
A very attractive fan-trained large shrub, although it requires time to reach any true stature.

Origin From southern Europe through to the Orient.
Use As a fan-trained or freestanding large shrub for walls.
Description *Flower* Numerous purple/rose pea-shaped flowers ½–1 in (1–2.5 cm) long, borne as leaves are produced, on both young and old branches in late spring, early summer. *Foliage* Deeply veined, broad, heart-shaped leaves, purple/green with a blue sheen. Good yellow autumn colours. *Stem* Dark brown to almost black stems. Very twiggy and branching. Good growth from base. Forms a large fan-trained shrub. Moderately slow growing. *Fruit* Pods, 3–4 in (7.5–10 cm) long, light grey/green, follow the flowers, ageing to grey/brown in autumn and retained in winter.
Hardiness Tolerates a minimum winter temperature of 4°F (−15°C).
Soil requirements Does best on neutral to acid soil types, but will tolerate moderate alkalinity.
Sun/Shade aspect Tolerates a moderately exposed aspect. Full sun to medium shade, with light shade for preference.
Pruning Cut young plants hard back in mid spring in second year of planting, which will induce strong shoots. Select five to seven to form a fan-trained shrub. Continue to tie in these shoots through their life. Any large protruding branches can be removed in winter.
Training Will require tying to wires or individual anchor points for fan-training, or allow to grow freestanding.
Propagation and nursery production From seed or layers. Purchase container grown or root-balled (balled-and-burlapped). Some of the latter are grown in peat soil and may require careful weaning to become accustomed to normal soil. Plant young plants from 18 in (45 cm) to 4 ft (1.2 m) tall; established or trained trees are rarely available and not recommended.

Cercis siliquastrum in flower

Problems This shrub takes a number of years to reach any significant size. Some forms are very scarce in production and are difficult to find.

Similar forms of interest *C. canadensis* (Redbud) Large leaves and clusters of pale rose pink flowers in early summer. Less hardy than average. From central and eastern USA; limited in production outside its native environment. *C. c.* **'Forest Pansy'** Heart-shaped deep purple leaves maintained throughout summer, turning bright scarlet in autumn. Flowers inconspicuous. Two thirds average height and spread. Only obtainable from specialist nurseries. *C. chinensis* Flowers purple/pink. Slightly more than average height and spread. From China. Seldom seen in production. *C. occidentalis* Rose-coloured flowers on short stalks. Two thirds average height and spread. From California. Rarely found outside its native environment. *C. racemosa* Flowers red/pink, produced in racemes 4 in (10 cm) long in late spring. Less hardy. From China. Somewhat scarce in production. *C. siliquastrum* **'Alba'** A pure white-flowering form from Europe and the Orient. A plant that is very scarce in commercial production in Europe but is more readily available in North America.

Average height and spread
Five years
5 × 5 ft (1.5 × 1.5 m)
Ten years
10 × 10 ft (3 × 3 m)
Twenty years
20 × 20 ft (6 × 6 m)
Eventually reaches 39 ft (12 m) but extremely slowly, taking 50 years or more in most northerly locations. Protrudes up to 4 ft (1.2 m) from support if fan-trained, 12 ft (3.5 m) untrained.

CESTRUM ELEGANS
(C. purpureum)

KNOWN BY BOTANICAL NAME

Solanaceae   *Tender Wall Shrub*
Evergreen
A tender shrub for mild areas and benefiting from the protection of a wall.

Origin From Mexico.
Use As a wall shrub in mild areas or for conservatories and greenhouses in large containers or in a border.
Description *Flower* Pendent panicles, up to 8 in (20 cm) long and 4 in (10 cm) wide at base, red/purple to pink, each floret up to 1 in (2.5 cm) long and ¾ in (2 cm) wide, with pointed lobes at the ends. Flowers throughout summer. *Foliage* Lanceolate to oblong, up to 5 in (12 cm) long with a downy covering. Grey/green. *Stem* Grey/green, upright becoming arching at ends with weight of flowers. Medium growth rate. *Fruit* Rarely fruits, but if it does will produce globe-shaped, red/purple berries, ½ in (1 cm) wide.
Hardiness Tolerates a minimum winter temperature of 12°F (−5°C) in very sheltered locations. Dislikes wind chill conditions.
Soil requirements If grown in containers, use a good quality potting compost. If grown in the soil provide a well drained, average garden soil, either alkaline or acid.
Sun/Shade aspect Requires a very sheltered aspect or the protection of a greenhouse or conservatory. Full sun to very light shade.
Pruning None, but individual limbs can be removed if required.
Training Freestanding. May need tying to anchor points for support with age.

Cestrum elegans in flower

Propagation and nursery production From cuttings taken from side shoots up to 3 in (7.5 cm) long in mid summer. Will require bottom heat of 65–70°F (18–21°C) to encourage rooting. Always purchase container grown, will have to be sought from specialist nurseries. Best planting height 6 in–2 ft (15–60 cm) tall.
Problems Often not winter hardy. Difficult to find.
Similar forms of interest *C. roseum* Attractive rose/pink flowers.
Average height and spread
Five years
3 × 3 ft (91 × 91 cm)
Ten years
5 × 5 ft (1.5 × 1.5 m)
Twenty years
7 × 7 ft (2.1 × 2.1 m)
Protrudes up to 5 ft (1.5 m) from support.

CHAENOMELES

ORNAMENTAL QUINCE, JAPANESE FLOWERING QUINCE, JAPONICA

Rosaceae   *Wall Shrub*
Deciduous
A fine flowering shrub, very attractive when pruned correctly as a fan-trained wall shrub.

Origin From China, most varieties being of garden origin.
Use As a fan-trained shrub for walls and fences.
Description *Flower* Single flowers shaped and sized like apple blossom borne in profusion on wood two years old or more, early to mid spring. Colours range through white, pink, apricot, flame, orange and red, depending on variety. *Foliage* Leaves elliptic, medium-sized, 3–4 in (7.5–10 cm) long, light to dark green. Some yellow autumn colour. *Stem* Upright when young and light green/brown, becoming dark brown, more twiggy and producing isolated large rigid thorns. Medium rate of growth. *Fruit* Large, pear-shaped fruits follow the flowers, ripening to an attractive bright yellow.
Hardiness Tolerates a minimum winter temperature of 0°F (−18°C)

Chaenomeles speciosa **'Moerloosii'** in fruit

Soil requirements Does well on any soil but liable to chlorosis in very alkaline areas.
Sun/Shade aspect Tolerates all aspects. Does well in full sun to deep shade.
Pruning Apart from growth required for fan shape, remove all previous season's growth back to two buds in spring before flowering, making sure that flowering buds are not removed.
Training Requires wires or individual anchor points to secure and encourage the fan-trained shape.
Propagation and nursery production From semi-ripe cuttings taken in mid summer. Best planting height 15–30 in (38–76 cm). Always purchase container grown. Wide range of forms generally available, or obtain from specialist nurseries.
Problems Intermittently produces very sharp thorns. May suffer fungus disease such as canker; prune out affected wood.
Forms of interest *C. japonica* Orange/red flowers. *C. j.* **'Alpina'** Orange/red flowers borne freely, late spring. A little shy to fruit due to its less vigorous habit. *C. j.* **'Issai Red'** Small red flowers in abundance. *C. j.* **'Issai White'** Many small white flowers. *C. speciosa* **'Atrococcinea'** Large, deep crimson flowers. *C. s.* **'Brilliant'** Large brilliant red to clear scarlet flowers. *C. s.* **'Cardinalis'** Crimson-scarlet flowers. *C. s.* **'Geisha Girl'** Very attractive deep apricot flowers. Later flowering. *C. s.* **'Moerloosii'** (Apple Blossom) Pink and white flowers, more sparsely produced than some forms. *C. s.* **'Nivalis'** A pure white-

Chaenomeles speciosa 'Moerloosii' in flower

flowered variety, green/white on first opening. Fewer flowers than average, but growth more vigorous. *C. s.* **'Rosea Plena'** Double rich rose-pink flowers. *C. s.* **'Simonii'** Deep blood red flowers freely produced. Low growing. *C. s.* **'Snow'** Snow-white flowers. A good variety. *C. s.* **'Umbilicata'** Deep pink flowers, larger than most. *C. s.* **'Eximia'** Upright deep brick-red flowers. *C. s.* **'Verbooms Vermillion'** Upright growing, bright red flowers. *C. × superba* **'Aurora'** Peach/pink flowers, unusual. *C. × sup.* **'Ballerina'** Large deep red flowers. *C. × sup.* **'Boule de Feu'** Vermillion flowers, strong-growing. Good yellow fruit. *C. × sup.* **'Choshan'** Semi-double, peach/apricot flowers; low-growing. Easy to find. *C. × sup.* **'Coral Sea'** Coral-pink good sized flowers and good fruits. *C. × sup.* **'Crimson and Gold'** Bright red flowers with pronounced golden anthers. Good fruit production. *C. × sup.* **'Elly Mossel'** Large, bright scarlet flowers, good fruit. *C. × sup.* **'Ernest Finken'** Upright brilliant red flowers. *C. × sup.* **'Etna'** Rich vermillion flowers, good colour. *C. × sup.* **'Fascination'** Vivid orange flowers. *C. × sup.* **'Fire Dance'** Rich, orange/scarlet flowers, good fruit. *C. × sup.* **'Hever Castle'** Shrimp pink flowers. *C. × sup.* **'Knap Hill Scarlet'** Smaller, brilliant orange/scarlet flowers, freely borne. Height slightly less than average. *C. × sup.* **'Hollandia'** An excellent scarlet/red flowering variety with good fruits. *C. × sup.* **'Nicoline'** Large red flowers, average height but with more spread. *C. × sup.* **'Pink Lady'** Good deep pink flowers and good fruits. *C. × sup.* **'Port Elliot'** Large red flowers, good growth.

Chaenomeles speciosa 'Simonii' in flower

Chaenomeles × superba 'Crimson and Gold' in flower

C. × sup **'Ohld'** Large red flowers of good stature. *C. × sup.* **'Rowallane'** Brilliant crimson flowers and small fruits. *C. × sup.* **'Taxus Scarlet'** Scarlet red flowers. *C. × sup.* **'Vermillion'** Vermillion red flowers. *C. × sup.* **'Vesuvius'** Scarlet red flowers.

There are many varieties of *C. speciosa* and *C. × superba*. Those listed are a good representative selection.

Average height and spread
Five years
7 × 7 ft (2.1 × 2.1 m)
Ten years
12 × 12 ft (3.7 × 3.7 m)
Twenty years
14 × 14 ft (4.3 × 4.3 m)
Protrudes 3–4 ft (91 cm–1.2 m) from support.

CHIMONANTHUS PRAECOX (*C. fragrans*)

FRAGRANT WINTERSWEET
Calycanthaceae   *Wall Shrub*
Deciduous
An interesting scented flowering shrub for winter display.

Origin From China.
Use As a freestanding wall shrub or for fan-training on sunny walls.
Description *Flower* Lemon yellow, waxy, hanging, bell-shaped flowers with purple anthers, frost-hardy, borne in late winter on mature branches three to four years old. *Foliage* Leaves light green to yellow green, medium-sized, elliptic, 3–7 in (7.5–18 cm) long, some yellow autumn colour. *Stem* Light green, strong, upright when young, ageing into brittle, twiggy branches. Medium growth rate, slowing with age. *Fruit* Insignificant.

Hardiness Tolerates a minimum winter temperature of 4°F (−15°C) but expect some die-back on growth produced in late autumn.
Soil requirements Does well on most soils, especially alkaline.
Sun/Shade aspect All but the most severe aspects. Full sun ripens the wood best for flowering. Tolerates light shade.
Pruning Normally not required.
Training Requires wires or individual anchor points to secure and encourage the fan-trained shape or can be allowed to grow freestanding.
Propagation and nursery production From semi-ripe cuttings taken in mid summer. Best planting height 15–30 in (38–76 cm). Purchase container grown from specialist nurseries.
Problems Can be slow to flower, especially in years when wood is slow to ripen. Looks unattractive in a container but grows rapidly once planted out.

Chimonanthus praecox in flower

Similar forms of interest *C. p.* **'Grandiflora'** Deeper yellow flowers with an interesting red stain in the throat. More difficult to find. *C. p.* **'Luteus'** Clear bright yellow flowers with even more waxy texture, more open than in the parent. Not easy to find but worth pursuing.
Average height and spread
Five years
6 × 6 ft (1.8 × 1.8 m)
Ten years
8 × 8 ft (2.4 × 2.4 m)
Twenty years
10 × 10 ft (3 × 3 m)
Protrudes up to 4 ft (1.2 m) from support if fan-trained, 10 ft (3 m) untrained.

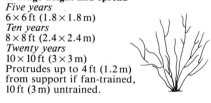

CHOISYA TERNATA

MEXICAN ORANGE BLOSSOM
Rutaceae   *Wall Shrub*
Evergreen
A very attractive, scented, late spring to early summer flowering shrub.

Origin From Mexico.
Use As an evergreen shrub for summer flowering, but with training can become an interesting wall shrub.
Description *Flower* Fragrant, single, ½ in (1 cm) wide, white, orange-scented flowers, borne in flat-topped clusters, late spring to early summer. *Foliage* Leaves glossy, mid to dark green, trifoliate, 3–6 in (7.5–15 cm) long, which when crushed give off an aromatic scent. *Stem* Light to bright green, glossy, upright, becoming spreading and twiggy with age, forming a fan-shaped shrub. Fast to medium rate of growth when young or pruned back, slowing with age. *Fruit* Insignificant.
Hardiness Tolerates a minimum winter temperature of 14°F (−10°C). Leaf damage

can occur in lower temperatures or in severe wind chill. In some winters, may die back to ground level but can normally rejuvenate itself the following spring.

Soil requirements Does well on most, although very severe alkaline soils may lead to chlorosis.

Sun/Shade aspect Tolerates all but the most exposed aspects. Equally good in full sun or deep shade.

Pruning Two methods of pruning are advocated; cut back to within 12 in (30 cm) of ground level after three to four years so it can rejuvenate itself and repeat process every third or fourth year following. This keeps the foliage glossy and encourages flowering. Otherwise, on mature shrubs, remove one third of the oldest wood to ground level after flowering to encourage rejuvenation from centre and base and repeat annually.

Training Requires wires or individual anchor

Choisya ternata in flower

points to secure and encourage the fan-trained shape.

Propagation and nursery production From softwood cuttings taken in summer. Best planting height 1–2 ft (30–60 cm). Purchase container grown. Available from most garden centres and nurseries.

Problems If pruning is neglected, plant becomes old, woody and unproductive. Plants are always relatively small when purchased but quickly mature when planted out.

Similar forms of interest *C. t.* 'Sundance' Yellow/green foliage in spring, quickly becoming golden yellow which persists through winter. Slightly more tender. Two thirds average height and spread. Requires very light shade.

Average height and spread

Five years
5 × 5 ft (1.5 × 1.5 m)
Ten years
6 × 6 ft (1.8 × 1.8 m)
Twenty years
7 × 7 ft (2.1 × 2.1 m)
Protrudes up to 3 ft (91 cm) from support.

CISTUS

ROCK ROSE

Cistaceae   *Wall Shrub*
Evergreen

A tender shrub worth experimenting with for the beauty it can give in its summer display of flowers when fan-trained on a wall.

Origin From Southern Europe and North Africa.

Use As a fan-trained shrub for walls and fences.

Description *Flower* Single, 1½–2½ in (4–6 cm) wide, flat flowers, lasting only for one day but followed by new buds opening in rapid succession, early to late summer. White or white with brown or purple spots, through shades of pink to dark purple-pink. *Foliage* Leaves ovate or lanceolate, medium sized,

Cistus × *purpureus* in flower

1–2 in (2.5–5 cm) long. Light green or grey, glossy surfaced in green-leaved forms, grey-leaved having a grey down or bloom. Leaf buds and new growth are often sticky. *Stem* Light green or grey/green. Some forms grow upright, others are of spreading habit. Medium growth rate.

Hardiness Tolerates a minimum winter temperature of 23°F (−5°C).

Soil requirements Does well on all soil types, tolerating quite high alkalinity.

Sun/Shade aspect Requires a sheltered aspect. Best in full sun for free flowering.

Pruning Remove one third of oldest growth to ground level after flowering on plants established more than three years, or cut the plants hard back in spring to within 4 in (10 cm) from ground level every three to four years.

Training Requires wires or individual anchor points to secure and encourage the fan-trained shape.

Propagation and nursery production From softwood cuttings taken early to mid summer. Purchase container grown. A wide range of forms normally obtainable in mild areas, otherwise must be sought from specialist sources. Best planting height 8–30 in (20–76 cm).

Problems Container grown plants often look leggy and unsightly but are the best choice because the wood is harder. Plants looking soft and fleshy at purchase have been grown under glass and are less reliable, but for early to mid summer planting shrubs of any age are suitable.

Forms of interest *C.* × *aguilari* Large white flowers throughout early and mid summer. Grey/green foliage. *C.* × *a.* 'Maculatus' Large, flat flowers with a central ring of crimson blotches on each of the five petals. Dark green, glossy foliage 2–4 in (5–10 cm) long. Upright. *C. algarvensis* Yellow flowers

Cistus aguilari in flower

with brown central discs. Grey upright foliage. Tender. *C.* 'Anne Palmer' Pink flowers, dark green crinkled foliage. Attractive. *C.* 'Barnsley Pink' Pale pink flowers, green foliage. Dense habit. Spreading in nature. *C.* × *corbariensis* Small, 1 in (2.5 cm) wide, pure white flowers, opening from crimson-tinted buds. Small, light green to grey/green leaves. Hardier than most. *C.* × *cyprius* Large white flower with crimson blotches on each of the five petals. Shiny green foliage, 4–6 in (10–15 cm) long. Upright and tall-growing. Said to be one of the hardiest. *C.* × *c.* 'Albiflora' Pure white flowers, otherwise similar to parent plant. *C.* 'Greyswood Pink' A profusion of pink flowers. Downy grey to grey/green foliage. *C. ladanifer* (Gum Cistus) White flowers up to 4 in (10 cm) in width with chocolate stains at base of each crimped petal. Leaves narrow, lanceolate, 3–4 in (7.5–10 cm) long, bright to mid green with glossy surface. Strong-growing. *C. l.* 'Albiflorus' A pure white form of the above. *C. laurifolius* Flat, white flower with yellow marking in centre. Very leathery, dark blue/green leaves, 4–5 in (10–12 cm) long. A hardier variety. *C.* × *lusitanicus* Large, white flowers with crimson basal blotches, green leaves. Height and spread 12–24 in (30–60 cm). *C.* × *l.* 'Decumbens' Covered in small, white flowers, again with crimson basal blotches. *C.* 'Peggy Sannons' Flowers a soft shade of pink contrasting well with grey/green foliage with a downy texture, which is repeated on the upright stems. *C. populifolius* White flowers with yellow staining at the base of each petal. Rounded, poplar-shaped, hairy leaves produced on an erect, upright shrub. One of the hardiest. *C.* × *pulverulentus* (syn. *C. albidus* × *crispus*, *C.* 'Warley Rose') Cerise flowers, foliage sage green and waxy-textured. A low spreading shrub. *C.* × *purpureus* Flowers rosy crimson, each with a chocolate basal blotch. Narrow, green to grey/green foliage on strong, upright stems. *C. salvifolius* White flowers with a yellow basal stain to each petal, sage green leaves forming a foil. Height 12–24 in (30–60 cm); spread 24 in (60 cm). *C.* 'Silver Pink' Silver-pink flowers borne on long clusters, very attractive grey foliage. *C.* × *skanbergii* Clear pink flowers and small grey leaves make this one of the most attractive forms. *C.* 'Sunset' Deep cerise-pink flowers, grey foliage. Upright. *C.* 'Alan Fradd' White flowers with purple blotches. Good grower.

Average height and spread

Five years
3 × 3 ft (91 × 91 cm)
Ten years
4 × 4 ft (1.2 × 1.2 m)
Twenty years
5 × 5 ft (1.5 × 1.5 m)
Protrudes 1½–2 ft (45–60 cm) from support.

CLEMATIS ALPINA

ALPINE CLEMATIS, COLUMBINE
Ranunculaceae   *Woody Climber*
Deciduous
With its good range of colours and delicate flowers, this group of clematis enhances any spring garden.

Origin From northern Europe, northern Asia and of garden origin.
Use For walls, fences, pillars, trellis and pergolas and to ramble through large shrubs. Can be used as a ground cover with or without support.

Clematis alpina in flower

Description *Flower* Pendent, nodding flowers in shades from violet blue to purple, pink and white, carried singly on stalks up to 4 in (10 cm) long. No petals but four coloured sepals up to 1½ in (4 cm) long. Some double-flowered varieties. Produced from early to late spring with spasmodic later flowering in early summer, but not reliable. *Foliage* Leaves comprise nine leaflets, each ovate to lanceolate, up to 2 in (5 cm) long, forming a total length of 6 in (15 cm) with a width of 3 in (7.5 cm). Light green with yellow/brown autumn colour. *Stem* Twining, leaf stalks acting as supporting tendrils. Light green, ageing to grey/brown. Medium growth rate. *Fruit* Attractive, silky white seedheads up to 1½ in (4 cm) long produced after flowering and maintained well into summer/early autumn.

Clematis alpina 'Ruby' in flower

Clematis alpina 'White Moth' in flower

Hardiness Tolerates a minimum winter temperature of 0°F (−18°C).
Soil requirements Does well on all soil types with no particular preference, but must have adequate moisture throughout the year to induce good growth.
Sun/Shade aspect Tolerates all but the most exposed aspects. Requires its roots to be shaded and prefers its growth in the sun, but will tolerate very light shade.
Pruning Cut all current season's growth to within 6–12 in (15–30 cm) of its origin after main flowering period to produce new flowering growth for next spring throughout the summer; alternatively, lightly trim and tidy after flowering. The latter method will suffice for one to five years, but the plant will become old and woody and will need hard cutting back every five to six years.
Training Requires wires or a trellis on walls and fences. Allow to ramble freely through shrubs and trees.
Propagation and nursery production From semi-ripe internodule cuttings taken late spring/early summer. Always purchase container grown, best planting height 1½–3 ft (45–91 cm). Most varieties readily available from good garden centres and specialist nurseries, although some may need searching for.
Problems If not pruned correctly can become very woody and poor in growth and flowers.

Similar forms of interest *C. a.* 'Co[...]' Pale blue flowers. One third mor[...] average height and spread. *C. a.* 'Fr[...] Rivis'* Mid blue flowers with white centres to [...] lantern-shaped flowers, which are larger tha[n] other varieties. *C. a.* 'Pamela Jackson'* Mid blue, attractive, lantern-shaped flowers. *C. a.* 'Ruby'* Purple/pink flowers with white centres. Generally reliable second late summer flowering. *C. a.* 'Siberica'* (syn. *C. a.* 'Alba'*) White flowers, flushed pink/mauve at base. Good flowering performance. Scarce. *C. a.* 'White Moth'* Pure white, double, nodding flowers. Most attractive.
Average height and spread
Five years
8 × 8 ft (2.4 × 2.4 m)
Ten years
8 × 8 ft (2.4 × 2.4 m)
Twenty years
8 × 8 ft (2.4 × 2.4 m)
Protrudes up to 2 ft (60 cm) from support.

CLEMATIS ARMANDII

EVERGREEN CLEMATIS
Ranunculaceae   *Woody Climber*
Evergreen to semi-evergreen
Given enough space, this evergreen climber produces an abundant display of pure white flowers in mid to late spring.

Origin From China.
Use As a climber for large walls or fences, to cover pergolas and roofs on small buildings. Can be allowed to grow through large shrubs or small trees.
Description *Flower* Saucer-shaped flowers up to 2 in (5 cm) wide, produced profusely in clusters at the leaf joints on wood two years old or more. Four to six narrow, oblong sepals, each ½ in (1 cm) wide, normally pure white, with some pale pink varieties, in mid to late spring. *Foliage* Trifoliate leaves with ovate to lanceolate leaflets, each 3–5 in (7.5–12 cm) long. Dark, glossy green with blue/silver undersides and prominent veins. Normally evergreen, but in severe winters may become semi-evergreen. *Stem* Light green, ageing to dark green. Limited branching; gains height very quickly and is reluctant to produce lower shoots. Twining, leaf tendrils giving some additional support. Medium to fast rate of growth. *Fruit* May produce small white fluffy seedheads.
Hardiness Requires a minimum winter

Clematis armandii in flower

°F (−15°C), although may be
...ere wind chill at this temper-

s Does well on all soil types,
...lkaline and acid conditions,
...moisture-retentive yet well

Sun/Shade aspect Requires a sheltered aspect
with protection from severe cold winds.
Needs stem, leaves and flowers in full sun with
roots in the shade.
Pruning Normally requires no pruning, but
old shoots can occasionally be reduced to
encourage rejuvenation.
Training Tie to wires or trellis, or allow to
ramble along the top of a wall or through
large shrubs and small trees.
Propagation and nursery production From
semi-ripe cuttings or by grafting; the former
method is difficult. Always purchase
container grown; will have to be sought from
specialist nurseries and named varieties may
be very scarce in production and sometimes
difficult to find. Best planting height 9 in–3 ft
(23 cm–91 cm).
Problems Foliage may be completely
defoliated by severe, cold winds. Size and
production of flower may vary according to
individual plants. Named varieties extremely
scarce.
Similar forms of interest. *C. a.* **'Apple
Blossom'** Flowers suffused with pale mother-
of-pearl pink. *C. a.* **'Everest'** A good, strong-
growing variety with pure white flowers. *C. a.*
'Snowdrift' Profusely borne snow-white
flowers.
Average height and spread
Five years
10 × 10 ft (3 × 3 m)
Ten years
20 × 20 ft (6 × 6 m)
Twenty years
25 × 25 ft (7.6 × 7.6 m)
Protrudes up to 2 ft (60 cm)
from support.

CLEMATIS CAMPANIFLORA

CAMPANULA FLOWERING CLEMATIS
Ranunculaceae   ***Woody Climber***
Deciduous
A clematis with charming growth and
foliage, bearing flowers which are among
the most delicate found in the genus.

Origin From Portugal.
Use To ramble through wall shrubs and other
climbers.

Clematis campaniflora **in flower**

Clematis cirrhosa balearica **in flower**

Description *Flower* Small, nodding, bell-
shaped flowers with wide open mouths,
carried singly on stalks up to 3 in (7.5 cm)
long. White with delicate violet/blue-tinged
sepals. Flowering from mid to late summer.
Foliage Pinnate, with five to nine divisions to
each of the three ovate to lanceolate leaflets.
Each leaflet up to 3 in (7.5 cm) long. Very wide
range of leaf shapes produced on a single
plant. Clinging leaf tendrils. *Stem* Wispy,
ranging, of thin constitution. Moderate rate
of growth. *Fruit* No fruit of interest.
Hardiness Tolerates a minimum winter temperature of 14°F (−10°C).
Soil requirements Tolerates a wide range of
soil types, only requiring adequate moisture
and food retention.
Sun/Shade aspect Requires a sheltered
aspect. Prefers light shade but will tolerate
full sun as long as roots are shaded.
Pruning Requires only a light trim in early
spring.
Training Allow to ramble through wall shrubs
or other climbers or through a framework of
wires. Rarely needs tying as is self-clinging by
leaf tendrils.
Propagation and nursery production From
semi-ripe internodal cuttings taken early to
mid summer. Always purchase container
grown, best planting height 6 in–3 ft
(15–91 cm). Will have to be sought from
specialist nurseries.
Problems Not a strong grower, although not
delicate in constitution. Can be difficult to
arrange and often grows into positions not
intended, although not invasive.
Similar forms of interest. None.
Average height and spread
Five years
6 × 6 ft (1.8 × 1.8 m)
Ten years
12 × 12 ft (3.7 × 3.7 m)
Twenty years
18 × 18 ft (5.5 × 5.5 m)
Protrudes up to 2 ft (60 cm)
from support.

CLEMATIS CIRRHOSA
(*C. calycina*)

WINTER-FLOWERING EVERGREEN CLEMATIS
Ranunculaceae   ***Woody Climber***
Evergreen
With both attractively shaped evergreen
foliage and winter flowers, this clematis is
rightly gaining recognition as a good
garden plant.

Origin From southern Europe.
Use For walls, fences, pillars, or to ramble

through large shrubs. Can be used as a
ground cover with or without support.
Description *Flower* Up to 1 in (2.5 cm) wide,
pendent, cup-shaped flowers, produced singly
at leaf joints on stalks up to 1 in (2.5 cm) long.
Yellow/white with red spots. Produced from
early to late winter, whenever the weather is
mild. *Foliage* Up to 3 in (7.5 cm) long and
wide. Five individual leaflets, deeply lobed or
toothed along the edges, giving a fern-like
appearance. Bright green in spring, turning
purple/bronze in winter. Shiny, evergreen
surface. *Stem* Very twining, forming an
interlocking mat. Light green when young,
turning brown/grey. Medium rate of growth.
Fruit May produce small, feathery seedheads
after flowering, but they are of no real merit.
Hardiness Tolerates a minimum winter
temperature of 14°F (−10°C).
Soil requirements Tolerates both acid and
alkaline, but requires adequate moisture
content to induce good growth.
Sun/Shade aspect Sheltered aspect for best
winter flowering results. Resents strong,
frost-laden winds, which cause foliage and
flower damage. Requires its roots shaded and
prefers its growth in light shade, although will
tolerate full sun.
Pruning Trim the plants lightly after flowering
each year for up to five years. Every fifth year
prune hard back into the main structure to
encourage a new head of growth. This may
slightly reduce the flowering effect in the
winter following such pruning, but it
generally has the effect of encouraging better
growth throughout.
Training Requires wire or trellis on walls or
fences, or can be allowed to ramble through
medium to large shrubs.
Propagation and nursery production From
semi-ripe internodal cuttings taken late
spring/early summer. Always purchase
container grown; best planting height 1–3 ft
(30–91 cm). May have to be sought from
specialist nurseries, but not normally hard to
find from such sources.
Problems Always crowns out on the top of a
wall or shrub; rarely produces any low stem
growth.
Similar forms of interest *C. c. balearica*
(Fern-leaved clematis) Possibly slightly more
tender. Pale yellow flowers with brown
specks. Foliage slightly more cut. *C. c.*
'Wisley' Lighter green foliage, otherwise
identical to its parent.
Average height and spread
Five years
6 × 6 ft (1.8 × 1.8 m)
Ten years
8 × 8 ft (2.5 × 2.5 m)
Twenty years
12 × 12 ft (3.7 × 3.7 m)
Protrudes up to 3 ft (91 cm)
from support.

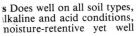

CLEMATIS
(Double and Semi-Double)

DOUBLE CLEMATIS

Ranunculaceae   *Woody Climber*
Deciduous

Attractive clematis with semi-double or double flowers in a wide range of colours, adding an extra dimension to this beautiful garden plant.

Origin Of garden or nursery origin.
Use As climbers for fences, walls, pillars, to ramble through medium-sized shrubs or over brushwood or pea-sticks. Can be used in large tubs and containers.
Description *Flower* Numerous sepals in a wide range of colours and flowering times, depending on variety, make up either semi-double or double flowers. Some varieties produce double flowers for the first crop and later flowering may well be single. *Foliage* Sometimes single ovate leaves, sometimes three to five lanceolate to ovate leaflets, each up to 4 in (10 cm) long, make up a single pinnate leaf. Mid green to grey/green. Tendril-type leaf stalks aid support. *Stem* Light green when young, ageing to green/brown and finally brown. Twining, with additional support from leaf tendrils. Medium to fast growth rate. *Fruit* Some varieties may produce white, tufted seedheads of some winter attraction.
Hardiness Tolerates a minimum temperature of 4°F (−15°C).
Soil requirements Tolerates all soil conditions except for extremely alkaline, but will produce average results even in the latter given a moisture-retentive soil with adequate organic material. For best results a higher degree of organic compost is advised than the normal planting recommendations for climbers and wall shrubs. When grown in tubs and containers use a soil-based potting compost, allow for adequate drainage and choose a container not less than 21 in (53 cm) wide and 18 in (45 cm) deep.
Sun/Shade aspect Tolerates all aspects, except extremely exposed. Full sun to light shade with full sun for preference. Roots should be shaded.
Pruning There are three different pruning methods, each particular to an individual variety. These are as follows:
1 Simply tidy and thin end shoots back to main framework after flowering.
2 Reduce by one third the growth made in the previous season in late winter, early spring.
3 Prune to within 12 in (30 cm) all growth produced in previous year during late winter, early spring.

It is important that the recommended pruning methods are carried out on an annual

Clematis **'Vyvyan Pennell'** in flower

basis, otherwise flowering will decrease and the overall well-being of the plant will suffer. The pruning method for each variety is given in 'Forms of Interest'. If the variety is not known use Method 2 as a safe option.
Training Allow to ramble through wires, trellis, branches of large shrubs or trees or any other support where the leaf tendrils can wrap around to anchor.
Propagation and nursery production From internodal cuttings taken in early to late summer, inserted into a sand/peat mixture, with some bottom heat to encourage rooting. Best planting height 6 in–3 ft (15–91 cm). Clematis is often available in a choice of 3–4 in (7.5–10 cm) or 1 litre (5–7 in/12–18 cm) pots; both sizes are equally good as long as the plants have been well hardened off and are not purchased before mid spring. Plant from mid spring through until late summer. Plants propagated in the spring are ripe enough for planting from mid autumn through until mid spring; these are normally offered in 3–4 in (7.5–10 cm) or 1 litre (5–7 in/12–18 cm) pots. Many varieties are standards and will be readily available, others will need searching for from specialist nurseries.
Problems Clematis wilt is an airborne fungus disease for which there is no prevention. The entire plant, both leaves and stem, turns black in early to late summer. Once an attack is seen, cut all growth to ground level, wash walls, fences or trellis with a mild disinfectant and protect any other plants growing below with plastic sheeting. There is then a 60 per

cent chance that new, uninfected shoots will develop from below ground level from the root system. Replanting with a new clematis in the same position is not a risk, but the area should be washed with mild disinfectant first.

The main reason for the failure of clematis plants is that they are often placed too close to the wall (see 'Planting Climbers and Wall Shrubs on p.168) and that not enough organic material such as garden compost, well rotted farmyard manure or mushroom compost is added to the soil. They will also fail to thrive if the roots are subject to direct summer sunshine. Blackfly can also be a problem and should be treated with a proprietary control. Where certain varieties are grown in association with other climbers such as roses pruning can be difficult and this should be taken into account before planting.
Forms of interest *C.* **'Beauty of Worcester'** Double, rich, deep mauve/blue flowers with bold creamy-white anthers from early to mid summer, followed by single flowers from late summer to early autumn. Two thirds average height and spread. Tolerates all but the most shady of aspects. Pruning Code 2. Readily available. *C.* **'Countess of Lovelace'** Large, violet-blue, rosette-shaped flowers, double in early summer, becoming single in late summer. Central white stamens. Tolerates all aspects. No pruning required. Readily available. *C.* **'Glynderek'** Double, deep blue flowers with central dark stamens late spring or early summer, late summer and early autumn flowers becoming single. Tolerates all but the most shady of aspects. No pruning required. Will have to be sought from specialist nurseries. *C.* **'Jackmanii Alba'** First flowering large, off-white, double in early summer, second flowering single with pronounced brown anthers from late summer to early autumn. Reaches one third more than average height and spread. Tolerates all aspects. Pruning Code 2. Normally readily available. *C.* **'Jackmanii Rubra'** Double crimson flowers carried on old wood in early summer, with attractive central creamy anthers. Late summer flowers become single. Pruning Code 2 or 3, although the latter will deter some of the double flowers. Will have to be sought from specialist nurseries. *C.* **'Jim Hollis'** Early spring flowers double, lavender-blue, followed in mid to late summer by single lavender-blue flowers. Tolerates all but the most shady of aspects. Pruning Code 2. Will have to be sought from specialist nurseries. *C.* **'Kathleen Dunford'** Large, rich rosy-purple flowers. Semi-double. Late spring to early summer, becoming single in late summer/ early autumn. Does not always flower continuously. Pruning Code 2. Will have to be sought from specialist nurseries. *C.* **'Louise Rowe'** Pale mauve flowers with golden stamens, single, semi-double and

Clematis **'Beauty of Worcester'** in flower

double all at the same time from early to mid summer. Late summer and early autumn flowers are all single. Tolerates all but the most shady of aspects. No pruning required. Will have to be sought from specialist nurseries. *C.* **'Lady Caroline Nevill'** Mauve flowers, large, semi-double, early to mid summer, becoming single in late summer. Tolerates all but the most shady of aspects. Pruning Code 2. Normally readily available. *C.* **'Mrs George Jackman'** Large creamy-white flowers with beige anthers. Semi-double in early spring to early summer, single in late summer and early autumn. Tolerates all but the most shady of aspects. No pruning required. Will have to be sought from specialist nurseries. *C.* **'Mrs Spencer Castle'** Good, medium-sized double flowers, heliotrope pink with golden stamens, in late spring, early summer, becoming single in late summer and early autumn. Tolerates all aspects. No pruning required. Will have to be sought from specialist nurseries. *C.* **'Proteus'** Mauve-pink double flowers, large, with green anthers, in late spring, early summer, becoming single in late summer. Dislikes deep shade. Pruning Code 2. Will have to be sought from specialist nurseries. *C.* **'Sylvia Denny'** Medium-sized, semi-double pure white flowers with pink anthers from late spring to early summer, becoming single in late summer. Good, tight growth habit. Tolerates all but the most shady of aspects. Pruning Code 2. Will have to be sought from specialist nurseries. *C.* × **'Vyvyan Pennell'** Large, truly double flowers, deep violet-blue with tinges of red, in late spring early summer. Late summer flowers single lavender-blue. Tolerates all but the most shady of aspects. Pruning Code 2. Readily available. *C.* **'Walter Pennell'** Deep pink flowers with mauve tinge, large, double, in late spring early summer; single flowers in late summer and early autumn. Tolerates all aspects. Readily available.

Average height and spread
Five years
5 × 5 ft (1.5 × 1.5 m)
Ten years
7 × 7 ft (2.1 × 2.1 m)
Twenty years
9 × 9 ft (2.7 × 2.7 m)
Protrudes up to 18 in (45 cm) from support.

CLEMATIS × DURANDII

KNOWN BY BOTANICAL NAME

Ranunculaceae   *Perennial Climber*
Deciduous

An interesting cross between the perennial clematis *C. integrifolia* and the woody clematis *C.* × *jackmanii*.

Origin Of garden origin.
Use As a climber for walls and fences and to ramble through large shrubs, up poles and pillars, or as ground cover, with or without supports.
Description *Flower* Four to six oval dark-blue/violet sepals with yellow stamens from early summer to mid autumn. Flowers up to 4½ in (11 cm) across. *Foliage* Attractive dark green, oval and pointed leaves, up to 6 in (15 cm) long. *Stem* Light grey/green, angled, predominantly upright but lax in habit without support. *Fruit* No fruit of any interest.
Hardiness Tolerates a minimum winter temperature of up to 4°F (−15°C), lower if given adequate root protection.
Soil requirements Tolerates a wide range of soil conditions as long as adequate organic material and plant nutrients are available. Dislikes waterlogging or very dry conditions.
Sun/Shade aspect Tolerates a wide range of aspects but not the most exposed. Full sun to medium shade with light shade for preference.
Pruning If any growth has survived the winter cut it back to ground level in early spring.
Training Tie to wires or individual anchor

points or allow to ramble through netting or large shrubs.
Propagation and nursery production From semi-ripe cuttings taken in early summer. Should always be purchased container grown; may have to be sought from specialist nursery. Best size to purchase; root-clumps to 2½ ft (76 cm).
Problems Suffers from attacks of its own specific mildew which is difficult to control but responds to perseverance.
Similar forms of interest None.
Average height and spread
One year
8 × 8 ft (2.4 × 2.4 m)
Protrudes up to 2 ft (60 cm) from support.

CLEMATIS × ERIOSTEMON (C. 'Hendersonii', C. intermedia)

KNOWN BY BOTANICAL NAME

Ranunculaceae   *Perennial Climber*
Deciduous

Although a perennial, in a good growing year it can reach a height of 6–10 ft (1.8–3 m), therefore it is worthy of consideration.

Origin Of garden origin.
Use As an attractive climber for small areas on walls and fences or to ramble through small to medium shrubs or other climbing plants.
Description *Flower* Deep blue, up to 1¼ in (3.5 cm) long, fragrant, nodding flowers carried on stalks up to 4 in (10 cm) long, giving a most attractive and delicate display in mid summer to early autumn. *Foliage* Single or pinnate leaves, each leaf oval and up to 2 in (5 cm) long, sparsely produced. Mid green with a slightly purple hue. *Stem* Wispy, ranging, forming no solid structure. Medium annual growth rate. *Fruit* Attractive small silver tufted seedheads in late summer/early autumn.
Hardiness Dies to ground level, therefore tolerates a minimum winter temperature of 4°F (−15°C), as long as roots are protected by a layer of organic material.
Soil requirements Tolerates all soils, except extremely waterlogged, but requires moisture retention and good organic material.
Sun/Shade aspect Requires a sheltered aspect. Best in light shade, although will tolerate full sun as long as roots are shaded.
Pruning Dies to ground level in winter and

therefore pruning is not required, but if shoots should be sustained over winter it is advisable to cut these hard back in spring.
Training Allow to ramble through trees or over wires. Very open in habit and therefore difficult to train.
Propagation and nursery production From internodal cuttings taken in early summer. Should always be purchased container grown; will have to be sought from specialist nurseries. Best planting height 6 in–3 ft (15–91 cm).
Problems None.
Similar forms of interest None.
Average height and spread
Five years
6 × 6 ft (1.8 × 1.8 m)
Ten years
6 × 6 ft (1.8 × 1.8 m)
Twenty years
6 × 6 ft (1.8 × 1.8 m)
Protrudes up to 2 ft (60 cm) from support.

Clematis × *eriostemon* **in flower**

CLEMATIS FLAMMULA

FRAGRANT VIRGIN'S BOWER

Ranunculaceae   *Woody Climber*
Deciduous

A charming, late summer/early autumn flowering clematis worthy of wider planting for its delicate foliage and flowers.

Origin From southern Europe.
Use As a late summer/early autumn flowering climber for walls, fences, archways and pillars. Can be allowed to grow through large shrubs and small trees to good effect.

Clematis × *durandii* **in flower**

Description *Flower* Very fragrant, up to 1 in (2.5 cm) wide, in large, loose bunches, each bunch up to 12 in (30 cm) long. Pure white in colour, varieties with red/purple markings, produced mid summer to mid autumn. *Foliage* Leaves bright green when young, becoming more grey/green with age; up to 1½ in (4 cm) long, composed of three to five lanceolate to almost round leaflets. Some bronze then yellow autumn colour. *Stem* Grey/green, ageing to grey/brown, finally grey. Graceful, twining, leaf tendrils assisting support. Fast rate of growth. *Fruit* Small, white, tufted seedheads follow flowers, providing interest for a limited time.

Hardiness Tolerates a minimum winter temperature of 4°F (−15°C).

Soil requirements Tolerates all soil types, as long as they are moisture-retentive.

Sun/Shade aspect Requires a sheltered aspect. Best in full sun, but will tolerate very light shade; roots must be in the shade.

Pruning Can either be left unpruned to attain more size and reduced every five years by very hard cutting back, or can be trimmed in early spring.

Training Will require wires or trellis or individual anchor points to train over any given area.

Propagation and nursery production From semi-ripe, internodal cuttings taken in early summer or from seed. Always purchase container grown; best planting height 1–2½ ft (30–76 cm). Normally available from good garden centres and specialist nurseries.

Problems May seem a little weak when purchased and often takes two or three years to gain any real stature.

Clematis flammula **in flower**

Clematis fargesii souliei **in flower**

Clematis flammula **'Rubra' in flower**

Similar forms of interest *C. f.* **'Rubra'** (syn. *C. × triternata* **'Rubromarginata'**) White flowers tipped with red to violet. Fragrant and extremely attractive but less vigorous. More difficult to find. *C. apiifolia* Small white flowers in abundance from mid to late summer. One third additional height and spread. Tolerates all areas but possibly best in a wild garden. *C. fargesii souliei* Medium-sized white flowers, strong-growing and free-flowering. Tolerates all aspects. *C. paniculata* (syn. *C. maximowicziana)* Large numbers of very small, white, scented flowers from late summer to early autumn. Prefers a sheltered, sunny aspect.

Average height and spread
Five years
5 × 5 ft (1.5 × 1.5 m)
Ten years
10 × 10 ft (3 × 3 m)
Twenty years
15 × 15 ft (4.6 × 4.6 m)
Protrudes up to 18 in (45 cm) from support.

CLEMATIS FLORIDA 'BICOLOR' (*C. f.* 'Sieboldii')

PASSION FLOWER CLEMATIS

Ranunculaceae   *Woody Climber*
Deciduous to semi-evergreen

A most beautiful and interesting flower, but a plant often of a weak, insipid constitution which necessitates some pampering.

Origin From China.

Use To ramble through wires, medium sized shrubs or other climbers and wall shrubs. It benefits from being grown under the protection of a conservatory or greenhouse.

Description *Flower* Up to 3 in (7.5 cm) wide with two leaf bracts in the centre and four to six oval sepals surrounding. Creamy-white with a green stripe and purple stamens. Carried singly on stalks up to 4 in (10 cm) from May to June. *Foliage* Leaves consisting of three segments of oval to lanceolate shape up to 2 in (5 cm) long, with toothed or lobed edges and downy undersides. Light green. Attractive, but sparsely produced. *Stem* Light green, ageing to green/brown, finally grey/brown. Ranging, wispy, of normally weak constitution. Medium growth rate. *Fruit* No fruit of any interest.

Hardiness Tolerates a minimum winter temperature of 14°F (−10°C).

Soil requirements Tolerates all but the most alkaline of soils, but does need a moisture retentive soil with additional organic material incorporated to encourage root growth. Suffers in drought conditions.

Sun/Shade aspect Requires a sheltered aspect in full sun to light shade. Roots should be in the shade.

Pruning Cut hard back in late winter or early spring to induce new flowering growth.

Training Allow to ramble over walls, through shrubs or other climbers, or tie to wires or individual anchorage points.

Propagation and nursery production From semi-ripe internodal cuttings taken in early summer. Extremely difficult to propagate. May be scarce in supply and will have to be sought from specialist nurseries. Always purchase container grown; best planting height 1–3 ft (30–91 cm).

Clematis florida **'Bicolor' in flower**

Problems Its weak constitution often causes it to die before becoming established, although additional organic material will go some way towards preventing this. Commands a premium price.

Similar forms of interest *C. f.* **'Alba'** Pure white flowers. Requires the protection of a conservatory or greenhouse in all but the most favoured areas.

Average height and spread
Five years
5 × 5 ft (1.5 × 1.5 m)
Ten years
10 × 10 ft (3 × 3 m)
Twenty years
12 × 12 ft (3.7 × 3.7 m)
Protrudes up to 18 in (45 cm) from support.

CLEMATIS × JOUINIANA PRAECOX

KNOWN BY BOTANICAL NAME

Ranunculaceae   *Perennial Climber*
Deciduous

A vigorous perennial clematis with attractive autumn flowers.

Origin Of garden origin.
Use As a fast-growing perennial climber for walls and fences, to cover large uninteresting shrubs, tree stumps or small sheds.
Description *Flower* Yellow/white, four-sepal flowers up to ¾in (2 cm) wide, carried in panicles up to 2 ft (60 cm) long from late summer to mid autumn. In full sun flowers will be white/yellow, in light to medium shade flowers will be pale blue. *Foliage* Large leaves composed of three to five leaflets, oval in shape, each up to 4 in (10 cm) long with very coarsely toothed edges. Mid green with attractive light silver reverse. *Stem* Light green, ageing to grey/green. Rigid, upright, becoming more spreading with age. Fast growth rate. *Fruit* May produce small clusters of white, fluffy seedheads of some limited interest in autumn and retain into early winter.

Clematis × jouiniana praecox **in flower**

Hardiness Tolerates a minimum winter temperature of 4°F (−15°C). Dies to ground level in winter to be regenerated in following spring.
Soil requirements Tolerates all soils provided they are well-fed and moisture retentive.
Sun/Shade aspect Tolerates all aspects in full sun to medium shade. Roots should be in the shade.
Pruning Normally dies to ground level in winter. If it does not, in a mild winter, remove top growth to ground level to induce new, vigorous summer growth and autumn flowers.
Training Allow to ramble over large shrubs or tie to wires or individual anchorage points. When used through shrubs it may, in time, kill its host.
Propagation and nursery production From semi-ripe cuttings taken early to mid summer. Should always be purchased container grown; may have to be sought from specialist nurseries, although it is becoming more widely available. Best planting height 6 in–3 ft (15–91 cm).
Problems It dies to ground level in winter when in pot which can deter potential purchasers.
Similar forms of interest *C.* × 'Mrs Robert Brydon' Dark blue, very attractive flowers and dark green foliage.
Average height and spread
Five years
8 × 8 ft (2.4 × 2.4 m)
Ten years
12 × 12 ft (3.7 × 3.7 m)
Twenty years
12 × 12 ft (3.7 × 3.7 m)
Protrudes up to 3 ft (91 cm) from support.

CLEMATIS (Large-flowered Hybrids)

KNOWN BY BOTANICAL NAME

Ranunculacee   *Woody Climber*
Deciduous

The clematis is one of the jewels of all summer flowering climbers and rightly takes its place as the most well-known of all climbing plants.

Origin Of garden or nursery origin.
Use As a flowering climbing plant for walls, fences, trellis, pergolas, bowers or similar lattice-type constructions, or to be part of walkways, in particular laburnum. If provided with a low wire frame, can be used as ground cover. Some varieties can be encouraged to grow through trees or large shrubs. Can be grown in large tubs or containers.
Description *Flower* Depending on variety, four to eight oval sepals make up a flat, plate-shaped flower 3–8 in (7.5–20 cm) wide, many with attractive stamens. Colours range through white, pink, purple, red, blue, mauve and yellow, some varieties with a pronounced coloured bar through the centre of each sepal. The flowers are borne singly on flowering shoots. *Foliage* Three to five lanceolate to ovate leaflets, each up to 4 in (10 cm) long, make up a leaf, mid green to grey/green, with tendril-type leaf stalks which aid support. *Stem* Light green when young, ageing to green/brown, finally brown. Twining. Medium to fast growth rate. *Fruit* Some varieties may produce white tufted seedheads of some winter attraction.
Hardiness Tolerates a minimum temperature of 4°F (−15°C).
Soil requirements Tolerates all soil conditions, except for extremely alkaline, but even in the latter, with adequate organic material added to the soil and moisture retention being achieved, average results can be expected. Overall, the more preparation and the more organic material added – up to 50 per cent of the volume – the better the results. When grown in tubs and containers, use a soil-based potting compost, allow for adequate drainage and choose a container not less than 21 in (53 cm) wide and 18 in (45 cm) deep.
Sun/Shade aspect Tolerates all aspects, except extremely exposed. Full sun to light shade with full sun for preference. Roots should be in the shade.

Pruning There are three different pruning methods, each particular to an individual variety. The three methods are as follows:
1 Simply tidy and thin end shoots back to main framework after flowering.
2 Reduce by one third the growth made in the previous season in late winter/early spring.
3 Remove all last season's growth to within 12 in (30 cm) of its origin during late winter/early spring.

It is important the recommended pruning methods are carried out on an annual basis, otherwise flowering will decrease and the overall well-being of the plant will suffer. The individual pruning for each variety is given in 'Forms of Interest'. If the variety is not known use method 2 as a safe option.

Clematis **'Dr Ruppel' in flower**

Training Allow to ramble through wires, trellis, branches of large shrubs or trees or any other support where the leaf tendrils can wrap round to anchor.
Propagation and nursery production From internodal cuttings taken in early to late summer, inserted into a sand/peat mixture, with some bottom heat to encourage rooting. Best planting height 6 in–3 ft (15–91 cm). Clematis is often sold in a choice of 3–4 in (7.5–10 cm) or 1 litre (5–7 in/12–18 cm) pots; both sizes are equally good as long as the plants have been well hardened off and are not purchased before mid spring. Plant from mid spring through until late summer. Plants propagated

Clematis **'Comtesse de Bouchard' in flower**

Clematis 'Edith' in flower

in the spring are ripe enough for planting from mid autumn through until mid spring; these are normally offered in 3–4 in (7.5–10 cm) or 1 litre (5–7 in/12–18 cm) pots. Many varieties will be readily available, others will need searching for from specialist nurseries.

Problems Clematis wilt is an airborne fungus disease for which there is no prevention. The entire plant, both leaves and stem, turns black in early to late summer. Once an attack is seen, cut all growth to ground level, wash walls, fences or trellis with a mild disinfectant and protect any other plants growing below with plastic sheeting. There is then a 60 per cent chance that new, uninfected shoots will develop from below ground from the root system. Planting a new clematis in the same position is not a risk, but the area should be washed with mild disinfectant first.

The main reason for the failure of clematis hybrids is that they are often planted too close to the wall (see 'Planting Climbers and Wall Shrubs' on p.168) and that not enough organic material such as garden compost, well-rotted farmyard manure or mushroom compost is added to the soil. Problems may also be experienced if roots are subject to direct summer sunshine. Blackfly is a common pest but can be treated with a proprietary control. Where certain varieties are grown in association with other climbers such as roses, the requisite pruning can be difficult and this should be taken into account when planting is planned.

Forms of interest C. 'Alice Fisk' Large, pointed sepals with wavy edges, mid to pale blue. Dark brown stamens. Late spring to early summer, with repeat flowering in late summer, early autumn. Any aspect. Reaches two thirds average height and spread. No pruning required. Will have to be sought from specialist nurseries. C. 'Allanah' Large, ruby-red flowers with well-spaced sepals and dark brown anthers produced from early summer to early autumn. Tolerates all but the most shady of aspects. Two thirds average height and spread. Pruning code 3. Will have to be sought from specialist nurseries. C. 'Annabel' Large blue flowers, white stamens. Will have to be sought from a specialist nursery. Pruning code 2. C. 'Asao' Large red/pink sepals with white bar. Free-flowering from late spring to early summer, with repeat flowering from late summer to early autumn. Tolerates any aspect. No pruning required. Will have to be sought from specialist nurseries. C. 'Ascotiensis' Large sepals, long and pointed, bright blue with central green stamens, produced continously from mid summer to early autumn. Tolerates any aspect. Pruning code 3. Will have to be sought from specialist nurseries. C. 'Barbara Dibley' Large, deep red flowers with purple/red central anthers from late spring to

early summer. Good on all aspects. Two thirds average height and spread. Pruning code 2. Readily available. C. 'Barbara Jackman' Large blue flowers with deep pink bar through each sepal and creamy-yellow anthers from late spring to early summer. Tolerates all aspects, although shade will enhance the coloured bar. Two thirds average height and spread. Pruning code 2. Readily available. C. 'Beauty of Richmond' Large, lavender-blue flowers with chocolate-coloured central anthers from early to late summer. A variety for any aspect. Pruning code 2. Will have to be sought from specialist nurseries. C. 'Bees Jubilee' Central brown anthers contrast well with deep pink sepals, each having a deep rose-pink bar. Tolerates all aspects, but the flower contrast colour is best in light shade. Pruning code 2. Readily available. C. 'Blue Gem' Purple anthers contrast with large lavender-blue flowers in late spring to early autumn. Good on any aspect. Pruning code 2. Will have to be sought from specialist nurseries. C. 'Belle Nantaise' Lavender-blue flowers, very large, with central white stamens, from early summer to early autumn. Tolerates any aspect. Pruning code 2 or 3. Will have to be sought from specialist nurseries. C. 'Bracebridge Star' Lavender-blue sepals with deep crimson bar

Clematis 'Ernest Markham' in flower

and red stamens. Large flowers from late spring to early summer. Pruning code 2. Will have to be sought from specialist nurseries. C. 'Captain Thuilleaux' Large, crimson sepals with strawberry-pink bar, contrasting with brown anthers, from late spring to early summer. Tolerates any aspect. Pruning code 2. Readily available. C. 'Cardinal Wyszynski' Large, crimson flowers with brown stamens from early summer to early autumn. Tolerates all but the most shady of aspects. Pruning code 3. Will have to be sought from specialist nurseries. C. 'Carnaby' Attractive crimped edges to raspberry-pink flowers and a central deep pink bar. Flowers from late spring to early summer. Two thirds average height and spread. A variety with a neat growth habit, making it ideal for confined spaces. Pruning code 2. Readily available. C. 'Charissima' Cerise-pink pointed sepals make up a large flower, each sepal with a deep pink bar and delicate but pronounced vein markings. Flowers from early summer to early autumn. Tolerates all aspects. No pruning required. Will have to be sought from specialist nurseries. C. 'Comtesse de Bouchard' One of the most attractive medium-sized flowering clematis. Mauve-pink in colour with cream anthers, very free-flowering throughout summer. Tolerates any aspect. Two thirds average height and spread. Pruning code 3. Readily available. C. 'Corona' Sepals with a velvety texture, purple pink in colour with deep red anthers, from late spring to early summer. Extremely free-flowering.

Clematis 'Jackmanii Rubra' in flower

Good compact habit. Tolerates any aspect. Pruning code 2. Will have to be sought from specialist nurseries. C. 'Crimson King' Large crimson sepals with brown stamens from early summer to early autumn. Tolerates all but the most shady of aspects. Pruning code 2 or 3. Will have to be sought from specialist nurseries. C. 'C.W. Dowman' Lavender flowers shaded pink from centre, carmine bar. Pruning code 2. Will have to be sought from specialist nurseries. C. 'Dawn' Very large pearly-pink flowers from late spring to early summer. Close growing, tidy plant. Avoid full sun, otherwise any aspect. Pruning code 2. Will have to be sought from specialist nurseries. C. 'Dr Ruppel' Carmine bar boldly presented on rose-pink sepals. Gold anthers in centre. Flowers from late spring to early summer, repeating in late summer, early autumn. Good in any aspect. Pruning code 2. Readily available. C. 'Duchess of Sutherland' A lighter red bar down a wine-red sepal makes a medium-sized flower with golden stamens, from early summer to early autumn. Tolerates all but the most shady of aspects. Pruning code 2 or 3. Will have to be sought from specialist nurseries. C. 'Edith' Red/brown anthers show off the large white sepals. Good flowering performance from late spring to early autumn. Tolerates any aspect. Pruning code 2. Will have to be sought from specialist nurseries. C. 'Edouard de Fosse' Red/purple anthers show off large, deep mauve/purple sepals in late spring to early summer. Tolerates any aspect. Pruning code 2. Will have to be sought for specialist nurseries. C. 'Elizabeth Foster' Delicate pink flowers, deep carmine bar, maroon centre. Pruning code 2. Will have to be sought from specialist nurseries. C. 'Elsa Spath' Large, deep violet-blue sepals surround red/purple anthers from early summer to early autumn. Tolerates any aspect. Pruning code 2. Will have to be sought from specialist nurseries. C. 'Ernest Markham' Glowing red flowers of medium size with golden anthers from mid summer to mid autumn. Dislikes exposed aspects. Pruning code 3. Readily available. C. 'Etoile de Paris' Large, pointed, mauve/blue sepals with red central bar and deep red anthers in centre from late spring to early summer. Good in all aspects. Pruning code 2. Will have to be sought from specialist nurseries. C. 'Fairy Queen' Large flesh-pink flowers with deep rose bar from early to late summer. Dislikes full sun. Pruning code 2. Will have to be sought from specialist nurseries. C. 'Fargesii Soulei' Medium-sized flower, pure white. Free-flowering and very strong growing, reaching 40 per cent more than average height and spread, making it ideal for growing through trees or large shrubs. Tolerates any aspect. Pruning code 3. Will have to be sought from specialist nurseries. C. 'Four Star' Lavender-coloured sepals with deeper blue bar make up a medium to large flower from late spring to early summer with repeat flowering late summer, early autumn. Tolerates all aspects. Pruning not normally required. Will have to be sought from specialist nurseries. C. 'General Sikorski' Crinkled edges to mid blue sepals with central golden anthers from early summer through until early autumn. Prefers a sheltered aspect. Pruning code 3. Will have to be sought from specialist nurseries. C. 'Gipsy Queen' Red/purple anthers surrounded by medium-sized rich violet/purple sepals. Very free-flowering from mid summer through to mid autumn. Tolerates any aspect. Pruning code 3. Readily available. C. 'Guiding Star' Blue/purple sepals making a large flower with brown anthers from late spring to early summer. Young foliage bronze in colour. Good compact habit for confined spaces. Tolerates any aspect. Pruning code 2. Will have to be sought from specialist nurseries. C. 'Hagley Hybrid' Medium-sized flowers, cup-shaped, shell-pink with brown anthers from early to late summer. Dislikes full sun which will fade the colour. Compact and good for restricted areas. Pruning code 3. Readily available. C. 'Haku Ookan' Very attractive deep violet-blue flowers with white central anthers from late spring to early summer. Tolerates any aspect. Pruning code 2. Will have to be sought from specialist nurseries. C. 'Henryii'

Clematis 'Nellie Moser' in flower

Medium-sized creamy-white flowers with coffee-coloured central anthers from early to late summer. A variety grown for many years. Pruning code 2. Will have to be sought from specialist nurseries. C. 'Herbert Johnson' Very large red/mauve flowers, maroon centre. Pruning code 2. Will have to be sought from specialist nurseries. C. 'H. F. Young' Wedgwood blue sepals make up large flowers with cream-coloured anthers. Free-flowering late spring to early summer, repeating in late summer, early autumn. Tolerates any aspect. Pruning code 2. Readily available. C. 'Horn of Plenty' Cup-shaped, rich rosy-purple flowers, large, with red anthers, produced from late spring to early summer with repeat flowering in late summer, early autumn. Reaches two thirds average height and spread. Good on any aspect. Pruning code 2. Will have to be sought from specialist nurseries. C. 'Hybrida Sieboldii Ramona' Overlapping sepals make a very round flower, lavender-blue, large, with dark coloured anthers, from early summer to early autumn. Good in any aspect. Pruning code 2. Readily available. C. 'Ishobel' Wavy edges to large white sepals with dark stamens from late spring to early summer, repeated in late summer to early autumn. Tolerates all but the most shady of aspects. Pruning not normally required. Will have to be sought from specialist nurseries. C. 'Jackmanii' Divided, deep purple blue sepals from mid summer to early autumn. Tolerates any aspect. Pruning code 3. Readily available. C. 'Jackmanii Superba' An improved form of the well known C. 'Jackmanii'. Larger sepals, more rounded,

dark purple, from mid summer to early autumn. Tolerates any aspect. Pruning code 3. Readily available. C. 'Jim Hollis' Vigorous, double lavender flowers. Pruning code 2. Will have to be sought from specialist nurseries. C. 'Joan Picton' Large flowers the colour of wild lilac with a white bar down each sepal and brown stamens produced from mid spring to early summer with repeat flowering in autumn. Tolerates all aspects. Pruning not normally required. Will have to be sought from specialist nurseries. C. 'John Paul II' Large, extremely attractive sepals, creamy white with pink shading which becomes deeper as summer passes and forms a pink bar. Sepals have creased edges and overlap. Flowers late spring, early summer with repeat flowering late summer, early autumn. Toler-

Clematis 'Niobe' in flower

ates all aspects. Pruning not normally required. Will have to be sought from specialist nurseries. C. 'John Warren' Extremely large flowers, consisting of pale pink sepals with dark pink bar surrounding central cluster of brown anthers; from early to late summer. Dislikes strong sunlight, otherwise good on all aspects, particularly shady. Pruning code 2. Readily available. C. 'Kaoper' Large, deep violet, crinkly-edged sepals with violet stamens from late spring to early summer, repeated in late summer, early autumn. Tolerates all aspects. Pruning not normally required. Will have to be sought from specialist nurseries. C. 'Kathleen Wheeler' Very attractive large plum/mauve-coloured flowers with pronounced golden anthers, early autumn. Tolerates any aspect. Pruning code 2. Will have to be sought from specialist nurseries. C. 'Ken Donson' Large, deep blue flowers, golden anthers. Pruning code 2. Will have to be sought from specialist nurseries. C. 'King Edward VII' Large, violet/puce sepals with

Clematis 'Mrs Cholmondeley' in flower

crimson bar and brown anthers from early to late summer. Pruning code 2. Will have to be sought from specialist nurseries. **C. 'King George V'** Large, flesh-pink sepals with bright pink bar surrounding brown anthers from mid to late summer. Tolerates any aspect. Pruning code 2. Will have to be sought from specialist nurseries. **C. 'Lady Betty Balfour'** Royal purple sepals make up a large flower with a central cluster of yellow anthers from late summer to early autumn. Very strong growing, 25 per cent more than average height and spread. Requires full sun to encourage flowering, dislikes shady aspects. Pruning code 3. Readily available. **C. 'Lady Londesborough'** Red anthers surrounded by medium-sized sepals, pale mauve/blue in colour, from late spring to early summer. Good compact growth habit; two thirds average height and spread. Tolerates all aspects, except extremely exposed. Pruning code 2. Readily available. **C. 'Lady Northcliffe'** Medium-sized sepals of Wedgwood blue, surrounding yellow anthers, from early to late summer. Good compact growth, only reaching two thirds average height and spread. Tolerates any aspect. Pruning code 2. Readily available. **C. 'Lasurstern'** Creamy-white anthers surrounded by large, pale mauve sepals from early spring to early summer with repeat flowering in late summer to early autumn. Tolerates any aspect. Pruning code 2. Readily available. **C. 'Lawsoniana'** Sky-blue sepals flushed with mauve and pale brown anthers make up a large flower from late spring to early summer, with repeat flowering in late summer. Tolerates any aspect. Pruning code 2. Readily available. **C. 'Lilacina Floribunda'** Large, very rich purple flowers from mid summer through until early autumn. Tolerates any aspect. Pruning code 3. Will have to be sought from specialist nurseries. **C. 'Lincoln Star'** Raspberry-pink sepals make up a large flower with deep red anthers from late spring to mid summer. The repeat flowers in late summer are paler pink but the bar is of a deeper colour. Two thirds average height and spread. Tolerates all aspects, except those in strong sunlight. Pruning code 2. Readily available. **C. 'Lord Neville'** Red anthers surrounded by a ring of dark blue sepals, making a large flower from early to late summer. Tolerates any aspect. Pruning code 2. Readily available. **C. 'Madame Baron Veillard'** Medium-sized flowers consisting of rosy/lilac sepals from late summer through to early autumn. Tolerates all aspects except exremely exposed or shady. Pruning code 3. Readily available. **C. 'Madame Edouard André'** Dusky red sepals of medium size with attractive velvety texture, creamy anthers. Early to late summer, good flowering performance. Tolerates any aspect. Pruning code 2. Readily available. **C. 'Madame Grange'** Sepals have silvery underside with dusky purple top,

Clematis **'Rouge Cardinale' in flower**

making up a medium-sized flower with dark anthers produced from late summer to early autumn. Tolerates any aspect. Pruning code 3. Will have to be sought from specialist nurseries. **C. 'Margaret Hunt'** Good-sized, dusky pink flowers carried from early to late summer. Strong growing, reaching one third more than average height and spread. Tolerates any aspect. Pruning code 3. Will have to be sought from specialist nurseries. **C. 'Marcel Moser'** Large, delicate mauve sepals with crimson bar and red/purple stamens. Flowers from late spring to early summer with repeat flowering late summer to early autumn. Tolerates all aspects. Pruning not normally required. Will have to be sought from specialist nurseries. **C. 'Marie Boisselot'** (syn. **C. 'Madame le Coultre'**) Very large white flowers with beige-coloured anthers from early to late summer. Very free-flowering. Tolerates all aspects. Pruning code 3. Readily available. **C. 'Maureen'** Light brown anthers surrounded by red/purple sepals, making a large flower from early to late summer. Tolerates any aspect. Pruning code 2. Will have to be sought from specialist nurseries. **C. 'Miss Bateman'** Very pretty medium-sized creamy-

white flowers with chocolate-coloured anthers from mid spring to early summer. Two thirds average height and spread. Tolerates all but the most exposed or shady aspects. Pruning code 2. Readily available. **C. 'Moonlight'** (syn. **C. 'Yellow Queen'**) Primrose-yellow sepals with yellow anthers from late spring to early summer. Glossy green foliage of interesting shape. Dislikes full sun or deep shade. Pruning code 2. Readily available. **C. 'Mrs Bush'** Very large, deep lavender sepals with light chocolate anthers from late spring to early summer. Tolerates all aspects. Pruning code 2. Will have to be sought from specialist nurseries. **C. 'Mrs Cholmondeley'** Long, narrow, lavender-blue sepals make up a large flower with brown central anthers. Long flowering period from late spring to early autumn, not necessarily continuous. Tolerates any aspect. Pruning code 2. Readily available. **C. 'Mrs N. Thompson'** Large blue sepals with a red bar and red anthers from late spring to early summer. Some repeat flowering in late summer. Tolerates any aspect. Pruning code 2. Readily available. **C. 'Mrs Spencer Castle'** Single and double flowers, pale mauve/pink, from June to October. Pruning code 2. Will have to be sought from specialist nurseries. **C. 'Mrs P. B. Truax'** Mid to deep blue medium-sized flowers with yellow anthers from late spring to early summer. Tolerates all but the most shady of aspects. Makes a compact plant, ideal for small gardens. Pruning code 2. Will have to be sought from specialist nurseries. **C. 'Myojo'** Large, velvety red sepals with deep red bar and attractive cream-coloured stamens from late spring to early summer, repeated in late summer, early autumn. Tolerates all aspects. Pruning not normally required. Will have to be sought from specialist nurseries. **C. 'Nellie Moser'** Large, pale pink/mauve sepals with a crimson-coloured bar and red/brown anthers from late spring to early summer. Repeat flowering late summer, early autumn. A very popular variety, suspected of not being easy to establish, but this is normally attributable to bad planting (see 'Planting Climbers and Wall Shrubs' on p.168). Good on exposed, shady aspects. Pruning code 2. Readily available. **C. 'Niobe'** Large, velvety textured deep ruby red sepals with yellow anthers from early to late summer. Tolerates all aspects. Plant against a light background to show off flowers to full extent. Pruning code 2. Readily available. **C. 'Patens Yellow'** Creamy yellow se-

Clematis **'Perle d'Azur' in flower**

pals and yellow stamens. Pruning code 2. Will have to be sought from specialist nurseries. C. 'Perle d'Azur' Delicate sky-blue sepals make up a medium-sized, semi-pendent flower, each sepal edge slightly corrugated, with green/yellow anthers. Good grower in any aspect. Flowers from mid summer to early autumn. Pruning code 3. Normally readily available. C. 'Pennell's Purity' White flowers with firm, crimped sepals, golden centre. Pruning code 2. Will have to be sought from specialist nurseries. C. 'Peveril Pearl' Violet-tipped creamy stamens, ringed by lilac sepals, each with a pink bar, making a large flower from late spring to early summer with repeat flowering early autumn. Strong growing. Tolerates any aspect. Pruning code 2. Will have to be sought from specialist nurseries. C. 'Pink Champagne' An interesting new large-flowering variety from Japan with strong pink petals. Pruning code 2. Readily available. C. 'Pink Fantasy' Large, shell pink sepals with deep pink bar and wavy edges; brown stamens. Flowers from early summer to early autumn. Tolerates all but the most shady of aspects. Pruning code 3. Will have to

Clematis 'The President' in flower

be sought from specialist nurseries. C. 'Prince Charles' Mauve-blue sepals make up medium-sized flowers which cover the entire plant from early summer to early autumn, although not necessarily continuously. Tolerates all but the most shady of aspects. Two thirds average height and spread. Pruning code 2. Will have to be sought from specialist nurseries. C. 'Princess of Wales' Satin mauve flowers from early summer to early autumn, not necessarily continuous. Tolerates all aspects. Strong growing. Named after Queen Alexandra when she was Princess of Wales in the 1800s. Pruning not normally required. Will have to be sought from specialist nurseries. C. 'Proteus' Rosy lilac, semi-double flowers with yellow stamens. Pruning code 2 on established plants. Will have to be sought from specialist nurseries. C. 'Richard Pennell' Pronounced red and cream anthers show off the large rosy/purple sepals from late spring to early summer. Repeat flowering late summer. Tolerates any aspect. Pruning code 2. Will have to be sought from specialist nurseries. C. 'Rouge Cardinale' Large, rich-textured, crimson square-tipped sepals around yellow anthers. Long flowering period from early summer to early autumn. Two thirds average height and spread. Tolerates all aspects. Pruning code 2. Readily available. C. 'Sally Cadge' Deep crimson bar runs down centre of large, mid blue sepals produced from late spring to early summer, with repeat flowering late summer, early autumn. Tolerates all aspects. Pruning not required. Will have to be sought from specialist nurseries. C. 'Saturn' Lavender blue sepals with maroon bar. White stamens. Pruning code 2. Will have to be sought from specialist nurseries. C. 'Scartho Gem' Attractive, large, deep pink sepals with deeper pink bar surrounding golden stamens. Very free flowering from early summer to

early autumn. Tolerates all aspects. Pruning not required. Normally readily available. C. 'Scotiensis' Attractive purple/blue flowers with yellow/green central anthers in mid to late summer. Tolerates any aspect. Pruning code 2. Will have to be sought from specialist nurseries. C. 'Sealand Gem' A deep mauve bar down the centre of rosy/mauve sepals makes up an attractive medium-sized flower with brown central stamens. Flowers early summer to early autumn, but not necessarily continuously. Tolerates any aspect. Pruning code 2 or 3. Normally readily available. C. 'Seranata' Deep purple flowers with bright yellow anthers from early summer to early autumn. Tolerates any aspect. Pruning code 3. Will have to be sought from specialist nurseries. C. 'Sir Garnet Wolseley' Mauve/blue sepals with a pale purple bar make up a medium-sized flower with red anthers produced from late spring to early summer. Good tight growth habit. Tolerates all aspects. Pruning code 2. Will have to be sought from specialist nurseries. C. 'Silver Moon' Large pale lilac flowers from early summer to early autumn. Good in exposed aspects but will flower in all conditions. Pruning code 2. Will have to be sought from specialist nurseries. C. 'Snow Queen' Medium- to large-sized flowers, pure white with blue-tinted edges, from early to mid summer. Tolerates all but the most shady of aspects. Pruning not required. Will have to be sought from specialist nurseries. C. 'Star of India' Deep purple sepals with a red bar, making up a medium-sized flower from early summer to early autumn. Tolerates any aspect. Pruning code 3. Will have to be sought from specialist nurseries. C. 'Susan Allsop' Large, rosy-purple flowers with red bar down each sepal and magenta-red centre shading, surrounding golden yellow anthers from early summer to early autumn. Tolerates any aspect. Pruning code 2. Will have to be sought from specialist nurseries. C. 'The President' Medium sized blue/purple flowers with a paler stripe and velvety texture, saucer-shaped in formation. Anthers red/purple. Flowers from late spring to early autumn, not necessarily continuously. Tolerates all aspects. Grown for many years and well established. Pruning code 2. Readily available. C. 'Twilight' Large, dark mauve flowers with yellow stamens from mid summer to early autumn, often continuous. Tolerates all but the most shady of aspects. Pruning code 3. Will have to be sought from specialist nurseries. C. 'Veronica's Choice' Large, semi-double lavender flowers with crimped edges. Pruning code 2. Will have to be sought from specialist nurseries. C. 'Victoria' Buff-coloured anthers surrounded by rosy/purple sepals, making up a large flower from early summer to early autumn. Strong growing, tolerates any aspect. Pruning code 3. Will have to be sought from specialist nurseries. C.

Clematis 'Ville de Lyon' in flower

Clematis 'William Kennet'

'Ville de Lyon' Carmine-pink sepals with crimson shading around their edges surround golden anthers to make up a medium-sized flower from early summer to mid autumn, often flowering continuously in good conditions. Dislikes full sun, otherwise tolerates a wide range of aspects. A well proven form. Pruning code 3. Readily available. C. 'Violet Charm' Long, rich violet/blue sepals with pointed ends and wavy edges with beige-coloured stamens from early summer to early autumn, not necessarily continuous. Tolerates all but the most shady of aspects. Two thirds average height and spread. Pruning code 2 or 3. Will have to be sought from specialist nurseries. C. 'Voluceau' Medium-sized red flowers with yellow anthers from early summer to early autumn, often continuous. Good strong grower, tolerating any aspect. Pruning code 3. Will have to be sought from specialist nurseries. C. 'Wadas Primrose' Pale primrose-yellow flowers with deeper central bar through each sepal from late spring to early summer with repeat flowers in early autumn. Strong growing. Prefers a shady position. Pruning code 2. Will have to be sought from specialist nurseries. C. 'Warsaw Nike' Good, glowing purple with central golden stamens on large flowers. Free-flowering from early summer to early autumn, not necessarily continuous. Tolerates all but the most shady of aspects. Pruning code 3. Readily available. C. 'W. E. Gladstone' Purple stamens surrounded by lilac blue sepals. Very large flowers from early summer to early autumn, not necessarily continuous. Tolerates all but the most shady of aspects. Pruning code 2 or 3. Readily available. C. 'Wilhelmina Tull' A broad crimson bar down the centre of large, deep violet blue sepals with central golden stamens from late spring to early summer, repeated late summer to early autumn. Two thirds average height and spread. Tolerates all but the most shady of aspects. Said to be an improved form of C. 'Mrs N. Thompson'. Pruning not normally required. Will have to be sought from specialist nurseries. C. 'Will Goodwin' Wavy edges to lavender blue sepals make up a large flower with golden central stamens from early summer to early autumn, not necessarily continuous. Tolerates all but the most shady of aspects. Pruning code 2 or 3. Will have to be sought from specialist nurseries. C. 'William Kennett' Crimped margins to the large, lavender blue flowers with dark blue anthers from early to late summer. Tolerates any aspect. Pruning code 2. Readily available.

Average height and spread
Five years
8 × 8 ft (2.4 × 2.4 m)
Ten years
12 × 12 ft (3.7 × 3.7 m)
Twenty years
15 × 15 ft (4.6 × 4.6 m)
Protrudes up to 18 in (45 cm) from support.

CLEMATIS MACROPETALA

KNOWN BY BOTANICAL NAME

Ranunculaceae   ***Woody Climber***
Deciduous

One of the stars of the spring flowering clematis with a wide range of colours and extremely attractive flowers.

Origin From China and Siberia and of garden origin.

Use As a climber for walls, fences, pillars, pergolas and trellis, or to ramble through large shrubs. Can be used as ground cover with or without support.

Description *Flower* Nodding flowers carried singly on stalks 2 in (5 cm) long. Each has four blue sepals. *Foliage* Nine coarsely toothed, ovate to lanceolate leaflets, each $\frac{1}{2}$–$1\frac{1}{2}$ in (1–4 cm) long, making up a total size of 4 in (10 cm) long and 2 in (5 cm) wide. Light to mid green. Yellow/brown autumn colour. *Stem* Light green when young, ageing to grey/brown. Twining. Leaf tendrils act as additional anchorage. Medium rate of growth. *Fruit* May, in hot summers and mild locations, produce small silver/white fluffy seedheads.

Hardiness Tolerates a minimum winter temperature of 4°F (−15°C).

Soil requirements Does well on all soil types with no particular preference, but must have adequate moisture throughout the year to induce good growth.

Clematis macropetala **in flower**

Sun/Shade aspect Tolerates all but the most exposed of aspects. Requires its roots in the shade and prefers its top in the sun but will tolerate very light shade.

Pruning Cut all current season's growth to within 6–12 in (15–30 cm) of its origin after main flowering period so that through the summer new flowering growth will be produced for next spring, or lightly trim and tidy after flowering. The latter method is normally suitable over one to five years, but the plant will become old and woody and will need hard cutting back every five to six years.

Training Requires wires or trellis on walls and fences. Allow to ramble freely through large shrubs. Good as ground cover, with or without support.

Propagation and nursery production From semi-ripe internodal cuttings taken late spring/early summer. Always purchase container grown; best planting height 1$\frac{1}{2}$–3 ft (45–91 cm). Most varieties readily available from good garden centres and specialist nurseries, although some varieties may need searching for.

Problems If not pruned correctly can become very woody and uninteresting in its growth.

Clematis montana '**Elizabeth**' **in flower**

Similar forms of interest *C. m.* '**Blue Bird**' Large flowers, up to 4 in (10 cm) wide, lavender blue in colour. Strong growing, reaching one third more than average height and spread. *C. m.* '**Maidwell Hall**' Deep blue flowers. A decided improvement on the parent plant. *C. m.* '**Markham's Pink**' (syn. *C. m.* '**Markhamii**') Pink flowers 3 in (7.5 cm) wide, pendent and nodding. Can produce a later summer display of flowers. *C. m.* '**Rosie O'Grady**' Pink flowers up to 3 in (7.5 cm) wide in spring with an occasional late summer flowering. *C. m.* '**Snowbird**' Pure white flowers 3 in (7.5 cm) across. *C. m.* '**White Lady**' Masses of star-shaped white flowers. Will have to be sought from specialist nurseries. *C. m.* '**White Swan**' Double white pendent flowers up to 2 in (5 cm) across. Extremely attractive.

Average height and spread

Five years
10 × 10 ft (3 × 3 m)
Ten years
10 × 10 ft (3 × 3 m)
Twenty years
10 × 10 ft (3 × 3 m)
Protrudes up to 18 in (45 cm) from support.

CLEMATIS MONTANA

KNOWN BY BOTANICAL NAME

Ranunculaceae   ***Woody Climber***
Deciduous

A well-known and very widely planted clematis which offers great value as a flowering climbing plant.

Origin From the Himalayas.

Use As a free-flowering, rambling climber for large walls or fences, or to grow over large shrubs and small trees. Ideal for pergolas, trellis, archways, in fact wherever a climber is required. It is also good as a widespreading ground cover with or without support.

Description *Flower* White, borne singly on stalks up to 5 in (12 cm) long, with up to five stalks at each leaf joint. Flowers 2–2$\frac{1}{2}$ in (5–6 cm) across with four sepals in a star formation. *Foliage* Three ovate to lanceolate leaflets on a stalk up to 4 in (10 cm) long. Each leaflet up to 4 in (10 cm) long, making a total leaf size of 4 × 5 in (10 × 12 cm). Bright mid green on white flowering forms or purple/green to quite deep purple on pink or purple flowering forms. *Stem* Light green ageing to purple/green, finally purple/brown. Twining with leaf petioles giving extra anchorage. Fast growth rate. *Fruit* May produce small, uninteresting seedheads following flowering.

Hardiness Tolerates a minimum winter temperature of 4°F (−15°C).

Soil requirements Does well on all soil types with no particular preference, but must have adequate moisture throughout the year to induce good growth.

Sun/Shade aspect Prefers its roots in the shade but its top growth will tolerate from full sun through to medium shade, although in medium shade the plant may become more open and lax and flower less.

Pruning Normally requires no pruning until five years after planting and then can be heavily reduced after flowering. Quickly rejuvenates itself, giving a better display of foliage in the following season and good flowering performance in the following spring. This treatment should be repeated every four to five years for best results.

Training Requires wires or trellis on walls and fences. Allow to ramble freely through shrubs and trees.

Propagation and nursery production From semi-ripe internodal cuttings taken in late spring/early summer. Always purchase container grown, best planting height 1$\frac{1}{2}$–3 ft (45–91 cm). Most varieties readily available from good garden centres and specialist nurseries, although some varieties may need searching for.

Problems Often outgrows the area intended for it. An extremely vigorous climber, needing care and attention regarding its ultimate size. May self-seed in the garden but resulting seedling will not be true to parent.

Similar forms of interest *C. m.* '**Alexandria**' Creamy white flowers 3 in (7.5 cm) wide with attractive scent and yellow stamens. Light green foliage. *C. m.* '**Elizabeth**' Scented, soft pale pink flowers up to 3 in (7.5 cm) wide. Extremely attractive. Light bronze foliage. *C. m.* '**Freda**' Cherry pink flowers with each sepal having a crimson red edge. Bronze foliage. *C. m. grandiflora* Flowers up to 4 in (10 cm) wide, white with yellow centres. Strong growing. *C. m.* '**Lilacine**' Purple/green foliage and blue/lilac flowers. *C. m.* '**Marjorie**' Semi-double, creamy pink flowers with orange tint. A most unusual variety. Two thirds average height and spread. *C. m.* '**Mayleen**' Deep pink flowers up to 3 in (7.5 cm) across with golden stamens. Bronze foliage. *C. m.* '**Odorata**' Possibly the original form of *C. montana* with soft pink flowers and some scent, produced in late spring/early summer. Tolerates all aspects. *C. m.* '**Picton's Variety**' Strawberry-pink flowers with golden centres. Purple to purple/green foliage. Reaches only half average height and spread. *C. m.* '**Pink Perfection**' Smaller flowers than most, but attractive pink colour with round-ended sepals. Two thirds average height and spread. Purple/green foliage. *C. m.* '**Rubens**' Purple/green foliage. Pale mauve pink flowers. Most reliable. *C. m.* '**Tetrarose**' Bronze foliage. Medium deep rose/mauve

Clematis montana **in flower**

flowers of good size. Half average height and spread. *C. m.* **'Vera'** Foliage dark green with large, pink, fragrant flowers. *C. m.* **'Wilsonii'** Creamy white flowers with yellow anthers. Later flowering than most varieties, not producing its flowers until early to mid summer. Two thirds average height and spread. *C. chrysocoma* Strong-growing attractive foliage with downy surface. Small soft pink flowers in late spring/early summer. Tolerates all aspects. *C.c. sericea* (syn. *C.c. spooneri*) Pure white flowers up to 3 in (7.5 cm) in diameter with bold yellow anthers, produced from late spring to early summer. Tolerates all aspects. *C. vedrariensis* Medium-sized bold rosy/mauve flowers borne in profusion from late spring to early summer. Tolerates all aspects. *C. v.* **'Hidcote'** Small, deep pink flowers from late spring to early summer. Tolerates all positions. Wide-ranging, rambling habit. *C. v.* **'Highdown'** Large pink flowers very similar to others in its group. Tolerates all aspects.

Average height and spread
Five years
15 × 15 ft (4.6 × 4.6 m)
Ten years
30 × 30 ft (9 × 9 m)
Twenty years
40 × 40 ft (12 × 12 m)
Protrudes up to 3 ft (91cm) from support. These heights and spreads are only achieved when the vine is unpruned, but over ten years or more this can lead to deterioration in flower and foliage size and colour.

CLEMATIS ORIENTALIS
(*C. graveolens*)

ORIENTAL CLEMATIS

Ranunculaceae	*Woody Climber*
Deciduous	

An attractive, late summer flowering clematis with a charm all of its own. Excellent for rambling over walls, fences and buildings but also a good ground cover plant.

Origin From Northern Asia.
Use For walls, fences, pillars, pergolas, roofs of small buildings or to ramble through large shrubs or small trees. Can be used as ground cover with or without support.
Description *Flower* Four oval, pointed, downy covered sepals carried on up to 4 in (10 cm) long flower stalks. Each flower 11-12 in (2.5-5 cm) wide, yellow in colour. Flowers late summer, early autumn. Attractive when in bud, forming a small balloon shape, opening to a more reflexed shape. *Foliage* Light green, dissected, ferny leaves offer-

ing some yellow autumn colour until the first hard frost. *Stem* Light green, becoming grey/green, finally grey/brown. Twining. More fragile than most. Additional support supplied by leaf tendrils. Medium rate of growth. *Fruit* Small, white, tufted seedheads follow flowers.
Hardiness Tolerates a minimum winter temperature of 14°F (−10°C).
Soil requirements Tolerates both alkaline and acid conditions, but must have a moist soil high in organic material. Resents drought.
Sun/Shade aspect Tolerates all but the most severe of aspects. Full sun to very light shade. Roots must be in the shade.
Pruning Cut hard back by at least two thirds or more in early to mid spring. Rapid regrowth follows pruning and the plant quickly gains its full height. It is sometimes suggested that no pruning is necessary unless it becomes too large, but this can lead to a very woody structure.
Training Will require wires on walls or fences, or can be allowed to ramble through large shrubs and small trees.
Propagation and nursery production From seed or, for named varieties, semi-ripe internodal cuttings taken early to mid summer. Should always be purchased container grown, best planting height 1-3 ft (30-91cm). Named varieties will need searching for from specialist nurseries.
Problems If not pruned as suggested can become old and woody, with resulting decrease in foliage and flower production. Stems in early spring often look dead.

Similar forms of interest *C. o.* **'Bill McKenzie'** The largest flowering of all the varieties and possibly the most spectacular. Yellow flowers followed by very attractive silver/white seedheads. *C. o.* **'Burford Variety'** One of the strongest-growing varieties with good-sized flowers of deep lemon yellow. *C. o.* **'L. & S. 13342'** Orange flowers with thick sepals in a nodding formation. *C. o.* **'Orange Peel'** Grey/green foliage, finely cut. Nodding, cup-shaped flowers with yellow, waxy sepals. Derives its name from the fact that the sepals are the same thickness as orange peel. L. & S. 13342 and 'Orange Peel' may well be the same plant masquerading under two different names. *C. o.* **'Sherriffii'** Very attractive grey/green foliage with deep yellow, cowslip-scented flowers in mid summer. *C. tangutica* Lemon yellow nodding flowers with silver/white stamens in mid summer to late autumn.

Average height and spread
Five years
7 × 7 ft (2.1 × 2.1 m)
Ten years
12 × 12 ft (3.7 × 3.7 m)
Twenty years
18 × 18 ft (4.5 × 4.5 m)
Protrudes up to 2 ft (60 cm) from support.

CLEMATIS REHDERIANA
(*C. nutans thyrsoidea*)

KNOWN BY BOTANICAL NAME

Ranunculaceae	*Woody Climber*
Deciduous	

One of the choicest of all clematis and other flowering climbing plants, not without its problems but worthy of perseverance.

Origin From China.
Use As a large spreading climber for walls, fences or pergolas and to ramble through medium-sized uninteresting shrubs and small trees.
Description *Flower* Bell-shaped, nodding, fragrant flowers 1½-2½ in (4-6cm) wide carried in upright panicles. Each flower panicle up to 9 in (23 cm) long and 5 in (12 cm) wide. Sepals pale yellow, ¾ in (2 cm) long with recurved tips. Flowers in late summer to mid autumn. *Foliage* Pinnate leaves 6-9 in (15-23 cm) long, each with seven or nine wide, ovate, veined, light green leaflets up to 3 in (7.5 cm) long, deeply lobed with toothed edges and downy texture. *Stem* Light grey/green, becoming grey/ brown. Vigorous, upright habit. Limited twining. *Fruit* No fruit of interest.

Clematis orientalis **'Bill McKenzie' – flowers and seedheads**

Hardiness Tolerates a minimum winter temperature of 14°F (−10°C).
Soil requirements Does well on all soil types with no particular preference other than a high degree of good organic material and moisture retention.
Sun/Shade aspect Sheltered aspect. Full sun to very light shade. Roots must be in the shade.
Pruning Lightly trim in spring. Every five to ten years prune hard to induce new growth.
Training Will require tying to wires on walls or fences. Allow to ramble through large shrubs and small trees.
Propagation and nursery production From seed sown soon after fruiting or semi-ripe internodal cuttings taken in early to mid summer. Should always be purchased container grown, best planting height 9 in–3 ft (23–91 cm) Will have to be sought from specialist nurseries.

Clematis rehderiana

Problems Can take up to three years to establish. Unless adequate organic material is available in the soil, may often give poor results.
Similar forms of interest None.
Average height and spread
Five years
8 × 8 ft (2.4 × 2.4 m)
Ten years
12 × 12 ft (3.7 × 3.7 m)
Twenty years
20 × 20 ft (6 × 6 m)
Protrudes up to 3 ft (91 cm) from support.

CLEMATIS TEXENSIS

KNOWN BY BOTANICAL NAME
Ranunculaceae   *Woody Climber*
Deciduous
A gem of a clematis but lacking the vigour and robustness of many of its stronger growing relations and needing care with siting.

Origin From Texas, USA.
Use Best allowed to ramble through medium to large shrubs but can also be used for walls and fences or small pillars.
Description *Flower* Single, urn-shaped flowers carried on slender, graceful stalks up to 6 in (15 cm) long, each flower up to 1¼ in (3.5 cm) long and 1 in (2.5 cm) wide in shades of red. Sepals thick and reflexed at tips. *Foliage* Leaves composed of four to eight broadly ovate leaflets up to 3 in (7.5 cm) long with two or three lobes. *Stem* Light grey/green to grey/brown. Fragile, sparse, medium to fast growth rate. Twining. *Fruit* Small tufts of silver/white seedheads follow flowers.

Hardiness Tolerates a minimum winter temperature of 14°F (−10°C).
Soil requirements Tolerates all soil types including alkaline but requires a good moisture-retentive soil with high organic content.
Sun/Shade aspect Needs a sheltered aspect. Stems, leaves and flowers in full sun and roots in shade.

Clematis texensis 'Gravetye Beauty' in flower

Pruning Cut hard back to within 6 in (15 cm) of previous season's point of origin in early to mid spring.
Training Allow to ramble through large shrubs or, if used on walls and fences, tie to wires.
Propagation and nursery production From semi-ripe cuttings. Difficult to propagate. Always purchase container grown; best planting height 9 in–3 ft (23–91 cm). Will have to be sought from specialist nurseries.
Problems Its sparse, wispy growth pattern is not always understood. Should not be compared with other forms of clematis, in particular the *montana* or large-flowering forms.
Similar forms of interest *C. t.* **'Duchess of Albany'** Flowers deep pink with red stripe through each sepal. Can be semi-herbaceous, often dying to ground level in winter. *C. t.* **'Etoile Rose'** Cherry pink flowers with silver margins. Semi-herbaceous. *C. t.* **'Gravetye Beauty'** Small ruby-red flowers. Ends of flowers open wide. Semi-herbaceous. *C. t.* **'Pagoda'** Early pink flowers. Semi-herbaceous. *C. t.* **'Princess of Wales'** Deep pink, attractive flowers.
Average height and spread
Five years
7 × 7 ft (2.1 × 2.1 m)
Ten years
10 × 10 ft (3 × 3 m)
Twenty years
12 × 12 ft (3.7 × 3.7 m)
Protrudes up to 2 ft (60 cm) from support.

Clematis texensis 'Princess of Wales' in flower

CLEMATIS VITALBA

TRAVELLER'S JOY, OLD MAN'S BEARD
Ranunculaceae   *Woody Climber*
Deciduous
Although this is considered in many regions to be a wild plant, the beauty of its seedheads should allow it a wider use within gardens.

Origin From Europe and North Africa.
Use To ramble through large shrubs and small trees, as large-scale ground cover or to climb large walls, fences and pergolas.
Description *Flower* Off-white, ¾ in (2 cm) wide, carried at the ends and from the side shoots of stems. Almond scented, flowering from mid summer to early autumn. *Foliage* Pinnate, between 3–10 in (7.5–25 cm) long, depending on geographical location. Five ovate to lanceolate leaflets, each up to 4 in (10 cm) long, with coarsely toothed edges and downy grey/green appearance. *Stem* Grey/green, becoming grey/brown. Free-ranging and vigorous, making up to 16 ft (4.9 m) of growth per year. *Fruit* Attractive silky-white, ageing to grey/white, finally grey seedheads of very feathery texture, carried en masse. Often retained well into winter.

Clematis vitalba in flower

Hardiness Tolerates a minimum winter temperature of 0°F (−18°C).
Soil requirements Does extremely well on soils with high alkaline content but will tolerate all conditions. Requires a moist soil high in organic material for best results.
Sun/Shade aspect All aspects with foliage and flowers in light shade to full sun and roots in the shade.
Pruning Normally requires no pruning, but can be drastically reduced in size if required on a five or ten year basis. Pruning is best carried out in early spring.
Training Allow to ramble through large shrubs and trees.
Propagation and nursery production From seed or from semi-ripe cuttings taken early summer. Always purchase container grown; although common, it may be difficult to find and will have to be sought from specialist nurseries. Best planting height 9 in–3 ft (23–91 cm).
Problems Does require a very large area to reach its full potential.
Similar forms of interest None.
Average height and spread
Five years
8 × 8 ft (2.4 × 2.4 m)
Ten years
12 × 12 ft (3.7 × 3.7 m)
Twenty years
20 × 20 ft (6 × 6 m)
Protrudes up to 3 ft (91 cm) from support.

CLEMATIS VITICELLA

VINE BOWER

Ranunculaceae   *Woody Climber*
Deciduous

A species with a large number of varieties covering a whole range of colours, but all retaining the delicate charm of the flowers.

Origin From south-east Europe.

Use For walls, fences, pillars and pergolas or to ramble through medium to large shrubs. Good for ground cover with support or through small, low-growing shrubs such as heathers.

Description *Flower* Broadly bell-shaped violet or purple/red flowers, 1½–2½ in (4–6 cm) across, presented singly on 3–4 in (7.5–10 cm) stems from mid summer to early autumn. *Foliage* Up to 5 in (12 cm) long dark green leaves composed of numerous ovate leaflets. *Stem* Thin, wispy, limited number of shoots, twining. Leaves offer support by leaf tendrils. Light green when young, ageing to grey/brown. Slow to medium rate of growth. *Fruit* May produce small silver seedheads of limited attraction.

Hardiness Tolerates a minimum winter temperature of 4°F (−15°C). Although some stem die-back may be suffered at this temperature, spring rejuvenation normally occurs.

Clematis viticella 'Alba Luxuriens' in flower

Soil requirements Tolerates all types but must have substantial organic content. Resents drying out.

Sun/Shade aspect Tolerates all but the most exposed of situations. Foliage and flowers should be in full sun to very light shade and roots in shade.

Pruning Either allow to grow unpruned for one to ten years and then cut hard back every subsequent ten years and only lightly trim in interim years, or cut hard back each spring to induce new production of flowering growth. The latter pruning will reduce the overall size and possibly the architectural features of a mature climber.

Training Will require wires on walls and fences.

Propagation and nursery production From semi-ripe internodal cuttings taken in early summer. Should always be purchased container grown; best planting height 1–3 ft (30–91 cm). Many varieties will require searching for from specialist nurseries.

Problems Its sparse growth must be appreciated. May suffer attacks of mildew in late summer/early autumn but a proprietary control will normally eradicate this. Availability of some varieties may be extremely scarce. Difficult to propagate.

Similar forms of interest *C. v.* **'Abundance'** Extremely attractive, light red to purple flowers. Responds well to hard pruning in

Clematis viticella 'Abundance' in flower

spring. *C. v.* **'Alba Luxuriens'** One of the most interesting clematis with twisted, creamy white sepals with green bands of colour through each. Colour variegations will occur according to season. *C. v.* **'Albiflora'** White flowers, medium size. May be scarce. *C. v.* **'Caerulea'** Deep blue/violet flowers borne in profusion. Scarce. *C. v.* **'Elvan'** Purple flowers with cream edging. Extremely good when allowed to ramble through shrubs. Scarce. *C. v.* **'Etoile Violet'** Violet flowers of good size with pale yellow anthers. Very free-flowering throughout late summer and early autumn. Good for ground cover. *C. v.* **'Flora Plena'** Double, rose-coloured flowers. A very old variety scarce in production. *C. v.* **'Huldine'** Most attractive white flowers, suffused with mother-of-pearl pink, carried in large clusters. Well recommended. *C. v.* **'Kermesina'** Wine-red flowers up to 3 in (7.5 cm) across. Well recommended. *C. v.* **'Little Nell'** Small mauve flowers with cream central bar down each sepal. *C. v.* **'Madame Julia Correvon'** Wine-red flowers up to 2½ in (6 cm) across. Up to six twisted sepals with central golden anthers. Less vigorous than most. Flowers from early summer to early autumn. *C. v.* **'Margot Koster'** Mauve-pink flowers of medium size with pure white anthers. Sepals well spaced. Two thirds average height and

spread. *C. v.* **'Minuet'** White flowers, small, with each sepal having pronounced mauve edging. Two thirds average height and spread. Extremely attractive. *C. v.* **'Purpurea Plena Elegance'** Violet-purple, double flowers resembling a small chrysanthemum. Two thirds average height and spread. Grow through medium to large shrubs for best display. *C. v.* **'Royal Velours'** Royal purple, velvety textured, medium-sized flowers with deep black anthers. Position carefully to show off flowers to best advantage. *C. v.* **'Rubra'** Wine-red flowers, small, with contrasting black anthers. Good for ground cover. *C. v.* **'Venosa Violacea'** Sepals boat-shaped, medium-sized, purple with bold white and purple veined centres.

Average height and spread

Five years
8 × 8 ft (2.4 × 2.4 m)
Ten years
12 × 12 ft (3.7 × 3.7 m)
Twenty years
12 × 12 ft (3.7 × 3.7 m)
Protrudes up to 2 ft (60 cm) from support.

Clematis viticella 'Minuet' in flower

Clematis viticella 'Etoile Violet' in flower

Cleyera fortunei

CLEYERA FORTUNEI

KNOWN BY BOTANICAL NAME

Theaceae   *Wall Shrub*
Evergreen

An attractive foliage shrub responding
well to fan-training or planting in
association with walls or fences where it
derives some protection.

Origin from Japan.
Use As a fan-trained foliage shrub for sheltered walls and fences both in favourable
open areas and under the protection of greenhouses or conservatories.
Description *Flower* Flowers up to $\frac{1}{2}$ in (1 cm)
across, pale yellow with red/brown calyxes,
presented in clusters or singly in late sum-
mer/early autumn. *Foliage* Ovate to lanceolate, up to 4 in (10 cm) long, bright green with
golden yellow and scarlet variegation around
the edges. *Stems* Mid to dark green, semi-
rigid, adapting well to fan-training. Slow to
medium growth rate. *Fruit* No fruit of
interest.
Hardiness Tolerates a minimum winter temperature of 14°F (−10° C) with the protection
of a wall or fence.
Soil requirements Neutral to acid, although
its full range of tolerance of alkalinity has not
yet been fully tested. Requires a soil high in
organic material and plant nutrients for best
growth and foliage.
Sun/Shade aspect Sheltered aspect. Light
shade for preference but will tolerate full sun
to medium shade.
Pruning Not normally required other than for
training.
Training Fan-train on to wires or individual
anchor points or allow to grow freestanding.
Propagation and nursery production From
semi-ripe cuttings. Should always be purchased container grown; will have to be
sought from specialist nurseries. Best
planting height 9 in–2 ft (23–60 cm).
Problems Its range of hardiness, soil conditions and growth have not yet been fully
tested outside its native environment.
Similar forms of interest None.
Average height and spread
Five years
4 × 4 ft (1.2 × 1.2 m)
Ten years
8 × 8 ft (2.4 × 2.4 m)
Twenty years
12 × 12 ft (3.7 × 3.7 m)

Protrudes up to 2$\frac{1}{2}$ ft (76 cm) from support if
fan-trained, 5 ft (1.5 m) untrained.

CLIANTHUS PUNICEUS

PARROT'S BILL, LOBSTER CLAW, KAKA BEAK

Leguminosae   *Tender Wall Shrub*
Evergreen

An attractive and interesting flowering
wall shrub requiring a very mild planting
location to achieve any results.

Origin From New Zealand.
Use As a tender wall shrub for very warm
sheltered walls or fences or under the protection of a conservatory or greenhouse.
Decription *Flower* 4 in (10 cm) long clusters of
six or more brilliant scarlet flowers from early
summer onwards. *Foliage* Pinnate, up to 6 in
(15 cm) long, with 12–24 oblong leaflets each
up to 1$\frac{1}{4}$ in (3.5 cm) long. Mid green. *Stem*
Mid green, semi-rigid, forming fan shape.
Not self-clinging. Medium growth rate. *Fruit*
Produces no fruit of interest.

Clianthus puniceus **in flower**

Hardiness Tolerates a minimum winter
temperature of up to 23°F (−5°C) but only in
very sheltered locations.
Soil requirements Tolerates all soil types but
resents very dry conditions.
Sun/Shade aspect Requires a very warm,
sheltered aspect in full sun to very light shade.
Pruning Not normally required but individual
branches can be removed if necessary.
Training Fan-train on to wires or individual
anchorage points.
Propagation and nursery production Seed or
semi-ripe cuttings inserted into sand with
some additional bottom heat. Always purchase container grown; will have to be sought
from a specialist nursery or from florists,
where it is sometimes sold as a house plant.
Best planting height 6 in–2 ft (15–60 cm).
Problems Its hardiness is always suspect and
even in the most sheltered of areas it is at risk
in winter. Availability scarce.
Similar forms of interest *C. p.* 'Albus' Pure
white, less hardy. Very scarce. *C. p.* 'Flamingo' Deep rose pink flowers. Less hardy. *C. p.*
'Red Cardinal' Bright scarlet. Less hardy. *C.
p.* 'White Heron' Ivory white flowers with
green shading. Less hardy.
Average height and spread
Five years
4 × 4 ft (1.2 × 1.2 m)
Ten years
8 × 8 ft (2.4 × 2.4 m)
Twenty years
12 × 12 ft (3.7 × 3.7 m)
Protrudes up to 2 ft (60 cm)
from support.

COBAEA SCANDENS

CLIMBING CATHEDRAL BELLS

Polemoniaceae   *Annual Climber*
Deciduous

An attractive annual climber producing
fascinating flowers when a hot summer
prevails.

Origin From Central South America, including Mexico.
Use As an annual climber for walls and fences, to cascade through medium to large
shrubs, or as a greenhouse or conservatory
climber in large containers.
Description *Flower* Large, bell-shaped
flowers, up to 2–3 in (5–7.5 cm) long, carried
singly on leaf stalks up to 8 in (20 cm) long
from May to October. Green inner colouring
towards the base, violet/purple on outer side.
Rounded, lobed ends. *Foliage* Pinnate leaves
with three pairs of leaflets, up to 4 in (10 cm)
long and 2 in (15 cm) wide. Grey/green with
purple hue. Attractive. *Stem* Self-clinging by
twining and tendrils. Light green. Fast annual
growth produced from seedlings. *Fruit* No
fruit of interest.
Hardiness Tolerates a minimum winter temperature of 32°F (0°C).
Soil requirements Any average garden soil
with adequate moisture retention and nutrients. For plants grown in containers in conservatories and greenhouses, a good quality
soil-based potting compost should be used.
Sun/Shade aspect Requires a sheltered summer planting area to prevent wind and rain
damage to flowers. Full sun, dislikes shade in
which it will be very shy to flower.
Pruning Not required. Of an annual nature
and dies in autumn.
Training Allow to ramble through large
shrubs, up pillars and posts. May need wires
or strings where adequate training material is
unavailable.
Propagation and nursery production From
seed raised under protection and not planted
out until all danger of spring frosts has passed. Purchase seed from specialist seed merchants. If plants are available in spring from
nurseries, garden centres or other sources,
best planting height is 2–6 in (5–15 cm).
Problems The requirement to grow it annually can be a little frustrating, but it is well
worth the effort.

Cobaea scandens

Similar forms of interest *C. s.* **'Alba'** Pure white form. Seed extremely scarce. *C. s.* **'Variegata'** Variegated foliage. Seed extremely scarce.

Average height and spread
One year
15 × 15 ft
(4.6 × 4.6 m)
Protrudes up to
12 in (30 cm)
from support.

COLLETIA CRUCIATA

ANCHOR PLANT
Rhamnaceae   *Wall Shrub*
Evergreen

An unusual shrub without foliage but viciously armed with cactus-like spikes so must be carefully sited and handled.

Colletia cruciata

Origin From Brazil and Uruguay.
Use As a curiosity shrub for growing against walls and fences where it benefits from the protection.
Description *Flower* Small, white, fragrant, pitcher-shaped, borne in profusion on mature shrubs mid summer to early autumn. *Foliage* None. *Stem* Light grey/green stems, surmounted by branches which take on a flat, triangular shape, each triangulation topped by a very sharp spike. Slow-growing. *Fruit* Insignificant.
Hardiness Tolerates a minimum winter temperature of 14°F (−10°C), but susceptible to frost when young and needs protection in early stages.

Soil requirements Any soil, including dry to very dry.
Sun/Shade aspect Sheltered aspect. Full sun to light shade.
Pruning None required.
Training No training necessary, simply grow against a wall.
Propagation and nursery production From seed. Purchase container grown. Not easy to find. Best planting height 8–15 in (20–40 cm).
Problems Its spines are vicious, so handle with due care.
Similar forms of interest *C. armata* Vanilla-scented flowers, borne profusely late summer to early autumn. Shoots form rounded spines, each tipped with a single thorn. From Chile. *C. a.* **'Rosea'** A stronger-growing, very scarce form with flowers pink in bud, opening to pink-tinged white.

Average height and spread
Five years
3 × 3 ft (91 × 91 cm)
Ten years
4 × 4 ft (1.2 × 1.2 m)
Twenty years
8 × 8 ft (2.4 × 2.4 m)
Protrudes up to 5 ft (1.5 m) from wall or fence.

CORNUS FLORIDA
(*Benthamidia florida*)

NORTH AMERICAN FLOWERING DOGWOOD
Cornaceae   *Wall Shrub*
Deciduous

A large shrub not always recognized as being suitable for a wall, but in such situations, particularly if lightly shaded, makes a handsome specimen.

Origin From eastern USA.
Use As a large, fan-trained flowering and autumn foliage shrub against walls and fences.
Description *Flower* A 3 in (7.5 cm) wide head with four medium-sized white bracts resembling petals, late spring to early summer, bracts being slightly twisted and curled. Some pink flowering forms. *Foliage* Leaves oblong, 2–3 in (5–7.5 cm) long, purple-green, giving good red/orange autumn colour. Some white, yellow and pink variegated forms. *Stem* Upright when young, becoming branching with age. Medium to fast growth rate when young, slowing with age. *Fruit* Insignificant.
Hardiness Tolerates a minimum winter temperature of 14°F (−10°C).
Soil requirements Prefers neutral to acid soil, dislikes any alkalinity.
Sun/Shade aspect Tolerates all but the most severe aspect. As a wall shrub best in light shade.
Pruning None, apart from that required for training.

Training Requires wires or individual anchor points to secure and encourage a fan-trained shape.
Propagation and nursery production From softwood cuttings taken in mid summer or from layers. Purchase container grown. Readily available in its native environment, scarce elsewhere. Best planting height 2–2½ ft (60–76 cm).
Problems None, given suitable conditions.
Similar forms of interest *C. f.* **'Apple Blossom'** Apple blossom pink bracts. Good autumn colour. *C. f.* **'Cherokee Chief'** Flower bracts deep rose red. Good autumn colour. *C. f.* **'Cherokee Princess'** Large, round, white flower bracts. Good autumn colour. *C. f.* **'Pendula'** White flower bracts. Good autumn colour. An interesting weeping form, of less than average height but with more spread. *C. f.* **'Rainbow'** White flower bracts. Golden-margined dark green leaves, in autumn turning plum/purple. Slightly less hardy and less than average height and

Cornus florida in flower

spread. *C. f.* **'Rubra'** One of the most sought-after varieties, with rosy-pink flower bracts in spring. Leaves red when young. Slightly less hardy and less than average height and spread. *C. f.* **'Spring Song'** Deep rose-red flower bracts. *C. f.* **'Tricolor'** White flower bracts in spring. Foliage green with white irregular margin, flushed rose-pink, turning purple in winter with rose-red edges. Less than average hardiness, height and spread. *C. f.* **'White Cloud'** Large white flower bracts freely borne. Foliage bronze/green.
Average height and spread
Five years
7 × 7 ft (2.1 × 2.1 m)
Ten years
15 × 15 ft (4.6 × 4.6 m)
Twenty years
18 × 18 ft (5.5 × 5.5 m)
Protrudes up to 4 ft (1.2 m) from support.

Cornus florida 'Rubra' in flower

CORNUS KOUSA

CHINESE DOGWOOD, JAPANESE DOGWOOD, KOUSA DOGWOOD

Cornaceae   *Wall Shrub*
Deciduous

A truly magnificent late spring flowering shrub with good autumn colour, adapting well as a large fan-trained specimen.

Origin From Japan and Korea.
Use As a large, spreading, fan-shaped wall or fence shrub.
Description *Flower* Four 2in (5cm) wide, large creamy-white bracts surround purple-green flower clusters in late spring, early summer. *Foliage* Leaves elliptic, slightly curled, 2–3in (5–7.5cm) long, olive-green with some purple shading, giving exceptional orange/red autumn colour. Foliage in autumn is retained well and is not usually damaged or destroyed by wind. *Stem* Upright, light green to grey/green, becoming grey/brown and branching with age. With training forms a wide, spreading, fan-shaped shrub. Slow growth rate at first, then medium, finally again becoming less vigorous. *Fruit* Attractive dull red, strawberry-like fruits on mature shrubs.
Hardiness Tolerates a minimum winter temperature of 4°F (−15°C).
Soil requirements Neutral to acid, in moist conditions and light shade, however, may be happy on slightly alkaline soils.
Sun/Shade aspect Tolerates all aspects, except extremely severe. Prefers light shade, tolerates medium shade to full sun.
Pruning None required, other than for training.
Training Requires wires or individual anchor points to secure and encourage the fan-trained shape.
Propagation and nursery production From layers or softwood cuttings taken in mid summer. Purchase container grown. Moderately easy to find. Best planting height 2–3ft (60–91cm).

Cornus kousa **in flower**

Problems Slow to establish, taking three to four years to flower really well.
Similar forms of interest *C. k. chinensis* A Chinese form which produces larger flowering bracts than its parent. *C. k.* 'Gold Spot' A variety with white flower bracts and with the green foliage mottled with golden variegation. Hard to find. *C. k.* 'Milky Way' An American variety of garden origin with larger white flower bracts. *C. k.* 'Norman Haddon' Light grey/green foliage with good autumn colour. Pink bracts in late spring. Fruits insignificant.
Average height and spread
Five years
5 × 5 ft (1.5 × 1.5 m)
Ten years
10 × 10 ft (3 × 3 m)
Twenty years
15 × 15 ft+ (4.6 × 4.6 m+)
Protrudes up to 3 ft (91 cm) from support.

COROKIA COTONEASTER

WIRE-NETTING BUSH

Cornaceae   *Wall Shrub*
Evergreen

An interesting shrub that fan-trains well against a wall and often benefits from the protection.

Origin From New Zealand.
Use As a low, spreading, fan-trained shrub with interesting stems, foliage and flowers for walls and fences.
Description *Flower* Very small, single, bright yellow, star-like flowers, late spring to early summer. *Foliage* Leaves very small, ovate, ½–¾ in (1–2 cm) long, dark green to purple/green. Some yellow autumn colour. *Stem* Contorted, very twiggy branchlets, forming an intricate tracery. When trained, forms a fan-shape. Stems purple/green. Very slow rate of growth. *Fruit* In hot summers, produces small, round, orange fruits.

Corokia cotoneaster **in flower**

Hardiness Tolerates a minimum winter temperature of 14°F (−10°C).
Soil requirements Alkaline to acid. Prefers a well-drained soil.
Sun/Shade aspect Sheltered aspect. Best in full sun or very light shade.
Pruning None, other than that required for training.
Training Allow to grow against a wall. Normally needs no fixing.
Propagation and nursery production From softwood cuttings taken in early summer. Purchase container grown. Not easy to find. Best planting height 4–12 in (10–30 cm).
Problems Extremely slow-growing. Young plants often look weak and insipid before being planted out, but gradually acquire an interesting, contorted form.
Similar forms of interest *C. c.* 'Little Prince' Black bark, green leaves with silver sheen. Small star-shaped yellow flowers. *C. buddleioides* Upright lanceolate grey leaves with silver reverse. Clusters of bright yellow star-shaped flowers. *C.* 'Coppershine' foliage turns purple in sun. Yellow flowers.
Average height and spread
Five years
2½ × 2½ ft (76 × 76 cm)
Ten years
3½ × 3½ ft (1 × 1 m)
Twenty years
4 × 4 ft (1.2 × 1.2 m)
Protrudes up to 2 ft (60 cm) from support.

COROKIA × VIRGATA

WIRE NETTING PLANT

Cornaceae   *Wall Shrub*
Evergreen

A shrub benefiting from the protection of a wall or fence where it can show off its small yellow flowers to the best advantage.

Origin From New Zealand.
Use As a freestanding or fan-trained shrub for walls and fences. Good as a container-grown plant for greenhouses and conservatories in colder areas.
Description *Flower* Small, star-shaped yellow flowers up to ½ in (1 cm) wide, normally presented in threes at the ends of branches in mid to late spring. *Foliage* Lanceolate, up to 1¾ in (4.5 cm) long and ½ in (1 cm) wide. Grey/green shiny upper surface, white downy undersides. Attractive. *Stem* Grey/green, becoming grey/brown. Rigid, branching. Attractive. Slow to medium growth rate. *Fruit* In hot summers may produce oval, ¼ in (5 mm) long, orange/yellow fruits.
Hardiness Tolerates a minimum winter temperature of up to 23°F (−5°C) but needs shelter from cold winds.
Soil requirements Tolerates all soil types except extremely waterlogged and very dry.
Sun/Shade aspect Requires a sheltered aspect in full sun to light shade, with full sun for preference.
Pruning Normally not required but individual branches can be removed if necessary.
Training Allow to grow freestanding or fan-train on to wires or individual anchorage points.
Propagation and nursery production From semi-ripe cuttings taken in mid to late summer. Should always be purchased container grown; may have to be sought from specialist nurseries. Best planting height 6 in–2 ft (15–60 cm).

Corokia × virgata **in flower**

Problems Its hardiness can be suspect. Availability is scarce and the plants offered are normally small.
Similar forms of interest *C. × v.* 'Bronze King' Bronze lanceolate leaves and small yellow star-shaped flowers. *C. × v.* 'Red Wonder' Bronze/green leaves, yellow star-shaped flowers. May produce deep red berries. *C. × v.* 'Yellow Wonder' Green leaves. Yellow fruits follow yellow star-shaped flowers.
Average height and spread
Five years
3 × 4 ft (91 cm × 1.2 m)
Ten years
8 × 8 ft (2.4 × 2.4 m)
Twenty years
10 × 12 ft (3 × 3.7 m)
Protrudes up to 18 in (45 cm) from support if fan-trained, 5 ft (1.5 m) untrained.

CORONILLA GLAUCA

KNOWN BY BOTANICAL NAME

Leguminosae   *Wall Shrub*
Evergreen

Although long cultivated, certainly in Europe, too rarely used as a wall shrub today.

Origin From southern Europe.
Use As a freestanding shrub against walls and fences or up pillars.
Description *Flower* Yellow pea-flowers, ½ in (1 cm) wide and long, very freely produced, mid to late spring, with further intermittent flowering through summer and early autumn. *Foliage* Leaves round to ovate, 1–1½ in (2.5–4 cm) long, grey/green, giving some yellow autumn colour on older leaves. *Stem* Grey/green. Upright, becoming branching, forming a flat-backed, arching shrub. Can be fan-trained if required. *Fruit* Small, grey/green pea pods.
Hardiness Tolerates a minimum winter temperature of 23°F (−5°C).
Soil requirements Any soil, including very alkaline.
Sun/Shade aspect Sheltered aspect in full sun to very light shade.
Pruning Remove some three to four year old branches to ground level occasionally to help annual rejuvenation.
Training May need tying to anchor points or wires to prevent it falling forward.
Propagation and nursery production From softwood cuttings taken mid summer. Purchase container grown. Often looks weak when purchased, but quickly establishes itself. Best planting height 2–2½ ft (60–76 cm). Available from specialist nurseries and good garden centres.

Coronilla glauca in flower

Problems May suffer from blackfly but not a major problem.
Similar forms of interest *C.g.* **'Variegata'** Grey/green leaves with white variegation when old. Yellow flowers. Slightly more tender. *C. emerus* Dark yellow pea-flowers produced mainly in spring, but continuing intermittently into summer and early autumn. A slightly more hardy form. *C. valentina* Bright golden yellow fragrant flowers. Grey/green foliage. Slightly more tender.
Average height and spread
Five years
6 × 6 ft (1.8 × 1.8 m)
Ten years
7 × 7 ft (2.1 × 2.1 m)
Twenty years
9 × 9 ft (2.7 × 2.7 m)
Protrudes 2½–3 ft (76–91 cm) from wall or fence.

CORYNABUTILON VITIFOLIUM
(*Abutilon vitifolium*)

FLOWERING MAPLE, VINE-LEAVED ABUTILON

Malvaceae   *Wall Shrub*
Deciduous

A tall, impressive plant but susceptible to winter cold. In very mild areas it may be considered a semi-evergreen. Recently reclassified as *Corynabutilon vitifolium*, this shrub is often still available under the name *Abutilon vitifolium*.

Origin From Chile.
Use As a tall flowering shrub for mild areas grown on a wall, or in large conservatories for colder areas.
Description *Flower* Large, saucer-shaped, deep to pale mauve or white flowers, depending on variety, borne freely late spring through to early summer. *Foliage* Vine-shaped leaves, 4–6 in (10–15 cm) long with a grey, downy covering. Some yellow autumn colour. *Stem* Upright, grey/green with a grey downy covering. Fast to medium rate of growth. *Fruit* Insignificant.
Hardiness Tolerates a minimum winter temperature of 23°F (−5°C).
Soil requirements Most soils, although thin alkaline soils will cause chlorosis.

Corynabutilon vitifolium **'Album'** in flower

Corynabutilon vitifolium **'Suntense'** in flower

Sun/Shade aspect Sheltered aspect in full sun. Resents any shade.
Pruning None required, although individual branches or limbs may be removed.
Training Tie upright shoots to individual anchor points.
Propagation and nursery production The basic form from seed, named varieties may be produced from softwood cuttings taken mid to late summer. Purchase container grown, often difficult to find. Best planting height 14 in–3 ft (40–91 cm).
Problems Stems at risk to severe temperature changes in winter and to wind chill factor. If stems die off, regeneration from the base is possible.
Similar forms of interest *C. v.* **'Album'** A white flowering form. *C. v.* **'Veronica Tennant'** Produces masses of large mauve flowers, deeper in colour than those of the parent. *C. v.* **'Suntense'** Slightly later-flowering, with mauve flowers. More tender than parent.
Average height and spread
Five years
8 × 6 ft (2.4 × 1.8 m)
Ten years
16 × 12 ft (5 × 3.7 m)
Twenty years
24 × 18 ft (7.3 × 5.5 m)
Protrudes up to 4 ft (1.2 m) from support.

COTINUS COGGYGRIA

SMOKE TREE, SMOKE BUSH, BURNING BUSH, CHITAM WOOD, VENETIAN SUMACH

Anacardiaceae   *Wall Shrub*
Deciduous

A shrub for summer and autumn display, producing fine foliage colours, profuse feathery flowers and good structural shape.

Origin From central and southern Europe.
Use As a foliage and flowering shrub fan-trained against a wall or fence.
Description *Flower* Large, open, pale pink inflorescences resembling plumes 6–8 in (15–20 cm) long, borne profusely on all wood three years old or more in summer, persisting into early and late autumn, turning smoky grey. *Foliage* Leaves ovate to oblong, 1½–2 in (4–5 cm) long, grey/green when young, opening to mid green, turning vivid orange/yellow in autumn; purple-leaved varieties turning scarlet-red. *Stem* Light green, becoming streaked with orange or red shading, finally grey/brown. Fast growing and upright when

young, becoming slower and very branching and twiggy, forming a fan-shaped shrub when trained. *Fruit* Feathery flowers change to seedheads.

Hardiness Tolerates a minimum winter temperature of 4°F (−15°C). Some winter dieback may occur at tips of new growth.

Soil requirements Prefers rich, deep soil, but tolerates most.

Sun/Shade aspect Tolerates all but the most severe of aspects. Green-leaved varieties tolerate very light shade to full sun; purple-leaved varieties must have full sun, otherwise they turn green.

Pruning Remove some mature shoots one to three years old each spring, so inducing some foliage rejuvenation and improved flowering.

Training Requires wires or individual anchor points to secure and encourage the fan-trained shape.

Propagation and nursery production From layers. Purchase container grown. Relatively easy to find in nursery production, some varieties will be found in garden centres. Best planting height 15 in–2½ ft (38–76 cm).

Problems Some purple-leaved varieties susceptible to mildew. Slow to establish, taking two to three years after planting to gain full stature.

Similar forms of interest *C. c.* 'Flame' One of the best varieties for autumn colour. Pink flowers and bright orange-red foliage in autumn. Hard to find and often confused with the parent plant. *C. c.* 'Foliis Purpureis' Pink inflorescence, young foliage rich plum/purple, ageing to lighter red to purple/red, late summer. Good autumn colours. *C. c.* 'Notcutt's Variety' Pink to purple-pink inflorescence with good red/purple autumn colours. Very deep purple leaves, slightly larger than those of its parent. Of slightly less height and spread. *C. c.* 'Royal Purple'

Cotinus coggygria 'Royal Purple' in leaf

Purple/pink inflorescence, purple/wine foliage, almost translucent when seen with sunlight behind it, becoming duller purple towards autumn, finally red. Slightly smaller than *C. coggygria*. Of garden origin. *C. c.* 'Rubrifolius' Pink inflorescence, deep wine red leaves when young, translucent in sunlight, becoming red/green towards autumn. Good autumn colour. *C. obovatus* (syn. *C. o. americanus*) (Chitam Wood). Light pink inflorescence. Round, ovate, light to mid green foliage with some orange shading, brilliant orange-red in autumn. Leaves much larger than *C. coggygria*. A large, spreading shrub from south-eastern USA.

Average height and spread
Five years
7 × 7 ft (2.1 × 2.1 m)
Ten years
12 × 12 ft (3.7 × 3.7 m)
Twenty years
20 × 20 ft (6 × 6 m)
Protrudes up to 4 ft (1.2 m) from support.

Cotoneaster horizontalis in fruit

COTONEASTER HORIZONTALIS

FISHBONE COTONEASTER, HERRINGBONE COTONEASTER

Rosaceae *Wall Shrub*
Deciduous

An excellent foliage, flowering and fruiting shrub ideal for fan-training against exposed walls and fences where height is limited.

Origin Possibly a native of Western China or of garden origin.

Use A deciduous shrub with attractive autumn foliage and fruit. Ideal for fan-training on low exposed walls or fences.

Description *Flower* Masses of small, white, four-petalled, cup-shaped flowers, borne singly at leaf joints, each with a red calyx, in late spring to early summer. *Foliage* Leaves ovate, ½–1 in (1–2.5 cm) long and wide, dark green to grey/green, with white edge variegation, depending on variety. Good autumn colours. *Stem* Upright when young, becoming branching, twiggy and spreading with age. Soft grey/green when young ageing to grey/brown. Medium growth rate. *Fruit* Small, red, round, glossy fruits in autumn.

Hardiness Tolerates a minimum winter temperature of 4°F (−15°C).

Soil requirements Tolerates all soil types.

Sun/Shade aspect Good in exposed situations. Full sun to medium shade.

Pruning None required but can be reduced in size in early spring if necessary.

Training Normally requires individual anchor points or wires to secure main branches. Side branches form a fish-bone pattern without assistance.

Propagation and nursery production From semi-ripe cuttings taken in mid summer or seed sown in spring. Purchase container grown for best results. Best planting height 12–18 in (30–45 cm).

Problems Relatively slow growing.

Similar forms of interest *C. h.* 'Major' Very similar in growth and habit to its parent but slightly more vigorous, with larger, rounder leaves and larger but fewer fruit. *C. h.* 'Robusta' A larger, faster-growing variety in which the herringbone pattern is more widely spaced. Leaves larger, rounder, more cup-shaped. Good red, round autumn fruits. One third more average height and spread. Not always easy to find. *C. h.* 'Variegatus' Herringbone growth pattern. Light grey/green foliage, round, with creamy white margins and lined with red round the outer edge. White flowers and red fruit, less glossy and less freely produced. Two thirds average height and spread. Of garden origin. *C.*

Cotoneaster 'Coral Beauty' in flower

'Coral Beauty' A similar variety with small, round, grey/green, ovate leaves giving good orange autumn colour. White flowers followed by coral red fruits in autumn. Slightly less than average height and spread. Of garden origin.

Average height and spread
Five years
3 × 4 ft (91 cm × 1.2 m)
Ten years
5 × 6 ft (1.5 × 1.8 m)
Twenty years
8 × 6 ft (2.4 × 1.8 m)
Protrudes up to 18 in (45 cm) from support.

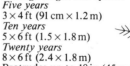

COTONEASTER × HYBRIDUS PENDULUS

WEEPING COTONEASTER

Rosaceae *Wall Shrub*
Semi-evergreen to evergreen

A fast-growing shrub that when grown as a fan-trained specimen provides a brilliant display of berries against walls and fences.

Origin Of garden origin.

Use As a fan-trained shrub for large walls and fences where its rapid growth provides quick cover.

Description *Flower* Numerous small white flowers produced in clusters in early summer. *Foliage* Ovate, 2–3 in (5–7.5 cm) long, dark green, with reddish veins on silver undersides. Often retained well into winter. *Stem* Light green ageing to purple/brown, finally grey/

brown. Fast growing, slowing with age. *Fruit* Clusters of red fruits in autumn carried along full length of mature stems.

Hardiness Tolerates a minimum winter temperature of 0°F (−18°C).

Soil requirements Any good soil, but shows some resistance on severe alkaline types by being slower growing.

Sun/Shade aspect Tolerates a wide range of aspects. Full sun to light shade, preferring full sun.

Pruning None required other than that for fan-training.

Training Tie to wires or individual anchor points in a fan shape.

Propagation and nursery production From cuttings or by grafting or budding on to *C. bullatus*. Best purchased container-grown; tree-trained plants of 6 ft (1.8 m) or more are available from garden centres and general nurseries. Both plants grown for ground cover and tree-trained can be used for fan-training.

Cotoneaster × *hybridus pendulus* in fruit

Problems Susceptible to stem canker, which can kill entire branches. On poor soils may well lose its vigour. Also susceptible to fire blight; if this disease is confirmed the tree must be completely destroyed by burning and its occurrence should be reported to the appropriate government agency.

Similar forms of interest None.

Average height and spread

Five years
6 × 6 ft (1.8 × 1.8 m)
Ten years
9 × 9 ft (2.7 × 2.7 m)
Twenty years
15 × 15 ft (4.6 × 4.6 m)
Protrudes up to 3 ft (91 cm) from support.

COTONEASTER
(Low-growing, Spreading, Evergreen Forms for Walls)

KNOWN BY BOTANICAL NAME

Rosaceae   *Wall Shrub*
Evergreen

Useful flowering and fruiting evergreens for growing as wall shrubs.

Origin Mainly native to China, but many varieties now of garden or nursery origin.

Use As low, spreading, fan-trained shrubs for walls and fences.

Description *Flower* Small, white, four-petalled flowers with red calyxes, borne singly or in clusters, depending on variety, late spring to early summer. *Foliage* Leaves ½–¾ in (1–2 cm) long, lanceolate to ovate and in some varieties round. Dark shiny green with grey undersides, veins and stalks often red-shaded. *Stem* Green to dark brown, spreading, forming a fan-shape. Slow to medium growth rate. *Fruit* Round to ovate, glossy fruits, normally red, some purple/red depending on variety. **Hardiness** Tolerates a minimum winter temperature of 4°F (−14°C).

Cotoneaster congestus in fruit

Soil requirements Tolerant of any soil.

Sun/Shade aspect Tolerates all aspects. Good in full sun to medium shade.

Pruning None required other than keeping within bounds.

Training Requires wires or individual anchor points to secure and encourage the fan-trained shape.

Propagation and nursery production From semi-ripe cuttings taken early to mid summer. Purchase container grown. Best planting height 8–15 in (20–38 cm). There is a wide range of varieties, most easy to find.

Problems Relatively small when purchased and rather slow-growing.

Forms of interest *C. adpressus* 'Praecox' Small, round, semi-evergreen, ovate leaves, giving some contrasting autumn red and orange colour from old leaves which are discarded. Orange/red, good-sized fruits in autumn. Also known sometimes as *C.* 'Nanshan'. From western China. *C. buxifolius* A very dense dwarf evergreen variety with white flowers and grey to dull green round foliage. Oval to round red fruits in autumn. From south-western India. *C. congestus* A very thick, creeping form with white flowers and blue/green foliage. Good red round fruits. From the Himalayas. *C. dammeri* Wide-spreading, with long ranging shoots. White flowers, bright red fruits in autumn. Leaves ovate, dark green above with grey/green underside, some having slight purple shading on veins and outer edges. Quite free in habit and has self-rooting tips. From China. *C. d.* 'Radicans' A vigorous variety with ovate leaves and flowers borne closely together, often in pairs. Red fruits in autumn. Slightly less than average height and spread.

Average height and spread

Five years
4 × 4 ft (1.2 × 1.2 m)
Ten years
6 × 6 ft (1.8 × 1.8 m)
Twenty years
7 × 7 ft (2.1 × 2.1 m)
Protrudes up to 4 ft (1.2 m) from support.

COTONEASTER
(Medium Height, Spreading Evergreen and Semi-Evergreen Forms for Walls)

KNOWN BY BOTANICAL NAME

Rosaceae   *Wall Shrub*
Evergreen or semi-evergreen

Useful, medium height flowering and fruiting shrubs to cover low exposed areas.

Origin Mostly native to China or of garden origin.

Use As medium size, fan-trained shrubs, often useful in difficult positions.

Description *Flower* Small ¼ in (5 mm) wide, white, four-petalled flowers with small red calyxes, borne singly or in clusters, late spring to early summer, depending on variety.

Foliage Leaves small, 1–1½ in (2.5–4 cm) long, round to broad ovate, dark green or grey/green, depending on variety. *Stem* Upright when young, becoming spreading with age forming a fan-shape. Medium growth rate. *Fruit* Round to ovate, glossy, normally red, but some purple/red varieties.

Hardiness Tolerates a minimum winter temperature of 0°F (−18°C).

Soil requirements Any soil conditions.

Sun/Shade aspect Tolerates all aspects. Full sun to medium shade.

Pruning None required but may be cut back to keep within bounds.

Training Requires wires or individual anchor points to secure and encourage the fan-trained shape.

Cotoneaster microphyllus in fruit

Propagation and nursery production From semi-ripe cuttings taken in mid summer. Purchase container grown. Most varieties relatively easy to find. Best planting height 1–2 ft (30–60 cm).

Problems May suffer from fire blight, for which there is no control or prevention. The plant should be burnt and the relevant government agency should be informed, since this is a notifiable disease.

Forms of interest *C. conspicuus* Arching branches with small, ovate, grey to grey/green foliage, covered in small white flowers, late spring to early summer. Bright red fruits freely borne. From south-eastern Tibet. *C. c.* 'Decorus' Equal to the parent in flowers and fruit, lower growing, height up to 4 ft (1.2 m) at maturity, spread 8 ft (2.4 m). *C. salicifolius* 'Autumn Fire' Narrow, ovate, dark green leaves, white flowers followed by orange-red fruit borne in clusters. Some foliage dies in winter, turning scarlet and enhancing the

Cotoneaster 'Skogholm' in flower

overall effect of fruit and colour. *C.* **'Donards Gem'** Small, round, ovate leaves, semi-ever-green. Good red autumn fruits. *C. microphyllus* Round, dark, glossy grey/green leaves, $\frac{1}{2}$ in (1 cm) long, very thickly produced along very twiggy branches. Round, dark scarlet fruits in autumn. Very hardy. Slower growth rate than average. From the Himalayas and south-western China. *C. m.* **'Cochleatus'** Slower than its parent and lower growing. Dull grey/green, ovate leaves and dull grey/red, round fruits in autumn. Of less height and vigour but of equal hardiness. From western China, south-eastern Tibet through eastern Nepal. *C. m.* **'Thymifolius'** Very small, narrow, ovate, shiny, dark green leaves produced very thickly and close to stems and branches. Purple/red berries in autumn. Not easy to find. *C. salicifolius* **'Gnome'** Small, elliptic to round, dark grey/green leaves. Small red fruits. Of garden origin. *C. s.* **'Parkteppich'** (Park Carpet) Leaves evergreen, narrow to medium width, lanceolate, dark green upper surface with grey underside, purple marking on veins. Round, red fruit, borne singly and in clusters. Of garden origin. *C.* × **'Skogholm'** Leaves small, lanceolate to oval, mid green to dark green. Large, oval to round, coral red fruits in autumn. Attractive weeping habit. From western China.

Average height and spread
Five years
4 × 4 ft (1.2 × 1.2 m)
Ten years
8 × 8 ft (2.4 × 2.4 m)
Twenty years
12 × 12 ft (3.7 × 3.7 m)
Protrudes up to 4 ft (1.2 m) from support depending on variety.

COTONEASTER
(Tall Deciduous Forms)

KNOWN BY BOTANICAL NAME

Rosaceae   *Wall Shrub*
Deciduous

A group of shrubs often overlooked which can give attractive autumn foliage and fruit effects.

Origin Mostly from China and the Himalayas, or of garden origin.
Use As a fanned or spreading, fruiting shrub for large walls and fences.
Description *Flower* White, four-petalled flowers with prominent red calyxes, borne either singly or in clusters, 3 in (7.5 cm) across, in late spring to early summer. *Foliage* Basically elliptic, 1–1$\frac{1}{2}$ in (2.5–4 cm) long, normally green to grey/green with good autumn colours. *Stem* Strong, quick-growing, upright, becoming spreading with age. *Fruit* Red fruits, borne singly or in clusters, depending on variety.
Hardiness Tolerates a minimum winter temperature of 4°F (−15°C).
Soil requirements Any soil, except very dry.
Sun/Shade aspect Tolerates exposed aspects. Full sun to medium shade.
Pruning None required, but can be reduced in size.
Training Requires wires or individual anchor points to secure and encourage a fan-trained shape.
Propagation and nursery production From softwood cuttings, grafting or seed, depending on variety. Purchase container grown. Best planting height 2–4 ft (60 cm–1.2 m).
Problems The variety *C.* × 'Firebird' is normally grafted on to understock of *C. bullatus* which can sucker and, given time, kill the variety. Keep a careful watch for suckering growth and remove from the plant immediately when seen.
Forms of interest *C. bullatus* Foliage large, round to oblong, dark green with corrugated surfaces, giving good autumn colour. 2 in (5 cm) clusters of white flowers give way to dark red fruit, enhancing autumn colour of foliage. Often used as grafting understock for

Cotoneaster simonsii **in fruit**

many of the large-leaved, evergreen forms. From western China. *C. distichus* Foliage very distinct, round, $\frac{3}{4}$–1 in (2–2.5 cm) long and wide, glossy green with red autumn colour. Bright red elliptic-shaped fruits borne singly in each leaf axil, being held well into early spring. Two thirds average height and spread. Often found in commercial production under the incorrect name of *C. rotundifolius*. From the Himalayas and south-western China. *C. divaricatus* Very good orange-red autumn foliage, contrasting with some later held green leaves. Many fruits, dark red and glossy. From western China. *C.* × **'Firebird'** Foliage dark grey/green, 3–4 in (7.5–10 cm) long, oval to oblong, giving good autumn colour. Large, round, orange/red fruits borne in thick clusters in autumn. Possibly more spreading than average and very hardy. Not easy to find but obtainable. A hybrid of *C. bullatus*, probably being a cross between this and *C. franchetii*. *C. simonsii* Semi-evergreen, round to elliptic leaves, borne on upright stems, covered in late spring with single or small clusters of white flowers in each leaf axil, culminating in red fruits. Adapts well to training. Very good for propagation from seed. From Assam.

Average height and spread
Five years
8 × 8 ft (2.4 × 2.4 m)
Ten years
12 × 12 ft (3.7 × 3.7 m)
Twenty years
15 × 15 ft (4.6 × 4.6 m)
Protrudes up to 4 ft (1.2 m) from support.

COTONEASTER
(Tall Evergreen Forms)

KNOWN BY BOTANICAL NAME

Rosaceae   *Wall Shrub*
Evergreen

A very useful group of large evergreen flowering and fruiting shrubs that can be trained against walls and fences.

Origin Mostly native to western China or of garden origin.
Use As wide-spreading, evergreen shrubs for flower, foliage and fruit effect on large walls and fences.
Description *Flower* White flowers with red calyxes borne either in clusters 3 in (7.5 cm) across, or singly, depending on variety, in early summer. *Foliage* Ovate, lanceolate to round, 2–4 in (5–10 cm) long, dark to mid or grey/green, depending on variety. *Stem* Strong, upright, green to green/red or grey/green, becoming branching with age. Fast rate of growth. *Fruit* Yellow, red or

orange fruits, produced in clusters in early autumn. Not normally attacked by birds until late in the winter.
Hardiness Tolerates a minimum winter temperature of 4°F (−15°C)
Soil requirements Most soil conditions, but may show distress on very thin alkaline types.
Sun/Shade aspect Tolerates exposed aspects. Full sun to medium shade.
Training Tie to wires or to individual anchor points in a spreading fan shape.
Pruning None required but may be reduced in size in early spring, if necessary.
Propagation and nursery production From semi-ripe cuttings taken in early summer or by grafting in winter. Purchase container grown. Most varieties fairly easy to find in nurseries and in some garden centres. Best planting height 2–4 ft (60 cm–1.2 m).
Problems *C.* 'Cornubia', *C.* 'Exburiensis', *C.* 'Inchmery' and *C.* 'Rothschildianus' may be grafted on to understocks of *C. bullatus* which can sucker and, given time, kill the variety. If suckers are seen they should be removed as soon as possible. Certain varieties are susceptible to the fungus disease fire blight, while others are liable to stem canker. In areas where the fire blight problem cannot be controlled, some named varieties are likely to be withdrawn from commercial production. Stem canker can be dealt with by cutting back affected shoots and treating with pruning compound.

Cotoneaster lacteus **in fruit**

Forms of interest *C.* **'Cornubia'** Broad, lanceolate leaves. Large clusters of white flowers followed by bright red fruits. Of garden origin. *C.* **'Exburiensis'** Light to mid green, broad, lanceolate leaves. White flowers followed by clusters of bright yellow fruits. Two thirds average height and spread. Raised in Exbury Gardens, Hampshire, England. *C. franchetii sternianus* (syn. *C. wardii*) Round, silver/grey to grey/green foliage. White flowers followed by good orange fruits. Two thirds average height and spread. From southern Tibet and northern Burma. *C. henryanus* Leaves long, lanceolate, dark green, slightly corrugated, with duller grey undersides. Clusters of white flowers borne on brown/red, strong, upright shoots, followed by red fruits. *C.* **'Inchmery'** Foliage light green, slightly broader, lanceolate. Clusters of white flowers, followed by yellow fruit with coral shading in autumn. Two thirds average height and spread. Raised in the Inchmery Gardens, Hampshire, England. *C. lacteus* Elliptic, dark green foliage, clusters of white flowers followed by dark red rounded fruits borne profusely and held sometimes until they rot. Very good on large walls. From China. *C.* **'Rothschildianus'** Large clusters of yellow fruit set off against light green, broad, lanceolate leaves, 4–6 in (10–15 cm) long, spectacular in autumn. Raised at Exbury Gardens, Hampshire, England. *C. salicifolius floccosus* Long, graceful, pendulous branches with narrow, elliptic, shiny-surfaced leaves, green with white undersides, giving a drooping, fan-like appearance. Clusters of white flowers give way to small, dull, red fruits. Very good for using on an exposed, shady wall. Two thirds average height and spread. From China.

Average height and spread
Five years
8 × 8 ft (2.4 × 2.4 m)
Ten years
12 × 12 ft (3.7 × 3.7 m)
Twenty years
15 × 15 ft (4.6 × 4.6 m)
Protrudes up to 3 ft (91 cm) from support.

CRATAEGUS
(Autumn Foliage Forms)

ORNAMENTAL THORN

Rosaceae **Hardy Tree**
Deciduous
Not normally thought of for fan-training but their ability to make regrowth allows them to be used for this purpose with good results, particularly in exposed areas.

Origin Throughout the northern hemisphere.
Use As a large fan-trained tree for walls, particularly in exposed locations.
Description *Flower* Small white florets, ½ in (1 cm) across, produced in clusters 2–3 in (5–7.5 cm) wide in early summer, often with a musty scent enjoyed by bees. *Foliage* Ovate, 2–3 in (5–7.5 cm) long, light or mid green, sometimes glossy, depending on variety. Good yellow or orange autumn colour. *Stem* Medium rate of growth, forming a large fan-shaped tree with training. Very closely branched. Stems grey/green and attractive in winter. Most varieties have large thorns, normally curved and mahogany brown. *Fruit* Clusters up to 6 in (15 cm) in diameter of round, orange or crimson fruits produced in autumn; in some varieties very late to ripen.
Hardiness Tolerates a minimum winter temperature of 0°F (−18°C).
Soil requirements Most soil conditions, except very dry.
Sun/Shade aspect Tolerates all aspects. Full sun to medium shade, preferring light shade.
Pruning Prune young trees hard in the spring following planting. Select and train resulting five to seven shoots and tie into a fan-trained shape. In subsequent years, remove all side growths back to two points from their origin

and maintain original main branches in fan shape.
Training Will require tying to wires or individual anchor points.
Propagation and nursery production From budding or grafting on to understock of *C. monogyna*. Purchase container grown or bare-rooted; most varieties relatively easy to find from general nurseries. Select trees of 6 ft (1.8 m), ensuring that they have been either bottom budded or grafted.
Problems Slow to establish and may need two full springs to recover from transplanting. Sharp thorns can be a hazard in close garden planting.
Forms of interest *C.* **'Autumn Glory'** Excellent yellow and orange autumn colour; white flowers and red berries. Of garden origin. *C. crus-galli* (Cockspur thorn) A flat-topped tree of more spreading habit and slightly less height. Foliage ovate to narrowly ovate, up to 3 in (7.5 cm) long, with toothed edges. Good orange/yellow autumn colours. White flowers in May followed by large clusters of long-lasting red fruits. Large thorns up to 3 in (7.5 cm) long. From North America. *C. durobrivensis* Leaves ovate with good autumn colours. White flowers followed by shining crimson berries maintained well into winter. Two thirds average height and spread and may also be grown as a large shrub. Limited in commercial production outside its native environment of North America. *C. × grignonensis* Leaves ovate, up to 2½ in (6 cm) long, very glossy upper surface, downy grey underside. Large clusters of white flowers followed by oval to globe-shaped red fruits in autumn. Two thirds average height and spread. Originating in France. Not readily available. *C. × lavallei* (syn. *C. carrierei*) Ovate, dark glossy green foliage with downy, paler undersides. Good autumn colour. White flowers in clusters with dominant anthers of red and yellow in June. Fruits orange/red, globe-shaped, ripening in September/October and maintained well into winter. Two thirds average height and spread. *C. mollis* Ovate leaves up to 4 in (10 cm) long with double-toothed edges. Light downy grey/green at first, ageing to light green. Good autumn colours. Flowers white with yellow anthers followed by large, globe-shaped red fruits, with downy texture. From North America. *C. pedicellata* (syn. *C. coccinea*) (Scarlet haw) Foliage light to mid green, slightly glossy, with toothed edges. Good yellow/orange autumn colour, ageing to red. Numerous short thorns. White flowers in early to mid spring, followed in autumn by bunches of scarlet fruits. Two thirds average height and spread. From north-eastern USA. *C. pinnatifida* Interesting crimson fruits with small, dark, red/brown to black dots over their surface. Leaves light to mid green, slightly glossy, with deeply cut lobes. Good orange/red autumn colour. Few thorns, in some cases none at all. Two thirds average

height and spread. From northern China. Not readily available and must be sought from specialist nurseries. *C. prunifolia* Dark green, glossy foliage, round to ovate, with slightly downy undersides. Round clusters of white flowers up to 2½ in (6 cm) across, on downy stalks, followed by rounded crimson fruits which are rarely maintained far into winter. Two thirds average height and spread. Thought to be a cross between *C. macrantha* and *C. crus-galli*. *C. submollis* Similar to *C. mollis*, but not reaching such a height. Plants may be intermixed in nursery production and difficult to differentiate; *C. submollis* has 10 stamens to the flower and *C. mollis* has 20.

Average height and spread
Five years
13 × 13 ft (4 × 4 m)
Ten years
20 × 20 ft (6 × 6 m)
Twenty years
26 × 26 ft (8 × 8 m)
Protrudes up to 5 ft (1.5 m) from support.

CRATAEGUS OXYACANTHA
(*C. laevigata*)

THORN, MAY, HAWTHORN

Rosaceae **Hardy Tree**
Deciduous
A tree responding well to hard pruning and forming a close fan-trained wall specimen.

Origin From Europe.
Use As a large, flowering, fan-trained specimen for large, exposed walls.
Description *Flower* Clusters up to 2 in (5 cm) across of white flowers produced in late spring. Musty scent attractive to bees. *Foliage* Basically ovate, 2 in (5 cm) long, very deeply lobed with three or five indentations. Grey/green with some yellow autumn tints. *Stem* Light grey/green, becoming grey/brown. Strong, upright when young, quickly branching. Armed with small, extremely sharp spines up to ½ in (1 cm) long. Medium rate of growth. *Fruit* Clusters 2–4 in (5–10 cm) wide of small, dull red, round to oval fruits containing two stone seeds, produced in autumn.
Hardiness Tolerates a minimum winter temperature of 0°F (−18°C).
Soil requirements Any soil conditions, but shows signs of distress on extremely dry areas, where growth may be stunted.
Sun/Shade aspect Tolerates all aspects. Full sun to medium shade, preferring light shade.
Pruning Prune young trees hard in the spring following planting. Select and train resulting five to seven shoots and tie into a fan-trained

Crataegus crus-galli in fruit

shape. In subsequent years remove all side growths back to two points from their origin and maintain original main branches in fan shape.
Training Will require tying to wires or individual anchor points.
Propagation and nursery production From seed from the parent; all varieties budded or grafted. Purchase bare-rooted or container grown as young trees 3–6 ft (91 cm–1.8 m) tall, ensuring that they are grafted or budded at the base.
Problems The sharp spines can make cultivation difficult. Suckers of understock may appear and must be removed.

Crataegus oxyacantha 'Coccinea Plena' in flower

Similar forms of interest *C. o.* **'Alba Plena'** Double white flowers in mid spring, followed by limited numbers of red berries in autumn. *C. o.* **'Crimson Cloud'** Single, dark pink to red flowers with yellow eyes profusely borne in late spring. Good yellow/bronze/orange autumn colour. *C. o.* **'Gireoudii'** New foliage on new growth mottled pink and white, ageing to green. New foliage on old wood green. Two thirds average height and spread. Shy to flower, but can produce white, musty-scented blooms. Limited fruit production. Difficult to find and must be sought from specialist nurseries. *C. o.* **'Paul's Double Scarlet Thorn'** (syn. *C. o.* **'Coccinea Plena'**) Dark pink to red double flowers produced in late spring, early summer. Limited red berries in autumn. *C. o.* **'Rosa Plena'** Double pink flowers, produced late spring, early summer. Some limited berrying. *C. laciniata* (syn. *C. orientalis*) Attractive, dark grey/green, cut-leaved foliage, light grey undersides. White

flowers and large dull orange/red fruits. Two thirds average height and spread. Somewhat scarce in production. From the Orient. *C. monogyna* (Hedgerow thorn, singleseed hawthorn) Single white flowers. Red, round fruits containing one stone. Foliage dark green. Rarely offered as a tree, normally used as a hedgerow plant. From Europe. *C.* × *mordenensis* **'Toba'** Double, creamy white flowers in the spring, followed by red berries in autumn.
Average height and spread
Five years
13 × 4 ft (4 × 1.2 m)
Ten years
20 × 10 ft (6 × 3 m)
Twenty years
20 × 20 ft (6 × 6 m)
Protrudes up to 3 ft 91 cm from support.

CRINODENDRON HOOKERIANUM
(*Tricuspidaria lanceolata*)

LANTERN TREE
Elaeocarpaceae   *Wall Shrub*
Evergreen
A beautiful shrub responding well when grown against walls and fences where it will derive some additional protection.

Origin From Chile.
Use As a freestanding or fan-trained shrub for walls and fences on acid soils.
Description *Flower* Crimson, lantern-shaped flowers, 1–1¼ in (2.5–3.5 cm) long, hanging from stalks along underside of branches, on mature wood only, late spring to early summer. *Foliage* Leaves dark green, lanceolate, 1½–2 in (4–5 cm) long, with silver undersides. *Stem* Dark green, upright. Slow to medium growth rate. *Fruit* Rarely fruits, but occasionally produces brown, leathery capsules.
Hardiness Tolerates a minimum winter temperature of 14°F (−10°C), but some leaf scorch may be suffered in severe wind chill conditions.
Soil requirements Acid soil; dislikes any alkalinity.
Sun/Shade aspect Sheltered to moderately sheltered aspect. Full sun to light shade.
Pruning Not normally required.
Training Grow freestanding or tie to wires or individual anchor points for fan-training.
Propagation and nursery production From softwood cuttings taken in early summer. Purchase container grown; may be rather hard to find. Best planting height 15 in–2½ ft (38 – 76 cm).

Crinodendron hookerianum in flower

Problems Slow to establish and achieve full beauty and may take some years to become fan-trained.
Similar forms of interest *C. patagua* (syn. *Tricuspidaria dependens*) White bell-shaped flowers, late summer. Attractive round purple/green foliage. A stronger growing shrub, reaching greater height and spread. More tender. Very hard to find.
Average height and spread
Five years
4 × 3 ft (1.2 × 91 cm)
Ten years
7 × 4 ft (2.1 × 1.2 m)
Twenty years
12 × 7 ft (3.7 × 2.1 m)
Protrudes up to 2 ft (60 cm) from support if fan-trained, 5 ft (1.5 m) untrained.

CYDONIA OBLONGA

QUINCE
Rosaceae   *Hardy Fruit Tree*
Deciduous
Beautiful spring-flowering trees, with autumn fruits both edible and attractive, adapting well to fan-training.

Origin Parent from northern Iran and Turkestan; many varieties of garden origin, particularly from France.
Use As fan-trained edible fruit-producing trees for large walls and fences.
Description *Flower* Saucer-shaped flowers coloured delicate mother-of-pearl to light rose-pink, up to 2 in (5 cm) wide, produced in good numbers in mid to late spring. Slightly scented. *Foliage* Leaves ovate, mid to dark green with silver undersides, 3–6 in (7.5-15 cm) long and 1½–2½ in (4–6 cm) wide. Good yellow autumn colour. *Stem* Attractive

Crataegus oxyacantha 'Rosa Plena' in flower

Cydonia oblonga 'Vranja' in flower

Cydonia oblonga 'Vranja' in fruit

growth formation even when fan-trained. Branches dark brown to purple/ brown. Medium to fast rate of growth. *Fruit* Medium-sized, round or pear-shaped yellow fruits, 2–5 in (5–12 cm) long and 2–3 in (5–7.5 cm) wide, depending on variety, abundantly produced in late summer, early autumn. Used to make quince jelly.
Hardiness Tolerates a minimum winter temperature of 4°F (−15°C).
Soil requirements Most soil conditions, only dislikes extremely dry or very waterlogged areas.
Sun/Shade aspect Tolerates all but the most exposed of aspects. Best in full sun to allow the fruit to ripen.
Pruning Prune young trees hard in spring following planting. Select and train resulting five to seven shoots and tie into a fan-trained shape. In subsequent years remove all side growths back to two points from their origin and maintain original main branches in fan shape.
Training Will require tying to wires or individual anchor points.
Propagation and nursery production *C. oblonga* from seed; all named varieties by budding or grafting. Purchase bare-rooted or container grown from specialist nurseries. Best planting height 3–5 ft (91 cm–1.5 m). Always select young trees that have been grafted or budded at the base.
Problems Fruiting can be a little erratic, especially after hard, late spring frosts at flowering time. Trees tend to look misshapen and irregular when young.
Similar forms of interest *C. o.* 'Meech's Prolific' Round, squat, pear-shaped fruits produced in good quantities. Flowers not the best feature. *C. o.* 'Portugal' Small, pear-shaped fruits in profusion; a good culinary variety. Generous flower production. *C. o.*

'Vranja' Large, pear-shaped, yellow fruits. Large flowers, somewhat sparsely produced, but the tree is a fine ornamental form.
Average height and spread
Five years
10 × 10 ft (3 × 3 m)
Ten years
16 × 16 ft (4.9 × 4.9 m)
Twenty years
23 × 23 ft (7 × 7 m)
Protrudes up to 4 ft (1.2 m) from support.

CYTISUS BATTANDIERI

MOROCCAN BROOM, PINEAPPLE BROOM
Leguminosae   *Wall Shrub*
Deciduous
An elegant, summer-flowering shrub, which in mild areas may be semi-evergreen. In exposed gardens prefers a wall position.

Origin From Morocco.
Use As a fan or spreading large shrub for high walls and fences.
Description *Flower* Upright racemes 4 in (10 cm) long, 2 in (5 cm) wide, of bright yellow, pineapple-scented flowers, early to mid summer. *Foliage* Trifoliate silvery green leaves, up to 4 in (10 cm) long and wide, comprising three leaflets 1½ in (4 cm) long. *Stem* Silvery grey when young, ageing to grey/green to grey/brown. Strong, upright, becoming branching and spreading with age. Fast-growing when young, slowing with age. *Fruit* Insignificant.
Hardiness Tolerates a minimum winter temperature of 14°F (−10°C).
Soil requirements Does well on moist soils but unhappy on very thin chalk types.
Sun/Shade aspect Sheltered, warm aspect in full sun.
Pruning None required, best planted where it can attain full maturity without pruning. If size must be restricted, cut young wood after flowering. Cutting into old wood may lead to die-back.
Training Requires wires or individual anchor points to secure and encourage the fan-trained shape.
Propagation and nursery production From seed, grafting or semi-ripe cuttings taken in mid summer. Available from most good garden centres. Best planting height 2–4 ft (60 cm–1.2 m).
Problems None, if given space to attain its full height and spread.
Similar forms of interest None.
Average height and spread
Five years
12 × 12 ft (3.7 × 3.7 m)
Ten years
16 × 16 ft (5 × 5 m)
Twenty years
25 × 25 ft (7.6 × 7.6 m)
Protrudes up to 4 ft (1.2 m) from support.

DECAISNEA FARGESII

KNOWN BY BOTANICAL NAME
Lardizabalaceae   *Wall Shrub*
Deciduous
Interesting green flowers which produce turquoise blue seed pods after a good summer.

Origin From China.
Use A tall, unusual, upright shrub for growing as a specimen against a wall, producing better flowers and fruit in this situation than when grown in the open.

Decaisnea fargesii in fruit

Description *Flower* Open panicles, up to 12 in (30 cm) long, of lime-green to yellow-green tubular flowers, produced at ends of upright shoots, late spring to early summer. *Foliage* Large leaves, 2–3 ft (60–91 cm) long, with six to 12 pairs of opposite leaflets each 3–6 in (7.5–15 cm) long. Light grey/green with yellow autumn colour. *Stem* Upright, becoming leaning with age, forming an upright central clump with some spreading side growths. Medium to fast growth rate. *Fruit* Metallic blue bean pods up to 15 in (38 cm) long in autumn following dry, hot summers.
Hardiness Tolerates a minimum winter temperature of 14°F (−10°C).
Soil requirements Does well on most soils but very moist, well-drained soil produces better growth and therefore more flowers and, in favourable years, fruit.
Sun/Shade aspect Requires some protection. Prefers light shade, but tolerates full sun provided adequate moisture is available.
Pruning None required. Weak, unattractive stems may be removed.
Training Normally grown in front of the wall and not necessarily against it, therefore needs no training or fixing.
Propagation and nursery production From seed. Purchase container grown plants or root-balled (balled-and-burlapped). Available from specialist nurseries. Best planting height 15 in–3 ft (38–91 cm).
Problems Can take several years to produce fruit.
Similar forms of interest None.
Average height and spread
Five years
6 × 6 ft (1.8 × 1.8 m)
Ten years
10 × 13 ft (3 × 4 m)
Twenty years
13 × 13 ft (4 × 4 m).
Protrudes up to 6 ft (1.8 m) from wall or fence.

Cytisus battandieri in flower

DECUMARIA BARBARA

KNOWN BY BOTANICAL NAME

Saxifragaceae   *Woody Climber*
Deciduous to semi-evergreen
An interesting climbing plant related both
to the climbing hydrangea and
schizophragma but possibly a little less
hardy.

Origin From USA.
Use As a self-clinging climber for lightly
shady walls and fences.
Description *Flower* 2–3 in (5–7.5 cm) wide
clusters of white, sterile flowers up to ¼ in
(5 mm) across, carried at the ends of each
branch in mid to late summer. *Foliage* Oval,
pointed, up to 5 in (12 cm) long. Initially grey
in colour, quickly becoming bright green ageing to dark green. Yellow autumn colour.
Stem Light grey/green, becoming maho-
gany/brown, finally brown/grey. Short-
branching, clinging by aerial roots. Slow to
medium growth rate. *Fruit* Fruiting not
reliable but may produce white ¼ in (5 mm)
long fruits in early autumn.
Hardiness Tolerates a minimum winter
temperature of 14°F (−10°C) although will
require additional protection from cold
winds.
Soil requirements Tolerates all types of soil
including dry, once established.
Sun/Shade aspect Light to medium shade,
dislikes full sun.
Pruning Requires no pruning but can be
reduced in size if required and will slowly
rejuvenate.
Training Normally self-clinging but may need
additional tying to individual anchor points
or wires, particularly when young.
Propagation and nursery production From
layers or cuttings, rooted into sand under the
protection of glass. Always purchase
container grown; will have to be sought from
a specialist nursery. Best planting height
6 in–2 ft (15–60 cm).
Problems Slow to establish and availability
may be scarce.
Similar forms of interest *D. sinensis* A very
similar variety except that it reaches 50 per
cent less height and spread. Not readily
available.
Average height and spread
Five years
5 × 5 ft (1.5 × 1.5 m)
Ten years
10 × 10 ft (3 × 3 m)
Twenty years
20 × 20 ft (6 × 6 m)
Protrudes up to 12 in (30 cm) from support.

Desfontainea spinosa **in flower**

Decumaria barbara **in flower**

DESFONTAINEA SPINOSA

KNOWN BY BOTANICAL NAME

Potaliaceae   *Wall Shrub*
Evergreen
A moderately hardy shrub which will
nevertheless benefit from the protection of
a wall or fence.

Origin From Chile and Peru.
Use As a freestanding or fan-trained shrub
for walls and fences.
Description *Flower* Scarlet, 1½ in (4 cm) long,
tubular flowers, yellow shaded in mouth, mid
summer. *Foliage* Leaves oval, 1–2 in (2.5–
5 cm) long, dark green, glossy, holly-like with
silver undersides. *Stem* Moderately stout,
dark green, forming a clump of upright
flowering shoots. Slow growth rate. *Fruit*
Insignificant.
Hardiness Tolerates a minimum winter temperature of 14°F (−10°C) but may suffer
foliage damage in severe wind chill
conditions.
Soil requirements Acid soil, dislikes any
alkalinity or waterlogging. Thrives on soil
high in organic content such as in woodland.
Sun/Shade aspect Requires a sheltered
aspect. Prefers light to medium shade, dislikes full sun.
Pruning None required.
Training Allow to grow freestanding or fan-
train by tying to individual anchor points.
Propagation and nursery production From
semi-ripe cuttings taken mid summer or from
rooted suckers from outer edges of mature
clumps. Purchase container-grown. Hard to
find; may be available from specialist
nurseries. Best planting height 8–15 in
(20–38 cm).
Problems Often takes a number of years to
settle down. Slow to form a fan-trained habit
but worthy of the effort once established.
Similar forms of interest *D. s.* 'Harold
Comber' A variety collected from the wild,
with varying flower colour, from vermillion to
orient red. Very scarce.
Average height and spread
Five years
2 × 2½ ft (60–80 cm)
Ten years
3 × 4 ft (1 × 1.2 m)
Twenty years
7 × 5 ft (2.2 × 1.5 m)
Protrudes up to 2 ft (60 cm) from support if
fan-trained, 4 ft (1.2 m) untrained.

DRIMYS WINTERI

WINTER'S BARK

Winteraceae   *Wall Shrub*
Evergreen
An evergreen which often prefers the
protection of a wall, making a tall,
interesting shrub.

Origin From South America.
Use As a freestanding, large shrub for walls
and fences.
Description *Flower* White to ivory-white
loose clusters of jasmine-scented flowers, mid
spring. *Foliage* Leaves large, 5–10 in
(12–25 cm) long, ovate, grey/green with glaucous undersides and leathery texture. *Stem*
Upright, light to bright green to grey/green,
becoming branching and spreading with age.
Medium growth rate. *Fruit* Insignificant.

Drimys winteri **in flower**

Hardiness Tolerates a minimum winter
temperature of 23°F (−5°C). Foliage resents
severe wind chill.
Soil requirements Acid, preferably open,
woodland, leafy soil, dislikes any alkalinity.
Sun/Shade aspect Requires a sheltered
aspect. Best in light or dappled shade.
Pruning None required, but any arching,
spreading branches may be removed to
confine the shrub to the planting area.
Training Main stems will require fixing to
individual anchor points for support.

Propagation and nursery production From layers or semi-ripe cuttings taken late summer. Purchase container grown or rootballed (balled-and-burlapped). Rather hard to find and must be sought from specialist nurseries. Best planting height 2–2½ ft (60–76 cm).
Problems Wind chill may cause extensive defoliation and some die-back.
Similar forms of interest None.
Average height and spread
Five years
6 × 6 ft (1.8 × 1.8 m)
Ten years
10 × 8 ft (3 × 2.4 m)
Twenty years
15 × 10 ft (4.6 × 3 m)
Protrudes up to 6 ft (1.8 m) from support.

ECCREMOCARPUS SCABER

CHILEAN GLORY FLOWER
Bignoniaceae   Annual/Perennial Climber
Evergreen
A somewhat tender climber worthy of effort but may need to be propagated annually from seed.

Origin From Chile.
Use As an annual climber for sunny walls and fences or for rambling over an uninteresting shrub. Good for training up pillars.

Eccremocarpus scaber **'Rubra' in flower**

Description *Flower* Racemes of narrow tubular flowers, deep orange/red in colour, up to 1 in (2.5 cm) long. Yellow and deep red flowering varieties also available. *Foliage* 1½ in (4 cm) long light green pinnate leaves; may be evergreen in very mild areas, although in less favourable conditions may be damaged and replaced in following spring by foliage on new basal growth. *Stem* Angular with ribbed edges, light green becoming mid green, not readily forming a woody structure except in the mildest areas. Rambling, not self-clinging. Medium to fast growing. *Fruit* None of interest, although seeds are required for annual propagation.
Hardiness Tolerates a minimum winter temperature of 23°F (−5°C). Not winter hardy except in the most favourable areas and best repropagated on an annual basis.
Soil requirements Alkaline to acid well drained soil with good plant food and adequate moisture retention to achieve good rate of annual growth.
Sun/Shade aspect Very sheltered aspect if overwintering is required. Full sun to light shade.
Pruning Normally killed over winter, therefore no pruning required other than cleaning away damaged material. If not killed by winter weather, a light trim in spring will secure new growth and good flowering in the following summer.

Eccremocarpus scaber **in flower**

Training Allow to ramble through a framework of wires, trellis or netting stretched over areas to be covered. Can be allowed to ramble over an uninteresting shrub to good effect.
Propagation and nursery production From seed collected after flowering in late summer/early autumn, sown in trays with a good quality potting compost under cover in late winter/early spring and then planted out on an annual basis once danger of frost has passed. Always purchase container grown, best planting height 3 in–2 ft (7.5–60 cm). Available from specialist nurseries and good garden centres.
Problems The possible need to produce this plant annually can be a disadvantage but its flowering display is sufficiently interesting to make the effort well worthwhile.
Similar forms of interest *E. s.* 'Aureus' Golden yellow flowers. Not readily available. *E. s.* 'Rubra' Orange/red flowers. Not readily available.
Average height and spread
One year
6 × 6 ft (1.8 × 1.8 m)
Protrudes up to 2 ft (60 cm) from support.

ELAEAGNUS COMMUTATA (*E. argentea*)

SILVER BERRY
Elaeagnaceae   *Wall Shrub*
Deciduous
Interesting, useful, silver-foliage shrub attractive when fan-trained on a large wall.

Origin From North America.
Use As an attractive foliage shrub for training on large walls and fences.

Elaeagnus commutata **in leaf**

Description *Flower* Small, inconspicuous, scented, pale yellow flowers in mid spring. *Foliage* Ovate, deep silver green leaves. *Stem* Grey/green, upright, becoming arching. Medium to fast growing. *Fruit* Small, oval, ½ in (1 cm) long, silver fruits in early to mid summer, often retained into autumn.
Hardiness Tolerates a minimum winter temperature of 4°F (−15°C).
Soil requirements Does well on all soil types, tolerating quite dry areas.
Sun/Shade aspect Tolerates all but the most exposed aspects. Prefers full sun.
Pruning None required, but can be cut back and will rejuvenate.
Training Requires wires or individual anchor points to secure and encourage a fan-trained shape.
Propagation and nursery production From softwood cuttings taken in early summer. Purchase container grown. Easy to find. Best planting height 1½–4 ft (45 cm–1.2 m).
Problems Root disturbance may lead to die-back with foliage dropping and stems dying back to ground level, but often rejuvenates again.
Forms of interest See further entries.
Average height and spread
Five years
5 × 5 ft (1.5 × 1.5 m)
Ten years
10 × 10 ft (3 × 3 m)
Twenty years
15 × 15 ft (4.6 × 4.6 m)
Protrudes up to 5 ft (1.5 m) from support.

ELAEAGNUS × EBBINGEI

KNOWN BY BOTANICAL NAME
Elaeagnaceae   *Wall Shrub*
Evergreen
Very useful, quick-growing evergreen with hidden scented flowers, adapting well to use on walls.

Origin Of garden origin; a hybrid of *E. macrophylla* and *E. pungens*, both from Japan.
Use As a fan-trained evergreen to give winter foliage colour on exposed walls and fences.

Elaeagnus × ebbingei **in flower**

Description *Flower* Sulphur yellow petals with silver calyx in late summer to late autumn. *Foliage* Leaves ovate, 3–6 in (7.5–15 cm) long, grey/green with some gold-variegated varieties. *Stem* Upright when young, becoming twiggy and dense with age. Can be trained into a fan or spreading shape. Normally grey/green when young, ageing to grey/brown. Medium to fast rate of growth. *Fruit* Small, egg-shaped red/orange fruits on mature shrubs in hot summers.
Hardiness Tolerates a minimum winter temperature of 4°F (−15°C).
Soil requirements Tolerates most soils, although unhappy on extremely alkaline or dry soils.

Sun/Shade aspect Tolerates all aspects. Full sun to deep shade, although shrub may be more lax and loose in shape in deep shade.
Pruning Trim hard back by two thirds in spring to encourage bushy habit once main structure has been trained.
Training Requires wires or individual anchor points to secure and encourage a fan-trained shape.
Propagation and nursery production From semi-ripe cuttings taken in early summer or by grafting. Purchase container grown; most forms fairly easy to find. Best planting height 1½–4 ft (45–1.2 m).
Problems Roots very susceptible to any dramatic change in soil conditions such as drought or waterlogging; whole areas of root may die, resulting in death of limb or even whole side of shrub directly related to damaged root area. Cultivation damage can also lead to this demise. If gold-variegated foliage varieties start to revert, producing all green foliage, remove this once seen.
Similar forms of interest *E.* × *e.* 'Limelight' Centres of leaves irregularly splashed gold to pale gold, variegation best in spring and summer, declining slightly in autumn. Upright habit. *E.* × *e.* 'Salcombe Seedling' Fragrant white flowers produced in good numbers in autumn. Foliage dark green with silver reverse. *E. macrophylla* Slightly broader, larger, grey/green leaves with silver undersides. Less hardy than *E.* × *ebbingei* and rather hard to find in colder areas.
Average height and spread
Five years
6 × 6 ft (1.8 × 1.8 m)
Ten years
8 × 8 ft (2.4 × 2.4 m)
Twenty years
12 × 12 ft (3.7 × 3.7 m)
Protrudes up to 4 ft (1.2 m) from support.

ELAEAGNUS PUNGENS

THORNY ELAEAGNUS

Elaeagnaceae   *Wall Shrub*
Evergreen

Foliage shrub for winter colour and for flower arrangements.

Origin From Japan. Most variegated forms of garden origin.
Use As a green or golden variegated fan-trained shrub for walls and fences.
Description *Flower* Small, inconspicuous, fragrant sulphur yellow or silvery-white flowers, mid to late autumn. *Foliage* Leaves 2–3 in (5–7.5 cm) long, ovate with pointed ends, dark olive-green with glossy upper surfaces and duller undersides. The young leaves of golden variegated forms, grey/brown in spring, do not become variegated until early summer. *Stem* Grey/green, ageing to brown/green. Upright when young, quickly becoming spreading, branching and twiggy, forming a wide, spreading shrub. Medium rate of growth. *Fruit* Insignificant.
Hardiness Tolerates a minimum winter temperature of 0°F (−18°C). Foliage may be damaged in severe wind chill conditions.
Soil requirements Tolerates most soils but unhappy on extremely alkaline or dry conditions.
Sun/Shade aspect Tolerates all but the most exposed aspects in full sun to deep shade, but may be lax and poorly shaped in deep shade.
Pruning Prune and train new shoots into fan or spreading shape on wall or fence. Cut back all forward-growing growths in spring to encourage a thick covering of branches and foliage.
Training Will require the support of wires, trellis or individual anchor points to form a fan-trained shape.
Propagation and nursery production By grafting in winter or semi-ripe cuttings taken late spring/early summer. Purchase container grown or root-balled (balled-and-burlapped). Best planting height 1½–4 ft (45 cm –1.2 m).

Elaeagnus pungens 'Maculata'

Problems May suffer from aphid attack. Shoots of variegated forms showing reversion to green should be cut out once seen. On grafted shrubs, rip out any suckers of understock.
Similar forms of interest *E. p.* 'Dicksonii' Leaves narrow, almost holly-like, with bright gold margins. Two thirds average height and spread. Slightly less hardy than *E. pungens*. Of garden origin. *E. p.* 'Fredericia' Light green, cream-splashed, narrow, very pointed leaves. Very branching habit. Slightly less than average height and spread. *E. p.* 'Gold Rim' A European variety, having round to ovate leaves with extensive gold variegation.

Elaeagnus pungens 'Gold Rim'

Two thirds average height and spread. *E. p.* 'Maculata' Dark leaves with central gold patches. Reaching just less than average height and spread. Very susceptible to green reversion, remove any reverted shoots once seen or golden colouring will be destroyed. Of garden origin and very widely grown. *E. p.* 'Variegata' Foliage margined creamy white. Some sulphur yellow fragrant flowers on very old plants. Prune back old limbs occasionally to preserve foliage size and quality. Two thirds average height and spread. Of garden origin. *E.* × *ebbingei* 'Gilt Edge' Attractive gold-margined leaves. Severe wind chill and extreme waterlogging may damage foliage. Slightly tender – minimum winter temperature 23°F (−5°C). Two thirds average height and spread. Of garden origin.
Average height and spread
Five years
5 × 5 ft (1.5 × 1.5 m)
Ten years
8 × 8 ft (2.4 × 2.4 m)
Twenty years
14 × 14 ft (4.3 × 4.3 m)
Protrudes up to 4 ft (1.2 m) from support.

ERIOBOTRYA JAPONICA (*Photinia japonica, Mespilus japonica*)

JAPANESE LOQUAT

Rosaceae   *Tender Tree*
Evergreen

A tree normally grown as a shrub outside its native environment for its attractive, large, evergreen foliage, benefiting well from the protection of a wall.

Origin From China.
Use As a freestanding, large, multi-stemmed shrub or tree for sheltered large walls, or in very large conservatories and greenhouses.
Description *Flower* Terminal panicles up to 6 in (15 cm) long consisting of yellow/white, ¾ in (2 cm) wide, fragrant, closely packed flowers in late summer, early autumn, rarely flowers outside its native environment. *Foliage* Leathery, lanceolate leaves, up to 12 in (30 cm) long and 6 in (15 cm) wide on young growth, smaller on older shoots. Dark glossy green above, with pronounced veins and silver/white, woolly undersides. Attractive. *Stem* Light green when young, becoming darker green with age. Stiff,

Eriobotrya japonica

upright, glossy surface, forming a round, upright pillar. Medium growth rate. *Fruit* Pear-shaped, yellow, edible fruits up to 1½ in (4 cm) long, but rarely fruits outside its native environment.
Hardiness Tolerates a minimum winter temperature of 14°F (−10°C) in sheltered wall locations.
Soil requirements Tolerates all types of soil as long as it is well drained.

Sun/Shade aspect Requires a very sheltered aspect. Best in a sunny, sheltered corner.
Pruning Normally requires no pruning for its own well-being but individual limbs can be removed if becoming an obstruction.
Training Allow to grow freestanding in front of walls. May need securing to individual anchor points.
Propagation and nursery production From seed sown in spring or autumn individually in pots, or by semi-ripe cuttings taken in late summer, in both cases under protection. Always purchase container grown; may be difficult to find, except from specialist nurseries. Best planting height 6–18 in (15–45 cm).
Problems Often outgrows the area allowed for it. Its availability may be scarce and its hardiness is suspect.
Average height and spread
Five years
5 × 3 ft (1.5 × 91 cm)
Ten years
15 × 6 ft (4.6 × 1.8 m)
Twenty years
20 × 12 ft (6 × 3.7 m)
Protrudes up to 12 ft (3.7 m) from wall or fence.

ERYTHRINA CRISTA-GALLI

CORAL TREE, COXCOMB

Leguminosae   *Wall Shrub*
Deciduous
An interesting shrub for a sun-facing wall.

Origin From Brazil.
Use As a medium-sized, summer-flowering sub-shrub for sunny walls and fences.
Description *Flower* Racemes of deep scarlet florets, waxy-textured, borne in large clusters at ends of shoots, mid to late summer. *Foliage* Leaves medium-sized, trifoliate, 4–5 in (10–12 cm) long, leaflets ovate. Grey/green, giving some yellow autumn colour. *Stem* Strong, upright, becoming arching with weight of flowers, grey to grey/green. Small sharp spines at each leaf axil. Dies to ground level each winter, regenerating following spring. Fast-growing, annually produced stems. *Fruit* Insignificant.
Hardiness Tolerates a minimum winter temperature of 23°F (−5°C).
Soil requirements Good, light, open soil.
Sun/Shade aspect Plant facing full sun, in a protected position against a wall or fence.
Pruning None required, but in early spring remove any old shoots retained through winter.
Training Requires no training, freestanding.
Propagation and nursery production Produced by root division and from seed. Purchase container-grown without stems while dormant, if available, or as plants up to

12–18 in (30–45 cm). Extremely scarce, should be sought from specialist nurseries.
Problems Difficult to establish, taking some years to flower.
Similar forms of interest None.
Average height and spread
Five years
5 × 5 ft (1.5 × 1.5 m)
Ten years
6 × 8 ft (1.8 × 2.4 m)
Twenty years
6 × 10 ft (1.8 × 3 m)
Protrudes up to 3 ft (91 cm) from wall or fence.

ESCALLONIA

KNOWN BY BOTANICAL NAME

Escalloniaceae   *Wall Shrub*
Evergreen
Handsome early summer flowering shrubs with an attractive range of flower colours.

Origin From South America. Nearly all varieties offered are of garden or nursery origin.
Use As a loose, fan-trained or spreading shrub for walls or fences. Can be grown as a pillar subject.

Escallonia 'Crimson Spire' in flower

Description *Flower* Short racemes of bell-shaped flowers in various shades of pink to pink/red. Some white forms. Late spring through to early summer, with intermittent flowering through late summer and early autumn. *Foliage* Leaves ovate, 1–1½ in (2.5–4 cm) long, with indented edges. Light to dark green glossy upper surfaces, grey undersides. Size of foliage varies according to form. *Stem* Upright when young, becoming arching according to species and variety, and branching with age. Grey/green. Fast rate of growth when young, slowing with age. *Fruit* Insignificant.

Hardiness Tolerates a minimum winter temperature of 4°F (−15°C).
Soil requirements Tolerates most soils but liable to chlorosis on extremely alkaline types.
Sun/Shade aspect Tolerates all aspects, except extremely exposed. Full sun through to medium shade.
Pruning Remove one-third of old flowering

Escallonia 'Iveyi' in flower

wood after main flowering period. If cut to ground level will rejuvenate after second or third spring.
Training Wires, trellis or individual anchor points will be required for training.
Propagation and nursery production From softwood cuttings taken mid summer. Purchase container-grown; most varieties comparatively easy to find. Best planting height 2–2½ ft (60–76 cm).
Problems Susceptible to severe wind chill which may kill leaves and stems completely. Normally rejuvenates from ground level but may take two to three years to reach previous height.
Forms of interest *E.* 'Apple Blossom' Flowers apple blossom pink, large and normally borne singly. Slightly upright. *E.* 'C. F. Ball' Rich red flowers and medium-sized foliage. Slightly arching. *E.* 'Crimson Spire' Crimson flowers and medium-sized foliage. Upright. Slightly less than average spread. *E.* 'Donard Beauty' Large rose-carmine flowers and large green foliage. Slightly arching. *E.* 'Donard Brilliance' Large rose-red flowers and large foliage. Arching, becoming spreading with age. *E.* 'Donard Radiance' Medium-sized, rich pink flowers and large foliage. Slightly arching. *E.* 'Donard Seedling' Medium-sized flowers, pink in bud, opening to white tinted rose. Large leaves. Slightly arching. *E.* 'Edinensis' Medium-sized, carmine-pink flowers. Large foliage. Arching. *E.* 'Gwendolyn Anley' Small flowers, pink in bud, opening to paler pink. Small foliage. Arching, spreading and very twiggy. Two-thirds average height and spread. Best planting height 12–15 in (30–40 cm). *E.* 'Ingramii' Rose-pink flowers, medium size. Large foliage. Arching. *E.* 'Iveyi' Large pure white flowers. Large, dark green, shiny foliage. Upright, becoming slightly spreading with age. *E.* 'Langleyensis' Small, bright carmine-rose flowers in profusion along arching branches. Small-leaved. *E.* 'Peach Blossom' Good-sized clear pink flowers. Large foliage. Arching. *E.* 'Slieve Donard' Small pale pink flowers in profusion, borne on long, arching branches. Slightly less than average height and spread. *E. macrantha* Medium-sized, rose-carmine flowers, large, scented. Dark green foliage. Upright and branching. Good in coastal areas. Less than average hardiness. Height and spread slightly larger than average in favourable areas.
Average height and spread
Five years
8 × 8 ft (2.4 × 2.4 m)
Ten years
14 × 14 ft (4.3 × 4.3 m)
Twenty years
14 × 14 ft (4.3 × 4.3 m)
Protrudes up to 3 ft (91 cm) from support.

Erythrina crista-galli **in flower**

Eucalyptus gunnii in flower (juvenile foliage)

EUCALYPTUS

EUCALYPTUS, GUM TREE

Myrtaceae   *Semi-hardy Tree*
Evergreen

Attractive, blue-leaved and ornamental-stemmed trees good for growing in association with walls in mild locations.

Origin From Australia and Tasmania.
Use As a freestanding or fan-trained ornamental foliage tree for growing against large walls, where it can gain protection.
Description *Flower* White or cream tufted clusters 1–3 in (2.5–7.5 cm) long in autumn, early winter. *Foliage* The main attraction. Ovate to broadly linear, depending on variety. Stiff leathery texture, blue/green to glaucous blue. Adult foliage often different from juvenile in shape and form. *Stem* Grey/green to blue/green, often with peeling bark, revealing primrose-yellow underskin. Winter stems attractive. Often very fast-growing. *Fruit* Small, spinning-top-shaped fruit, glaucous blue ageing to brown, but rarely fruits outside its native environment.
Hardiness Tolerates a minimum winter temperature of 4°F (−15°C). Wind chill and very hard frosts can cause severe damage.
Soil requirements Light, well-drained soil for best results; tolerates a wide range of conditions.
Sun/Shade aspect Tolerates all but the most exposed of aspects. Full sun to light shade, preferring full sun.
Pruning Prune young trees hard in spring following planting. Select and train resulting five to seven shoots and tie into a fan-trained shape. In subsequent years, remove all side growths back to two points from their origin and maintain original main branches in fan shape. Alternatively, cut hard back in spring to induce a multi-stemmed large shrub effect.
Training Requires either tying to wires or individual anchor points or can be grown freestanding.
Propagation and nursery production From seed. Purchase container-grown, best planting height between 15 in (38 cm) and 4 ft (1.2 m). Transplanting larger trees is not recommended. Hardiest varieties generally available; outside favourable locations, more tender varieties must be sought from specialist nurseries.
Problems May look weak when young in nursery or garden centre, but develops rapidly once planted out. Reacts badly very quickly to poor planting; requires good preparation for speedy results.
Forms of interest *E. coccifera* Juvenile foliage glaucous blue, round to oval, up to 1½ in (4 cm) long. Adult foliage grey/green, narrow, oblong to lanceolate, up to 4 in (10 cm) long. Yellow flower umbels, produced in clusters late autumn, early winter. May produce conical fruits. One-third average height and spread. From Tasmania. *E. dalrympleana* Attractive foliage and patchwork bark, light brown with grey/white undercolour progressing in area as tree matures. Young foliage light green; mature grey/green, broadly lanceolate, up to 5 in (12 cm) long. *E. globulus* (Blue gum) Juvenile foliage glaucous white, up to 6 in (15 cm) long and 2½ in (6 cm) wide. Adult foliage is dark, shiny green, lanceolate, up to 12 in (30 cm) long and 2 in (5 cm) wide. Tufted clusters of three individual white florets produced late autumn, early winter. From Tasmania. In its native environment can exceed 100 ft (30 m) but usually achieves around 48 ft (15 m) in height. Tender; for use in non-mild areas only as annual foliage bedding plant. *E. gunnii* (Cider gum) Juvenile foliage orbicular, up to 2 cm (5 in) across, glaucous white to blue/green, produced on short stalks. Adult foliage green, lanceolate, up to 4 in (10 cm) long. White flowers in threes produced late autumn to early winter. May reach more than average height and spread in mild areas. From Tasmania and southern Australia. One of the hardiest of all eucalyptus. *E. niphophila* (Snow gum) Slow-growing with large, leathery, grey/green, ovate to lanceolate leaves 8 in (20 cm) long. Attractive trunk patched with grey/green, red/brown and cream. Relatively hardy. From Australia. *E. parvifolia* Narrow, lanceolate, blue/green leaves, up to 6 in (15 cm) long. Tolerates more alkalinity than most. Moderately hardy. *E. pauciflora* (syn. *E. coriacea*) (Cabbage gum) Juvenile foliage round to broadly lanceolate, glaucous green, up to 8 in (20 cm) long and 6 in (15 cm) wide. Adult foliage produced on long stalks up to 8 in (20 cm) long and 1 in (2.5 cm) wide. White flowers in tufted clusters of five to twelve. From Australia and Tasmania. Relatively hardy. *E. perriniana* Juvenile foliage small, silver/blue, ovate to round. Adult foliage lanceolate, glaucous blue. Stems white with dark purple/brown blotches. Tender. *E. pulverulenta* Attractive peeling bark. Juvenile foliage ovate to round, sometimes kidney-shaped, up to 2½ in (6 cm) long. Adult foliage similar, slightly larger. Tufted clusters of three white florets produced late autumn, early winter. Two thirds average height and spread. From New South Wales. Tender.

There are a large number of available eucalyptus forms. Those listed are among the most hardy, but even so, careful selection is required to suit the plant to any particular location.

Average height and spread
Five years
16 × 16 ft (4.9 × 4.9 m)
Ten years
25 × 25 ft (7.6 × 7.6 m)
Twenty years
35 × 35 ft (10.5 × 10.5 m)
Protrudes up to 5 ft (1.5 m) from support if fan-trained, 13 ft (4 m) untrained.

EUCRYPHIA

BRUSH BUSH

Eucryphiaceae   *Wall Shrub*
Evergreen or deciduous

A magnificent specimen shrub if a suitable site can be found with enough height and breadth.

Origin Native to South America, Australia and Tasmania but many forms of garden origin and garden crosses.
Use As a freestanding specimen shrub to be grown against a wall for protection, producing late summer flowers of interest, and ultimately reaching the proportions of a small tree.
Description *Flower* White, single, saucer-shaped flowers with pronounced stamens, freely borne. Size depends on variety, from numerous small flowers to flowers up to 2 in (5 cm) across, late summer to early autumn. *Foliage* Mostly evergreen. Ovate, 1½–3 in (4–7.5 cm) long, some with indented outer edges. Glossy upper surfaces, grey undersides. *Stem* Upright, becoming branching with age, but maintaining upright effect. Grey/green ageing to green/brown. Medium growth rate. *Fruit* Insignificant.
Hardiness Tolerates a minimum winter temperature of 4°F (−15°C).
Soil requirements Neutral to acid soil, tolerating low alkalinity provided soil is rich, deep and moist.
Sun/Shade aspect Prefers a moderately sheltered, shady location but will tolerate full sun.

Eucryphia × *nymansensis* 'Nymansay'

Pruning None required. Individual limbs can be cut back in late spring, encouraging new growth.
Training Normally freestanding but may be secured to the wall by individual anchor points.
Propagation and nursery production From semi-ripe cuttings taken in late summer. Purchase container grown; some varieties may have to be sought from specialist nurseries. Best planting height 15 in–3 ft (38–91 cm). May be available taller but normally very slow to establish.
Problems In severe cold, especially with high wind chill, foliage can be damaged and branches denuded. New growth normally appears in late spring.
Forms of interest *E. cordifolia* (syn. *E. ulmo*) White flowers and heart-shaped evergreen leaves. Possibly tolerates more alkalinity than most. Slightly less hardy than average and slightly less in height and spread. *E. glutinosa* White flowers 2½–2¾ in (6–7 cm) across, mid to late summer. Foliage deciduous, pinnate, grey/green, giving good autumn colour. A very upright form. From Chile. *E.* × *intermedia* 'Rostrevor' Produces a very good display of fragrant white flowers from 1–2 in

(2.5–5 cm) across, with yellow centres. Branches more pendulous and graceful than in most varieties. Fast growth rate. *E. lucida* Fragrant, white, hanging flowers 2 in (5 cm) across, mid to late summer. Very thick, dark, grey/green evergreen foliage, oblong with glaucous underside. Slightly less hardy. From Tasmania. *E. milliganii* Flowers 1–1½ in (2.5–4 cm) across, white and cup-shaped, often produced freely on young shrub. Small dark grey/green leaves open from sticky buds. Half average height and spread. From Tasmania. *E.* × *nymansensis* 'Nymansay' The most popular of all the varieties. Pure white flowers, 2½ in (6 cm) across, late summer to early autumn. Interesting dark green evergreen foliage. Raised in the Nymans Gardens, Sussex, England.

Average height and spread
Five years
8 × 4 ft (2.4 × 1.2 m)
Ten years
15 × 8 ft (4.6 × 2.4 m)
Twenty years
30 × 15 ft (9 × 4.6 m)
Protrudes 6 ft (1.8 m) or more from wall or fence.

EUONYMUS FORTUNEI
(*E. radicans*)

WINTERCREEPER EUONYMUS
Celastraceae   **Wall Shrub**
Evergreen

A very useful climbing foliage shrub for shady, exposed sites.

Origin From China. Most modern varieties of garden origin.
Use As an evergreen climbing shrub for exposed and shady positions. Tolerates dry conditions once established.
Description *Flower* Small, rather inconspicuous, green flowerheads. *Foliage* Leaves small, ovate, ¾–1 in (2–2.5 cm) long, ranging from green through to golden and silver variegated depending on variety, some changing to pink in winter. *Stem* Close-growing, spreading, grey/green when young ageing to grey/brown. Medium rate of growth. *Fruit* Sometimes produces small, round, red fruits, but rarely seen in variegated forms.
Hardiness Tolerates a minimum winter temperature of 0°F (−18°C). May suffer foliage loss in extremely cold conditions.
Soil requirements Accepts a wide range of soil conditions. Once established, will tolerate quite dry areas.
Sun/Shade aspect Tolerates all but the most exposed of aspects. Full sun to fairly deep shade, although golden varieties prefer full sun to medium shade.
Pruning None required, although old shoots may be removed occasionally to help rejuvenation.
Training Normally self-supporting by forming a bushy habit, but when reaching considerable height may need some individual anchor points.

Euonymus fortunei 'Emerald 'n' Gold'

Euonymus fortunei 'Silver Queen'

Propagation and nursery production From softwood cuttings. Purchase container grown; most varieties easy to find. Best planting height 8–18 in (20–45 cm).
Problems Container grown shrubs sometimes appear weak when purchased, but once planted grow quickly.
Similar forms of interest *E. f.* 'Coloratus' Green leaves, turning purple in winter, becoming green again in spring. Best effect is achieved if grown on dry or starved soils. One of the quickest growing varieties. *E. f.* 'Emerald Gaiety' Round grey/green leaves with white margins, turning pink in very cold winter weather. *E. f.* 'Emerald 'n' Gold' Round to ovate, dark grey/green leaves with gold margins. Variegation turns pink/red in very cold conditions. One of the most popular varieties. *E. f.* 'Gold Spot' Dark green foliage with bright gold splashes. Branches more upright and stronger than most. Very attractive in winter and early spring. *E. f.* 'Silver Queen' Elliptic leaves, creamy yellow in spring, becoming green with creamy white margin through summer. Two thirds average height and spread. *E. f.* 'Sunshine' Bold gold edges, grey/green leaves. Slightly quicker growth rate than most variegated forms. *E. f.* 'Sunspot' Foliage splashed gold on dark green. Attractive. *E. f.* 'Variegatus' A small-leaved variety with grey/green ovate foliage, margined white, tinged pink in cold winter weather. *E. f.* 'Vegetus' Leaves ovate to round, very thick, dull green; bears profuse round, red fruits in autumn.

Average height and spread
Five years
3 × 4 ft (91 cm × 1.2 m)
Ten years
4 × 6 ft (1.2 × 1.8 m)
Twenty years
6 × 10 ft (1.8 × 3 m)
Protrudes 1–2 ft (30–60 cm) from wall or fence.

EUONYMUS JAPONICUS

JAPANESE EUONYMUS
Celastraceae   **Wall Shrub**
Evergreen

A useful range of evergreens including green and variegated forms, most of which should be treated as slightly tender and therefore benefiting from a wall or fence for protection.

Origin From Japan, with many forms of garden origin.
Use As an evergreen shrub to grow against walls and fences where it will benefit from protection in colder areas.
Description *Flower* Clusters of green/yellow flowers, late spring and early summer. *Foliage*

Leaves medium-sized, elliptic, up to 2½ in (6 cm) long, shiny upper surfaces, dull, matt undersides. All-green, or some silver or gold variegation, depending on variety. *Stem* Upright, becoming branching with age; becoming spreading after ten years or more. Light to dark green. Slow growth rate in cold areas, faster in warmer regions. *Fruit* Pink capsules with orange, hanging seeds if the shrub is planted in an ideal situation.
Hardiness Tolerates a minimum winter temperature of 14°F (−10°C). In many cold areas the protection of a wall or fence is imperative, particularly with the variegated forms.
Soil requirements Any soil conditions, including sandy, coastal locations.

Euonymus japonicus 'Albomarginatus'

Sun/Shade aspect Requires a sheltered aspect. Full sun to moderately deep shade; variegated forms may resent very deep shade and lose some variegation.
Pruning None required, but may be clipped and trimmed.
Training Normally requires no training, growing as a freestanding shrub in front of a wall or fence.
Propagation and nursery production From softwood cuttings taken in early summer. Purchase container grown; most forms easy to find. Best planting height 15 in–3 ft (38–91 cm).
Problems Very severe wind chill may damage foliage, but new foliage is normally regenerated the following spring. Some variegated forms, especially golden varieties, may revert to green, but this can be controlled by pruning.

Similar forms of interest *E. j.* 'Albomarginatus' Leaves 2–2½ in (5–6 cm) long, mid to dark green with white outer margins. Slightly less than average height and spread. *E. j.* 'Aureopictus' Dark green foliage, with bold gold centre. *E. j.* 'Robusta' A green-leaved, strong growing variety with good fruiting. *E. kiautschovicus* (syn. *E. patens*) (Spreading euonymus) Light green foliage, small yellow/green flowers, followed by pink autumn fruits.
Average height and spread
Five years
6 × 6 ft (1.8 × 1.8 m)
Ten years
10 × 10 ft (3 × 3 m)
Twenty years
15 ft × 15 ft (4.6 × 4.6 m)
Protrudes up to 6 ft (1.8 m) from wall or fence.

EXOCHORDA × MACRANTHA 'THE BRIDE'

KNOWN BY BOTANICAL NAME
Rosaceae   *Wall Shrub*
Deciduous
A late spring flowering shrub which is not always thought of as a fan-trained wall shrub.

Origin Of garden origin.
Use For fan-training on walls and fences.
Description *Flower* 4 in (10 cm) long by 2 in (5 cm) wide racemes of bold, single, white, saucer-shaped flowers ¾ in (2 cm) across, arching outwards and downwards from main stem in late spring. *Foliage* Leaves medium-sized, lance-shaped, 1½–3 in (4–7.5 cm) long, grey/green, offering some yellow autumn colour. *Stem* Forms an arching, cascading wall shrub. Grey/green. Medium rate of growth. *Fruit* Sometimes produces small, red, round fruits.

Exochorda × macrantha 'The Bride' in flower

Hardiness Tolerates a minimum winter temperature of 4°F (−15°C).
Soil requirements Does well on most soil conditions, but extreme alkalinity will lead to chlorosis which, if not fatal to the shrub, will certainly curtail its performance.
Sun/Shade aspect Tolerates all but the most exposed aspects. Prefers full sun to light shade. May become leggy and spreading in medium to deep shade.
Pruning Remove one third of old flowering wood after flowering to encourage new growth for flowering in subsequent seasons.
Training Requires wires or individual anchor points to encourage a fan-trained shape.

Propagation and nursery production From layers or softwood cuttings taken in early summer. Purchase container grown or root-balled (balled-and-burlapped); comparatively easy to find.
Problems None, apart from its dislike of extremely alkaline soils.
Similar forms of interest None.
Average height and spread
Five years
7 × 7 ft (2.1 × 2.1 m)
Ten years
9 × 9 ft (2.7 × 2.7 m)
Twenty years
12 × 12 ft (3.7 × 3.7 m)
Protrudes up to 3 ft (91 cm) from support.

FABIANA IMBRICATA

KNOWN BY BOTANICAL NAME
Solanaceae   *Wall Shrub*
Evergreen
An attractive shrub benefiting greatly from the protection of a wall or fence.

Origin From Chile.
Use As a freestanding or fan-trained shrub against walls and fences in areas where acid soils are available.
Description *Flower* White tubular flowers covering the branches so thickly when in full bloom the entire branch appears to be a flower spike; late spring. *Foliage* Lanceolate leaves ½ in (1 cm) long, bright green to grey/green, bunched closely on stems. *Stem* Upright at first, quickly becoming arching, forming a wide spreading shrub or fan-shape if trained. Bright green to light grey/green. Slow growth rate. *Fruit* Insignificant.
Hardiness Tolerates a minimum winter temperature of 14°F (−10°C).
Soil requirements Must have an acid soil, dislikes any alkalinity.
Sun/Shade aspect Requires a moderately sheltered aspect. Prefers full sun or very light shade. Resents deeper shade.

Fabiana imbricata in flower

Pruning None required other than occasional cutting back of any overlong branches.
Training Allow to grow freestanding or tie to wires or individual anchor points.
Propagation and nursery production From softwood cuttings taken in early summer. Purchase container grown; rather difficult to find. Best planting height 4 in–2 ft (10–60 cm).
Problems Its need for a sheltered aspect and acid soil restrict its possible locations.
Similar forms of interest None.
Average height and spread
Five years
3 × 6 ft (91 cm × 1.8 m)
Ten years
5 × 9 ft (1.5 × 2.7 m)
Twenty years
5 × 12 ft (1.5 × 3.7 m)
Protrudes up to 18 in (45 cm) from support if fan-trained, 4 ft (1.2 m) untrained.

× FATSHEDERA LIZEI

ARALIA IVY
Araliaceae   *Wall Shrub*
Evergreen
Very good for large-scale fence, wall or stump covering in shade, as long as adequate moisture is available.

Origin Of garden origin. Said to be a cross between *Hedera helix* 'Hibernica' and *Fatsia japonica* 'Moseri'.
Use As a spreading, rambling evergreen for shady walls and fences. Can also be fan-trained.

× *Fatshedera lizei* 'Aureovariegate'

Description *Flower* Clusters of round, green flowers on 2–2½ in (5–6 cm) stalks, borne almost year-round, either as buds, flowers or dead flowers, only produced on mature branches three to four years old. *Foliage* Leaves large, palmate, 4–10 in (10–25 cm) wide, dark green, leathery textured with shiny upper surfaces and duller undersides. *Stem* Allow to ramble. Light to dark green. Fast rate of growth in favourable conditions. *Fruit* Round clusters of black fruits follow flowers.
Hardiness Tolerates a minimum winter temperature of 14°F (−10°C).
Soil requirements Prefers rich, moist soils but does well on all types.
Sun/Shade aspect Requires some protection from exposed aspects. Very good in deep shade, but tolerates medium to light shade. Unhappy in full sun, unless adequate moisture is available.
Pruning None required, although very old shoots can be removed.
Training Tie to wires or individual anchor points or allow to ramble over shrubs or stumps.
Propagation and nursery production From softwood cuttings taken in late spring to early summer. Purchase container grown; normally easy to find. Best planting height 15 in–2½ ft (38–76 cm).

× *Fatshedera lizei*

Problems When purchased in container may look weak and floppy but grows quickly once planted out.
Similar forms of interest × *F. l.* **'Variegata'** Grey/green leaves with creamy white margins. May be hard to find. More tender than the parent. × *F. l.* **'Aureovariegata'** Grey/green leaves with dull gold edges. May be hard to find. More tender than its parent.
Average height and spread
Five years
6 × 6 ft (1.8 × 1.8 m)
Ten years
13 × 13 ft (4 × 4 m)
Twenty years
20 × 12 ft (6 × 3.7 m)
Protrudes up to 4 ft (1.2 m) from support.

FATSIA JAPONICA

CASTOR OIL PLANT, JAPANESE FATSIA
Araliaceae   *Wall Shrub*
Evergreen
One of the best of all large, shade-loving wall shrubs for quick effect.

Origin From Japan.
Use As a freestanding evergreen shrub against walls and fences, requiring space.
Description *Flower* 2 in (5 cm) wide clusters of silver-green opening to milk white flowers; produced in spring from round clusters of buds developed in previous autumn and maintained over a long period. *Foliage* Leaves large to very large, dark to mid-green, 2½–6½ in (6–16 cm) wide and 9–18 in (23–45 cm) long, palmate, with seven, nine, or 11 leaflets. Glossy upper surface and paler underside. *Stem* Light to mid green, strong, stout, upright, forming a tall, rigid structure. Fast growth rate in the right conditions. *Fruit* Large clusters of black fruits follow flowers. Removal will increase leaf size.
Hardiness Tolerates a minimum winter temperature of 4°F (−15°C).
Soil requirements Does well on most types, but rich, deep, moist soil produces largest leaves.
Sun/Shade aspect Requires a partially protected aspect. Best in deep to medium shade, dislikes full sun.
Pruning None required but can be reduced in size and will rejuvenate itself from below pruning cuts.
Training Normally requires no training and is freestanding.
Propagation and nursery production From semi-ripe cuttings taken in early summer. Purchase container grown; easy to find. Best planting height 1½–3 ft (45–91 cm).

Fatsia japonica **'Variegata'**

Problems When purchased may look weak and sickly but once planted out it soon flourishes.
Similar forms of interest *F. j.* **'Variegata'** White to creamy white variegation to lobes and tips of foliage. Slightly less than average height and spread. More tender but wall planting will give added protection.
Average height and spread
Five years
8 × 8 ft (2.4 × 2.4 m)
Ten years
12 × 12 ft (3.7 × 3.7 m)
Twenty years
15 × 15 ft (4.6 × 4.6 m)
Protrudes up to 8 ft (2.4 m) from wall or fence.

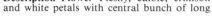

FEIJOA SELLOWIANA

GUAVA, PINEAPPLE GUAVA
Myrtaceae   *Wall Shrub*
Evergreen
An interesting, attractive, foliage evergreen, even without its summer flowers, worthy of a sheltered wall or fence.

Origin From Brazil and Uruguay.
Use As a freestanding or fan-trained wall shrub for sheltered walls and fences or for use in a conservatory or greenhouse.
Description *Flower* Fleshy, edible, crimson and white petals with central bunch of long

crimson stamens, but shy to flower in most areas. *Foliage* Leaves round to ovate, 1½–3 in (4–7.5 cm) long, grey/green with white felted undersides and grey leaf stalks. Some older leaves die in autumn, giving contrasting colour. *Stem* Grey/green when young, ageing to grey/brown, forming a loose fan-trained shrub on a wall or fence. Slow to medium rate of growth. *Fruit* Good-sized, egg-shaped, yellow fruits, edible, with aromatic flavour. Rarely fruits outside its native environment.
Hardiness Tolerates a minimum winter temperature of 23°F (−5°C).
Soil requirements Does well on most soils, disliking only extreme alkalinity.

Feijoa sellowiana

Sun/Shade aspect Requires a very sheltered aspect. Prefers light shade, tolerates full sun.
Pruning None required.
Training Requires wires or individual anchor points for fan-training or allow it to grow freestanding.
Propagation and nursery production From softwood cuttings. Purchase container grown; difficult to find.
Problems None.
Similar forms of interest *F. s.* **'David'** A large-foliage variety from New Zealand. *F. s.* **'Variegata'** Foliage variegated creamy white. Two thirds average height and spread; more tender than the parent.
Average height and spread
Five years
5 × 5 ft (1.5 × 1.5 m)
Ten years
9 × 9 ft (2.7 × 2.7 m)
Twenty years
15 × 15 ft (4.6 × 4.6 m)
Protrudes up to 3 ft (91 cm) from support if fan-trained, 13 ft (4 m) untrained.

FICUS CARICA

COMMON FIG, FIG
Moraceae   *Wall Shrub*
Deciduous
A very decorative fruiting shrub, and there is nothing better on a late summer or early autumn afternoon than picking the ripe figs from your own plants.

Origin From western Asia.
Use As a wall or fence grown specimen to protect and encourage its edible fruits to ripen. Train horizontally or in a fan shape. Can be grown in large containers against walls and fences with less height and spread.
Description *Flower* Pale green, insignificant. *Foliage* Leaves large, palmate, 8–10 in (20–25 cm) long and wide, mid green to grey/green, abundantly produced, giving good yellow autumn colour. Attractive. *Stem* Light green when young, becoming spreading and arching with time, needing support. Fast

Fatsia japonica **in flower**

Ficus carica 'Brown Turkey' in fruit

growing. *Fruit* Large, green-skinned, becoming edible after two years. Fruits become wrinkled and purple/black when ripe in late summer to early autumn. Leave on shrub and use as required.
Hardiness Tolerates a minimum winter temperature of 4°F (−15°C). In cold winters or cold areas, stems should be protected with bracken or other open material.
Soil requirements Does well on most soil types. For best fruiting, roots must be restricted within a 6 ft (1.8 m) box sunk in soil, or the shrub will grow too vigorously and not fruit adequately. This treatment is imperative when it is grown against a wall or fence.
Sun/Shade aspect Requires a warm, protected aspect. Full sun to light shade needed to ripen fruit.
Pruning Reduce thin, weak growth either in winter or summer. Train fan or horizontal but avoid hard cutting back as this will only lead to stronger, unfruiting growth.
Training Requires wires or individual anchor points for training in a fan shape.
Propagation and nursery production From softwood cuttings taken in late summer or from layering, suckers, or grafting. Purchase container grown; easy to find. Best planting height 1½–2½ ft (45–76 cm).
Problems Can become invasive unless root development is restrained.
Similar forms of interest *F. c.* 'Brown Turkey' Large, brown to purple-skinned pear-shaped fruits. Flesh creamy white with red tinge. *F. c.* 'Brunswick' Pear-shaped, yellow-skinned fruits, flesh white flushed red. Hard to find, but not impossible. *F. c.* 'White Marseilles' Round, white-skinned fruits, flesh almost translucent. Very sweet and juicy. Very scarce.
Average height and spread
Five years
10 × 10 ft (3 × 3 m)
Ten years
15 × 15 ft (4.6 × 4.6 m)
Twenty years
20 × 20 ft (6 × 6 m)
Protrudes up to 8 ft (2.4 m) from support.

FORSYTHIA SUSPENSA

CLIMBING FORSYTHIA, WEEPING FORSYTHIA
Oleaceae   *Wall Shrub*
Deciduous

A long, arching, ranging shrub requiring space to mature to its full potential.

Origin From China, but many forms of garden origin.
Use As a rambling, spreading, permanent wall or fence shrub, requiring space.
Description *Flower* Clear yellow to golden yellow, hanging, bell-shaped flowers covering all mature stems in early to mid spring. Last

season's shoots do not flower. *Foliage* Leaves ovate, 2–4 in (5–10 cm) long, tooth-edged. Light to mid-green. Yellow autumn colour. *Stem* Green to grey/green to grey/brown. Long, arching, ranging branches. Medium to fast growing. *Fruit* Insignificant.
Hardiness Tolerates a minimum winter temperature of 4°F (−15°C).
Soil requirements Does well on all soil types.
Sun/Shade aspect Tolerates all aspects. Full sun to medium shade. In deep shade becomes very open, lax and shy to flower.
Pruning Sometimes very difficult to prune because it forms a very woody structure, but if possible remove one third of oldest flowering wood to ground level, or to lowest young, strong shoot, after flowering.
Training Will require tying to wires, trellis or individual anchor points.
Propagation and nursery production From semi-ripe cuttings taken mid summer or hardwood cuttings taken in winter. Purchase bare-rooted or container grown. Most varieties easy to find, some must be sought from specialist nurseries. Best planting height 1–3 ft (30–91 cm).
Problems Unlike other forsythias it may look loose and weak in constitution when young, but quickly generates new growth once planted out.
Similar forms of interest *F. s. atrocaulis* Pale lemon yellow flowers produced on black/purple stems, arching in habit in early spring. One of the earliest to flower. More open than most varieties in its habit. *F. s.* 'Nymans' Flowers primrose yellow, of good size and borne on an open arching shrub. Early flowering. From Nymans Gardens, England.
Average height and spread
Five years
8 × 8 ft (2.4 × 2.4 m)
Ten years
12 × 12 ft (3.7 × 3.7 m)
Twenty years
18 × 18 ft (5.5 × 5.5 m)
Protrudes up to 3 ft (91 cm) from support.

FREMONTODENDRON CALIFORNICUM

FREMONTIA
Sterculiaceae   *Wall Shrub*
Evergreen

One of the most spectacular shrubs for planting against a high sunny wall.

Origin From California and Arizona, USA.
Use As a fan-trained wall shrub where it will reach a height of at least 26–30 ft (8–9 m) relatively quickly, flowering from late spring until well into late autumn.

Description *Flower* No actual petals, large, saucer-shaped yellow calyxes form flowers up to 3 in (7.5 cm) wide with golden yellow stigma and stamens protruding from centre, profusely borne in late spring through to late autumn. *Foliage* Trifoliate leaves with heart-shaped leaflets, three- to seven-lobed, 2–4 in (5–10 cm) long, grey/green. *Stem* Upright when young, becoming more spreading to form a fan-shaped shrub. Grey/green, down-covered. Fast growth rate. *Fruit* Insignificant.
Hardiness Tolerates a minimum winter temperature of 4°F (−15°C), although often wrongly considered more tender.
Soil requirements Any soil type, tolerating high alkalinity.
Sun/Shade aspect Tolerates all but the most exposed of aspects. Prefers full sun, tolerates very light shade.
Pruning Prune current season's growth back by two thirds in mid to late summer. This will generate new growth and more flowers. The height of the plant cannot be easily controlled by pruning.

Fremontodendron californicum 'California Glory' in flower

Training Requires wires or individual anchor points to achieve a fan-trained shape.
Propagation and nursery production From softwood cuttings taken in early spring, or from seed. Purchase container grown. May not be easy to find outside its native environment. Best planting height 15 in–3 ft (38–91 cm).
Problems When young, susceptible to severe winter weather, but after reaching 5 ft (1.5 m) rarely affected by cold. Often outgrows the area allowed for it. The dusty down from the stems can be very painful if it gets into the eyes or on the skin.

Forsythia suspensa in flower

Similar forms of interest *F. c.* 'California Glory' The best variety to try, with good large yellow flowers. *F. mexicanum* Orange/yellow flowers, more tender, requiring a very sheltered site.

Average height and spread

Five years
10 × 6 ft (3 × 1.8 m)
Ten years
20 × 10 ft (6 × 3 m)
Twenty years
30 × 15 ft (9 × 4.6 m)
Protrudes up to 3 ft (91 cm) from support.

GARRYA ELLIPTICA

TASSEL BUSH, SILK TASSEL TREE

Garryaceae   *Wall Shrub*
Evergreen

It is hard to imagine a finer sight than *Garrya elliptica* fully clothed with its catkins in late spring.

Origin From California and Oregon, USA.
Use A shrub for shady walls and fences. Produces evergreen foliage and attractive mid to late winter catkins; good in maritime areas.
Description *Flower* Male plants have long, grey/green, hanging catkins, up to 5 in (12 cm) long, made up of a series of bell-shaped flowers. Female plants have insignificant flowers in short catkins so are not normally considered as attractive. *Foliage* Leaves broadly ovate, 1½–3 in (4–7.5 cm) long, dark green, glossy upper surfaces, glaucous undersides and of leathery texture. *Stem* Upright, becoming branching and spreading with age. Grey/green to green/brown. Medium growth rate. *Fruit* Small, round, purple/brown fruits in long clusters produced by female plants when there is a male plant nearby.
Hardiness Tolerates a minimum temperature of 4°F (−15°C).
Soil requirements Prefers fertile soil, but does well on all types.

Garrya elliptica in flower

Sun/Shade aspect Requires a partially sheltered aspect in full sun to medium shade. In deep shade becomes long, open and straggly and catkins diminish in number.
Pruning None required but can be reduced by removing major branches in late winter or early spring and will rejuvenate itself in following spring.
Training Requires a limited number of individual anchor points to assist training and give support.
Propagation and nursery production From semi-ripe cuttings taken in early to mid summer. Purchase container grown; available from good garden centres and nurseries. Best planting height 1½–3 ft (45–91 cm).

Ginkgo biloba in autumn

Problems Rather untidy habit of growth. Black spots often appear on old foliage just before it drops in late winter and early spring. In cold springs there may be a delay between fall of old evergreen foliage and growth of new leaves, leaving the plant temporarily defoliated. This can also sometimes happen after planting.
Similar forms of interest *G. e.* 'James Roof' Good, bright, leathery leaves, with catkins twice the length of *G. elliptica* and thicker in texture. Strong-growing. Worth looking for. *G. fremontii* Similar to its parent but with more ovate, twisted leaves and short catkins. From western USA.

Average height and spread

Five years
8 × 8 ft (2.4 × 2.4 m)
Ten years
12 × 12 ft (3.7 × 3.7 m)
Twenty years
15 × 15 ft (4.6 × 4.6 m)
Protrudes up to 4 ft (1.2 m) from support.

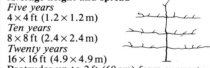

GINKGO BILOBA

MAIDENHAIR TREE

Ginkgoaceae   *Conifer*
Deciduous

A deciduous conifer that adapts itself well to training horizontally or in a fan shape, producing a very attractive display of foliage.

Origin From northern China.
Use As a wide spreading, horizontal or fan-trained wall shrub for large walls and fences.
Description *Flower* Male flowers are short yellow catkins, appearing at the same time as the leaves; female flowers grow in pairs after hot summers. Flowering is rare except in the most favourable sunny positions or at great maturity. *Foliage* Fan-shaped, 2 in (5 cm) wide and long, with a cleft in the centre and irregular, notched, indented edges. Almost leathery in texture. Extremely attractive. Grey/green with beautiful yellow autumn colour. *Stem* Light grey/green when young, becoming grey/brown. Attractive both in summer and in winter. Rigid. Medium growth rate. *Fruit* Rarely fruits outside its native environment, but may produce plum-shaped yellow fruits which are edible and sweet tasting.
Hardiness Tolerates a minimum winter temperature of 0°F (−18°C).
Soil requirements Tolerates all soil conditions with no particular preference, although a high degree of organic material incorporated at planting time will encourage the root system to grow quickly and to support good top growth.

Sun/Shade aspect Tolerates all aspects with no particular preference, although may be more likely to flower and fruit in sunny positions.
Pruning Cut newly purchased plants in spring to within 12 in (30 cm) of ground level and the resulting two or three shoots can be trained horizontally or in a fan shape. Additional side branches as they arise can also be fan-trained. In subsequent springs, shorten back surplus side branches not needed for framework to within 2 in (5 cm) of their origin. The shortening back of side branches then becomes an annual process to encourage new growth and attractive foliage.
Training Tie to wires or individual anchor points.
Propagation and nursery production From seed. Should always be purchased container grown or root-balled (balled-and-burlapped). Young plants of trainable age will normally be found in garden centres but may have to be sought from general and specialist nurseries. Best planting height not more than 3 ft (91 cm) and ideally not more than three years old.
Problems Will take up to five years to produce a good fan-trained or horizontal shape and from then on will increase in size to cover a large area which must be allowed for.
Similar forms of interest *G. b.* 'Autumn Gold' Golden-yellow foliage in autumn. Neat habit. *G. b.* 'Saratoya' Very hardy. Good yellow autumn tints.

Average height and spread

Five years
4 × 4 ft (1.2 × 1.2 m)
Ten years
8 × 8 ft (2.4 × 2.4 m)
Twenty years
16 × 16 ft (4.9 × 4.9 m)
Protrudes up to 2 ft (60 cm) from support.

GLEDITSIA TRIACANTHOS 'SUNBURST'

GOLDEN-LEAVED HONEYLOCUST

Leguminosae   *Hardy Tree*
Deciduous

An attractive foliage tree responding well to fan-training.

Origin From North America.
Use As a fan-trained tree for large walls and fences.
Description *Flower* Green/white male flowers in pendent racemes 2 in (5 cm) long. Female flowers limited and inconspicuous. Borne in mid summer but may be shy to flower. *Foliage* Pinnate or bipinnate, up to 8 in (20 cm) long with up to 32 leaflets 1 in (2.5 cm) long. Golden-yellow becoming lime-green then deep

yellow in autumn. *Stem* Light grey/green, somewhat fragile. May suffer from wind damage. Mature bark grey and deeply channelled, of architectural interest. Medium rate of growth. *Fruit* Small, pea-shaped, grey/green pods, sword-shaped and twisted, often retained well into winter, but may be shy to fruit in all but the most favourable areas. Poisonous.

Hardiness Tolerates a minimum winter temperature of 4°F (−15°C).

Soil requirements Best results on well-drained, deep, rich soil. Tolerates limited amount of alkalinity through to fully acid types.

Sun/Shade aspect Tolerates all but the most exposed of aspects. Full sun to very light shade.

Gleditsia triacanthos 'Sunburst' in leaf

Pruning Prune young trees hard in spring following planting. Select and train resulting five to seven shoots and tie into a fan-trained shape. In subsequent years remove all side growths back to two points from their origin and maintain original main branches in fan shape.

Training Will require fixing to wires or individual anchor points.

Propagation and nursery production Grafted on to *G. triacanthos*. Best purchased container grown although root-balled (balled-and-burlapped) or bare-rooted plants can be successful if planted between late autumn and early spring. Should be sought from general or specialist nurseries and garden centres. Best planting height 3–5 ft (91 cm–1.5 m). Always choose young trees for preference.

Problems Normally slow growing and young plants may often look irregular and weak in constitution in nurseries and garden centres.

Similar forms of interest *G. t.* 'Elegantissima' Compact, only reaching one third ultimate height and spread; can be considered as large shrub. Interesting light green, fern-like foliage. Yellow autumn colour. *G. t.* 'Ruby Lace' Foliage purple to purple/green in spring; new growth red/purple. Some yellow/bronze autumn colour. White flowers, but rarely occurring. Reaches only one third average height and spread.

Average height and spread

Five years
7 × 7 ft (2.1 × 2.1 m)
Ten years
14 × 14 ft (4.3 × 4.3 m)
Twenty years
25 × 25 ft (7.6 × 7.6 m)
Protrudes up to 3 ft (91 cm) from support.

HALESIA

MOUNTAIN SILVERBELL, MOUNTAIN SNOWBALL TREE, CAROLINA SILVERBELL

Styracaceae   *Wall Shrub*
Deciduous

A very attractive large shrub that adapts well to being grown fan-trained on a wall or fence, showing off its flowers to the best effect.

Origin From south-eastern USA.

Use As a shrub for fan-training on walls and fences where the protection helps its performance.

Description *Flower* Small to medium-sized, hanging, nodding, bell-shaped flowers borne in 3 in (7.5 cm) long clusters of three or five along the underside of each branch in mid to late spring. *Foliage* Broad, ovate, 2–5 in (5–12 cm) long, light grey/green, giving good yellow autumn colour. *Stem* Upright when young, becoming branching and twiggy with age. Grey to grey/green. Medium growth rate. *Fruit* Small, green, winged fruits in autumn.

Hardiness Tolerates a minimum winter temperature of 4°F (−15°C).

Soil requirements Does well on most types but best on well-drained soil.

Sun/Shade aspect A sheltered aspect. Prefers full sun to light shade.

Pruning None required.

Training Requires individual anchorage points or wires to secure plant to wall or fence to achieve a fan shape.

Propagation and nursery production From layers or semi-ripe cuttings taken in early summer. Purchase container grown; must be sought from specialist nurseries. Best planting height 1½–2½ ft (45–76 m).

Problems Often looks weak when purchased; begins to achieve full potential only after three to five years.

Forms of interest *H. carolina* (syn. *H. tetraptera*) (Carolina Silverbell) White, bell-shaped nodding flowers, grouped along branches, early to mid spring. Fruits are four-winged and narrowly pear-shaped. *H. monticola* (Mountain Silverbell) A variety with larger flowers and fruit, fruit clusters being up to 2 in (5 cm) in length. From the mountain regions of south-eastern USA. *H. m.* 'Vestita' A large-flowering form with flower clusters up to 1–1½ in (2.5–4 cm) across, sometimes pink-tinged. When mature, the leaves are downy with a glabrous covering.

Average height and spread

Five years
6 × 6 ft (1.8 × 1.8 m)
Ten years
13 × 13 ft (4 × 4 m)
Twenty years
20 × 20 ft (6 × 6 m)
Protrudes up to 3 ft (91 cm) from support.

HAMAMELIS

WITCH HAZEL, CHINESE WITCH HAZEL

Hamamelidaceae   *Wall Shrub*
Deciduous

A shrub not normally considered for fan-training on a wall but when used in this form it is very attractive in winter.

Origin Most forms originating from Japan, with many varieties now of garden origin.

Use As a large, fan-trained shrub for walls and fences.

Hamamelis × *intermedia* 'Diane' in autumn

Description *Flower* Clusters of strap-like 1–1½ in (2.5–4 cm) long petals ranging from lemon-yellow through gold, brown, orange to dark red, according to variety, borne in winter through early spring, withstanding harsh weather conditions undamaged. Some varieties fragrant. Exact flowering time depends on winter temperatures; the first mild spell after the shortest day of the year often triggers the first flower bud to open. *Foliage* Leaves ovate, 3–5 in (7.5–12 cm) long, with good orange/yellow autumn colours. *Stem* Upright when young, becoming spreading with age when it can be adapted to become fan-shaped. Grey to grey/green. Medium growth rate.

Hardiness Tolerates a minimum winter temperature of 4°F (−15°C).

Soil requirements Neutral to acid; moderate to heavy alkalinity will rapidly cause signs of chlorosis. Mulch annually with peat or garden compost to a depth of 2 in (5 cm) over 1–2 sq yd (1–2 sq m) to maintain health and encourage flowering.

Sun/Shade aspect Tolerates all aspects. Prefers full sun to light shade; too much shade will spoil shape and reduce flowers.

Halesia carolina in flower

Best planted where winter sunlight can enhance flowering effect.
Pruning None required.
Training Requires wires or individual anchor points to secure and encourage a fan-trained shape.
Propagation and nursery production H. virginiana, grown from seed, is the understock on to which all other varieties are grafted. Purchase container grown or root-balled (balled-and-burlapped). Best planting height 2–4 ft (60 cm–1.2 m).

Hamamelis mollis in flower

Problems Young grafted plants often fail so it is advisable to purchase plants four years old or more, although these are expensive.
Forms of interest *H.* × *intermedia* **'Diane'** Flowers 1–1½ in (2.5–4 cm) across, rich copper-red. Good autumn foliage colours. Slightly less than average height and spread. *H.* × *i.* **'Jelena'** Flowers 1½ in (4 cm) across, bright copper-orange. *H.* × *i.* **'Ruby Glow'** Flowers 1 in (2.5 cm) across, copper-red. Narrow foliage with good autumn colour. *H.* × *i.* **'Westersteide'** Flowers 1 in (2.5 cm) across, clear yellow and freely borne, produced later than most. Small to medium sized foliage. Good autumn colour. *H. japonica* **'Zuccariniana'** (Japanese witch hazel) Grey, curled flower buds open to release pale yellow, lemon-scented flowers in early spring. Flowers less than 1 in (2.5 cm) across but borne profusely. Growth habit makes it extremely good for fan-training. *H. mollis* (Chinese witch hazel) Pure golden yellow, very fragrant flowers 1½ in (4 cm) across, late winter. Large, oval to round leaves with good autumn colour. *H. m.* **'Brevipetala'**

Scented, bronze-yellow flowers, 1½ in (4 cm) across, borne on strong upright branches, more vigorous than most. Broad ovate leaves with good autumn colour. Spreading habit. One of the most beautiful forms. *H. virginiana* (Common witch hazel) Slightly scented, golden yellow flowers, 1 in (2.5 cm) across. Good golden yellow autumn colour. Apart from its use as understock, this is the basic form from which the essence known as witch hazel is distilled. Its growth makes it extremely good for fan-training.
Average height and spread
Five years
8 × 8 ft (2.4 × 2.4 m)
Ten years
15 × 15 ft (4.6 × 4.6 m)
Twenty years
20 × 20 ft (6 × 6 m)

Protrudes up to 3 ft (91 cm) from support.

HEDERA CANARIENSIS

CANARY ISLAND IVY
Araliaceae   *Woody Climber*
Evergreen
Amongst one of the most attractive of all evergreen climbing plants.

Origin From the Canary Islands and North Africa.
Use As a free-growing climber for all aspects, growing up walls and fences, through trees and for covering large areas where required. Can be adapted to creep along the ground as an evergreen ground-covering carpet.
Description *Flower* Small clusters of green flowers in late winter on very mature plants. *Foliage* Up to 8 in (20 cm) wide with five to seven lobes and of leathery texture, matt dark green in colour with silver reverse. *Stem* Light green becoming dark green and glossy, twining and twisting, partially self-clinging. Medium to fast growing. *Fruit* Mature plants may carry clusters of dark blue/black fruits in early to late autumn.
Hardiness Tolerates a minimum winter temperature of 4°F (−15°C). Requires protection from north and east winds to stop leaf scorch.
Soil requirements All soil types, both alkaline and acid, only showing signs of distress in extremely dry conditions.
Sun/Shade aspect Full sun to deep shade, although in deep shade may be more lax and open in habit. Good in all aspects except for those exposed to severe winds in winter.
Pruning No pruning for its own well-being but can be contained in a specific area if required by cutting back.

Hedera canariensis

Training Allow to ramble over trellis and wires. Weight of leaf and stems will need support when used on walls and fences.
Propagation and nursery production From semi-ripe cuttings or rooted natural layers. Purchase container grown; readily available from good garden centres and general nurseries. Best planting height 1–4 ft (30 cm–1.2 m).
Problems It is susceptible to very cold winds and extreme conditions but if it is damaged it normally recovers quite quickly.
Similar forms of interest *H. c.* **'Azorica'** Good grower, attractive formation, matt green. *H. c.* **'Ravensholst'** Tender, needing protection, but strong growing. *H. c.* **'Variegata'** (syn. **'Gloire de Marengo'**) Oval, leathery, dark green leaves with silvery reverse and bold creamy white margins. Smaller than the parent.
Average height and spread
Five years
7 × 7 ft (2.1 × 2.1 m)
Ten years
12 × 12 ft (3.5 × 3.5 m)
Twenty years
30 × 30 ft (9 × 9 m)
Protrudes up to 3 ft (91 cm) from support.

HEDERA COLCHICA

PERSIAN IVY
Araliaceae   *Woody Climber*
Evergreen
Amongst the most attractive of all the green-leaved ivies. Not startling in its display but able to present a bold appearance.

Origin From Persia.
Use As a dark green climber for covering all types of construction to give an evergreen attraction. Good as ground cover.

Hedera colchica

Hedera canariensis **'Variegata'**

Hedera colchica **'Sulphur Heart'**

Description *Flower* Clusters of dark green buds open to petal-less flowers throughout autumn and winter. Produced mainly on very mature plants and of some limited attraction. *Foliage* Oval to elliptic in shape, leathery texture, dark matt green in colour. *Stem* Vigorous red/brown stems becoming grey/brown with age. Self-clinging but some initial

Hedera colchica **'Dentata Variegata'**

support needed in exposed positions or following heavy snow or rain. Medium to fast growing. *Fruit* Produces poisonous dark blue to black fruits through winter and early spring.
Hardiness Tolerates a minimum winter temperature of 14°F (−10°C). Hardy but may show signs of foliage damage in extremely severe winters.
Soil requirements Does well on all soil types.
Sun/Shade aspect Prefers light shade but will tolerate full sun to deep shade.
Pruning No pruning for its own well-being but can be maintained within bounds by removing offending shoots as and when required.
Training Partially self-clinging but will need some support to climb walls or fences.
Propagation and nursery production From semi-ripe cuttings or rooted natural layers. Always purchase container grown; although relatively common it may be difficult to find. Best planting height 1–4 ft (30 cm–1.2 m).

Problems Often becomes larger than the area intended, although slow to establish – will take up to three years before vigorous growth becomes apparent.
Similar forms of interest *H. c.* **'Amur River'** Dark green, leathery texture. May be less hardy. *H. c.* **'Blair Castle'** Dark green with indentations on outer edges of leaves. *H. c.* **'Dentata'** Foliage larger, good strong grower. *H. c.* **'Dentata Variegata'** Mid green foliage with yellow/cream variegation. *H. c* **'Sulphur Heart'** (syn. **'Paddy's Pride'**) Central yellow splash on pale to mid green leaves. Tolerates a minimum winter temperature of 4°F (−15°C).
Average height and spread
Five years
6 × 6 ft (1.8 × 1.8 m)
Ten years
12 × 12 ft (3.7 × 3.7 m)
Twenty years
25 × 25 ft (7.5 × 7.5 m)
Protrudes up to 2 ft (60 cm) from support.

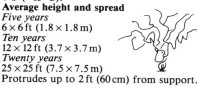

HEDERA HELIX

ENGLISH IVY, COMMON IVY

Araliaceae   *Woody Climber*
Evergreen
Although common, this still has a place for planting where an evergreen climber is needed in the most inhospitable areas, as it tolerates both shade and exposure to the extreme.

Origin From Europe, Asia Minor and into Persia.
Use A climber for all aspects, up walls, fences or banks. Can be trained both up or down a wall. Is also useful as a spreading ground cover.
Description *Flower* Round, ball-shaped clusters of dark green flower buds open to lighter green in late winter/spring, attracting many bees and other insects. *Foliage* Young leaves are three- to five-lobed, dark green with white undersides and some white veining. Adult foliage is oval to oval-triangular in shape. Some forms have interesting leaf shapes and green colour variations. *Stem* Light green turning dark green, finally grey-brown, self-clinging by suckering aerial roots on undersides of stems. Medium rate of growth. *Fruit* Clusters of poisonous black fruits produced in spring and summer on mature stems.
Hardiness Tolerates a minimum winter temperature of 0°F (−18°C).

Soil requirements Does well on all soil types, although it dislikes dry conditions until established.
Sun/Shade aspect Tolerates all aspects. Deep shade to full sun.
Pruning No pruning for its own well-being but can be cut back in spring to contain, as required.
Training Allow to form a self-clinging, area-defining climber. Normally requires no additional support.
Propagation and nursery production From semi-ripe cuttings taken in early summer or from self-rooted layers. May also be grown from seed. Always purchase container-grown, available all year round; may have to be sought from a specialist nursery. Those purchased as house plants will make useful climbers, once hardened off. Best planting height 1–3 ft (30–91 cm).
Problems Can become invasive. In Europe it is commonly believed to damage walls and trees, but this is only the case with very poor brickwork or trees that are relatively unhealthy, although climbing of trees should be discouraged.
Similar forms of interest *H. h.* **'Atropurpurea'** Dark green leaves changing to purple/black in winter. Sparse open habit. *H. h.* **'Brokamp'** Good dark green narrow leaves. Slow growing. *H. h.* **'Chicago'** Strong grower. Soft green foliage of good shape. *H. h.* **'Deltoides'** Interesting blunt leaf shape, dark green turning purple in winter. Growth thick and stiff. *H. h.* **'Digitata'** Good large leaf shape, dark green. *H. h.* **'Glymii'** (syn. *H. h.* **'Tortuosa'**) Leathery, average-sized, dark glossy green juvenile foliage, shaped more than when older. Turns purple to purple/green in winter. *H. h.* **'Gracilis'** Mid green leaves supported on red stems, open habit, turning wine red in winter. *H. h.* **'Green Ripple'** Dark green leathery texture, deeply lobed edges, strong grower. Copper colouring in winter. *H. h.* **'Hamilton'** Strong growth, large, interestingly shaped, mid green leathery leaves. Very good overall shape. *H. h.* **'Hibernica'** (Irish ivy) Average-sized, glossy dark green, five-lobed leaves. *H. h.* **'Ivalace'** Small, dark green, leathery, curly-edged, five-lobed leaves, turning copper/orange in cold winters. *H. h.* **'Manda's Crested'** (syn. *H. h.* **'Curly Locks'**) Pale green, soft-textured, five-pointed average-sized leaves, becoming blood red in cold winters. *H. h.* **'Marmorata Minor'** (syns. *H. h.* **'Discolor'**, *H. h.* **'Minor Marmorata'**) Leaves mid green with darker green blotches. *H. h.* **'Meagheri'** Open, trailing nature, presenting three-lobed, small, mid green leaves over a wide area. Trim in spring to encourage a lighter stem formation. *H. h.* **'Minima'** (syn. *H. h.* **'Spetchley'**) Very small,

Hedera helix **'Green Ripple'**

Hedera helix

Hedera helix angularis 'Aurea' in summer

three- or five-lobed, dark green foliage turning bronze to dull orange in winter. *H. h.* **'Nymans'** The centre lobe is long compared with the other four. Bright green in colour, good white veins in summer. Slow to attain any size. *H. h.* **'Neilsonii'** (syn. *H. h.* **'Neilson'**) Coppery red in winter, bright green in summer. Five-lobed interesting shape. Shrubby habit. Slower growing than its parent. *H. h.* **'Palmata'** Brown/red winter colour, mid green palm-shaped leaves of average size. *H. h.* **'Pittsburgh'** Medium-sized, five-lobed, bright green leaves, attaining a copper shading in winter. Strong growing. *H. h.* **'Poetica'** (syn. *H. h.* **'Chrysocarpa'**) Stiff upright grower with bright green, average-sized leaves. *H. h.* **'Russelliana'** (syn. *H. h.* **'Erecta'**) Very stiff, upright grower, covered with leathery dark green leaves of average size. *H. h.* **'Très Coupé'** Slow growing. Narrow, mid green, five-lobed leaves with pronounced points to ends of lobes.

Average height and spread
Five years
6 × 6 ft (1.8 × 1.8 m)
Ten years
12 × 12 ft (3.5 × 3.5 m)
Twenty years
25 × 25 ft (7.6 × 7.6 m)
Protrudes up to 18 in (45 cm) from support.

HEDERA HELIX ANGULARIS 'AUREA'

KNOWN BY BOTANICAL NAME

Araliaceae   *Woody Climber*
Evergreen

One of the most attractive of all the golden-foliaged ivies with an irregular yet interesting growth pattern.

Origin From Europe.
Use As a self-clinging climber for walls and fences, useful for growing over old stumps and other similar features. Can be used as a spreading ground cover.
Description *Flower* Small round clusters up to 1 in (2.5 cm) across of mid to dark green round flower heads produced through autumn and winter on mature growth. *Foliage* Three- to five-fingered, triangular, curly, wavy leaves up to 1½ in (4 cm) wide by 2 in (5 cm) long, green ageing to bright yellow, turning to an attractive chocolate brown in cold winters. *Stem* Light green/gold aging to

dark green, finally brown. Self-clinging, often more irregular in habit than many small-leaved ivies. Small, suckering, hanging aerial roots produced from underside of branches. Slow to medium growing. *Fruit* Round clusters of black poisonous fruit may be produced in spring on mature plants.
Hardiness Tolerates a minimum winter temperature of 4°F (−15°C). Foliage may be damaged by severe wind chill in winter in exposed positions, although it normally rejuvenates the following spring.
Soil requirements Both alkaline or acid but with a good moisture content to assist production of new golden foliage.
Sun/Shade aspect All but the most exposed aspects. Must be in full sun, deep shade will turn foliage green.
Pruning Not normally required other than for retaining within bounds which is best carried out in spring.
Training Self-clinging on both stone and brick walls, tying-in may be required on timber fences and posts.
Propagation and nursery production From semi-ripe cuttings taken in early summer. Self-rooted layers may be available at ground level on established plants. Always purchase

container grown in early autumn to early summer, may have to be sought from specialist nurseries. Best planting height 6 in–3 ft (15–91 cm).
Problems Its requirement for full sun to prevent fading. Can be irregular in its growth habit, particularly in the early years.
Similar forms of interest None.
Average height and spread
Five years
12 × 5 ft (3.7 × 1.5 m)
Ten years
15 × 10 ft (4.6 × 3 m)
Twenty years
25 × 20 ft (7.6 × 6 m)
Protrudes up to 2 ft (60 cm) from support.

HEDERA HELIX 'BUTTERCUP'

BUTTERCUP IVY

Araliaceae   *Woody Climber*
Evergreen

One of the few shrubs to improve its foliage colour in winter.

Origin Of garden origin.
Use As a climber for walls, fences, pillars and large banks.
Description *Flower* On mature plants, round ball-shaped clusters of dark green flower buds open to lighter green in late winter/spring. *Foliage* Three- to five-lobed leaves, bright golden-yellow in autumn, winter and spring, may turn green/yellow in summer but regain their full yellow colouring in following

Hedera helix angularis 'Aurea' in winter

autumn/winter. *Stem* Grey/green ageing to yellow/green, finally green/brown, twining. Self-clinging. Medium rate of growth. *Fruit* Shy to fruit, only very mature shrubs may produce the round, dark red fruits typical of ivy in clusters during late winter.

Hardiness Tolerates a minimum winter temperature of 4°F (−15°C).

Soil requirements Tolerates both acid and alkaline soil with no particular preference. Requires moisture to establish and then will tolerate drier soil conditions.

Hedera helix 'Buttercup'

Sun/Shade aspect All but the most exposed aspects. Full sun to medium shade, although sun improves colour. In early to late summer, some shade protection should be given during midday sun to prevent scorching.

Pruning Normally requires no pruning for its own well-being but can be cut back in late winter/early spring if required.

Training Self-clinging pads attach to bricks. On fences will require wires or individual anchor points to assist training.

Propagation and nursery production From semi-ripe cuttings taken in early summer. Should always be purchased container grown; best planting height 1–3 ft (30–91 cm). Normally available from good garden centres and nurseries.

Problems May scorch in direct, strong, mid-day sunlight, but nevertheless will require sunny conditions to maintain good golden colouring. Although these two elements may seem contradictory, they are normally possible with a little attention to detail.

Similar forms of interest *H. h.* 'Clotted Cream' Soft cream-coloured foliage all year round. *H. h.* 'Light Fingers' (syn. 'Tampa Gold') All golden yellow foliaged leaves, may be susceptible to scorching in strong sunlight.

Average height and spread
Five years
8 × 8 ft (2.4 × 2.4 m)
Ten years
16 × 16 ft (4.9 × 4.9 m)
Twenty years
20 × 20 ft (6 × 6 m)
Protrudes up to 12 in (30 cm) from support.

HEDERA HELIX 'CRISTATA'

CRESTED IVY, PARSLEY CRESTED IVY

Araliaceae　　　　*Woody Climber*
Evergreen

Leaves uncharacteristic for its species, offering an attractive alternative to the more familiar ivies.

Origin Sport of common English ivy.
Use As an attractive winter-foliaged shrub for walls, fences, pillars and pergolas.

Hedera helix 'Cristata'

Description *Flower* Round clusters of dark green flower buds open to lighter green in late winter/spring, attracting bees and other insects. *Foliage* Uncharacteristically round, with curled edges; 2–2½ in (5–6 cm) in diameter, shiny, pale-green, turning red on both sides, with more pronounced red blotching on upper surface in cold winters. *Stem* Twining. Brown/green to red/brown when young, becoming grey/green, finally green/brown. Medium rate of growth. *Fruit* Rarely fruits but may produce the round dark red fruits typical of ivy on mature shrubs.

Hardiness Tolerates a minimum winter temperature of 0°F (−18°C).

Soil requirements No particular preference, tolerating both acid and alkaline conditions. Will tolerate dry types, once established.

Sun/Shade aspect Tolerates all but the most exposed aspects. Prefers light shade but will tolerate full sun to deep shade, although in deep shade may become more lax in habit.

Pruning Requires no pruning for its own well-being but can be reduced in size if required, normally in spring.

Training Partially self-clinging. Allow to ramble over wires and trellis, secure individual branches to anchor points.

Propagation and nursery production From semi-ripe cuttings taken in early summer. Purchase container grown all the year round or plant those purchased as house plants, once hardened off. Will have to be sought from specialist nurseries and garden centres. Best planting height 1–3 ft (30–91 cm).

Problems Can become invasive. May be slightly difficult to obtain.

Similar forms of interest None.

Average height and spread
Five years
8 × 8 ft (2.4 × 2.4 m)
Ten years
12 × 12 ft (3.7 × 3.7 m)
Twenty years
16 × 16 ft (4.9 × 4.9 m)
Protrudes up to 2 ft (60 cm) from support.

HEDERA HELIX 'GLACIER'

KNOWN BY BOTANICAL NAME

Araliaceae　　　　*Woody Climber*
Evergreen

A useful variegated climber with attractive winter colour brightening the dullest of corners.

Origin Of garden origin.
Use A variegated, close-growing, self-clinging climber for most situations including exposed. Can be used as a spreading ground cover.

Description *Flower* Small clusters, 1½ in (4 cm) across, of green-yellow flower heads produced on very mature plants from autumn through until spring, not normally of great attraction. *Foliage* Three- to five-fingered triangular leaves up to 1½ in (4 cm) across and 1¾ in (4.5 cm) long; silver/grey/green with silvery white edges. *Stem* Self-clinging, tight formation, attractive red colouring on new growth, older wood becoming grey/green to grey/brown. Upright to fan-shaped formation on wall. Medium rate of growth. *Fruits* Clusters of poisonous black to blue/black fruits in spring on mature plants.

Hedera helix 'Glacier'

Hardiness Tolerates a minimum winter temperature of 4°F (−15°C). Hardy, although some juvenile and adult foliage may be damaged in severe wind chill conditions; rejuvenation is normal the following spring.

Soil requirements Does well on all soil types, only disliking extremely dry soil conditions.

Sun/Shade aspect All but the most exposed aspect. Medium shade to full sun.

Pruning Requires no pruning for its own well-being but can be reduced in size if required, in early to mid spring.

Training Self-clinging to most types of support; may need some tying in when young.

Propagation and nursery production From semi-ripe cuttings taken in early summer or from self-rooted layers. Always purchase container grown, in early autumn to early summer; readily available from most good garden centres and nurseries. Best planting height 9 in–3 ft (23–91 cm).

Problems In extremely dry summers may show some signs of distress by foliage drying; will normally rejuvenate the following spring.
Similar forms of interest *H. h.* 'Adam' Silver variegated with the edges of leaves turning pink in extremely cold weather. *H. h.* 'Cavendishii' (syns. *H. h.* 'Tricolor', *H. h.* 'Silver Sheen') White to silver variegation, some pink colouring in winter. *H. h.* 'Colebri' Foliage mottled silver, attractive. *H. h.* 'Heise' Silver variegation, more bushy habit.
Average height and spread
Five years
5 × 5 ft (1.5 × 1.5 m)
Ten years
10 × 10 ft (3 × 3 m)
Twenty years
20 × 20 ft (6 × 6 m)
Protrudes up to 12 in (30 cm) from support.

HEDERA HELIX 'GOLD HEART' (*H. h.* 'Jubilee')

GOLD HEART IVY
Araliaceae　　　　*Woody Climber*
Evergreen
Rightly amongst the most popular of all the small-leaved golden variegated ivies.

Origin Possibly of Italian garden origin.
Use As a self-clinging climber for walls, will cling to timber fences and timber posts but will need some support. When young can be used as a spreading ground-cover.
Description *Flower* Small clusters, 1½ in (4 cm) across, of green-yellow flower heads produced on mature shrubs from autumn through until spring. *Foliage* Juvenile foliage three- or five-pointed, very regular in shape, dark green with golden splashes of yellow in centre; adult foliage often has no indentations and variegation is more irregular. **Stem** Smooth light green ageing to dark green, finally to grey/brown. Very close formation with little or no forward growth except on very mature plants. Small, suckering climbing aerial roots produced from underside of branches. Medium rate of growth. *Fruit*

Mature plants may produce clusters of poisonous black to blue/black round fruits in spring.
Hardiness Tolerates a minimum winter temperature of 4°F (−15°C). Hardy, although some juvenile and adult foliage may be damaged in severe wind chill conditions; rejuvenation is normal the following spring.
Soil requirements Does well on both alkaline and acid soils, requires adequate moisture for establishment and good growth.
Sun/Shade aspect All aspects. Medium shade to full sun with no particular preference.
Pruning Remove any very mature forward-facing shoots and any green reverting shoots. Otherwise prune to maintain within desired area in early to late spring.
Training It normally requires no support on stone and brick walls, but on timber fences and posts it may need some assistance by tying in when young.
Propagation and nursery production From semi-ripe cuttings taken in early to mid summer or by self-propagated layers at ground level. Always purchase container grown, in early autumn to early summer; readily obtainable from all garden centres and nurseries. Best planting height 6 in–3 ft (15–91 cm).
Problems May, in some situations, become slightly invasive and allowance must be made for its ultimate size. On acid soils there will be a greater degree of reversion and production of green shoots, which must be removed.
Similar forms of interest *H. h.* 'Chicago Variegata' Leaves green with cream variegation below; average-sized leaves, three- to five-lobed, soft textured on strong-growing climbers. *H. h.* 'Eva' Interesting, small, pointed-lobed, green, cream-edged leaves. Bushy habit. *H. h.* 'Gold Child' Foliage golden-edged, may have to be sought from specialist nurseries. *H. h.* 'Herald' Shiny yellow/green variegated leaves of average size. Yellow ageing to cream.
Average height and spread
Five years
12 × 5 ft (3.7 × 1.5 m)
Ten years
15 × 10 ft (4.6 × 3 m)
Twenty years
25 × 20 ft (7.6 × 6 m)
Protrudes up to 12 in (30 cm) from support.

Hedera helix 'Gold Heart'

HEDERA HELIX 'LUZII'

GOLDEN SPECKLED IVY
Araliaceae　　　　*Woody Climber*
Evergreen
An interesting colour variation within the variegated ivies, often attractive all year round but of particular interest in winter.

Origin Of garden origin.
Use As an evergreen variegated climber to cover walls, fences, pillars and banks.
Description *Flower* Round ball-shaped clusters of dark green flower buds, opening to light green in late winter/spring. *Foliage* Leaves 1½–1¾ in (4–4.5 cm) wide and long, three- to five-lobed. Light gold to light yellow leaves with green blotching and marbled effect. Very attractive in winter. **Stem** Grey/green ageing to grey/brown. Twining, self-clinging, but may require additional support. Medium rate of growth. *Fruit* Mature shrubs may, in hot summers, produce small clusters of round black fruits but not reliable.
Hardiness Tolerates a minimum winter temperature of 14°F (−10°C).
Soil requirements Does well on all soil conditions but requires good moisture to establish.
Sun/Shade aspect All but the most exposed aspects. Full sun to very light shade; deep shade will spoil coloration.
Pruning None required but can be cut back to contain in early spring, if required.
Training Partially self-clinging, may need support by tying in when young or heavy at maturity.

Hedera helix 'Luzii'

Propagation and nursery production From semi-ripe cuttings taken in early summer. Always purchase container grown; available from good garden centres and nurseries. Plants purchased for the house can be planted in the garden between late spring and late summer and will usually establish. Best planting height 1–3 ft (30–91 cm).
Problems May suffer some summer scorching if adequate moisture is not available.
Similar forms of interest *H. h.* 'Bodil' White and yellow leaves blotched with green; three pointed lobes. *H. h.* 'Hibernica Pallida' Cream mottling on shiny, five-lobed, blunt-ended, dark green leaves. *H. h.* 'Masquerade' Yellow blotched variegation. Small leaved. *H. h.* 'Sicilia' Attractive crinkly edged leaves with creamy yellow variegation ageing to white.
Average height and spread
Five years
5 × 5 ft (1.5 × 1.5 m)
Ten years
10 × 10 ft (3 × 3 m)
Twenty years
15 × 15 ft (4.6 × 4.6 m)
Protrudes up to 18 in (45 cm) from support.

Hedera helix sagittifolia

HEDERA HELIX SAGITTIFOLIA

CROW'S FOOT IVY, ARROWHEAD IVY

Araliaceae   *Woody Climber*
Evergreen

A compact, fan-shaped, evergreen climber with attractive and interesting foliage.

Origin Possibly of Italian garden origin.
Use As a close-clinging, spreading climber for all walls, including exposed situations.
Description *Flower* Only very mature plants may occasionally produce typical ivy flowers. *Foliage* Five-fingered, arrow-shaped leaves 3 in (7.5 cm) long by 2½ in (6 cm) wide, forming an overall triangular shape. Mid to dark green with some light purple or silver veining, depending on season. *Stem* Very close, self-clinging, purple-green when young becoming dark green and finally brown/ green. Upright at first, becoming spreading with age. Slow to medium growing. *Fruits* Rarely fruits.
Hardiness Tolerates a minimum winter temperature of 4°F (−15°C).
Soil requirements Does well on all soil types, only resenting extremely dry conditions until established.
Sun/Shade aspect All but the most exposed positions. Full sun to deep shade.
Pruning Normally requires no pruning but can be cut back if required.
Training Allow to spread by self-clinging stems to the area it is required to cover.

Hedera helix sagittifolia 'Variegata'

Propagation and nursery production From semi-ripe cuttings taken in early summer or from self-rooted layers. Always purchase container grown, in early autumn to early summer; will have to be sought from specialist nurseries and good garden centres. Best planting height 1–3 ft (30–91 cm).
Problems Slow to establish, can take up to three years to form a good-sized covering plant.
Similar forms of interest *H. h. s.* 'Variegata' (syn. *H. h. s.* 'Konigers Variegated') Cream and green variegated form. Very attractive. *H. h. pedata* 'Heron' Somewhat sparse in its green foliage presentation. *H. h. caenwoodiana* (syn. *H. h.* 'Grey Arrow') Grey/ green leaves, attractive white veins down centre, upright growth. *H. h.* 'Silver Diamond' Attractive distinctive, silver/white-edged foliage.
Average height and spread
Five years
4 × 2 ft (1.2 m × 60 cm)
Ten years
8 × 4 ft (2.4 × 1.2 m)
Twenty years
16 × 8 ft (4.9 × 2.4 m)
Protrudes up to 6 in (15 cm) from support.

HEDERA (Shrubby Forms)

SHRUBBY IVIES

Araliaceae   *Wall Shrub*
Evergreen

Attractive and useful upright evergreen shrubs when used against walls and fences.

Origin From various areas of the northern hemisphere.
Use As slow-growing, upright, shrub-forming evergreens; suitable for growing against walls and fences. Ideal for under windows.
Description *Flower* 2 in (5 cm) wide heads of green to lime-green flowers, borne mainly in early to late spring but either in bud or open throughout year. *Foliage* Leaves small to large, diamond-shaped, 1½–5 in (4–12 cm) long, with glossy upper surfaces, duller underside, ranging from dark through mid green to golden and silver variegated forms. *Stem* Densely foliaged, upright stems. Some varieties with slightly looser habit. Slow growth rate. *Fruit* Round clusters of black poisonous fruits, 1½ in (4 cm) wide, in autumn and winter.
Hardiness Tolerates a minimum winter temperature of 4°F (−15°C).
Soil requirements Any soil, including very alkaline and very acid. Tolerates both dry and wet areas, although forms more growth on moister soils. In very dry areas should be watered to help it establish itself.

Sun/Shade aspect Tolerates all but the most exposed aspects. Prefers medium shade but good in deep shade through to full sun.
Pruning None required, but can be cut to contain or train. Best done in early spring.
Training Self-clinging. Normally needs no additional support but the larger leaved varieties may require individual anchor points to prevent damage from snow or heavy rain.
Propagation and nursery production From semi-ripe cuttings or rooted natural layers. Purchase container grown; best planting height 4–15 in (10–38 cm). May be difficult to find.
Problems Can be slow to attain any substantial size.

Hedera colchica arborescens

Similar forms of interest *H. colchica arborescens* (Shrubby Persian ivy) Foliage light green, oblong to ovate, up to 3 in (7.5 cm) in width and length, forming a dense, upright wall shrub. Good for flower and fruit production. *H. c. a.* 'Variegata' Attractive, white-edged variegated foliage. *H. helix* 'Arborescens' (Shrubby common ivy) Dark green, broad, spreading, tightly growing in fan shape. *H. h.* 'Conglomerata' (Shrubby common ivy) Small foliage, no more than 1–1½ in (2.5–4 cm) in width, lobed with wavy edges. Dark green upper surface, silvery underside. Forms a tight, fan-trained shape or column to be grown adjacent to a wall or fence. Very slow growth rate.
Average height and spread
Five years
3 × 3 ft (91 × 91 cm)
Ten years
5 × 5 ft (1.5 × 1.5 m)
Twenty years
7 × 7 ft (2.1 × 2.1 m)
Protrudes up to 2 ft (60 cm) from wall or fence.

HEDYSARUM MULTIJUGUM

KNOWN BY BOTANICAL NAME

Leguminosae   *Wall Shrub*
Deciduous

An attractive shrub in which rose-purple flowers are enhanced by soft green foliage.

Origin From Mongolia.
Use As an interesting fan-trained summer flowering shrub on walls and fences where it can gain protection in more hostile winter areas.
Description *Flowers* Racemes 4 in (10 cm) long by 2 in (5 cm) wide of openly spaced, small, rose-purple pea-flowers, borne mainly during mid to late summer but produced intermittently into early autumn. *Foliage* Leaves pinnate, 4–6 in (10–15 cm) long, with narrow leaflets, grey/green to sea-green, some yellow autumn colour. *Stem* Upright at first, becoming arching with age. Grey/green

Hedysarum multijugum in flower

to green. Growth rate fast when new, slowing with age. **Fruit** Insignificant.
Hardiness Tolerates a minimum winter temperature of 14°F (−10°C) but stems may die back in winter. Rejuvenation from base usually occurs the following spring.
Soil requirements Prefers light, open soil, dislikes extremely waterlogged, but tolerates both alkalinity and acidity.
Sun/Shade aspect Requires a sheltered aspect in full sun to very light shade.
Pruning None required but one third or more of oldest wood may be removed in early spring to encourage new shoots for flowering in late summer.
Training Secure by individual anchor points or wires.
Propagation and nursery production From softwood cuttings taken in early summer. Purchase container grown from specialist nurseries; best planting height 1–2 ft (30–60 cm).
Problems Rather slow to establish. In areas where its hardiness may be suspect, best not planted before late spring.
Similar forms of interest None.
Average height and spread
Five years
7 × 7 ft (2.1 × 2.1 m)
Ten years
10 × 10 ft (3 × 3 m)
Twenty years
12 × 12 ft (3.7 × 3.7 m)
Protrudes up to 2 ft (60 cm) from support.

HOHERIA

KNOWN BY BOTANICAL NAME

Malvaceae   *Wall Shrub*
Deciduous

An interesting, very free-flowering, handsome shrub.

Origin From New Zealand.
Use As a tall, mid summer flowering shrub benefiting in winter from the protection of a wall or fence.
Description *Flower* Clusters of round, white, saucer-shaped, fragrant flowers in mid summer. *Foliage* Leaves ovate, 2–4½ in (5–11 cm) long, sometimes toothed and lobed, especially when young. Grey to grey/green, giving some yellow autumn colour; some variegated and purple-leaved forms. *Stem* Upright, becoming branching and spreading with age, forming a tall, upright wall shrub. Grey/green to grey/brown. Medium growth rate. *Fruit* Insignificant.

Hardiness Tolerates a minimum winter temperature of 4°F (−15°C).
Soil requirements Prefers deep, rich, light soil, acid to neutral but tolerates some alkalinity.
Sun/Shade aspect Requires a sheltered aspect. Prefers light shade but will tolerate full sun.
Pruning None required other than for training or removing any over-sized branches.
Training Allow to stand free or secure to wall or fence by individual anchor points or wires.
Propagation and nursery production From softwood cuttings or layers. Purchase container grown; all varieties must be sought from specialist nurseries. Best planting height 15 in–3 ft (38–91 cm).
Problems Appears quite tough, so its tenderness is not always appreciated. Stems can be damaged quite severely in winter.
Forms of interest *H. lyallii* (syn. *Gaya lyallii*, *G. lyallii ribifolia*, *Plagianthus lyallii*) Clusters of white flowers borne in profusion in mid summer. Foliage more glabrous grey than most. Somewhat variable in growth, forming a large fan-trained shrub. *H. populnea* Pure white flowers 1 in (2.5 cm) across, in large clusters, flowering later than most varieties. Large, broad, ovate leaves, very similar to poplar leaves. *H. p.* 'Foliis

Purpureis' White flowers. Leaves plum-coloured on undersides. Very scarce. *H. p.* 'Variegata' White flowers. Leaves yellow/green, ageing to white with deep green margins. Benefits greatly from being grown against a wall or fence. Very scarce.
Average height and spread
Five years
6 × 6 ft (1.8 × 1.8 m)
Ten years
9 × 9 ft (2.7 × 2.7 m)
Twenty years
15 × 15 ft (4.6 × 4.6 m)
Protrudes up to 4 ft (1.2 cm) from support.

HOYA CARNOSA

WAX FLOWER

Asclepiadaceae   *Tender Greenhouse Climber*

Evergreen

An attractive greenhouse or conservatory climber which is not winter hardy and always needs protection.

Origin From Queensland, Australia.
Use As a climbing vine for heated greenhouses and conservatories.
Description *Flower* Round clusters 3 in (7.5 cm) wide of waxy, very fragrant pink/white flowers throughout summer. *Foliage* Ovate, pointed, 3 in (7.5 cm) long and 1½ in (4 cm) wide, leathery, thick leaves, grey/green with slight purple hue. *Stem* Round, brown/green, trailing, limited branching, supporting by twisting. Slow to medium rate of growth. *Fruit* No fruit of interest.
Hardiness Not winter hardy. Tolerates a temperature of 32°F (0°C) but under protection.
Soil requirements If grown in large containers, a good quality potting compost is required. If grown in soil in greenhouse beds, add liberal quantities of sharp sand and sedge peat to lighten.
Sun/Shade aspect Must be under protection of greenhouse or conservatory. Light shade to full sun.
Pruning Remove overcrowded shoots in spring.
Training Allow to twine around wire or timber supports.
Propagation and nursery production From cuttings of previous year's growth taken in early to late spring and encouraged to root in a protecting frame with some bottom heat, or by layering from the parent plant into a pot containing good-quality potting compost; the latter method normally takes two to three years for rooting to occur. Always purchase container grown; will normally have to be

Hoheria lyalli in flower

Hoya carnosa in flower

sought from specialist nurseries or flower shops selling house plants. Best planting height 6 in–3 ft (15–91 cm).
Problems Its availability may be scarce. The correct temperature balance must be achieved to encourage good flowering; it does not necessarily need heat, but it must not be allowed to be frosted.
Similar forms of interest *H. carnosa* 'Variegata' A form with variegated leaves. Extremely scarce, but worth looking for.
Average height and spread
Five years
7 × 7 ft (2.1 × 2.1 m)
Ten years
14 × 14 ft (4.3 × 4.3 m)
Twenty years
20 × 20 ft (6 × 6 m)
Protrudes up to 6 in (15 cm) from support.

HUMULUS LUPULUS 'AUREUS' (*H. l. 'Luteus'*)

GOLDEN HOP
Urticaceae   *Perennial Climber*
Deciduous
Amongst one of the most attractive of all fast-growing, hardy perennials with attractive golden foliage and yellow/green fruits.

Origin Most of Europe, Asia and North America.
Use As a fast-growing, golden foliaged perennial useful for growing over walls, buildings and trees and up poles. Good when used to cover a 10–12 ft (3–3.7 m) high tripod of poles. The young shoots can be blanched and used as a culinary herb.
Description *Flower* Green-yellow male flowers are in small panicles and the female flowers are in spikes; neither are of any real attraction. *Foliage* Leaves trifoliate, each leaflet round to oval, deeply veined with toothed edges, 5 in (12 cm) wide and 6 in (15 cm) long. *Stem* Light grey/green, twining, self-supporting, ageing to grey/brown. Dies back in winter. Very fast growing. *Fruit* Green panicles of round fruits each consisting of many overlapping scales, up to 10–12 in (25–30 cm) in size, ageing to yellow/brown. Can be used for brewing of beer.
Hardiness Root clumps hardy, all growth above ground level dies in winter to be replaced in following spring.
Soil requirements Does well on acid, neutral and moderately alkaline soils, may show some distress on extremely alkaline types. Requires a deep, moist, well-fed soil to achieve best results.
Sun/Shade aspect All but the most exposed aspects. Full sun to very light shade to maintain golden foliage.

Pruning All top growth should be removed to within 9 in (23 cm) of ground level in autumn to afford winter protection, remaining 9 in (23 cm) removed to ground level the following spring.
Training Requires some form of easily accessible wire, pole or branch to twine on.
Propagation and nursery production By division of root-stools in spring. Purchase bare-rooted in early spring or container grown in spring and early summer, the latter for preference. Will have to be sought from specialist nurseries.

Humulus lupulus 'Aureus' in leaf

Problems Can often over-exceed the intended area allocated for it. In all but light shade, the leaves will turn green. The need to cut down a large amount of growth each year could be considered a disadvantage.
Similar forms of interest *Humulus lupulus* The green leaf brewer's hop with attractive yellow autumn fruits, not readily available outside hop growing areas.
Average height and spread
Five years
12 × 12 ft (3.7 × 3.7 m)
Ten years
20 × 20 ft (6 × 6 m)
Twenty years
25 × 25 ft (7.6 × 7.6 m)
Protrudes up to 2½ ft (76 cm) from support.

HYDRANGEA (Large-leaved Forms)

LARGE-LEAVED HYDRANGEA
Hydrangeaceae   *Wall Shrub*
Deciduous
The aristocrats of the hydrangea group and a truly delightful sight when in full flower in late summer.

Origin From China, Taiwan and the Himalayas.
Use As a wall or fence fan-trained shrub where flowers show to best advantage.
Description *Flower* Large, porcelain blue clusters with ring of lilac, pink or white florets on outer edges in late summer, maintained into early autumn. *Foliage* Leaves large to very large, 4–9 in (10–23 cm) long and 3–6 in (7.5–15 cm) wide, ovate, purple/green, down-covered with silver undersides. *Stem* Cream and brown to cream and purple/brown stems. Upright when young, producing attractive coloured bark and becoming branching, gnarled and spreading, forming a fan-shape with training. Stem formation and colour provides interest in winter. Medium growth rate. *Fruit* None, but may retain old flower-heads with ray florets turning brown.
Hardiness Tolerates a minimum winter temperature of 14°F (−10°C).
Soil requirements Neutral to acid soil, tolerates some alkalinity.
Sun/Shade aspect Requires a sheltered aspect in medium to light shade. Dislikes full sun and deep shade may spoil shape.
Pruning None required and may resent it.
Training Train branches when young into a fan-shaped shrub, tying to individual anchor points or to wires.
Propagation and nursery production From semi-ripe cuttings taken in early summer. Purchase container grown; rather hard to find, must be sought from specialist nurseries. Best planting height 15 in–2½ ft (38–76 cm).
Problems Often looks uninteresting when purchased but grows rapidly once planted out.
Forms of interest *H. aspera* Purple/blue florets around central light blue clusters. Foliage purple/green, down-covered. *H. sargentiana* (Sargent's hydrangea) Foliage up to 6–10 in (15–25 cm) long. Flat flower up to 8 in (20 cm) wide. Blue central fertile petals, outer white ray florets, slightly pink on alkaline soils. Mid summer.
Average height and spread
Five years
5 × 5 ft (1.5 × 1.5 m)
Ten years
8 × 8 ft (2.4 × 2.4 m)
Twenty years
12 × 12 ft (3.7 × 3.7 m)
Protrudes up to 3 ft (91 cm) from support.

Hydrangea aspera in flower

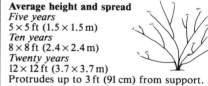

HYDRANGEA PANICULATA

PANICK HYDRANGEA
Hydrangeaceae   *Wall Shrub*
Deciduous
Spectacular, late summer flowering shrub, requiring specific pruning to do well.

Origin From Japan, China and Taiwan.
Use As a fan-trained shrub for walls and fences.
Description *Flower* Large panicles of sterile white bracts, mid to late summer, fading to pink, finally to brown. *Foliage* Leaves broad, ovate, 3–6 in (7.5–15 cm) long and 1½–3 in (4–7.5 cm) wide, light green, giving yellow autumn colour. *Stem* Upright and brittle. Light green to green/brown, becoming mahogany-brown with age. Fast growth rate. *Fruit* None, but dead flowerheads maintained into early winter.
Hardiness Tolerates a minimum winter temperature of 4°F (−15°C).

Hydrangea paniculata 'Tardiva' in flower

Soil requirements Prefers rich, deep soil, tolerates a wide range including alkaline or acid, but dislikes extreme alkalinity.
Sun/Shade aspect Tolerates all but the most exposed aspects. Prefers light shade but will tolerate full sun. Deep shade spoils shape.
Pruning Once a fan framework of branches has been formed, ensure new growth and improved flowering by cutting back hard each spring, reducing previous year's wood back to two buds from point of origin, otherwise the shrub becomes old, woody and very brittle, with small flowers.
Training As new shoots emerge tie them to wires or individual anchor points in fan-trained formation. The reduction of the previous season's growth by pruning will entail retying each year.
Propagation and nursery production From softwood cuttings taken in early summer. Purchase container grown or root-balled (balled-and-burlapped). Easy to find, especially when in flower. Best planting height 15 in–3 ft (38–91 cm).
Problems As the shrub is very brittle, take care to avoid damage.
Similar forms of interest *H. p.* 'Grandiflora' (Pee gee hydrangea) Very large white panicles of flowers, fading to pink. The most common form. *H. p.* 'Kyushu' Large white flowers. Said to be an improvement on *H. p.* 'Grandiflora'. *H. p.* 'Praecox' Earlier, white flowers, although slightly less profuse, larger foliage and stronger stems. *H. p.* 'Tardiva' A later-flowering form, with slightly more open flowers and a wider base to the panicles.
Average height and spread
Five years
6 × 6 ft (1.8 × 1.8 m)
Ten years
10 × 10 ft (3 × 3 m)
Twenty years
13 × 13 ft (4 × 4 m)
Protrudes up to 2 ft (60 cm) from support.

HYDRANGEA PETIOLARIS
(*H. p. scandens*)

CLIMBING HYDRANGEA
Hydrangeaceae   *Wall Shrub*
Deciduous
Rightly deserving its widespread use as a vigorous wall shrub but its full potential is not always appreciated.

Origin From Japan.
Use Ideal as a self-clinging climber for exposed, shady walls, for adorning the trunks of trees, or as a free-growing pillar. Will spread to form a ground-cover.
Description *Flower* White, round florets, up to ¾ in (2 cm) wide, form a flat lace-cap flower up to 10 in (25 cm) wide with central clusters of tufted, creamy white, fertile flowers, each consisting of up to 20 stamens in each cluster; profusely borne from June onwards, ageing to pink/brown in late autumn, finally turning brown in winter and retained in good order until late winter. *Foliage* Oval, tapering, slightly curled shape, up to 5 in (12 cm) long and 1½ in (4 cm) wide, light green turning a good yellow in autumn. *Stem* Light green ageing to light brown, becoming mahogany brown in winter with peeling bark; very attractive. Clinging aerial roots produced on undersides of shoots and branches. Slow growing at first, becoming faster with time. *Fruit* No fruits of interest, but brown flowerheads have winter attraction.
Hardiness Tolerates a minimum winter temperature of 4°F (−15°C).
Soil requirements Does well on both alkaline or acid soils but requires adequate moisture for establishment when young.
Sun/Shade aspect All aspects. Medium shade to full sun with no particular preference.
Pruning No pruning required although can be cut back in spring to keep within bounds as required.
Training Self-clinging but young plants will appreciate being tied to some form of cane framework to assist their initial establishment.
Propagation and nursery production From layers. Purchase container grown or root-balled (balled-and-burlapped) from late summer through to early spring; generally available from most good garden centres and nurseries. Best planting height 6 in–3 ft (15–91 cm).
Problems Slow to establish, often taking up to three years to produce any amount of new

growth, but from then on quickly establishes. Can become larger than anticipated.
Similer forms of interest None.
Average height and spread
Five years
6 × 6 ft (1.8 × 1.8 m)
Ten years
20 × 20 ft (6 × 6 m)
Twenty years
40 × 40 ft (12 × 12 m)
Protrudes up to 2½ ft (76 cm) from support.

HYDRANGEA QUERCIFOLIA

OAK LEAF HYDRANGEA
Hydrangeaceae   *Wall Shrub*
Deciduous
A very good autumn-flowering shrub with interestingly shaped foliage giving good autumn colours.

Origin From south-eastern USA.
Use Good as a fan-trained climber for shady walls and fences.
Description *Flower* Panicles of white florets produced from mid summer, maintaining their white texture well into early autumn when they begin to turn pink and finally, in winter, brown. *Foliage* Leaves round to ovate, 4–8 in (10–20 cm) long and 2–4 in (5–10 cm) wide, with large pointed lobes simi-

Hydrangea quercifolia in flower

Hydrangea petiolaris in flower

Hydrangea villosa in flower

lar in shape to oak leaves. Dark green, deeply veined, turning vivid orange/red in autumn. *Stem* Upright when young, becoming lax and ranging. Brown, peeling bark. Very brittle in constitution. Medium growth rate. *Fruit* None, but dead flowerheads retained into winter.
Hardiness Tolerates a minimum winter temperature of 14°F (−10°C).
Soil requirements Does well on most soils, both alkaline and acid.
Sun/Shade aspect Tolerates all but the most exposed aspects in full sun to deep shade.
Pruning None, other than that required for training.
Training Secure to individual anchor points or wires to form a fan-trained formation.
Propagation and nursery production From semi-ripe cuttings taken in mid summer. Purchase container grown; easy to find in nurseries, less common in garden centres. Best planting height 15–20 in (38–60 cm).
Problems The wood is brittle. Young plants when purchased look extremely misshapen but, once trained, quickly form an attractive all-round shape.
Similar forms of interest None.
Average height and spread
Five years
6 × 6 ft (1.8 × 1.8 m)
Ten years
8 × 8 ft (2.4 × 2.4 m)
Twenty years
10 × 12 ft (3 × 3.7 m)
Protrudes up to 2 ft (60 cm) from support.

HYDRANGEA VILLOSA
(*H. rosthornii*)

KNOWN BY BOTANICAL NAME

Hydrangeaceae   *Wall Shrub*
Deciduous

Has always been one of the most interesting of hydrangeas but its use as a fan-trained specimen is often overlooked although it is a form in which it does extremely well.

Origin From western China.
Use As a fan-trained shrub for walls and fences.
Description *Flower* Round, flat, lilac-blue clusters with toothed outer marginal sepals up to 6 in (15 cm) wide in late summer to early autumn. May be more pink on alkaline soils. *Foliage* Leaves narrow, elliptic, 4–9 in (10–23 cm) long, purple/green, velvet textured. Some autumn yellow colours. *Stem* Numerous upright stems, surmounted by slight branching, each branch producing a terminal flower. Grey/green when young, ageing to creamy/brown, attractive in winter.

Fast growth rate when young, becoming slower with age. *Fruit* None. Flowers retained into winter as brown flowerheads.
Hardiness Tolerates a minimum winter temperature of 14°F (−10°C). Foliage may be destroyed by late spring frosts, although a wall or fence will offer some protection; recovery is normal.
Soil requirements Prefers acid soil, but tolerates considerable alkalinity. Does best on rich, deep, moist woodland leaf mould.
Sun/Shade aspect Preferably an aspect which gives protection from late spring frosts to prevent foliage damage. Light dappled shade; dislikes full sun. Very useful in exposed, shady positions if wind protection is provided.
Pruning Remove one third of oldest stems on established plants in early spring to encourage good basal rejuvenation and maintain foliage and flower size.
Training Tie to individual anchor points or to wires to achieve a fan shape.
Propagation and nursery production From softwood cuttings taken in early summer or from micropropagated nursery stock. Purchase container grown or root-balled (balled-and-burlapped). Best planting height 15 in–2 ft (38–60 cm).
Problems Stock often appears short and deformed when purchased.
Similar forms of interest None.
Average height and spread
Five years
4 × 4 ft (1.2 × 1.2 m)
Ten years
8 × 8 ft (2.4 × 2.4 m)
Twenty years
12 × 12 ft (3.7 × 3.7 m)
Protrudes up to 3 ft (91 cm) from support.

ILEX × ALTACLAERENSIS

ALTACLAER HOLLY, HIGHCLERE HOLLY

Aquifoliaceae   *Wall Shrub*
Evergreen

A beautiful range of evergreen shrubs with female plants producing interesting berries and foliage.

Origin Basic form raised in Highclere, Berkshire, England as a cross between *I. aquifolium* and *I. perado*; from this came all the varieties.
Use As an attractive shrub for growing against walls and fences where it can be allowed to grow free or can be trimmed and clipped.
Description *Flower* Small clusters of small white flowers with prominent stamens in late spring and early summer. *Foliage* Leaves ovate, 2–4 in (5–10 cm) long and 2–3 in

(5–7.5 cm) wide, some spines at outer lobed edges. Glossy, waxy upper surfaces, dull undersides. Mainly green, but with silver and golden variegated forms. *Stem* With pruning, forms a tight, upright wall shrub for all year round attraction. Light to mid green, glossy. Medium rate of growth. *Fruit* Round berries, green at first, becoming bright glossy red, borne on female plants in autumn and maintained into winter. Male shrubs do not fruit. Male and female specimens must be planted together to achieve fruits on the female.
Hardiness Tolerates a minimum winter temperature of 4°F (−18°C).
Soil requirements Prefers rich, moist, open soil but does well on most types.
Sun/Shade aspect Tolerates all aspects in full sun to medium shade. In deep shade it will lose its compact shape and become sprawling and less likely to fruit.
Pruning None required, but can be reduced in size, or trimmed to shape in early spring.
Training Normally freestanding but may need securing to individual anchor points.
Propagation and nursery production From semi-ripe cuttings taken in early summer. Purchase container grown or root-balled (balled-and-burlapped). Availability varies. Best planting height 1½–4 ft (45 cm–1.2 m).
Problems Although less spiny than most hollies, handling can be uncomfortable. When purchased, young plants often look uninteresting, but shape improves once planted out. Newly planted shrubs may lose their leaves entirely in early spring following planting.

Ilex × altaclaerensis 'Lawsoniana'

Similar forms of interest *I. × a.* 'Atkinsonii' Large, dark green, glossy foliage with spiny edges. A male form often used as a pollinator for other forms. *I. × a.* 'Camelliifolia' Large, camellia-like foliage, red/purple when young, becoming dark green and shiny with age. A female form with large clusters of dark red fruits and purple stems. *I. × a.* 'Golden King' Almost round, shiny, spineless leaves, green with bright yellow to gold margins. A female form producing red to orange/red fruit. One of the finest of all golden variegated hollies. Slightly less than average height. *I. × a.* 'Hodginsii' Dark green, oval leaves with some spines produced irregularly. A male form useful as a pollinator. *I. × a.* 'Lawsoniana' Spineless leaves, dark green with bright yellow centres. A female form with orange/red fruit. Reversion may be a problem and any completely green shoots should be removed at once. *I. × a.* 'Silver Sentinel' Creamy white to yellow margins around pale green to grey/green, narrow, elliptic leaves. Very few spines. A female form with orange/red fruit. Quick-growing and upright in habit. Slightly less than average height and spread.
Average height and spread
Five years
6 × 6 ft (1.8 × 1.8 m)
Ten years
13 × 10 ft (4 × 3 m)
Twenty years
20 × 13 ft (6 × 4 m)
Protrudes up to 13 ft (4 m) from wall or fence.

73

ILEX AQUIFOLIUM

COMMON HOLLY, ENGLISH HOLLY

Aquifoliaceae   *Wall Shrub*
Evergreen

An extremely interesting and useful range of very hardy evergreen shrubs.

Origin From Europe and western Asia.
Use As an evergreen shrub planted to grow up against a wall or fence, either trimmed and shaped or left free-growing.
Description *Flower* Small clusters of small white flowers with prominent stamens in late spring to early summer. *Foliage* Leaves ovate, lobed, 1–3 in (2.5–7.5 cm) long and 1–2 in (2.5–5 cm) wide, with very spiny edges. Glossy green, golden or silver variegated, depending on variety. *Stem* Upright, becoming very spreading, forming an individual upright shrub against a wall or fence. Mid to dark green, glossy. Fast to medium growth rate when young, slowing with age. *Fruit* Female forms, if pollinated by a male form nearby, produce round, red fruits in autumn, maintaining them into winter.
Hardiness Tolerates a minimum winter temperature of 4°F (−15°C).
Soil requirements Does well on any soil except extremely dry.
Sun/Shade aspect Tolerates all aspects in full sun to medium shade. In deep shade will lose its compact shape, becoming sprawling and less likely to fruit.
Pruning None required, but can be reduced in height and spread, or closely trimmed and shaped, in early spring.
Training Normally freestanding but may need individual anchor points.
Propagation and nursery production From semi-ripe cuttings taken in early summer. Purchase container-grown or root-balled (balled-and-burlapped). Most varieties easy to find in nurseries and some offered through garden centres. Best planting height 1½–4 ft (45 cm–1.2 m).
Problems Newly planted shrubs may lose leaves entirely in early spring following transplanting. Young plants when purchased often look thin and sparse but shape quickly improves once planted out.
Similar forms of interest *I. a.* '**Argenteo-marginata**' (Broad-leaved silver holly) White margins on dark green or grey/green spiny leaves. Normally offered in female form, but can also be found as a male plant so care should be taken to ascertain sex before purchasing. Fruit orange to orange/red in female form, retained into mid winter, but fruit production requires a nearby male shrub for pollination. *I. a.* '**Bacciflava**' (syn. *I. a.* '**Fructu-luteo**') (Yellow-fruited holly) Female form with dark green to mid green spiny leaves and good bright yellow fruits maintained into winter. *I. a.* '**Golden Milkboy**' (syn. *I. a.* '**Aurea Mediopicta Latifolia**') Leaves flat in presentation, green with large golden centre variegation and spiny edges. May revert and

all-green shoots should be removed when seen. Male form, no fruits. Very attractive foliage. *I. a.* '**Golden Queen**' (syn. *I. a.* '**Aurea Regina**') Very dark green leaves with broad, bright golden yellow margins. Male form so no fruits. Slightly less than average height and spread. *I. a.* '**Golden van Tol**' Foliage less spiny than most forms, more ovate to lanceolate, and with very good golden margins. Female form producing red fruits, maintained into winter. *I. a.* '**Handsworth New Silver**' Narrow, ovate leaves with creamy white margins around deep green to grey/green centres. Female, producing orange to orange/red fruits. *I. a.* '**J.C. van Tol**' Narrow, ovate, dark green foliage, almost spineless. Female, producing large regular crops of red fruits. *I. a.* '**Madame Briot**' Glossy, dark yellow to gold margins around dark green leaves, presented on purple stems. Female, producing orange/red fruits. *I. a.* '**Myrtifolia Aureomaculata**' Smaller foliage than most, narrow and ovate, very dark green with central golden variegation. Male form, no fruit. Slightly less than average height and spread. *I. a.* '**Silver Milkboy**' Flattish, spiny leaves, dark green with central creamy white variegation. Some reversion may occur and all-green shoots should be removed when seen. Male form, no fruit. Slightly less than average height and spread. *I. a.* '**Silver Queen**' Young shoots purple to black in colour. Creamy white margins to dark green leaves. Male form, no fruit.
Average height and spread
Five years
6 × 6 ft (1.8 × 1.8 m)
Ten years
14 × 14 ft (4.3 × 4.3 m)
Twenty years
20 × 20 ft (6 × 6 m)
Protrudes up to 20 ft (6 m) from wall or fence.

Indigofera heterantha in flower

INDIGOFERA HETERANTHA
(*I. gerardiana*)

INDIGO BUSH

Leguminosae   *Wall Shrub*
Deciduous

An attractive, mid to late summer flowering shrub useful for its ability to adapt to dry conditions.

Origin From the north-western Himalayas.
Use As a mid summer, early autumn flowering fan-trained or freestanding wall or fence shrub, especially suitable for colder areas.
Description *Flower* Moderately open racemes of purple/pink pea-flowers in mid summer through to early autumn. *Foliage* Leaves pinnate, 2–4 in (5–10 cm) long with 13–21 leaflets up to ½ in (1 cm) long. Grey/green, giving some good yellow autumn colour. *Stem* Long, arching, becoming twiggy in second year in milder areas. Grey/green. Fast growth rate when young, slowing with age. *Fruit* May produce small, grey/green pea-pods of some winter interest.
Hardiness Tolerates a minimum winter temperature of 14°F (−10°C). Stems may die back to ground level in severe winters, but normally rejuvenate in the spring.
Soil requirements Does well on all soil conditions, especially dry areas, once established.
Sun/Shade aspect Requires a sheltered aspect in full sun to very light shade.
Pruning If they are not destroyed by winter cold, reduce long arching stems by two thirds or more in spring to encourage new growth.
Training Allow to stand free or secure to wall or fence by individual anchor points or wires.
Propagation and nursery production From softwood cuttings taken in late spring/early summer. Purchase container grown; may need to be sought from specialist nurseries. Best planting height 15 in–2½ ft (38–76 cm).
Problems Often very late to produce new leaves and growth, which may not appear until early summer. May look weak and insipid when purchased.
Similar forms of interest *I. potaninii* Longer racemes of pink flowers, up to 4–5 in (10–12 cm) long, late summer to early autumn. Slightly less than average height and spread. From north-western China.
Average height and spread
Five years
6 × 6 ft (1.8 × 1.8 m)
Ten years
8 × 8 ft (2.4 × 2.4 m)
Twenty years
12 × 12 ft (3.7 × 3.7 m)
Protrudes up to 4 ft (1.2 m) from support if fan-trained, 11 ft (3.4 m) untrained.

Ilex aquifolium 'Golden Queen'

IPOMOEA HEDERACEA

MORNING GLORY

Convolvulacaea   *Annual Climber*
Deciduous

One of the most spectacular of all the annual climbing plants, needing some care for good results, but worth the effort.

Origin From northern Australia.
Use As an annual climber for walls and fences, to ramble over large shrubs and ideal for growing up the south side of conifers or in containers or greenhouses.
Description *Flower* Five intense blue petals make up a 2½ in (6 cm) wide, reflex-mouthed trumpet with white central eye. *Foliage* Broad, ovate, up to 5 in (12 cm) long and 1 in (2.5 cm) wide. Light to mid green, showing off the flowers to good advantage. *Stem* Light green, twining, self-supporting. Fast rate of growth. *Fruit* No fruit of any interest.
Hardiness Not winter hardy. Must be planted when all danger of spring frosts has passed. Will be killed by autumn frosts. Seeds do not overwinter in soil.
Soil requirements Tolerates all soil conditions, but an addition of a good quantity of organic material will aid root run and therefore good growth above ground.
Sun/Shade aspect Requires a sheltered aspect with protection from wind and heavy rain if possible. Can be grown in greenhouses or conservatories. Best in full sun. Will tolerate light shade, although flowering will be reduced the greater the amount of shade.

Ipomoea hederacea **in flower**

Pruning Not required. Is killed in autumn by frosts.
Training Allow to twine over wires, trellis or through the branches of medium to large shrubs. If used for growing up the face of conifers a cane or pole may be needed against the tree to give the vine additional support.
Propagation and nursery production From seeds planted under protection with bottom heat in early spring; do not plant out until all danger of frosts has passed, normally early summer. Always purchase container grown; often found in garden centres in late spring, early summer with the bedding plants. Best planting height 2–4 in (5–10 cm).
Problems Its need for annual planting does make it less appealing than some other climbers, but it is well worth the effort. Can be difficult to establish unless adequate organic material is introduced into the soil prior to planting.
Similar forms of interest None.
Average height and spread
One year
12 × 12 ft (3.7 × 3.7 m)
Protrudes up to 12 in (30 cm) from support.

Itea ilicifolia **in flower**

ITEA ILICIFOLIA

KNOWN BY BOTANICAL NAME

Iteaceae   *Wall Shrub*
Evergreen

One of the most spectacular late summer flowering shrubs to benefit from the protection of a wall or fence in cold conditions.

Origin From central China.
Use As a fan-trained shrub for large walls and fences in sheltered positions.
Description *Flower* Racemes up to 15 in (38 cm) long of fragrant green to green/white flowers, ageing to yellow/green, reminiscent of large catkins, late summer. *Foliage* Leaves lobed, dark green, glossy, ovate, 2–5 in (5–12 cm) long, similar to those of holly, with purple hue underlying base colour and silver undersides. *Stem* Strong and upright when young, becoming weeping with age, forming a cascading effect as a weeping shrub when grown against a wall or fence. Light green to purple/green. Fast growth rate when young, slowing with age. *Fruit* Insignificant.
Hardiness Tolerates a minimum winter temperature of 14°F (−10°C). Leaves easily damaged by severe wind chill.
Soil requirements Does well on all soil types.
Sun/Shade aspect Requires a sheltered aspect. Prefers light shade, tolerates full sun to medium shade.
Pruning None required.
Training Requires wires or individual anchor points to secure and encourage a fan-trained shape.
Propagation and nursery production From semi-ripe cuttings taken in early summer. Purchase container grown from garden centres and specialist nurseries. Best planting height 15 in–2 ft (38–60 cm).
Problems Gives the appearance of poor rooting and irregular shape when young but soon grows away once planted.
Average height and spread
Five years
3 × 3 ft (91 × 91 cm)
Ten years
6 × 6 ft (1.8 × 1.8 m)
Twenty years
12 × 12 ft (3.7 × 3.7 m)
Protrudes up to 3 ft (91 cm) from support.

JASMINUM FRUTICANS

KNOWN BY BOTANICAL NAME

Oleaceae   *Wall Shrub*
Evergreen to semi-evergreen

An interesting, shrubby jasmine, presenting itself more attractively when used against a wall or fence than when free-growing.

Origin From the Mediterranean region.
Use As a freestanding shrub or fan-trained against walls or fences.
Description *Flower* Clusters of small yellow flowers carried in early to mid summer. Little individual attraction but effective en masse. *Foliage* Narrowly lanceolate up to ¾ in (2 cm) long, with rounded ends. Deep green, blue/green towards edges, sparse in number, some yellow autumn colour. *Stem* Light green when young, becoming mid green and finally grey/green. Arching, ranging, semi-rigid. Medium to fast growth. *Fruit* Black, globe-shaped fruits up to ¼ in (5 mm) wide carried in late summer/early winter.
Hardiness Tolerates a minimum winter temperature of up to 0°F (−18°C).

Jasminum fruticans **in flower**

Soil requirements Tolerates a wide range of soils with no particular preference, except it dislikes very dry or waterlogged conditions.
Sun/Shade aspect Requries a sheltered aspect. Full sun to medium shade, full sun for preference.
Pruning If freestanding, remove one third of oldest growth to ground level after flowering. If fan-trained, do the same as far as is practical.
Training Tie to wires or individual anchor points or allow to grow freestanding.
Propagation and nursery production From semi-ripe cuttings taken in early summer. Should always be purchased container-grown; may have to be sought from specialist nurseries. Best planting height 6 in–3 ft (15–91 cm).
Problems Its open habit does not appeal to all. Flowers and foliage are limited but are of interest.
Similar forms of interest None.
Average height and spread
Five years
4 × 4 ft (1.2 × 1.2 m)
Ten years
8 × 8 ft (2.4 × 2.4 m)
Twenty years
8 × 8 ft (2.4 × 2.4 m)

Protrudes up to 18 in (45 cm) from support if fan-trained, 4 ft (1.2 m) untrained.

JASMINUM HUMILE REVOLUTUM

SHRUBBY JASMINE
Oleaceae   **Wall Shrub**
Evergreen
An attractive, late-summer flowering wall shrub often overlooked and not planted as widely as it deserves.

Origin From the Himalayas.
Use As a freestanding wall shrub for walls and fences where it benefits from the protection offered.

Jasminum humile revolutum **in flower**

Description *Flower* Small, five-petalled, ½ in (1 cm) wide bright yellow flowers are intermittently produced in small clusters through late summer and early autumn. *Foliage* Attractive foliage, bright green, glossy, 1½ in (3.5 cm) long and ½ in (1 cm) wide. *Stem* Light, bright green. Upright, becoming branching. Produces underground suckers which in some circumstances become invasive. *Fruit* No fruits of any significance.
Hardiness Tolerates a minimum winter temperature of 4°F (−15°C).
Soil requirements Tolerates all soil conditions, with no particular preference, only disliking extremely dry soil when becoming established.

Sun/Shade aspect Moderately sheltered aspect in light shade to full sun.
Pruning Remove one third of oldest growth to ground level in early to mid spring to encourage rejuvenation.
Training Allow to stand free, growing against a wall or fence.
Propagation and nursery production From semi-ripe cuttings taken in early to mid summer. Purchase container grown from good garden centres and specialist nurseries. Best planting height 1–2½ ft (30–76 cm).
Problems Can outgrow the area allowed for it, particularly in a forward direction.
Similar forms of interest None.
Average height and spread
Five years
4 × 3 ft (1.2 m × 91 cm)
Ten years
6 × 6 ft (1.8 × 1.8 m)
Twenty years
8 × 6 ft (2.4 × 1.8 m)

Protrudes up to 6 ft (1.8 m) from wall or fence.

JASMINUM MESNYI
(*J. primulinum*)

PRIMROSE JASMINE
Oleaceae   **Tender Woody Climber**
Deciduous to semi-evergreen
An attractive climber but requires protection in all but the mildest areas.

Origin From China.
Use As a rambling climber for very sunny, hot walls but best grown under the protection of a greenhouse or conservatory.
Description *Flower* Small, solitary flowers are up to 1¾ in (4.5 cm) long, bright yellow, with seven to eight petals carried at each leaf joint during mid to late summer, earlier under protection. *Foliage* Trifoliate, leaflets 1–3 in (2.5–7.5 cm) long and ½–¾ in (1–2 cm) wide. The degree of evergreen will depend on its location. *Stem* Shoots four-angled, bright green, loosely twisting. Very ranging and spreading in habit. Fast growing. *Fruit* Does not normally fruit outside its native environment.
Hardiness Tolerates a minimum winter temperature of 32°F (0°C).
Soil requirements Any average soil as long as adequate moisture is available. If grown in tubs they must be at least 21 in (53 cm) in diameter and filled with a good soil-based potting compost.
Sun/Shade aspect Protected aspect in full sun to light shade.
Pruning Not normally required, but can be reduced in size if necessary.
Training Semi-self-twining, but will need tying to train over wires or similar support system.

Jasminum mesnyi **in flower**

Propagation and nursery production From semi-ripe cuttings taken in early spring to mid summer. Best planting height 1–3 ft (30–91 cm). Always purchase container grown; will have to be sought from specialist nurseries or may be found in florists.
Problems Its tenderness must always be allowed for, and its overall size, particularly when grown in confined spaces under protection.
Similar forms of interest None.
Average height and spread
Five years
6 × 6 ft (1.8 × 1.8 m)
Ten years
12 × 12 ft (3.7 × 3.7 m)
Twenty years
18 × 18 ft (5.5 × 5.5 m)
Protrudes up to 3 ft (91 cm) from support.

JASMINUM NUDIFLORUM

WINTER JASMINE
Oleaceae   **Wall Shrub**
Deciduous
One of the most widely planted of all wall shrubs, well deserving its rightful place as a true gem for its winter flowers.

Origin From western China.
Use As a winter flowering shrub for walls, fences and pillars.
Description *Flower* Five-petalled, ¾ in (2 cm) wide, butter-yellow in colour, carried at the leaf joints in profusion from early winter to early spring whenever mild weather persists. *Foliage* ¾ in (2 cm) long and ¼ in (5 mm) wide, dark bright green, carried in groups of three.

Jasminum nudiflorum **in flower**

Stem Angled, arching, possibly lax in habit, ribbed. Bright green in winter. Medium rate of growth, slowing with age. *Fruit* Insignificant.
Hardiness Tolerates a minimum winter temperature of 4°F (−15°C).
Soil requirements Any soil, often tolerating extremely poor conditions, both acid and alkaline.
Sun/Shade aspect Tolerates all but the most exposed of aspects in full sun through to medium shade and even deep shade in some circumstances.
Pruning Remove one third of old flowering shoots to ground level on shrubs established more than three years as an annual operation to encourage regrowth.
Training Allow to ramble through wires and trellis. May need some initial support by tying in.
Propagation and nursery production From semi-ripe cuttings taken in early summer. Purchase container grown; most forms easy to find. Best planting height 15 in–2½ ft (38–76 cm).
Problems Can often outgrow the desired area because it is assumed to be smaller than it truly is. Some winter die-back may be experienced and flowers may be damaged in severe cold spells, but new buds normally open once warmer conditions arrive.
Similar forms of interest None.
Average height and spread
Five years
5 × 5 ft (1.5 × 1.5 m)
Ten years
10 × 10 ft (3 × 3 m)
Twenty years
10 × 15 ft (3 × 4.6 m)
Protrudes up to 3 ft (91 cm) from support.

JASMINUM OFFICINALE

COMMON JASMINE

Oleaceae   *Woody Climber*
Deciduous
A vigorous, sweetly-scented, summer flowering climber to cover large areas.

Origin From Persia, North India and China.
Use As a very free-growing climber, quickly spreading in all directions both sidewards and forward through large shrubs, small trees, over fences, walls and buildings.
Description *Flower* Small clusters of three to eight small white flowers at the ends of branches, each flower made up of four to five ¾ in (2 cm) wide petals, flowering from mid summer to early autumn. Very fragrant. *Foliage* Pinnate leaves 4–6 in (10–15 cm) long and 3 in (7.5 cm) wide with five, seven or nine leaflets, oval in shape and from 1½–2½ in (4–6 cm) long and ½ in (1 cm) wide; end leaflet on short stalk. Mid to grey-green, some good yellow autumn colour. *Stem* Grey-green when young, becoming darker with age, angled, partially twining in habit. Very vigorous, able to produce in excess of 10 ft (3 m) of growth in one year. *Fruit* Produces no fruit of interest.
Hardiness Tolerates a minimum winter temperature of 14°F (−10°C). Tips of new growth often killed in winter but replaced in following spring.
Soil requirements Does well on all soil types but requires adequate moisture to sustain vigorous growth.
Sun/Shade aspect Good in all but the most severe, exposed aspects. Sull sun to very light shade.
Pruning Prune hard in late winter and early spring, cutting back growth as much as is required for training; will reflower on current season's new growth.
Training Allow to ramble through shrubs and trees, provide wires or other suitable support for twining over walls and fences. Long shoots may need some tying in, especially in windy situations.
Propagation and nursery production From semi-ripe cuttings taken in early summer. Always purchase container-grown from early

Jasminum officinale in flower

to late summer; best planting height 1½–4 ft (45 cm–1.2 m). Normally available from good garden centres and nurseries.
Problems Its ultimate size and rate of growth are often underestimated. Requires a large area to show itself off to best advantage.
Forms of interest See further entries.
Average height and spread
Five years
12 × 12 ft (3.7 × 3.7 m)
Ten years
24 × 24 ft (7.3 × 7.3 m)
Twenty years
36 × 36 ft (11 × 11 m)
Protrudes up to 4 ft (1.2 m) from support.

JASMINUM OFFICINALE (Variegated Forms)

VARIEGATED SUMMER-FLOWERING JASMINE
Oleaceae   *Woody Climber*
Deciduous
Given some protection, these are amongst the finest of both ornamental foliage and summer-flowering climbers.

Origin From north India and China.
Use As a climber for walls, fences, pillars and pergolas where protection can be given. Can be planted in large conservatories and greenhouses.
Description *Flower* White, five-petalled, small flowers up to ½ in (1 cm) across and long, carried in small open clusters. Very frag-

Jasminum officinale 'Aureum' in leaf

rant. *Foliage* Pinnate with up to five leaflets, each leaflet grey/green, splashed boldly with yellow and golden or silver variegation. More intense on new foliage than old. *Stem* Light grey/green to mid green, ridged. Partially twining. Medium to fast growing. *Fruit* Insignificant.
Hardiness Tolerates a minimum winter temperature of 23°F (−5°C).
Soil requirements Alkaline to acid. Needs a rich, moist soil type.
Sun/Shade aspect Requires a sheltered aspect. Full sun to very light shade.
Pruning Remove one third of oldest growth to ground level in early spring on plants more than three years old. Repeat annually.
Training Semi-twining. Will need some additional support by tying into wires, trellis or individual anchor points when young and when becoming heavy at maturity.
Propagation and nursery production From semi-ripe cuttings taken in early to mid summer. Best planting height 1–3 ft (30–91 cm). Always purchase container grown; will have to be sought from specialist nurseries.
Problems Can be slow to establish, taking up to three years to promote any new growth. Occasionally branches may revert to all-green and should be removed at point of origin as soon as seen. Some frost die-back may be experienced but rejuvenation normally occurs the following spring.
Forms of interest *J. o.* 'Argentea' White variegated foliage. White, very fragrant flowers. *J. o.* 'Aureum' Golden variegated foliage. White, very fragrant flowers.
Average height and spread
Five years
5 × 5 ft (1.5 × 1.5 m)
Ten years
10 × 10 ft (3 × 3 m)
Twenty years
18 × 18 ft (5.5 × 5.5 m)
Protrudes up to 2 ft (60 cm) from support.

JASMINUM POLYANTHUM

FLORIST'S JASMINE
Oleaceae   *Tender Woody Climber*
Deciduous, semi-evergreen or evergreen depending on location and cultivation
Although this beautiful climber requires an extremely sheltered position or, ideally, the protection of a conservatory or greenhouse, it is well worth consideration.

Origin From China.
Use As a climber for very sheltered walls in very mild areas, or to adorn the roof of a conservatory or large greenhouse.

Description *Flower* Small, five-petalled flowers up to $\frac{3}{4}$ in (2 cm) long and wide with reflexed petals, white on the inside and rosy-white on the outside. Produced in panicles at the leaf joints, each panicle up to 2–4 in (5–10 cm) long. Very fragrant. Flowers from late spring to late summer, but may be earlier depending on location. *Foliage* Light green, pinnate, with five to seven curling leaflets, each 2 in (5 cm) long. Overall size of leaf 5 in (12 cm) long by 4 in (10 cm) wide. *Stem* Bright green when young ageing to mid-green. Semi-twining. Fast growing. *Fruit* Insignificant.

Jasminum polyanthum in flower

Hardiness Tolerates a minimum winter temperature of 32°F (0°C).
Soil requirements Moderately alkaline to acid, with a good degree of organic material and moisture retention. If grown in pots in conservatories, requires a pot with a diameter of not less than 21 in (53 cm), filled with a good quality soil-based potting compost.
Sun/Shade aspect Must be in a very warm, sheltered position. Full sun to light shade.
Pruning Plants establishd for three years should have one third of the oldest growth removed to ground level in late winter when under protection or in early spring when outside to encourage rejuvenation. Repeat annually.
Training Will twine around wires and timber structures. When young may need some additional support by tying in. May also need tying in for training in a specific direction.
Propagation and nursery production From semi-ripe cuttings taken in late spring and early summer. Always purchase container grown; will have to be sought from specialist nurseries, good garden centres or florists. Can be planted out in the greenhouse or con-

servatory once the plant has finished flowering and it will grow away well. Best planting height 1–3 ft (30–91 cm).
Problems Its tenderness and its ability to outgrow a conservatory or greenhouse in a very short time.
Similar forms of interest None.
Average height and spread
Five years
8 × 8 ft (2.4 × 2.4 m)
Ten years
16 × 16 ft (4.9 × 4.9 m)
Twenty years
30 × 30 ft (9 × 9 m)
Protrudes up to 2 ft (60 cm) from support.

JASMINUM × STEPHANENSE

PINK FLOWERING SUMMER JASMINE
Oleaceae　　　　　*Woody Climber*
Deciduous
An attractive, summer-flowering climber with strongly scented blooms; often sadly overlooked.

Origin Of garden origin.
Use For climbing walls, fences and pillars and for rambling through medium-sized shrubs.
Description *Flower* Five-petalled, pale pink flowers up to $\frac{1}{2}$ in (1 cm) across and long; carried in small open clusters of three to five flowers. Very fragrant. *Foliage* Pinnate, with up to five leaflets $1\frac{1}{2}$–2 in (4–5 cm) long. Dull green to grey/green, with downy undersides. When young, each leaf has an attractive yellow/orange margin around the edge. *Stem* Light green when young, becoming dark green and eventually green/brown. Smooth, ridged, semi-twining. Medium growth rate. *Fruit* None.
Hardiness Tolerates a minimum winter temperature of 14°F (−10°C). Below this temperature some damage may be caused in winter but rejuvenation is normal in spring.
Soil requirements Alkaline to acid. Moist, rich, well-fed soil for best results.
Sun/Shade aspect Tolerates all but the most exposed aspect. Best in full sun to light shade.
Pruning Remove one third of oldest growth to ground level in early spring to induce rejuvenation on plants more than three years old and continue on annual basis.
Training Will require the support of wires or trellis through which it will twine.
Propagation and nursery production From semi-ripe cuttings taken in early to mid summer. Always purchase container grown; normally available from good garden centres and nurseries. Best planting height 15 in–3 ft (38–91 cm).

Problems Can be slow to establish unless soil conditions are satisfactory.
Similar forms of interest *J. beesianum* A darker red/pink variety.
Average height and spread
Five years
6 × 6 ft (1.8 × 1.8 m)
Ten years
10 × 10 ft (3 × 3 m)
Twenty years
15 × 15 ft (4.6 × 4.6 m)
Protrudes up to 18 in (45 cm) from support.

KERRIA JAPONICA

JAPANESE KERRIA, JEW'S MALLOW, BACHELOR'S BUTTON, SAILOR'S BUTTON
Rosaceae　　　　　*Wall Shrub*
Deciduous
A shrub of attractive flowers, foliage and stems, rather invasive because of its suckering habit but useful for dense cover against walls and fences on poor soils.

Origin From China and Japan.
Use As a spring-flowering shrub that can be grown in close association with walls and fences.
Description *Flower* Yellow buttercup-shaped flowers, single or double, dependent on variety, mid to late spring. *Foliage* Leaves oval with narrow pointed ends, $1\frac{1}{2}$–3 in (4–7.5 cm) long, bright green, giving some yellow autumn colour. *Stem* Glossy green, strong, upright, spreading. Lateral underground shoots are produced which emerge some distance from parent. Good winter stem attraction if pruned as suggested. Medium to fast rate of growth. *Fruit* Insignificant.
Hardiness Tolerates a minimum winter temperature of 0°F (−18°C).
Soil requirements Any soil type and condition, often tolerating extremely poor areas.

Kerria japonica 'Pleniflora' in flower

Sun/Shade aspect Tolerates all aspects in full sun to medium shade.
Pruning Cut back one third to half of oldest flowering wood to ground level, after flowering.
Training Allow to stand free or secure to wall or fence by individual anchor points or tying to wires.
Propagation and nursery production From rooted underground suckers or from hardwood cuttings taken in winter or semi-ripe cuttings taken in early summer. Purchase container grown; all forms easy to find. Best planting height 2–3 ft (60–91 cm).
Problems Needs space to perform to best advantage.
Similar forms of interest *K. j.* 'Pleniflora' (syn. *K. j.* 'Flore Pleno') Double, golden

yellow flowers on an upright, vigorous shrub. Good green stems in winter. **K. j. 'Splendens'** A single-flowered form with buttercup yellow flowers larger than most varieties.
Average height and spread
Five years
10 × 5 ft (3 × 1.5 m)
Ten years
10 × 8 ft (3 × 2.4 m)
Twenty years
10 × 12 ft (3 × 3.7 m)
Protrudes up to 4 ft (1.2 m) from support.

KOLKWITZIA AMABILIS

BEAUTY BUSH

Caprifoliaceae   ***Wall Shrub***
Deciduous

An often overlooked shrub for late spring to early summer flowering, but a real beauty, as its common name implies. Adapts well, if given space, as a fan-trained wall shrub.

Origin From western China.
Use As a medium- to large-sized shrub for walls and fences where adequate space can be allowed for it to be fan-trained.
Description *Flower* Bell shaped, ¾ in (2 cm) long and ½ in (1 cm) wide, soft pink with yellow throat, hanging in small clusters 3 in (7.5 cm) wide and long along wood three years old, late spring, early summer and mid summer. *Foliage* Leaves medium to small, ovate, 1–1½ in (2.5–4 cm) long, slightly toothed-edged, light olive-green to grey/green with red shading and silver undersides. Yellow autumn colour. *Stem* Young shoots light green to green/brown, strong and upright, produced mainly from ground level. Growth more than two years old becomes slightly arched, spreading and twiggy. Fast to medium rate of growth. *Fruit* Small, grey/brown, slightly translucent seeds.
Hardiness Tolerates a minimum winter temperature of 4°F (−15°C).
Soil requirements Any soil, no preferences.
Sun/Shade aspect Tolerates all aspects in full sun to light shade.
Pruning Remove one third of older flowering wood by cutting to ground level after the flowering period and retraining in its fan shape.
Training Allow to stand free or secure to wall or fence by individual anchor points and wires.
Propagation and nursery production From soft to semi-ripe cuttings taken mid summer or from hardwood cuttings taken in winter. Plant bare-rooted or container grown. Best planting height 1½–2½ ft (45–76 cm).

Kolkwitzia amabilis in flower

Laburnocytisus × adamii in flower

Problems When purchased, container grown plants present a very fragile appearance but rapidly become robust once planted out.
Similar forms of interest K. a. 'Pink Cloud' A cultivar of garden origin with large, strong pink flowers, possibly better for garden planting than its parent.
Average height and spread
Five years
5 × 7 ft (1.5 × 2.1 m)
Ten years
8 × 10 ft (2.4 × 3 m)
Twenty years
10 × 12 ft (3 × 3.7 m)
Protrudes up to 5 ft (1.5 m) from support if fan-trained, 10 ft (3 m) untrained.

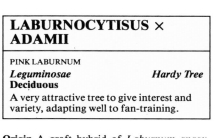

LABURNOCYTISUS × ADAMII

PINK LABURNUM

Leguminosae   ***Hardy Tree***
Deciduous

A very attractive tree to give interest and variety, adapting well to fan-training.

Origin A graft hybrid of *Laburnum anagyroides* and *Cytisus purpureus* originated in the early 1800s in France.
Use As a fan-trained tree for large walls.
Description *Flower* Individual limbs bear either racemes of yellow *Laburnum anagyroides* flowers 9–12 in (23–30 cm) long or shorter racemes of the pink *Cytisus purpureus* flowers 4–6 in (10–15 cm) long. Some limbs may even present both flowers, one type interspersed with the other. Small areas of true *Cytisus purpureus* may occur in small clusters at the end of older branches. *Foliage* Light grey/green trifoliate leaves, rather untidy. On mature trees tend to be yellow and sickly. Some yellow autumn colour. *Stem* Grey/green, rubbery texture. Slow to medium rate of growth. *Fruit* Small, poisonous pea-pods sometimes produced.
Hardiness Tolerates a minimum winter temperature of 0°F (−18°C).
Soil requirements Does well on most soil conditions; tolerates heavy alkalinity or acid types. Dislikes wet conditions, when root damage may cause poor anchorage.
Sun/Shade aspect Tolerates all aspects. Best in full sun; tolerates light shade.
Pruning Resents pruning, therefore plant only young or bush trees.
Training Tie branches as they appear into a fan-trained shape on wires or individual anchor points.
Propagation and nursery production By grafting or budding on to *Laburnum vulgaris*

understocks. Purchase bare-rooted or container grown. Best planting height: one- or two-year-old grafted trees 3 ft (91 cm) high or bush trees with multiple stems two years old and up to 5 ft (1.5 m) high.
Problems Root systems often feeble at time of purchase.
Similar forms of interest None.
Average height and spread
Five years
7 × 7 ft (2.1 × 2.1 m)
Ten years
14 × 14 ft (4.3 × 4.3 m)
Twenty years
28 × 28 ft (8.5 × 8.5 m)
Protrudes up to 3 ft (91 cm) from support.

LABURNUM × WATERERI 'VOSSII'

GOLDEN CHAIN TREE, WATERER LABURNUM

Leguminosae   ***Hardy Tree***
Deciduous

A well-known flowering tree adapting well to fan-training, particularly useful for exposed aspects, but care must be taken with its poisonous fruits.

Origin Of garden origin.
Use As a large fan- or upright-trained flowering tree for walls and fences.
Description *Flower* Long, pendent racemes up to 12 in (30 cm) long of numerous deep yellow to golden-yellow pea-flowers produced

Laburnum × watereri 'Vossii' in flower

in late spring. *Foliage* Leaves trifoliate, each leaflet up to 3 in (7.5 cm) long. Grey/green to dark green, glossy upper surfaces and lighter, often hairy undersides. *Stem* Dark glossy green with a slight grey sheen. Strong, upright when young, branching and twiggy with age; finally a spreading tree of medium vigour. Medium rate of growth. *Fruit* Grey/green, pendent pods containing poisonous, black, pea-shaped fruits. Produces fewer seed pods than other laburnum.

Hardiness Tolerates a minimum winter temperature of 0°F (−18°C).

Soil requirements Any soil conditions; tolerates high alkalinity.

Sun/Shade aspect Tolerates all aspects. Full sun to light shade, preferring full sun.

Pruning Prune young trees hard in spring following planting. Select and train resulting five to seven shoots and tie into a fan-trained shape. In subsequent years remove all side growths back to two points from their origin and maintain original main branches in fan shape.

Training Will require tying to wires or individual anchor points.

Propagation and nursery production By grafting. Plant bare-rooted or container grown; stocked by most garden centres and nurseries. Choose bush or young trees of one to two years old.

Problems All laburnums have poor root systems and require permanent staking. Relatively short-lived trees, showing signs of distress after 40 or more years. Poisonous fruits can be dangerous to children.

Similar forms of interest None.

L. alpina (Scotch laburnum) Dark glossy foliage, short racemes of yellow flowers. Adapts well to training.

Average height and spread
Five years
10 × 10 ft (3 × 3 m)
Ten years
20 × 20 ft (6 × 6 m)
Twenty years
28 × 28 ft (8.5 × 8.5 m)
Protrudes up to 3 ft (91 cm) from support.

LAGERSTROEMIA INDICA

CRAPE MYRTLE

Lythraceae   *Tender Tree*
Deciduous

An attractive tender tree, benefiting from the protection of a wall both in very warm sheltered areas and when grown under protection of a greenhouse or conservatory.

Origin From China.

Use As a large fan-trained wall shrub for very sheltered positions or under glass.

Description *Flower* Six crescent-shaped crinkle-edged stalked petals make up a round flower, petunia-pink to deep red, carried in panicles 7–8 in (17–20 cm) long and 4–5 in (10–12 cm) wide in summer/early autumn. *Foliage* Lanceolate leaves up to 2½ in (6 cm) long and 1 in (2.5 cm) wide, presented in threes on short stalks. Mid-green, with pronounced veining. Yellow autumn colour. *Stem* Grey/green, rigid, branching, interesting in winter. Medium rate of growth. *Fruit* No fruit of interest.

Hardiness Tolerates a minimum winter temperature of 23°F (−5°C) but requires shelter from cold winds.

Soil requirements Tolerates most soil conditions with no particular preference, except dislikes extreme alkaline types.

Sun/Shade aspect A sheltered aspect in full sun.

Pruning Flowering shoots should be shortened back to within two buds of their origin in early spring to induce new flowering growth.

Training Fan-train on walls by fixing wires or individual anchor points.

Propagation and nursery production From seed or semi-ripe cuttings. Always purchase

Lagerstroemia indica in flower

container grown; best planting height 1–3 ft (30–91 cm). Not readily available, will have to be sought from specialist nurseries.

Problems Its tenderness must not be underestimated and it does require a very sheltered position for any degree of success. May be hard to find.

Similar forms of interest *L. i.* 'Alba' Pure white flowers, more tender and even scarcer in commercial production.

Average height and spread
Five years
4 × 4 ft (1.2 × 1.2 m)
Ten years
6 × 6 ft (1.8 × 1.8 m)
Twenty years
10 × 10 ft (3 × 3 m)
Protrudes up to 2 ft (60 cm) from support.

LAPAGERIA ROSEA

KNOWN BY BOTANICAL NAME

Philesiaceae   *Tender Woody Climber*
Evergreen

Of all tender climbing plants, has among the most spectacular flowers.

Origin From Chile.

Use As a climbing plant for very sheltered gardens or for use in conservatories and greenhouses where it is possibly more at home.

Lapageria rosea 'Nashcourt' in flower

Description *Flower* Large, 3 in (7.5 cm) long, bell-shaped, fleshy, pendent pink flowers from late summer to early autumn. *Foliage* Broad, ovate, pointed leaves, leathery, grey/green, up to 3 in (7.5 cm) long, borne either singly or in twos and threes. *Stem* Grey/green, loosely twining, not self-clinging or supporting. Medium rate of growth. *Fruit* May produce oblong to oval berries containing many seeds in late summer/early autumn.

Hardiness Tolerates a minimum winter temperature of 32°F (0°C).

Soil requirements If grown in containers use a good-quality potting compost. If grown in soil add additional sharp sand and peat to provide well-drained soil with moisture retention.

Sun/Shade aspect Very sheltered aspect or under the protection of a conservatory or greenhouse. Light shade, dislikes full sun. Also requires a moist atmosphere.

Pruning Not normally required but can be cut back if necessary in early spring.

Training Encourage to twine around wires. Ideal when allowed to climb above walkways, where the pendent flowers can be seen to full advantage.

Propagation and nursery production From seed, from cuttings taken from semi-ripe wood in mid summer, or layered. Always purchase container grown; will have to be

Lapageria rosea in flower

sought from specialist nurseries. Best planting height 6 in–3 ft (15–91 cm).

Problems Can be attacked by greenfly, mealy bug, scale insects and thrips. Eradicate with a proprietary control. In some circumstances can become invasive by underground shoots appearing some considerable distance from parent, although this is normally only seen in greenhouse or conservatory beds.

Similar forms of interest *L. r.* 'Albiflora' Pure white flowers. *L. r.* 'Flesh Pink' Mother-of-pearl to very pale pink flowers. *L. r.* 'Nashcourt' Dark pink to red flowers.

Average height and spread
Five years
7 × 7 ft (2.1 × 2.1 m)
Ten years
14 × 14 ft (4.3 × 4.3 m)
Twenty years
20 × 20 ft (6.6 × 6.6 m)
Protrudes up to 6 in (15 cm) from support.

Lathyrus latifolius in flower

LATHYRUS LATIFOLIUS

EVERLASTING PEA

Leguminosae **Deciduous**   *Perennial Climber*

When allowed to grow free and wild, one of the most spectacular of flowering climbers.

Origin From Europe.
Use As a climbing perennial for walls, fences, pillars and pergolas but at its best when allowed to ramble through large shrubs. Useful for ground cover with or without support.
Description *Flower* A large back shield, with two wings either side and two forward-facing petals, forming a typical sweet-pea flower, 1½ in (4 cm) wide and deep. Rose-pink in colour and scented, produced from June to September. *Foliage* Grey/green, elliptic, 1½–2 in (4–5 cm) long, normally in pairs, with clinging tendrils from the stalk. Some scent. *Stem* Heavily angled stems, almost square, with ribs. Grey/green to mid green. Ranging. Fast rate of growth. *Fruit* Small, grey/green pea pods containing poisonous black fruits.
Hardiness Roots tolerate a minimum winter temperature of 14°F (−10°C). Top growth dies to ground level in winter.
Soil requirements Tolerates both alkaline and

acid conditions. Requires moisture retention and a high degree of organic material for best results.
Sun/Shade aspect Tolerates all aspects. Full sun to light shade for preference.
Pruning Dies to ground level in winter.
Training Tie to wires or individual anchor points or allow to ramble through wires, trellis or large shrubs.
Propagation and nursery production From seed sown in early spring under protection, or from division of root clump. Should always be purchased container grown; relatively easy to find in garden centres and specialist nurseries. Best planting height: either pot-grown clumps in early spring with no top growth, or up to 18–20 in (45–55 cm) tall in later spring, early summer.
Problems Often outgrows the position allocated for it. If happy can be invasive.
Similar forms of interest *L. l. albus* Pure white flowers. Scarce. *L. l. a.* **'Snow Queen'** A very good form. Extremely scarce. *L. l. roseus* Becoming more plentiful. Attractive bright flowers. *L. l. splendens* A form sometimes seen, with large flowers.
Average height and spread
One year
6–10 ft × 5–6 ft
(1.8–3 m × 1.5–1.8 m)
Protrudes up to
2 ft (60 cm) from
support.

LATHYRUS ODORATUS

SWEET PEA

Leguminosae **Deciduous**   *Annual Climber*

Rightly well loved by every gardener for its summer display of delicately coloured, fragrant flowers.

Origin From Sicily.
Use As a climber for walls, fences, pillars and pergolas, supported by brushwood or twigs, or grown up netting. Allow to ramble through large shrubs. Grown individually for flower size against canes. Use for ground cover where wire supports are provided.
Description *Flower* Two wings stand either side of a large back flower up to 1½ in (4 cm) wide and deep in a range of colours from white, blue, mauve, purple, pink, red and yellow from mid summer to early autumn. Highly fragrant, carried in clusters at the end of long flower stalks. *Foliage* Grey/green, ovate leaves, normally in pairs, the stalk ending in a clinging tendril. *Stem* Angular, grey/green, loosely twining. Fast rate of growth. *Fruit* Small, grey/green pea pods of little attraction containing black, poisonous fruits.
Hardiness Seeds do not overwinter in soil.
Soil requirements Requires a deep, well prepared soil with liberal quantities of organic material, moisture retaining yet well drained. Both alkaline and acid.
Sun/Shade aspect Tolerates most aspects but requires protection from wind and driving rain which will damage the flowers. Full sun to light shade.
Pruning Allow to ramble or reduce to a central cordon stem on which the flowers will be larger and on long flowering stalks. Plants will die with the first winter frosts.
Training Allow to grow over nets, up strings, poles or wires, or to ramble through brushwood. Clings by leaf tendrils, as well as loosely twining habit.
Propagation and nursery production From seed grown under protection and planted out in mid to late spring. Best grown in pots, either singly or in threes using good-quality soil-based potting compost. Seeds may also be sown in late autumn or early winter and overwintered under protection or sown directly into the soil in early spring in their flowering position, although the flowers may not be as large when grown this way. Container grown plants can be purchased from garden centres and nurseries, best planting size 2–4 in (5–10 cm).
Problems May suffer attacks of blackfly, greenfly or mildew. May well run out of energy unless adequate moisture and plant food are available.
Forms of interest SPENCER HYBRIDS **'Aerospace'** Pure white flowers. **'Air Warden'** Cerise-scarlet flowers. **'Alan Williams'** Large, mid blue flowers. **'Apricot Queen'** Orange/pink flowers. **'Beaujolais'** Burgundy flowers. **'Blue Danube'** Deep blue, frilled flowers. **'Blue Ripple'** White flowers, flushed lavender. **'Carlotta'** Brilliant carmine flowers. **'Corinne'** Rose-pink and carmine flowers with white blotch at base. **'Cream Beauty'** Frilled cream flowers. **'Dorothy Sutton'** Rose-pink on cream ground. **'Elizabeth Taylor'** Clear mauve, strongly fragrant flowers. **'Garden Party'** Wavy flowers, bright red with orange tinge. **'Geranium Pink'** Deep rose-pink flowers. **'Grace of Monaco'** Soft pink on white ground. Slightly waved petals. **'Hunter's Moon'** Large, creamy yellow, frilled blooms. **'Lady Diana'** Pale violet-blue flowers. **'Lady Fairbairn'** Lavender/rose flowers. **'Larkspur'** Soft blue to lavender flowers. **'Leamington'** Deep lavender flowers. **'Lilac Ripple'** Pure white flowers splashed with purple. **'Lillie Langtry'** Deep cream, wavy flowers. **'Maggie May'** Sky-blue flowers flushed white. **'Marietta'** Rose/mauve flowers on strong stems. **'Mrs Bernard Jones'** Large, frilled, cerise on white flowers. **'Mrs C. Kay'** Lavender flowers. **'Mrs R. Bolton'** Almond-

Lathyrus latifolius albus in flower

Lathyrus odoratus in flower

blossom pink. **'Noel Sutton'** Large, rich blue flowers. **'North Shore'** Navy blue flowers with pale violet wings. **'Pageantry'** Large, red/purple flowers. **'Pennine Floss'** Large, wavy, red/purple flowers. **'Princess Elizabeth'** Salmon-pink on cream flowers. **'Radar'** Salmon-pink flowers. **'Red Ensign'** Red flowers on long stems. **'Rosy Frills'** Large, frilled white flowers with deep rose edge. **'Royal Flush'** Salmon-pink on cream flowers. **'Royal Wedding'** Large, snow-white flowers on long stems. **'Snowdonia Park'** Pure white, frilled flowers. **'Superstar'** Deep rose-pink flowers with white base. **'Swan Lake'** White flowers. **'Welcome'** Deep scarlet flowers. **'Wiltshire Ripple'** White flowers flushed claret red. **'Winston Churchill'** Rich crimson flowers.

GRANDIFLORA VARIETIES (old-fashioned scented types) Very fragrant, flowers smaller than average, with a good range of colours. **'Jet Set Mixed'** Large flowers on good stems in a range of colours including scarlet, crimson, blue, salmon, cerise and mauve. **'Old Spice Mixed'** Old variety in a wide range of colours. Very strongly scented flowers, small compared with modern varieties. **'Romance'** Bicoloured flowers, each delicately frilled around outer edges, with very pleasant perfume. **'Royals Mixed'** Good mixture for cutting. Strong plants with very attractive blooms on long stems. **'Ruffle-edged Mixed'** Sweetly scented. Ruffled edges to petals in pinks, white and creams. **'Summer Breeze Mixed'** Soft pastel colours. Some deep red and blue bi-colours. Good scent. Wavy petals with frilled edges.

OLD 18th CENTURY VARIETY **'Fragrant Beauty'** Royal blue and rich violet purple. Fewer flowers. Highly scented.

MIXED SEED COLLECTIONS **'Candyman'** A range of colours, with some striped flowers. Large flowers with good fragrance. **'Early-bird Mammoth Mixed'** Early flowering, fragrant variety, with a wide range of colours. Good for greenhouses or outdoor display. **'Early Multiflora Gigantea Mixed'** Good range of colours. Strong growing, flowers produced over a long period. **'Floriana Mixed'** Similar to Spencer Hybrids. Good number of blooms on individual stems. Good range of colours. **'Galaxy Mixed'** Very vigorous and prolific in flower. Frilled petals. Very fragrant and good stems.

Average height and spread
One year
9 × 3 ft (2.7 m × 91 cm)
Protrudes up to 2 ft (60 cm) from support.

LAURUS NOBILIS

BAY, SWEET BAY, BAY LAUREL, POET'S LAUREL
Lauraceae   *Wall Shrub*
Evergreen
A useful evergreen shrub with protection gained from winter cold by wall planting.

Origin From the Mediterranean region.
Use A large, freestanding evergreen for mild locations, planted in front of walls and fences.
Description *Flower* Small $\frac{1}{2}$ in (1 cm) wide tufts of almost petalless flowers with very prominent stamens, yellow/green. Flowers are either male or female, the latter being more commonly produced. *Foliage* Elliptic leaves 2–4 in (5–10 cm) long, dark green, glossy upper surfaces with dull grey/green undersides. *Stem* Upright, becoming branching. Mid green sometimes tinged purple. Medium to fast growth rate, slowing with age. *Fruit* Small, shiny, black fruits sometimes produced on mature shrubs growing in mild areas. Fruit not always an asset as it can mean that the shrub is maturing, when the leaves become small and uninteresting, or even in ill health.

Laurus nobilis in flower

Hardiness Tolerates a minimum winter temperature of 14°F (−10°C). Susceptible to leaf scorch in cold winter winds.
Soil requirements Prefers light open sc..., but tolerates most types, including considerable degrees of alkalinity and acidity.
Sun/Shade aspect Requires a moderately protected aspect in full sun to light shade but will tolerate deep shade.
Pruning Can be clipped hard, as required. If reduced to ground level it rejuvenates but takes some years to reach former height.
Training Allow to stand free in front of walls and fences.
Propagation and nursery production From semi-ripe cuttings taken mid summer. Purchase container grown; if not found in garden centres and nurseries, may be sought from suppliers of culinary herbs. Best planting height 1½–6 ft (45 cm–1.8 m).
Problems Often outgrows its intended space; may be damaged in winter.
Similar forms of interest *L. n.* **'Aurea'** An attractive variety with golden yellow evergreen leaves. Slightly less than average height and spread and slightly more tender.

Average height and spread
Five years
7 × 4 ft (2.1 × 1.2 m)
Ten years
10 × 7 ft (3 × 2.1 m)
Twenty years
20 × 15 ft (6 × 4.6 m)
Protrudes up to 7 ft (2.1 m) from wall or fence.

LAVATERA OLBIA

TREE MALLOW, TREE LAVATERA
Malvaceae   *Wall Shrub*
Deciduous
A tall-growing, rather tender shrub which adapts well to being grown against a wall where some protection is afforded against wind damage to flowers.

Lavatera olbia in flower

Origin From southern France.
Use As a freestanding wall shrub.
Description *Flower* Single, 3 in (7.5 cm) wide, saucer-shaped flowers, pink to silvery/pink, produced from early summer through until autumn frosts. Flowers open, progressively from midway down flowering shoot, last for a short period and then perish as the next two or three flowers open, continuing in this way to the end of flowering spike. *Foliage* Leaves broad, elliptic, five-lobed, 3–4 in (7.5–10 cm) long and wide, light green to grey/green. *Stem* Strong, upright, grey/green shoots produced from a central crown in spring. Very fast annual growth of new shoots. *Fruit* Insignificant.

Hardiness Tolerates a minimum winter temperature of 14°F (−10°C).
Soil requirements Light, open, dry soil. Requires adequate feeding to encourage production of long flower shoots.
Sun/Shade aspect Requires a sheltered aspect in full sun. Tolerates very light shade.
Pruning All previous year's shoots should be cut hard back annually in early spring. Hard pruning encourages flowering.
Training Allow to stand free in front of a wall or fence.
Propagation and nursery production From hardwood cuttings taken in winter or from semi-ripe cuttings taken in early summer. Purchase container grown; normally found in specialist nurseries. Best planting height 15 in–2 ft (40–60 m).
Problems Can be late to break into growth and may show little life until early summer, but grows rapidly once dormancy is broken. Plants in containers tend to look unsightly and sickly. Flower colour and size is dependent on maximum sunlight – the duller the summer, the less showy the flowers.
Similar forms of interest *L. o.* **'Barnsley'** Attractive light purple/pink flowers in abundance. Slightly less height and spread. May be more tender. *L. o.* **'Variegata'** Bright pink flowers. Foliage golden variegated. Requires protection.
Average height and spread
Five years
8 × 6 ft (2.4 × 1.8 m)
Ten years
10 × 10 ft (3 × 3 m)
Twenty years
10 × 10 ft (3 × 3 m)
Protrudes up to 7 ft (2.1 m) from wall or fence.

LIGUSTRUM LUCIDUM

GLOSSY PRIVET, CHINESE PRIVET, WAXLEAF PRIVET
Oleaceae   *Wall Shrub*
Evergreen
A useful group of evergreen shrubs with some striking variegated varieties, not so widely planted as they deserve. Adapts well to wall-training.

Origin From China.
Use As an upright evergreen shrub for walls and fences, suitable for trimming and shaping if required.
Description *Flower* Good-sized, 6 in (15 cm) long and 4 in (10 cm) wide, triangular-shaped panicles of musty scented flowers on mature wood in late summer. *Foliage* Pointed ovate leaves, 3–6 in (7.5–15 cm) long, glossy green upper surfaces, duller undersides, some

Ligustrum lucidum **'Tricolor'**

white, silver and gold variegated forms. *Stem* Strong, vigorous, upright, becoming branching and spreading with age. Light green to green/purple. Medium to fast rate of growth.
Fruit Clusters of dull blue to blue/black fruits in late summer, early autumn.
Hardiness Tolerates a minimum winter temperature of 4°F (−15°C).
Soil requirements Any soil, but dislikes very dry, alkaline conditions or extremely waterlogged areas.
Sun/Shade aspect Tolerates all aspects. Full sun to medium shade. Tolerates deep shade but may become slightly deformed.
Pruning None required. Can be cut hard back and will quickly rejuvenate, even from very old stems.
Training Allow to stand free or secure to wall or fence by individual anchor points or tying to wires.
Propagation and nursery production From semi-ripe cuttings taken in mid to late summer, or hardwood cuttings taken in late autumn to early winter. Purchase container grown or root-balled (balled-and-burlapped); quite easy to find. Best planting height 1½–2½ ft (45–76 cm).
Problems The green form is vigorous and may outgrow the area allowed for it. Golden-leaved varieties may suffer sun scorch in strong sunlight.
Similar forms of interest *L. l.* **'Aureum'** Bright yellow to golden spring foliage, this colouring declining as summer progresses. Two thirds average height and spread and less hardy than the parent. May be hard to find. *L. l.* **'Excelsum Superbum'** Foliage margined and mottled with deep yellow or creamy

white. Two thirds average height and spread. May be hard to find. *L. l.* **'Tricolor'** White to cream variegation, leaf margins tinged pink when young, making a very pleasant colour combination. Two thirds average height and spread. Slightly less hardy than the parent. May be hard to find.
Average height and spread
Five years
8 × 8 ft (2.4 × 2.4 m)
Ten years
15 × 15 ft (4.6 × 4.6 m)
Twenty years
26 × 26 ft (8 × 8 m)
Protrudes up to 5 ft (1.5 m) from support if fan-trained, 20 ft (6 m) untrained.

LIGUSTRUM OVALIFOLIUM

OVAL-LEAVED PRIVET, HEDGING PRIVET, CALIFORNIA PRIVET
Oleaceae   *Wall Shrub*
Deciduous to semi-evergreen
In its gold and silver form can make an interesting fan-trained shrub. The green form will grow against walls but is of little attraction, other than for clipping to a specific shape.

Origin From Japan.
Use As a freestanding or fan-trained shrub for walls and fences.

Ligustrum ovalifolium **'Aureum'** in leaf

Description *Flower* 3 in (7.5 cm) long and 1½ in (4 cm) wide panicles of off-white flowers with a musty scent, borne only on untrimmed shrubs in mid summer. *Foliage* Leaves ovate, pointed, 1–1½ in (2.5–4 cm) long, mid to dark green with glossy upper surfaces and lighter, duller green undersides. Often maintained to mid winter in mild conditions, but cannot be relied upon as a full evergreen. *Stem* Strong, grey/green to green/brown, upright, vigorous, becoming very branching with age. Fast growth rate. *Fruit* Small, 2 in (5 cm) long and 1½ in (4 cm) wide, clusters of dull black berries produced only on mature, untrimmed shrubs.
Hardiness Tolerates a minimum winter temperature of 4°F (−15°C).
Soil requirements Most soils, but distressed by extremely dry or very alkaline types.
Sun/Shade aspect Tolerates any aspect in full sun to deep shade, but the latter leads to very open and lax habit.
Pruning May be reduced to ground level and will rejuvenate quite quickly, or may be trimmed back hard. Both operations decrease flowering on mature plants.
Training Allow to stand free or secure to wall or fence by individual anchor points or tying to wires.
Propagation and nursery production From semi-ripe cuttings taken in late spring or early summer, or hardwood cuttings taken in

Ligustrum lucidum **in flower**

winter. Plant bare-rooted or container grown. Availability varies. Best planting height 15 in–3 ft (38–91 cm).

Problems Privet roots are extremely invasive and draw all plant nutrients out of surrounding soil up to 6–10 ft (1.8–3 m) from base of shrub. Consequently it is difficult for other plants to grow in its immediate vicinity. Golden-leaved varieties may suffer sun scorch in strong sunlight.

Similar forms of interest *L. o.* **'Argenteum'** Leaves grey/green with creamy white margins. Mature, unpruned shrubs may produce off-white flowers not particularly visible against foliage. Current season's growth should be cut by half or more in early spring to encourage prolific regeneration of creamy white foliage. Two thirds average height and spread. *L. o.* **'Aureum'** (Golden privet) Rich golden yellow leaves with green centres. If required for foliage effect, current season's growth should be cut back by half or more in early spring to encourage regeneration of golden foliage. Two thirds average height and spread. *L.* × **'Vicaryi'** Attractive all-golden foliage. May be semi-evergreen in some areas. White flowers.

Average height and spread
Five years
10 × 10 ft (3 × 3 m)
Ten years
13 × 13 ft (4 × 4 m)
Twenty years
20 × 20 ft (6 × 6 m)
Protrudes up to 6 ft (1.8 m) from support if fan-trained, 20 ft (6 m) untrained.

LIGUSTRUM QUIHOUI

KNOWN BY BOTANICAL NAME

Oleaceae   *Wall Shrub*
Deciduous

An attractive, graceful privet adapting well to being fan-trained on walls and fences.

Origin From China.
Use As a late summer flowering shrub for large walls and fences where it can be grown freestanding or trained into a fan shape.
Description *Flower* Large, 10–12 in (25–30 cm) long, white to creamy white flower panicles produced profusely, mid to late summer. *Foliage* Leaves narrow, ovate, 1–1½ in (2.5–4 cm) long, somewhat sparsely produced on branches. Grey to olive-green giving some yellow autumn colour. *Stem* Upright at first, quickly becoming ranging and arching, producing an informal, open and somewhat lax effect. Light grey/green when young, becoming dark green to green/brown with age. Medium growth rate, slowing with age. *Fruit* Clusters of blue to blue/black fruits, early to late summer.

Ligustrum quihoui in flower

Ligustrum sinense in flower

Hardiness Tolerates a minimum winter temperature of 4°F (−15°C).
Soil requirements Most soils, but may be distressed by very alkaline or waterlogged conditions.
Sun/Shade aspect Tolerates all but the most exposed aspects in full sun to medium shade.
Pruning None required. May be cut back hard but will rejuvenate.
Training Allow to stand free or secure to wall or fence by individual anchor points or wires.
Propagation and nursery production From semi-ripe cuttings taken in mid summer or hardwood cuttings taken in early winter. Purchase container grown; rather hard to find, should be sought from specialist nurseries. Best planting height 2–2½ ft (60–76 cm).
Problems The young plant gives no indication of its true flowering potential.

Average height and spread
Five years
5 × 5 ft (1.5 × 1.5 m)
Ten years
7 × 7 ft (2.1 × 2.1 m)
Twenty years
15 × 15 ft (4.5 × 4.5 m)
Protrudes up to 4 ft (1.2 m) from support if fan-trained, 15 ft (4.6 m) untrained.

LIGUSTRUM SINENSE

CHINESE PRIVET

Oleaceae   *Wall Shrub*
Deciduous

A handsome shrub, with an attractive variegated form providing useful material for flower arranging. Adapts well to fan-training.

Origin From China.
Use As a tall, freestanding shrub or as a fan-trained specimen against walls and fences.
Description *Flower* 3–4 in (7.5–10 cm) long panicles of white flowers freely produced in mid summer. *Foliage* Leaves narrow, pointed, ovate, 1–3 in (2.5–7.5 cm) long, mid green, giving some limited autumn colour. *Stem* Strong and upright when young, becoming branching with age, forming a high, wide-spreading clump or fan-trained specimen. Medium growth rate. *Fruit* Clusters of black to blue/black fruits follow flowers in early autumn and are often retained into winter.
Hardiness Tolerates a minimum winter temperature of 4°F (−15°C).
Soil requirements Most soils but dislikes extremely dry, very alkaline or waterlogged conditions.
Sun/Shade aspect Tolerates all aspects in full sun to medium shade. In deep shade may become open, lax and shy to flower.

Pruning None required other than for training. May be trimmed very hard and will regenerate rapidly; can even be cut to ground level.
Training Allow to stand free or secure to wall or fence by individual anchor points or wires.
Propagation and nursery production From semi-ripe cuttings taken in mid summer or hardwood cuttings taken in late winter. Purchase container grown or bare-rooted; variegated forms easy to find, green form less often seen. Best planting height 2–2½ ft (60–76 cm).
Problems The true beauty of this privet is not always appreciated, because it is often kept trimmed and not allowed to reach full stature.
Similar forms of interest *L. s.* **'Variegatum'** Narrow, ovate, grey/green leaves, with white to creamy white margins, white flowers. Slightly less than average height and spread. Current season's growth may be cut back by half in early spring to encourage new, prolific growth of variegated leaves.

Average height and spread
Five years
10 × 10 ft (3 × 3 m)
Ten years
20 × 20 ft (6 × 6 m)
Twenty years
20 × 26 ft (6 × 8 m)
Protrudes up to 3 ft (91 cm) from support if fan-trained, 8 ft (2.4 m) untrained.

LIPPIA CITRIODORA
(*Aloysia triphylla*)

LEMON VERBENA, SHRUBBY VERBENA, LEMON PLANT

Verbenaceae   *Tender Wall Shrub*
Deciduous

A very attractive shrub with lemon-scented foliage and stems, benefiting from the protection of a wall or fence in many areas.

Origin From Chile.
Use As a fan-trained shrub on a sunny wall or fence. In cold areas can be grown in conservatories or greenhouses. Can be used as a culinary herb.
Description *Flower* 6 in (15 cm) long and 3 in (7.5 cm) wide, open terminal panicles of small pale blue/mauve florets in mid summer. *Foliage* Leaves lanceolate, 3–4 in (7.5–10 cm) long, grey/green to sea/green, giving off lemony, aromatic scent when crushed. *Stem* In cooler areas dies back completely in winter, in milder areas is maintained as a loose, open shrub. Grey/green, lemon-scented. *Fruit* Insignificant.
Hardiness Tolerates a minimum winter temperature of 23°F (−5°C).

Lippia citriodora **in flower**

Soil requirements Open, well-drained, warm soil.

Sun/Shade aspect Requires a sheltered aspect in full sun to very light shade.

Pruning Either cut to ground level or remove one third of oldest wood each spring to encourage new strong shoots with good aromatic foliage.

Training Allow to stand free or secure to wall or fence by individual anchor points or wires.

Propagation and nursery production From semi-ripe cuttings taken in mid summer for overwintering under cover and planting out in spring, or earlier if planting area is completely frost-free. Purchase container grown. Best planting height 15 in–2 ft (38–60 cm).

Problems Often a poor-looking specimen when purchased container grown but grows rapidly once planted.

Average height and spread
Five years
4 × 4 ft (1.2 × 1.2 m)
Ten years
5 × 5 ft (1.5 × 1.5 m)
Twenty years
7 × 7 ft (2.1 × 2.1 m)
Protrudes up to 4 ft (1.2 m) from support.

LOMATIA MYRICOIDES
(*L. longifolia*)

KNOWN BY BOTANICAL NAME

Proteaceae   *Wall Shrub*
Evergreen

A shrub which tolerates lower temperatures and a larger geographical range when given the protection of a wall or fence.

Origin From Chile.

Use As a large, fan-trained or freestanding foliage shrub for walls or fences, requiring an acid soil.

Description *Flower* Long, strap-like white petals, very fragrant, borne in late summer. *Foliage* Long, narrow, light grey/green leaves up to 8 in (20 cm) long and ½ in (1 cm) wide. *Stem* Upright, erect stems with red/brown velvety texture. Medium growth rate. *Fruit* Insignificant.

Hardiness Tolerates a minimum winter temperature of 14°F (−10°C), although at this temperature there may be some wind chill scorch to foliage.

Soil requirements Acid soil, dislikes any alkalinity. Must have good drainage.

Sun/Shade aspect Sheltered aspect in full sun to light shade.

Pruning None required, other than that for fan-training.

Training Allow to grow freestanding or tie to wires or individual anchorage points in a fan shape.

Propagation and nursery production From softwood cuttings taken in late summer, or from seed. Purchase container grown; rather hard to find. Best planting height 1½–2 ft (45–60 cm).

Problems Often looks very poor and weak in containers but on correct soil quickly presents itself attractively.

Similar forms of interest *L. ferruginea* Attractive foliage and flowers, possibly slightly stronger growing. *L. tinctoria* A variety with pinnate to double pinnate leaves with very narrow, long leaflets, light to mid green. Flowers sulphur yellow in bud, becoming creamy white, produced in long racemes at the terminals of each shoot. Half average height and spread. From Tasmania.

Average height and spread
Five years
7 × 7 ft (2.1 × 2.1 m)
Ten years
12 × 12 ft (3.7 × 3.7 m)
Twenty years
15 × 15 ft (4.6 × 4.6 m)
In favourable conditions may eventually reach 26 ft (8 m) height and spread. Protrudes up to 3 ft (91 cm) from support if fan-trained, 8 ft (2.4 m) untrained.

Lomatia myricoides **in flower**

LONICERA ×
AMERICANA
(*L. grata, L. italica*)

HONEYSUCKLE

Caprifoliaceae   *Woody Climber*
Deciduous

The attractive flower colouring and strong scent make this a notable honeysuckle worthy of a place in any garden.

Origin From south-east Europe.

Use As a mid summer to early autumn flowering, strong-growing climber for trellis, wires, walls, fences, poles, large shrubs and small trees. Can be grown as a weeping standard.

Description *Flower* Clusters of funnel-shaped trumpets up to 2 in (5 cm) long, carried in panicles up to 12 in (30 cm) long and 8 in (20 cm) wide at the ends of the branches. Yellow with purple shading. The tubular trumpets have two distinct lips at their ends up to 1–1½ in (2.5–4 cm) in diameter. Flowering is from early to mid summer with some later flowers in late summer and early autumn. *Foliage* Oval, up to 3 in (7.5 cm) long and 1½ in (4 cm) wide, carried in pairs along the stems. Light green with some purple shading. *Stem* Light yellow/green when young, ageing to yellow/brown, finally grey/brown. Twining and twisting, making it self-supporting. Medium to fast growing. *Fruit* Small, red, almost translucent fruits are produced in hot summers.

Lonicera americana **in flower**

Hardiness Tolerates a minimum winter temperature of 4°F (−15°C). Young foliage may be damaged by spring frosts but normally rejuvenates.

Soil requirements Does well on all soil types, although may show distress on very severe alkaline or dry conditions.

Sun/Shade aspect Tolerates all aspects. Performance is enhanced in light shade but will tolerate full sun to medium shade with varying degrees of success. Requires its roots to be shaded.

Pruning Once plants are established more than three years, remove one third of the oldest growth to ground level in early spring.

Training Allow to ramble and twine over wire trellis or branch supports. Normally needs no tying in except when young.

Propagation and nursery production From semi-ripe cuttings taken in mid summer or hardwood cuttings taken in mid to late winter. Always purchase container grown; best planting height 1½–3½ ft (45 cm–1.1 m)

from late summer through to early autumn. Normally available from good garden centres and specialist nurseries.
Problems May suffer attacks of blackfly and mildew. Protect with a proprietary control.
Similar forms of interest None.
Average height and spread
Five years
12 × 12 ft (3.7 × 3.7 m)
Ten years
20 × 20 ft (6 × 6 m)
Twenty years
25 × 25 ft (7.6 × 7.6 m)
Protrudes up to 2 ft (60 cm) from support.

LONICERA × BROWNII

SCARLET TRUMPET HONEYSUCKLE

Caprifoliaceae   *Woody Climber*
Deciduous

A most attractive group of honeysuckles, with unusual orange-red flowers.

Origin From North America.
Use Attractive climbers with all the characteristics of honeysuckle but with an interestingly different flower colour. Can be grown as a weeping standard.
Description *Flower* Red to scarlet-red, tubular trumpets up to 1–1½ in (2.5–4 cm) long are produced together at the ends of flowering shoots from early summer to early autumn. Moderately scented. *Foliage* Oval, up to 3½ in (9 cm) long and 1–1½ in (2.5–4 cm) wide. Downy, blue undersides, light fresh green upper. Carried in pairs along the shoots. *Stem* Grey/green when young, ageing to yellow/brown, finally grey/brown. Twining. Self-supporting. Medium to fast growing. *Fruit* May produce small, round, red fruits ⅛ in (2mm) in diameter following hot summers.
Hardiness Tolerates a minimum winter temperature of 14°F (−10°C). May suffer foliage damage from late spring frosts in excess of 23°F (−5°C).
Soil requirements Requires a moist, deep, rich soil to produce adequate growth and flowers. Tolerates moderately alkaline to acid soil.
Sun/Shade aspect Best on a slightly protected aspect in light shade, although will tolerate full sun to medium shade, as long as roots have adequate moisture and shade.
Pruning Remove one third of oldest growth to ground level in early spring on plants established more than three years. To restrict growth, prune offending shoots in early spring.
Training Self-twining over trellis, wires and branches and normally requires no other support, except tying in when young.
Propagation and nursery production From

semi-ripe cuttings in early summer or hardwood cuttings in winter. Always purchase container grown from late spring through to early summer; normally available from good garden centres and specialist nurseries. Best planting height 1½–3½ ft (45 cm–1.1 m).
Problems May suffer from attacks of blackfly and mildew. Protect with a proprietary control. May be slow to establish. Make sure adequate organic material is available to retain moisture to produce best growth results.
Similar forms of interest *L.* × *b.* **'Dropmore Scarlet'** Bright scarlet-red tubular flowers from mid summer to early autumn. The main and best form offered by garden centres and nurseries. *L.* × *b.* **'Fuchsoides'** A variety with larger flowers. May be slightly less hardy but not to any marked degree. Scented. May have to be sought from specialist nurseries. *L.* × *b.* **'Plantierensis'** Coral-red flowers. Will have to be sought from specialist nurseries.
Average height and spread
Five years
7 × 7 ft (2.1 × 2.1 m)
Ten years
14 × 14 ft (4.3 × 4.3 m)
Twenty years
21 × 21 ft (6.4 × 6.4 m)
Protrudes up to 2½ ft (76 cm) from support.

LONICERA CAPRIFOLIUM
(*L.* 'Early Cream')

PERFOLIATE HONEYSUCKLE

Caprifoliaceae   *Woody Climber*
Deciduous

Amongst the most pleasant of all the scented honeysuckles, but it may be a little difficult to find the true plant.

Origin From Europe.
Use As a useful scented climber for wires, trellis, walls and fences or for rambling through large shrubs. Can be grown as a weeping standard.
Description *Flower* One to two clusters carried at the ends of flowering shoots, made up of a number of tubular trumpet-shaped florets, each 1½–2 in (4–5 cm) long. Yellow/white with pink tinge. Two lips at the end of each floret up to 1 in (2.5 cm) across. Very fragrant. *Foliage* Oval, up to 4 in (10 cm) long and 1½ in (4 cm) wide. Grey/green. End pairs of shoots may be united, forming an attractive saucer-shaped leaf. *Stem* Light grey/green, ageing to yellow/brown, finally grey/brown. Twining. Medium to fast in growth. *Fruit* In autumn following hot summers may produce red fruits up to ¼ in (5mm) across, in clusters.

Hardiness Tolerates a minimum winter temperature of 4°F (−15°C).
Soil requirements Does well on all soil types, but prefers a moist soil, high in organic material. Tolerates both alkalinity and acidity, only showing distress on extremely alkaline soil types.
Sun/Shade aspect Light shade for preference, but will tolerate full sun to medium shade as long as roots are shaded. Does well on all aspects.
Pruning Remove one third of oldest growth to ground level in early spring on plants established more than three years.
Training Self-twining over trellis, wires and branches and requires no other support except tying in when young.

Lonicera caprifolium in flower

Propagation and nursery production From semi-ripe cuttings in early summer or hardwood cuttings in winter. Always purchase container grown; best planting height 1½–3½ ft (45 cm–1.1 m). Normally available from garden centres and specialist nurseries.
Problems May suffer from attacks of blackfly and mildew. Protect with a proprietary control.
Similar forms of interest *L. c.* **'Alba'** (syn. *L. praecox*) All white flowers. Not readily available and will have to be sought from specialist nurseries. *L. c.* **'Pauciflora'** Rose-tinged outer colouring to flowers.
Average height and spread
Five years
6 × 6 ft (1.8 × 1.8 m)
Ten years
12 × 12 ft (3.5 × 3.5 m)
Twenty years
18 × 18 ft (5.5 × 5.5 m)
Protrudes up to 2½ ft (45 cm) from support.

LONICERA ETRUSCA

ETRUSCAN HONEYSUCKLE

Caprifoliaceae   *Woody Climber*
Deciduous to semi-evergreen

The grey/green foliage of this very strong-growing honeysuckle, combined with the fragrant, creamy-yellow flowers, makes it a must for the larger gardens.

Origin From the Mediterranean region.
Use As a strong-growing climber for larger walls, fences, trellis, poles, pillars or for growing over large shrubs and medium-sized trees.
Description *Flower* Clusters of very fragrant tubular florets up to 1¾ in (4.5 cm) long. Creamy-yellow in colour with purple/red shading, produced from late summer to early autumn. *Foliage* Up to 3½ in (9 cm) long, blue/grey with downy undersides and light grey/green upper. End pairs of leaves join at the base. Some yellow autumn colouring.

Lonicera × *brownii* 'Fuchsoides' in flower

Lonicera etrusca 'Superba' in flower

Stem Grey/green when young, becoming yellow/brown, finally grey/brown. Twining. Medium to fast growing. *Fruit* May in very hot summers produce small red fruits in clusters.
Hardiness Tolerates a minimum winter temperature of 4°F (−15°C).
Soil requirements Requires a moist, deep soil high in organic material. Tolerates moderately alkaline to acid.
Sun/Shade aspect Tolerates all aspects. Best in light shade, although will tolerate full sun to medium shade as long as adequate shade and moisture are provided for the roots.
Pruning Remove one third of oldest growth to ground level in spring once plants are established more than three years.
Training Allow to ramble over wire, trellis or branches. Self-supporting and only requires tying in when young.
Propagation and nursery production From semi-ripe cuttings in early summer or hardwood cuttings in winter. Always purchase container grown; best planting height 1½–3½ ft (45 cm–1.1 m). Normally available from garden centres and specialist nurseries.
Problems May suffer from attacks of blackfly and mildew. Protect with a proprietary control. Often underestimated for its ultimate height and spread.
Similar forms of interest *L. e.* **'Pubescens'** Downy surface to leaves. Yellow flowers. *L. e.* **'Superba'** Creamy-yellow flowers turning orange. More tender than its parent. The variety most frequently offered in garden centres and nurseries.
Average height and spread
Five years
6 × 6 ft (1.8 × 1.8 m)
Ten years
12 × 12 ft (3.5 × 3.5 m)
Twenty years
18 × 18 ft (5.5 × 5.5 m)
Protrudes up to 2½ ft (76 cm) from support.

LONICERA FRAGRANTISSIMA

HONEYSUCKLE, WINTER HONEYSUCKLE, SHRUBBY HONEYSUCKLE

Caprifoliaceae   ***Wall Shrub***
Semi-evergreen
A delightful, scented winter shrub, adapting well to training against walls and fences.

Origin From China.
Use As a shrub for growing against a wall or fence to show off its highly scented winter flowers.
Description *Flower* Small, ¼ in (5 mm) long

and wide, sweetly scented, creamy white flowers, produced on almost leafless branches in mild spells, late autumn through to mid spring, standing up well to light to moderate frosts. *Foliage* Leaves ovate, 1–2½ in (2.5–6 cm) long, dark green tinged purple with lighter undersides. Some autumn colour.
Stem Upright when young, becoming branching and spreading with age. Light grey/green when young, becoming darker green with some purple veining. Medium growth rate when young, becoming slower with age. *Fruit* May produce bunches of red fruits in early to mid spring.
Hardiness Tolerates a minimum winter temperature of 0°F (−18°C).
Soil requirements Any soil, tolerating quite dry areas.
Sun/Shade aspect Tolerates all but the most exposed aspects, full sun to medium shade.
Pruning None required, but may be reduced in size or trained.
Training Allow to stand free or secure to wall or fence by individual anchor points or wires, or fan-train.
Propagation and nursery production From semi-ripe cuttings taken in early summer. Purchase container grown; quite easy to find. Best planting height 15 in–2½ ft (38–76 cm).
Problems Young plants give no indication of their true potential.
Similar forms of interest *L. × purpusii* Fragrant white flowers, early winter to early spring. Slightly more vigorous than *L. fragrantissima* and larger leaves but fewer flowers. *L. × p.* **'Spring Purple'** White

Lonicera fragrantissima in flower

fragrant flowers in winter. New foliage purple/green and stems purple when young. *L. standishii* Fragrant white flowers in winter, produced on stems covered in fine downy hair. Red fruits in early summer.
Average height and spread
Five years
6 × 6 ft (1.8 × 1.8 m)
Ten years
8 × 10 ft (2.4 × 3 m)
Twenty years
10 × 13 ft (3 × 4 m)

Protrudes up to 3 ft (91 cm) from support if fan-trained, 4 ft (1.2 m) untrained.

LONICERA × HECKROTII
(*L. × heckrotii* 'Gold Flame')

SHRUBBY HONEYSUCKLE, EVER-FLOWERING HONEYSUCKLE

Caprifoliaceae   ***Woody Climber***
Deciduous
A shrubby, pillar-forming honeysuckle without the characteristic twining branches, but with attractive flowers.

Origin Not known.
Use As a shrubby climber for pillars and against walls and fences.
Description *Flower* Clusters of slender, tubular flowers up to 2 in (5 cm) long, produced on long stalks. Orange/yellow in colour with purple/crimson shading on the outside. Flowering in early to mid summer. *Foliage* Oblong to oval, up to 2½ in (6 cm) long. Grey/blue underside. End pairs of leaves join at the base. *Stem* Grey/green to grey/brown, twining. Medium to fast growth rate. *Fruit* May produce small red clusters of fruits in very hot summers but not reliable.
Hardiness Tolerates a minimum winter temperature of 4°F (−15°C).
Soil requirements Does well on all soil conditions except very dry.
Sun/Shade aspect All but the most exposed of aspects. Light shade for preference but will tolerate full sun with root shading.

Lonicera × heckrotii in flower

Pruning Not normally required, but to assist rejuvenation of foliage and flowers remove one third of oldest growth on three-year-old plants and repeat every three to five years.
Training Will need tying to an upright support. Normally not twining.
Propagation and nursery production From semi-ripe cuttings taken in early summer. Should always be purchased container grown; best planting height 1½–3 ft (45–91 cm). Available from good garden centres and specialist nurseries.
Problems May suffer from attacks of blackfly and mildew. Protect with a proprietary control. Its non-climbing habit is not always understood.

Similar forms of interest Although it should truly be called *Lonicera × heckrotii*, it is often offered in nurseries and garden centres as *L. × h.* 'Gold Flame'.
Average height and spread
Five years
5 × 3 ft (1.5 × 91 cm)
Ten years
8 × 5 ft (2.4 × 1.5 m)
Twenty years
10 × 6 ft (3 × 1.8 m)
Protrudes up to 2½ ft (76 cm) from support.

LONICERA JAPONICA 'AUREORETICULATA'

GOLDEN VARIEGATED JAPANESE HONEYSUCKLE

Caprifoliaceae   *Woody Climber*
Semi-evergreen

Given the right conditions an attractive climber for all aspects except those extremely exposed.

Origin From Japan, Korea and China.
Use As an ornamental foliage climber for walls, fences, trellis, wires, pergolas, stumps of old trees and for rambling through medium to large shrubs.
Description *Flower* Somewhat inconspicuous, fragrant, bright yellow flowers, up to 1¼ in (3 cm) long in clusters. Purple in bud and ageing to yellow in early to mid summer, but often not noticeable due to the golden variegated foliage. *Foliage* Oval to round. Green to blue/green, splashed yellow to gold. Normally semi-evergreen, but in favourable

Lonicera japonica 'Aureoreticulata' in leaf

conditions can be evergreen. *Stem* Light grey/green ageing to grey/brown. Twining, partially self-supporting. Medium rate of growth. *Fruit* Clusters of small black fruits mainly produced following hot summers.
Hardiness Tolerates a minimum winter temperature of 14°F (−10°C). Severe wind chill in winter may cause damage to the foliage. Rejuvenation is normal the following spring.
Soil requirements Alkaline to acid. Must always be moist and rich in organic material.
Sun/Shade aspect Does well in all aspects except extremely exposed. Full sun to light shade.
Pruning When plants are established for more than three years, remove one third of oldest growth to ground level in early spring to encourage rejuvenation of new, good-coloured foliage and feed with a liquid fertilizer in mid summer. Every five to ten years it may be advantageous to cut plants back to within 2 ft (60 cm) of ground level to induce new regrowth.
Training Self-twining over wires and trellis but may need some initial tying in when young.

Propagation and nursery production From semi-ripe cuttings taken in early summer. May require a little bottom heat for good root development. Always purchase container grown; normally available from garden centres and nurseries. Best planting height 1½–3 ft (45–91 cm).
Problems Can be a little shy in its growth in early years. Growth without pruning can be old and woody.
Similar forms of interest None.
Average height and spread
Five years
5 × 5 ft (1.5 × 1.5 m)
Ten years
10 × 10 ft (3 × 3 m)
Twenty years
15 × 15 ft (4.6 × 4.6 m)
Protrudes up to 2 ft (60 cm) from support.

LONICERA JAPONICA 'HALLIANA'

EVERGREEN HONEYSUCKLE

Caprifoliaceae   *Woody Climber*
Evergreen

Whenever a quick-growing, flowering evergreen climber is required, this vigorous honeysuckle is ideal.

Origin From Japan.
Use As an evergreen climber for fences, trellises and pillars. Can be allowed to ramble over large shrubs and through small trees. Useful, with support, as an evergreen climbing screen.
Description *Flower* Borne in pairs at the leaf joints; five to seven tubular florets ½ in (1 cm) long. White, sometimes tinged purple, ageing to yellow, from early to mid summer. *Foliage* Oval to oblong, pointed. Up to 3½ in (9 cm) long and 1¾ in (4.5 cm) wide. Light spring green to light grey/green with a downy covering on both sides. *Stem* Light green ageing to dark green, finally green/brown. Twining. Fast growing. *Fruit* Clusters of small, black, round fruits produced after hot summers.
Hardiness Tolerates a minimum winter temperature of 4°F (−15°C). Foliage may be damaged in severe wind chill conditions, but is normally replaced in the following spring. Some stem damage may also be caused under these conditions.
Soil requirements Does well on both moderately alkaline and acid. Requires a moist, rich, organic type for best results.
Sun/Shade aspect Does well on all aspects. Light shade for preference, although will tolerate full sun to medium shade as long as roots are in a shady, moist position.
Pruning Allow to grow for four to five years and then shear off all forward growing shoots

to a height of 6 ft (1.8 m) or more after flowering. Rejuvenation is rapid. This process should be repeated every four to six years.
Training Allow to twine through wires, trellis, and branches of large shrubs and small trees. May need tying in when young.
Propagation and nursery production From semi-ripe cuttings taken in early to mid summer. Always purchase container grown; best planting height 2–4 ft (60 cm–1.2 m). Normally available from all garden centres and nurseries.
Problems Foliage can look a little damaged after winter, making the plant appear untidy, but is quickly rejuvenated in spring with fresh, soft, light green growth.
Similar forms of interest None.
Average height and spread
Five years
8 × 8 ft (2.4 × 2.4 m)
Ten years
16 × 16 ft (4.9 × 4.9 m)
Twenty years
30 × 30 ft (9 × 9 m)
Protrudes up to 3 ft (91 cm) from support.

LONICERA JAPONICA HENRYII

EVERGREEN HONEYSUCKLE

Caprifoliaceae   *Woody Climber*
Evergreen

Possibly the most attractive of the evergreen honeysuckles with good foliage and interesting flowers.

Origin From China.
Use As an evergreen climber for trellis, wires, fences, walls, pergolas and pillars, for growing over large shrubs and small trees and for a screen which is attractive all year round.
Description *Flower* Clusters up to 3 in (7.5 cm) wide of small, tubular, purple/red to yellow/red flowers, ¾ in (2 cm) long with reflexed lips at outer edges, normally in pairs at ends of flower shoots. Produced in early to mid summer. Scented. *Foliage* Ovate to lanceolate, light green ageing to mid green. Some yellow autumn colour. *Stem* Grey/green to green, finally grey/brown. Twining. Fast growing. *Fruit* In hot summers small clusters of blue/black fruits are produced.
Hardiness Tolerates a minimum winter temperature of 4°F (−15°C). In extremely cold wind chill conditions the evergreen foliage will be damaged, but is normally replaced in the following spring. Some stem damage also may be suffered in such conditions.
Soil requirements Does well on both moderately alkaline and acid soils where a moist, high organic content is found.
Sun/Shade aspect Does well on all aspects

Lonicera japonica 'Halliana' in flower

except extremely exposed. Light shade for preference, but will tolerate from full sun to medium shade as long as roots are adequately shaded.

Pruning None required until five years after established, then it can be heavily pruned, with the removal of all branches up to 4 ft (1.2 m) from ground level in early spring. It will quickly rejuvenate and cover the same space from which it was cut. Repeat every five years.

Training Twining in habit but may need some initial support when young by tying in. It can also develop a very heavy head of evergreen foliage which may need tying in to prevent damage in heavy snow.

Lonicera japonica henryii in flower

Propagation and nursery production From semi-ripe cuttings taken in early to mid summer. Should always be purchased container grown; normally available from garden centres and nurseries. Best planting height 1½–3 ft (45–91 cm).

Similar forms of interest *L. similis delavayi* (*L. delavayi*) Fragrant white flowers, ageing to pale yellow, produced in late summer, early autumn. From western China. Scarce and will have to be sought from specialist nurseries.

Average height and spread
Five years
10 × 10 ft (3 × 3 m)
Ten years
20 × 20 ft (6 × 6 m)
Twenty years
25 × 25 ft (7.6 × 7.6 m)
Protrudes up to 3 ft (91 cm) from support.

LONICERA JAPONICA REPENS (*L. flexuosa*)

JAPANESE HONEYSUCKLE

Caprifoliaceae   **Woody Climber**
Deciduous to semi-evergreen

One of the most attractive of the Japanese flowering honeysuckles, with good flowers and attractive purple-tinged foliage.

Origin From Japan.
Use For covering trellis, walls, fences, pillars and for growing through large shrubs. Can be trained into a small weeping standard if required.
Description *Flower* Borne in pairs at leaf joints, up to 2 in (5 cm) long. Five to six tubular florets, heavily scented; purple/red and pink/white. *Foliage* Oval, up to 2½ in (6 cm) long and 1⅜ in (3.5 cm) wide. Olive green to purple/olive green. Leaves have a distinct purple veining, contrasting well with the flowers. *Stem* Red/purple when young, ageing to purple/green, finally grey/green. Twining. Fast growing. *Fruit* May produce small clusters of black fruits following hot summers, but not reliable.
Hardiness Tolerates a minimum winter tem-

Lonicera japonica repens in flower

perature of 0°F (−18°C). Although its semi-evergreen habit may be turned fully deciduous by severe winters, spring rejuvenation normally follows.
Soil requirements Does well on moderately alkaline to acid soils. Requires a moist, rich, organic type.
Sun/Shade aspect Happy in all aspects. Light shade for preference but will tolerate full sun to medium shade as long as roots are adequately shaded.
Pruning Allow to grow free for up to five years and then prune heavily in early spring. This process should be repeated every five years.
Training Normally self-supporting by twining around wires and trellis but may need some tying in when young.
Propagation and nursery production From semi-ripe cuttings taken in early summer or hardwood cuttings taken in winter. Always purchase container grown; best planting height 2–4 ft (60 cm-1.2 m). Normally available from good garden centres and specialist nurseries.
Problems May suffer from attacks of blackfly and mildew. Protect with a proprietary control.
Similar forms of interest *L. j. r.* 'Halls Prolific' Heavily scented, creamy/white flowers produced even on young plants. *L. j. chinensis* Attractive rose/pink flowers. Not entirely hardy. Is scarce and will have to be sought from specialist nurseries. *L. reflexa* Flowers red and white in mid summer, foliage dark red/purple. Fragrant.
Average height and spread
Five years
8 × 8 ft (2.4 × 2.4 m)
Ten years
16 × 16 ft (4.9 × 4.9 m)
Twenty years
28 × 28 ft (8.5 × 8.5 m)
Protrudes up to 3 ft (91 cm) from support.

LONICERA NITIDA

BOXLEAF HONEYSUCKLE, POOR MAN'S BOX

Caprifoliaceae   **Wall Shrub**
Evergreen

A useful evergreen shrub that can be trimmed and shaped into pillars adjacent to walls and fences. Both the green and golden-leaved varieties are attractive in winter.

Origin From western China.
Use As a trimmed or untrimmed freestanding specimen adjacent to walls or fences.
Description *Flower* Inconspicuous, small, scented, sulphur-yellow flowers. *Foliage* Leaves small, ovate, ¼–½ in (5 mm–1 cm) long, mid green, shiny, with silver undersides, freely produced along branches and shoots. Slight purple tinge when young. *Stem* Upright

and branching when young, becoming very full and twiggy with age. Purple/green when young, becoming dark green with purple shading. Fast growth rate. *Fruit* Insignificant.
Hardiness Tolerates a minimum winter temperature of 4°F (−15°C).
Soil requirements Tolerates most soils but dislikes extreme dryness or waterlogging.
Sun/Shade aspect Tolerates all aspects except very dry. Full sun to deep shade.
Pruning Remove one third of old wood each spring to rejuvenate. May be cut to ground level and will regrow. Trim as required to almost any shape.
Training Normally requires no support other than possibly securing with individual anchor points when plants become mature.
Propagation and nursery production From semi-ripe cuttings taken in late summer or hardwood cuttings in mid winter. Purchase bare-rooted or container grown, best planting height 1–2 ft (30–60 cm).
Problems Becomes woody and uninteresting as it ages, although hard pruning corrects this. Mature plants may become lax and suffer damage from heavy snow.

Lonicera nitida 'Baggesen's Gold'

Similar forms of interest *L. n.* 'Baggesen's Gold' Yellow foliage, often turning more golden in winter when in full sun. In light shade turns yellow/green in autumn. Dislikes dry or waterlogged soils and shows ill effects immediately by losing foliage. Two thirds average height and spread. *L. n.* 'Yunnan' (syn. *L. yunnanensis*) A green-leaved variety with large foliage, more freely flowering and fruiting. Upright, typically offered by nurseries for hedging.
Average height and spread
Five years
6 × 6 ft (1.8 × 1.8 m)
Ten years
8 × 12 ft (2.4 × 3.7 m)
Twenty years
9 × 16 ft (2.7 × 4.9 m)
Protrudes up to 8 ft (2.4 m) from wall or fence.

Lonicera periclymen 'Belgica' in flower

LONICERA PERICLYMENUM (Hybrids)

HONEYSUCKLE

Caprifoliaceae **Woody Climber**
Deciduous

The hybrid varieties are a decided improvement on the wild parent, offering large, fragrant flowers.

Origin Of nursery origin.
Use As a twining climber for trellis, walls, fences and pergolas and to grow over medium to large shrubs or small trees. Can be grown as a small standard or used as loose, flowing ground cover.
Description *Flower* Tubular florets, each up to 2 in (5 cm) long, make up a cluster up to 2½–3 in (6–7.5 cm) across in May and June. See 'Forms of interest' for colour. Depending on location, very fragrant. *Foliage* Oval to oblong. Up to 2½ in (6 cm) long and 1¾ in (4.5 cm) wide. Blue/grey undersides, light to mid green upper with a purple hue. *Stem* Light grey/green, ageing to grey/brown. Twining, fast growing. *Fruit* Small clusters of red fruits may sometimes be formed following hot summers.
Hardiness Tolerates a minimum winter temperature of 4°F (−15°C).
Soil requirements Moderately alkaline to acid. Must have a deep, moist, organic soil for best results.
Sun/Shade aspect Tolerates all but the most exposed aspects. Best in light shade but will

Lonicera periclymen 'Serotina' in flower

tolerate full sun to medium shade as long as roots are shaded.
Pruning Remove one third of oldest growth to ground level in early spring on all shrubs established more than three years and repeat annually.
Training Allow to twine through wires and trellis. May need some support in early years by tying in.
Propagation and nursery production From semi-ripe cuttings taken in early summer. Always purchase container grown, normally readily available from all garden centres and nurseries. Best planting height 2–4 ft (60 cm–1.2 m).
Problems May suffer from attacks of blackfly and from mildew. Protect with a proprietary control.
Forms of interest *L. p.* 'Belgica' (Early Dutch honeysuckle) flowers tubular, up to 2 in (5 cm) long in May and June, deep purple/red, fading to yellow/red. Fragrant. *L. p.* 'Graham Thomas' Large, yellow, scented flowers from mid summer through to early autumn. *L. p.* 'Red Gables' Attractive, large, red/yellow flowers. Strong grower. *L. p.* 'Serotina' (Late Dutch honeysuckle). Red/purple flowers, creamy white inside, from July to October. *L. p.* 'Serotina Winchester' Flowers red/purple outside, pale cream inside. From USA.
Average height and spread
Five years
6 × 6 ft (1.8 × 1.8 m)
Ten years
12 × 12 ft (3.7 × 3.7 m)
Twenty years
20 × 20 ft (6 × 6 m)
Protrudes up to 2 ft (60 cm) from support.

LONICERA SPLENDIDA

SPANISH HONEYSUCKLE

Caprifoliaceae **Woody Climber**
Evergreen

An interesting honeysuckle but only useful in mild locations or under protection.

Origin From Spain.
Use As an evergreen climber for favoured positions against walls.
Description *Flower* Semi-open, yellow, tubular flowers, 1½–2 in (4–5 cm) long, with two red lips at the ends up to 1 in (2.5 cm) across, produced from mid summer to early autumn. *Foliage* Oval to oblong, grey/blue to green/blue. Somewhat sparsely produced. *Stem* Blue/grey, ageing to grey/green. Loosely twining, not normally self-supporting. Downy texture. Slow to medium rate of growth. *Fruit* Small grey/blue fruits may be produced, but not reliable.

Hardiness Tolerates a minimum winter temperature of 23°F (−5°C).
Soil requirements Moderately alkaline to acid. Must have a moist, deep, rich soil.
Sun/Shade aspect Will require protection in all aspects, except those which are very warm. Light shade or full sun, provided roots are shaded.
Pruning Does not normally require pruning.
Training Not completely self-clinging and will require tying to wires or trellis.
Propagation and nursery production From semi-ripe cuttings taken in early summer. Very difficult to propagate. Always purchase container grown; will have to be sought from specialist nurseries. Best planting height 1–3 ft (30–91 cm).

Lonicera splendida in flower

Problems Not completely hardy and requires specific degrees of shade and good soil to get good results, but worth an attempt for collectors. Scarce in production.
Similar forms of interest None.
Average height and spread
Five years
5 × 5 ft (1.5 × 1.5 m)
Ten years
10 × 10 ft (3 × 3 m)
Twenty years
15 × 15 ft (4.6 × 4.6 m)
Protrudes up to 2 ft (60 cm) from support.

LONICERA TATARICA

TATARIAN HONEYSUCKLE

Caprifoliaceae **Wall Shrub**
Deciduous

An interesting mid spring, early summer flowering shrub, provided mildew attacks are controlled. Not often thought of as a wall shrub.

Origin From the USSR.
Use As a freestanding or fan-trained shrub for large walls and fences.
Description *Flower* Small, ½ in (1 cm) long, tubular, pink flowers profusely borne in mid spring to early summer. White and red flowering varieties also available. *Foliage* Elliptic, grey/green, somewhat sparsely produced. *Stem* Upright, becoming branching with age, grey/green. Medium growth rate when young, becoming slower with age. *Fruit* Small, red fruits, late summer, early autumn.
Hardiness Tolerates a minimum winter temperature of 0°F (−18°C).
Soil requirements Any soil type except very dry.
Sun/Shade aspect Tolerates all aspects. Prefers light shade, but will tolerate full sun to medium shade.
Pruning Remove one third of old wood after flowering period to induce new growth.
Training Will require wires or individual anchor points for fan-training.
Propagation and nursery production From semi-ripe cuttings taken in early summer. Purchase container grown; quite easy to find in nurseries and some garden centres, especi-

Lonicera tatarica in flower

ally when in flower. Best planting height 15 in–2½ ft (38–76 cm).
Problems Suffers badly from attacks of mildew which can lead to complete defoliation. Use a proprietary control.
Similar forms of interest *L. t.* 'Alba' White flowers and red fruits. *L. t.* 'Hack's Red' Deep rose pink flowers and red fruits.
Average height and spread
Five years
10 × 10 ft (3 × 3 m)
Ten years
10 × 13 ft (3 × 4 m)
Twenty years
10 × 20 ft (3 × 6 m)
Protrudes up to 2 ft (60 cm) from support if fan-trained, 6 ft (1.8 m) untrained.

LONICERA × TELLMANNIANA

KNOWN BY BOTANICAL NAME
Caprifoliaceae   *Woody Climber*
Deciduous
Its unusual colouring makes it possibly one of the most interesting of flowering honeysuckles.

Origin From Hungary.
Use As a summer-flowering climber for walls, fences and pillars.
Description *Flower* 2 in (5 cm) long, coppery yellow in colour, when in bud flushed red. Produced in good-sized clusters from early to mid summer. *Foliage* Oval, produced in pairs opposite each other at source, forming an interesting double shield effect. Grey/green in colour. *Stem* Light grey/green to grey/brown in colour. Not self-supporting but does cling by twisting growth. Medium to fast growing. *Fruit* Small red fruits may be produced in hot summers.
Hardiness Tolerates a minimum winter temperature of 14°F (−10°C).
Soil requirements Alkaline to acid. Requires a well drained but good, moisture retentive soil. The inclusion of large quantities of organic material will help growth and keep roots in the cool.
Sun/Shade aspect Best on a south-west wall. Flowers in full sun to light shade, roots in deep shade.

Pruning Not normally required, but can be reduced in size if necessary with no ill effects. The occasional removal of lower growth will encourage new shoots.
Training Allow to twine through wires and trellis. Normally needs no assistance other than when young or heavy at maturity.
Propagation and nursery production From semi-ripe cuttings taken in mid summer. Should always be purchased container grown; best planting height 1½–2½ ft (45–76 cm). Available from most garden centres and nurseries.
Problems Can be attacked by mildew in warm, humid summers. Control with a proprietary control.
Similar forms of interest None.
Average height and spread
Five years
5 × 5 ft (1.5 × 1.5 m)
Ten years
12 × 12 ft (3.7 × 3.7 m)
Twenty years
15 × 15 ft (4.6 × 4.6 m)
Protrudes up to 3 ft (91 cm) from support.

Lonicera × tellmanniana in flower

LONICERA TRAGOPHYLLA

CHINESE WOODBINE
Caprifoliaceae   *Woody Climber*
Deciduous
A most spectacular, tall, climbing plant when given the correct environment.

Origin From western China.
Use As a tall, vigorous climber to grow through large shrubs and trees.
Description *Flower* Terminal whorls of 10–20 bright yellow, tubular flowers up to 3½ in (9 cm) long in June and July. Slender in shape with a 1–1½ in (2.5–4 cm) lobed mouth. Not fragrant. *Foliage* Ovate to lanceolate, up to 5 in (12 cm) long and 1⅜ in (3.5 cm) wide. Light grey/green. Some yellow autumn colour. *Stem* Light green to yellow/brown, smooth textured. Loosely twining, fast growing, up to 9 ft (2.7 m) per year. *Fruit* Small clusters of bright red fruits up to ⅛ in (5 mm) across may be produced following hot summers.
Hardiness Tolerates a minimum winter temperature of 14°F (−10°C).
Soil requirements Alkaline to acid; a rich, moist soil for best results.
Sun/Shade aspect Requires protection from exposed aspects and light shade.
Pruning Normally impractical to prune due to

Lonicera tragophylla in flower

its height and rambling nature.
Training Allow to ramble and twine through large shrubs and trees.
Propagation and nursery production From semi-ripe cuttings. May be difficult to propagate without specialist equipment. Always purchase container grown; will have to be sought from specialist nurseries. Best planting height 1½–4 ft (45 cm–1.2 m).
Problems Its requirement for a shady woodland situation must not be overlooked, or its performance will be disappointing.
Similar forms of interest *L. hildebrandiana* (Giant honeysuckle) Tender, requiring very favourable conditions. Up to 80 ft (25 m) with fragrant, creamy-white flowers, which deepen to orange with age. Flowering from mid summer to early autumn. From Burma.
Average height and spread
Five years
15 × 10 ft (4.6 × 3 m)
Ten years
30 × 20 ft (9 × 6 m)
Twenty years
40 × 30 ft + (12 × 9 m +)
Protrudes up to 2 ft (60 cm) from support.

LYCIUM BARBARUM

DUKE OF ARGYLL'S TEA TREE

Solanaceae   *Wall Shrub*
Deciduous

A very useful shrub for coastal areas,
standing up to salt-laden winds and
adapting well to fan-training.

Origin From China, but naturalized throughout Europe and western Asia.
Use As a fan-trained shrub for walls and
fences.
Description *Flower* Small, ½ in (1 cm) long,
purple, trumpet-shaped flowers in clusters
1¼–3 in (4.5–7.5 cm) in diameter, produced
from each leaf axil from early to mid summer.
Foliage Leaves narrow, 1–4 in (2.5–10 cm)
long, sea green, giving some yellow autumn
colour. *Stem* Upright when young, quickly
forming a spreading, arching wall shrub.
Grey to grey/green with sparsely distributed
small spines. Medium to fast growth rate.
Fruit Small, egg-shaped, orange/red fruits in
autumn.
Hardiness Tolerates a minimum winter
temperature of 4°F (−15°C).
Soil requirements Light, open, sandy soil.
Dislikes waterlogging.
Sun/Shade aspect Tolerates all but the most
severe of aspects, including salt-laden winds.
Full sun, dislikes shade.
Pruning Reduce one third of oldest shoots on
mature shrubs to ground level in early spring
to encourage growth of new shoots for
following year.

Lycium chilense **in flower**

Training Requires wires or individual anchor
points to secure and encourage a fan-trained
shape.
Propagation and nursery production From
seed or semi-ripe cuttings taken in early
summer. Purchase container grown; availability varies but may be found in coastal
areas. Best planting height 15 in–2 ft (38–
60 cm).
Problems Can become a little invasive if
happily situated, but if not, may be difficult to
establish.
Similar forms of interest *L. chilense* Spreading branches covered with yellow, white and
purple funnel-shaped flowers, mid to late
summer, followed by red, egg-shaped fruits.
A spineless variety more open and of slightly
less than average height and spread. Less
hardy than *L. barbarum*. From Chile.
Average height and spread
Five years
8 × 8 ft (2.4 × 2.4 m)
Ten years
12 × 12 ft (3.7 × 3.7 m)
Twenty years
16 × 16 ft (4.9 × 4.9 m)
Protrudes up to 4 ft (1.2 m) from support.

Magnolia grandiflora **in flower**

MAGNOLIA GRANDIFLORA

EVERGREEN MAGNOLIA, LAUREL MAGNOLIA,
SOUTHERN MAGNOLIA, BULL BAY

Magnoliaeceae   *Wall Shrub*
Evergreen

When grown in the correct position, given
space and time to mature, this is a truly
spectacular evergreen flowering shrub.

Origin From south-eastern USA.
Use As a freestanding shrub or even small
tree, grown adjacent to large walls or fences,
where it benefits from the protection in colder
areas.
Description *Flower* Up to 10 in (25 cm) across,
creamy white, very fragrant flowers, produced in late spring, summer and early autumn. Late flowers susceptible to early
autumn frost damage. *Foliage* Leaves elliptic,
8–10 in (20–25 cm) long, attractive bright
green when young, maturing to duller green,
with brown, felted undersides. *Stem* Strong,
upright, becoming branching with age,
forming a tall shrub. Mid to dark green.
Medium rate of growth. *Fruit* Green fruit
pods 4 in (10 cm) long, following flowering.
Hardiness Tolerates a minimum winter temperature of 14°F (−10°C).
Soil requirements Does well on most soils
including alkaline as long as there is 6 ft
(1.8 m) of good topsoil above underlying
alkaline soil.
Sun/Shade aspect Requires a sheltered aspect
in full sun to mid shade.
Pruning None required but can be trimmed to
control size.

Magnolia grandiflora **'Exmouth' in flower**

Training Individual anchor points will be required to secure main stems as they develop.
Propagation and nursery production From
semi-ripe cuttings taken in early summer.
Purchase container grown; one or other of
the varieties likely to be found in most general
nurseries and some good garden centres. Best
planting height 2–4 ft (60 cm–1.2 m).
Problems May take five to six years to come
into flower.
Similar forms of interest *M. g.* 'Exmouth'
Richly scented, large, creamy white flowers,
produced at a relatively early age in its life
span. Dark green, polished, narrow foliage
with red or brown felted undersides. A useful
variety for colder areas. *M. g.* 'Ferruginea'
Scented, large, white flowers. Leaves elliptic
to ovate, dark shiny green, brown and heavily
felted undersides. Upright and of average
height but slightly less spread. More tender
than other varieties and should be planted
only in very mild areas. *M. g.* 'Goliath'
Scented, white, globe-shaped flowers, produced three to five years after planting. Foliage elliptic, slightly concave with rounded
ends; dark glossy green to light green,
grey/green undersides. Slightly less than average spread. Not suited to temperatures below
23°F (−5°C). *M. g.* 'Maryland' Large, fragrant white flowers of more open shape, produced two years after planting. Foliage elliptic to ovate, mid green, shiny upper surfaces
and grey/brown undersides. Slightly less than
average height and spread. *M. g.* 'Russet'
Russet brown buds to leaves. Creamy white
flowers. Less hardy. *M. g.* 'Samuel Sommer'
Good flowering variety but difficult to obtain.
Less hardy.
Average height and spread
Five years
6 × 6 ft (1.8 × 1.8 m)
Ten years
12 × 12 ft (3.7 × 3.7 m)
Twenty years
26 × 26 ft (8 × 8 m)
Protrudes up to 12 ft (3.7 m)
from wall or fence.

MAGNOLIA (Large-growing, Star-flowered Forms)

STAR MAGNOLIA

Magnoliaceae   *Wall Shrub*
Deciduous

Large, early spring flowering shrubs for a
very attractive flower display. Even more
spectacular when fan-trained.

Origin From Japan
Use As a freestanding shrub grown adjacent
to large walls and fences or for fan-training.
Description *Flower* Multi-petalled, star-
shaped, white or pink depending on variety,

fragrant flowers produced in small numbers for 15–20 years after planting, after which flowering increases to give a glorious display in mid to late spring. *Foliage* Leaves elliptic, 2½–4in (6–10cm) long, light to mid green. Some yellow autumn colour. *Stem* Strong, upright, becoming branching with age, eventually forming a very dense, twiggy framework. Dark green to green/brown. Medium growth rate. *Fruit* Small green fruit capsules in late summer.

Hardiness Tolerates a minimum winter temperature of 0°F (−18°C).

Soil requirements Most soil types, tolerates alkaline conditions provided 18in (45 cm) of topsoil is provided.

Sun/Shade aspect Tolerates all but the most severe of aspects. Requires protection from early morning sun. Prefers full sun, tolerates light shade.

Pruning None required.

Training Requires individual anchor points or wires to achieve a fan-trained effect or allow to grow freestanding.

Propagation and nursery production From layers or semi-ripe cuttings taken in early summer. Purchase container grown or root-balled (balled-and-burlapped); best planting height 1½–3 ft (60–91 cm). Generally available from garden centres and nurseries.

Problems Some varieties, such as *M. kobus*, are very slow to come into flower and can take as long as 15 years to produce a full display of blooms.

Forms of interest *M. kobus* (Northern Japanese magnolia, Kobus magnolia) Fragrant white flowers produced only after 10–15 years from date of planting. *M.* × *loebneri* A cross between *M. kobus* and *M. stellata*, which from an early age produces a profusion of multi-petalled, fragrant white flowers in early to mid spring. Does well on all soil types, including alkaline. Reaches two thirds average height and spread. Of garden origin. *M.* × *l.* 'Leonard Messel' Fragrant, multi-petalled flowers are deep pink in bud, opening to lilac/pink. Said to be a cross between *M. kobus* and *M. stellata* 'Rosea'. Of garden origin. *M.* × *l.* 'Merrill' Large, fragrant, star-shaped flowers produced from an early age on a shrub two thirds average height and spread. From USA. *M. salicifolia* Fragrant, white, star-shaped flowers with six narrow petals in mid spring. Slightly more than average height but slightly less spread. Leaves, bark and wood are lemon-scented if bruised. From Japan.

Average height and spread
Five years
8 × 8 ft (2.4 × 2.4 m)
Ten years
15 × 15 ft (4.6 × 4.6 m)
Twenty years
26 × 26 ft (8 × 8 m)
Protrudes 3 ft (91 cm) from support if fan-trained, 15 ft (4.6 m) or more untrained.

Magnolia × *soulangiana* in flower

MAGNOLIA × SOULANGIANA

SAUCER MAGNOLIA, TULIP MAGNOLIA
Magnoliaceae   *Wall Shrub*
Deciduous
Very popular flowering shrubs which must be given adequate space to develop. None of the beautiful varieties surpasses the splendour of *M.* × *soulangiana* itself.

Origin From France.

Use As a fan-trained or freestanding shrub grown adjacent to large walls or fences.

Description *Flower* Light pink with purple shading in centre and at base of each petal. Flowers produced before leaves in early spring; buds large with hairy outer coat. Some secondary flowering in early summer. *Foliage* Leaves elliptic to ovate, 3–6 in (7.5–15 cm) long, light green to grey/green. Some yellow autumn colour. *Stem* Upright, strong when young and light grey/green. In maturity branches become very short, twiggy and almost rubbery in texture. Medium rate of growth. *Fruit* May produce long, orange/red, pod-shaped fruits in hot summers.

Hardiness Tolerates a minimum winter temperature of 4°F (−15°C).

Soil requirements Does well on heavy clay soils and most other types, except extremely alkaline areas which will lead to chlorosis.

Sun/Shade aspect Requires a moderately sheltered aspect and must be planted away from early morning spring sun, otherwise

flowers frozen by late spring frosts thaw too quickly and cell damage causes browning.

Pruning None required, but remove any small crossing branches in winter to prevent rubbing.

Training Will require individual anchor points or wires for tying in when grown fan-trained.

Propagation and nursery production From layers or semi-ripe cuttings taken in early summer. Purchase container grown or root-balled (balled-and-burlapped). *M.* × *soulangiana* easy to find but some varieties must be sought from specialist nurseries. Best planting height 2–4 ft (60 cm–1.2 m)

Problems Can take up to five years or more to flower well.

Magnolia × *soulangiana* 'Alba Superba' in flower

Similar forms of interest *M. s.* × 'Alba Superba' (syn. *M.* × *s.* 'Alba') Large, scented, pure white, erect, tulip-shaped flowers, flushed purple at base. Growth upright and strong, but forms slightly less spread than the parent. *M.* × *s.* 'Alexandrina' Large, upright, white flowers with purple-flushed bases. A good, vigorous, upright, free-flowering variety, sometimes difficult to obtain. *M.* × *s.* 'Amabilis' Ivory white, tulip-shaped flowers, flushed light purple inside at base of petals. Upright habit. May have to be obtained from specialist nurseries. *M.* × *s.* 'Brozzonii' Longer than average white flowers with purple shading at the base. May have to be sought from specialist nurseries. *M.* × *s.* 'Lennei' Flowers goblet-shaped with fleshy petals rose purple outside, creamy white stained purple on inside, in mid to late spring. Sometimes limited repeat flowering in autumn. Broad, ovate leaves, up to 10–12 in (25–30 cm) long. *M.* × *s.* 'Lennei Alba' Ivory white, extremely beautiful goblet-shaped flowers, presenting themselves upright along branches. May need to be obtained from specialist nurseries. Slightly more than average spread. *M.* × *s.* 'Picture' Purple outer colouring to petals, white inside. Flowers

Magnolia × *loebneri* 'Merrill' in flower

Magnolia × soulangiana 'Lennei' in flower

Magnolia stellata in flower

borne erect, often appearing early in the shrub's lifespan. Leaves up to 10 in (25 cm) long. Somewhat upright branches, reaching less than average spread. Best sought from specialist nurseries. *M. × s.* **'Speciosa'** White flowers with very little purple shading, leaves smaller than average. Slightly less than average height and spread. Best sought from specialist nurseries. *M. liliiflora* **'Nigra'** Buds resemble slender tulips, gradually opening to a reflexed star shape. Flowers deep purple outside, creamy white stained purple inside, late spring through to early summer. From Japan.

Average height and spread
Five years
8 × 8 ft (2.4 × 2.4 m)
Ten years
16 × 16 ft (4.9 × 4.9 m)
Twenty years
26 × 26 ft (8 × 8 m)
Protrudes up to 3 ft (91 cm) from support if fan-trained, 20 ft (6 m) untrained.

MAGNOLIA STELLATA

STAR MAGNOLIA, STAR-FLOWERED MAGNOLIA

Magnoliaceae   **Wall Shrub**
Deciduous

A well-loved, exceptionally beautiful early spring-flowering garden shrub which, when grown on a wall or fence, gains an added dimension.

Origin From Japan.
Use As a freestanding or fan-trained wall or fence shrub where it gains extra protection.
Description *Flower* Slightly scented, white, multi-petalled, star-shaped flowers 2–2½ in (5–6 cm) wide, borne in early spring before leaves. Usually flowers within two years of planting. *Foliage* Leaves medium-sized, elliptic, 2–4 in (5–10 cm) long, light green, giving some yellow autumn colouring. *Stem* Upright when young, quickly branching and spreading. Can be trained into a fan shape or close-branched network adjacent to walls and fences. Grey/green. Slow growth rate.
Fruit Insignificant.
Hardiness Tolerates a minimum winter temperature of 4°F (−15C°).
Soil requirements Any soil type except extremely alkaline.
Sun/Shade aspect Plant in a position where the shrub will not get early morning sun in early spring, so allowing frozen flowers to thaw out slowly and incur less tissue damage and browning. Prefers full sun to light shade.
Pruning None required.
Propagation and nursery production From layers or cuttings taken in early summer. Purchase container grown or root-balled (balled-and-burlapped); normally available from

garden centres and nurseries, especially in spring when in flower. Best planting height 15 in–2½ ft (38–76 cm).
Training Will require individual anchor points or wires for tying in when grown fan-trained.
Problems Young plants when purchased may look small and misshapen due to their slow growth rate, and are expensive, but the investment is well worthwhile.
Similar forms of interest *M. s.* **'King Rose'** A variety with good pink flowers. *M. s.* **'Rosea'** Star-shaped flowers deep pink in bud, opening to flushed pink. *M. s.* **'Royal Star'** Slightly larger white flowers with numerous petals making a very full star shape. *M. s.* **'Rubra'** Flowers multi-petalled and purple/pink, deeper colouring while in bud. Rather scarce in production. *M. s.* **'Water Lily'** Larger flowers with more petals. Extremely attractive but usually a little weaker in constitution than the parent.

Average height and spread
Five years
4 × 4 ft (1.2 × 1.2 m)
Ten years
7 × 7 ft (2.1 × 2.1 m)
Twenty years
15 × 15 ft (4.6 × 4.6 m)
Protrudes up to 3 ft (91 cm) from support if fan-trained, 10 ft (3 m) untrained.

MAGNOLIA
(Summer-flowering Forms)

KNOWN BY BOTANICAL NAME

Magnoliaceae   **Wall Shrub**
Deciduous

Summer-flowering magnolias are among the most magnificent of summer shrubs and adapt well to fan-training on walls and fences.

Origin From western China.
Use As a fan-trained or freestanding shrub adjacent to large walls and fences.
Description *Flower* Hanging, egg-shaped buds, opening into outward-facing, 3–4 in (7.5–10 cm) wide, white, fragrant, cup-shaped flowers. Flowers mainly in late spring and early summer, then intermittently until late summer. *Foliage* Leaves elliptic, 4–5 in (10–12 cm) long, light grey/green giving some autumn colours. Liable to be blackened by hard early autumn frosts, making them unsightly. *Stem* Strong, forming a goblet-shaped shrub. Grey/green. Medium growth rate. *Fruit* Crimson-red fruit clusters in late summer, early autumn.
Hardiness Tolerates a minimum winter temperature of 4°F (−15°C).

Soil requirements Does well on most soils, only disliking extreme alkalinity.
Sun/Shade aspect Requires some protection in exposed aspects. Best in full sun through to medium shade.
Pruning None required other than that needed for training. May be reduced in size with care; best done in late autumn or early winter.
Training Will require individual anchor points or wires for tying when grown fan-trained.

Magnolia × watsonii

Propagation and nursery production From layers. Purchase container grown or root-balled (balled-and-burlapped); fairly easy to find in nurseries, less often stocked by garden centres. Best planting height 1½–4 ft (45 cm –1.2 m).
Problems Often planted in areas where it is unable to reach its full size and potential.
Forms of interest *M. denudata* (syn. *M. conspicua*) Fragrant, cup-shaped, pure white flowers, with broad, thick, fleshy petals, produced mid spring to early summer. Foliage ovate with rounded ends, 3–6 in (7.5–15 cm) long, mid to grey/green. Upright habit, becoming rounded with time. Benefits well from a wall or fence. *M. × highdownensis* Fragrant, white, hanging flowers with purple central cone 4 in (10 cm) across. Good on very chalky soils. Of slightly less than average height and spread. Rather hard to find except in specialist nurseries. Possibly a clone of *M. wilsonii*. *M. hypoleuca* (syn. *M. obovata*) Fragrant, white to creamy white flowers up to 6 in (15 cm) across with central crimson stamens, early summer, followed by interesting fruit clusters in late summer, early autumn. Obovate leaves up to 6 in (15 cm) long, grey/green. Dislikes alkaline soils, best on neutral to acid types. Benefits from the protection of a wall or large fence. From

Japan. *M. sieboldii* (syn. *M. parviflora*) Fragrant, white, cup-shaped flowers 3–3½ in (7.5–9 cm) across, with rose pink to crimson central stamens. Stems upright when young, spreading with age. Foliage grey/green with some yellow autumn colour. Two thirds average height and spread. *M. sinensis* Lemon-scented, white, hanging flowers with red central cones, 4–6 in (10–15 cm) across, early summer. Foliage grey/green, 5 in (12 cm) long, obovate. Slightly less than average height and slightly more than average spread. From western China. *M. virginiana* (Swamp bay, sweetbay magnolia) Fragrant creamy white flowers 2 in (5 cm) across, globular and slightly hanging, early to late summer. Ovate to elliptic, semi-evergreen leaves with glossy upper surfaces and blue/white undersides. Tolerates some alkalinity as long as 18 in (45 cm) of good topsoil is available. Rather hard to find. From eastern USA. *M. × watsonii* Strongly scented, creamy white, saucer-shaped flowers facing upwards, with rosy crimson anthers and pink sepals, 5½–6 in (13–15 cm) across, early to mid summer. Grey/green, oval, leathery leaves. Will tolerate some alkalinity provided 18 in (45 cm) of good topsoil is available. Extremely difficult to find. Benefits well from wall or fence protection. *M. wilsonii* Slightly scented, hanging, white, saucer-shaped flowers with crimson stamens, in late spring to early summer. Foliage elliptic to lanceolate, 4–5 in (10–12 cm) long, grey/green. A wide, spreading shrub. Will tolerate a limited amount of alkalinity, provided 18 in (45 cm) of topsoil is available. Scarce in production. From western China.

Average height and spread
Five years
7 × 7 ft (2.1 × 2.1 m)
Ten years
15 × 15 ft (4.6 × 4.6 m)
Twenty years
26 × 26 ft (8 × 8 m)
Protrudes up to 3 ft (91 cm) from support if fan-trained, 13 ft (4 m) untrained.

MAHONIA × 'CHARITY'

KNOWN BY BOTANICAL NAME

Berberidaceae   **Wall Shrub**
Evergreen
Among the aristocrats of tall-growing, winter-flowering shrubs, particularly adaptable for growing against walls or fences where a tall evergreen is required.

Origin Of garden origin.
Use As a freestanding or fan-trained tall-growing shrub for large walls and fences.

Mahonia × 'Charity' in flower

Description *Flower* Circular groups of bright yellow racemes, up to 8–10 in (20–25 cm) long, in late autumn through to mid winter. Flowers borne at terminals of upright shoots, upright at first, becoming more arching with age. *Foliage* Eight to 16 spined leaflets, each 1½–2 in (4–5 cm) long, make up a pinnate leaf in excess of 12 in (30 cm) in length and 4 in (10 cm) in width. Light grey/green in colour. *Stem* Rigid, upright, light grey/green becoming grey/brown. Medium growth rate. *Fruit* Racemes of blue/black fruits with white downy covering follow flowers in mid to late winter.
Hardiness Tolerates a minimum winter temperature of 4°F (−15°C). Young foliage may suffer leaf scorch in severe winters, but normally rejuvenates the following spring. Some damage may be caused to new foliage by late spring frosts.
Soil requirements Prefers open, leafy, moist, peaty soil. Tolerates wide range of types but may show distress on very dry, alkaline soils.
Sun/Shade aspect Tolerates all aspects. Full sun to very light shade. In deeper shade will become more open and lax in habit.
Pruning It is very important that young plants have terminal clusters of foliage removed after flowering to encourage branching, otherwise growth becomes very tall and upright, often placing the flowers at a height where they cannot be appreciated to the full.
Training Normally requires no support and is freestanding but may also be fan-trained.
Propagation and nursery production From semi-ripe cuttings taken in early summer. Very slow to root. Purchase container grown or root-balled (balled-and-burlapped). Easy to find from good garden centres and nurseries. Best planting height 12–15 in (30–38 cm).
Problems None if pruning advice is followed.
Similar forms of interest *M.* 'Buckland' Good, thick racemes of yellow flowers in late autumn to early winter, followed by blue/black fruits. Flowers are initially upright in habit but become lax with age. Foliage pinnate, mid green and 10 in (25 cm) long, but with smaller leaflets than *M.* × 'Charity'. Upright form, slightly more than average spread. Obtainable from specialist nurseries. *M.* 'Lionel Fortescue' Upright racemes of yellow scented flowers in clusters of up to 15. Good large foliage, up to 12 in (30 cm) long and pinnate. One third more than average spread. Obtainable from specialist nurseries. *M. lomariifolia* Flowers deep yellow, produced from terminal clusters of up to 20 flower spikes, racemes retaining an upright habit, 6–10 in (15–25 cm) high. Leaves pinnate, dark to olive-green, up to 2 ft (30 cm) long, with moderately small leaflets. Minimum winter temperature 23°F (−5°C). Benefits from the protection of a wall or

fence. Reaches one third more than average height. *M.* 'Winter Sun' Upright racemes of scented yellow flowers in winter. Dark green, pinnate leaves. Slightly less than average height and spread. Usually found in specialist nurseries.
Average height and spread
Five years
7 × 4 ft (2.1 × 1.2 m)
Ten years
12 × 6 ft (3.7 × 1.8 m)
Twenty years
16 × 10 ft (4.9 × 3 m)
Protrudes up to 3 ft (91 cm) from support if fan-trained, 10 ft (3 m) untrained.

MAHONIA FREMONTII

KNOWN BY BOTANICAL NAME

Berberidaceae   **Tender Wall Shrub**
Evergreen
Given the right conditions, this attractively-foliaged mahonia offers a great deal of all-year-round interest.

Origin From south-west USA.
Use As a wall shrub for sheltered walls and fences.
Description *Flower* Racemes up to 2 in (5 cm) long of yellow flowers in mid to late spring. *Foliage* Up to 4 in (10 cm) long, consisting of two to three pairs of leaflets, curled when juvenile, often with coarsely toothed edges. Grey/green with white undersides. *Stem*

Mahonia fremontii

Grey/green becoming grey/brown. Predominantly upright. Slow growth rate. *Fruit* Blue/black, oval-shaped berries follow flowers.
Hardiness Tolerates a minimum winter temperature of 14°F (−10°C) as long as there is adequate shelter from wind.
Soil requirements Tolerates all soil conditions except extremely dry.
Sun/Shade aspect Must have a sheltered aspect with protection from cold winds. Performs best in light shade but will tolerate full sun.
Pruning Not normally required but individual branches can be removed if necessary.
Training Tie to individual anchorage points or wires.
Propagation and nursery production From semi-ripe cuttings taken in early to mid summer. Should always be purchased container grown; will have to be sought from specialist nurseries. Best planting height 6 in–2 ft (15–60 cm).
Problems Slow to establish and scarce in production.
Similar forms of interest None.
Average height and spread
Five years
3 × 3 ft (91 × 91 cm)
Ten years
6 × 4 ft (1.8 × 1.2 m)
Twenty years
8 × 6 ft (2.4 × 1.8 m)
Protrudes up to 18 in (45 cm) from support if fan-trained, 4 ft (1.2 m) untrained.

MALUS
(Fruiting Forms)

FRUITING CRAB, CRAB APPLE

Rosaceae   *Hardy Tree*
Deciduous

A group of trees not often enough used for
fan-training even though they adapt well
for the purpose.

Origin Some varieties of natural origin,
others of garden or nursery extraction.
Use As large, fan-trained, fruiting trees for
walls and fences.
Description *Flower* White, pink or wine-red,
depending on variety. Flowers 1–1½ in (2.5–
4 cm) across, produced singly or in multiple
heads of five to seven flowers in mid spring.
Foliage Ovate, tooth-edged, 2 in (5 cm) long.
Green or wine-red, depending on variety.
Some yellow autumn colour. *Stem* Light
green to grey/green when young, becoming
green/brown. Moderately upright, becoming
spreading and branching. Moderate rate of
growth. *Fruit* Colours from yellow,
orange/red, through to purple/red. Shaped
like miniature apples, 1–2 in (2.5–5 cm) wide.
Produced in late summer and early autumn,
all edible and used for making jelly.
Hardiness Tolerates a minimum winter temperature of 4°F (−15°C).
Soil requirements Tolerates most soil conditions; dislikes extreme waterlogging.
Sun/Shade aspect Tolerates all but the most
severe of aspects. Full sun to light shade.
Pruning Prune young trees hard in spring
following planting. Select and train resulting
five to seven shoots and tie into a fan-trained
shape. In subsequent years, remove all side
growths back to two points from their origin
and maintain original main branches in fan
shape.
Training Requires tying to wires or individual
anchorage points.
Propagation and nursery production Mainly
grafted or budded on to wild apple understock. Purchase bare-rooted or container
grown; most varieties readily available from
general or specialist nurseries, also sometimes
from garden centres. Choose one- to two-
year-old trees 3–6 ft (91 cm–1.8 m) in height,
ensuring that they are grafted at the base.
Problems Liable to fungus diseases such as
apple scab and apple mildew, damaging both
foliage and fruit. Some stem canker may
occur; remove by pruning and treat cuts with
pruning compound.

Forms of interest *M.* **'Dartmouth'** White
flowers followed by sizeable red/purple
fruits. Green foliage. *M.* **'Dolgo'** A white-
flowering form with yellow fruits held well
into autumn. Foliage mid green, often with
light purplish hue. Used as a universal pollinator for garden or orchard trees. *M.*
'Golden Hornet' White flowers, followed by a
good crop of bright yellow fruits which may
remain on the tree well into winter. Green
foliage. Can be used as a universal pollinator
for garden or orchard trees. *M.* **'John
Downie'** Pear-shaped fruits, 1 in (2.5 cm)
long, bright orange shaded scarlet. One of the
best for making jelly. Green foliage. More
susceptible to apple scab and mildew than
most varieties. *M.* **'Professor Sprenger'**
Flowers pink in bud, opening to white. Good
crop of amber fruits retained until mid
winter. Green foliage. Half average height
and spread. *M.* **'Red Sentinel'** White flowers
followed by deep red fruits maintained
beyond mid winter. Green foliage. *M.* ×
robusta (Siberian crab) Two forms available,
both with pink-tinged white flowers: *M.* × *r.*
'Red Siberian' Large crop of red fruits, green

foliage; *M.* × *r.* **'Yellow Siberian'** Yellow
fruits, green foliage; *M. sylvestris* (Common
crab apple) Flowers white shaded with pink.
Fruits yellow/green, sometimes flushed red,
1–1½ in (3–4 cm) wide. Light green foliage.
Not readily available; must be sought from
specialist nurseries. The parent of many ornamental crabs and the garden apple. *M.*
'Wintergold' White flowers, pink in bud.
Good crop of yellow fruit retained into
winter. Green foliage with autumn colour. *M.*
'Wisley' Strong-growing tree with limited
purple/red to bronze/red flowers, with
reddish shading and slight fragrance. Large
purple/red fruits in autumn which, although
sparse, are attractive for their size. Purple to
purple/green foliage.
Average height and spread
Five years
12 × 12 ft (3.7 × 3.7 m)
Ten years
24 × 24 ft (7.3 × 7.3 m)
Twenty years
30 × 30 ft (9 × 9 m)
Protrudes up to 3 ft (91 cm)
from support.

Malus floribunda **in flower**

Malus **'John Downie'** in fruit

MALUS
(Green-leaved Flowering Forms)

FLOWERING CRAB, CRAB APPLE

Rosaceae   *Hardy Tree*
Deciduous

A group of trees responding well to fan-
training, giving a good flowering display in
a wide range of aspects.

Origin Mostly of garden origin; a few direct
species.
Use As a fan-trained tree for walls and fences.
Description *Flower* White, pink or bi-
coloured pink and white flowers 1½ in (4 cm)
across, singly or in clusters of five to seven
flowers, producing a mass display. *Foliage*
Green, ovate, 2 in (5 cm) long, tooth-edged,
giving some yellow autumn colour. *Stem*
Purple/red to purple/green. Upright when
young, but very trainable. Medium to fast
rate of growth. *Fruit* Normally green to
yellow/green and of little attraction.
Hardiness Tolerates a minimum winter temperature of 4°F (−15°C).
Soil requirements Tolerates most soil conditions; dislikes waterlogging.
Sun/Shade aspect Tolerates all aspects and
full sun to light shade, preferring full sun.

Pruning Prune young trees hard in spring following planting. Select and train resulting five to seven shoots and tie into a fan-trained shape. In subsequent years, remove all side growths back to two buds from their origin and maintain main branches in fan shape.

Training Secure to wires or individual anchor points.

Propagation and nursery production From budding or grafting on to wild under-stock. Best planting height for fan-training 3–5 ft (91 cm–1.5 m). Purchase bare-rooted or container grown one- to two-year-old trees, ensuring they are grafted at the base; most varieties readily available from garden centres and general nurseries.

Problems Can suffer from severe attacks of apple mildew and lesser attacks of apple scab.

Forms of interest *M. baccata* White flowers up to 1½ in (4 cm) across in mid spring, followed by bright red, globe-shaped fruits. One third more than average height and spread. From eastern Asia and north China. Normally sold in the form *M. baccata mandshurica*, which has slightly larger fruits. *M. floribunda* A pendulous variety, branches on mature trees reaching to the ground. Flowers rose-red in bud, opening to pink, finally fading to white, produced in mid to late spring in great profusion. Foliage smaller than most, ovate and deeply toothed. *M. hupehensis* Fragrant flowers soft pink in bud, opening to white. Fruits yellow with red tints. Two thirds average height and spread. Somewhat upright in habit. From China and Japan. *M.* 'Katherine' Semi-double flowers, pink in bud, finally white. Bright red fruits with yellow flushing. Two thirds average height and spread. Not readily found in production, but worth searching for. *M.* 'Lady Northcliffe' Carmine-red buds, opening to white with blush shading. Fruits small, yellow and round. Two thirds average height and spread. Not always available. *M.* 'Magdeburgensis' A tree similar to cultivated apple. Flowers deep red in bud, opening to blush-pink, finally becoming white. Insignificant fruits, light green to green/yellow. Two thirds average height and spread. Not readily available. *M. sargetii* Foliage oblong with three lobes up to 2½ in (6 cm) long. Some yellow autumn colour. Flowers pure white with greenish centres in clusters of five and six; petals overlap. Fruits bright red. Very floriferous. One third average height and spread. From Japan. *M. spectabilis* Grey/green foliage susceptible to apple scab. Flowers rosy red in bud, opening to pale blush pink, up to 2 in (5 cm) across and borne in clusters of six to eight in early spring. Fruits yellow and globe-shaped. From China. *M.* 'Strathmore' Light green foliage and a profusion of pale pink flowers. *M. toringoides* Foliage ovate to lanceolate, up to 3 in (7.5 cm) long, deeply lobed when new; that produced on older wood is less indented. Pastel autumn colours. Flowers light pink in bud opening to creamy-white, produced in clusters of six to eight. Fruit globe-shaped, yellow with scarlet flushing. Two thirds average height and spread. From China. *M. transitoria* Small-lobed foliage, small pink/white flowers and rounded yellow fruits. Excellent autumn colour. Two thirds average height and spread. From north-west China. *M. trilobata* Leaves maple-shaped, deeply lobed, mid to dark green with good autumn colour. White flowers, followed by infrequently produced yellow fruits. Two thirds average height and spread. Scarce in production and will have to be sought from specialist nurseries. From eastern Mediterranean and north-eastern Greece. *M.* 'Van Eseltine' Flowers rose/scarlet in bud, opening to shell-pink, semi-double. Small yellow fruits. Two thirds average height and spread.

Average height and spread
Five years
12 × 12 ft (3.7 × 3.7 m)
Ten years
18 × 18 ft (5.5 × 5.5 m)
Twenty years
25 × 25 ft (7.6 × 7.6 m)
Protrudes up to 3 ft (91 cm) from support.

MALUS
(Purple-leaved Forms)

PURPLE-LEAVED CRAB APPLE

Rosaceae　　　　　　　　　*Hardy Tree*
Deciduous

These attractive foliage trees respond well to fan-training where pruning encourages even better foliage display but may lessen flowering.

Origin Of garden or nursery origin.

Use As fan-trained trees for large walls and fences.

Description *Flower* Wine-red to purple/red flowers up to 1 in (2.5 cm) across in clusters of five to seven, produced in great profusion in mid spring. *Foliage* Ovate, sometimes toothed, purple/red to purple/bronze. *Stem* Purple/red to purple/green. Upright when young, quickly becoming spreading and branching, particularly with training. Moderate rate of growth. *Fruit* Small, wine-red fruits in early autumn, sometimes inconspicuous against the purple foliage.

Hardiness Tolerates a minimum winter temperature of 4°F (−15°C).

Soil requirements Does well on most soils; dislikes very poor or waterlogged types.

Sun/Shade aspect Tolerates all aspects. Full sun to very light shade. Deeper shade spoils foliage colour and shape of tree.

Pruning Prune young trees hard in spring following planting. Select and train resulting five to seven shoots and tie into a fan-trained shape. In subsequent years, remove all side growths back to two buds from their origin and maintain original main braches in fan shape.

Malus 'Royalty' in flower

Training Requires tying to wires or individual anchor points.

Propagation and nursery production From budding or grafting on to wild apple under-stocks. For fan-training best purchased 3–5 ft (91 cm–1.5 m) high as one- to two-year-old trees, ensuring that they are grafted at the base. Available from garden centres and nurseries.

Problems Can suffer severe attacks of apple mildew, lesser attacks of apple scab.

Forms of interest *M.* × *eleyi* Large red/purple flowers, followed by conical, purple/red fruits. Foliage red/purple, up to 4 in (10 cm) long. Initial growth somewhat weak. *M.* × *lemoinei* An early nursery cross of merit. Purple foliage, crimson/purple flowers, bronze/purple fruits. *M.* 'Liset' Modern hybrid with good foliage and flowers,

adequate dark red fruit. *M.* 'Neville Copeman' Foliage dull wine red, flowers pink/purple, fruits purple. Not as intensely coloured as some, but worth consideration. Not easy to find in commercial production. *M.* 'Profusion' An early nursery cross. Good purple/wine flowers, purple/red fruits and copper/crimson spring foliage. Originally robust but recently appears to be losing its overall vigour. *M.* 'Red Glow' Wine red flowers, large leaves and fruit. A good introduction, but not readily available. *M.* 'Royalty' Possibly the best purple/red leaf form. Large, disease-resistant, wine-coloured foliage and wine-red flowers followed by large purple/red fruits. Becoming more widely available.

Average height and spread
Five years
12 × 12 ft (3.7 × 3.7 m)
Ten years
24 × 24 ft (7.3 × 7.3 m)
Twenty years
30 × 30 ft (9 × 9 m)
Protrudes up to 3 ft (91 cm) from support.

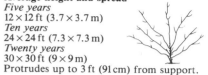

MALUS PUMILA
(Apple Hybrids)

APPLE

Rosaceae　　　　　　　　　*Fruit Tree*
Deciduous

Trained fruit trees have for a long time been recognized as attractive wall specimens, not only for their fruit but also their flowers.

Origin Of orchard, garden and nursery origin.

Use As fan-trained, horizontal-trained or cordon-shaped trees for walls and fences.

Description *Flower* Five oval to round petals make up a saucer-shaped flower ½–¾ in (1–2 cm) wide carried in clusters on two-year-old growth or more, from white through shades of pink, profusely borne in mid spring. Specific varieties cross-pollinate each other and in 'Forms of Interest' (UK) each variety is given a pollination number. For best results varieties of the same number should be planted together, but in many cases numbers to either side will also produce good pollination. *Malus* 'Golden Hornet' in close proximity to any variety will also encourage fruiting as it is a universal pollinator. *Foliage* Oval, up to 4 in (10 cm) long, some with toothed edges. Mid green with yellow autumn colour. *Stem* Grey/green, becoming brown to grey/brown. Stiff, branching. Medium to fast growing. *Fruit* Round edible apples in a wide range of varieties, each with its own texture, colour, flavour and usage for dessert or culi-

Malus pumila 'Discovery'

nary purposes. Green, yellow or shaded orange, red or striped depending on variety.

Hardiness Tolerates a minimum winter temperature of 0°F (−18°C), although late spring frosts may damage flowers and consequently fruiting.

Soil requirements Tolerates a wide range of soil conditions. Some varieties may show distress on extremely wet soils.

Sun/Shade aspect Tolerates all aspects. Best in full sun to very light shade to aid ripening of fruit. Will grow in deeper shade but flowering and fruiting will be decreased.

Pruning For all three shapes of fan, horizontal (espalier) and cordon: shoots produced in late spring and early summer are reduced to two buds from their point of origin in late summer, early autumn.

Malus pumila 'Ellison's Orange'

Training Tie to wires. Purchase pre-trained trees or one-year-old trees for training. For fan-training, cut back to within 12 in (30 cm) of their graft union to induce numerous side shoots which are then trained into a fan shape. For horizontal training, cut back to 18 in (45 cm) from their graft union. This will induce three shoots, two of which are trained horizontally either side of the main stem and the third upwards. After one year the upward shoot is again cut back to 18 in (45 cm) from the lower tier. This again produces three new shoots and the process continues until up to five or six tiers are formed. Once a tier is formed, all growth made between early and late summer is cut back in early autumn to two buds from its origin, so forming a fruiting spur. For cordon fruit trees, all side growth is cut back to two buds from its origin each year in late summer/early autumn to form fruiting spurs.

Propagation and nursery production Should always be grafted or budded on to an understock with a known characteristic. There are many combinations, but in the main, fan, horizontal and cordon fruit trees are propagated on to semi-dwarfing root stocks. Can be planted bare-rooted from early autumn to early spring or container grown as available, with autumn and early spring planting for preference. Pre-trained trees in each of the shapes or young trees can be purchased at a height of 3–5 ft (91 cm–1.5 m) from a garden centre or from a specialist nursery.

Problems May suffer from attacks of apple mildew and apple scab, but a proprietary spray will normally control these diseases. Greenfly and blackfly may be a problem in some circumstances, but again proprietary sprays can be used. Codling moth may attack fruit; prevention is by grease bands applied to the trees in early to mid summer. Apple trees are also susceptible to stem and bud canker; remove affected wood immediately.

Forms of interest

UK

The numbers in brackets denote the pollination group.

Malus pumila 'James Grieve'

LATE SUMMER DESSERT APPLES Harvest in late summer and eat within ten days. **'Beauty of Bath'** (2) Fruit mottled orange, scarlet or yellow. Sharp, crisp, sweet, juicy apple. **'Discovery'** (2) Scarlet flushed. Juicy fruit with good flavour. Resistant to apple scab. **'George Cave'** (2) Crisp, good flavoured fruit, green with orange flush. Gives a good crop. **'Greensleeves'** (2) Green apples with sweet flavour. Can be small in some years. Cross between 'James Grieve' and 'Golden Delicious'. **'Scarlet Pimpernel'** (syn. **Stark Earliest'**) (1) An American variety. Pale green or white with scarlet shading, crisp and juicy. Scab resistant.

EARLY AUTUMN DESSERT APPLES Ripening early autumn and keeping until mid autumn. Eaten immediately after picking, although late varieties will keep for up to 14 days. **'Ellison's Orange'** (4) Very similar to 'Cox's Orange Pippin'. Strong-scented apple with pleasant flavour. Attractive orange/yellow speckling to fruit. **'Fortune'** (3) Very good flavour. Very heavy crop of fruit, needs thinning for best results. **'James Grieve'** (3) Juicy and sharp flavoured. Handsome round fruits with orange stripes. Dislikes waterlogged conditions. Susceptible to canker. **'Laxton's Fortune'** (3) Crisp, well-flavoured fruit with good orange/red striped colouring. May fruit only every other year. Attractively shaped tree resistant to apple scab. **'Merton Worcester'** (3) A 'Cox's Orange Pippin' cross with the colour of Cox and the flavour of 'Worcester Pearmain'. **'Tydeman's Early Worcester'** (3)

Juicy fruit of good colour and a tree of good garden merit. **'Worcester Pearmain'** (3) Crisp, juicy fruit, strawberry flavoured. Allow to ripen on tree and eat immediately.

LATE AUTUMN DESSERT APPLES Ripening in mid autumn and keeping through late autumn into early winter. Pick the fruit when ripe and store until required. **'Charles Ross'** (3) Large, round fruit, shiny, juicy, pleasant flavour. Does not keep well. Scab resistant. Extremely good on alkaline soils. **'Egremont Russet'** (2) Golden russet-skinned with good flavour. Will keep until mid winter in good conditions. Upright growing. Resistant to scab. **'Lord Lambourne'** (2) Bright coloured fruit, juicy and tender with good mellow flavour. Good cropping. **'Spartan'** (3) Dark crimson, almost black fruit when ripe. Crisp, juicy with good flavour. Scab resistant. A variety from Canada. **'Sunset'** (3) Considered by many to be better than Cox, crisp with a rich Cox flavour. Resistant to scab and tolerates a wider soil range than Cox, its parent.

MIDWINTER DESSERT APPLES Ripening late autumn to late winter with good storage. Pick in mid autumn and store until required. **'Blenheim Orange'** (3) Crisp, acid-flavoured orange/yellow fruit. Makes a large, spreading tree. **'Cox's Orange Pippin'** (3) Flavour and texture are unsurpassed, but it is susceptible to all fungus, bacteria and soil deficiencies and can be a most disappointing and difficult tree to grow. Consider 'Sunset' as an alternative. Using as a fan-trained or horizontal tree can improve its growth performance.

Malus pumila 'Worcester Pearmain'

'**Crimson**' (syn. '**Mutsu**') (2) Green/yellow and shiny, juicy and hard with good flavour. Strong growing. From Japan. '**Jupiter**' (3) A Cox cross. Very similar to its parent but larger fruit. Strong grower. '**Kidd's Orange Red**' (3) A derivative of Cox with bright-coloured, good-flavoured fruit. Resistant to both scab and mildew. '**Merton Russet**' (3) Russet-flavoured. Good russet foliage and crimson pink flowers. Small growing and upright in habit. '**Queen Cox**' (3) An improved form of 'Cox's Orange Pippin' with brightly coloured fruit. '**Ribston Pippin**' (2) Strong flavour, crisp, juicy and aromatic. Suffers from canker on poor soils. Strong growing, does well as a cordon. '**Suntan**' (3) Cox flavour. Very similar to 'Cox's Orange Pippin'.

Malus pumila '**Egremont Russet**'

NEW YEAR DESSERT APPLES Harvest in late autumn and store through the winter until required. '**Midwinter**' (3) Often keeping until early spring, with good storage, but may become somewhat shrivelled towards the end. '**Claygate Pearmain**' (3) Rich flavour. Small apple, greenish, carried in profusion. Upright growth and resistant to scab. '**Laxton's Pearmain**' (4) Similar to a red-coloured Cox. Crisp, with a pleasant flavour. '**Laxton's Superb**' (4) Good apple which has a dual purpose, both culinary and dessert, with the flavour and colouring of Cox, but a larger fruit. Well recommended. '**Orleans Reinette**' (4) Golden yellow with brown red shading. Good fruiting but susceptible to scab in poor soil conditions. '**Rosemary Russet**' (3) Russet flavour. Keeps well. Somewhat light in cropping performance. '**Winston**' (5) An improved form of 'Laxton's Superb'. Fruit small, highly coloured but flavour not always of the best. Resistant to scab. Upright growth.

Malus pumila '**Lord Lambourne**'

SPRING DESSERT APPLES Harvest in late autumn/early winter and keep in store until required. '**Granny Smith**' (2) An Australian variety with bright green fruit. Benefits well from the extra warmth afforded by a wall or fence. '**Sturmer Pippin**' (3) Thrives on the extra warmth provided by a wall or fence. Pale green, russet-flavoured fruit. Harvest as late as possible in the year. '**Tydeman's Late Orange**' (3) A form of Cox. Bright orange/red with russety markings. Good Cox flavour, crisp. Stores well. '**Wagener**' (3) An American variety of some standing. Crisp and juicy, with good flavour. Keeps well until early spring. Golden yellow in colour with carmine shading when ripe. Free fruiting and free from scab.

SUMMER AND AUTUMN COOKING APPLES Use as required from the tree. '**Arthur Turner**' (3) Late summer to mid autumn. Green/yellow fruit, turning to orange/brown on sun side. Good cropper. '**Early Victoria**' (syn. '**Emneth Early**') (3) Mid summer to early autumn. Pale yellow fruit of average size. Cooks well. '**George Neal**' (2) Early to mid autumn. Pale golden fruit with rosy red shading on sun side. Good for cooking, becoming golden in colour. Good cropping and disease free. '**Grenadier**' (3) Late summer to mid autumn. Large green fruit. Good cropping and disease free. '**Lord Derby**' (5) Mid autumn to early winter. Green fruit, turning red with cooking. Heavy cropper. Disease free. '**Peasgood's Nonesuch**' (3) Early to late autumn. Very large golden fruit with attract-

ive orange/red stripe. Sweet. '**Rev. W. Wilks**' (2) Early to late autumn. Creamy white in colour, becoming pale yellow with cooking. Good cropper.

LATE KEEPING COOKING APPLES Harvest in late autumn/early winter and store until required. '**Annie Elizabeth**' (4) Mid winter to early summer, with good storage. Large fruit, golden yellow in colour with red shading. Cooks well with crisp flavour. '**Bramley Seedling**' (3) Must be one of the best known of all cooking apples. Late autumn to early spring. Large fruit, cooking exceedingly well and very high in vitamin C. Will require a large wall or fence for results. '**Crawley Beauty**' (8) Mid winter to early spring. Fruit pale yellow/green with red striping. Cooks well, with good flavour. Self-fertile. Scab re-

Malus pumila '**Cox's Orange Pippin**'

sistant. '**Edward VII**' (6) Mid winter to mid spring. Pale yellow, turning red with cooking. '**Howgate Wonder**' (4) Mid autumn to late spring. Fruit creamy yellow with red shading. Heavy cropping. Cooks well. Scab resistant. '**Newton Wonder**' (5) Late autumn to early spring. Golden yellow with red stripes and shading. Strong grower.

USA

All varieties are self-fertile unless otherwise stated; however, pollination is improved by planting any two varieties together.

EARLY SEASON DESSERT APPLES Use from the tree in mid to late summer. '**Akane**' A crisp, red-skinned, juicy apple with white flesh. Good flavour. Ideal variety for areas where the fungus disease fire blight is a problem. From Japan. '**Anna**' A variety for Florida and Southern California. Green skin with red

Malus pumila '**Spartan**'

blush. Ripens in July but may produce a second crop of flowers giving late fruits. Requires pollination from 'Dorset Golden' or 'Ein Shemer'. A low-chill variety. From Israel. **'Dorset Golden'** Large fruit, reminiscent of 'Golden Delicious'. Cannot tolerate any degree of frost or winter chill. Good for eating or cooking. Use 'Anna' or 'Ein Shemer' as pollinators. A low-chill variety. From Bahamas. **'Ein Shemer'** A derivative of 'Golden Delicious', does best in the deep South, Texas and Southern California. Early fruiting. Use 'Dorset Golden' as a pollinator.

Malus pumila **'Laxton's Superb'**

Malus pumila **'Jupiter'**

A low-chill variety. From Israel. **'Jerseymac'** Moderately firm, juicy, red-skinned fruit of good quality ripening in August. From New Jersey. **'Liberty'** An apple of medium size, sweet and juicy but can be coarse-grained in its texture. Skin shaded red, often over entire area. Resistant to rust, scab, mildew and attacks of fire blight. From New York. **'Tydeman's Early Worcester'** Juicy fruit of good colour and a tree of good garden merit. From the UK.

EARLY TO MID SEASON DESSERT APPLES Use from the tree from mid summer to early fall. **'Gravenstein'** Large, light green fruit with red shading. Yellow/green flesh. Good texture. Firm, crisp and juicy. Strong-growing, spreading habit. From Germany. **'Jonamac'** A 'McIntosh' type apple with very good flavour and texture. From New York. **'McIntosh'** One of the best of all the apple varieties. Medium to large in size, with sweet, tender, juicy white flesh. The skin is yellow, flushed red. Good as a dessert and as a cooking apple. From Ontario.

MID SEASON DESSERT APPLES Harvest in mid fall to early winter. May store for a short period. **'Empire'** Medium-sized fruit, red striped skin. Flesh white to cream. Good texture, crisp and juicy. Trees moderately vigorous and spreading. From New York.

'Jonathon' A widely grown variety, both by the amateur and in commercial orchards. Fruit of medium size, skin shaded red and pale yellow. Crisp, juicy, firm fruit with good flavour. Good for dessert or cooking. Very heavy crop. From New York. **'Winter Banana'** Large, attractive fruit. Pale skin colour of waxy texture with a pink blush which spreads as it ripens. Tender flesh. Very attractive perfume and interesting flavour. Use 'Red Astrachan' as a pollinator. A low-chill variety. From Indiana. **'Winter Pearmain'** Large green-skinned apples with moderately firm flesh of very good quality. For use in southern California. A low-chill variety. Origin unknown.

Malus pumila **'Grenadier'**

MID TO LATE SEASON DESSERT APPLES Harvest in mid fall to early winter. Will keep in store until required. **'Golden Delicious'** Fruit medium to large in size. Yellow/green skin, sometimes with a bright pink blush. Crisp, juicy and sweet. From West Virginia. **'Honeygold'** Good flavoured fruit of medium to large size, similar to 'Golden Delicious'. Yellow to golden yellow skin. Yellow flesh which is crisp, smooth and juicy. Extra hardy. From Minnesota. **'Jonagold'** This cross between 'Jonathon' and 'Golden Delicious' produces large yellow/green fruit shaded red, with crisp, juicy, cream-coloured flesh of good flavour. Can be used as a dessert and cooking apple. From New York. **'Red Delicious'** A popular variety with fruit of medium to large size, either striped or solid red skin colour. Flesh moderately firm, sweet and juicy. From Iowa.

LATE SEASON DESSERT APPLES Harvest in late fall to late winter and keep in store until

required. **'Fuji'** Can be left on the tree to ripen for at least 200 days, can also be ripened in store. Medium to large fruit, fresh, tart flavour. Can be used for dessert or cooking. From Australia. **'Idared'** This cross between 'Jonathon' and 'Wagner' produces large, bright red apples with smooth, glossy skin. Good flavoured sweet white flesh. Stores well. From Idaho. **'Regent'** A medium-sized variety with red skin. Crisp, juicy, creamy-white flesh. Can be used for dessert and cooking. Maintains its quality well into winter. Extra hardy. From Minnesota. **'Stayman'** Very late to ripen, a good keeper. Fruit juicy with tart flavour and bright red skin. Can be used for dessert and cooking. From Kansas.

COOKING APPLES Use from the tree in late fall or store until required. **'Beverley Hills'** An early-cropping variety with small to medium sized fruit. Skin striped or splashed with red on a yellow background. Tender, juicy with a tart flavour. Best production achieved in coastal areas of California and other southern states. A low-chill variety. From California.

Malus pumila **'Bramley Seedling'**

'Courtland' Said by many growers to be even an improvement on McIntosh, both as a dessert and cooking apple. Skin red striped, flesh white and of good flavour. Mid season fruiting. From New York. **'Paulard'** Fruit red, flushed bright yellow, ripening late summer/early fall. White flesh, sometimes cream. Possible tart flavour. Can be used for cooking or dessert. From Michigan. **'Yellow Newton'** Medium-sized fruit with green to

Malus pumila **'Golden Delicious'**

yellow skin for dessert or cooking. Firm, crisp flesh of good flavour. Strong growth, vigorous habit. Mid season to late fruiting. From New York.

Average height and spread
Fan-trained
Five years
8 × 8 ft   (2.4 × 2.4 m)
Ten years
10 × 12 ft   (3 × 3.7 m)
Twenty years
12 × 16 ft   (3.7 × 4.9 m)
Protrudes up to 3 ft (91 cm) from support.

Horizontal (3 trained tiers)
Five years
6 × 8 ft   (1.8 × 2.4)
Ten years
8 × 12 ft   (2.4 × 3.7 m)
Twenty years
10 × 20 ft   (3 × 6 m)
Protrudes up to 3 ft (91 cm) from support.

Cordon
Five years
8 × 2 ft   (2.4 × 60 cm)
Ten years
9 × 3 ft   (2.7 × 91 cm)
Twenty years
9 × 3 ft   (2.7 × 91 cm)
Protrudes up to 2 ft (60 cm) from support.

MANDEVILLA SPLENDENS

ACHILLEAN JASMINE

Apocynaceae   *Tender Greenhouse Climber*

Evergreen

Possibly one of the most charming of tender flowering climbers but its need for protection must be appreciated.

Mandevilla 'Alice du Pont'

Origin From Argentina.
Use As a climber for very sheltered favourable conditions or for preference under protection of a greenhouse or conservatory.
Description *Flower* Five bold petunia-pink or white flowers 2 in (5 cm) across make a tubular, trumpet-shaped flower arrangement carried in clusters. Flowers through summer to early autumn or, if grown under protection, over a wider timespan. Fragrant. *Foliage* Oblong, up to 3½ in (9 cm) long, with pointed ends. Dark green, glossy, attractive, borne well apart on short stalks along the stems. *Stem* Twisting, twining, self-supporting to suitable wires or string. Light green to mid green. Medium to fast rate of growth, depending on planting position *Fruit* Slender seeds, often up to 15 in (38 cm) long, presented in pairs in ideal growing conditions.

Melianthus major

Hardiness Tolerates a minimum winter temperature of 32°F (0°C).
Soil conditions Tolerates a wide range of soil conditions except extremely alkaline. Dislikes drying out.
Sun/Shade aspect Very sheltered, warm aspect or under protection. Light shade for preference, will tolerate full sun but may show signs of scorching in very open positions.
Pruning Requires no pruning other than that to keep it within bounds.
Training Allow to ramble up wire supports by twining its branches around the support.
Propagation and nursery production From cuttings of well-ripened side-shoots taken approximately 2–3 in (5–7.5 cm) long and rooted into a sand mixture in a propagating case. Always purchase container grown; best planting height 6 in–2 ft (15–60 cm). Will have to be sought from specialist nurseries.
Problems Rarely succeeds for any great length of time in a container, so if planted in a conservatory or greenhouse should be planted into soil beds rather than pots or tubs.
Similar forms of interest *M. 'Alice Du Pont'* Petunia-pink, scented, large flowers. Good climbing habit. *M. suaveolens* White, scented flowers. The original plant in commercial production but today often superseded in interest by the pink-flowering forms.
Average height and spread
Five years
10 × 10 ft (3 × 3 m)
Ten years
20 × 20 ft (6 × 6 m)
Twenty years
25 × 25 ft (7.6 × 7.6 m)
Protrudes up to 2 ft (60 cm) from support.

MELIANTHUS MAJOR

HONEY BUSH

Melianthaceae   *Tender Wall Shrub*
Evergreen

A useful evergreen shrub suitable for only very mild areas and benefiting from the protection of walls and fences.

Origin From South Africa.
Use As a wall shrub for warm, sunny, sheltered walls and fences. In colder areas, for conservatories and greenhouses.
Description *Flower* Crimson to tawny/crimson, tubular flowers in erect terminal racemes up to 6 in (15 cm) long, borne on mature shrubs throughout summer, but only in very favourable areas. *Foliage* Leaves pinnate, up to 12–18 in (30–45 cm) long, with nine to 11 leaflets 3–4 in (7.5–10 cm) long. Deeply

toothed edges. Sea-green to glaucous blue. *Stem* Hollow, upright stems, grey/green. In cold areas may die back to ground level in winter but can show a fast rate of growth in following spring. *Fruit* Insignificant.
Hardiness Tolerates a minimum winter temperature of 23°F (−5°C) when given the protection of a wall or fence.
Soil requirements Rich, moist, deep soil to produce good foliage growth.
Sun/Shade aspect Requires a very sheltered aspect in full sun to very light shade, otherwise leaf colour and shrub shape are spoiled.
Pruning None required.
Training Normally freestanding, but may need individual anchor points for securing.
Propagation and nursery production From root division or from seed. Purchase container grown; very hard to find outside mild areas and even in these locations available only from specialist nurseries. Best planting height 4 in–2 ft (10–60 cm).
Problems Only suitable for very mild areas.
Average height and spread
Five years
5 × 5 ft (1.5 × 1.5 m)
Ten years
8 × 8 ft (2.4 × 2.4 m)
Twenty years
12 × 12 ft (3.7 × 3.7 m)
Protrudes up to 6 ft (1.8 m) from wall or fence.

MORUS

MULBERRY

Moraceae   *Hardy Tree*
Deciduous

Although not often seen as a fan-trained wall tree, it should be considered more widely for this use.

Origin From China, North America and western Asia, depending on variety.
Use As a large fan-trained tree for large walls.
Description *Flower* Very short, male or female catkins of little interest; produced in early spring. *Foliage* Ovate, lobed or unlobed, grey/green leaves. Individual branches may carry both leaf shapes. Good yellow autumn colour. The lighter green leaves of *Morus alba* are used to feed silkworms. *Stem* Grey/green, corky, almost rubbery texture. Slow to medium rate of growth. *Fruit* Blackberry-shaped, dark red to black clusters of fruit. Edible and very juicy.
Hardiness Tolerates a minimum winter temperature of 4°F (−15°C).
Soil requirements Best results on rich, moist, deep soil. Must be well drained.
Sun/Shade aspect Tolerates all but the most

Morus nigra in fruit

severe of aspects. Best in full sun to allow ripening of fruit, but tolerates light shade.

Pruning Purchase bush trees to encourage branches to become fan-trained. Remove forward growing branches after fruiting to two buds from their point of origin. After 10–20 years thin out some of the major branches.

Training Secure to wires or individual anchor points.

Propagation and nursery production From hardwood cuttings taken in early winter. Purchase container grown bush or young trees not more than 3 ft (91 cm) in height from garden centres and nurseries.

Problems Roots very fleshy and often poorly anchored.

Forms of interest *M. alba* (White mulberry) Fast-growing. Light grey/green stems with large, ovate, light green foliage. Black fruits in autumn. One third more than average height and spread and slightly more tender.

Morus nigra in autumn

From China. *M. a.* 'Laciniata' Leaves deeply cut and toothed. Good autumn colour. Fruits as parent. *M. nigra* (Common or black mulberry) Good fruiting ability in all areas. Of reliable hardiness. From western Asia. *M. rubra* (Red mulberry) Fruits red to dark purple and sweet. May exceed average height and spread by one third or more. From North America and not always successful as a garden tree elsewhere.

Average height and spread
Five years
8 × 8 ft (2.4 × 2.4 m)
Ten years
16 × 16 ft (4.9 × 4.9 m)
Twenty years
24 × 24 ft (7.3 × 7.3 m)
Protrudes up to 3 ft (91 cm) from support.

102

MYRTUS COMMUNIS

COMMON MYRTLE
Myrtaceae   **Wall Shrub**
Evergreen

An attractive flowering evergreen shrub for mild locations which benefits from the protection of a wall or fence.

Origin From southern Europe and the Mediterranean region.

Use As a freestanding evergreen shrub for planting in front of walls and fences.

Description *Flower* White, round, tufted flowers, single or double depending on variety, mid to late summer. *Foliage* Leaves round to ovate, 1–2 in (2.5–5 cm) long, dark green with duller undersides, aromatic and very profusely borne. *Stem* Upright, becoming branching with age. Purple green to dark green. Fast growth rate when young, slowing with age. *Fruit* Small purple/black fruits in autumn.

Hardiness Tolerates a minimum winter temperature of 14°F (−10°C).

Soil requirements Does best on well-drained soil, tolerating both alkalinity and acidity.

Sun/Shade aspect Requires a sheltered aspect in full sun to mid shade.

Pruning None required but can be cut back hard or trimmed.

Training Allow to grow freestanding; normally needs no additional support.

Propagation and nursery production From semi-ripe cuttings taken in early summer. Purchase container grown; easy to find but varieties must be sought from specialist nurseries. Best planting height 15 in–2 ft (38–60 cm).

Problems Sometimes thought to be hardier than it actually is, but a wall will give it protection.

Similar forms of interest *M. c.* 'Variegata' A form with broad, creamy white margins to the foliage. A tender variety which will not withstand temperatures below freezing. *M. c. tarentina* White tufted flowers in summer with white berries in autumn. Leaves narrower than those of *M. communis*. From the Mediterranean region. *M. c. t.* 'Variegata' Flowers white, fragrant, produced in good numbers. Fruits black, foliage edged creamy white. *M. apiculata* (syn. *M. luma*) Tufted white flowers borne singly at each leaf axil cover the entire shrub during late summer and early autumn, followed by red to black fruits which are edible and sweet. Foliage oval, dark, dull green, ending in an abrupt point. Bark cinnamon-coloured and peels off in patches, showing creamy under surface. In

mild sheltered locations reaches size of small tree. From Chile.

Average height and spread
Five years
4 × 4 ft (1.2 × 1.2 m)
Ten years
8 × 8 ft (2.4 × 2.4 m)
Twenty years
15 × 10 ft (4.6 × 3 m)
Protrudes up to 8 ft (2.4 m) from wall or fence.

NERIUM OLEANDER

OLEANDER
Apocynaceae   **Tender Wall Shrub**
Evergreen

Although tender, this shrub is worthy of mention, especially for wall-trained use in conservatories and large heated greenhouses.

Nerium oleander in flower

Origin From the Mediterranean region.

Use As a wall shrub under protection in greenhouses or conservatories.

Description *Flower* Medium-sized, flat, five-petalled flowers ranging from white through yellow, buff and various shades of pink in mid summer to mid autumn. *Foliage* Leaves lanceolate, 3–6 in (7.5–15 cm) long, borne in clusters. Grey/green to sea-green with some silver and gold variegated forms. *Stem* Upright stems, becoming branching at extremities, forming a narrow-based, wide-headed shrub. Grey/green to sea-green. *Fruit* Insignificant.

Myrtus communis in flower

Nerium oleander **in flower**

Hardiness Tolerates a minimum winter temperature of 32°F (0°C).
Soil requirements Requires a light, open soil, tolerates both alkalinity and acidity.
Sun/Shade aspect Requires the protection of a conservatory or greenhouse or may be planted outside in areas where the minimum temperature can be guaranteed year long. Full sun to light shade.
Pruning None required. Individual branches may be shortened and will rebranch.
Training Can either be allowed to grow freestanding or trained into a fan shape using individual anchor points or wires.
Propagation and nursery production From softwood cuttings taken in early spring. Scarce, normally found in the house-plant sections of larger garden centres. Purchase container grown; best planting height 15 in–2 ft (38–60 cm).
Problems Scarce in production.
Similar forms of interest None.
Average height and spread
Five years
3 × 3 ft (91 × 91 cm)
Ten years
6 × 6 ft (1.8 × 1.8 m)
Twenty years
13 × 13 ft (4 × 4 m)
Protrudes up to 3 ft (91 cm) from support.

OSMANTHUS

KNOWN BY BOTANICAL NAME
Oleaceae   *Wall Shrub*
Evergreen
A useful group of evergreen shrubs with scented flowers adapting well to wall training.

Origin Most varieties from western China or Japan.
Use As a freestanding shrub to grow in front of walls or fences, or to train in a fan shape.
Description *Flower* Small, white or cream, trumpet-shaped flowers, sweetly scented, late autumn or early spring, depending on variety. *Foliage* Leaves elliptic, ovate or oblong, ½–1½ in (1–4 cm) long, some larger according to variety, some with toothed, spiny edges. White and gold variegation in some forms. *Stem* Upright, becoming branching. Dark green to grey/green. Slow to medium growth rate. *Fruit* Broad seedheads may be formed after flowering.
Hardiness Tolerates a minimum winter temperature of 14°F (−10°C).
Soil requirements Tolerates most soils, but resents waterlogging.
Sun/Shade aspect Tolerates all but the most exposed aspects. Prefers light dappled shade but tolerates full sun through to medium shade.
Pruning Some pruning will be required to achieve a fan-trained shrub. May be cut and trimmed after flowering to keep within bounds.

Training Allow to stand free or secure to walls or fences by individual anchor points or wires.
Propagation and nursery production From semi-ripe cuttings taken in early summer. Purchase container grown; most varieties fairly easy to find. Best planting height 15 in–2½ ft (38–76 cm).
Problems Liable to leaf scorch in cold winters.
Forms of interest *O. americanus* (Devil wood) A variety reaching more than one third average height and spread. White fragrant flowers borne in short panicles in axils of each leaf joint in spring. Dark blue fruits, late summer. Slightly tender. Outside its native environment needs a warm, sheltered position, or can be grown in a conservatory. From south-eastern USA. *O. armatus* White, sweetly scented flowers in autumn. Elliptic, oblong or lanceolate leaves, thick and rigid in texture, from 3–8 in (7.5–20 cm) long. Edges of leaves have a series of hooked spiny teeth. From western China. *O. × burkwoodii* Round to ovate leaves, 1 in (2.5 cm) long. Dark, shiny upper surface, leathery textured, silvery undersides with toothed edges. Clusters of tubular, white, very fragrant flowers, early to mid spring. Will tolerate shallow chalk soils. A nursery hybrid formerly known as *Osmarea burkwoodii*. *O. delavayi* Dark grey/green foliage. Reaches two thirds average height and spread. Covered with a good display of very sweetly scented white flowers, early to mid spring. Foliage may be damaged by severe wind chill. *O. heterophyllus* (syns. *O. aquifolium, O. ilicifolius*) (Holly osmanthus, false holly) Small to medium holly-shaped leaves, dark green, shiny upper surface, spined and toothed edges, 1½ in (4 cm) long. White, scented, tubular flowers in small clusters in autumn. From Japan. *O.h.* **'Aureomarginatus'** Holly-like leaves with golden yellow to deep yellow variegated margins. White flowers. Two thirds average height and spread. *O.h.* **'Gulftide'** Leaves twisted and lobed with strong spines. White scented flowers. Very dense habit of growth. Slightly less than average height and spread. *O.h.* **'Purpureus'** Young growth holly-shaped, purple, later becoming very dark green tinged purple. White flowers in autumn. Two thirds average height and spread. *O.h.* **'Rotundifolius'** Almost round, tooth-edged, leathery, dark green foliage on dark, green/black stems. White trumpet flowers, scented, freely borne in spring. Very scarce but not impossible to find. *O.h.* **'Variegatus'** Holly-like leaves, grey/green with creamy

white bold bordered edges. Shy to flower. Grows slowly to two thirds average height and spread.
Average height and spread
Five years
6 × 6 ft (2 × 2 m) freestanding
8 × 8 ft (2.5 × 2.5 m) fan-trained
Ten years
10 × 10 ft (3 × 3 m) freestanding
12 × 12 ft (3.5 × 3.5 m) fan-trained
Twenty years
13 × 13 ft (4 × 4 m) freestanding
15 × 15 ft (4.5 × 4.5 m) fan-trained
Protrudes up to 2 ft (60 cm) from support if fan-trained, 7 ft (2.1 m) untrained.

PALIURUS SPINA-CHRISTI

CHRIST'S THORN, JERUSALEM THORN
Rhamnaceae   *Wall Shrub*
Deciduous
An interesting shrub for specimen planting, traditionally reputed to have been used in Christ's crown of thorns.

Paliurus spina-christi **in flower**

Origin From southern Europe to the Himalayas and through to northern China.
Use As a fan-trained or freestanding wall shrub where it will benefit from the protection afforded.
Description *Flower* Small, open racemes of yellow to green/yellow flowers, late summer. *Foliage* Leaves ovate, ¾–1½ in (2–4 cm) long, slightly tooth-edged, light yellow/green, giving good yellow autumn colour. *Stem* Upright when young, quickly becoming

Osmanthus delavayi **in flower**

branching, twiggy and spreading. Mid green to green/yellow. Armed with numerous pairs of thorns. Slow to medium growth rate. *Fruit* Rounded, curiously shaped, green/yellow fruits in autumn and early winter.
Hardiness Tolerates a minimum winter temperature of 14°F (−10°C).
Soil requirements Most soils, provided adequate feeding is supplied.
Sun/Shade aspect Tolerates all but the most exposed aspects in full sun to very light shade. Dislikes deeper shade.
Pruning None required, but may be reduced in size or fan-trained if necessary.
Training Allow to stand free or secure to wall or fence with individual anchor points or wires.
Propagation and nursery production From semi-ripe cuttings taken in late spring/early summer, or from layers. Difficult to propagate. Purchase container grown; hard to find. Best planting height 8–18 in (20–45 cm).
Problems A little slow to develop into an interesting plant.
Similar forms of interest None.
Average height and spread
Five years
3 × 3 ft (91 × 91 cm) freestanding
5 × 5 ft (1.5 × 1.5 m) fan-trained
Ten years
6 × 6 ft (1.8 × 1.8 m) freestanding
8 × 8 ft (2.4 × 2.4 m) fan-trained
Twenty years
13 × 13 ft (4 × 4 m) freestanding
16 × 16 ft (5 × 5 m) fan-trained
Protrudes up to 2 ft (60 cm) from support if fan-trained, 10 ft (3 m) untrained.

PARTHENOCISSUS HENRYANA (*Vitis henryana*)

CHINESE VIRGINIA CREEPER
Vitaceae　　　　　*Woody Climber*
Deciduous
One of the most attractive ornamental vines, both in summer and autumn.

Origin From central China.
Use As a free-growing climber for walls, fences, trellises, pergolas and to cover large shrubs and small trees. Can be used as a loose-flowing ground cover.
Description *Flower* Insignificant, minutely petalled, green to green/yellow flowers carried in clusters through spring and summer. *Foliage* Three to five leaflets, each up to 5 in (12 cm) long and 1½ in (4 cm) wide, form a hand-shaped leaf. Leaflets oval to narrowly oval, with tapered ends and toothed edges. Dark green when young, with distinct silver-white veining, turning more purple/red during summer, finally vivid orange/scarlet in autumn. *Stem* Purple/green with red/purple leaf stalks. Becoming brown/grey. Twining. Fast growing. *Fruit* May produce small

clusters of round blue/black fruits in late summer and early autumn.
Hardiness Tolerates a minimum temperature of 0°F (−18°C).
Soil requirements Tolerates both alkaline and acid conditions. Requires a rich, moisture-retaining soil.
Sun/Shade aspect Tolerates all aspects with no particular preference. Best in light to medium shade; will tolerate full sun but the variegation will be reduced.
Pruning No pruning required for its own wellbeing but previous season's growth can be cut back to within two buds of its origin to allow the build-up of a fan-trained shape. Pruning is normally carried out in early spring and should be commenced on an annual basis as early as possible to achieve a good fan-trained shape. Alternatively can be allowed to ramble with no pruning although foliage may decrease in size.
Training Produces tendrils which make it self-clinging, but may need some additional support when young or very heavy with age.
Propagation and nursery production From cuttings taken in mid summer. Always purchase container grown; best planting height 1½–4 ft (45 cm–1.2 m). Generally available from good garden centres and nurseries.
Problems None.
Similar forms of interest *P. thomsonii* (syn. *Vitis thomsonii*) Five oval leaflets make up a hand-shaped leaf with a length and width of up to 4½ in (11 cm), with teeth indents along the outer edges. Glossy dark green. Leaf shoots purple when young, becoming a duller purple with age. Very good red/purple autumn colours, black fruits. From the Himalayas and China. Not readily available.
Average height and spread
Five years
5 × 5 ft (1.5 × 1.5 m)
Ten years
10 × 10 ft (3 × 3 m)
Twenty years
20 × 20 ft (6 × 6 m)
Protrudes 9–12 in (23–30 cm) from support.

PARTHENOCISSUS QUINQUEFOLIA (*Vitis quinquefolia, V. hederacea*)

VIRGINIA CREEPER
Vitaceae　　　　　*Woody Climber*
Deciduous
Few other climbing plants can surpass this fast growing climber for autumn colour.

Origin From eastern North America.
Use For covering large walls, fences and hedges, will ramble through large shrubs and trees; can be allowed to fall down banks to make a spreading ground cover.

Description *Flower* Insignificant green to green/yellow flowers, minutely petalled, carried in clusters through spring and summer. *Foliage* Five leaflets form a hand shape, with each leaf up to 4 in (10 cm) long and 6 in (15 cm) wide. Oval in shape with slender points and closely toothed edges. Dull to mid-green when young with grey/blue undersides, turning vivid orange and crimson in autumn. *Stem* Light brown/red when young, becoming deep brown to grey/brown with age. Small sucker pads make it self-clinging. Fast growth rate. *Fruit* In hot seasons may produce small blue/black fruits.
Hardiness Tolerates a minimum winter temperature of 0°F (−18°C).
Soil requirements Does well on all soil types with no particular preference.
Sun/Shade aspect Tolerates all aspects. Best in full sun but will tolerate light shade.

Parthenocissus quinquefolia in autumn

Pruning Allow to cover a desired area and then reduce its extremities by up to 2 ft (60 cm) to expose windows, doors or roofs; will rejuvenate in following spring/summer. Will also respond to cutting down to ground level and over the next two to three years will rejuvenate itself.
Training Self-clinging with tendrils and pads. May need some assistance by tying in when young or when excessively heavy with age.
Propagation and nursery production From cuttings taken in early to mid summer, or self-rooted layers from undersides of established plants. Always purchase container grown; best planting height 1–3 ft (30–91 cm). Normally available from all good garden centres and nurseries.
Problems Often outgrows the area allowed for it. Can take up to two years to establish before any real growth is seen.
Similar forms of interest *P. q.* 'Engelmannii' Smaller leaved. Good autumn colour. *P. q.* 'Murorum' Very similar. Found in central and southern European nurseries and garden centres and occasionally in the UK.
Average height and spread
Five years
8 × 8 ft (2.4 × 2.4 m)
Ten years
16 × 16 ft (5 × 5 m)
Twenty years
32 × 32 ft (10 × 10 m)
Protrudes up to 12 in (30 cm) from support.

PARTHENOCISSUS TRICUSPIDATA 'VEITCHII' (*Ampelopsis veitchii, Vitis inconstans* 'Purpurea')

BOSTON IVY
Vitaceae　　　　　*Woody Climber*
Deciduous
An attractive self-clinging climber for covering all walls, including the most inhospitable.

Origin From Japan, Korea, China and also Taiwan.
Use As a fast-growing, close, self-clinging climber for all large walls and fences.

Parthenocissus henryana in leaf

Parthenocissus tricuspidata 'Veitchii' in autumn

Description *Flower* Insignificant, minutely petalled, green to green/yellow flowers produced only on mature growth. *Foliage* Leaves vary according to age; on young plants ovate and toothed, sometimes carried in threes, becoming three-lobed with pointed fingers on older plants. Glossy upper surface, downy underside. Mid to dark green in spring and summer, turning vivid crimson and scarlet in autumn. *Stem* Light green, becoming green/purple, particularly on outer sides, finally brown/grey. Covered with self-clinging pads. Very tight formation, hand-shaped effect achieved naturally. Medium to fast growth rate. *Fruit* Round, blue-black with downy covering, produced on mature wood in warm seasons. Often hidden by foliage.
Hardiness Tolerates a minimum winter temperature of 0°F (−18°C).
Soil requirements Does well on all soil types with no particular preference, except it must have adequate moisture and organic material at the roots to produce good growth.
Sun/Shade aspect Tolerates all aspects. Full sun to light shade.
Pruning Normally requires no pruning, but can be reduced at its extremities by up to 2 ft (60 cm) with no harm and will rejuvenate very quickly. Can be cut down to within 3 ft (91 cm) of the base and will regain its original size over three to four years.
Training Self-clinging, requires no support.

Parthenocissus tricuspidata 'Beverley Brook' in summer

Propagation and nursery production From cuttings taken in mid summer. Best planting height 1–3 ft (30–91 cm). Always purchase container grown; normally available from most garden centres and nurseries.
Problems Slow to establish, often taking up to two years, but then very rapid in its further development.
Similar forms of interest *P. t.* 'Lowii' Three- to seven-lobed leaves when young, becoming three-lobed with age. Very good dark foliage both in summer and autumn. *P. t.* 'Beverley

Brook' Almost purple foliage in summer with very good orange/scarlet autumn tints. A decided improvement on the parent plant. *P. t.* 'Green Spring' Smaller-growing with small leaves. Good autumn colour. Not readily available outside southern Europe. *P. t.* 'Purpurea' Green leaves in summer with purple/red autumn tints. *P. t.* 'Boskoop' Purple/green leaves in summer, turning red in autumn. A central European variety but sometimes found outside this region.
Average height and spread
Five years
6 × 6 ft (1.8 × 1.8 m)
Ten years
15 × 15 ft (4.6 × 4.6 m)
Twenty years
30 × 30 ft (9 × 9 m)
Protrudes up to 6 in (15 cm) from support.

PASSIFLORA CAERULEA

PASSION FLOWER, BLUE PASSION FLOWER
Passifloraceae   *Perennial Climber/Woody Climber*
Deciduous
This woody climber is technically a perennial plant, but because of its woody nature is now considered a woody climber. May revert back to the perennial form in severe winters.

Origin From Brazil.
Use As a climber for walls, fences, to cover archways or pillars and to grow over pergolas.

Passiflora caerulea 'Constance Elliott' in flower

Description *Flower* Borne singly, up to 4 in (10 cm) wide. Sepals and petals white or pink-white. Central area 2 in (5 cm) across with blue spiky filaments, white in the middle and purple at the base. Fragrant. Flowers produced from mid to late summer. *Foliage* Mid green, palmate with five to seven lobed leaflets, each oblong to lance-shaped, 4–7 in (10–18 cm) long and 2 in (5 cm) wide. Yellow autumn colouring. *Stem* Twining, light green when young ageing to dark green, may turn light grey in winter. Fast growing. *Fruit* Oval, up to 1¼ in (3.5 cm) long. Turning yellow to orange/yellow from mid summer through until autumn. Edible, but not necessarily palatable.
Hardiness Tolerates a minimum winter temperature of 23°F (−5°C).
Soil requirements No particular soil preference, only disliking extremely alkaline and dry types.
Sun/Shade aspect Requires a very sheltered, warm aspect in full sun to very light shade.
Pruning The entire shrub can be cut to within

Passiflora caerulea in flower

3 ft (91 cm) of ground level every five to six years and will quickly rejuvenate itself with young, fresher foliage. Best carried out in early spring.
Training Allow to ramble through wires, over trellis or similar support. Can be tied to individual anchor points if required, but this is not normally the best method.
Propagation and nursery production From seed sown in autumn or semi-ripe cuttings taken in early summer. Always purchase container grown; normally available from good garden centres and nurseries. Best planting height 1–3 ft (30–91 cm).
Problems May die back in severe winters but rejuvenates from ground level the following spring.
Similar forms of interest *P. c.* 'Constance Elliott' White flowers with pale blue spiky filaments. Produced mid summer through until autumn. Slight fragrance.
Average height and spread
Five years
8 × 8 ft (2.4 × 2.4 m)
Ten years
16 × 16 ft (4.9 × 4.9 m)
Twenty years
20 × 20 ft (6 × 6 m)
Protrudes up to 12 in (30 cm) from support.

PELARGONIUM

ZONAL AND IVY-LEAF GERANIUMS
Geraniaceae   *Tender Greenhouse Climber*
Deciduous
Many zonal and ivy-leaf geraniums adapt well to fan-training in very favourable sheltered areas or under protection.

Origin Of garden origin.
Use As fan-trained plants for sheltered warm walls and fences or in conservatories or greenhouses.

Pelargonium 'Gustave Emich' in flower

Description *Flower* Five or more petals, ends indented, make up either a single or double flower up to 1–1½ in (2.5–4 cm) across, carried in clusters on the ends of 4 in (10 cm) long flower stalks, normally from mid summer to mid autumn, often longer, particularly when under protection. Colours range through white, pink, red, and purple with some bi-colours, particularly in ivy-leaf varieties. *Foliage* Three-lobed, each lobe heart-shaped, grey/green to red/green on zonal varieties, glossy green on ivy-leaf varieties. Some variegated varieties in both forms. Leaves 1½–4 in (4–10 cm) in width and length, depending on variety. *Stem* Light green becoming darker green, finally grey/green. Vigorous growth, rigid formation; can be easily broken. *Fruit* No fruit of interest.
Hardiness Tolerates a minimum winter temperature of 32°F (0°C) but may survive lower winter temperatures in very sheltered areas.
Soil requirements Tolerates a wide range of soil conditions as long as adequate plant nutrients and organic material are available on an annual basis. Dislikes waterlogging.
Sun/Shade aspect Very sheltered aspect or under protection. Light shade for preference but will tolerate full sun to medium shade.
Pruning Remove all forward-growing shoots in early winter, only retaining those required to form a fan-shaped framework.
Training Train into a fan-shaped form, securing to wires or individual anchor points. Ivy-leaf and thin-stemmed varieties may need the assistance of small canes between wires or anchorage points.
Propagation and nursery production From semi-ripe cuttings taken in early summer or in late autumn. Should always be purchased container grown; an extremely wide range of varieties is normally available from garden centres and nurseries. Best planting height 2 in–2 ft (5–60 cm).
Problems Under protection of greenhouse or conservatory may suffer from attacks of whitefly. Can be slow to form fan-shaped formation and will need patience.
Forms of interest Almost any variety of zonal or ivy-leaf geraniums can be fan-trained on a wall but the following would be my first choices:
ZONAL *P.* 'Gustave Emich' Double bright red flowers. *P.* 'Mrs Lawrence' Double pink

flowers. *P.* 'Paul Crampel' Single red flowers; one of the best varieties. *P.* 'Queen of the Whites' Single white flowers.
IVY-LEAF *P. peltatum* 'Abel Carrière' Magenta flowers. *P. p.* 'L'Elegante' Pink flowers; white-edged foliage. *P. p.* 'La France' Mauve flowers. *P. p.* 'Galilee' Pink flowers.
Average height and spread
Five years
4 × 4 ft (1.2 × 1.2 m)
Ten years
8 × 8 ft (2.4 × 2.4 m)
Twenty years
12 × 12 ft (3.7 × 3.7 m)
Protrudes up to 2 ft (60 cm) from support.

PHASEOLUS COCCINEUS

RUNNER BEAN, SCARLET RUNNER

Leguminosae **Annual Climber**
Deciduous

Normally considered as a vegetable but equally attractive when grown as a flowering climber with the added bonus of its edible bean pods.

Origin From North America.
Use As an annual climber against walls and fences, up a pyramidal support or can be trained into walkways and arches. Produces edible runner beans.
Description *Flower* Racemes up to 12 in (30 cm) long of pea-shaped flowers each ½ in (1 cm) wide and long, bright scarlet with some white and pink varieties. *Foliage* Three oval to round leaflets each 3–4 in (8–10 cm) long and wide make up a leaf up to 6–8 in (15–20 cm) long and wide, on long leaf stalks. Larger size depends on available moisture. Light green with yellow autumn colour. *Stem* Light grey/green, fast-growing, self-climbing by twining habit. *Fruit* Long green bean pods up to 18 in (45 cm) long and 1 in (2.5 cm) wide, toxic when raw but edible cooked.
Hardiness Tolerates a minimum winter temperature of 32°F (0°C). Seeds are not winter hardy in soil.
Soil requirements Does well on all soil types with no particular preferences although adequate moisture and plant food must be

available for maximum growth.
Sun/Shade aspect Tolerates all aspects. Full sun to light shade with full sun for preference.
Pruning Requires no pruning. Growth dies back totally in winter.
Training Provide supports on wires, canes, poles or other solid structures to form a framework.
Propagation and nursery production From seed planted in early to mid spring under protection and transplanted into final position after all danger of frost has passed, or planted in situ as seed in mid spring and protected if frosts are likely. Purchase container grown plants from garden centres and nurseries; best planting height 4–5 in (10–12 cm).
Problems Suffers attacks from blackfly. Dislikes drought and poor soils; supply extra feed and irrigation in such conditions.
Similar forms of interest *P. c.* 'Achievement' Red flowers. Good flavoured variety, good for freezing. *P. c.* 'Best of All' Good, heavy crop of bean pods. Orange/red flowers. *P. c.* 'Butter' Stringless pods of medium length. Red flowers. *P. c.* 'Bokkie' Early cropping in large amounts. Red flowers. *P. c.* 'Crusader' Red flowers. Long pods. *P. c.* 'Enoma' Very heavy cropper, beans have good shape and colour. Red flowers. *P. c.* 'Erecta' White flowers. Tolerant of wide range of growing conditions. *P. c.* 'Goliath' (Prize Taker) Bright orange/red flowers. Very long beans and heavy crop. *P. c.* 'Kelvedon Marvel' Red flowers, good as ground cover. *P. c.* 'Gower Emperor' Good early variety with good pod production. Red flowers. *P. c.* 'Mergoles' Beans are stringless and of good length. Red flowers. *P. c.* 'Painted Lady' Attractive flowers, both red and white. *P. c.* 'Polestar' Stringless, fleshy pods. Good cropper. Red flowers. *P. c.* 'Prizewinner' Well tested variety with good pod production. Red flowers. *P. c.* 'Purple Podded' Red flowers. Pods attractive

Phaseolus coccineus in flower

deep blue to purple colour. *P. c.* 'Red Knight' Stringless pods. Red flowers. *P. c.* 'Scarlet Emperor' Can be used up supports or as large-scale ground cover. Red flowers. *P. c.* 'Stringline' Smooth podded variety. Very strong growing. Red flowers. *P. c.* 'Sunset' Pale pink flowers. Early cropping, *P. c.* 'White Achievement' White flowers with good pod production
Average height and spread
One year
12 × 3 ft (3.7 m × 91 cm)
Protrudes up to 18 in (45 cm) from support.

PHILADELPHUS
(Medium-sized Forms)

MOCK ORANGE, SYRINGA

Philadelphaceae **Wall Shrub**
Deciduous

A group of plants not often thought of as wall shrubs, but if fan-trained or allowed to grow freestanding adjacent to a wall or fence will make a very elegant display.

Origin Most varieties of garden origin.
Use To be planted freestanding in front of a wall or fence or fan-trained.

Philadelphus 'Belle Etoile' in flower

Description *Flower* White, often fragrant flowers, ¾–1½ in (2–4 cm) wide, single or double depending on variety, some with purple throat markings, borne in mid summer. *Foliage* Leaves ovate, 1½–4 in (4–10 cm) long, slightly tooth-edged, light to mid green with good yellow autumn colour. Some varieties variegated. *Stem* Forming an upright, round-topped shrub if freestanding or can be fan-trained. Grey/green. Medium to fast growth rate. *Fruit* Insignificant.
Hardiness Tolerates a minimum winter temperature of 4°F (−15°C).
Soil requirements Most soils, including alkaline and acid types.
Sun/Shade aspect Tolerates all aspects and full sun through to medium shade.
Pruning On established plants three years old or more, remove one third of older flowering shoots to ground level after flowering each year.
Training Will require tying to wires or individual anchor points if fan-trained.
Propagation and nursery production From semi-ripe cuttings taken in early summer, or from hardwood cuttings taken in winter. Purchase container grown or bare-rooted from garden centres and nurseries; best planting height 15 in–2½ ft (38–76 cm).
Problems Harbours blackfly, which can transfer to other plants.

Philadelphus 'Virginal' in flower

Forms of interest *P.* 'Avalanche' Small, pure white, single, scented flowers borne in profusion. An upright-growing shrub with smaller than average foliage. *P.* 'Belle Etoile' White, single, fragrant flowers with maroon central blotches. *P. coronarius* 'Variegatus' Attractive white-margined green/grey foliage and scented white flowers. Must have light shade and protection from strong midday sun to avoid scorching. Round bushy habit if freestanding but can also be fan-trained. *P.* 'Erectus' Pure white, single, scented flowers, very free-flowering. Distinct upright branches. *P.* 'Galahad' Single, scented, white flowers. Stems mahogany-brown in winter. Rather hard to find. *P.* 'Innocence' Single, white, fragrant flowers. Foliage sometimes has creamy white variegation. *P.* 'Sybille' Almost square, purple-stained, single, white flowers, orange-scented, on arching branches.
Average height and spread
Five years
3 × 3 ft (91 × 91 cm) freestanding
5 × 5 ft (1.5 × 1.5 m) fan-trained
Ten years
5 × 5 ft (1.5 × 1.5 m) freestanding
7 × 7 ft (2.1 × 2.1 m) fan-trained
Twenty years
5 × 6 ft (1.5 × 1.8 m) freestanding
9 × 9 ft (2.7 × 2.7 m) fan-trained
Protrudes up to 3 ft (91 cm) from support if fan-trained, 6 ft (1.8 m) untrained.

PHILADELPHUS
(Tall-growing Forms)

MOCK ORANGE, SYRINGA

Philadelphaceae **Wall Shrub**
Deciduous

These fragrant, summer-flowering shrubs make a spectacular display on walls and fences.

Origin Most varieties of garden origin.
Use As large, freestanding shrubs to be planted adjacent to walls or fences or for fan-training.
Description *Flower* Single or double, depending on variety, very fragrant, ¾–1½ in (2–4 cm) wide, white with purple throat markings, borne in clusters in early to mid summer. *Foliage* Leaves ovate, 1½–4 in (4–10 cm) long, slightly tooth-edged, light to mid green, good yellow autumn colour. Some varieties with golden foliage. *Stem* Forms an upright, round-topped shrub or large fan-trained specimen. Grey/green. Fast growth rate. *Fruit* Insignificant.
Hardiness Tolerates a minimum winter temperature of 4°F (−15°C).
Soil requirements Most soils, including alkaline and acid types.
Sun/Shade aspect Tolerates all aspects in full sun through to medium shade.
Pruning Remove one third of old flowering

wood to ground level annually after flowering on plants established three years or more.
Training Will require tying to wires or individual anchor points if grown fan-trained.
Propagation and nursery production From semi-ripe cuttings taken in early summer or hardwood cuttings in winter. Plant bare-rooted or container grown from garden centres and nurseries; best planting height 15 in–3 ft (38–91 cm).
Problems Harbours blackfly which can transfer to other plants.
Forms of interest *P.* 'Beauclerk' Large, somewhat square, fragrant, single, white flowers with pink centres. *P.* 'Burfordensis' Large, fragrant, semi-double, white flowers with yellow stamens. More upright in growth than most. *P.* 'Burkwoodii' Very fragrant, single, cup-shaped white flowers with pink-stained centres. *P. coronarius* Single, white to creamy white, scented flowers. The form from which many garden hybrids derived. *P.* 'Aureus' Single, white, scented flowers, somewhat obscured by lime green to golden-yellow foliage, which is susceptible to late frost damage and strong summer sun scorching. Plant in light dappled shade – in deeper shade foliage turns green. *P.* 'Minnesota Snowflake' Large, double, fragrant, white flowers, weighing down branches. *P.* 'Norma' Single, large, white flowers, less fragrant than most, on long arching branches. *P.* 'Virginal' Fragrant, pure white, double flowers up to 1½ in (4 cm) across, covering upright branches in mid summer. The most popular variety. It is worth looking out for a very rare variegated form, *P.* 'Virginal Variegata'. *P.* 'Voie Lactée' Strong-growing, broad-petalled, pure white, single, scented flowers up to 2 in (5 cm) across.
Average height and spread
Five years
5 × 3 ft (1.5 m × 91 cm)
freestanding
5 × 5 ft (1.5 × 1.5 m)
fan-trained
Ten years
8 × 6 ft (2.4 × 1.8 m)
freestanding
8 × 8 ft (2.4 × 2.4 m)
fan-trained
Twenty years
13 × 13 ft (4 × 4 m) freestanding
15 × 15 ft (4.6 × 4.6 m) fan-trained
Protrudes up to 4 ft (1.2 m) from support if fan-trained, 12 ft (3.7 m) untrained.

PHILLYREA

JASMINE BOX

Oleaceae **Wall Shrub**
Evergreen

A group of evergreen shrubs with small but fragrant spring flowers adapting well to fan training which shows off their elegant evergreen foliage to the full.

Origin From Africa, southern Europe and the Mediterranean regions.
Use As a large, fan-trained or freestanding shrub for large walls and fences.
Description *Flower* Small, tubular, 1 in (2.5 cm) fragrant flowers, borne in clusters 5 in (12 cm) long on mature shrubs in late spring/early summer. *Foliage* Leaves ovate to lanceolate, small or medium-sized, 2–5 in (5–12 cm) long and ½–¾ (1–2 cm) wide, leathery textured. Dark glossy green upper surfaces, duller glabrous undersides. *Stem* Branching from an early age to form a dome-shaped or fan-trained specimen. Light olive-green to green/brown. Medium growth rate. *Fruit* Small, oval, purple to purple/black fruits in autumn.
Hardiness Tolerates a minimum winter temperature of 4°F (−15°C)
Soil requirements Tolerates most soils but distressed by extremely alkaline or very wet conditions.
Sun/Shade aspect Tolerates all but the most severe of aspects. Prefers light shade, tolerates full sun to medium shade.

Pruning None required but may be clipped and shaped.

Training Will require tying to wires or individual anchor points if grown fan-trained.

Propagation and nursery production From semi-ripe cuttings taken in early summer. Purchase container-grown; normally available from specialist nurseries but becoming more widely stocked. Best planting height 15 in–2½ ft (38–76 cm).

Problems Young plants when purchased often look misshapen and require time to develop.

Forms of interest *P. angustifolia* Flowers creamy yellow, fragrant, produced in clusters at leaf axils in late spring, early summer on mature shrubs. Foliage narrow ovate, 1½–2 in (4–5 cm) long, mid grey/green, lighter green when young. Very good for coastal planting. *P. decora* (syn. *P. medwediewii*) Small clusters of fragrant white flowers in mid to late spring. Foliage large, ovate to lanceolate, leathery texture, dark glossy green upper surfaces and paler glabrous undersides. The best variety for general garden use. Now classified as

Phillyrea decora

Osmarea decora by some authorities. *P. latifolia* Flowers white, some fragrance, but less interesting than most, borne in late spring, sometimes followed by small, blue/black fruits. Small, glossy green leaves presented opposite each other on arching stems. Slightly less than average height.

Average height and spread
Five years
4 × 4 ft (1.2 × 1.2 m) freestanding
6 × 6 ft (1.8 × 1.8 m) fan-trained
Ten years
6 × 6 ft (1.8 × 1.8 m) freestanding
8 × 8 ft (2.4 × 2.4 m) fan-trained
Twenty years
10 × 10 ft (3 × 3 m) freestanding
12 × 12 ft (3.7 × 3.7 m) fan-trained
Protrudes up to 3 ft (91 cm) from support if fan-trained, 10 ft (3 m) untrained.

PHLOMIS FRUTICOSA

JERUSALEM SAGE

Labiatae   *Wall Shrub*
Evergreen

An attractive, silver-leaved, summer flowering shrub which benefits from the protection of a wall or fence.

Origin From the Mediterranean region.

Use As a loose, open, summer flowering shrub using a wall or fence to give added height and protection.

Description *Flower* Yellow, interestingly shaped flowers up to 2 in (5 cm) wide and 3 in (7.5 cm) long in June and July. *Foliage* Leaves oval, pointed, 3 in (7.5 cm) long and 2 in (5 cm) wide, with grey/green downy surface, giving some yellow autumn colour. *Stem* Upright when young, grey/green and downy, becoming open and straggly with age, forming a loose fan shape. Old growth of less interest. Fast rate of growth in spring, slowing with season. *Fruit* Insignificant.

Phlomis fruticosa **in flower**

Hardiness Tolerates a minimum winter temperature of 14°F (−10°C).

Soil requirements Dry, open soil, dislikes any waterlogging.

Sun/Shade aspect Requires a moderately protected aspect in full sun. Dislikes any degree of shade.

Pruning As the best foliage and flowers are borne on new wood, trim by one-third in late spring to induce new growth.

Training Requires tying to wires on individual anchor points if grown fan-trained or allow to grow freestanding.

Propagation and nursery production From softwood cuttings taken in mid to late summer. Purchase container grown; normally stocked by garden centres and general nurseries. Best planting height 8–18 in (20–45 cm).

Problems May die off in a severe winter so rooted cuttings should be over-wintered under protection to ensure replacements for following spring.

Average height and spread
Five years
3 × 3 ft (91 × 91 cm)
Ten years
3 × 4 ft (91 cm × 1.2 m)
Twenty years
3 × 4 ft (91 cm × 1.2 m)
Protrudes up to 4 ft (1.2 m) from support if fan-trained, 5 ft (1.5 m) untrained.

PHOTINIA × FRASERI 'RED ROBIN'
(*P. glabra* 'Red Robin')

KNOWN BY BOTANICAL NAME

Rosaceae   *Wall Shrub*
Evergreen

An attractive winter foliage shrub not normally considered for its attractive wall-training ability.

Origin From New Zealand and Australia.

Use As a short or tall fan-trained shrub for walls and fences, adapting well to hard pruning to maintain it within a metre of the ground, but exceeding this if required.

Description *Flower* Clusters of 3 in (7.5 cm) long, white flowers in late spring but outside its native environment rarely flowers except in very warm areas. *Foliage* Leaves large, ovate to lanceolate, 4–8 in (10–20 cm) long and 1½–3½ in (4–9 cm) wide, often tooth-edged. Dark glossy green when mature. Young growth, produced from late autumn, starts as dark or brilliant red and increases in intensity through winter into early spring, becoming bronze during mid spring to early summer. *Stem* Upright, becoming branching with age,

forming a close-foliaged, fan-trained wall shrub. Dark green tinged red. Medium growth rate. *Fruit* Rarely fruits outside its native environment or very hot climates, where it produces clusters of red or orange/red fruits.

Hardiness Tolerates a minimum winter temperature of 4°F (−15°C), although young foliage may become slightly misshapen or split in severe cold.

Soil requirements Does well on most soils, only disliking extreme alkalinity.

Sun/Shade aspect Tolerates all but the most severe aspects in full sun to light shade.

Photinia × fraseri 'Red Robin' (juvenile foliage)

Pruning Can be cut hard to maintain within a required area through late spring and early summer. Responds by producing large amounts of new red foliage growth in late summer, autumn and winter.

Training Will require tying to wires or individual anchor points if grown fan-trained.

Propagation and nursery production From semi-ripe cuttings taken in early summer. Purchase container-grown; normally stocked by good garden centres and nurseries. Best planting height 15 in–3 ft (38–91 cm).

Problems Often on sale as a single shoot plant but soon grows thicker.

Similar forms of interest *P. × f.* 'Birmingham' Very dark coppery red to dark red new growth. Slightly broader foliage. Raised in North America. *P. × f.* 'Pink Lady' Foliage pink variegated. An attractive plant for sheltered aspects. *P. glabra* 'Rubens' Foliage

shorter but broader than many of the hybrid types. Can be more reliable in its production of clusters of white flowers followed by red fruits. Young growth and foliage brilliant red in winter and spring. Slightly more tender. From Japan. *P. serrulata* (Chinese Hawthorn) Upright coppery red foliage from mid winter through spring and maintained over a long period. Sometimes bears clusters of white flowers in mid to late spring, followed by red fruits in early autumn.
Average height and spread
Five years
7 × 7 ft (2.1 × 2.1 m)
Ten years
9 × 9 ft (2.7 × 2.7 m)
Twenty years
15 × 15 ft (4.6 × 4.6 m)
Protrudes up to 3 ft (91 cm) from support.

PHOTINIA STRANVAESIA

CHINESE STRANVAESIA

Rosaceae   *Wall Shrub*
Semi-evergreen

An interesting, semi-evergreen, fruiting shrub not always thought of as a potential fan-trained wall shrub.

Origin From western China.
Use As a wall-trained specimen for large walls and fences, where it can display its flowers and berries to the fullest effect.
Description *Flower* Clusters of 3 in (7.5 cm) wide white to off-white flowers borne on wood two years old or more, in early summer. *Foliage* Leaves lanceolate to broad lanceolate, 2–4 in (5–10 cm) long, leathery-textured, mid green with duller, lighter undersides. Some bright red autumn colour, contrasting with remaining semi-evergreen leaves, extent of evergreen depending upon severity of winter. Better foliage on young shoots, decreasing in interest and colour intensity on older wood. *Stem* Upright, vigorous stems, dark green tinged red, becoming spreading and branching with age and will form a good fan-shape with training. Fast growth rate when young, slowing with age. *Fruit* Dull red/orange fruits, resistant to birds, produced in clusters in late summer through to early autumn.
Hardiness Tolerates a minimum winter temperature of 4°F (−15°C) but some stem damage may be suffered.
Soil requirements Does well on most, but performs less well on very poor soils.
Sun/Shade aspect Tolerates most aspects in full sun to medium shade.
Pruning Cut as required for training and from time to time reduce young shoots. Prune shoots more than four years old to ground level in early spring, to induce new, upright,

Photinia stranvaesia 'Palette'

Phygelius capensis 'Coccineus' in flower

very leafy shoots, improve overall appearance and still maintain older fruiting branches.
Training Will require wires or fixing to individual anchor points.
Propagation and nursery production From semi-ripe cuttings taken in early summer or by layering. Purchase container-grown. Some nurseries offer plants from seed, but resulting shrubs can be extremely variable, so check the method of propagation with nursery staff. Availability varies. Best planting height 2–3 ft (60–91 cm).
Problems This shrub and its forms are susceptible to the fungus disease fire blight. Its future is uncertain, since production may be discontinued on this account. Affected shrubs should be destroyed immediately by burning and the appropriate government agency should be notified. Also liable to stem canker fungus, especially older stems, which are strangled by the collar-like effect of the canker.
Similar forms of interest *P. s.* '**Fructu-luteo**' Yellow fruits in autumn but somewhat sparser than the parent. Two thirds average height and spread. *P. s.* '**Palette**' Attractive foliage splashed creamy white or pink. Fruits red. *P. s. var. undulata* Slightly later flowering than the species, but otherwise very similar. Two-thirds average height and equal spread. *P. × stranvinia* '**Redstart**' Foliage red to dark red. Flowers white. Fruits red and yellow.
Average height and spread
Five years
7 × 7 ft (2.1 × 2.1 m)
Ten years
10 × 10 ft (3 × 3 m)
Twenty years
20 × 20 ft (6 × 6 m)
Protrudes up to 4 ft (1.2 m) from support.

PHYGELIUS

CAPE FIGWORT

Scrophulariaceae   *Wall Shrub*
Deciduous

Interesting, late summer flowering sub-shrubs that adapt well to wall conditions.

Origin From South Africa.
Use As a fan-trained or trailing wall shrub for walls, fences and pillars or through shrubs.
Description *Flower* Yellow or orange tubular flowers, up to 1½ in (4 cm) long, hanging from upright panicles, late summer/early autumn. *Foliage* Leaves ovate to lanceolate, 2–3 in (5–7.5 cm) long, tooth-edged, dark glossy green upper surfaces, grey undersides. Some yellow autumn colour. *Stem* Upright shoots may be annually produced after die-back in winter but against a wall or fence may become permanent. Dark green. Fast annual spring and summer growth. *Fruit* Insignificant.
Hardiness Tolerates a minimum winter temperature of 14°F (−10°C).
Soil requirements Does well on all soil types except very dry.
Sun/Shade aspect Requires a sheltered aspect. Prefers full sun, tolerates light shade.
Pruning Should be lightly trimmed in early spring and new growths tied in as they appear.
Training Will require tying to wires or individual anchor points if fan-trained.
Propagation and nursery production From seed or semi-ripe cuttings taken in mid summer. In cold areas young plants may be overwintered under cover in case replacements are needed. Purchase container-grown. Fairly easy to find; yellow-flowering forms less often available. If purchased when in flower keep under cover until next spring. Best planting height 8–15 in (20–38 cm).
Problems As sub-shrubs may die back in winter or become very woody; if so, cut hard back in spring to encourage rejuvenation.
Forms of interest *P. aequalis* '**Yellow Trumpet**' Large, yellow, tubular flowers, up to 1½ in (4 cm) long, hanging from upright panicles, 12–18 in (30–45 cm) in mid summer to early autumn. Light green foliage. May not withstand any frost. *P. capensis* '**Coccineus**' Crimson-scarlet, hanging, tubular flowers, 1 in (2.5 cm) long, produced from terminal panicles 12 in (30 cm) long in late summer, early autumn. *P. c.* '**Indian Chief**' Good-sized red tubular flowers with yellow throats.
Average height and spread
Five years
4 × 4 ft (1.2 × 1.2 m)
Ten years
7 × 7 ft (2.1 × 2.1 m)
Twenty years
8 × 8 ft (2.4 × 2.4 m)
Protrudes up to 2½ ft (76 cm) from support.

PILEOSTEGIA VIBURNOIDES

CLIMBING VIBURNUM

Hydrangeaceae   *Woody Climber*
Evergreen

An interesting climbing evergreen if given adequate protection.

Origin From China, Taiwan and India.
Use For covering large walls and fences where it can be trained in a fan shape.
Description *Flower* Many small flowers, creamy-white in bud, opening to white, with prominent stamens in the centre. Carried in panicles up to 4–6 in (10–15 cm) long at ends of shoots during late summer to early autumn. *Foliage* Narrow oblong or lanceolate leaves 2½–6 in (6–15 cm) long. Leathery in texture, dark green above with pitted· silver underside and prominent veins. *Stem* Green ageing to brown. Slow to medium rate of growth. Aerial roots on underside. *Fruit* No fruits of interest.
Hardiness Tolerates a minimum winter temperature of 14°F (−10°C). Foliage may be damaged by severe winter chill.
Soil requirements Does well on all soil types with no particular preference, except needing adequate moisture.
Sun/Shade aspect Does well on all aspects, only disliking extreme degrees of wind chill and draught. Full sun to light shade with no particular preference.

Pileostegia viburnoides **in flower**

Pruning Normally does not require pruning, but can be retained within an area by cutting back the offending shoots in early spring.
Training Best fan-trained, using individual pins or wires to train branches or canes. Clings by aerial roots which need additional support when young and when plants become heavy with age, particularly during snowfalls.
Propagation and nursery production From semi-ripe cuttings taken in early to mid summer or self-produced layers. Always purchase container grown; will have to be sought from specialist nurseries. Best planting height 9–18 in (23–45 cm).
Problems Some foliage may be damaged by severe winters. This is normally replaced the following spring. Slow to establish, taking up to five years to become a plant of any substance.
Similar forms of interest. None.
Average height and spread
Five years
3 × 3 ft (91 × 91 cm)
Ten years
6 × 6 ft (1.8 × 1.8 m)
Twenty years
18 × 18 ft (5.5 × 5.5 m)
Protrudes up to 2 ft (60 cm) from support.

Piptanthus laburnifolius **in flower**

PIPTANTHUS LABURNIFOLIUS
(*P. nepalensis*)

EVERGREEN LABURNUM

Leguminosae   *Wall Shrub*
Evergreen

An interesting evergreen shrub, particularly useful as a wall specimen.

Origin From the Himalayas.
Use As a fan-trained or spreading specimen for walls and fences.
Description *Flower* Bright yellow pea-flowers in 4 in (10 cm) long, 2 in (5 cm) wide racemes, in mid to late spring. *Foliage* Leaves trifoliate, 3–6 in (7.5–15 cm) long, with dark glossy green upper surfaces and duller undersides. Old leaves drop in autumn giving some good autumn colour. *Stem* Upright with some branching, forming a narrow-based, wide-headed, fan-shaped shrub. Dark glossy green. Medium growth rate. *Fruit* Medium to long pea-pods, grey to grey/brown in autumn and winter.
Hardiness Tolerates a minimum winter temperature of 14°F (−10°C) but may be defoliated in severe winters, with some stem die-back.
Soil requirements Prefers a well-drained soil but accepts most, tolerating high alkalinity.
Sun/Shade aspect Tolerates all but the most exposed aspects in full sun or shade, but may be slightly taller in shade.
Pruning Each year shorten back one or two stems on established shrubs after flowering to encourage new wood.
Training Will require tying to wires or individual anchor points if grown fan-trained or allow to grow freestanding.
Propagation and nursery production From seed. Purchase container grown; easy to find in some areas, otherwise obtainable from specialist nurseries. Best planting height 15 in–2½ ft (38–76 cm).
Problems Apart from possible winter die-back, occasional shoots can die from drought, waterlogging, or mechanical damage to roots.
Average height and spread
Five years
6 × 5 ft (1.8 × 1.5 m)
Ten years
10 × 8 ft (3 × 2.4 m)
Twenty years
13 × 12 ft (4 × 3.7 m)
Protrudes up to 2½ ft (76 cm) or more from support if fan-trained, 6 ft (1.8 m) untrained.

PITTOSPORUM

PITTOSPORIUM, KOHUHA

Pittosporaceae   *Wall Shrub*
Evergreen

Attractive foliage shrubs, in most areas benefiting from the protection of a wall or fence.

Origin From New Zealand.
Use As freestanding shrubs to be grown adjacent to walls and fences, both in the open and in the protection of conservatories and greenhouses. Foliage useful for flower arranging.
Description *Flower* Small, ¼–½ in (5 mm–1 cm) wide, unusual, chocolate brown to purple, honey-scented flowers in late spring, only on very mature shrubs in favourable areas. *Foliage* Leaves ovate to oblong, 1–2½ in (3–6 cm) long, glossy, thick textured, in varying shades of olive-green, purple, silver, gold or variegated. *Stem* Upright stems, becoming branching and twiggy with age, forming an upright, pyramidal shrub. Dark brown to almost black. Medium growth rate. *Fruit* Insignificant.
Hardiness Tolerates a minimum winter temperature of 23°F (−5°C).
Soil requirements Well-drained soil.

Pittosporum tenuifolium

Sun/Shade aspect Requires a sheltered, protected aspect in full sun to very light shade.
Pruning None required but can be trimmed quite harshly in early spring. If cut to ground level will rejuvenate.
Training Normally freestanding and requires no additional support.
Propagation and nursery production From semi-ripe cuttings taken in early summer. Purchase container grown; easy to find, especially in mild coastal areas. Best planting height 1–3 ft (30–91 cm).
Problems Often purchased in mild coastal areas and taken inland for planting in the open, where it rarely succeeds.

Pittosporum tenuifolium 'Wendle Channon'

Forms of interest *P.* 'Margaret Turnbull' Mid green foliage edged with yellow. *P. tenuifolium* Attractive grey/green foliage, leaves slightly twisted with good black twigs. Flowers well in mild areas. One of the hardiest forms. *P. t.* 'Garnettii' Round, white-variegated leaves, flushed pink in winter. One of the hardiest of variegated forms. Slightly less than average height and

Pittosporum tenuifolium 'Purpureum'

spread. Of garden origin. *P. t.* 'Irene Paterson' Marbled, creamy white foliage. Interesting leaf display, forming a slightly rounder shrub than most. Half average height and spread. *P. t.* 'James Stirling' Small, silver/green, rounded or oval leaves, very densely presented on black/purple twigs. Tender and will not withstand frost. Slightly less than average height and spread. *P. t.* 'Purpureum' Young pale green leaves turning to deep bronze/purple, ageing to purple/green, giving an outer canopy of good purple foli-

age. Two thirds average height and spread. *P. t.* 'Saundersii' Foliage golden variegated. *P. t.* 'Silver Queen' Narrow, ovate leaves, pointed and tightly bunched on black stems, forming a neat, conical shape. Foliage variegated silver/grey, black twigs. Two thirds average height and spread. *P. t.* 'Tresederi' Amber leaves, mottled gold when young. *P. t.* 'Warnham Gold' Yellow to yellow/green young foliage, ageing to golden yellow. Half average height and spread. Of garden origin. *P. t.* 'Wendle Channon' Attractive mid to dark green foliage with yellow edging ageing to off-white, sometimes gold. *P. tobira* (Japanese pittosporum, tobiri pittosporum) Large, obovate, bright glossy green leaves, presented in whorls, bearing orange-blossom scented, creamy-coloured flowers in mid summer. Good in mild coastal areas; in less favourable conditions use as a conservatory specimen. Two thirds average height and spread. From China, Taiwan and Japan, now frequently seen in southern Europe. *P. t.* 'Variegatum' Variegation irregular, with creamy white margins and central patches. Needs a favourable, mild location. In colder areas use as a conservatory shrub.

Average height and spread
Five years
5 × 3 ft (1.5 m × 91 cm)
Ten years
10 × 6 ft (3 × 1.8 m)
Twenty years
20 × 10 ft (6 × 3 m)
Protrudes up to 8 ft (2.4 m) from wall or fence.

PLUMBAGO CAPENSIS

BLUE PLUMBAGO, PLUMBAGO, CAPE LEADWORT

Plumbaginaeceae   **Tender Greenhouse Climber**

Deciduous

A well distributed climber with attractive flowers but requiring greenhouse or conservatory protection in winter.

Origin From South Africa.
Use As a large climbing shrub for conservatories and greenhouses, either in large containers or planted into greenhouse beds.
Description *Flower* Large panicles up to 5 in (12 cm) across, consisting of numerous ½ in (1 cm) wide, five-petalled flowers of a delicate

pale blue from April to November. Clusters supported on flower shoots up to 4–6 in (10–15 cm) long. *Foliage* Light grey/green, elliptic, pointed, soft in texture. Some yellow autumn colour. *Stem* Light green to grey/green. Upright, branching, twiggy. Not self-clinging or supporting after 3 ft (91 cm) in height. Medium to fast rate of growth. *Fruit* No fruit of interest.
Hardiness Tolerates a minimum winter temperature of 32°F (0°C). Requires the protection of conservatory or greenhouse in areas experiencing frost.
Soil requirements No particular preference. If planted in greenhouse beds, additional grit, sand and sedge peat should be added in liberal quantities. If grown in containers, a good-quality proprietary soil-based potting compost should be used.
Sun/Shade aspect Needs the protection of a conservatory or greenhouse in all but the most favourable of areas. Can be grown in containers, given winter protection and moved out in spring or summer. Prefers light shade but will tolerate a wide range of sun/shade conditions, except for deep shade.
Pruning Shorten back flowering shoots after flowering to encourage new production for following year's blooms. Thin main branches once area required has been covered. Can be cut hard back if required and will rejuvenate.
Training Secure to wires or individual anchor points.
Propagation and nursery production From semi-ripe cuttings taken late spring/early summer and rooted by providing some bottom heat in a propagating frame. Best purchased container grown at a height of 6 in–3 ft (15–91 cm). Will have to be sought from specialist nurseries or from florists where it is sold as a house plant when in flower in late summer.
Problems Requires a large root run or large container. Top growth can quickly outgrow the space it is intended for; pruning will control it to a certain extent, but it can become invasive. Can be attacked by whitefly.
Similar forms of interest *P. c.* 'Alba' Pure white flowers. Scarce. More tender.
Average height and spread
Five years
5 × 5 ft (1.5 × 1.5 m)
Ten years
8 × 8 ft (2.4 × 2.4 m)
Twenty years
16 × 16 ft (4.9 × 4.9 m)
Protrudes up to 2 ft (60 cm) from support.

Plumbago capensis in flower

POLYGONUM BALDSCHUANICUM

RUSSIAN VINE, MILE A MINUTE
Polygonaceae   *Woody Climber*
Deciduous
Possibly one of the quickest growing of all climbing plants, even to the extent of becoming invasive.

Origin From south-eastern USSR.
Use As a fast-growing climber for walls, fences and to grow through trees or large shrubs. Ideal for covering an ugly building.
Description *Flower* Small white flowers in panicles 10–18 in (25–45 cm) long and 3 in (7.5 cm) wide entirely covering the whole framework of branches from late summer to early autumn and then ageing to pink and finally brown by mid winter. *Foliage* Oval-shaped, up to 2 in (5 cm) long and 1 in (2.5 cm) wide. Light green, ageing to a yellow/green with veins and edges turning to orange/brown, then good autumn colour of yellow and bronze. *Stem* Smooth, light grey/green when young, ageing to light brown and finally dark grey/brown. Loosely twining and very fast growing – can make up to 15 ft (4.6 m) of growth in one season. *Fruit* The ageing flowers, as they turn brown, are retained as seed heads and have some attraction in certain winter light.
Hardiness Tolerates a minimum winter temperature of 0°F (−18°C).
Soil requirements Does well on all soil types, only disliking extremely dry types when first planted.
Sun/Shade aspect Does well in all aspects, including very exposed. Full sun to medium shade, although will flower best in a sunny position.
Pruning Requires no pruning for its own well being but often needs containing within an allotted area. Prune back in early spring.
Training Not self-clinging but its loose, twining habit secures it to wires, trellis, open fences or through the branches of trees and large shrubs. Normally needs no other form of support.
Propagation and nursery production From seed or semi-ripe cuttings taken in summer. Can also be produced from hardwood cuttings taken in winter. Always purchase container grown, normally available from good

Poncirus trifoliata **in flower**

garden centres and nurseries. Best planting height 2–4 ft (60 cm–1.2 m).
Problems Almost always underestimated for its rate and spread of growth. This variety is often confused in commercial horticulture with *P. aubertii*.
Similar forms of interest *P. aubertii* (Silver lace or fleece vine) A variety flowering in mid summer, otherwise indistinct.
Average height and spread
Five years
20 × 20 ft (6 × 6 m)
Ten years
40 × 40 ft (12.2 × 12.2 m)
Twenty years
60 × 60 ft (18.3 × 18.3 m)
Protrudes up to 2 ft (60 cm) from support.

PONCIRUS TRIFOLIATA
(*Citrus trifoliata*)

HARDY ORANGE, JAPANESE BITTER ORANGE, TRIFOLIATE ORANGE
Rutaceae   *Wall Shrub*
Deciduous
An interesting shrub forming a round, rigid, architectural shape with attractive scented flowers and yellow autumn fruit. Now referred to by some authorities as *Aegle sepiara*.

Origin From northern China.
Use As a freestanding or fan-trained shrub of interest for walls and fences.
Description *Flower* Very sweetly scented, white, orange-blossom type flowers 1½–2 in (4–5 cm) across in mid to late spring. *Foliage* Leaves somewhat sparsely presented, obovate, 1–2½ in (2.5–6 cm) long, light, bright green, yellow autumn colour. *Stem* Branching, stout, armed with spines 1 in (2.5 cm) long, grey to bright green. Forms a ball-shaped shrub or can be fan-trained. Slow growth rate. *Fruit* Green, ripening to yellow, globular, miniature orange fruits 1½–1¾ in (4–4.5 cm) across.
Hardiness Tolerates a minimum winter temperature of 14°F (−10°C).
Soil requirements Well-drained, open, light soil, tolerates alkaline and acid types.
Sun/Shade aspect Tolerates all but the most severe of aspects in full sun to light shade.
Pruning None required.
Training Free-standing or, if fan-trained, will require wires or individual anchor points.
Propagation and nursery production From seed. Purchase container grown from specialist nurseries. Best planting height 8–18 in (20–45 cm).
Problems Relatively short-lived, can deteriorate after 25 years. Dislikes soil cultivation close to roots.
Average height and spread
Five years
3 × 3 ft (91 × 91 cm)
Ten years
6 × 6 ft (1.8 × 1.8 m)
Twenty years
10 × 10 ft (3 × 3 m)
Protrudes up to 2 ft (60 cm) from support if fan-trained, 6 ft (1.8 m) untrained.

Polygonum baldshuanicum **in flower**

PRUNUS ARMENIACA
(Apricot Hybrids)

APRICOT

Rosaceae   *Fruit Tree*
Deciduous

A fruiting tree that benefits greatly from
being grown against a warm wall or fence,
possibly the only location in which it will
produce any fruit of use, other than under
protection.

Origin From China.
Use As a fan-trained tree for large walls and
fences, both in the open and under the protection of conservatory or greenhouse.
Description *Flower* Five-petalled, 1 in (2.5 cm)
wide, saucer-shaped pink flowers produced in
clusters on short spurs on the naked branches
in early spring. Self fertile. *Foliage* Oval, 3 in
(7.5 cm) long by 2 in (5 cm) wide, dark green
with some yellow autumn colour. *Stem* Mid
green when young, quickly ageing to
mahogany brown. Shiny, attractive, rigid.
Medium rate of growth. *Fruit* Edible, round,
yellow flushed, sweet-flavoured, with a stone.
Hardiness Tolerates a minimum winter temperature of 4°F (−15°C).
Soil requirements Tolerates all types, but
prefers an alkaline soil. Requires large
amounts of organic compost applied prior to
planting and an annual mulch to achieve best
results.
Sun/Shade aspect Requires a sheltered aspect. Full sun or fruits will not ripen.
Pruning Remove old fruiting shoots in
autumn and avoid pruning at other times.
Training Purchase already fan-trained and tie
to wires and individual anchor points.
Propagation and nursery production From
grafting or budding of chosen variety on to a
seedling understock. Seedling understocks do
not control vigour or ultimate size. Best size
to purchase: minimum of five pre-trained
shoots, overall size 3–5 ft (91 cm–1.5 m). Can
be planted bare-root from mid autumn to
early spring or container grown as available,
with autumn and winter for preference.
Problems May suffer attacks of silver leaf
disease, so take care not to prune other than
in autumn. Severe attacks of blackfly may
occur; control with a proprietary spray.
Mildew may be another problem. Some
bleeding on established plants may be found;
normally this is a sign of extreme age and im-
pending demise.
Forms of interest
UK
'Alfred' A canadian variety with mid summer
fruiting. 'Farmindale' A Canadian variety
which is gaining in popularity. Mid summer
fruiting. 'Moorpark' Possibly the best variety
to attempt. Mid to late summer.
USA
All varieties are self-fertile unless otherwise
stated but pollination is improved by planting
two varieties. **'Blenheim'** ('Royal') A very
good variety for eating or drying. Used ex-
tensively in California for canning. Medium
sized, dull orange fruit. May produce green
shoulders to the fruit which is detrimental.
Can only tolerate temperatures up to 90°F at
harvesting stage. From the UK. **'Chinese'**
('Morman') A good variety for the West
Coast and cooler regions. Late flowering
allows blossom to escape the worst of spring
frosts. Heavy crops of small, sweet, juicy
fruit. From Utah. **'Flora Gold'** A dwarf-
growing variety. Medium-sized, good quality
fruit. Used as a dessert and also for canning.
Heavy cropping. Requires relatively cool conditions when at harvest stage. From California. **'Goldcot'** A hardy variety which will
survive temperatures down to −20°F. Late
flowering and late cropping. Good in Eastern
and Midwestern states. Produce medium to
large-sized, good flavoured fruit with tough
skins. Good for canning or for dessert. From
Michigan. **'Harcot'** A variety for cool conditions, late flowering but earlier ripening than
most. Heavy crops of large to medium good
flavoured fruits, on good-shaped, compact

Prunus armeniaca 'Moorpark'

trees. Resistant to bacterial spot and brown
rot. From Ontario, Canada. **'Harogem'**
Fruits shaded bright red over an orange background. Small to medium-sized with firm
flesh. Mid-season ripening and good long-
lasting qualities, once picked. The tree is
resistant to perennial canker and brown spot.
From Ontario, Canada. **'Moorpark'** Large
orange fruit with deep blush shading. Orange
flesh with good flavour and scent. Thought by
many to be the best variety and is the most
reliable for all areas. From the UK. **'Perfection'** ('Goldbeck') Very large, light orange-
yellow, oval fruits. Flesh bright orange and of
moderate quality. Strong-growing tree,
flowering early and therefore possibly frost-
prone. Requires another variety for pollination to be grown with it. Crops possibly
light. Good for the South and West. From
Washington. **'Rival'** Large, firm, mild-flavoured fruit, heavily blushed. Good variety
for canning. Tree large and spreading. Use
'Perfection' as a pollinating variety. Good in
Northwestern States. From Washington.
'Royal Rosa' Bright yellow, firm-fleshed fruit
with strong aromatic scent and tart to sweet
flavour. Best eaten fresh from the tree. Large
crops. Medium-sized, early in its fruiting.
Good in Southern States. From California.
'Scout' Medium to large bronze-skinned fruit
with deep yellow flesh. Good as dessert, for
canning or as jam. Trees strong-growing, upright in habit and hardy. Midsummer
fruiting, good in the Midwest. From Mani-
toba, Canada. **'Sungold'** Round, medium-
sized, tender fruit with a golden skin, blushed
orange. Mild, sweet flavour. Good as dessert
or for jam. Strong-growing, upright habit,
medium-sized tree. Good in all areas and
zones. From Minnesota. **'Tilton'** Yellow-
orange fruit, can tolerate high temperatures.
It has a high-chill requirement of over
1,000 hours below 45°F. From California.
'Wenatchee' Large, oval fruit with orange-
yellow skin and flesh of good flavour. Trees
have a lifespan of up to 30 years. Good on the
Pacific Northwest coast and in the West.
From Washington.
Average height and spread
Five years
7 × 7 ft (2.1 × 2.1 m)
Ten years
15 × 15 ft (4.6 × 4.6 m)
Twenty years
15 × 20 ft (4.6 × 6 m)
Protrudes up to 2½ ft (76 cm) from support.

PRUNUS AVIUM,
P. CERASUS, P. MAHALEB
(Fruiting Cherry Hybrids)

FRUITING CHERRIES

Rosaceae   *Fruit Trees*
Deciduous

The fan-training of cherries on walls will
aid the ripening of the fruit and will help
protect it from the ravages of birds.

Origin Of nursery origin.
Use As fan-trained trees with edible fruits for
large walls and fences.
Description *Flower* Five-petalled, ½–¾ in
(1–2 cm) wide, saucer-shaped white flowers in
mid spring. Carried in clusters at leaf joints
on mature wood. *Foliage* Oval, 4 in (10 cm)
long and 2 in (5 cm) wide, mid to dark green.
Some yellow autumn colour. *Stem* Brown
when young, ageing to brown/grey, finally
grey. Strong, unbranching. Medium to fast
growth rate. *Fruit* Clusters of round, white,
red or black stoned fruits in mid to late
summer depending on variety.
Hardiness Tolerates a minimum winter temperature of 4°F (−15°C).
Soil requirements Tolerates all soil conditions, except very waterlogged. Ideal for
alkaline soils.
Sun/Shade aspect Tolerates all aspects, but
fruit ripens best in full sun.
Pruning Normally not required other than the
removal of dead or crossing branches. This is
best carried out in late summer/early autumn
to avoid attacks of silver leaf.
Training Purchase fan-trained trees and tie to
wire or individual anchor points.
Propagation and nursery production From
grafting or budding of a main variety on to a
seedling understock. Seedling understocks do
not control vigour or ultimate size but some
dwarfing rootstocks which do are now
available. Best size to purchase: minimum of
five pre-trained shoots, overall size 3–5 ft
(91 cm–1.5 m). Can be planted bare-rooted
from mid autumn to early spring, or
container grown as available, with autumn
and winter for preference.
Problems Susceptible to silver leaf. Fruit
often ravaged by birds and once ripe requires
netting to protect.

113

Forms of interest
UK
More than one variety normally has to be used for pollination. The letters A–N indicate suitable pollinating varieties.

DESSERT CHERRIES **A 'Early Rivers'** Pollinator J. Heart-shaped black fruits with rich flavour and tender flesh. **B 'Florence'** Pollinators E, L. Heart-shaped white fruits with sweet flavour. Late summer. **C 'Frogmore'** Pollinators D, I, J, L, M. Round white fruits with good flavour. A well established variety. Mid summer. **D 'Governor Wood'** Pollinators C, E, F, G, I, L, M, H, K. Round white fruits of good flavour. Mid summer. **E. 'Kent Bigarreau'** Pollinators F, G, D, B, I. Round white fruits of good flavour. Mid to late summer. **F 'Merton Bigareau'** Pollinators D, E, I, J, L, M, K. Round black fruits of good colour. Mid summer. **G 'Merton Bounty'** Pollinators D, E, I, J, L, M, K. Black fruits. Mid summer. Can be used as a universal pollinator. **H 'Merton Crane'** Pollinators D, I, K. Round black fruits with good flavour. Mid summer. **I 'Merton Glory'** Pollinators F, G, D, C, E, J, L, M. White fruits. Mid summer. Can be used as a universal pollinator. **J 'Merton Heart'** Pollinators A, C, F, G, I, M. Heart-shaped black fruit with good flavour. Early to mid summer. **K 'Merton Late'** Pollinators D, F, G, H. White fruits of good flavour. Mid to late summer. **L 'Napoleon Bigarreau'** Pollinators B, C, D, F, G, I. White fruits. Late summer. A well established variety. **M 'Roundel'** Pollinators C, D, F, I, J, L. Black fruits. Mid summer.

SELF-FERTILE VARIETIES **'Stella'** Large red fruits with firm flesh. Mid summer. Can be used as a universal pollinator. **'Van'** Large red fruits with sweet flavour. Mid summer. Fruits at only three years old and is very hardy. **'Morello'** Fruits with an acid flavour, ideal for culinary purposes. A universal pollinator except for 'Early Rivers' and 'Merton Heart'.

USA
EARLY SEASON VARIETIES **'Black Tartarian'** Medium-sized, sweet black cherry. Early to fruit. A useful pollinator for many other varieties and easily pollinated itself. Good for all areas. From California. **'May Duke'** Dark red fruit of medium size with very good flavour. Best used for cooking or preserving. Most other varieties of cherry will pollinate it and it is a good pollinator for other varieties. Good for the Western states. From France. **'Northstar'** A morello-type, sour cherry of dwarf constitution. Red fruit and flesh, rarely cracking, presented on a small yet vigorous and hardy tree. Resists diseases such as brown rot. Self fertile. Good for all areas. From Minnesota. **'Sam'** Medium to large sweet, black fruits which are juicy and firm. Good dessert variety. Use varieties 'Bing', 'Lam-

Prunus 'Morello Cherry' in autumn

bert' or 'Van' as pollinators. Very vigorous and heavy cropping. Good for the North and West. From British Columbia, Canada.

MID SEASON VARIETIES **'Bing'** Heavy crops of sweet, juicy, black cherries. May suffer from bacterial leaf spot in humid climates. Use varieties 'Sam', 'Van' or 'Black Tartarian' as pollinators. Good for the West. From Oregon. **'Chinook'** Large, sweet, heart-shaped fruit with mahogany skin and deep red flesh. Produces good crops. Use varieties 'Bing', 'Sam' or 'Van' as pollinators. Good in Western states. From Washington. **'Corum'** A sweet cherry particularly good for pollinating the variety 'Royal Ann'. Fruit yellow, sweet and firm. Use 'Royal Ann', 'Sam' or 'Van' as pollinators. Extremely good in Western areas. From Oregon. **'Emperor Francis'** Large, yellow blushed cherry red. Firm, sweet flesh. Heavy cropping and hardy stature. Use 'Rainier' or 'Hedelfingen' as pollinators. Particularly good in the North. From Europe. **'Garden Bing'** Sweet, dark red fruit. A dwarf form of the variety 'Bing', not reaching more than 8 ft (2.4 m) in height. Self-fertile. Good in Western areas. From California. **'Kansas Sweet'** ('Hansen Sweet') A sweet form of the pie cherry. Fruit red with a firm flesh. Best used for pies, where it has a fresh flavour. Both blossom and tree are hardy in Kansas. Self-fertile. From Kansas. **'Meteor'** A dwarf amarelle sour cherry, only

reaches up to 10 ft (3 m). Large, bright red fruit with yellow flesh. Good for pies. Very hardy but tolerating milder conditions well. Self-fertile. Good in all areas. From Minnesota. **'Montmorency'** A sour cherry for both commercial and home use. Brilliant red fruits with yellow, firm flesh. Self-fertile. Good in all areas. From France. **'Rainier'** Fruit blushed yellow with firm, sweet, juicy flesh. Use 'Bing', 'Sam' or 'Van' as pollinators. Ideal for the South and West. From Washington. **'Royal Ann'** ('Napoleon') Blushed yellow fruits with firm juicy flesh. Mostly used commercially for candies and maraschino cherries. Not entirely hardy. Use 'Corum', 'Windsor' or 'Hedelfingen' as pollinators. Good in all areas. From France. **'Schmidt'** Large, mahogany coloured fruit with thick skin and wine-red sweet flesh. Fruit buds may suffer from spring frosts. Use 'Bing', 'Lambert' or 'Royal Ann' as pollinators. Good for the North and South. From Germany. **'Stella'** Large red fruits with firm flesh. A strong-growing tree. Self-fertile and can be used as a universal pollinator. From the UK. **'Van'** Large red fruits with sweet flavour. Fruits at only three years old and is very hardy. From the UK.

LATE SEASON VARIETIES **'Angela'** Large, sweet, dark red fruits. The tree is vigorous and produces large crops. Use 'Emperor Francis' or 'Lambert' as pollinators. From Utah. **'Black Republican'** ('Black Oregon') Very dark, sweet, firm fruits. Heavy cropping. Any other variety of cherry will act as a pollinator. From Oregon. **'Hedelfingen'** Medium sized, sweet dark fruits with firm flesh. Very heavy cropping. Any sweet cherry variety will act as pollinator. Good for North and South. From Germany. **'Lambert'** Large, dark, sweet fruits. Use 'Van' or 'Rainier' as pollinators. Good in all areas. From British Columbia, Canada. **'Late Duke'** Large, light red fruits. Best for cooking or preserving. Normally self-fertile but in colder climates requires any other sour variety to pollinate. Good for the West. From France. **'Morello'** Black fruits with acid flavour, ideal for culinary purposes. Good in cold locations. From the UK. **'Windsor'** Small, sweet, dark red fruits. Often succeeds where other varieties may fail. Any sweet variety will pollinate with the exception of 'Van' and 'Emperor Francis'. Ideal for easterly areas as well as North and South. Origin unknown.

Average height and spread
Five years
7 × 7 ft (2.1 × 2.1 m)
Ten years
15 × 12 ft (4.6 × 3.7 m)
Twenty years
15 × 18 ft (4.6 × 5.5 m)
Protrudes up to 3 ft (91 cm) from support.

Prunus 'Morello Cherry' in fruit

PRUNUS DOMESTICA
(Damson Hybrids)

DAMSON

Rosaceae **Fruit Tree**
Deciduous

As long as adequate space can be given, damsons make extremely fine fan-trained specimens, the ripening of the fruit being enhanced by the warmth afforded by the wall.

Origin Most hybrids of garden origin.
Use As a large fan-trained tree for walls and fences.
Description *Flower* Five-petalled, 1 in (2.5 cm) wide white flowers in profusion in mid spring. Plums can be used to pollinate and corresponding numbers of both plums or damsons can be considered. *Foliage* Oval, 1½–2 in (4–5 cm) and ¾ (2 cm) wide, mid to dark grey/green with some yellow autumn colour of attraction. *Stem* Twiggy, branching. Green/brown when young, becoming mahogany brown with age. Medium growth rate. *Fruit* Round to oval, blue skinned, yellow flesh with stones. Sweet and juicy when ripe.
Hardiness Tolerates a minimum winter temperature of 0°F (−18°C) but flowers may be damaged by spring frosts.
Soil requirements Tolerates all soil conditions, responding particularly well to alkaline types.
Sun/Shade aspect Tolerates all aspects but benefits from some protection from wind to encourage pollinating insects. Full sun to enhance ripening, but will tolerate light shade.
Pruning Rarely requires pruning other than removal of dead, damaged or crossing branches in late summer/early autumn.
Training One-year-old trees should be cut to within 12 in (30 cm) of graft union and will make up to three to five new shoots. These can then be trained into a fan shape. Trees can be purchased pre-trained, which is possibly the best solution. Will require wires or individual anchor points for support.
Propagation and nursery production From grafting or budding on to 'St Julien A' rootstock. Can be planted bare-rooted from mid autumn to early spring or container grown as available. Purchase one-year-old trees of 2½–4 ft (76 cm–1.2 m) or pre-trained trees with not less than five branches up to 3–4 ft (91 cm–1.2 m). Not readily available either as one-year-old or pre-trained trees and will have to be sought from specialist nurseries.

Prunus domestica (greengage) in flower

Problems Suffers from attacks of silver leaf. May take up to five to eight years to come into full fruit production.
Forms of interest 'Farleigh Damson' (2) Mid autumn. When in full crop, large numbers of small blue-black fruits with very good flavour. Can be used either as a dessert or cooking damson. Most other varieties of plum, if in flower at the correct time, will pollinate this variety. **'Merryweather'** (3) Early to mid autumn. The main variety worthy of consideration and often the only variety available. Large, blue/black fruits with good damson flavour. Sweet and juicy. Self-fertile but benefits from additional pollination from other plum varieties. **'Shropshire Prune'** (Prune Damson) (5) Oval, blue/black fruits. Very good flavour, particularly when cooked. Reliable cropper.

Average height and spread
Five years
8 × 8 ft (2.4 × 2.4 m)
Ten years
12 × 12 ft (3.7 × 3.7 m)
Twenty years
15 × 15 ft (4.6 × 4.6 m)
Protrudes up to 3 ft (91 cm) from support.

PRUNUS DOMESTICA
(Gage Hybrids)

GAGES, GREENGAGES

Rosaceae **Fruit Tree**
Deciduous

Attractive flowering and fruiting trees, adapting well to fan-training on walls, where the warmth aids their ripening.

Origin Most varieties of garden or nursery origin.
Use As a large fan-trained tree for walls and fences.
Description *Flower* Small, five-petalled white flowers, 1 in (2.5 cm) wide, carried in profusion in early to mid spring. Consideration has to be given to the selection of varieties for cross-pollination. *Foliage* 1–1½ in (2.5–4 cm) long and ½–¾ in (1–2 cm) wide, light green, often with notched edges. Good yellow autumn colour. *Stem* Twiggy, light green, ageing to brown/green. Medium growth rate. *Fruit* Round, 1 in (2.5 cm) across, normally light green to yellow. Edible and sweet, with stones.
Hardiness Will tolerate a minimum winter temperature of 0°F (−18°C) but flowers may be damaged by spring frost.
Soil requirements Tolerates all soil conditions, particularly benefiting from alkaline types. Dislikes waterlogging.
Sun/Shade aspect Tolerates all aspects, but pollination may be better in sheltered positions, where strong wind does not deter pollinating insects. Best in full sun to aid the ripening of the fruit.
Pruning Dead, crossing and congested branches may be removed in late summer/early autumn. No other pruning except that required for training.
Training Purchase fan-trained trees or train one-year-old plants by cutting to within 12 in (30 cm) of graft union and tying in subsequent growth in following season. Will require wires or individual anchor points for support.
Propagation and nursery production From budding or grafting on to an understock, normally 'St Julien A'. Some dwarfing stocks are becoming available but are not recommended for fan-training. Purchase bare-rooted from mid autumn to early spring or container grown as available. Fan-trained trees should not have less than five shoots and should be 3–6 ft (91 cm–1.8 m) high. Young trees for training should be no more than one

Prunus domestica 'Merryweather' in fruit

year old. Will have to be sought from specialist nurseries and young trees may be difficult to find.

Problems Suffers from attacks of silver leaf. Can be slow to fruit. Poor availability.

Forms of interest Two trees, of appropriate varieties, will be needed for pollination. Choose varieties with the same number or numbers to either side except in the case of self-fertile forms.

LATE SUMMER VARIETIES **'Denniston's Superb'** (2) Very reliable, tough variety with true gage fruit of good flavour. Self-fertile. **'Early Transparent Gage'** (4) Very sweet and good flavoured fruit, apricot yellow with white shading. Self-fertile. **'Cambridge Gage'** (4)

Prunus domestica (Greengage) in fruit

Good cropper. Yellow/green fruits with sweet and good flavour. **'Old Greengage'** (5) The original variety of greengage. Small green fruit with green/yellow flesh. Attractive scent and very rich, sweet flavour. May be shy to fruit. **'Oullins Gage'** (4) Neither a true plum nor a gage but, due to its shape, its golden gage colour and sweet flavour, listed here.

MID AUTUMN VARIETIES **'Jefferson'** (1) Considered by many to be a plum, but listed here because of its strong greengage flavour. Oval, green, plum-shaped fruit. A very tough dessert variety. **'Reine Claude De Bavay'** (2) Large, yellow/green fruit. Strong gage flavour. Self-fertile.

Average height and spread
Five years
7×7 ft (2.1×2.1 m)
Ten years
10×10 ft (3×3 m)
Twenty years
12×16 ft (3.7×4.9 m)
Protrudes up to 3 ft (91 cm) from support.

PRUNUS DOMESTICA (Plum Hybrids)

PLUM

Rosaceae   *Fruit Tree*
Deciduous

Flowering and the ripening of the plums are enhanced by growing the trees as fan-trained specimens

Origin Of garden and nursery origin.
Use As fan-trained trees for walls and fences where adequate space can be allowed.
Description *Flower* Small, 1 in (2.5 cm) wide, five-petalled white flowers carried along branches in early to mid spring. Consideration has to be given to the selection of varieties for cross pollination. *Foliage* Oval, pointed, grey/green, up to $2\frac{1}{2}$ in (6 cm) long

Prunus domestica 'Victoria' in fruit

and $1\frac{1}{2}$ in (4 cm) wide. Yellow autumn colour. *Stem* Green to green/brown when young, ageing to brown. Shiny. Medium rate of growth. *Fruit* Oval, 2 in (5 cm) long, thin skinned, yellow or purple, with stones. Juicy, sweet, edible.

Hardiness Tolerates a minimum winter temperature of 0°F (−18°C) but flowers may be damaged by spring frosts.

Soil requirements Tolerates most soil conditions, particularly benefiting from alkaline types. Dislikes waterlogging.

Sun/Shade aspect Tolerates all aspects but pollination may be better in sheltered positions where strong wind does not deter pollinating insects. Best in full sun to aid ripening of fruit.

Pruning Dead, crossing and congested branches may be removed in late summer/early autumn. No other pruning except that required for training.

Training Purchase fan-trained trees or train one-year-old plants by cutting to within 12 in (30 cm) of graft union and tying in subsequent growth in following season. Will require wires or individual anchor points for support.

Propagation and nursery production From budding or grafting on to an understock,

Prunus domestica 'Coe's Golden Drop'

normally 'St Julien A'. Some dwarfing stocks are available but not recommended for fan-training. Purchase bare-rooted from mid autumn to early spring or container grown as available; one-year-old trees for training, fan-trained trees with not less than five shoots. 'Victoria' may be available from good garden centres and nurseries. Other varieties will have to be sought from specialist nurseries. Young trees may be hard to find.

Problems In the UK the Ministry of Agriculture annually destroy young plum trees due to their extreme susceptibility to many diseases, including plum pox, silver leaf and plum canker. This can, in certain seasons, make their availability extremely scarce. These diseases are also suffered by mature trees and in most cases there are no controls. Plum gall mite and red plum maggot may also attack, but to a certain extent these can be deterred by proprietary controls.

Forms of interest
UK
Consideration has to be given to selecting cross-pollinating trees. For best results varieties of the same number should be planted together but in many cases numbers to either side will also give good pollination. The numbers are indicated alongside each variety.

MID TO EARLY SUMMER RIPENING VARIETIES **'Czar'** (3) Very heavy cropper. Purple/black fruits. Only suitable for cooking. **'Early Laxton'** (3) Small golden yellow fruits, round with rosy pink shading to skin. Good flavour, juicy. **'River's Early Prolific'** (3) A cooking plum with violet/purple fruits. Can be used as a dessert variety and is sweet when ripe.

LATE SUMMER RIPENING VARIETIES **'Belle De Louvain'** (5) Purple fruit for cooking. **'Goldfinch'** (3) Golden yellow dessert plum with greengage flavour. **'Victoria'** (3) Possibly the most reliable of all the varieties. Oval, red plums of very good flavour. Sweet and juicy when ripe. Can be cooked. Self-pollinating therefore the best tree to choose if there is room for only one.

EARLY AUTUMN RIPENING VARIETIES **'Kirke's Blue'** (3) Sweet, juicy, violet/red fruit. Ideal for wall use. **'Warwickshire Drooper'** (2) Yellow fruit. Best variety for preserving.

MID AUTUMN RIPENING VARIETIES **'Coe's Golden Drop'** (2) Amber-yellow fruits with apricot texture. Sweet when ripe. Only does well when grown as a wall-trained tree. Does not cross-pollinate with 'Jefferson' gage (see *P. domestica* Gage Hybrids). **'Marjorie's Seedling'** (5) Black cooking plum often retained on tree well into autumn. Can be used when ripe as a dessert variety. **'Pond's Seedling'** (4) Red, dry flavoured cooking plum. Not recommended for dessert. **'Severn Cross'** (3) Good dessert variety. Sweet flavour. Oval with golden skin.

USA

EARLY SEASON VARIETIES **'Bruce'** Large, red-skinned fruit, red-fleshed with good flavour. Ripens in early summer. A Japanese plum. Use 'Santa Rosa' as a pollinator. Good for the North and South. From Texas. **'Earliblue'** Blue skinned with tender green/yellow flesh. Medium production. Ideal for home garden use. Hardy. Ripens mid summer. Good for the North. Self-fertile. Origin unknown. **'Early Golden'** Round yellow fruit of medium quality. Can be biennial bearing. A Japanese plum. Use 'Shiro' or 'Burbank' as pollinators. Fruit ripening in Michigan area in mid summer. Good for Northern areas. From Canada. **'Mariposa'** Large, heart-shaped, yellow-skinned fruit with red mottling. Sweet red flesh. Good for dessert and cooking. Ripening mid summer. Requires winter cold to aid pollination. A Japanese plum. Use 'Late Santa Rosa', 'Santa Rosa' or 'Wickson' as pollinators. From California. **'Methley'** Medium-sized, red/purple fruit with red flesh of very good flavour. A Japanese plum. Use 'Shiro' or 'Burbank' as pollinators. Mid summer ripening but needs several pickings. Good for the North. From South Africa. **'Santa Rosa'** Large fruit with deep crimson skin and purple flesh, streaked yellow towards the centre. Good for dessert or canning. An early or mid season plum will pollinate. Early to mid summer ripening. A Japanese plum. Good for all areas. From California.

EARLY MID SEASON VARIETIES **'Abundance'** Purple/red skin and yellow flesh. Use for dessert or cooking. Bears fruit biennially from an early age. Use 'Methley' or 'Shiro' as pollinators. Ripens mid summer. A Japanese plum. Good for the North. From California. **'Satsuma'** Small to medium fruit with dull, dark red skin and red flesh. Use either as a dessert or for preserves. Use 'Santa Rosa' or 'Wickson' as pollinators. A Japanese plum. Good in all areas. From California. **'Shiro'** Medium to large round yellow fruit with very good flavour. Use as a dessert or for cooking. Very heavy crops. Use 'Early Golden', 'Methley', or 'Santa Rosa' as pollinators. A Japanese plum. Mid to late summer ripening, depending on area. Good for all areas. From California.

MID SEASON VARIETIES **'Burbank'** Large, red-skinned fruit with amber flesh with very good flavour. Use for dessert or canning. Use 'Early Golden' or 'Santa Rosa' as pollinators. A Japanese plum. Late summer ripening. Good for all areas. From California. **'Ozark Premier'** Very large, red fruit with yellow flesh. Very productive. Disease resistant and hardy. Ripening late summer. A Japanese plum. Good for the North, Midwest, and South. Self-fertile. From Missouri. **'Queen Ann'** Large purple fruit with golden orange flesh. Very juicy and sweet with good flavour. Ripens in mid summer. Use 'Santa Rosa' as a pollinator. A Japanese plum. Less vigorous than many. From California. **'Stanley'** Large, dark blue fruit with yellow, good flavoured flesh. Heavy cropping. Hardy. Self-fertile. A European plum. Ripening late summer/early autumn. Good for the North but also very popular in the East, Midwest and South. From New York. **'Sugar'** Dark blue, medium-sized, sweet fruit in mid to late summer. Good for drying and canning. Self-pollinating. Biennial bearing with some limited cropping in intermediate years. A European plum. Good in all areas. From California. **'Yellow Egg'** Thick golden-yellow skin and yellow flesh. Self-fertile. A European plum. Late summer/early autumn ripening. Good for the North and West. Origin unknown.

LATE SEASON VARIETIES **'Bluefre'** Large blue-skinned fruit with yellow flesh in early fall. Self-fertile. A European plum. May suffer from attacks of brown rot. Good for the North. From Missouri. **'French Prune'** Small, red to purple/black fruit with very sweet flesh and mild flavour. A European plum. Ripening late summer/early autumn. Good for the South and West. From France. **'Italian Prune'** ('Fellenberg') Dark blue fruit with sweet yellow flesh in late summer/early fall. Use for dessert, canning or drying. A European plum. Self-fertile. Good for the South and West. From Germany. **'President'** Dark blue fruit with amber flesh in early fall. Flavour somewhat indifferent, but good for cooking and canning. Use any late European plum as pollinator. A European plum. Good for the North. From the UK.

HARDY PLUMS Varieties suitable for the coldest Northern areas. **'Pipestone'** Large, well-flavoured red fruit with yellow flesh. Use 'Toka' or 'Superior' as pollinators. From Minnesota. **'Superior'** Large red fruit with russet dots. Firm yellow flesh with very good flavour. Use 'Toka' as a pollinator. From Minnesota. **'Toka'** Large pointed fruit with red/orange skin. Firm yellow flesh with a good flavour. Very heavy crops. Use 'Superior' as a pollinator. From Minnesota. **'Underwood'** Very large red fruit with golden yellow flesh. Very good for dessert. Fruits become available over a long ripening period from mid-summer onwards. Use 'Superior' as a pollinator. From Minnesota.

Average height and spread

Five years
8 × 8 ft (2.4 × 2.4 m)
Ten years
12 × 12 ft (3.7 × 3.7 m)
Twenty years
15 × 15 ft (4.6 × 4.6 m)
Protrudes up to 3 ft (91 cm) from support.

Prunus domestica **'Victoria' in flower**

PRUNUS PERSICA (Nectarine Hybrids)

NECTARINE

Rosaceae   *Fruit Tree*
Deciduous

Not always reliable for their fruiting achievements out of doors and will benefit from the protection of a greenhouse or large conservatory in all but the most southerly of areas.

Origin Of garden origin
Use As fan-trained trees for large, sheltered walls and fences or under protection.
Description *Flower* Five-petalled, ¾ in (2 cm) wide, saucer-shaped flowers in early spring, sugar pink in colour. Self-fertile. *Foliage* Lanceolate, 2–4 in (5–10 cm), mid-green with silvery reverse. Some red hue towards autumn. *Stem* Green when young with orange/red shading towards the sun,

Prunus persica **'Lord Napier'**

becoming purple/red. Rigid. Medium to fast growth rate. *Fruit* Smooth, sometimes glossy, yellow stone fruit with bold patches of dark red shading. Edible. Mid to late summer. May be hard and unripe in all but the sunniest of positions.
Hardiness Tolerates a minimum winter temperature of 4°F (−15°C).
Soil requirements Tolerates all soil conditions, preferring alkaline types.
Sun/Shade aspect Requires a sheltered aspect. Needs a position in full sun for fruit to ripen.
Pruning Remove all old fruiting or flowering shoots after fruiting.
Training Tie to wire on walls or fences. Plant pre-trained trees for preference. Alternatively, one-year-old trees 3–4 ft (91 cm–1.2 m) tall should be cut hard back to within 12 in (30 cm) of their graft union. This will induce numerous side branches, which can then be tied into a fan-trained shape. Tie in annually produced growths as they become large enough.
Propagation and nursery production From budding or grafting. Can be planted bare-rooted from late autumn to early spring or container grown as available. Best size to purchase: fan-trained trees with five or more branches, one-year-old trees 3–5 ft (91 cm–1.5 m) high. Pre-trained trees normally available from garden centres. Younger trees may have to be sought from specialist nurseries.
Problems Suffers from peach leaf curl, which is extremely difficult to control; possibly only a physical barrier, such as a polythene sheet stretched over the tree in early spring, will prevent, and even this is not infallible. Also susceptible to silver leaf disease.

Forms of interest '**Early Rivers**' Mid summer fruiting. Reliable. '**Humbolt**' Late summer fruiting. Scarce but worth consideration. '**Lord Napier**' Late summer fruiting. Good variety. '**Pineapple**' Late summer, early autumn fruiting. Interesting flavour. Scarce.

Average height and spread
Five years
7 × 7 ft (2.1 × 2.1 m)
Ten years
12 × 15 ft (3.7 × 4.6 m)
Twenty years
15 × 18 ft (4.6 × 5.5 m)
Protrudes up to 2 ft (60 cm) from support.

PRUNUS PERSICA
(Peach Hybrids)

PEACH
Rosaceae   *Fruit Tree*
Deciduous

In many areas peaches demand a wall or fence for best fruiting performance.

Origin Of garden origin.
Use As fan-trained trees for large walls and fences, both in the open and under protection of greenhouse or conservatory.
Description *Fruit* Five-petalled, ½ in (1 cm) wide, saucer-shaped flowers, attractive sugar-pink in colour in early spring. Produced close to the stems on two-year-old shoots. Self-fertile. *Foliage* Lanceolate, 2–4 in (5–10 cm) long, mid green with silvery reverse. Some red hue towards autumn. *Stem* Green when young with orange/red shading towards the sun, becoming purple/red. Rigid. Medium to fast growth rate. *Fruit* Round, orange/red to red fruits with stone, edible and juicy. Fruiting early autumn.
Hardiness Tolerates a minimum winter temperature of 4°F (−15°C).
Soil requirements Tolerates all soil, except heavily waterlogged.
Sun/Shade aspect Requires a sheltered aspect. Must be in full sun or fruits will not ripen.
Pruning Remove all old fruiting or flowering shoots after fruiting.
Training Tie to wires on walls or fences. Buy fan-trained trees for preference. Alternatively, one-year-old trees can be cut hard back to within 12 in (30 cm) of their graft union. This will induce numerous side branches, which can then be tied into a fan-trained shape. Tie in annually produced growths as they become large enough to become fruiting shoots for following year.

Prunus persica '**Peregrine**' in flower

Propagation and nursery production From budding or grafting. Can be planted bare-rooted from late autumn to early spring or container grown as available. Best size to purchase: fan-trained trees with five or more shoots, one-year-old trees for training 3–5 ft (91 cm–1.5 m) high. Pre-trained trees normally available from garden centres. One-year-old trees may have to be sought from specialist nurseries.
Problems Suffers from peach leaf curl. Possibly only a physical barrier, such as a polythene sheet stretched over the tree in early spring, will prevent, and even this is not infallible. Also susceptible to silver leaf disease. Avoid planting dwarf patio peaches for fan-training on walls as they are too small.

Forms of interest
UK
'**Duke of York**' Large yellow fruits, flushed crimson. Excellent flavour. Mid summer. '**Peregrine**' The best of all varieties and most reliable. Good colour and flavour. Late summer. '**Royal George**' A white-fleshed variety with good colour. Ripens late summer. Very scarce in production.

USA
EARLY SEASON VARIETIES '**Fairhaven**' A large peach with bright yellow skin with red sheen. Yellow flesh with a red centre. Good for Western states. From Michigan. '**Flavorcrest**' Large yellow fruit with good flavour. Skin has a red blush. From California. '**Garnet Beauty**' Medium to large firm fruit with yellow, red-streaked flesh. Heavy cropping but susceptible to bacterial leaf spot. Use in Northern states. From Ontario, Canada. '**Golden Jubilee**' Medium to large fruits with yellow, mottled red skin. Yellow flesh. Large cropper. Good in all areas. From New Jersey. '**Redhaven**' Medium-sized fruit, deep red skin on a yellow background. Yellow, firm flesh. Resistant to bacterial leaf spot. Good in all areas. From Michigan. '**Redtop**' Pinkish blush on yellow skin, flesh firm and yellow. May be susceptible to bacterial leaf spot. Good in Western states. From California. '**Reliance**' Large fruit with dark red skin over a yellow background. Flesh bright yellow. Winter hardy. Good for Northern and Western states. From New Hampshire. '**Springcrest**' Medium-sized, good flavoured fruits with yellow flesh. Good for Western states. From California. '**Sunhaven**' Large to medium-sized fruits, bright red skin over a golden background. Flesh yellow flecked with red. Good in all areas. From Michigan. '**Ventura**' Yellow skin with red blush. Firm, yellow, good flavoured flesh. Hardy. From California. '**Veteran**' Medium to large fruit with yellow skin splashed red. Soft yellow flesh. Heavy cropping. Good on Pacific coast. From Ontario, Canada. '**Babcock**' Small to medium-sized fruit, light pink with blush-red shading. Flesh white with red towards the centre. Juicy. Thin fruits for better performance. Ideal for Western states, particularly Southern California. From California. '**Early Elberta**' ('**Gleason Strain**') Large fruits with yellow flesh of good flavour. Can be used for canning and freezing. Good for the South and West. From Utah. '**J. H. Hale**' Very large yellow fruit with deep crimson shading. Golden yellow, firm flesh. Use a second variety for cross-pollination. Good in all areas. From Connecticut. '**July Elberta**' ('**Kim Elberta**') Medium-sized fruit with green/yellow skin and pink to dark red blush. Yellow, good quality flesh. Reliable large crops. May be susceptible to bacterial leaf spot. Good for the West. From California. '**Loring**' Medium-sized fruit, blush red over a yellow background. Firm yellow flesh of good texture. Said to be resistant to bacterial leaf

Prunus persica '**Peregrine**'

spot. Good for the North and South. From Missouri. **'Suncrest'** Large firm fruit with a red blush covering to the yellow skin. Susceptible to bacterial leaf spot and for this reason should only be grown in the West and other areas where the disease is not prevalent. Hardy enough for Northern areas. From California.

LATE SEASON VARIETIES **'Belle of Georgia'** (**'Georgia Belle'**) A white peach with red blush. Firm white flesh with very good flavour. Use for dessert and freezing but not suitable for canning. Susceptible to brown rot. Good for North and South. From Georgia. **'Blake'** Red skin and firm yellow flesh. Use mainly for freezing and canning. Susceptible to bacterial canker. Good for North and South. From New Jersey. **'Cresthaven'** Medium to large golden fruit with bright red shading. Yellow flesh. Hardy. Good for North and South. From Michigan. **'Elberta'** Deep golden skin with red blush. Fruits may drop from the tree at maturity.

Prunus persica **in flower**

Said to be resistant to brown rot. Good in all areas. From Georgia. **'Fay Elberta'** In its own state of California rates amongst one of the most reliable and widely-planted varieties. Skin yellow with red blush. Useful for all purposes of eating, cooking, canning and freezing. Not entirely winter-hardy. **'Jefferson'** Orange skin with bright red blush. Yellow, firm flesh. Good for canning and freezing. Said to be resistant to brown rot. Good in areas where late spring frosts are experienced and in Northern and Southern states. From Virginia. **'Madison'** Medium-sized orange/

yellow fruit with bright red blush. Flesh orange/yellow with good texture and flavour. Good in the North and South. From Virginia. **'Raritan Rose'** Red skin with white flesh. Very good flavour. Strong growing and hardy. Best used in the East and North. From New Jersey. **'Redskin'** Red-skinned fruit with good yellow flesh. Ideal for freezing, canning and dessert. Well-established in the East and North. From Maryland. **'Rio Oso Gem'** Large fruit with yellow skin and red shading. Yellow flesh. Can be used for dessert and freezing. Best in the South and West. From California. **'Sunhigh'** Medium to large fruit with bright red blush over a yellow skin. Yellow flesh. Said to be very susceptible to bacterial leaf spot and must have protection throughout the summer. Good in North and South. From New Jersey.

Average height and spread
Five years
7 × 7 ft (2.1 × 2.1 m)
Ten years
12 × 12 ft (3.7 × 3.7 m)
Twenty years
15 × 15 ft (4.6 × 4.6 m)
Protrudes up to 2 ft (60 cm) from support.

PYRACANTHA

PYRANTHA, FIRETHORN

Rosaceae   *Wall Shrub*
Evergreen
This attractive fruiting shrub is most often seen against walls and fences where it is generally found as a fan-trained shrub.

Origin Most forms originate in China; many varieties of garden origin.
Use As a large, fan-trained or lattice formation, flowering and fruiting shrub for walls and fences; can also be grown up pillars. Although it is well-known as a wall shrub, its other possibilities as a freestanding, small, mop-headed shrub or even as a hedging plant should not be overlooked.
Description *Flower* Good-sized clusters of white, hawthorn-like flowers up to 5 in (12 cm) across with a musty scent in early summer. Loved by bees. *Foliage* Leaves ovate, 1–2 in (2.5–5 cm) long and ½–¾ in (1–2 cm) wide. Some grey and variegated leaved varieties. *Stem* ½–1 in (1–2.5 cm) long, sharp spines at most leaf axils. Red/brown, ageing to dark green to brown. Forms a flat, fan-shaped shrub on walls and fences. Some attractive pendulous stem forms. Fast growth rate. *Fruit* Clusters of round, good-sized fruits, yellow, orange or red depending on variety,

early autumn, maintained well into winter.
Hardiness Tolerates a minimum winter temperature of 4°F (−15°C) although severe wind chill may damage some leaves and tips of younger growth. Damage is usually corrected the following spring.
Soil requirements Most soils, but distressed on extremely alkaline types.
Sun/Shade aspect Tolerates all aspects, only needing protection from very exposed winter wind conditions. Full sun to deep shade, but produces fewer fruit in deeper shade, and may also become more open.
Pruning None required other than that needed for fan-training. Can be drastically reduced in size, although following year's flowering and fruiting will be poorer. Pruning is best carried out in late winter to early spring to avoid attacks of fungus disease. Can be trimmed and shaped as desired.
Training Will require tying to wires or individual anchor points to achieve a fan-trained shape.
Propagation and nursery production From semi-ripe cuttings taken in early summer. Propagates readily from seed, but seed-raised plants are variable in fruit quality and colour. Purchase container grown; easy to find a good range of named varieties. Best planting height 15 in–3 ft (38–91 cm).

Pyracantha atalantoides **in flower**

Problems Subject to the airborne fungus disease fire blight in summer months which completely destroys all foliage. There is no cure or prevention. All affected or suspect shrubs should be burnt and the appropriate government agency informed of its occurrence.
Forms of interest *P.* **'Alexander Pendula'** A variety with interesting, long, weeping branches, forming a somewhat unruly shrub. Fruit coral red. *P. angustifolia* Grey/green, long, narrow, oblong leaves with grey, felted undersides. Fruit orange/yellow, may be maintained into winter. *P. atalantioides* (syn. *P. gibbsii*) (Gibbs firethorn) Strong, fast-growing variety with good-sized, oval, dark, glossy green leaves. Scarlet fruits produced late in autumn. Good for difficult shady walls, but may be withdrawn from production due to fire blight. *P. a.* **'Aurea'** (syn. *P. a.* **'Flava'**) A yellow-fruited form of the above, which may also be withdrawn for the same reason as its parent. *P. coccinea* **'Lalandei'** A somewhat upright but wide form with small, obovate leaves. Orange/red fruits in autumn, may be maintained into winter. *P. c.* **'Sparklers'** Rather small, narrow, ovate foliage variegated with white margins. Orange/red fruits. Reaches two thirds average height and spread. *P.* **'Golden Charmer'** Good dark foliage. Large clusters of golden-yellow fruits. *P.* **'Golden Sun'** Large golden-yellow fruits. Dark green foliage. *P.* **'Harlequin'** Grey/green foliage with silver/white edges, sometimes pink-tinged, especially in cold

Pyracantha **'Orange Charmer'** **in fruit**

Pyracantha rogersiana 'Flava' in fruit

weather. Small, orange/red fruits. Two thirds average height and spread. *P.* **'Mojave'** Good, large, mid to dark green foliage. Large orange/red fruits in autumn, may be maintained into winter. Very winter hardy and resistant to wind scorch. *P.* **'Orange Charmer'** Dark green foliage. Fruits large, deep orange in colour. *P.* **'Orange Glow'** Interesting dark green foliage with dark purple/black stems. Good clusters of orange/red fruits very freely produced in autumn. Smaller than average. *P.* **'Red Column'** Large red fruits. Upright habit. Good foliage. May have to be sought from specialist nursery. *P.* **'Red Cushion'** Light green foliage, ageing to grey/green. White flowers, followed by red fruits in autumn. Low-growing, reaching only 3 ft (91 cm) in height and 6 ft (1.8 m) spread. *P. rogersiana* Very dark, oblong to lanceolate leaves. Especially recommended for shaded walls, giving a display of orange/red fruits in autumn. *P. r.* **'Flava'** Small foliage, clusters of bright yellow fruits. Good for shaded walls. Somewhat weeping habit. *P.* **'Shawnee'**

Pyracantha 'Orange Glow'

Dense foliage and numerous spines. Fruit yellow to light orange, colouring early in season and maintained well into winter. Said to be resistant to fire blight and scab fungus. Raised in USA. *P.* **'Soleil d'Or'** Good mid to light green foliage. Very large clusters of deep yellow fruits. *P.* **'Teton'** Good, small, dark green foliage. Clusters of orange/yellow fruits. Upright growth.
Average height and spread
Five years
6 × 4 ft (1.8 × 1.2 m)
Ten years
12 × 6 ft (3.7 × 1.8 m)
Twenty years
13 × 10 ft (4 × 3 m)
Protrudes up to 3 ft (91 cm) from support.

PYRUS

ORNAMENTAL PEAR

Rosaceae   *Hardy Tree*
Deciduous

A group of ornamental pears responding well to fan-training on a wide range of aspects.

Origin From Europe through to Asia and Japan.
Use As medium to large fan-trained trees for walls and fences.
Description *Flower* Clusters of up to 3 in (7.5 cm) across composed of five to seven white, single, cup-shaped florets, each up to 1½ in (4 cm) across, produced in mid spring. *Foliage* Ovate to lanceolate. Either green or grey, depending on variety. Good autumn colours. *Stem* Grey/green to grey/brown. Upright, spreading or pendulous, depending on variety, and all easy to train. Medium rate of growth. *Fruit* Small, oval or rounded pears up to 2 in (5 cm) long, in autumn. Fruits not edible.
Hardiness Tolerates a minimum winter temperature of 4°F (−15°C).
Soil requirements Any soil type, but shows distress in extremely poor soils.
Sun/Shade aspect Tolerates all aspects. Green forms tolerate moderate shade, silver-leaved varieties prefer full sun.
Pruning Prune young trees hard in spring following planting. Select and train resulting five to seven shoots and tie into a fan-trained shape. In subsequent years remove all side growths back to two buds from their origin and maintain original main branches in fan shape.

Pyrus salicifolia

Training Secure to wires or individual anchor points.
Propagation and nursery production From grafting or budding on to understocks of quince or *P. communis*. Available bare-rooted or container grown. For fan-training choose trees of not more than two years old and 3–6 ft (91 cm–1.8 m) tall. Most forms easily found in garden centres and general nurseries; some must be sought from specialist nurseries.
Problems All varieties are poor-rooted, especially when young. Extra peat or other organic material should be added to the planting hole to encourage establishment of young roots. Also needs staking and extra watering in spring.
Forms of interest *P. amygdaliformis* Foliage grey/green and ovate, white undersides. Rarely available. *P. calleryana* **'Chanticleer'** Dark glossy green leaves maintained into late autumn and early winter, then turning orange/red. Narrow, columnar habit. *P. communis* (Wild pear) Attractive white flowers in spring. Light green, ovate foliage with good autumn colour. Limited in commercial production, must be sought from specialist nurseries. *P. c.* **'Beech Hill'** Dark green, round leaves; interesting leathery texture, glossy surface and wavy edges. Good autumn colours. *P. elaeagrifolia* Silver grey, ovate, sometimes lanceolate foliage. Interesting white flowers. Slightly more tender than most but above average height. *P. nivalis* Attractive, ovate, white to silver/grey foliage. Graceful white flowers. Small, globed, yellow/green fruits. Two thirds average height and spread. Must be sought from specialist nurseries. *P. salicifolia* **'Pendula'** (Weeping willow-leaved pear) Narrow, lanceolate leaves up to 2 in (5 cm) long. Not usually supplied as large as other forms.
Average height and spread
Five years
12 × 12 ft (3.7 × 3.7 m)
Ten years
18 × 18 ft (5.5 × 5.5 m)
Twenty years
22 × 22 ft (6.7 × 6.7 m)
Protrudes up to 3 ft (91 cm) from support.

PYRUS COMMUNIS (Pear Hybrids)

PEAR

Rosaceae   *Fruit Tree*
Deciduous

Flowering and fruiting fan-trained subjects for walls and fences, with attractive branch formation as an added bonus.

Origin Of garden origin.
Use As fan-trained, horizontal-trained (espalier) or cordon trees for walls and fences.
Description *Flower* Five-petalled, 1 in (2.5 cm) wide, pink in bud opening to white in early to mid spring. Consideration must be given to the selection of varieties for cross-pollination. *Foliage* Round to oval, mid green glossy foliage up to 2½ in (6 cm) long and 1½ in (4 cm) wide. Yellow autumn colour. *Stem* Light grey/green when young, becoming grey/brown, finally grey. Upright. Rigid. Medium growth rate. *Fruit* Oval, pointed, up to 5 in (12 cm) long and 2½ in (6 cm) wide, grey/green to green/brown, often with orange and red shading. Fruiting late summer to early winter depending on variety.
Hardiness Tolerates a minimum winter temperature of 0°F (−18°C) but spring frosts may damage flowers.
Soil requirements Tolerates all soil conditions with no particular preference.
Sun/Shade aspect Tolerates all aspects. Best in full sun to ripen fruit, but will tolerate very light shade.
Pruning Once trained, shorten all annual growth back to within 2 in (5 cm) of its origin in early autumn, without reducing the main framework.

Training Buy fan-trained, horizontal-trained (espalier) or cordon trees and tie to wires or individual anchor points.

Propagation and nursery production Should always be grafted or budded with understock of known varieties. There are many combinations, but in the main, fan, horizontal and cordon fruit trees are propagated on to a semi-dwarf rootstock. Can be planted bare-rooted from early autumn to early spring or container grown as available, with autumn and spring planting for preference. Pre-trained trees in each of the forms measure 3–5 ft (91 cm–1.5 m) overall and will normally have to be obtained from a specialist supplier, although some varieties are available from garden centres and general nurseries.

Problems May suffer from attacks of mildew and blackfly. Treat with a proprietary control. Susceptible to pear scab – again, treat with a proprietary control.

Pyrus communis 'Gorham'

Forms of interest
UK
The number in brackets denotes the pollination group. Each variety should be grown in proximity with one of a similar number for successful pollination.

EARLY TO LATE AUTUMN RIPENING PEARS These varieties should be picked from the tree while still green and stored in a cool dark room for seven to 14 days to ripen. '**Dr Jules Guyot**' (3) Pale golden fruit, often flushed scarlet. Interesting flavour. Mid autumn. '**Fertility Improved**' (3) Yellow with russet skin. Good flavour, sweet and juicy. Good red autumn foliage. Disease resistant. Mid to late autumn. '**Glow Red William**' (3) A form of

Pyrus communis 'Conference' in flower

'Williams' Bon Chrétien'. Very juicy fruit with a tart flavour and bright crimson skin. Resistant to scab. Mid autumn. '**Gorham**' (4) Pale yellow with russet shading. Long and narrow fruit shape. Mid to late autumn. A variety from America bred from 'Williams' Bon Chrétien', and inheriting its good flavour. '**Laxton's Foremost**' (4) Good-sized fruit with good flavour. Disease resistant. Mid to late autumn. '**Williams' Bon Chrétien**' (3) Pale yellow fruit. Very juicy and with a very good flavour. Will tolerate exposed positions. Susceptible to scab, but worthy of garden merit. Mid autumn.

LATE AUTUMN/EARLY WINTER RIPENING PEARS Harvest unripe in mid autumn, store to ripen, use as required. '**Beurre Hardy**' (4) Coppery colour with red shading. Good grower. Scab resistant. Attractive scarlet foliage in autumn. '**Beurre Superfin**' (3) Fruit long and yellow with russet patches on skin. Susceptible to scab. Late autumn. '**Conference**' (3) Long, pale green, bulbous-based fruit with russet skin. Very free fruiting. Self-fertile, but fruiting enhanced if another pollinating variety is used in association. Resistant to scab. '**Doyenne du Comice**' (4) Large golden fruit with some russeting. In good summers has a red shading. Fruiting can be unreliable and it is susceptible to scab unless regular control is applied. Early winter. '**Louise Bonne of Jersey**' (2) Fruits long, golden yellow with brown/red shading. Late autumn. Should not be considered for pollinating 'Williams' Bon Chrétien'. '**Packham's**

Triumph' (3) 'Williams' Bon Chrétien' type with golden yellow fruit. Early winter.

MID TO LATE WINTER RIPENING PEARS Harvest in mid to late autumn, store to ripen, use as required. '**Glou Morceau**' (4) Medium-sized green pears, becoming yellow when ripe. Benefits from training on a sunny wall or fence in a sheltered position. Mid to late winter. '**Joséphine de Malines**' (3) Green, becoming yellow when ripe. Benefits from use on a wall or fence. Will take some time to ripen in store. Early to mid winter. '**Winter Nellis**' (4) Green/yellow, small with some russeting to skin. Late autumn to mid winter.

Pyrus communis 'Williams' Bon Chrétien'

LATE COOKING PEARS Harvest in late autumn and allow to ripen in store. '**Pitmaston Duchess**' (4) Fruit pale yellow with a light brown russeting. Not of dessert flavour but good as a cooking pear. In wet, moist areas very susceptible to scab. Good red autumn colours. Late autumn to early winter.

USA
Most American varieties will pollinate each other, although the varieties 'Bartlett', 'Magness' and 'Seckel' are poor pollinators and should not be considered for such use.

EARLY SEASON VARIETIES Eat from the tree when ripe. '**Clapp's Favorite**' Large yellow fruit with red shading. Sweet soft flesh for dessert or canning. Attractively shaped tree very susceptible to fire blight. Hardy for all areas but particularly good for North and West. From Massachusetts. '**Gorham**' See UK varieties. '**Moonglow**' Large, soft, juicy fruit with attractive flavour. Use for dessert

Pyrus communis 'Fertility Improved'

Pyrus communis 'Pitmaston Duchess'

and canning. Heavy cropping from an early age. Resistant to fire blight. Good for all areas. From Maryland. **'Orient'** Almost round fruit with firm flesh. Good for canning but not to all tastes as a dessert. Moderate cropping. Resistant to fire blight. Good for Southen areas. From California. **'Red Clapp'** (**'Starkrimson'**) Good quality red-skinned fruit. Susceptible to fire blight. Good for the West and North. From Michigan.
MID SEASON VARIETIES Eat from the tree when ripe. **'Bartlett'** Yellow, medium to large fruit with thin skin. Very sweet and juicy, good for dessert and canning, and is commercially used in large quantities for this purpose. Subject to fire blight. Does not resent hot summers, assuming that there are cold winters. All varieties pollinate with the exception of 'Seckel' or 'Magness'. From the UK. **'Doyenne du Comice'** See UK varieties. **'Lincoln'** Large fruits carried in large numbers. Tree hardy and resistant to fire blight. Very reliable, particularly in the Midwest, but good for the North and South too. Origin unknown, possibly the Midwest. **'Magness'** Oval, medium sized fruit with russet skin and very attractive perfume. Fruit variable in its quality. Highly resistant to fire blight. Good for Southern and Western areas. From Maryland. **'Maxine'** (**'Starking Delicious'**) Large, good-looking fruit with firm, juicy, sweet white flesh. Moderately resistant to fire blight. Good in North and South. From Ohio. **'Parker'** Medium to large fruit, yellow-skinned with red blush. White, juicy, sweet flesh. Moderately hardy. Susceptible to fire

Pyrus communis 'Beurre Superfin'

blight. Good for northern areas. From Minnesota. **'Sensation Red Bartlett'** (**'Sensation'**) Yellow skins with heavy red blushing. White juicy flesh. Susceptible to fire blight. Good for the West. From Australia.
LATE SEASON VARIETIES Harvest in mid to late fall and allow to ripen in store. Can be used from the tree from mid fall onwards for cooking. **'Anjou'** Large green fruit with mild flavoured, firm flesh, somewhat on the dry side. Very good for storing. Can be eaten fresh or from store or used for canning. Susceptible to fire blight. Good for North and West. Variety 'Red Anjou' may also be worth consideration. From France. **'Bosc'** Long, narrow fruit with russet colouring. Crisp, firm flesh with good scent. Considered by many to be the best of all pears. Can be used for dessert, fresh from the tree, or canned. Cooks well. Susceptible to fire blight. Good for the North and West. From France.

Pyrus communis 'Doyenne du Comice'

'Duchess' Green/yellow, extremely large fruits with good-flavoured flesh. Good for Northern areas. From France. **'Keiffer'** Large yellow fruit, somewhat gritty texture to the flesh not universally well-liked. Good for keeping, cooks well and is ideal for canning. High resistance to fire blight. Needs some winter cold to encourage flowering and pollination, but will accept summer heat. Good for the East, North, South and Midwest. From Pennsylvania. **'Mericourt'** Green to yellow/green, sometimes blushed deep red. Creamy white flesh. Good for dessert or canning. Hardy, resistant to both fire blight and leaf spot. Good for the South. From Tennessee. **'Patten'** Large, juicy fruits. Good for dessert. Hardy, good for Northern areas. From Louisiana. **'Seckel'** Small yellow/brown fruits. Very good flavour and scent and an ideal pear for gardens. Either use for dessert directly from the tree or for preserving. Very

heavy crops. Resistant to fire blight. Good for all areas. From New York. **'Winter Nellis'** See UK varieties.
Average height and spread
Fan-trained
Five years
8 × 8 ft (2.4 × 2.4 m)
Ten years
10 × 12 ft (3 × 3.7 m)
Twenty years
12 × 16 ft (3.7 × 4.9 m)
Protrudes up to 3 ft (91 cm) from support

Horizontal (3 trained tiers)
Five years
6 × 8 ft (1.8 × 2.4 m)
Ten years
8 × 12 ft (2.4 × 3.7 m)
Twenty years
10 × 20 ft (3 × 6 m)
Protrudes up to 3 ft (91 cm) from support
Cordon
Five years
8 × 2 ft (2.4 m × 60 cm)
Ten years
29 × 3 ft (2.7 m × 91 cm)
Twenty years
9 × 3 ft (2.7 m × 91 cm)
Protrudes up to 2 ft (60 cm) from support.

RAPHIOLEPSIS UMBELLATA

KNOWN BY BOTANICAL NAME

Roseaceae   *Wall Shrub*
Evergreen

An attractive shrub which needs the protection of walls or fences against wind damage which can scorch and defoliate in winter.

Origin From Japan and Korea.
Use As a freestanding or fan-trained shrub for sheltered walls and fences.
Description *Flower* White suffused with pink, fragrant, ¾ in (2 cm) across, carried in terminal clusters 3–4 in (7.5–10 cm) across in late spring/summer. *Foliage* Oval leaves up to 3 in (7.5 cm) long. Grey/green with some red shading. *Stem* Short-branched, grey/green becoming green/ brown. Slow to medium growth rate. *Fruit* Pear-shaped, blue/black fruits in late summer/early autumn.
Hardiness Tolerates a minimum winter temperature of up to 14°F (−10°C) against a wall.
Soil requirements Requires a neutral to acid soil with adequate organic material and plant nutrient. Dislikes waterlogging or extremely dry conditions.
Sun/Shade aspect Requires a sheltered aspect. Tolerates full sun to medium shade, light shade for preference.
Pruning Normally not required other than that for training.
Training Allow to grow freestanding or fan-trained against walls or fences.

Raphiolepsis umbellata **in flower**

Rhamnus alaterna 'Argenteo-variegata'

Propagation and nursery production From semi-ripe cuttings taken in early summer and from seed. Should always be purchased container-grown; will have to be sought from specialist nurseries. Best planting height 3 in–2 ft (7.5–60 cm).
Problems Slow-growing and will not thrive in poor or alkaline soils. Full range of hardiness not yet explored.
Similar forms of interest *R.u.* 'Enchantress' Rose pink flowers, earlier than species and carried over a long period. Possibly less hardy than its parent.
Average height and spread
Five years
3 × 3 ft (91 × 91 cm)
Ten years
5 × 5 ft (1.5 × 1.5 m)
Twenty years
8 × 8 ft (2.4 × 2.4 m)
Protrudes up to 18 in (45 cm) from support if fan-trained, 3 ft (91 cm) untrained.

RHAMNUS ALATERNA 'ARGENTEO-VARIEGATA'

BUCKTHORN

Rhamnaceae   *Wall Shrub*
Evergreen

The variegated leaves of this moderately hardy shrub can add interest to any winter garden.

Origin From Europe and the Mediterranean region.
Use As a large, freestanding or fan-trained foliage shrub for large walls and fences.
Description *Flower* Inconspicuous, small, pale cream flowers in early summer. *Foliage* Leaves ovate, 1–2½ in (2.5–6 cm) long. Olive-green with white variegation. *Stem* Upright, becoming very branching with age. Dark purple to purple/brown. Fast growth rate. *Fruit* Produces small red fruits in autumn.
Hardiness Tolerates a minimum winter temperature of 4°F (−15°C).
Soil requirements Most soil types, but dislikes extremely wet conditions.
Sun/Shade aspect Requires a sheltered aspect in medium to full shade.
Pruning None required and is best left free-growing but may be trimmed or trained as necessary.
Propagation and nursery production From semi-ripe cuttings taken in summer. Purchase container grown; normally available from good garden centres and nurseries, particularly those in warm coastal areas. Best planting height 1–3 ft (30–91 cm).
Training Allow to stand free or secure to wires or individual anchor points to encourage a fan-trained shape.

Problems Its hardiness is suspect in cold winds and it often requires a larger space than anticipated.
Similar forms of interest None.
Average height and spread
Five years
6 × 3 ft (1.8 m × 91 cm)
Ten years
12 × 6 ft (3.7 × 1.8 m)
Twenty years
16 × 13 ft (4.9 × 4 m)
Protrudes up to 3 ft (91 cm) from support if fan-trained, 6 ft (1.8 m) untrained.

RHODOCHITON ASTROSANGUINEUM

PURPLE BELLS

Scrophulariaceae   *Climbing Perennial*
Deciduous

A tender, interesting, flowering climber for sheltered gardens, greenhouses and conservatories.

Rhodochiton atrosanguineum in flower

Origin From Mexico.
Use As a short climber for very warm, sunny positions in favourable locations, or as a greenhouse climber where the temperature is not allowed to fall below freezing.
Description *Flower* Blood-red to dark blood-red, ageing to purple-red. Five petals form a hanging bell-shaped flower arranged along the stems in early to mid summer. *Foliage* Narrow-pointed, with some small teeth and a

light downy covering. Mid green with purple hue around veins. *Stem* Dark green, dull, partially twining. Medium rate of growth. *Fruit* None of interest.
Hardiness Tolerates a minimum winter temperature of 32°F (0°C).
Soil requirements Moderately alkaline to acid with no particular preference. If grown in containers in conservatories, a container of at least 21 in (53 cm) in diameter, filled with a good quality soil-based potting compost, is required.
Sun/Shade aspect Requires a very sheltered, warm, sunny position with no frost. Best in full sun, but will tolerate light shade.
Pruning Normally requires no pruning.
Training Allow to ramble over wires or other similar constructions. May require some tying in, particularly when young. Can be worked around a wire framework in a circle when used in greenhouses and conservatories.
Propagation and nursery production From seed, which is often self-set on existing plants and germinates well when sown with a little bottom heat in early spring. Always purchase container grown; will have to be sought from specialist nurseries or as seed from a specialist seed merchant. Best planting height 5–18 in (12–45 cm).
Problems Its dislike of frost must always be considered, while its open habit of growth can make it difficult to accommodate in some greenhouses and conservatories.
Similar forms of interest None.
Average height and spread
Five years
4 × 4 ft (1.2 × 1.2 m)
Ten years
8 × 8 ft (2.4 × 2.4 m)
Twenty years
10 × 10 ft (3 × 3 m)
Protrudes up to 6 in (15 cm) from support.

RIBES GROSSULARIA (Gooseberry Hybrids)

GOOSEBERRY

Grossulariaceae   *Fruiting Shrub*
Deciduous

A fruiting bush not always considered for wall training but responding well, particularly in ripening, when used in such situations.

Origin The basic form is from the temperate regions of Europe, but most varieties today are hybrids of garden or nursery origin.
Use As single, double or treble cordons, fan-trained or upright bushes against a wall or fence.
Description *Flower* Small, pendent, silver/yellow, tubular flowers in mid to late spring.

Ribes grossularia 'Careless'

123

Ribes grossularia 'Whinham's Industry'

Not attractive. Self-fertile. *Foliage* Hand-shaped with lobed edges, ½–¾in (1–2cm) across, light green with yellow autumn colour. *Stem* Light grey/green, becoming grey to grey/brown. Thorned. Medium growth rate. Branching habit. *Fruit* Oval, ¾–1in (2–2.5cm) long, pendent, often covered with hairs. Green in colour, ripening either to yellow/green or red/green. Normally sweet and edible when ripe. Fruits mid to late summer on wood two years old or more. Good for freezing.
Hardiness Tolerates a minimum winter temperature of 0°F (−18°C).
Soil requirements Tolerates most soils, except very alkaline, dry or waterlogged conditions.
Sun/Shade aspect Tolerates all aspects. Full sun to light shade, with full sun for preference to ripen fruit to best advantage.
Pruning Once structure is trained, shorten all last season's growth back to two buds after fruiting to encourage formation of fruit spurs.
Training Purchase one-year-old rooted cuttings and train central upright stems for cordons. If double and treble cordons are required, stop initial shoot at 6in (15cm) from its origin; this will induce one, two or three shoots which can be trained. Continue to train, shortening back side growths. For fan-training, cut back central shoot to 18in (45cm) from ground level then train ensuing side shoots into a fan-trained shape. Cut back any side shoots not required for training to within two buds. Will require wires or individual anchor points for support.
Propagation and nursery production From hardwood cuttings taken in winter. Can be planted bare-rooted from mid autumn to early spring or container grown as available. One-year-old rooted cuttings are best for training. On very rare occasions, pre-trained cordons can be found; fan-trained shrubs are never available.
Problems Thorns can make cultivation uncomfortable. May suffer from American gooseberry mildew; a proprietary control will normally treat it, but do not apply during flowering period. There are a number of other mildews and rust fungus diseases which attack gooseberries and all can be treated as for American gooseberry mildew. Gooseberry sawfly and gooseberry red spider mite also can be problems requiring treatment with a proprietary control. The need to grow shrubs in situ for training may also be a drawback, but they are nevertheless worth persistence.
Forms of interest 'Careless' The most useful variety where only a few can be accommodated. Milky green skin when ripe in mid summer. Strong, upright growth. **'Keepsake'** Pale green when ripe in mid summer. **'Lancer'** Green when ripe. Mid to late summer fruiting. **'Leveller'** Yellow when ripe. Late summer fruiting. **'Whinhams Industry'** Dark red when ripe. Mid summer fruiting.
'Whitesmith' Pale green when ripe. Mid summer fruiting.
Average height and spread
Fan-trained
Five years
5 × 5 ft (1.5 × 1.5 m)
Ten years
7 × 7 ft (2.1 × 2.1 m)
Twenty years
9 × 9 ft (2.7 × 2.7 m)
Protrudes up to 18 in (45 cm) from support
Cordon
Five years
5 × 1 ft (1.5 m × 30 cm)
Ten years
7 × 3 ft (2.1 × 91 cm)
Twenty years
7 × 3 ft (2.1 m × 91 cm)
Protrudes up to 12 in (30 cm) from support.

RIBES LAURIFOLIUM

EVERGREEN WINTER FLOWERING CURRANT
Grossulariaceae   *Wall Shrub*
Evergreen
A unique evergreen, winter flowering variety deserving more attention.

Origin From western China.
Use As a winter-flowering and evergreen shrub for sheltered walls and fences.
Description *Flower* Small, hanging racemes of male flowers, 3 in (7.5 cm) long and 1½ in (4cm) wide, yellow to light green, are produced in mid to late winter at each leaf joint on mature shrubs. Female flowers are borne on shorter, erect racemes. *Foliage* Oval, 4 in (10 cm) long and 1½ in (4 cm) wide, pointed with slightly notched edges. Dull grey/green, lighter grey underside, contrasting well with flowers. *Stem* Light red/brown when young, ageing to darker brown, finally grey/brown with age. Branching. A little weak in constitution but this is overcome by fan-training. Slow to medium rate of growth. *Fruit* Rarely fruits, but may produce small, round black-currants in autumn and early winter.
Hardiness Tolerates a minimum winter temperature of 4°F (−15°C).
Soil requirements Most soils, only disliking extremely wet or dry conditions.
Sun/Shade aspect Requires a sheltered aspect in full sun to light shade.
Pruning Normally needs no pruning, other than that required to achieve a fan shape on walls or fences.
Training Will require tying to wires or individual anchor points to achieve a fan-trained shape.
Propagation and nursery production From semi-ripe cuttings taken in early summer or hardwood cuttings in winter. Always purchase container grown; will have to be sought from specialist nurseries. Best planting height 9 in–2 ft (23–60 cm).
Problems Slow to establish, often taking two years to produce new growth, but once established relatively fast growing.
Similar forms of interest None.
Average height and spread
Five years
5 × 3 ft (1.5 m × 91 cm)
Ten years
6 × 6 ft (1.8 × 1.8 m)
Twenty years
8 × 10 ft (2.4 × 3 m)
Protrudes up to 12 in (30 cm) from support.

RIBES SATIVUM (Red and White Currant Hybrids)

RED AND WHITE CURRANTS
Grossulariaceae   *Fruiting shrub*
Deciduous
Fruiting bushes which adapt very well to cultivation against a wall or fence, where they benefit from the protection and warmth.

Origin Of European origin. Possibly crosses between *Ribes sativum* and *R. rubrum* (Northern red currant). Most varieties of nursery or garden origin.
Use As fan-trained shrubs or single, double or treble cordons, upright or at an angle of 35°.

Ribes laurifolium in flower

Ribes sativum 'Laxton's No. 1'

Description *Flower* Small, inconspicuous sulphur-yellow flowers carried in small clusters at leaf axils in late spring. *Foliage* Hand-shaped, five-fingered, 3 in (7.5 cm) across and 3½ in (8.5 cm) long. Grey/green with silver reverse and yellow autumn colour. Currant-scented when crushed. *Stem* Grey/green, becoming grey, finally grey/brown. Upright. Limited branching. Currant-scented when crushed. *Fruit* Hanging clusters of red or white fruits, depending on variety, in mid summer. Sweet, edible, for dessert or culinary uses.
Hardiness Tolerates a minimum winter temperature of 0°F (−18°C).
Soil requirements Tolerates all soil conditions, except extremely waterlogged and extremely dry.
Sun/Shade aspect Tolerates all aspects but benefits from full sun to aid ripening of fruit.
Pruning Once trained shape has been achieved, remove all side growth back to within 2 in (5 cm) of its origin annually.
Training Purchase one-year-old plants or propagate as hardwood cuttings in winter. The second year, cut central shoot back to within 12 in (30 cm) of ground level in early to mid spring and fan-train the resulting side growths. If training as a single cordon, remove all but the central shoot. If required for two and three cordons, train two shoots horizontally and turn upwards once they have reached approximately 12–15 in (30–38 cm) from the central stem. Tie to wires or individual anchor points.
Propagation and nursery production From hardwood cuttings taken in mid to early spring. For preference purchase plants no more than one year old if required for training; these will normally be 12–18 in (30–45 cm) in height, bare-rooted, although some may be found container grown. Older plants can be used for training, but will require hard cutting back the first year after planting so that ensuing shoots can be trained and these may be slow to appear. Young plants may have to be sought from specialist growers but are sometimes found in garden centres.
Problems Apart from the need for careful training they have few problems except for mildew, which can be treated with a proprietary control.
Forms of interest
UK
RED CURRANTS **'Laxton's No. 1'** Still one of the best varieties. Large fruits. Reliable. **'Red Lake'** Very dark red fruits. Extremely good variety. **'Red Start'** Heavy cropping. Late season fruit of medium size. **'Rondon'** Cropping can be inconsistent but of good size. Late fruiting.
WHITE CURRANTS **'White Dutch'** White to yellow/white fruits. **'White Versailles'** Scarce but worth seeking out. Good sprays of fruits.

USA
RED CURRANTS **'Perfection'** Medium-sized fruits in open clusters. Vigorous growing and highly productive. Good for Washington and Oregon areas. From New York. **'Red Lake'** Very dark red fruits with good flavour. Good over a wide area. From the UK. **'Stephen's No. 9'** Medium-sized red berries in medium clusters. Spreading habit but highly productive. From Ontario, Canada. **'Wilder'** Large, firm, tender red berries with tart flavour. Plants vigorous, hardy and very long-lived. From Indiana.
WHITE CURRANTS **'Jumbo'** Large, pale green, sweet fruits. Strong-growing, upright habit. Origin unknown. **'White Grape'** Good quality and very widely used. From Europe.
Average height and spread
Five years
5 × 5 ft (1.5 × 1.5 m)
Ten years
7 × 7 ft (2.1 × 2.1 m)
Twenty years
9 × 9 ft (2.7 × 2.7 m)

Sizes shown are for fan, double and treble cordons. Single cordons will produce 60 per cent less spread. Protrudes up to 12 in (30 cm) from support prior to annual pruning.

RIBES SPECIOSUM

FUCHSIA-FLOWERING CURRANT

Grossulariaceae   *Wall Shrub*
Deciduous to semi-evergreen
This flowering gooseberry is an attractive shrub with interesting flowers and adapts well to fan-training.

Origin From California.
Use As a flowering fan-trained shrub of medium size for walls and fences.
Description *Flower* Small, tubular, 1–1½ in (2.5–4 cm) long, pendent, fuchsia-shaped flowers, dark red, carried very regimentally along branches in mid to late spring. Some later flowering. *Foliage* Three or five lobed, mid-green ovate to obovate leaves, 1½ in (4 cm) wide, but sometimes smaller on older wood. Some yellow autumn colour. Leaves may be retained through winter in favoured localities. *Stem* Grey/green, becoming grey/brown. Upright, becoming spreading. Limited branching. Armed with soft thorns. Good fan shape can be achieved with time. *Fruit* Bright red fruit with bristly surface, up to ½ in (1 cm) long. Not reliable and not generally of interest.
Hardiness Tolerates a minimum winter temperature of 4°F (−15°C).
Soil requirements Tolerates all soil types, except extremely dry and extremely waterlogged.

Sun/Shade aspect Tolerates any aspect. Full sun to medium shade with medium shade for preference.
Pruning Not normally required for this plant, but can be cut back if necessary after flowering.
Training Fan-train on to wires or individual anchor points.
Propagation and nursery production From semi-ripe cuttings. Should be purchased container grown, best planting height 6–18 in (15–45 cm). Normally available from garden centres and nurseries.

Ribes speciosum

Problem May be slow to establish.
Similar forms of interest None.
Average height and spread
Five years
4 × 4 ft (1.2 × 1.2 m)
Ten years
5 × 7 ft (1.5 × 2.1 m)
Twenty years
7 × 10 ft (2.1 × 3 m)
Protrudes up to 12 in (30 cm) from support.

ROBINIA (Pink-flowering Forms)

FALSE ACACIA

Leguminosae   *Hardy Tree*
Deciduous
A group of trees rapidly becoming appreciated for their adaptability to fan-training.

Origin From south-western USA, some named varieties from France.
Use As medium to large fan-trained trees for walls and fences.
Description *Flower* Clusters of pea-flowers, up to 3 in (75 cm) long, on wood two years old or more in early summer. *Foliage* Pinnate leaves, up to 6 in (15 cm) long, with nine to 11 oblong or ovate leaflets each 2 in (5 cm) long. Light grey/green with yellow autumn colour. *Stem* Light grey/green to grey/brown with small prickles. Upright when young, branching with age, easy to fan-train. Branches and twigs appear dead in winter, but produce leaves from apparently budless stems in late spring. Medium growth rate. *Fruit* Small, grey/green, bristly pea-pods up to 4 in (10 cm) long, in late summer and early autumn.
Hardiness Tolerates a minimum winter temperature of 4°F (−15°C). Stems may suffer some tip damage in severe winters.
Soil requirements Thrives in most soils; particularly tolerant of alkaline types. Resents waterlogging.
Sun/Shade aspect Tolerates all but the most

exposed of aspects. Full sun to very light shade.
Pruning Prune very young trees back to 9–12 in (23–30 cm) from the graft point in early spring following planting. Select and train resulting five to seven shoots and tie into a fan-trained shape. In subsequent years, remove all side growths back to two points from their origin and maintain original main branches in fan shape.
Training Will require securing to wires or individual anchor points.
Propagation and nursery production From seed or grafting. Purchase container grown. Choose either bush grown or young trees not more than two years old and between 3–5 ft (91 cm–1.5 m) tall. Must be sought from general or specialist nurseries; most varieties not offered by garden centres.
Problems Notorious for poor establishment; container grown trees provide best results. Branches may be damaged by high winds and need shelter.

Robinia kelseyi in flower

Forms of interest *R.* × *ambigua* Light pink flowers. Pinnate leaves with 13 to 21 light grey/green leaflets. Must be sought from specialist nurseries. *R.* 'Casque Rouge' Rose-pink to pink-red flowers. An interesting variety from France. Difficult to find. *R. fertilis* 'Monument' Rosy-red flowers. Half average height and spread. from south-eastern USA. *R.* × *hillieri* Slightly fragrant lilac-pink flowers. Originally raised in UK. *R. hispida* 'Macrophylla' Large flowers similar to those of wisteria. The variety most often planted. *R. kelseyi* Flowers white with purple/pink shading. Attractive pale grey/green foliage with nine to 11 leaflets. From south-eastern

USA. Must be sought from specialist nurseries. *R. luxurians* Rose-pink flowers. Leaves up to 12 in (30 cm) long, pinnate and with 15 to 25 ovate, bright green leaflets. Slightly more than average height and spread. Not readily available; must be sought from specialist nurseries. From south-western USA.
Average height and spread
Five years
12 × 12 ft (3.7 × 3.7 m)
Ten years
18 × 18 ft (5.5 × 5.5 m)
Twenty years
24 × 24 ft (7.3 × 7.3 m)
Protrudes up to 2 ft (60 cm) from support.

ROBINIA PSEUDOACACIA

ACACIA, BLACK LOCUST, FALSE ACACIA

Leguminosae   **Hardy Tree**
Deciduous

This tree makes an elegant fan-trained shape, as long as sufficient space can be provided.

Origin From the USA.
Use As a large fan-trained tree for walls.
Description *Flower* Racemes 4–7 in (10–18 cm) long of fragrant white flowers in early summer; florets have blotched yellow bases inside. Size varies with age of tree and location. *Foliage* Pinnate, up to 10 in (25 cm) long, with 11 to 23 ovate leaflets. Light grey/green with good yellow autumn colour. *Stem* Grey/green to grey/brown and sparsely covered in thorns. Fast-growing when young, slowing and branching with maturity. Appears completely dead in winter, breaks leaf from almost budless stems. *Fruit* Small, grey/green pea-pods up to 4 in (10 cm) long in autumn.
Hardiness Tolerates a minimum winter temperature of 4°F (−15°C). Some stem tip damage may occur in severe winters.
Soil requirements Tolerates most soil conditions but dislikes waterlogging. Good on dry, sandy soils.
Sun/Shade aspect Tolerates a moderately exposed aspect but may need wind protection. Full sun to medium shade, preferring full sun.
Pruning Prune young trees back to 9–12 in (23–30 cm) from base or graft point in early spring following planting. Select and train resulting five to seven shoots and tie into a fan-trained shape. In subsequent years, remove all growths back to two points from their origin and maintain original main branches in fan shape.
Training Secure to wires or individual anchor points.
Propagation and nursery production From seed. Named varieties from grafting on to

understock of *R. pseudoacacia*. Best purchased container grown or root-balled (balled-and-burlapped); difficult to establish bare-rooted. Plants for fan-training should not be more than two years old, either bush or single stem, between 3–5 ft (91 cm–1.5 m) tall. Stocked by general nurseries and specialist outlets.
Problems Subject to wind damage. Sometimes difficult to establish; extra organic or peat composts should be added to soil, and adequate watering supplied in first spring. Produces suckers at ground level, often far from the central stem.
Similar forms of interest *R. p.* 'Bessoniana' White flowers in early summer. Two thirds average height and spread; the best white-flowering form for small gardens. Possibly the best variety for fan-training.
Average height and spread
Five years
10 × 10 ft (3 × 3 m)
Ten years
20 × 20 ft (6 × 6 m)
Twenty years
30 × 30 ft (9 × 9 m)
Protrudes up to 4 ft (1.2 m) from support.

ROBINIA PSEUDOACACIA 'FRISIA'

GOLDEN ACACIA

Leguminosae   **Hardy Tree**
Deciduous

One of the most spectacular of all golden foliage wall specimens.

Robinia pseudoacacia 'Frisia' in leaf

Origin Of garden origin, from Europe.
Use As a medium to large fan-trained tree for walls and tall fences.
Description *Flower* Short racemes of white pea-flowers, produced only on very mature trees in mid summer. *Foliage* Pinnate, with seven to nine leaflets 6 in (15 cm) long. Bright yellow to yellow/green in spring, lightening in early summer. Turns deeper yellow in late summer to early autumn. *Stem* Brown to grey/brown. Strong shoots with definite red prickles on new growth. Wood may appear dead in winter but quickly grows away in late spring or early summer from apparently budless stems. Medium to fast growth rate. *Fruit* Insignificant.
Hardiness Tolerates a minimum winter temperature of 4°F (−15°C). Some stem-tip damage may occur in severe winters.
Soil requirements Most soil conditions; growth is limited on very alkaline, permanently wet or poor soils. Grows best on moist, rich, loamy soil.
Sun/Shade aspect Tolerates all but the most severe of aspects. Full sun to very light shade.
Pruning Prune young trees back to 9–12 in (23–30 cm) from the graft point in early spring following planting. Select and train resulting

Robinia pseudoacacia in flower

five to seven shoots and tie into a fan-trained shape. In subsequent years remove all side growths back to two points from their origin and maintain original main branches in fan shape.

Training Secure to wires or individual anchor points.

Propagation and nursery production From grafting on to *R. pseudoacacia*. Purchase container grown; best planting height for fan-trained trees between 2–5 ft (60 cm–1.5 m), using trees of not more than two years old. Normally available from general nurseries and garden centres.

Problems Branches may be brittle and easily damaged by severe weather conditions. Late to break leaf, often bare until early summer, but grows rapidly once started. Notoriously difficult to establish unless container grown.

Average height and spread
Five years
12 × 12 ft (3.7 × 3.7 m)
Ten years
18 × 18 ft (5.5 × 5.5 m)
Twenty years
24 × 24 ft (7.3 × 7.3 m)
Protrudes up to 4 ft (1.2 m) from support.

ROSA
(Climbing Musk Roses and Similar Forms)

KNOWN BY VARIETY NAME

Rosaceae   *Rose*
Deciduous

There are many beautiful white and off-white musk roses but many can, in all but the largest of spaces, be invasive, so alternative, less vigorous varieties have also been included in this entry.

Origin From the Himalayas and of garden origin.
Use Ideal for covering very large walls, fences, hedgerows, trellises and pergolas, or to climb through trees to give a cascading effect. Careful selection regarding size should be made as many are extemely vigorous.
Description *Flower* Single, semi-double or double, normally carried in clusters, each flower up to 1 in (2.5 cm) across, white to pale pink and flowering from mid summer to early autumn with attractive musk scent. *Foliage* Five, seven or nine small round leaflets make up a pinnate leaf, 5–7 in (12–18 cm) long. Normally light to mid green. Some good yellow autumn colour depending on variety. *Stem* Strong, ranging, arching, heavily thorned, thorns often attractive. Medium to

Rosa 'Francis E. Lester'

fast growth rate. *Fruit* Small, round, orange/red hips carried in clusters in many varieties offering winter attraction.
Hardiness Tolerates a minimum winter temperature of 0°F (−18°C).
Soil requirements Will grow on all soil types, including alkaline and acid, but needs a deep root run to achieve full growth potential.
Sun/Shade aspect Tolerates all aspects in full sun to medium shade.
Pruning Not normally required, but the occasional removal of an old branch almost to ground level in early spring will induce new growth and keep the rose in good order.
Training Tie to wires or individual anchor points. Allow to ramble through branches of large trees or hedgerows.
Propagation and nursery production Commercial production is by budding, which entails the insertion of a single bud into a pre-determined rootstock. Plants are normally sold 18 months on from this process. This group of roses can also be grown from hardwood cuttings. Purchase bare-rooted or root-wrapped from early autum to mid spring; may be available container grown from late spring to early autumn and beyond, but try to ensure the plant has not been potted for more than one year. Best planting height 1–3 ft (30–91 cm) depending on variety. Some varieties are available from garden centres and nurseries, but most may have to be sought from specialist growers.
Problems Often heavily thorned, many thorns with barbs. May suffer from mildew, although not normally to any great extent. Greenfly and blackfly may also be a problem, but normally pests and diseases are simply controlled by the great vigour of the plant, which can, in many cases, end in it growing out of its intended area.
Forms of interest 'Autumnalis' (syn. *Rosa moschata autumnalis*, *Rosa × noisettiana*, 'Champney's Rose') White flowers, single, flushed pink and red with central yellow stamens, carried in round clusters in mid summer. Needs some protection. Introduced prior to 1812. Average height and spread 8 × 8 ft (2.4 × 2.4 m). Protrudes up to 3 ft (91 cm) from support. **'Bleu Magenta'** Multiflora hybrid. Deep purple flowers in large clusters and bright green leaves. Rarely has thorns and is scentless. Ideal for growing up walls and trellis and through small trees or shrubs. Introduced 1899. Average height and spread 6 × 6 ft (1.8 × 1.8 m). Protrudes up to 2 ft (60 cm) from support. **'Bobbie James'** Creamy-white flowers, single, in large, pendent clusters in mid summer. Extremely vigorous. Introduced 1961. Average height and spread 30 × 20 ft (9 × 6 m). Protrudes up to 6 ft (1.8 m) from support. **'Brenda Colvin'** Soft pink flowers with yellow stamens, often appearing apricot overall. Very strong-growing. Ideal for growing in trees or for covering old buildings. Date of introduction

unknown. Average height and spread 30 × 30 ft (9 × 9 m). Protrudes up to 5 ft (1.5 m) from support. **'Francis E. Lester'** Flowers single, some white, most pink. Good hip production in autumn. Introduced 1946. Average height and spread 15 × 15 ft (4.6 × 4.6 m). Protrudes up to 5 ft (1.5 m) from support. **'Paul's Himalayan Musk'** Double, soft pink flowers, ageing to white, fragrant. Flowers in mid summer. Ideal for ground cover. Introduced in the late 19th century. Average height and spread 20 × 15 ft (6 × 4.6 m). Protrudes up to 5 ft (1.5 m) from

Rosa 'Rambling Rector'

support. **'Rambling Rector'** (syn. **'Shakespeare's Musk'**) Small, semi-double white flowers in clusters in mid summer. Origin is undetermined and has been in cultivation for many years. Average height and spread 20 × 20 ft (6 × 6 m). Protrudes up to 7 ft (2.1 m) from support. *R. brunonii* (syn. *R. b.* **'Himalayan Musk Rose'**, *R. moschata nepalensis*) Single white flowers in large clusters, larger than most, with golden yellow stamens, flowering mid summer. Long, ranging branches. Good hip production in autumn. Introduced 1822. Average height and spread 25 × 20 ft (7.6 × 6 m). Protrudes up to 7 ft (2.1 m) from support. *R. filipes* **'Kiftsgate'** Creamy-white flowers in huge trusses in mid summer. Extremely vigorous, flowering well in shade and producing good fruit. Tolerates full sun to almost full shade. Ideal for trees or hedgerows, but requires considerable space. Can also be allowed to grow as widespreading ground cover. Ideal for covering difficult banks, again where space can be allowed.

Rosa 'Paul's Himalayan Musk'

Introduced 1954. Average height and spread 30 × 30 ft (9 × 9 m). Protrudes up to 8 ft (2.4 m) from support. **R. helenae** The grey/green foliage shows off clusters of creamy-white single flowers. Introduced 1907. Average height and spread 20 × 18 ft (6 × 5.5 m). Protrudes up to 5 ft (1.5 m) from support. **R. moschata** Off-white flowers in trusses in mid summer to late summer. Strong-growing but not tall. Recorded as early as the 16th century. Average height and spread 12 × 12 ft (3.7 × 3.7 m). Protrudes up to 6 ft (1.8 m) from support. **R. mulliganii** (formerly known as *R. longicuspis*) Flowers white, single, banana-scented. Foliage coppery-tinted when young. Shoots and foliage glossy green, can be evergreen in some situa-

Rosa brunonii

tions. Good fruit production maintained into winter. Can be used as large-scale ground cover. Introduced 1917. Average height and spread 15 × 10 ft (4.6 × 3 m). Protrudes up to 5 ft (1.5 m) from support. **R. multiflora** Creamy-white single flowers with central yellow stamens, produced in large trusses in mid summer. Branches almost thornless. Bright, shiny mid green foliage. Date of introduction not known, but extremely old. Average height and spread 15 × 15 ft (4.6 × 4.6 m). Protrudes up to 5 ft (1.5 m) from support. **R. m. carnea** Flowers lilac/pink in hanging clusters, double and globe-shaped. Thin, ranging branches. Dark green foliage. Introduced 1804. Average height and spread 20 × 15 ft (6 × 4.6 m). Protrudes up to 6 ft (1.8 m) from support. **R. m. cathayensis** Single, flat, pink flowers, produced in mid summer. Introduced 1907. Average height and spread 15 × 15 ft (4.6 × 4.6 m). Protrudes up to 15 ft (4.6 m) from support. **R. m. platyphylla** (Seven Sisters Rose) Flowers deep lilac/pink to white, sweetly scented and flowering in mid summer. Thought to have been introduced from China prior to 1816. Average height and spread 15 × 15 ft (4.6 × 4.6 m). Protrudes up to 8 ft (2.4 m) from support. **R. m. watsoniana** Small, single

Rosa multiflora

flowers carried in large panicles in spring and again in mid summer, followed by small red hips. Very thin wispy growth. Leaves have wavy edges and stems are very thorny. Requires a sheltered aspect. Introduced 1870. Average height and spread 6 × 6 ft (1.8 × 1.8 m). Protrudes up to 3 ft (91 cm) from support. **R. sinowilsonii** Single white flowers, shown off well against glossy green foliage. Flowers mid summer. Strong-growing but needs a sheltered aspect. In existence for a great number of years. Average height and spread 12 × 10 ft (3.7 × 3 m). Protrudes up to 4 ft (1.2 m) from support. **'Seagull'** Truly a rambler, but closely resembles *R. brunonii* 'Himalayan Musk Rose'. Clusters of single, pure white flowers with bright golden-yellow stamens on vigorous-shooted plant. Introduced 1907. Average height and spread 25 × 20 ft (7.6 × 6 m). Protrudes up to 7 ft (2.1 m) from support. **'The Garland'** Semi-double, creamy-white, narrow petals, with age becoming tinged pink. Mid summer flowering. Good fragrance. Introduced 1835 and possibly the best Himalayan Musk type for a small garden. Average height and spread 15 × 12 ft (4.6 × 3.7 m). Protrudes up to 4 ft (1.2 m) from support. **'Treasure Trove'** Clusters of creamy-apricot flowers in mid summer, against good mid green foliage. Long red hips in autumn. Can be used for ground cover or woodland planting. Introduced 1979. Average height and spread 30 × 30 ft (9 × 9 m). Protrudes up to 8 ft (2.4 m) from support. **R. longicuspis 'Wedding Day'** Single white flowers with lemon and pink tinge, carried in clusters in mid summer.
Introduced 1950.
Average height and spread 30 × 20 ft (9 × 6 m). Protrudes up to 7 ft (2.1 m) from support.
Average height and spread Growth at ten years given for each variety.

Rosa felipes **'Kiftsgate'**

ROSA
(Climbing Species Roses)

KNOWN BY BOTANICAL NAME
Rosaceae   Rose
Deciduous
These varieties are gathered together under one heading and described in some detail. Some have specific requirements which are covered within 'Forms of interest', but all can be fan-trained as climbers.

Origin As per individual variety.
Use For large walls and fences, to cover pergolas and trellis. Some varieties suitable for cold greenhouse and conservatory use.
Description *Flower* Yellow or pink, 1–3 in (2.5–7.5 cm) across, early to mid summer, depending on variety. Some with fragrance. *Foliage* Five or seven leaflets, some light green, some darker, depending on variety, up to 5–7 in (12–18 cm) long. *Stem* Light green, ageing to brown, normally strong and upright. Medium to fast growth rate. *Fruit* Not normally produced.

Rosa chinensis mutabilis

Hardiness Tolerates a minimum winter temperature of 4°F (−15°C).
Soil requirements Tolerates all soil types, except for extremely alkaline, which may cause distress. Requires good moisture and plant food retention.
Sun/Shade aspect Sheltered aspect in full sun to light shade.
Pruning Not normally required, but after five to six years some old branches can be removed to within 2 ft (60 cm) of ground level. This will usually induce new shoots.
Training Tie to wires or individual anchor points, or to trellis.
Propagation and nursery production Always purchase container-grown with the exception of *R. chinensis* **'Climbing Cécile Brunner'**, which is also sold bare-rooted. Best planting height 1–3 ft (30–91 cm). Not always stocked by garden centres and will often have to be sought from specialist nurseries.
Problems May suffer from attacks of greenfly and blackfly; treat with a proprietary control. Mildew and blackspot may be a problem. Correct pruning, cultivation, feeding and treatment with a proprietary control will normally keep the disease to a minimum. Thorns can make handling uncomfortable and plants which are not pruned as suggested can become woody. Suckers from rootstocks may appear and are difficult to identify as they closely resemble the climbing variety. The indication is that if they develop from below ground level they are normally suckers.

Rosa banksiae lutea

Forms of interest *R. chinensis* **'Climbing Cécile Brunner'** Miniature hybrid tea flowers, mother-of-pearl pink, presented in large flowing sprays in mid summer. Extremely attractive. Tolerates all soil conditions and aspects in full sun to medium shade. Can be trained through trees. Introduced prior to 1904. Average height and spread 25 × 20 ft (7.6 × 6 m). Protrudes up to 5 ft (1.5 m) from support. *R. bracteata* **'Mermaid'** Single, large flowers, up to 4 in (10 cm) across, buff yellow with apricot shading and central russet-red stamens. Recurrent flowering, with main flowering period early to mid summer. Dark, almost purple/green foliage with glossy surface. Tolerates all aspects, in full sun to medium shade, but some die-back may be seen in very severe winters. Thorns are bright purple/red on purple/red foliage. Its natural habit is to climb high towards the sun and produce little or no basal growth. Dislikes severe alkalinity. Introduced 1917. Average height and spread 30 × 30 ft (9 × 9 m). Protrudes up to 5 ft (1.5 m) from support. *R. banksiae lutea* Double, almost carnation-like canary-yellow flowers 1 in (2.5 cm) across in large trusses. Flowering late spring, early summer, some later intermittent flowering. Attractive light green foliage and bright green stems with some winter attraction. Remove one-third of oldest flowering growth to ground level after flowering. Strong-growing. Requires a sheltered position; tolerates a minimum winter temperature of 14°F (−10°C). Introduced prior to 1824. Average height and spread 20 × 20 ft (6 × 6 m). Protrudes up to 4 ft (1.2 m) from support. *R. chinensis mutabilis* Flowers single, honey yel-

low, ageing to orange and finally red. Produced continuously from late spring to early or even late autumn, making an interesting contrast against dark wine-red, suffused dark green foliage. Flowers carried on attractive shoots, giving a flowing texture. Tolerates exposed positions and any soil in full sun to light shade. Introduced in the 18th century.
Average height and spread 7 × 7 ft (2.1 × 2.1 m).
Protrudes up to 2 ft (60 cm) from support.
Average height and spread Growth at ten years given for each variety.

ROSA
(Modern Hybrid Climbing)

KNOWN BY VARIETY NAME
Rosaceae   *Rose*
Deciduous
Still the paramount group of climbing plants to provide colour throughout the summer. This class of roses is defined as those that were brought into commercial production after 1920.

Origin Varied, but most of nursery origination.
Use For walls, fences, pillars, pergolas and trelliswork, for wire or timber frames in the open or to adorn the front of buildings. Can be grown in large containers.

Description *Flower* Either single or semi-double, with round-ended, triangular-shaped petals held open, closed or in cupped clusters. Many varieties with strong scent. Colours range from red, yellow, white, pink, blue and shades in between. Some bi-coloured and multi-coloured varieties. Flowers from early summer to late autumn, not continuously but repeating. *Foliage* Five ovate to round leaflets make up a pinnate leaf, dark green to mid green, some varieties with purple hue or purple backing. Ribs on leaves may have small thorns. *Stem* Light to dark green, becoming green/brown. Basically upright and branching. Frequent thorns, large, red to red/brown in colour. Medium to fast growth rate. *Fruit* Large orange to orange/red rose hips produced in autumn and often retained well into winter.
Hardiness Tolerates a minimum winter temperature of 4°F (−15°C).
Soil requirements Does well on all soils but may show some signs of chlorosis on severe alkaline types. Requires an annual mulch with spent mushroom compost, garden compost or farmyard manure.
Sun/Shade aspect Tolerates all aspects. Full sun to medium shade, but full sun to light shade for best performance. Some varieties will grow in a shady planting position, but may be shy to flower.

Rosa 'Schoolgirl'

Pruning Do not prune plants prior to planting as this may cause reversion to bush forms; just remove any very weak shoots or any dead tips. Apart from deadheading, the removal of any dead wood during the winter period and shaping, this group of roses needs little pruning for the first three to five years after planting. From then on it is a good practice to remove up to one-third of the oldest shoots to ground level or to near ground level in March, to encourage regrowth from the base. This can be carried out every two to three years thereafter to prevent the rose from becoming old and woody.
Training Tie to wires or individual anchor points, either upright or in a fan shape, depending on situation. Some varieties respond well to having their branches trained horizontally from the fan shape. This practice reduces sap flow and encourages flower buds to form.
Propagation and nursery production Commercial production is from budding, entailing the insertion of one single bud into a predetermined rootstock. Plants are normally sold 18 months on from this process. Can be grown from hardwood cuttings, but lifespan may be shortened due to lack of root vigour. Purchase bare-rooted from early autumn and beyond; if buying container grown plants try to ensure they have not been potted for more than one year. Best planting height 1–3 ft (30–91 cm), depending on variety. Many varieties readily available from garden centres

Rosa chinensis 'Climbing Cécile Brunner'

Rosa **'Superstar, Climbing'**

and nurseries, others may have to be sought from specialist growers.

Problems May suffer from attacks of greenfly and blackfly. Treat with a proprietary control. Mildew and blackspot may be a problem; correct pruning, cultivation and feeding and treatment with a proprietary control will normally keep to a minimum. Thorns can make handling uncomfortable and plants which are not pruned as suggested can become very woody. Newly planted modern hybrid climbing roses may be slow to produce strong shoots during the building up of a good root system.

Suckers from rootstocks may appear and are difficult to identify as they closely resemble the actual climbing variety. The indication is that if they develop from below ground they are normally suckers. Careful observation should, however, make it possible to differentiate between the two foliage patterns.

Many climbing roses in this group are sports of hybrid tea or floribunda roses and therefore care must be taken when purchasing to ensure that they are climbing and not bush forms.

Rosa **'White Cockade'**

Forms of interest 'Alchemist' Double yellow flowers with interspersed egg-yolk yellow petals in late spring and mid to late summer. Good scent. Attractive light green to mid green foliage. Strong growth. Good on all soils. Introduced in 1956. **'Alec's Red, Climbing'** Fragrant cherry red flowers, not strong growing but worthy of space. Good foliage. Ideal as a pillar rose. Introduced 1975. **'Allen Chandler'** Flowers up to 4 in (10 cm) across, single to semi-double, with central golden stamens setting off the vivid red petals. Repeat flowering. Requires a shel-

tered position with good, well prepared, moisture-retentive soil. Needs plenty of space. Introduced in 1923. **'Allgold, Climbing'** Double, golden yellow flowers carried in clusters from early to late summer, not necessarily continously. Slightly scented. Good growth. Mid green foliage. Good for all soil types. Introduced 1961. **'Aloha'** Very full, double, rich pink flowers with darker backs to petals. Very attractive. Flowering from late spring then almost continuously throughout summer. Leathery dark green foliage. Disease resistant. Tolerates all soil types. May be found in some garden centres in the shrub rose section. **'Altissimo'** Single, slightly scented, blood-red flowers, $3\frac{1}{2}$–4 in (9–10 cm) across, carried in large trusses. Spectacular. Almost continuous flowering throughout early summer to mid autumn. Good dark green, disease resistant foliage. Tolerates all soil types. Introduced 1966. **'Ash Wednesday'** Unusual double flowers, off-white to lilac/blue. Repeat flowering. Strong growing with good foliage. Can be grown in exposed aspects from full sun to medium shade. Introduced 1955. **'Bantry Bay'** Bold pink semi-

Rosa **'Aloha'**

double to double flowers presented in clusters. Repeat flowering. Tolerates all soils with adequate preparation and exposed aspects from full sun to medium shade. Introduced 1967. **'Bettina, Climbing'** Coppery-orange, fragrant, hybrid tea-shaped flowers. Repeat flowering from mid to late summer. Dark green leaves carried on strong, dark, upright stems. Needs a sheltered position for best results. Train branches horizontally to aid flowering. Introduced 1958. **'Blessings, Climbing'** Strongly fragrant, hybrid tea shaped-flowers from mid to late summer, salmon to bright pink in bud, opening to a full double clear pink. Dark green foliage on good, dark, upright stems. Introduced 1975. **'Blue Moon, Climbing'** Large, well-formed flowers, lilac to mid blue. Attractive in bud, opening to loose formation. Very heavily scented. Foliage susceptible to blackspot. Recurrent flowering. Requires full sun and good soil conditions. Introduced 1967. **'Breath of Life'** (syn. **'Harquanne'**) Large, fragrant, hybrid tea flowers of apricot/pink presented both singly and in sprays. Good foliage. Introduced 1982. **'Casino'** (syn. **'Gerbe d'Or'**) Very good yellow, double, scented flowers carried on strong stems. Repeat flowering. Good golden-green foliage. Tolerates a wide range of soils and exposed aspects in full sun to medium shade. Introduced 1963. **'Chaplin's Pink'** Well established variety with semi-double to single flowers, bright pink in colour, produced en masse from mid to late summer and more sparsely in early autumn. Good growth and foliage. Ideal for exposed aspects and for growing in trees. Introduced 1928. **'Chateau-de-Clos-Vougeot, Climbing'** Dark rich velvet crimson blooms, opening to

form a flat and wide flower. Very strongly scented. Possibly repeat flowering. Strong growing for trellis and walls. Introduced 1920. **'City of York'** Creamy-white flowers in clusters. Short flowering season. Clean foliage. Introduced 1945. **'Compassion'** Apricot to copper, fragrant flowers with yellow and pink highlights and shading. Repeat flowering. Good glossy foliage and strong

Rosa **'Altissimo'**

growth. Tolerates all soil conditions. Introduced 1974. **'Comtesse Vandal'** Orange in bud and opening to salmon. Reverse of petals orange/pink. Flowers from mid summer to early autumn, not necessarily continuously. Some scent. Introduced 1936. **'Coral Dawn'** Double, wide, balloon-shaped coral-pink flowers. Repeat flowering from mid summer to early autumn. Good dark green foliage and strong growth. Tolerates all soil conditions and aspects. Introduced 1952. **'Crimson Descant'** Fragrant, double, crimson flowers in good numbers. Good dark green foliage. No recorded date of introduction. **'Crimson Glory'** Possibly the most fragrant of all red roses. Double, attractively shaped flowers with a velvety texture from early to late summer. Foliage not of the best, subject to blackspot and mildew but worth perseverance. Introduced 1946. **'Danse de Feu'** (syn. **'Spectacular'**) Brick-red flowers, globe-shaped, opening to a looser formation. Almost continuous flowering from early summer to early autumn. Foliage dark green. Subject to attacks of blackspot and mildew but worth perseverance for its use on exposed and shady positions. Introduced 1952. **'Dream Girl'** Soft coral-pink, very attractively shaped flowers, rosette formation. Very strong characteristic rose scent. For pillars and trellis. Introduced

Rosa **'Compassion'**

Rosa 'Ena Harkness, Climbing'

1944. **'Dreaming Spires'** Bright golden yellow flowers with good scent. Dark green foliage and strong, upright growth. Introduced 1973. **'Dublin Bay'** Scented, bright crimson flowers in clusters from mid to early autumn, almost continuous. Two thirds average height and spread. Makes a good pillar rose for all soil types. Introduced 1976. **'Elegance'** Double, shapely flowers, mid yellow, ageing to lemon-yellow. Repeat flowering once established. Mid green, glossy foliage, strong growing. Tolerates all soil types. Introduced 1937. **'Elizabeth Harkness, Climbing'** Ivory to white flowers on upright growth. Ideal for pillars in all aspects and soils. Introduced 1975. **'Elizabeth Heather Grierson'** (syn. **'Mattnot'**) Fragrant, soft

Rosa 'Golden Showers'

pink hybrid tea flowers. Good growth and foliage. No recorded date of introduction. **'Ena Harkness, Climbing'** Double, velvety red, very highly scented, hybrid tea flowers carried on weak flower stalks which give the flowers a nodding effect. Flowers from early to late summer. Foliage may suffer from attacks of mildew and blackspot but worth perseverance. Tolerates all soil types. Ideal for exposed or shady walls. Introduced 1954. **'Fashion, Climbing'** A floribunda type rose. Large, fragrant, coral/peach flowers carried in clusters. Free-flowering from late summer to early autumn. Introduced 1951. **'Fragrant Cloud, Climbing'** Well-shaped coral-red flowers, very highly scented. Repeat flowering. Ideal for pillars in all aspects and soils. Introduced 1966. **'General MacArthur'** Flowers scented, loose in formation, rosy-red in colour, borne from mid summer to early autumn. Strong growing. Tolerates all soil types. Introduced 1923. **'Golden Showers'** Deep golden-yellow ageing to cream, loosely

floppy flowers with wavy-edged petals. Attractive and continuous flowering. Foliage dark green. Stems strong, upright, mid green with very few thorns. Ideal for exposed aspects from full sun to medium shade. Introduced 1956. **'Grand Hotel'** Bright red double flowers shaded scarlet. Medium-sized hybrid tea. Unfading good foliage and strong growth. Introduced 1973. **'Grand'mère Jenny, Climbing'** Hybrid tea flowers, creamy yellow with splashes of pink and red both through petals and on outer edges. Scented, flowering from mid summer to late summer. Leaves dark green. Strong growing, one third more than average height and spread. Introduced 1958. **'Guinée'** Very heavily scented, attractively shaped, deep wine-red petals opening to form a saucer-shaped flower. Repeat flowering. Suffers attacks of mildew which is difficult to control, but worth growing for its scent. Tolerates wide range of soil conditions as long as adequate preparation has been made. Introduced 1938. **'Handel'** Most attractive semi-double large flowers, white to silvery white with pink or red markings around each petal edge. Scented. Continuous flowering. Introduced 1956. **'Highfield'** Attractive buds open to medium-sized bright yellow flowers, often with peach tints. Good foliage and growth in all aspects. Introduced 1981. **'Iceberg, Climbing'** (syn. **'Schneewittchen'**) Floribunda type flowers in large sprays. Pure white semi-double, flowering from mid summer to early autumn. In wet conditions flower buds may spot pink, but still worthy of merit. Ideal for exposed aspects in full sun to medium shade. Introduced 1968. **'Joseph's Coat'** Flowers change

Rosa 'Handel'

from yellow through orange to red. Continuous flowering over a long period. Good on all aspects and soil types. Introduced 1954. **'Josephine Bruce, Climbing'** Extremely good, fragrant, deep velvet red flowers up to 4 in (10 cm) across. Flowers from mid summer to early autumn, not necessarily continuous. Good growth of dark green foliage but very thorny. Introduced 1954. **'Korona, Climbing'** Attractive buds open to semi-double orange/red flowers from mid summer to early autumn. Growth strong and upright in habit. Foliage dark green. Disease resistant. Tolerates exposed aspects in full sun to medium shade. Introduced 1957. **'Lady Sylvia, Climbing'** Hybrid tea flowers, rich pink with attractive perfume from early summer to early autumn, not necessarily continuous. Strong growing. Good foliage. Introduced 1933. **'La Rêve'** Mainly single, sometimes semi-double pale yellow flowers with attractive scent. Good glossy green foliage. Strong growing for trellis and walls. Introduced 1923. **'Lavinia'** Deep pink flowers, some scent. Strong growth and good foliage. Good on all soil types and aspects. Introduced 1983. **'Leaping Salmon'** Salmon-pink, good shaped, very fragrant flowers. Perpetual flowering. Good for trellis and pillars. Introduced 1986. **'Leverkusen'** Large sprays of semi-double, pale yellow flowers. Continuous flowering. Good light green foliage. Strong growing, tolerating exposed aspects in full sun to medium shade. Introduced 1954. **'Leys Perpetual'** Yellow and cream, flat, double flowers, scented and repeat flowering. Growth may be suspect and requires good soil conditions. Introduced 1937. **'Maigold'** Copper/yellow flowers, semi-double, somewhat open in habit, flowering from early summer to early autumn, not

Rosa 'Leverkusen'

necessarily continuously. Foliage mid green, glossy. Good growth. Tolerates a wide range of soil conditions in full sun to medium shade. Good for exposed aspects or for growing through trees. May be found in some garden centres in the shrub rose section. Introduced 1953. **'Masquerade, Climbing'** Clusters of semi-double saucer-shaped floribunda type flowers, first opening yellow, ageing to pink, finally red. Flowers from early to late summer. Dark green foliage, disease resistant. Strong growth. Tolerates all soil conditions. Introduced 1958. **'Meg'** Single buff-yellow to apricot flowers with central russet-red stamens. Scented. Repeat flowering from early summer to early autumn. Good dark green foliage, disease resistant. Tolerates a wide range of aspects. Introduced 1954. **'Mme Butterfly, Climbing'** Hybrid tea flowers in different shades of pink through to blush with lemon centres. Fragrant. Repeat flowering from early to late summer. Strong growth. Attractive foliage. Tolerates full sun to medium shade and most soil conditions. May benefit from horizontal training to induce more flowers. Introduced 1926. **'Mme**

Edouard Herriot, Climbing' Hybrid tea coral flowers with yellow shading. Semi-double, flowering from mid summer to early autumn. Good foliage. Tolerates all aspects and soils. Introduced 1921. **'Mme Grégoire Staechelin'** Large, open, double, pale pink flowers with deeper pink reverse and attractive veining. Flowers in early summer and intermittently thereafter. Good foliage. Tolerates all soil types in exposed locations in full sun to medium shade. Introduced 1927. **'Mme Henri Guillot'** Loose, semi-double, burnt orange flowers from mid to late summer. Some fragrance. Introduced 1942. **'Mrs Aaron Ward'** Strong, fragrant, bright yellow flowers, splashed with salmon pink. Weather will vary colour intensity. Flowers from mid to late summer. Introduced 1922. **'Mrs G. A. Van Rossem'** Orange/apricot, globe-shaped flowers with golden background, the reverse of petals deeper coloured. Repeat flowering. Tolerates exposed aspects in full sun to medium shade. Introduced 1937. **'Mrs Herbert Stevens'** Pure white, scented flowers. Very old variety still deserving consideration. Repeat flowering. Tolerates exposed aspects in full sun to medium shade. Introduced 1922. **'Mrs**

Rosa 'Maigold'

Sam McGredy, Climbing' Copper/orange scented flowers presented against a coppery-red foliage, making an attractive combination. Flowers from early to late summer. Strong growing, ideal for growing in trees. Tolerates all soil conditions. Introduced 1937. **'Malaga'** Repeat flowering, deep rose pink blooms with an interesting apple fragrance. Good growth and foliage. Good on all soil types. Introduced 1971. **'Morning Jewel'** Bright pink flowers of medium size produced in good numbers. Very good first flowering and some later flowers. Clean foliage. Good for walls, fences, trellis and pillars. Introduced 1968. **'New Dawn, Climbing'** Numerous repeat to almost continuous production of pale pink, perfumed flowers. Almost rambler-like growth. Tolerates exposed positions but dislikes shade. Introduced 1930. **'Night Light'** (syn **'Poullight'**) Fragrant, deep yellow flowers which age to orange/red. Strong growth and good foliage. Ideal for all aspects and soils. Introduced 1987. **'Norwich Pink'** Semi-double flowers, bright cerise, opening flat. Strong-growing for walls and trellis. Good clean foliage. Introduced 1962. **'Norwich Salmon'** Pale salmon-pink flowers in clusters. Dark green foliage. Strong growing, disease resistant. Good for all aspects on pillars, walls and trellis. Introduced 1962. **'Ophelia, Climbing'** Most beautifully shaped hybrid tea flowers in flesh pink with deeper shading, often with lemon tints towards the centre. Very fragrant. Repeat flowering. Good foliage. Growth may benefit from horizontal training to encourage flowering. Introduced 1920. **'Parade'** Deep rose pink flowers, sweetly scented and carried over a

Rosa 'Parade'

long period. Good on a wide range of aspects, including very exposed. Strong growing with good foliage. Introduced 1953. **'Parkdirektor Riggers'** Single, deep red flowers in large clusters. Continuous flowering. Strong growing with good foliage. Tolerates exposed aspects in full sun to medium shade. Introduced 1957. **'Paul's Scarlet'** One of the first of all the modern climbers and still worthy of merit. Repeat flowering with double scarlet flowers borne in clusters. Tolerates all soil conditions in exposed positions in full sun to medium shade. Introduced 1931. **'Picture, Climbing'** Fragrant hybrid tea flowers, pink with deeper shading and lemon at base, borne from mid to late summer. Strong growth which may benefit from being horizontally trained to encourage flowering. Good dark green foliage. Tolerates exposed positions in full sun to medium shade. Introduced 1942. **'Pink Perpetue'** Flowers in clusters, double, fragrant, deep pink in colour, borne in abundance in June and July and again in September. Good growth and dark green foliage. Tolerates all soil types and exposed aspects in full sun to medium shade. Introduced 1965. **'Queen Elizabeth, Climbing'** Extremely vigorous and often unruly by its sheer height. Double, silver/pink flowers of large proportions, carried in singles or up to five in a cluster from mid to late summer. Tolerates all soil types. Certainly needs horizontal training to encourage flowering, but will reach at least 20 ft (6 m) in width. Introduced 1956. **'Réveil Dijonnais'** Hybrid tea-shaped flowers, semi-double, crimson with yellow reverse. May be repeat flowering. Can be susceptible to blackspot. Introduced 1931. **'Ritter von Bramstedt'** Large, dark rose-pink flowers on strong, vigorous, upright growth. Repeat flowering.

Rosa 'Paul's Scarlet'

Requires careful placing due to its vigour. Date of introduction unknown. **'Rosy Mantle'** Double to semi-double mid pink flowers. Repeat flowering. Fragrant. Good dark glossy green foliage. Tolerates exposed aspects in full sun to medium shade and all soil types. Introduced 1968. **'Royal Gold'** Golden yellow flowers, scented. Continuous flowering. Good dark green foliage. Needs horizontal training to encourage maximum flower production. Requires good soil and dislikes extreme exposure. Introduced 1957. **'Schoolgirl'** Flowers copper/orange, double, good scent. Continuous flowering. Leaves and growth can be sparse. Requires good soil preparation and annual feeding for best results. Introduced 1964. **'Senateur Amic'** Strongly fragrant, semi-double to single, bright carmine flowers. Repeat flowering. Strong growing. Responds well to horizontal training to increase flowering. Introduced 1924. **'Shot Silk, Climbing'** Hybrid tea flowers of cherry cerise with golden yellow base. Flowers from early to late summer, not

Rosa 'Masquerade, Climbing'

necessarily continuously. Good growth responding to horizontal training to increase flower production. Disease resistant. Bright glossy green foliage. Tolerates exposed positions in full sun to medium shade. Introduced 1931. **'Souvenir de Claudius Denoyel'** Strongly fragrant double flowers, cup-shaped, rich red to scarlet. Repeat flowering. Strong growth but a little erratic and becoming somewhat ragged in formation. Introduced 1920. **'Speke's Yellow, Climbing'** Bright golden-yellow flowers, open in stature. Good flower production. Repeat flowering. Good for pillars and trellis on all aspects and soils. Date of introduction unknown. **'Sterling Silver, Climbing'** Hybrid tea flowers becoming loose when open, silver/lavender in colour. Mid to late summer flowering, highly fragrant. Foliage subject to blackspot and mildew and growth might be suspect without adequate preparation and good annual feeding. Nevertheless, worth consideration. Introduced 1963. **'Summer Wine'** (syn. **'Korizont'**) Semi-double coral pink flowers with bold red stamens. Good foliage and growth. Tolerates all

Rosa 'Pink Perpetue'

aspects and soils. Introduced 1984. **'Super Star, Climbing'** Bright vermillion, good shaped, fragrant flowers. Repeat flowering. For pillars and trellis. Dislikes shade, requires a good well-fed soil. Introduced 1965. **'Swan Lake'** Pure white with pale powdery pink shading on older flowers. Double. Continuous flowering. May spot pink in wet weather or in heavy dews or fog. Dark green foliage, disease resistant. Two thirds average height and spread. Introduced 1968. **'Sutters Gold, Climbing'** Fragrant yellow hybrid tea flowers with pink veining. Repeat flowering. Makes a good cut flower. Upright growth and good foliage. Introduced 1950. **'Sympathie'** Bright scarlet, fragrant, hybrid tea flowers on strong growths with good foliage. Tolerates a wide range of soils and aspects. Introduced 1964. **'Vicomtesse Pierre de Fou'** Rosette-shaped

Rosa 'Royal Gold'

coppery-pink flowers hanging down from branches. Good rose scent. Repeat flowering. Very strong growing for walls. Introduced 1923. **'White Cockade'** Pure white double flowers carried on upright thorny stems. Flowers continuously. Good dark foliage. Two thirds average height and spread. Introduced 1969.

Average height and spread
Five years
9 × 9 ft (2.7 × 2.7 m)
Ten years
15 × 15 ft (4.6 × 4.6 m)
Twenty years
15 × 15 ft (4.6 × 4.6 m)
Protrudes up to 3 ft (91 cm)
from support.

ROSA (Old Climbing Roses Prior to 1920)

KNOWN BY VARIETY NAME
Rosaceae   *Rose*
Deciduous
A group of climbing roses that have stood the test of time and still merit consideration for planting today.

Origin Mostly of garden or nursery origin.
Use As climbing roses for fences, walls, pergolas, trellis and archways.
Description *Flower* Single, semi-double and double in a range of colours through white, pink, red and apricot in sizes from 2–4 in (5–10 cm) across, many with fragrance, and carried from early summer to early autumn, depending on variety. *Foliage* Five round leaflets make up a pinnate leaf, up to 5–7 in (12–18 cm) long, normally dark to mid green. *Stem* Normally upright, becoming spreading. Mid green to dark green and covered with thorns. Medium to fast growth rate. *Fruit* May produce large, round rose hips, orange in colour and of some winter attraction.
Hardiness Tolerates a minimum winter temperature of 4°F (−15°C).
Soil requirements Tolerates all soil types, with no preference unless otherwise stated.
Sun/Shade aspect Tolerates all aspects and full sun to medium shade unless otherwise stated.
Pruning Requires no pruning when first planted. Remove one third of oldest wood to ground level after roses are established for more than three to four years.
Training Tie to wires or individual anchor points.
Propagation and nursery production Commercial production is from budding which entails the insertion of one single bud into a predetermined rootstock. Plants are normally sold 18 months on from this process. Can be grown from hardwood cuttings, but lifespan may be shortened due to lack of root vigour. Can be purchased bare-rooted or root-wrapped from early autumn onwards, but ensure that plants are one year old. May also be found container grown in spring, summer and autumn as two-year-old plant. Best planting height 1–3 ft (30–91 cm), depending on variety. Many varieties available from garden centres and nurseries, but some may have to be sought from specialist nurseries.
Problems Mildew and blackspot may be a problem, but correct pruning, cultivation, feeding and treatment with a proprietary control will normally keep the diseases to a minimum. May also suffer from attacks of greenfly and blackfly which should be treated

with a proprietary control. Thorns can make handling uncomfortable and plants which are not pruned as suggested can become very woody. Suckers may appear and are difficult to identify as they closely resemble the actual climbing variety. The indication is that if they develop from below ground level they are indeed suckers. Careful observation should, however, make it possible to differentiate between the two foliage patterns.
Forms of interest 'Adam' Peach/pink double flowers in clusters of three, sometimes produced singly. Good scent. Strong-flowering and recurrent. Introduced 1833. Average height and spread 7 × 7 ft (2.1 × 2.1 m). Protrudes up to 2 ft (60 cm) from support. **'Aimée Vibert'** (Noisette) Graceful sprays of scented double white flowers, showing yellow stamens when open. Repeat flowering. Good glossy foliage. For large trellises and walls. Introduced in 1823. Average height and spread 12 × 15 ft (3.7 × 4.6 m). Protrudes up to 5 ft (1.5 m) from support. **'Anemone Rose'** Flowers almost papery, single, silver/pink, sometimes with mauve shading. Recurrent flowering. Introduced 1895. Average height and spread 10 × 10 ft (3 × 3 m). Protrudes up to 2 ft (60 cm) from support. **'Ards Rover'** Crimson flowers with very strong scent. Normally flowers once in early summer, but may give later flowers. Introduced 1898. Average height and spread 10 × 8 ft (3 × 2.4 m). Protrudes up to 3 ft (91 cm) from support. **'Belle Portugaise'** (Hybrid) Semi-double, pale pink flowers in spring. Needs a sheltered position. Introduced 1900. Average height and spread 15 × 12 ft (4.6 × 3.7 m). Protrudes up to 3 ft (91 cm) from support. **'Blairi No.1'** (Bourbon) Large fluffy open flowers, soft pink and scented. Recurrent flowering. Introduced prior to 1845. Average height and spread 12 × 8 ft (3.7 × 2.4 m). Protrudes up to 3 ft (91 cm) from support. **'Blairi No.2'** (Bourbon) Pale pink, flat, almost saucer-shaped flowers with deeper coloured pink centres. Double and fragrant. Recurrent and profuse flowering. Introduced 1845. Average height and spread 18 × 10 ft (5.5 × 3 m). Protrudes up to 3 ft (91 cm) from support. **'Blush Boursault'** Double, blush-pink flowers, somewhat irregular in petal formation. Thornless stems, strong growing. Introduced 1848. Average height and spread 15 × 12 ft (4.6 × 3.7 m). Protrudes up to 3 ft (91 cm) from support. **'Captain Christy'** (Hybrid Tea) Soft pink with deeper pink centres, globe-shaped and good fragrance. Repeat flowering. Introduced 1881. Average height and spread 12 × 10 ft (3.7 × 3 m). Protrudes up to 3 ft (91 cm) from support. **'Céline Forestier'** (Noisette) Pale pink, silky textured, cabbage-like flowers. Good perfume. Repeat flowering. Requires a warm wall and regular feeding for good results. For pillars and trel-

Rosa 'Gloire de Dijon'

Rosa 'Anemone Rose'

lis. Introduced 1842. Average height and spread 9 × 9 ft (2.7 × 2.7 m). Protrudes up to 3 ft (91 cm) from support. **'Champney's Pink Cluster'** A hybrid of *R. chinensis* and *R. moschata*. Pink double flowers in large clusters in mid summer. Requires a sheltered position. Introduced 1802. Average height and spread 15 × 10 ft (4.6 × 3 m). Protrudes up to 3 ft (91 cm) from support. **'Claire Jacquier'** (Noisette) Yolk-yellow flowers, medium sized and fragrant. Recurrent flowering. Strong-growing for walls and large trellis. Introduced 1888. Average height and spread 15 × 15 ft (4.6 × 4.6 m). Protrudes up to 5 ft (1.5 cm) from support. **'Cooper's Burmese'** (*R. laevigata*) (Species) Creamy-white flowers, single, unscented, in mid summer. Good dark green foliage. Strong growing but requires a sheltered aspect. Introduced 1920. Average height and spread 20 × 20 ft (6 × 6 m). Protrudes up to 3 ft (91 cm) from support. **'Cupid'** (Hybrid Tea) Large single flowers, sometimes semi-double, up to 5 in (12 cm) across. Flesh-pink with apricot shading. Petals crinkly-edged. Strong growing. Not repeat flowering but produces good hips. Ideal for trees and large walls. Introduced 1915. Average height and spread 15 × 15 ft (4.6 × 4.6 m). Protrudes up to 5 ft (1.5 cm) from support. **'Desprez à Fleur Jaune'** (Noisette) Strongly fragrant, many petalled, silky-textured flowers of warm yellow, shaded with peach and apricot. Good perfume. Strong growing. Repeat flowering. Needs a warm situation. For walls and fences and for growing through trees. Introduced 1826. Average height and spread 18 × 18 ft (5.5 × 5.5 m). Protrudes up to 6 ft (1.8 m) from support. **'Devoniensis, Climbing'** (Tea) Large creamy-white flowers with apricot flushing. Strong tea scent. Perpetual flowering. Must have a warm wall. Strong growing for walls and large trellis. Introduced 1858. Average height and spread 15 × 15 ft (4.6 × 4.6 m). Protrudes up to 5 ft (1.5 m) from support. **'Etoile de Hollande'** Rich velvety crimson, highly scented flowers from early to late summer, carried on strong, well-foliaged shoots. Introduced 1919. Average height and spread 8 × 8 ft (2.4 × 2.4 m). Protrudes up to 2½ ft (76 cm) from support. **'General Schablikine'** (China) Pendent coppery carmine-pink flowers with some fragrance. For trellis and pillars with a warm aspect. Introduced 1878. Average height and spread 9 × 9 ft (2.7 × 2.7 m). Protrudes up to 3 ft (91 cm) from support. **'Gloire de Dijon'** (Noisette) Fragrant buff to peach flowers, tight in bud, opening to a more frothy nature. Repeat flowering. Introduced 1853. Average height and spread 12 × 10 ft (3.7 × 3 m). Protrudes up to 2 ft (60 cm) from support. **'Grüss an Teplitz'** An old fashioned rose with large, rich crimson flowers and very strong fragrance. Repeat flowering. For pillars and trellis. Introduced 1897. Average height and spread 8 × 8 ft (2.4 × 2.4 m). Protrudes up to 2 ft (60 cm) from support. **'Kathleen Harrop'**

(Bourbon) Soft pink flowers, scented, thornless. Spring flowering with recurrent blooms after. Tolerates exposed aspects and all soil types. Introduced 1919. Average height and spread 10 × 8 ft (3 × 2.4 m). Protrudes up to 3 ft (91 cm) from support. **'Lady Hillingdon'** (Tea Rose) Very popular. Apricot-yellow flowers carried on purple-coloured shoots with grey/green leaves. Fragrant and recurrent flowering. Introduced 1917. Average height and spread 10 × 10 ft (3 × 3 m). Protrudes up to 3 ft (91 cm) from support. **'Lady Waterlow'** (Hybrid Tea) Soft pink flowers to salmon semi-double flowers with deeper pink edges. Recurrent flowering. Strong climber with good foliage. Tolerates all aspects. Introduced 1903. Average height and spread 12 × 10 ft (3.7 × 3 m). Protrudes up to 3 ft (91 cm) from support. **'La France, Climbing'** Pale pink cupped flowers. Moderately strong-growing for walls and trellis. Introduced 1893. Average height and spread 10 × 10 ft (3 × 3 m). Protrudes 3 ft (91 cm) from support. **'Lawrence Johnston'** Yellow, semi-double with some tints of buff. Mid summer flowering. Tolerates all aspects. Vigorous. Introduced prior to 1900. Average height and spread 25 × 25 ft (7.6 × 7.6 m). Protrudes up to 4 ft (1.2 m) from support. **'Leys Perpetual'** (Noisette) Globe-shaped flowers, lemon-yellow in colour and fragrant. Strong-growing for trellis and walls. Date of introduction unknown. Average height and spread 12 × 12 ft (3.7 × 3.7 m). Protrudes 4 ft (1.2 m) from support. **'Maréchal Niel'** (Noisette) Bright golden yellow flowers, repeating. Fragrant. Attractive when in bud. Needs good protection, even to the extent of a greenhouse or conservatory. Introduced 1864. Average height and spread 15 × 10 ft (4.7 × 3 m). Protrudes up to 3 ft (91 cm) from support. **'Mme Abel Chatenay'** (Hybrid Tea) Soft silver/pink flowers plump when in bud, opening to a good shaped flower. Mid summer flowering. Less vigorous than some with weak foliage. Introduced 1917. Average height and spread 8 × 8 ft (2.4 × 2.4 m). Protrudes up to 2 ft (60 cm) from support. **'Mme Alfred Carrière'** (Noisette) Double, globe-shaped flowers, flesh pink/white, profusely borne. Continuous flowering. May need training horizontally to encourage best flowering performance. Strong growing, tolerating all soils and aspects. Can be grown through trees. Introduced 1879. Average height and spread 10 × 10 ft (3 × 3 m). Protrudes up to 3 ft (91 cm) from support. **'Mme Caroline Testout'** (Hybrid Tea) Satin-pink with deeper pink centre. Very large blooms carried on strong and upright stems with good foliage. Repeat flowering. Tolerates all aspects and soil types. Introduced 1890. Average height and spread 15 × 10 ft (4.6 × 3 m). Protrudes up to 3 ft (91 cm) from support. **'Mme Jules Gravereux'** Yellow/buff double flowers with some peach and pink shading. Repeat flowering. Some scent. Good dark green foliage. Introduced 1901. Average

height and spread 8 × 8 ft (2.4 × 2.4 m). Protrudes up to 3 ft (91 cm) from support. **'Paul Lédé'** (Tea Rose) Yellowish-buff flowers with carmine shading at the centre. Attractive sweet scent. Very free flowering from early to late summer. Introduced 1913. Average height and spread 6 × 6 ft (1.8 × 1.8 m). Protrudes up to 3 ft (91 cm) from support. **'Paul's Lemon Pillar'** (Hybrid Tea) Creamy lemon blooms tinged with green at the centre. Strongly fragrant. Flowering mid summer. Vigorous climber with strong upright branches and very good foliage. Tolerates all soil types and aspects. Introduced 1915. Average height and spread 15 × 12 ft (4.6 × 3.7 m). Protrudes up to 18 in (45 cm) from support. **'Pompon De Paris, Climbing'** A climbing form of the miniature rose, twiggy growth. Rose-pink, pompon-shaped flowers carried in good profusion in early to mid summer. Not repeat flowering. Foliage small and grey/green. For growing through shrubs, up pillars or wherever a small climber is required. Date of introduction unknown. Average height and spread 9 × 9 ft (2.7 × 2.7 m). Protrudes 3 ft (91 cm) from support. **'Richmond, Climbing'** (Hybrid Tea). Narrow, elegant, bright scarlet, ageing to crimson. Moderately strong-growing for trellis and walls. Introduced 1912. Average height and spread 12 × 12 ft (3.7 × 3.7 m). Protrudes 4 ft (1.2 m) from support. **'Sombreuil'** (Tea Rose) Pure white in humid conditions becoming flushed with pink. Flat, quartered flowers with delightful tea fragrance. Repeat flowering. Introduced 1850. Average height and spread 8 × 6 ft (2.4 × 1.8 m). Protrudes up to 3 ft (91 cm) from support. **'Souvenir de la Malmaison,**

Rosa 'Zéphirine Drouhin'

Climbing' (Bourbon) Blush-pink, globe-shaped flowers. Repeat flowering. Good foliage. Strong-growing for trellis and walls. Introduced 1893. Average height and spread 12 × 12 ft (3.7 × 3.7 m). Protrudes up to 3 ft (91 cm) from support. **'Souvenir de Madame Léonie Viennot, Climbing'** (Tea) Tea rose flowers, pale yellow, shaded to coppery-pink. Fragrant. Free-flowering. Tolerant of most aspects. For trellis and large walls. Introduced 1904. Average height and spread 12 × 12 ft (3.7 × 3.7 m). Protrudes up to 3 ft (91 cm) from support. **'Tea Rambler'** Salmon-pink, double, small, fragrant flowers in mid summer and carried in profusion on vigorous, strong-growing shrub. Tolerates all soils and aspects. Can be used to grow through trees. Introduced 1904. Average height and spread 12 × 10 ft (3.5 × 3 m). Protrudes up to 3 ft (91 cm) from support. **'Zéphirine Drouhin'** (Bourbon) Cerise-pink, semi-double, very fragrant flowers. Some spring flowers, after which continuous. Thornless. Tolerates all aspects and soil conditions. Introduced 1868. Average height and spread 10 × 10 ft (3 × 3 m). Protrudes up to 18 in (45 cm) from support.

Average height and spread
Growth at ten years given for each variety.

ROSA (Rambler Roses)

KNOWN BY VARIETY NAME

Rosaceae   *Rose*
Deciduous

Rambler roses have a pedigree that stretches back often more than 100 years. They had their heyday in the late 1800s to early 1900s followed by a period of unpopularity, but are now becoming rightly appreciated for their flower display.

Origin Mostly derivatives of *R. wichuraiana* with various crosses with other forms. Often of garden or nursery descent.

Use As large, rambling climbers for fences, walls, pergolas and archways, to ramble through trees or to be used for ground cover with or without support.

Description *Flower* Single or semi-double, carried in clusters, either single or repeat flowering. Individual flowers between ½–1½ in (1–4 cm) in diameter. Normally flowering mid to late summer in a range of colours through white, yellow, pink, red, mauve, all depending on variety. *Foliage* Five or seven round leaflets make up a pinnate leaf. Light green to mid green depending on variety. *Stem* Light green, rambling, branching, with thorns, degree according to variety. Fast to medium growth rate. *Fruit* Some varieties may produce clusters of small, red rose hips which have winter attraction.

Hardiness Tolerates a minimum winter temperature of 4°F (−15°C).

Soil requirements Tolerates all soil types, both alkaline and acid, but on severe alkaline soils may show signs of chlorosis. Good preparation and annual feeding and mulching will normally control this.

Sun/Shade aspect Tolerates all aspects. Best in full sun to light shade, but some varieties may tolerate deeper degrees of shade.

Pruning Prior to planting young plants the top growth should be reduced to 2–3 ft (60–91 cm), and any very weak shoots removed. Roses established more than 12 months should always be pruned in early to late autumn and all old flowering shoots cut to ground level. Tie in new shoots to supports to flower in following year. If production of new growth is limited, retain a proportion of older shoots, choosing the healthiest, but cut back all their lateral shoots to within 3 in (7.5 cm) of their point of origin.

Training Allow to ramble through trees or over wire or timber supports. On walls and fences tie to wires or individual anchor points. Up pillars and trelliswork some limited tying may be required.

Rosa 'Albertine'

Propagation and nursery production Commercial production is from budding, entailing the insertion of one single bud into a predetermined root stock. Plants are normally sold 18 months on from this process. Can be grown from hardwood cuttings, but lifespan may be shortened due to possible lack of root vigour. Can be purchased bare-rooted or root-wrapped from early autumn to mid spring. May be available container grown from late spring to early autumn and beyond, but ensure that the plant has not been potted for more than one year. Best planting height 1–3 ft (30–91 cm), depending on variety. Many varieties are readily available from garden centres and nurseries, but some have to be sought from specialist rose growers.

Problems Many varieties suffer from black spot and mildew. In the case of mildew, this is often specific to the particular plant and is hard to control, but worth the effort. Suckers from root stools may appear and are difficult to identify as they closely resemble the rambler variety. The indication is that if they develop from below ground they may be suckers and they should be ripped away from the root stool. Careful observation should, however, make it possible to differentiate between the two foliage patterns.

Forms of interest 'Abbandonata' (Sempervirens) Mid-pink flowers, strong-growing. Ideal for large walls and for growing through trees. Date of introduction unknown. 'Adeläide d'Orléans' (Sempervirens) Creamy-pink, semi-double, small, pendent flowers with attractive foliage. Primrose scent.

Moderately strong-growing in trees and on large walls. Introduced 1826. 'Albéric Barbier' Double, very fragrant flowers, creamy-white flushed yellow. Somewhat floppy when open. Flowering mid to late summer. Good dark glossy green foliage, in some years almost evergreen. Ideal for trees. Tolerates exposed aspects in full sun to medium shade, but may be shy to flower in shade. Introduced 1900. 'Albertine' The exquisitely fragrant rambler of cottage doors. Copper/orange in bud and opening to pink with gold shading. Flowering early to mid summer. Strong growing. Tolerates all soil conditions. Ideal for growing in trees. Introduced 1921. 'Alexandre Girault' Deep rose pink and copper double flowers with a raspberry fragrance in mid summer. Useful as ground cover. Tolerates full sun to medium shade. Two thirds average height and spread. Introduced 1909. 'Alister Stella Gray' (syn. 'Golden Rambler') Yellow with deeper yellow centre, ageing to creamy-white. Good scent over a long flowering period. Repeat flowering. Ideal for trees and can be grown in full sun to medium shade. Introduced 1894. 'American Pillar' Single flowers, pink with central white eye. Good dark green foliage. Strong and upright stems. Ideal for growing in trees. Will tolerate a wide range of conditions. Introduced 1909. 'Apple Blossom' Apple-blossom pink flowers, each petal with a crinkled edge, from mid to late summer. Tolerates all soil conditions in full sun to medium shade. Two thirds average height and spread.

Rosa 'American Pillar'

Unusual in being a rambler suitable for pillars. Introduced 1932. 'Auguste Gervais' Semi-double, fragrant, salmon-pink flowers with a coppery tinge, ageing to soft pink. Flowers mid summer. Mid green shiny foliage on good shoots. Tolerates all soil conditions and exposed positions, but dislikes shade. Ideal for growing up trees. Introduced 1918. 'Blush Rambler' Pink flowers in very large clusters, reminiscent of apple blossom, in mid summer. For walls, fences, trellis and trees. Introduced 1903. 'Breeze Hill' Clear pink flowers flushed tawny orange. Double to semi-double, cup-shaped. Mid summer flowering. Strong growing even to the extent of being gangly and gaunt. Tolerates all soil conditions and aspects. Full sun to medium shade. Ideal for growing in trees. Introduced 1926. 'Chaplin's Pink Climber' Attractive single or semi-double mid to deep pink flowers, in profusion mid summer. Tolerates all soil types. Good for use on fences, walls, pergolas and arches. Introduced 1928. 'Coralle' Coral-pink flowers in clusters in mid summer. Good green foliage. Two thirds average height and spread. Introduced 1919 and should be more widely grown. 'Crimson Conquest' Semi-double flowers, bright crimson, carried in clusters in mid summer.

Rosa 'Albéric Barbier'

Good foliage. Tolerates all aspects in full sun to medium shade and all soil conditions. Introduced 1932. **'Crimson Shower'** Semi-double crimson flowers in bold clusters from mid to late summer. Some later autumn flowers. Small glossy foliage. Introduced 1951. **'Debutante'** Fragrant, rose-pink flowers carried in clusters. Mid summer flowering. Foliage dark green, showing off the flowers to good advantage. Tolerates all soil types. Ideal for extensive ground cover or for growing through trees. Introduced 1902. **'Dorothy Perkins'** Clear pink double flowers in clusters. Mid summer flowering. Light green foliage on wispy stems. Widely planted but prone to its own specific strain of mildew which is difficult to control. Introduced 1902. **'Dr Van Fleet'** Double, fragrant, flesh-pink flowers, fading to white, with attractive texture to petals. Mid summer flowering. Strong growing with good foliage. Tolerates full sun to medium shade. Ideal for growing in trees. Introduced 1910. **'Easlea's Golden Rambler'** Rich yellow, double flowers in clusters on long, ranging flower stems. Mid summer flowering. Good mid green foliage and good growth. Ideal on all soil types in full sun to medium shade. Ideal for growing in trees. Introduced 1932.

Rosa 'Dorothy Perkins'

'Emily Gray' Large, fragrant, golden yellow flowers in mid summer showing off well against the glossy, deep green foliage. Tolerates all soil types in full sun to medium shade. Ideal for growing in trees. Introduced 1918. **'Ethel'** Mauve/pink flowers in clusters mid summer set against good foliage. Tolerates all soil types and exposed positions in full sun to medium shade. Ideal for growing in trees. Introduced 1912. **'Evangeline'** Creamy-white flowers diffused pink, flowering in late summer. Good, dark green, leathery foliage. Ideal for exposed positions in full sun to medium shade. Tolerates all soil conditions. Ideal for growing up trees. Introduced 1906. **'Excelsa'** Double, light crimson flowers carried in large trusses on thin wispy shoots. Flowers in mid summer. Strong growing. Tolerates exposed aspects in full sun to medium shade on all soil types. Ideal for ground cover or for climbing through trees. Introduced 1909. **'Félicité et Perpétue'** Fragrant, creamy-white flowers, small in size and globe-shaped, from mid to late summer. Light green foliage, almost evergreen. Tolerates all soil types. Ideal for climbing in trees. Introduced 1827. **'Flora'** Double flowers, off-white with lilac shading. Cup-shaped, scented, flowering mid to late summer. Good dark green foliage. Tolerates exposed positions in full sun to medium shade. Ideal for growing in trees. Introduced 1929. **'François Juranville'** Mid pink, double flowers in mid to late summer. Tolerates exposed conditions in full sun to medium shade and almost any soil type. Ideal for

Rosa 'François Juranville'

growing in trees or for ground cover. Introduced 1906. **'Goldfinch'** Large golden-yellow and primrose-yellow petals with golden central anthers. Double, fragrant flowers freely borne from late spring to mid summer. Good foliage. Tolerates full sun to medium shade but dislikes exposed positions. Less robust than some varieties. Two thirds average height and spread. Introduced 1907. **'Hiawatha'** Each single crimson flower has a white eye and pronounced golden anthers in the centre. Flowers produced in clusters from mid to late summer. Tolerates all soil conditions in full sun to medium shade. Ideal for climbing up trees. Introduced 1904. **'Kew Rambler'** Soft pink single flowers with deeper pink margins to each petal. Flowers from mid to late summer. Foliage grey to grey/green. Tolerates all aspects in full sun to medium shade. Ideal for growing in trees. Introduced 1912. **'Lykkefund'** Creamy-yellow, semi-double, fragrant flowers in large tight clusters from mid to late summer. Stems thornless, supporting glossy dark green foliage. Requires some protection but will tolerate full sun to medium shade on a wide range of soil conditions. Very good for woodland planting and for use in trees. Introduced 1930. **'Léontine Gervais'** Double flowers, clear pink

Rosa 'Easlea's Golden Rambler'

with copper shading. Fragrant. Foliage clean and attractive. Very strong growing; ideal for covering buildings or large walls or for growing through trees. Introduced 1903. **'May Queen'** Lilac/pink flowers, ageing to white, semi-double, produced in mid to late summer in an abundance of large clusters. Tolerates all aspects in full sun to medium shade. Ideal for growing through trees or for ground cover. Introduced 1898. **'Minnehaha'** Pale pink flowers ageing to white in large clusters from mid to late summer. Strong growing. Large quantity of small, dark green foliage. Tolerates full sun to medium shade in exposed positions on all soil types, ideal for growing through trees or for ground cover. Introduced 1905. **'Mme Alice Garnier'** Bright orange/pink flowers with orange centres and attractive scent from mid to late summer. Foliage dark green on slender, arching branches. Ideal for ground cover. Introduced 1906. **'Mme d'Arblay'** Blush-pink to white fragrant, cup-shaped flowers from mid to late summer. Strong growing and vigorous. Ideal for exposed positions. Can be grown in trees. One third more than average height and spread. Introduced 1835. **'Paul Transon'** Medium-sized double flowers, rich salmon with coppery shading and yellow base. Repeat flowering from mid summer to mid autumn. Foliage coppery when young, shiny, becoming light green, making a good contrast. Requires some protection. Tolerates full sun to medium shade and a wide range of soil types. Introduced 1901. **'Phyllis Bide'** Semi-double pink, salmon and gold flowers, continuous flowering. Some fragrance. Medium growth rate, reaching two thirds average height and spread. Introduced 1923. **'René André'** Semi-double, fragrant flowers with saffron and carmine tinges, paling with age. Flowers from mid to late summer. Tolerates exposed situations in full sun to medium shade on all soil types. Ideal for training in trees. Introduced 1901. **'Russelliana'** (syns. **'Old Spanish Rose'**, **'Russell's Cottage'**, **'Scarlet Grevillea'**) Was once called 'Souvenir de la Bataille de Marengo'. Magenta/crimson flat flowers borne in clusters in mid to late summer. Tolerates exposed situations in full sun to light shade on all soil types. Two thirds average height and spread. Ideal for growing in trees. Introduced 1840. **'Sanders White'** Distinct pure white rosette-shaped flowers, carried in cascading clusters. Scented and flowering from mid to late summer. Foliage bright green. Tolerates most soil conditions in full sun to light shade. Can be used to climb in trees. Introduced 1912. **'Silver Moon'**

Rosa 'Phyllis Bide'

Strongly fragrant, creamy-white single flowers with golden anthers. Flowers mid summer. Date of introduction unknown. **'Thelma'** Coral-pink and red large semi-double flowers, from mid to late summer. Stems have very few thorns. Tolerates full sun to light shade on all soil types. Ideal for training in trees. Introduced 1927. **'Veilchenblau'** (syn. **'Violet Blue'**) Semi-double, violet/purple flowers with white towards centre, fading to blue/lilac and lilac/grey with age. Good scent. Best in light to medium shade for flower colour, although will tolerate full sun if required, but may fade. Tolerates exposed aspects and all soil types. Ideal for training in trees. Introduced 1909. **'Violette'** Violet/purple very full double

Rosa 'Veilchenblau'

flowers carried in large trusses from mid to late summer. Strong growing. Tolerates full sun to medium shade on most soil types. Ideal for training in trees. Introduced 1921. **'White Flight'** Semi-double pure white flowers from mid to late summer. Light green foliage. Tolerates full sun to light shade in exposed positions and most soils. Introduced 1900.
Average height and spread
Five years
8 × 8 ft (2.4 × 2.4 m)
Ten years
15 × 15 ft (4.6 × 4.6 m)
Twenty years
20 × 20 ft (6 × 6 m).
Protrudes up to 3 ft (91 cm) from support.

ROSA
(Shrub and Species Roses for Fan-training)

KNOWN BY VARIETY NAME
Rosaceae   *Rose*
Deciduous
Apart from climbing and rambler roses there are many shrub and species roses which adapt extremely well to fan-training, often showing off their flowers to better advantage.

Origin Various.
Use As fan-trained shrubs for walls and fences.
Description *Flower* Either single, semi-double or double in a wide range of colours through pink, white, purple, red, flowering from spring through summer, depending on variety. Many are fragrant. *Foliage* Five or seven leaflets make up a pinnate leaf, 5–7 in (12–18 cm) long. Some yellow autumn colour. *Stem* Bushy habit, normally green thorny stems. Some may have winter attraction. Medium to fast growth rate. *Fruit* Some varieties may produce orange/red or scarlet hips in autumn.

Rosa 'Alba Maxima'

Hardiness Tolerates a minimum winter temperature of 4°F (−15°C).
Soil requirements Tolerates all soil conditions with no particular preference except that it must be moisture- and nutrient-retentive.
Sun/Shade aspect Tolerates all aspects in full sun to light shade.
Pruning Remove one third of oldest growth to ground level on roses established more than three years.
Training Tie to wires or individual anchor points.
Propagation and nursery production Commercial production is from budding, entailing the insertion of one single bud into a predetermined rootstock. Plants are normally sold 18 months on from this process. Some varieties can be grown successfully from hardwood cuttings. Purchase bare-rooted or root-wrapped from early autumn to mid spring; may be available container grown from late spring to early autumn and beyond. Best planting height 1–3 ft (30–91 cm). Many varieties readily available from garden centres and nurseries, but some may have to be sought from specialist nurseries.
Problems May suffer from greenfly and blackfly. Treat with a proprietary control. Mildew and blackspot may be a problem, but correct pruning, cultivation, feeding and treatment with a proprietary control will normally keep the disease to a minimum. Thorns can make handling uncomfortable and plants which are not pruned as suggested can become very woody. Suckers from rootstocks

may appear and are difficult to identify as they closely resemble the actual variety. The indication is that if they develop from below ground they are normally suckers. Careful observation should, however, make it possible to differentiate between the two foliage patterns.
Forms of interest The genetic group which each variety fits into is shown in brackets: **'Adam Messerich'** (Bourbon) Very bright pink, semi-double flowers in bold sprays. Continuous flowers, strong growing. Introduced 1920. Average height and spread 6 × 6 ft (1.8 × 1.8 m). Protrudes up to 2 ft (60 cm) from support. **'Alba Maxima'** (Alba) ('Jacobite Rose', 'White Rose of York') Flat double flowers, slightly incurved, white on outer edges, more creamy-white in centre. Early to late summer flowering. Leaves dark, almost grey/green. Flowers followed by a good crop of orange/red autumn fruits. Introduced prior to the 16th century. Average height and spread 6 × 6 ft (1.8 × 1.8 m). Protrudes up to 2 ft (60 cm) from support. **'Ballerina'** (Modern Shrub) Small, single flowers, up to ½ in (1 cm) across, pink with white centres, carried in sprays. Continuous flowering. Introduced 1937. Average height and spread 5 × 5 ft (1.5 × 1.5 m). Protrudes up to 18 in (45 cm) from support. Of garden origin. **'Belle de Crécy'** (Gallica) Flowers up to 3 in (7.5 cm) across, bright pink and mauve with good fragrance. Early to mid summer flowering, tolerating full sun to light shade. Stems almost thornless. Introduced mid 19th century. Average height and spread 4 × 4 ft (1.2 × 1.2 m). Protrudes up to 18 in (45 cm) from support. Of garden origin. **'Bloomfield Abundance'** (China Rose) Small, attractive,

Rosa 'Ballerina'

mid pink hybrid tea blooms, carried on large sprays. Continuous flowering. Introduced 1920. Average height and spread 6 × 6 ft (1.8 × 1.8 m). Protrudes up to 2 ft (60 cm) from support. Of garden origin. **'Blush Damask'** (Damask) Strongly fragrant flowers, pale pink with deeper pink centre. Early to mid summer flowering. An extremely old variety. Average height and spread 4 × 4 ft (1.2 × 1.2 m). Protrudes up to 12 in (30 cm) from support. Of garden origin. **'Bonn'** (Hybrid Musk) Large, double flowers up to 4 in (10 cm) across, orange/scarlet, fragrant, carried in clusters. Continuous flowering. Introduced 1915. Average height and spread 5 × 5 ft (1.5 × 1.5 m). Protrudes up to 18 ft (45 cm) from support. Of nursery origin. **'Buff Beauty'** (Hybrid Musk) Fragrant apricot/yellow flowers, ageing to buff-yellow, carried in large trusses, each flower up to 3 in (7.5 cm) across and semi-double. Continuous flowering. Tolerates full sun to medium shade. Introduced 1939. Average height and spread 7 × 7 ft (2.1 × 2.1 m). Protrudes up to 2 ft (60 cm) from support. Of garden origin.

'Capitaine John Ingram' (Moss) Dark crimson, but can be purple in some weather conditions. Very strongly scented. Flowers from early to mid summer. Introduced 1856. Average height and spread 7 × 7 ft (2.1 × 2.1 m). Protrudes up to 18 in (45 cm) from support. Of garden origin. 'Cardinal de Richelieu' (Gallica) Strongly fragrant purple flowers with a velvety texture in mid summer. Good foliage. Introduced 1840. Average height and spread 5 × 5 ft (1.5 × 1.5 m). Protrudes up to 18 ft (45 cm) from support. Of garden origin. 'Celestial' (syn. 'Celeste') (Alba) Semi-double, soft pink flowers from late spring to early summer. Foliage grey/green and attractive after flowering. Average height and spread 7 × 7 ft (2.1 × 2.1 m). Protrudes up to 12 ft (30 cm) from support. Origin not known, but a very old variety. 'Cerise Bouquet' (Modern Shrub) Flowers deep crimson pink, double and scented, borne from early to late summer with

Rosa 'Bloomfield Abundance'

main flowering period mid summer. Foliage grey to grey/green with indented edges to leaves. Tolerates full sun to medium shade. Often underestimated for its height and spread potential. Introduced 1958. Average height and spread 15 × 15 ft (4.6 × 4.6 m). Protrudes up to 6 ft (1.8 m) from support. 'Chapeau de Napoleon' (syns. 'Crested Moss', 'Cristata') (Centifolia) Large, double, lettuce-like flowers, silvery pink, very fragrant, from mid to late summer. Flower buds before opening have attractive moss covering. Introduced 1826. Average height and spread 7 × 7 ft (2.1 × 2.1 m). Protrudes up to 2 ft (60 cm)

Rosa 'Celestial'

Rosa 'Fruhlingsgold'

from support. Of garden origin. 'Charles de Mills' (Gallica) Flowers bi-coloured, purple and deep red. Mid summer flowering. Foliage attractive, mid-green, indented edges. Origin unknown. Average height and spread 5 × 5 ft (1.5 × 1.5 m). Protrudes up to 12 in (30 cm) from support. 'Constance Spry' (Modern Shrub) Flowers up to 5 in (12 cm) across, pink and very heavily scented. Mid summer flowering. Full sun to medium shade. Does best against a wall. Introduced 1960. Average height and spread 20 × 12 ft (6 × 3.7 m). Protrudes up to 2 ft (60 cm) from support. 'Copenhagen' (Shrub) Often considered as a climbing rose and stocked by garden centres and nurseries in that area, but technically is a shrub rose with its scarlet flowers borne in clusters. Continuous flowering. A truly handsome red rose for climbing or for pillars. Introduced 1964. Average height and spread 8 × 6 ft (2.4 × 1.8 m). Protrudes up to 2 ft (60 cm) from support. 'Cornelia' (Hybrid Musk) Apricot flowers with pink shading continuously from mid summer to early autumn. Foliage bronze when young. Flowers in full sun to medium shade. Introduced 1925. Average height and spread 7 × 7 ft (2.1 × 2.1 m). Protrudes up to 2 ft (60 cm) from support. 'Dortmund' (Hybrid Pimpinellifolia) Fragrant red flowers with white eye, opening from long, pointed, attractive buds and carried in clusters. often considered as a climber. Repeat flowering. Foliage glossy dark green, strong growing. Tolerates exposed aspects in full sun to medium shade. Introduced 1955. Average height and spread 12 × 12 ft (3.7 × 3.7 m). Protrudes up to 3 ft (91 cm) from support. 'Elmshorn' (Modern Shrub) Vivid pink blooms, repeat flowering from mid summer to early autumn. Tolerates full sun to medium shade. Introduced 1951. Average height and spread 7 × 7 ft (2.1 × 2.1 m). Protrudes up to 2 ft (60 cm) from support. 'Erfut' (Hybrid Musk) Pink and white flowers with central dull yellow stamens. Continuous flowering. Tolerates full sun to medium shade. Introduced 1939. Average height and spread 7 × 7 ft (2.1 × 2.1 m). Protrudes up to 2 ft (60 cm) from support. 'Fantin-Latour' (Centifolia) Pale pink scented flowers from early to mid summer. Introduced prior to 1890. Average height and spread 7 × 7 ft (2.1 × 2.1 m). Protrudes up to 2 ft (60 cm) from support. 'Felicia' (Hybrid Musk) Silver/pink fading to salmon-pink. Continuous flowering. One of the best. Introduced 1928. Average height and spread 6 × 6 ft (1.8 × 1.8 m). Protrudes up to 2 ft (60 cm) from support. 'Félicité Parmentier' (Alba) Soft pink petals, reflexed, forming a double flower. Scented. Early to mid summer flowering. Foliage grey/green, attractive. Full sun to medium shade. Intro-

duced 1834. Average height and spread 5 × 5 ft (1.5 × 1.5 m). Protrudes up to 18 in (45 cm) from support. 'Ferdinand Pichard' (Hybrid Perpetual) Double, deep pink flowers with lighter pink candy stripes, profusely borne. Recurrent flowering. Good foliage. Introduced 1921. Average height and spread 7 × 7 ft (2.1 × 2.1 m). Protrudes up to 18 in (45 cm) from support. 'Francesca' (Hybrid Musk) Single to semi-double apricot-coloured flowers produced in large sprays. Good scent. Continuous flowering. Strong growth with attractive foliage. Introduced 1921. Average height and spread 5 × 5 ft (1.5 × 1.5 m). Protrudes up to 2 ft (60 cm) from support. 'Fred

Rosa 'Dortmund'

Loads' (Modern Shrub) Orange to vermillion/orange, semi-double, scented, continuous flowering. Strong upright growth. Introduced 1968. Average height and spread 7 × 7 ft (2.1 × 2.1 m). Protrudes up to 2 ft (60 cm) from support. 'Fritz Nobis' (Modern Shrub) Pale pink flowers, semi-double with clove scent, from mid to late summer. Good hips in autumn. Introduced 1940. Average height and spread 7 × 7 ft (2.1 × 2.1 m). Protrudes up to 2 ft (60 cm) from support. 'Frühlingsanfang' (Hybrid Pimpinellifolia) Ivory-white, single flowers 4 in (10cm) across with attractive golden anthers. Scented. Flowers late spring to early summer. Strong growing. Introduced 1950. Average height and spread 10 × 10 ft (3 × 3 m). Protrudes up to 4 ft (1.2 m) from support. 'Frühlingsgold' (Hybrid Pimpinellifolia) Single pale yellow flowers, 4 in (10cm) across, from mid to late spring. May produce purple tomato-shaped fruits. Strong growing, with numerous thorns. Full sun to medium shade. Introduced 1951. Average height and spread 9 × 9 ft (2.7 × 2.7 m). Protrudes up to 2 ft (60 cm) from support. **'Frühlingsmorgen'** (Hybrid Pimpinellifolia) Very attractive single cherry-pink flowers with primrose-coloured centres. Flowers up to 4 in (10 cm) across pro-

Rosa 'Ferdinand Pichard'

duced in mid to late spring. Second flowering late summer to early autumn. Normally a good display of tomato-shaped purple hips. Introduced 1942. Average height and spread 8 × 8 ft (2.4 × 2.4 m). Protrudes up to 2 ft (60 cm) from support. **'Frühlingsschnee'** (Hybrid Pimpinellifolia) Double pure white flowers in mid summer in full sun to light shade. Good foliage, thorny stems. Introduced 1954. Average height and spread 8 × 8 ft (2.4 × 2.4 m). Protrudes up to 2 ft (60 cm) from support. **'Frühlingszauber'** (Hybrid Pimpinellifolia) Semi-double, silver/pink, scented flowers from late spring to early summer, shown off well against dark green foliage. Introduced 1942. Average height and spread 9 × 9 ft (2.7 × 2.7 m). Protrudes up to 2 ft (60 cm) from support. **'Gipsy Boy'** (syn. **'Zigeunerknabe'**) (Bourbon) Double, crimson to deep crimson fading to purple, with primrose yellow centres. Flowers mid summer. Full sun to light shade. Introduced 1909. Average height and spread 8 × 8 ft (2.4 × 2.4 m). Protrudes up to 2 ft (60 cm) from support. **'Golden Chersonese'** (*R. ecae* hybrid) Single flowers, bright yellow, 1½ in

Rosa 'Fred Loads'

Rosa 'Fritz Nobis'

(4 cm) across, carried singly at each leaf joint in mid to late spring. Foliage fern-like, attractive. Full sun to medium shade. Introduced 1963. Average height and spread 6 × 6 ft (1.8 × 1.8 m). Protrudes up to 18 in (45 cm) from support. **'Golden Wings'** (Modern Shrub) Single flowers, up to 4 in (10 cm) across, yellow with red central anthers. Continuous flowering. Can be prone to black-

Rosa 'Gipsy Boy'

spot, but worth consideration. Introduced 1953. Average height and spread 7 × 7 ft (2.1 × 2.1 m). Protrudes up to 3 ft (91 cm) from support. **'Helen Knight'** (*R. ecae* hybrid) 1 in (2.5 cm) wide, saucer-shaped flowers of deep, clear yellow, carried en masse close to stems in late spring to early summer in full sun to medium shade. Introduced 1953. Average height and spread 9 × 4 ft (2.7 × 1.2 m). Protrudes up to 12 in (30 cm) from support. **'Ispahan'** (Damask) Pink, semi-double flowers up to 2½ in (6 cm) across from mid to late summer. Attractive foliage. Introduced prior to 1842. Average height and spread 7 × 7 ft (2.1 × 2.1 m). Protrudes up to 2 ft (60 cm) from support. **'Kassel'** (Modern Shrub) Clusters of orange/scarlet, semi-double flowers contrasting well with dark green foliage. Continuous flowering from mid summer to early autumn. Introduced 1957. Average height and spread 7 × 7 ft (2.1 × 2.1 m). Protrudes up to 2 ft (60 cm) from support. **'La Noblesse'** (Centifolia) Soft silver/pink flowers, semi-double, with good scent. Flowering from mid to late summer, although not continuously. Introduced 1856.

Average height and spread 6 × 6 ft (1.8 × 1.8 m). Protrudes up to 2 ft (60 cm) from support. **'La Reine Victoria'** (Bourbon) Warm rose pink, cup-shaped flowers. Perpetual flowering. Attractive soft green foliage. Introduced 1872. Average height and spread 6 × 3 ft (1.8 × 91 cm). Protrudes up to 18 in (45 cm) from support. **'Maiden's Blush'** (syn. **'Cuisse de Nymphe'**) (Alba) Double, somewhat floppy, blush-pink, sweet-scented flowers from mid to late summer. Foliage grey/green. Tolerates full sun to medium shade. Introduced in the late 18th century. Average height and spread 12 × 12 ft

Rosa 'Buff Beauty'

(3.7 × 3.7 m). Protrudes up to 2 ft (60 cm) from support. **'Marguerite Hilling'** (Modern Shrub) Mid-pink, semi-double flowers. Recurrent flowering. Without good soil preparation and adequate organic material and additional feed, can be a little insipid in growth. Introduced 1959. Average height and spread 7 × 7 ft (2.1 × 2.1 m). Protrudes up to 2 ft (60 cm) from support. **'Mme Isaac Pereire'** (Bourbon) Large, purple/crimson rosette flowers. Continuous flowering in full sun to medium shade. Introduced in 1881. Average height and spread 8 × 8 ft (2.4 × 2.4 m). Protrudes up to 2 ft (60 cm) from support. **'Mme Lauriol de Barny'** (Bourbon) Flowers quartered, flat, with unusual fragrance. Silver/pink in colour. Recurrent flowering in full sun to medium shade. Introduced 1868. Average height and spread 8 × 8 ft (2.4 × 2.4 m). Protrudes up to

Rosa 'Helen Knight'

Rosa 'Marguerite Hilling'

2 ft (60 cm) from support. **'Mme Pierre Oger'** (Bourbon) Cup-shaped flowers, pale silver/pink with good scent. Continuous flowering. Dislikes shade. Introduced 1878. Average height and spread 6 × 6 ft (1.8 × 1.8 m). Protrudes up to 18 in (45 cm) from support. **'Moonlight'** (Hybrid Musk) Flowers single, lemon to white on attractive long stems. Continuous flowering in full sun to medium shade. Introduced 1913. Average height and spread 7 × 7 ft (2.1 × 2.1 m). Protrudes up to 18 ft (45 cm) from support. **'Mrs John Laing'** (Hybrid Perpetual) Good shaped, double, soft pink flowers. Recurrent flowering. Requires good soil preparation and additional organic material and food for best

Rosa 'Nevada'

results. Introduced 1887. Average height and spread 3 × 2 ft (91 × 60 cm). Protrudes up to 3 ft (91 cm) from support. **'Nevada'** (Modern Shrub) Large creamy-white blooms up to 3 in (7.5 cm) across with wavy edged petals. Repeat flowering through late spring to early summer. Introduced 1927. Average height and spread 10 × 10 ft (3 × 3 m). Protrudes up to 2 ft (60 cm) from support. **'Nozomi'** (Modern Shrub) Pearly-pink flowers, ageing to white, carried in profusion on long cascading sprays. Normally considered for ground cover, but with care can be persuaded to be an attractive low climbing wall shrub in full sun to medium shade. Introduced 1968. Average height and spread 7 × 6 ft (2.1 × 1.8 m). Protrudes up to 12 in (30 cm) from support. **'Penelope'** (Hybrid Musk) Creamy-pink, semi-double flowers with good scent. Recurrent flowering

from early summer to early autumn. Introduced 1924. Average height and spread 7 × 7 ft (2.1 × 2.1 m). Protrudes up to 18 in (45 cm) from support. **'Pink Prosperity'** (Hybrid Musk) Double pink flowers carried in small sprays. Continuous flowering. Introduced 1931. Average height and spread 7 × 7 ft (2.1 × 2.1 m). Protrudes up to 2 ft (60 cm) from support. **'Pomifera Duplex'** ('Wolly-Dod's Rose') (Pomifera) Soft clear pink flowers, semi-double, from mid to late summer contrasting well with light grey/green foliage. Attractive purple autumn hips. Ideal in full sun to medium shade. Tol-

Rosa complicata

erates exposed aspects. Introduced 1900. Average height and spread 7 × 7 ft (2.1 × 2.1 m). Protrudes up to 2 ft (60 cm) from support. **'Prince Charles'** (Bourbon) Maroon to lilac, scented, double flowers from mid to late summer but not necessarily continuous. Full sun to medium shade. Origin unknown. Average height and spread 7 × 7 ft (2.1 × 2.1 m). Protrudes up to 18 in (45 cm) from support. **'Prosperity'** (Hybrid Musk) Trusses of double, creamy-white flowers with strong scent. Recurrent flowering from summer to early autumn in both sun and medium shade. Introduced 1919. Average height and spread 7 × 7 ft (2.1 × 2.1 m). Protrudes up to 2 ft (60 cm) from support. *R. californica plena* (Species) Deep pink, small, semi-double flowers profusely borne from mid summer to early autumn, not necessarily continuous. Introduced 1894. Average height and spread 10 × 10 ft (3 × 3 m). Protrudes up

Rosa moyesii 'Geranium'

to 2 ft (60 cm) from support. *R. complicata* (Of Gallica origin) Possibly one of the most attractive of all species roses with large, pink, single flowers with a paler centre and bold golden stamens in early to mid summer. Strongly fragrant. Stems and foliage green to grey/green. Will flower in full sun to medium shade. Origin unknown. Average height and spread 11 × 11 ft (3.4 × 3.4 m). Protrudes up to 12 in (30 cm) from support. *R. ecae* (Species) Deep yellow flowers, up to 1 in (2.5 cm) across, from mid to late spring. Small, dark green foliage. Stems red/brown with attractive red/brown thorns. Introduced 1880. Average height and spread 6 × 6 ft (1.8 × 1.8 m). Protrudes up to 18 in (45 cm) from support. *R. farreri persetosa* ('Three-penny Bit Rose') (Species) Small lilac/pink flowers carried on graceful, heavily soft-thorned shoots with attractive fern-like foliage. Flowers from mid to late summer, not necessarily continuously. Small orange/red hips in autumn, making an all-round attraction. Tolerates full sun to medium shade. Introduced 1914. Average height and spread 7 × 7 ft (2.1 × 2.1 m). Protrudes up to 12 in (30 cm) from support. *R. fedtschenkoana* (Species) Flowers single, white, but main attraction is the grey/green to silver green foliage. Red hips in autumn. Flowers recurrent. Introduced 1880. Average height and spread 10 × 10 ft (3 × 3 m). Protrudes up to 5 ft (1.5 cm) from support. *R. foetida* (syn. **'Yellow Austrian Briar'**) (Species) Attractive single yellow flowers from mid to late spring. Dark glossy green foliage and brown stems. The protection of a

Rosa bicolor

wall adds to its overall vigour. Introduced earlier than the 16th century. Average height and spread 8 × 8 ft (2.4 × 2.4 m). Protrudes up to 18 in (45 cm) from support. **R. f. bicolor** (syn. **'Austrian Copper'**) (Species) Single, copper/scarlet with rich yellow reverse to petals in mid to late spring. Can be prone to diseases, such as mildew and blackspot; spraying can normally counteract this. Fan-training against a wall often enhances its growth. Introduced 1590. Average height and spread 7 × 7 ft (2.1 × 2.1 m). Protrudes up to 18 in (45 cm) from support. **R. f. persiana** (syn. **'Persian Yellow'**) (Species) Globe-shaped, bright yellow double flowers against dark, glossy green foliage and brown stems with brown thorns. Flowers from mid spring to mid summer. Fan-training against a wall enhances its growth. Introduced 1837.

Rosa × paulii

Average height and spread 7 × 7 ft (2.1 × 2.1 m). Protrudes up to 2 ft (60 cm) from support. **R. × highdownensis** (Hybrid) Light crimson flowers, followed in autumn by attractive bottle-shaped hips. Mid spring to early summer flowering. Strong growing. Introduced 1903. Average height and spread 9 × 9 ft (2.7 × 2.7 m). Protrudes up to 2 ft (60 cm) from support. **R. moyesii** (Species) Pink flowers in mid summer and good hips in autumn. Red, thorny branches and dark green foliage. Tolerates full sun to medium shade. Origin unknown. Average height and spread 10 × 10 ft (3 × 3 m). Protrudes up to 18 in (45 cm) from support. **R. m. 'Geranium'** (Species) Very bright scarlet flowers with good orange/red hip production. Flowers mid summer in full sun to medium shade. A good form. Introduced 1938. Average height and spread 9 × 9 ft (2.7 × 2.7 m). Protrudes up to 18 in (45 cm) from support. **R. m. 'Sealing Wax'** Deep pink flowers in mid summer. Good autumn hips. Introduced 1938. Average height and spread 9 × 9 ft (2.7 × 2.7 m). Protrudes up to 18 in (45 cm) from support. **R. omeiensis pteracantha** (syn. **R. sericea pteracantha**) (Species) Attractive bright red stems that age to brown in winter. Large bright red thorns of interesting shape. Single, small white flowers in late spring to early summer, followed by red hips in autumn. Tolerates full sun to medium shade. Will require an annual reduction of growth by one third, selecting oldest shoots and removing to ground level. This will entail an annual retying in to wires or individual anchorage points. Introduced 1890. Average height and spread 12 × 12 ft (3.7 × 3.7 m). Protrudes up to 18 in (45 cm) from support. **R. o. 'Red Wing'** (Species) Very similar to *R. o. pteracantha* but thorns are stronger red with yellow flowers in early summer. Full sun to medium shade. Origin unknown. Average height and spread 7 × 7 ft (2.1 × 2.1 m). Protrudes up to 18 in (45 cm) from support. **R. × paulii** (Hybrid) Single white flowers, 3 in (7.5 cm) across with bold

Rosa woodsii fendleri in fruit

yellow stamens, on very thorny branches. Flowers mid summer. Somewhat ranging in habit. Normally considered for ground cover, but very useful for covering large walls in difficult situations. Introduced prior to 1903. Average height and spread 15 × 15 ft (4.6 × 4.6 m). Protrudes up to 6 ft (1.8 m) from support. **R. × p. 'Rosea'** (Hybrid) Similar in all respects to *R. × p.* but with pink flowers. **R. rubrifolia** (syn. **R. glauca**) (Species) Attractive purple stems and purple foliage, covered in mid summer by numerous single, pink flowers 1 in (2.5 cm) across with white eyes. Some red hip production. Tolerates full sun to medium shade in exposed positions. Introduced prior to 1830. Average height and spread 8 × 8 ft (2.4 × 2.4 m). Protrudes up to 3 ft (91 cm) from support. **R. willmottiae** (Species) The fern-shaped foliage of this rose is its main attraction, but it does produce lilac/pink flowers ½ in (1 cm) across in mid summer. Introduced 1904. Average height and spread 8 × 8 ft (2.4 × 2.4 m). Protrudes up to 18 in (45 cm) from support. **R. woodsii fendleri** (Species) Lilac/pink flowers followed by good production of round, small hips. Mid summer flowering. Tolerates full sun to medium shade. Introduced prior to 1888. Average height and spread 7 × 7 ft (2.1 × 2.1 m). Protrudes up to 18 in (45 cm) from support. **'Scharlachglut'** (syn. **'Scarlet Fire'**) (Hybrid Gallica) Bright scarlet/crimson, single flowers 3 in (7.5 cm) across with scarlet golden stamens in early summer to late autumn, but not necessarily continuous. Flowers followed by urn-shaped hips which

Rosa 'Wilhelm'

are retained well into winter. Full sun to medium shade. Introduced 1952. Average height and spread 10 × 10 ft (3 × 3 m). Protrudes up to 3 ft (91 cm) from support. **'Souvenir de la Malmaison'** (Bourbon) Fragrant, pink/white mother-of-pearl flowers up to 3 in (7.5 cm) across with deeper shading. Continuous flowering through summer. Difficult in wet weather. Introduced 1843. Average height and spread 5 × 5 ft (1.5 × 1.5 m). Protrudes up to 18 in (45 cm) from support. **'Swany'** (Procumbens) Cup-shaped white flowers up to ½ in (1 cm) across, double. Continuous flowering. This variety is often considered for ground cover but makes an attractive climbing rose for small areas. Introduced 1978. Average height and spread 6 × 6 ft (1.8 × 1.8 m). Protrudes up to 12 in (30 cm) from support. **'Tuscany Superb'** (Gallica) Flowers deep crimson/purple, semi-double with central golden stamens, from mid summer to late summer. Introduced prior to 1848. Average height and spread 5 × 5 ft (1.5 × 1.5 m). Protrudes up to 18 in (45 cm) from support. **'Vanity'** (Hybrid Musk) Fragrant, semi-double, rose-pink flowers carried in large sprays. Recurrent flowering from mid summer to early autumn. Introduced 1920. Average height and spread 7 × 7 ft (2.1 × 2.1 m). Protrudes up to 2 ft (60 cm) from support. **'White Wings'** (Hybrid Tea) Beautiful large single white flowers with papery texture and chocolate-coloured anthers. Foliage thick, dark green. Repeat flowering. Tolerates all aspects, except extremely shady. May be susceptible to blackspot. Introduced 1947. Average height and spread 6 × 5 ft (1.8 × 1.5 m). Protrudes up to 3 ft (91 cm) from support. **'Wilhelm'** (syn. **'Skyrocket'**) (Hybrid Musk) Flowers semi-double, dark red and carried in large clusters. Repeat flowering with good autumn displays. Good foliage, although it does congregate towards the top ends of the branches. Tolerates all aspects. Introduced 1944. Average height and spread 7 × 6 ft (2.1 × 1.8 m). Protrudes up to 3 ft (91 cm) from support. **'William Lobb'** (syn. **'Old Velvet Moss'**) (Moss) Strong growing, needs a large wall. Buds have heavy moss effect. Flowers purple magenta, scented. Introduced 1855. Average height and spread 9 × 9 ft (2.7 × 2.7 m). Protrudes up to 4 ft (1.2 m) from support. **'Yesterday'** (Modern Shrub) Semi-double fragrant flowers, rose-pink, carried in sprays. Good as a cut flower. Continuous flowering. Introduced 1973. Average height and spread 5 × 5 ft (1.5 × 1.5 m). Protrudes up to 2 ft (60 cm) from support. **Average height and spread** Growth at ten years given for each variety.

ROSMARINUS

ROSEMARY

Labiatae　　　　　　　　　　*Wall Shrub*
Evergreen

Although these shrubs are well-known as aromatic herbs, their potential for fan-training is not often appreciated.

Origin From southern Europe and Asia Minor.
Use As medium height, fan-shaped, scented foliage shrubs with attractive flowers for walls and fences or up pillars.
Description *Flower* Small mauve/blue flowers of varying shades produced in leaf axils, often in small clusters, on branches two years old or more. Pink and white flowering varieties are less hardy. Flowers late spring to early summer, and intermittently later in summer and sometimes in autumn. *Foliage* Leaves linear $\frac{1}{4}$–$1\frac{1}{2}$ in (5 mm–3.5 cm) long, grey to grey/green with white undersides. Some golden variegated forms. Aromatic when crushed. *Stem* Upright, becoming arching and spreading with age, grey/green. Medium growth rate when young, slowing with age. *Fruit* Insignificant.
Hardiness Tolerates a minimum winter temperature of 14°F (−10°C).
Soil requirements Light open soils, dislikes waterlogging and liable to chlorosis on extreme alkalinity.
Sun/Shade aspect Requires protection from the most severe weather. Full sun, but tolerates light shade.
Pruning Remove one third of old wood each spring to ground level plus any pruning required for training.
Training Requires individual wires or anchor points to achieve a fan shape.
Propagation and nursery production From semi-ripe cuttings taken in late spring to early summer. Purchase container grown, most varieties easy to find. Best planting height 8 in–2 ft (20–60 cm).
Problems Can become very woody, but pruning should control this.
Forms of interest *R. angustifolia* (Narrow-leaved rosemary) Very narrow foliage and mauve/blue flowers. Not easy to find. *R. a.* **'Corsican Blue'** Narrow foliage, bright blue flowers. Difficult to find. *R. officinalis* (Common rosemary) Grey/green, aromatic foliage with white undersides. Pale to mid blue flowers produced in axillary clusters along wood two years old or more. One of the best forms for culinary use. *R. o.* **'Albus'** A variety with white flowers. More tender than most. Not easy to find. *R. o.* **'Aurea Variegata'** Foliage intermittently splashed pale

Rosmarinus angustifolia **in flower**

gold. Light blue flowers. *R. o.* **'Benenden Blue'** Bright blue flowers and dark green, narrow foliage. Reaches two thirds average height and spread. *R. o.* **'Fastigiatus'** (syn. *R. o.* **'Pyramidalis'**) Mid-blue flowers. An upright growing variety, forming an upright pillar. Often sold as 'Miss Jessop's Upright'. *R. o.* **'Roseus'** Lilac-pink flowers, more tender than average. Reaches two thirds average height and spread. *R. o.* **'Severn Sea'** Brilliant blue flowers. A low-growing variety, reaching one third average height and spread. *R. o.* **'Tuscan Blue'** Good bright blue flowers, broader leaves than most. One third average height and spread.

Average height and spread
Five years
2$\frac{1}{2}$ × 3 ft (76 × 91 cm)
Ten years
4 × 5 ft (1.2 × 1.5 m)
Twenty years
4 × 5 ft (1.2 × 1.5 m)
Protrudes up to 4 ft (1.2 m) from support.

RUBUS FRUTICOSUS
(Blackberry Hybrids)

BLACKBERRY, BRAMBLE

Rosaceae　　　　　　　　*Fruiting Canes*
Deciduous, Semi-evergreen or Evergreen

The wild blackberry and the many hybrids offer ornamental foliage, flowers and edible fruit.

Origin From Europe. Named hybrids of nursery and garden extraction.

Use As fan-trained canes for walls and fences and for the open garden when supported by posts and wires.
Description *Flower* Five-petalled, saucer-shaped flowers $\frac{3}{4}$ in (2 cm) wide in varying colours, from white to pink, carried in large, open clusters 4 in (10 cm) across during mid summer. *Foliage* Three- to five-lobed, 4 in (10 cm) wide and long, light to dark green, often with silver reverse. Some yellow autumn colour. *Stem* Either thorned or thornless, ranging, strong-growing. Light grey/green when young, quickly becoming red, particularly on sun side. Canes die after fruiting. *Fruit* Berries black to red/black in a range of sizes according to variety. Sweet, edible, fruiting in late summer to early autumn. Good for freezing.
Hardiness Tolerates a minimum winter temperature of 0°F (−18°C).
Soil requirements Tolerates all soil conditions with no particular preference, often succeeding on the poorest of environments.
Sun/Shade aspect Tolerates all aspects. Full sun; will grow in light to medium shade, but fruiting may be diminished.
Pruning In first year of establishment, cut plants to ground level in spring. In subsequent years, remove all fruiting canes to ground level after fruiting, retaining new growth for following year's fruit.
Training Tie to wires or individual anchor points. Must be planted at least 10 ft (3 m) apart for training against a wall and if planted in rows in the open garden the rows must be at least 8 ft (2.4 m) apart.
Propagation and nursery production Layer tips of stems into garden soil in early summer and remove in autumn for planting in final position. Purchase bare-rooted from mid autumn to early spring or container grown as available, with autumn, winter or spring planting for preference. Named varieties normally available from good garden centres and general nurseries, but wild form may be very difficult to purchase.
Problems The thorns can make cultivation difficult. Its habit of tip layering itself and spreading can become invasive. Removing old fruiting canes each year can be laborious, but is worthwhile for fruit production.
Forms of interest
UK
'Bedfordshire Giant' Large fruit with good flavour. **'Himalayan Giant'** Very large fruit. Possibly the most popular fruiting variety. One third more height and spread. **'Merton Thornless'** Thornless stems and semi-evergreen foliage. Good fruit with good flavour. **'Oregon Thornless'** ('Cut-leaved Bramble') Semi-evergreen to evergreen foliage, dark green and attractive. Good production of medium-sized fruit with good flavour. Two thirds average height and spread. **Wild varieties** are also good for fruiting; flowers, foliage and fruit are smaller.
USA
ERECT BLACKBERRIES Winter protection of canes, straw and burlap is required in Northern regions.
'Alfred' Large, firm, dark red berries. Good for the North. From Michigan. **'Bailey'** Large, good quality fruit. Good productivity. Good for the North and parts of the Pacific Northwest. From New York. **'Black Satin'** Thornless, semi-erect. Large crops of dark berries, good for eating directly from the cane or for cooking. Good for the South. Origin Maryland. **'Brainerd'** Large fruit of good quality. Very productive, strong-growing canes. Hardy. Good for the South. From Georgia. **'Brazos'** Large fruit carried over a long fruiting period. Strong-growing, resistant to disease. Good for the South. From Texas. **'Cherokee'** Upright canes, moderately thorny. Large crops of good quality fruit of medium size. Good for the South. From Arkansas. **'Comanche'** Large fruits, good for eating directly from the canes but can be cooked. Good for the South. From Arkansas. **'Darrow'** Large, somewhat irregular in shape, ripening over a long period. Good flesh. Hardy but dislikes the coldest areas. From New York. **'Ebony King'** Large, glossy,

Rosmarinus officinalis **in flower**

Rubus fruticosus 'Oregon Thornless'

black, sweet and tangy fruit. Early ripening. Resistant to orange rust. Good for the South, North and Pacific Northwest. From Michigan. **'Eldorado'** Extremely hardy. Good production of good dark red fruits. Resistant to orange rust. Good for the South and North. From Ohio. **'Flint'** Requiring only moderate winter chill. Large fruit in clusters of up to 15. Resistant to leaf spot and anthracnose. Good for the South. From Georgia. **'Hendrick'** Large fruit, medium firm, with a sharp flavour. Very productive. Good for the North. From New York. **'Humble'** Soft fruit and a limited number of thorns. Good for the South. From Texas. **'Jerseyblack'** Large, good flavoured fruits. Strong-growing. Rust resistant. Good for the South. From New Jersey. **'Ranger'** Large, firm fruit, best eaten when really ripe. Good in Virginia. From

Rubus fruticosus 'Himalayan Giant'

Maryland. **'Raven'** Large fruit of very good quality. Very productive. Tender. From Maryland. **'Smoothstem'** Soft, late ripening fruits. Good production in large clusters. Thornless. Hardy. Best from Maryland southwards. From Maryland. **'Thornfree'** Good, medium to large, sharp flavoured fruit. Canes semi-erect up to 10 ft (3 m). Very large cropping. Tender. From Maryland. **'Williams'** Medium-sized fruit, ripening early summer. Good flavour. Strong growing, semi-erect habit with thorns. Resistant to most diseases. Good for the South. From North Carolina.

TRAILING BLACKBERRIES **'Aurora'** Large, firm, early fruit of good flavour. Canes reach up to 6 ft (1.8 m). From Oregon. **'Boysen'** ('Nectar') Large, good flavoured, scented fruit produced over a long season. Strong-growing. Some thorns. In some Southern states can have a first crop in late spring/early summer and a second crop in late summer. Good for the South and Pacific Northwest. From California. **'Carolina'** A good strong-growing cane with large fruits. A dewberry. Resistant to leaf spot diseases. Good for the South. Origin North Carolina. **'Cascade'** Very good flavour. Good production but canes are tender. Good in milder parts of the Pacific Northwest. From Oregon. **'Early June'** Large round fruits of very good flavour. Good for jam, jelly and pies. A dewberry ripening in early summer. Limited number of thorns. Partially resistant to anthracnose and leaf spot. Good for the South. From Georgia. **'Floragrand'** Large, soft, rather tart fruit. Good for cooking and preserving. Early fruiting. Canes remain over winter. A dewberry. Requires 'Oklawaha' for pollination. Good for the South. From Florida. **'Himalayan Berry'** Very large fruits. One third more height and spread than average. Good over a wide area. From the UK. **'Lavaca'** Hardy, resistant to disease. Good fruits with acid flavour. Good for the South. Origin unknown. **'Lucretia'** Hardy, strong-growing, well-established variety. Heavily productive with early ripening, large, soft fruits. Will require protection in winter in the North. A dewberry. From North Carolina. **'Marion'** Medium to large, very good flavoured fruit. Mid season variety. Limited number of canes but extremely long, often up to 20 ft (6 m) or more. Very thorny. Requires mild areas for best results, particularly good in Pacific Northwest. From Oregon. **'Oklawaha'** Normally used as a pollination variety for 'Floragrand' but has a good fruit in its own right. Good for the South. **'Olallie'** Large, shiny black fruit of very high quality, sweet and good flavoured. The canes have thorns and are very productive. Resists verticillium wilt and mildew. Good for Southern California. From Oregon. **'Thornless Evergreen'** See 'Oregon Thornless' in UK varieties for full description. **'Young'** Large purple/black fruits of good flavour. A black dewberry making limited long canes. Anthracnose is a serious problem. Good for the South. From Louisiana.

Average height and spread
One year
8 × 8 ft (2.4 × 2.4 m)
Protrudes up to 5 ft (1.5 m) from support prior to training, 2 ft (60 cm) after training.

RUBUS (Hybrid Forms)

BOYSENBERRY, JOHN INNES BERRY, TAYBERRY, WORCESTER BERRY
Rosaceae   *Fruit Canes*
Deciduous to semi-evergreen
A group of fruit canes where the parentage is very diverse, listed together here due to their shared general characteristics.

Origin Various crosses between recognized soft fruit canes.
Use Fan-trained for walls and fences, or for growing over archways and similar constructions.
Description *Flower* Attractive white or pink flowers, up to $\frac{1}{2}$ in (1 cm) across, saucer-shaped, carried in short clusters in mid to late spring. *Foliage* Hand-shaped, dark green with silver reverse, 4 in (10 cm) wide and 5 in (12 cm) long. Some good yellow autumn colour. Deciduous or semi-evergreen according to variety. *Stem* Light green, becoming shaded red on sun side, finally red/brown. Mostly armed with thorns, but some varieties thornless. *Fruit* Either round or oblong fruits, normally dark red to purple red in colour. Sweet and edible.
Hardiness Tolerates a minimum winter temperature of 4°F (−15°C).

Rubus 'Tayberry'

Soil requirements Tolerates all soils, except for extremely waterlogged or dry conditions.
Sun/Shade aspect Tolerates all aspects, but best fruiting in sheltered, sunny positions where pollination and ripening can benefit.
Pruning In first spring following planting, cut all existing canes to ground level. This will induce a vigorous root development and build up a root stool from which will develop strong canes for the following year's fruiting. In subsequent years remove old fruiting canes to ground level after fruiting and tie in new canes to replace them.
Training Tie in new canes to a fan-shape formation as they develop through spring and summer.
Propagation and nursery production From stem top layers. Can be purchased bare-rooted from mid autumn to early spring or container grown as available. Some forms may have to be sought from specialist nurseries. Look for good root formation; stem size is irrelevant as it has to be removed in spring after planting.
Problems Thorny stems can make cultivation difficult. The need to cut hard back and lose the fruit in the first year is a drawback.
Forms of interest *Boysenberry* Large, dark red fruits, ageing to black. Good sharp distinct flavour. *Thornless boysenberry* A thornless variety with lighter stems. Possibly

less fruit production. *John Innes berry* Similar to a blackberry, sweetly flavoured. *Tayberry* A hybrid between a blackberry and a raspberry with large, deep purple, good flavoured fruit. Good for freezing. *Worcester berry* A cross between a gooseberry and a blackcurrant. Berries red/purple, sweet flavoured. Resistant to most diseases, such as mildew. Two thirds average height and spread.

Average height and spread
One year
10×10 ft (3×3 m)
New canes protrude up to 3 ft (91 cm) from wall or fence, 12 in (30 cm) once tied in.

RUBUS HENRYI BAMBUSARUM
(R. bambusarum)

KNOWN BY BOTANICAL NAME

Rosaceae   *Wall Shrub*
Evergreen
A somewhat unruly bramble but worthy of interest for its attractive foliage.

Origin From China.
Use As a rambling climber through other large wall shrubs. Normally not seen trained in its own right.
Description *Flower* Racemes 4 in (10 cm) long consisting of six to ten $\frac{3}{4}$ in (2 cm) wide pink sepals resembling long, thin tails, early summer. *Foliage* Attractive, three-lobed, up to 6 in (15 cm) wide and long. Light green when young, becoming mid to dark green. White felted undersides. *Stem* Light green becoming dark green, finally green/brown.

Rubus henryii bambusarum

Ranging and arching in habit. Stems die after flowering. Medium to fast annual growth rate. *Fruit* Round, black and shiny, of some limited interest.
Hardiness Tolerates a minimum winter temperature of 14°F (−10°C).
Soil requirements Requires a soil high in organic material and nutrients. Neutral to acid, although as long as adequate moisture is available, may tolerate degrees of alkalinity.
Sun/Shade aspect Requires a sheltered aspect. Full sun to medium shade with light to medium shade for preference.
Pruning Remove all flowering stems to ground level in winter.
Training Normally allowed to ramble through freestanding shrubs or through other wall specimens, although can be tied to wires or individual anchor points.
Propagation and nursery production From tip cuttings or semi-ripe cuttings taken in early summer. Should always be purchased container grown; will have to be sought from specialist nurseries. Best planting height: from root clumps to 3 ft (91 cm).

Problems Rarely looks attractive as a young plant and requires time to establish. Can become invasive in ideal situations.
Forms of interest None.
Average height and spread
Five years
6×6 ft (1.8×1.8 m)
Ten years
10×10 ft (3×3 m)
Twenty years
10×10 ft (3×3 m)
Protrudes up to 4 ft (1.2 m) from support.

RUBUS LOGANOBACCUS
(Loganberry Hybrids)

LOGANBERRY

Rosaceae   *Fruiting Canes*
Deciduous
A cane fruit that responds well to fan-training, but its robustness of growth must be taken into account.

Origin Raised in the USA in the late 1800s.
Use As a large, ranging, loosely fan-trained cane fruit for walls and fences. Ideal for growing in the open garden with the support of stakes and wires.
Description *Flower* White, $\frac{1}{2}$ in (1 cm) wide, five-petalled flowers carried in clusters in early summer; each cluster up to 5 in (12 cm) in width. *Foliage* Hand-shaped, attractive, light grey/green with silvery reverse. Often up to 8 in (20 cm) in width and length. Some yellow autumn colouring. *Stem* Both thorned and thornless varieties. Stems grey/green when young, quickly becoming shaded red, ageing to red/green, finally grey/brown. Upright at first, quickly becoming spreading, ranging, vigorous. After fruiting, canes die and must be removed. Fast rate of growth. *Fruit* Cone-shaped berries, red with grey sheen. Sweet, edible. Produced late summer/early autumn. Good for freezing.
Hardiness Tolerates a minimum winter temperature of 0°F (−18°C).
Soil requirements Tolerates all but the most alkaline. Dislikes excess waterlogging. Must contain a high degree of organic material and adequate plant nutrients both when planting and as an annual addition.
Sun/Shade aspect Tolerates all aspects, but adequate windbreaks should be provided so that pollinating insects are able to reach flowers. Full sun for fruit, but will tolerate very light shade although with decrease in fruiting.
Pruning In year of planting reduce all shoots to ground level in spring to induce the formation of root stool and strong shoots for fruiting in following year. Once established,

remove all fruiting canes to ground level after fruiting, tying in new canes into fan-trained shape.
Training Requires wires or individual anchor points. Tie in annually produced canes alternately to the left and right where they will flower and fruit the following year. Alternatively, gather all new canes loosely in the centre then retie to form the fan-trained shape when the old fruiting canes have been removed. Must be planted at least 12 ft (3.7 m) apart on any wall, fence or wire structure, and if more than one row is planted on wires rows must be at least 8 ft (2.4 m) apart.
Propagation and nursery production From self-rooted tips by inserting into the soil in mid summer and removing in following year for replanting in new positions. Purchase bare-rooted from mid autumn to early spring, container grown as available, with autumn, winter and spring for preference. Normally available from garden centres and general nurseries. Size is irrelevant and a good root system is the predominant factor.
Problems Suffers attacks of raspberry cane spot and mildew, otherwise is one of the most reliable amongst all of the fruiting canes.
Forms of interest 'LY59' The best of the thorned varieties, giving the biggest crop and best flavour. 'Loganberry Thornless' Canes without thorns. Fruiting good but crop may be slightly decreased in quantity.
Average height and spread
After one year
8×8 ft (2.4×2.4 m)
Protrudes up to 6 ft (1.8 m) from support prior to training, 2 ft (60 cm) after training.

RUBUS PHOENICOLASIUS

JAPANESE WINEBERRY

Rosaceae   *Woody Fruiting Climber*
Deciduous
An edible, fruiting shrub which can make an attractive display in the garden.

Origin From Japan.
Use As a fan-trained wall or fence shrub to show off its flowers, fruit, foliage and stems, all of which are of attraction. Can also be grown freestanding.
Description *Flower* Clusters up to 3 in (7.5 cm) across and 4 in (10 cm) long of single pink flowers produced in early summer. *Foliage* Trifoliate leaves, 6 in (15 cm) long and 4 in (10 cm) wide, with five leaflets, each 1$\frac{3}{4}$ in (4.5 cm) long and 1 in (2.5 cm) wide. Mid green with good yellow autumn colour. Felted

Rubus loganobaccus 'LY59'

Rubus phoenicolasius

texture with silver undersides. **Stem** Long, arching, orange/red in colour. Extremely attractive in winter. Downy, with soft thorns. Fast rate of growth. **Fruit** Small clusters, up to 6 in (15 cm) long and 4 in (10 cm) wide, of round, bright red, sweet, edible fruits in late summer, early autumn.

Hardiness Tolerates a minimum winter temperature of 0°F (−18°C). At this temperature some stem damage may be caused but is not terminal.

Soil requirements Most soils suitable.

Sun/Shade aspect Requires only light protection. Prefers light shade, tolerates full sun to deep shade.

Pruning Cut all old fruit canes to ground level after fruiting. Retain new shoots for next year's display and fruit. Young plants should be cut severely prior to planting to induce a good formation of root stool. This normally leads to no production of fruit in the subsequent year.

Training Tie to wires or individual anchor points.

Propagation and nursery production From semi-ripe cuttings taken in early summer. Purchase container grown from good nurseries and some garden centres. Best planting height 15 in–2½ ft (38–76 cm).

Problems Often requires more room than is anticipated. May be difficult to find.

Similar forms of interest None.

Average height and spread

Five years
3 × 3 ft (91 × 91 cm)
Ten years
6 × 6 ft (1.8 × 1.8 m)
Twenty years
10 × 10 ft (3 × 3 m)
Protrudes up to 2 ft (60 cm) from support if fan-trained, 10 ft (3 m) untrained.

RUBUS TRICOLOR

CREEPING BRAMBLE

Rosaceae　　　　　　　　***Wall Shrub***
Evergreen but may become deciduous in severe winters

A low-growing, carpeting shrub that can be easily adapted to a low climber for more inhospitable areas.

Origin From China.

Use As a low climber for walls, fences or pillars, or to ramble through medium-sized shrubs where many other climbers will not succeed.

Description *Flower* Single white flowers, ½ in (1 cm) wide, produced in early summer. *Foliage* Leaves oval, up to 4 in (10 cm) long

and 1½ in (4 cm) wide, with pronounced veins. Dark green with a silver sheen and silver reverse. *Stem* Arching, orange/red to orange/brown, covered with soft brown to grey/brown hairy thorns. Tips and buds root on contact with soil. Slow to medium growth rate. *Fruit* Round berries, up to ¼ in (5 mm) in diameter, bright red, edible, but with a bland taste.

Rubus tricolor

Hardiness Tolerates a minimum winter temperature of 0°F (−18°C).

Soil requirements Does well on all soil types with no particular preference, tolerating poor conditions if adequate moisture is available.

Sun/Shade aspect All aspects in full sun to deep shade, although deep shade may make it more lax in its habit.

Pruning Remove old fruiting wood after fruiting to encourage new growth.

Training Allow to ramble through shrubs or over wires.

Propagation and nursery production From layers or from semi-ripe cuttings taken in early summer. Purchase container grown; may have to be sought from specialist ground cover nurseries or from good garden centres. Best planting height 6–18 in (15–45 cm).

Problems May be shy to flower, particularly when in deep shade.

Similar forms of interest *R. idaeus* 'Aureus' A golden form of the raspberry, annually producing new golden shoots with white flowers. Red and yellow edible fruits. *R. microphyllus* 'Variegatus' Green foliage splashed cream and pink. Flowers magenta-rose in colour. Fragrant. Edible orange fruits.

Average height and spread

Five years
4 × 4 ft (1.2 × 1.2 m)
Ten years
6 × 6 ft (1.8 × 1.8 m)
Twenty years
6 × 6 ft (1.8 × 1.8 m)
Protrudes up to 18 in (45 m) from support.

RUBUS ULMIFOLIUS 'BELLIDIFLORUS' (Rusticanus bellidiflorus)

DOUBLE FLOWERING BLACKBERRY

Rosaceae　　　　　　　　***Wall Shrub***
Deciduous

A gem of a climber, tolerating the worst degrees of cultivation, yet still producing a flowering display.

Origin From Europe.

Use As a climber for fences and walls and for growing through large shrubs. Can be allowed to grow untrained, but requires some support.

Description *Flower* Attractive, mauve/pink, cylinder-shaped panicles, up to 12 in (30 cm) long and 5 in (12 cm) wide, consisting of numerous button-like, lacerated petals. Produced in mid to late summer. *Foliage* Three to five leaflets make up a pinnate leaf up to 3½ in (9 cm) long and 2 in (5 cm) wide, with white felted undersides and dark green upper. *Stem* Dark green, angular, thorny, ranging in habit, although not invasive. Flowering in second year. *Fruit* Small, black, inedible round berries produced in late summer to early autumn.

Hardiness Tolerates a minimum winter temperature of 0°F (−18°C).

Soil requirements Does well on all soil types with no particular preference, tolerating quite poor conditions as long as adequate moisture is available.

Sun/Shade aspect Tolerates all aspects with no particular preference. Full sun to deep shade, but in deep shade may be more lax in habit.

Pruning Remove all flowering shoots to ground level once flowering is finished, encouraging new shoots for following year.

Training Allow to grow freestanding against a wall or fan-train to wires or individual anchor points.

Rubus ulmifolius 'Bellidiflorus' in flower

Propagation and nursery production From layers or softwood cuttings taken in early summer. Purchase container grown; will have to be sought from specialist nurseries. Best planting height 6 in–3 ft (15–91 cm).

Problems Apart from its limited availability it has no problems.

Similar forms of interest None.

Average height and spread

Five years
5 × 5 ft (1.5 × 1.5 m)
Ten years
7 × 7 ft (2.1 × 2.1 m)
Twenty years
12 × 12 ft (3.7 × 3.7 m)
Protrudes up to 2 ft (60 cm) from support if fan-trained, 10 ft (3 m) untrained.

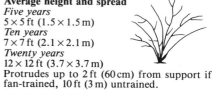

145

Schisandra grandiflora rubrifolia in flower

SCHISANDRA GRANDIFLORA RUBRIFOLIA (S. rubrifolia)

KNOWN BY BOTANICAL NAME

Magnoliaceae, syn. *Schisandraceae*   *Woody Climber*
Deciduous

An attractive climber which is not planted as often as it deserves.

Origin From China.
Use As a climber for walls, fences, poles and pergolas for its interesting flowers.
Description *Flower* Borne singly at the leaf joints. Pendulous, hanging on stalks 1–2 in (2.5–5 cm) long. Seven petals, deep crimson in colour. Mid to late spring. *Foliage* Ovate to lanceolate, 5½ in (14 cm) long and 2 in (5 cm) wide. Deep green with attractive autumn colour. *Stem* Green/brown, ageing to grey/brown, finally dark brown. Moderately twining. Slow to medium growth rate. *Fruit* Flower spikes give way to fruit spikes, with globe-shaped, round, red fruits borne in late summer/early autumn, although not always reliable.
Hardiness Tolerates a minimum winter temperature of 14°F (−10°C).
Soil requirements Does equally well on both moderately alkaline and acid soil, as long as adequate moisture is available to achieve good growth.
Sun/Shade aspect Tolerates all but the most exposed aspects. Best growth and flowers in light shade, but will tolerate full sun as long as roots have adequate shade and moisture.
Pruning Normally requires no pruning, but can be reduced in size in early spring if necessary.
Training Shoots semi-twining over wires, trellis or similar framework, but may need additional support by tying in when young or heavy with age.
Propagation and nursery production From seed sown in spring or semi-ripe cuttings taken in early to mid summer. In both instances propagation is not easy. Always purchase container grown; will have to be sought from specialist nurseries. Best planting height 1–3 ft (30–91 cm).
Problems Limited availability. Takes up to three to five years to reach any size and to give a good flowering display.
Similar forms of interest None.
Average height and spread
Five years
5 × 5 ft (1.5 × 1.5 m)
Ten years
10 × 10 ft (3 × 3 m)
Twenty years
18 × 18 ft (5.5 × 5.5 m)
Protrudes up to 3 ft (91 cm) from support.

SCHIZOPHRAGMA HYDRANGEOIDES

KNOWN BY BOTANICAL NAME

Hydrangeaceae   *Woody Climber*
Deciduous

This attractive climber that is closely related to *Hydrangea petiolaris* (climbing hydrangea) is worthy of inclusion in the garden, but its availability and the time it takes to mature must be considered.

Origin From Japan.
Use As an attractive climber for large walls and fences or to climb through large trees, over stumps or medium to large shrubs.
Description *Flower* Small yellow-white flowers ringed by 1½ in (4 cm) long white bracts make up a flat, lace-capped flower up to 10–12 in (25–30 cm) in diameter in late summer. Bracts age to brown and are retained until Christmas. *Foliage* Broad, oval-shaped leaves with coarsely toothed edges, up to 3–5 in (7.5–12 cm) long, supported on stalks 1–2 in (2.5–5 cm) long. Deep green above, glaucous pale green beneath. *Stem* Green/brown ageing to grey/brown, branching. Slow growing when young, faster with age. *Fruit* No fruit of interest.
Hardiness Tolerates a minimum winter temperature of 4°F (−15°C).
Soil requirements Does well on all soil types, only disliking extremely alkaline conditions.

Sun/Shade aspect Tolerates all but the most severe of aspects, benefiting from a small amount of protection. Best in full sun, but will tolerate very light shade.
Pruning Normally needs no pruning, but can be cut back if required in early spring.
Training Tie to wires, trellis or individual fixings to form a broad, fan-shaped formation.
Propagation and nursery production From semi-ripe cuttings taken in late summer. Can be layered if parent plant has young enough shoots. Propagation at times can be difficult, making it scarce. Should always be purchased container grown; may have to be sought from specialist nurseries. Best planting height 6 in–2 ft (15–60 cm).
Problems Slow to establish and not readily available but, once established, a true gem of a plant.
Similar forms of interest *S. h.* 'Roseum' A variety with pink bracts. Very scarce in commercial production. *S. integrifolia* Larger leaves and flower heads than *S. hydrangeoides*. Scarce in production. From China.
Average height and spread
Five years
5 × 5 ft (1.5 × 1.5 m)
Ten years
10 × 10 ft (3 × 3 m)
Twenty years
20 × 20 ft (6 × 6 m)
Protrudes up to 2 ft (60 cm) from support.

SOLANUM CRISPUM

CLIMBING POTATO, CHILEAN POTATO TREE

Solanaceae   *Wall Shrub*
Deciduous, semi-evergreen

One of the most attractive of all wall shrubs, requiring space to develop to its full potential but, if allowed, making a splendid display.

Origin From Chile.
Use As a freestanding wall shrub for walls and fences.
Description *Flower* Five purple/blue, fleshy petals, surmounted in the centre by an attractive bright yellow bunch of anthers, make up star-shaped flowers 1 in (2.5 cm) across, which are borne in 3–6 in (7.5–15 cm) wide clusters from June to September. *Foliage* Narrowly ovate leaves dark green above, paler beneath. Some yellow autumn colour. *Stem* Bright glossy green, upright, becoming branching. Medium to fast growing. *Fruit* Yellow/white, pea-sized, poisonous fruits.

Schizophragma hydrangeoides in flower

Hardiness Tolerates a minimum winter temperature of 14°F (−10°C).
Soil requirements Does well on most soils, except in very dry or poor conditions. Dislikes high degrees of alkalinity.
Sun/Shade aspect Requires a sheltered aspect in full sun to light shade.
Pruning Remove one third of oldest growth to ground level in early spring.
Training Tie to wires or trellis against walls or fences to obtain a fan-trained shape.

Solanum crispum **in flower**

Propagation and nursery production From semi-ripe cuttings taken in early summer. Always purchase container grown; best planting height 12 in–2 ft (30–60 cm). Relatively easy to find in garden centres and nurseries, particularly when in flower.
Similar forms of interest *S. c.* 'Glasnevin' Larger flower clusters of slightly darker blue.
Average height and spread
Five years
4 × 4 ft (1.2 × 1.2 m)
Ten years
6 × 6 ft (1.8 × 1.8 m)
Twenty years
12 × 12 ft (3.7 × 3.7 m)
Protrudes up to 4 ft (1.2 m) from support.

SOLANUM DULCAMARA 'VARIEGATUM'

VARIEGATED BITTERSWEET, VARIEGATED FELLONWOOD, VARIEGATED WOODY NIGHTSHADE
Solanaceae   *Perennial Climber*
Deciduous
An attractive variegated perennial climber which does not form a woody structure. Produces poisonous fruits.

Origin From Europe, Asia and Africa.
Use As an attractive foliage climber for covering walls, fences and pillars. Can be grown through large, uninteresting shrubs.
Description *Flower* Five-lobed petals, purple to purple/blue, each flower ½ in (1 cm) across, carried in clusters up to 4 in (10 cm) wide and long. *Foliage* Oval with three to five leaflets, each up to 3 in (7.5 cm) long, with narrow points. Olive/green, splashed with creamy-white variegation. *Stem* Mid green, semi-twining, spreading and lax in habit. Medium growth rate. *Fruit* Small, round, red, sometimes yellow, up to ½ in (1 cm) across, poisonous, produced in late summer/early autumn.
Hardiness Tolerates a minimum winter temperature of 4°F (−15°C). All top growth is killed annually to ground level and rejuvenates from root stool.
Soil requirements Does well on all soil conditions, with no particular preference.
Sun/Shade aspect Tolerates all aspects in full sun to light shade.

Solanum dulcamara 'Variegatum' **in flower**

Pruning Requires no pruning other than removal of dead growth above ground level in autumn or early spring.
Training Allow to ramble through wires, netting, trelliswork or over large uninteresting shrubs.
Propagation and nursery production From seed or semi-ripe cuttings taken in early summer. Always purchase container grown; best planting height 6 in–3 ft (15–91 cm). Normally available from good garden centres and nurseries.
Problems Fruits are poisonous, making it an inadvisable plant where there are young children.
Similar forms of interest None.
Average height and spread
Five years
8 × 8 ft (2.4 × 2.4 m)
Ten years
8 × 8 ft (2.4 × 2.4 m)
Twenty years
8 × 8 ft (2.4 × 2.4 m)
Protrudes up to 4 ft (1.2 m) from support.

SOLANUM JASMINOIDES

POTATO VINE, JASMINE NIGHTSHADE
Solanaceae   *Woody Climber*
Deciduous to semi-evergreen
Possibly too tender for most gardens, but if a sheltered position can be found it is well worth consideration as it is one of the most fragrant of all climbers.

Origin From South America.
Use As a climber for walls, fences or pillars in sheltered environments, or for greenhouses or conservatories.

Solanum jasminoides 'Album' **in flower**

Description *Flower* Blue/white to pale blue, each flower up to ¾ in (2 cm) across, consisting of five thick, fleshy petals with golden-yellow anthers. Fragrant. Flowers produced in branched clusters. *Foliage* Three leaflets, each oval, terminal leaflet up to 2 in (5 cm) long. Pair of lower lateral leaflets 1½ in (4 cm) long and wide. Grey/green, supported on short leaf shoot. *Stem* Dark grey/green, twining, not self-clinging. Medium rate of growth. *Fruit* No fruit of interest.
Hardiness Tolerates a minimum winter temperature of 23°F (−5°C).
Soil requirements Tolerates all soil conditions, except extremely dry.
Sun/Shade aspect Must have a sheltered aspect. Fully sun to light shade.

Solanum jasminoides **in flower**

Pruning Remove one third of oldest growth to ground level in early spring to induce rejuvenation.
Training Tie to wires or trelliswork when young. Quickly establishes itself with twining habit and becomes self-supporting until very old and heavy.
Propagation and nursery production From semi-ripe cuttings taken in early summer. Always purchase container grown; best planting height 1–3 ft (30–91 cm). Will have to be sought from specialist nurseries.
Problems Its lack of hardiness is not always appreciated and it may often die in winter.
Similar forms of interest *S. j.* 'Album' White flowers, more fragrant than the parent plant. Slightly smaller in height and spread.
Average height and spread
Five years
6 × 6 ft (1.8 × 1.8 m)
Ten years
12 × 12 ft (3.7 × 3.7 m)
Twenty years
18 × 18 ft (5.5 × 5.5 m)
Protrudes up to 2 ft (60 cm) from support.

SOLLYA FUSIFORMIS

AUSTRALIAN BLUEBELL CREEPER
Pittosporaceae **Tender Woody Climber**
Evergreen
An attractive climbing plant requiring protection in all but the most sheltered of areas.

Origin From Australia.
Use As a self-clinging climber for very sheltered walls and fences or for growing under the protection of a conservatory or greenhouse.
Description *Flower* Pendent clusters of four to 12 blue flowers each approximately $\frac{1}{2}$ in (1 cm) across, consisting of five small pointed petals. *Foliage* Ovate to lanceolate, pointed, up to 2$\frac{1}{2}$ in (6 cm) long and $\frac{3}{4}$ in (2 cm) wide. Light bright green when young, becoming darker with age. *Stem* Light green becoming dark green. Glossy, self-supporting by twining habit. Medium growth rate. *Fruit* No fruit of interest.

Sollya fusiformis in flower

Hardiness Requires a very sheltered sunny position or the protection of a greenhouse or conservatory. Tolerates a minimum winter temperature of 23°F (−5°C) but only in very sheltered, favourable areas.
Soil requirements Requires a soil high in organic material. Resents drying out.
Sun/Shade aspect Needs a sheltered aspect. Semi-shade for best results but will tolerate full sun.
Pruning Normally requires no pruning but can be reduced in size if necessary and will quickly rejuvenate.
Training Allow to twine through trellis or over a wire support.
Propagation and nursery production From semi-ripe cuttings, rooted into sharp sand, under the protection of a greenhouse. Should always be purchased container grown; may have to be sought from specialist nurseries, although sometimes available in good garden centres. Best size to purchase 6 in–3 ft (15–91 cm).
Problems Its lack of hardiness is often underestimated and attempts are made to grow it in areas where it cannot tolerate the low winter temperatures.
Similar forms of interest None.
Average height and spread
Five years
6 × 6 ft (1.8 × 1.8 m)
Ten years
9 × 9 ft (2.7 × 2.7 m)
Twenty years
15 × 15 ft (4.6 × 4.6 m)
Protrudes up to 2 ft (60 cm) from support.

Sophora tetraptera in flower

SOPHORA TETRAPTERA

NEW ZEALAND LABURNUM, KOWHAI
Leguminosae **Wall Shrub**
Evergreen
An interesting large shrub or small tree for foliage and flowers in mild locations provided the protection of a wall or fence is available.

Origin From New Zealand.
Use As an attractive foliage wall shrub for walls and fences in very mild areas, or for growing against walls in conservatories or large greenhouses.
Description *Flower* Small, yellow tubular flowers 1$\frac{1}{2}$–2 in (4–5 cm) long in pendent clusters in late spring. *Foliage* Pinnate leaves consisting of numerous pairs of small, ovate to oblong leaflets, light green to green/brown. *Stem* Upright, becoming attractively branched, slightly drooping. Light green/brown to brown. Slow to medium growth rate. *Fruit* Unusual seed pods looking like beads, each with four broad wings, late summer to early autumn.
Hardiness Tolerates a minimum winter temperature of 23°F (−5°C).
Soil requirements Light, open, well-drained soil, alkaline or acid.
Sun/Shade aspect Requires a very sheltered, warm aspect in full sun.
Pruning None required.
Training Requires wires or individual anchor points to achieve a good trained shape.
Propagation and nursery production From seed or semi-ripe cuttings taken in early summer. Purchase container grown; may need to be obtained from specialist nurseries. Best planting height 15 in–2$\frac{1}{2}$ ft (38–76 cm).
Problems Often purchased in mild areas for transplanting to colder regions where it rarely succeeds.
Similar forms of interest *S. t.* 'Early Gold' Fern-like foliage and lemon-yellow flowers. *S. microphylla* A very similar form to *S. tetraptera* but with smaller leaflets and flowers. Juvenile foliage may be dense and wiry. *S. m.* 'Early Gold' Yellow flowers and rich green leaves. Upright habit.
Average height and spread
Five years
3 × 3 ft (91 × 91 cm)
Ten years
6 × 6 ft (1.8 × 1.8 m)
Twenty years
10 × 10 ft (3 × 3 m)
Protrudes up to 3 ft (91 cm) from support.

SORBUS ARIA

WHITEBEAM
Rosaceae **Hardy Tree**
Deciduous
A tree which is easy to grow in most soils and situations and offers attractive berries and autumn foliage.

Sorbus aria 'Lutescens' in leaf

Origin From Europe.
Use As a fan-trained tree on large walls or on open wire fences.
Description *Flower* Clusters 4 in (10 cm) across of white fluffy flowers in late spring. *Foliage* Ovate, toothed leaves, up to 4 in (10 cm) long with downy white undersides and dark green to grey/green upper surfaces. Good russet and gold autumn colour. *Stem* Grey/green to grey/brown with downy covering. Strong, upright and fast-growing when young. Responds well to fan-training. Medium to fast growth rate. *Fruit* Clusters of scarlet-red, oval to globe-shaped fruits 4 in (10 cm) across in autumn.
Hardiness Tolerates a minimum winter temperature of 4°F (−15°C).
Soil requirements Any soil conditions; particularly tolerant of alkalinity.

Sun/Shade aspect Tolerates all aspects. Best in full sun to maintain colouring.
Pruning Prune young trees hard in the spring following planting. Select and train resulting five to seven shoots and tie into a fan-trained shape. In subsequent years, remove all side growths back to two points from their origin and maintain original main branches in fan shape.
Training Secure to wires or individual anchor points.
Propagation and nursery production Parent plant from seed; named varieties grafted or budded on to understocks of *S. aria*. Available bare-rooted or container grown. Select young trees of not more than two years old and 3–6 ft (91 cm–1.8 m) in height for fan-training. Usually available from specialist nurseries and garden centres.
Problems Young trees suitable for fan-training may be hard to find.
Forms of interest *S. a.* 'Chrysophylla' Leaves predominantly primrose yellow through summer with some silver undersides, turning buttercup yellow in autumn. White flowers. Orange/red fruits. *S. a.* 'Lutescens' Best of all silver whitebeams. Pale green foliage with silver down, white flowers and orange berries. Most adaptable variety for fan-training. *S. a.* 'Majestica' Large, round to ovate foliage 6 in (15 cm) long, grey upper surface with white, downy undersides. Orange fruits in autumn. *S. bristoliensis* Small, ovate, silver leaves. Little clusters of white flowers and orange/red berries. Not readily available but worth researching for a planting collection. Two thirds average height and spread. Originating in the UK. *S. folgneri* Slender growths with lanceolate to narrowly ovate, finely tapering leaves up to 4 in (10 cm) long. White felted undersides and dark grey upper surfaces. Good yellow autumn colour. Clusters of white flowers 4 in (10 cm) across, followed by red, oval fruits. Half average height and spread. Not easy to find and will have to be sought from specialist nurseries. From China. *S. hybrida* 'Gibbsii' Dark grey leaves with silver undersides, lobed with three to five indentations. Large clusters of white flowers up to 5 in (12 cm) across, followed by orange/red berries in autumn. Two thirds average height and spread. Not readily available and must be sought from specialist nurseries. *S. intermedia* (Swedish whitebeam) Lobed leaves up to 4 in (10 cm) long, with steel-grey upper surfaces and white undersides. White flowers and orange/red fruits. *S. latifolia* (Service tree of Fontainbleau) Large, silver/grey foliage with white, downy undersides, round to ovate, 4 in (10 cm) long or more, toothed edges. White flower clusters up to 3 in (7.5 cm) across, followed by globe-shaped, brown/red fruits. From Europe. *S.*

'Mitchellii' Among the largest of whitebeam foliage forms. Leaves up to 8 in (20 cm) long and 6 in (15 cm) wide, grey/green to silver/grey upper surfaces with white, downy, felted undersides. Good yellow autumn colour. White flower clusters up to 4 in (10 cm) across, followed by red fruits in autumn, more sparse than in most varieties. Stems brown, solid, stout. Two thirds average height and spread. Not readily available but found in specialist nurseries.
Average height and spread
Five years
10×10 ft (3×3 m)
Ten years
20×20 ft (6×6 m)
Twenty years
30×30 ft (9×9 m)
Protrudes up to 4 ft (1.2 m) from support.

STACHYURUS PRAECOX

KNOWN BY BOTANICAL NAME

Stachyuraceae   *Wall Shrub*
Deciduous

A winter-flowering shrub which deserves to be more widely planted and is not always considered for its use as a wall shrub.

Origin From Japan.
Use As a fan-trained wall shrub for its late winter and early spring flowers.
Description *Flower* Numerous pendent racemes, $1\frac{1}{2}$–4 in (4–10 cm) long, consisting of over 20 pale yellow, cup-shaped flowers, borne along branches from late winter through to early spring. Exact flowering time is dependent on winter temperatures. Flowers produced on wood two years old or more. Frost resistant. *Foliage* Leaves large, ovate, pointed, 3–6 in (7.5–15 cm) long and 2–3 in (5–7.5 cm) wide. Dark green tinged purple, with purple veining. Some yellow autumn colour. *Stem* Strong, upright, arching when young, becoming more branching in subsequent years. Purple/green. When fan-trained forms a large, interesting shrub. Medium to fast growth rate. *Fruit* Insignificant.
Hardiness Tolerates a minimum winter temperature of 0°F (−18°C).
Soil requirements Does well in most soils.
Sun/Shade aspect Requires some protection from cold winter winds to maintain flowers over a long period. Full sun to mid shade.
Pruning On established shrubs five years old or more, remove one third of old flowering wood to ground level following flowering to encourage rejuvenation.
Training Will require wires or individual

anchor points to achieve a fan-trained shape.
Propagation and nursery production From layers or semi-ripe cuttings taken early to mid summer. Purchase container grown; fairly easily found in nurseries. Best planting height 2–4 ft (60 cm–1.2 m).
Problems Young plants often appear lop-sided, with one or more strong shoots, but grow quickly once planted.
Similar forms of interest *S. chinensis* Foliage slightly narrower and possibly duller green than that of *S. praecox*. Racemes shorter but comprising more numerous small florets. Flowers dependent on weather, but can be slightly earlier. *S. c.* 'Magpie' White to creamy white margins on leaves. Often splashed with pale green mottling and tinged rose pink. Yellow flowers. Extremely scarce.
Average height and spread
Five years
8×8 ft (2.4×2.4 m)
Ten years
12×12 ft (3.7×3.7 m)
Twenty years
15×15 ft (4.6×4.6 m)
Protrudes up to 3 ft (91 cm) from support.

STAPHYLEA COLCHICA

BLADDERNUT, COLCHIS BLADDERNUT

Staphyleaceae   *Wall Shrub*
Deciduous

One of the aristocrats of flowering shrubs but not always thought of for its use as a large wall shrub, where it can show off its flowers and interesting fruits to the best advantage.

Staphylea colchica **in flower**

Origin From southern Caucasus.
Use As a very large, fan-trained wall shrub for its flowers and fruit.
Description *Flower* Small, white, fragrant flowers $\frac{1}{2}$ in (1 cm) wide with five reflexed outer petals and five central petals forming a loose trumpet shape. Borne in panicles over 5 in (12 cm) long in mid spring. *Foliage* Leaves ovate to oblong, composed of three to five leaflets up to 4 in (10 cm) long. Dull grey/green upper surfaces, glossy undersides. Some yellow autumn colour. *Stem* Upright with limited branching. Light green to grey/green, becoming grey/brown. Fast growth rate when young, slowing with age. *Fruit* Conspicuous, translucent, bladder-shaped capsules, 3–4 in (7.5–10 cm) long, in late summer/early autumn.
Hardiness Tolerates a minimum winter temperature of 4°F (−15°C).
Soil requirements Best in neutral to acid fertile soil, but tolerates moderate alkalinity.

Stachyurus praecox **in flower**

Sun/Shade aspect Requires a sheltered aspect in full sun or light shade.

Pruning None required for its well-being but for fan-training the previous season's growth can be cut back by two-thirds or more. Older shoots of four years or more should be cut hard to ground level to induce new foliage shoots which can be trained. This method can also be used to enhance the foliage production on varieties not fan-trained.

Training Will require wires or fixing to individual anchor points.

Propagation and nursery production From seed or layers. Purchase container grown; rather hard to find. Best planting height 2–2½ ft (60–76 cm).

Problems Susceptibility to severe winters can be a problem if the shrub is to establish and show its full potential. Must be provided with the right type of soil.

Similar forms of interest *S. holocarpa* Flowers pink in bud, opening to white, in short pendent panicles in mid to late spring. Foliage trifoliate, oblong to lanceolate leaflets, light grey/green. From central China. Difficult to find. *S. h.* 'Rosea' Flowers pink to soft pink, in pendent panicles mid to late spring. Young foliage trifoliate and bronze in colour, ageing to mid green. Yellow autumn colour. Difficult to find. *S. pinnata* (Antoney nut) White flowers in thin, pendent panicles in late spring to early summer. Foliage pinnate, grey/green, five to seven leaflets. Easy to find. From central Europe.

Average height and spread
Five years
6 × 6 ft (1.8 × 1.8 m)
Ten years
9 × 9 ft (2.7 × 2.7 m)
Twenty years
16 × 16 ft (4.9 × 4.9 m)
Protrudes up to 3 ft (91 cm) from support.

STAUNTONIA HEXAPHYLLA

KNOWN BY BOTANICAL NAME

Lardizabalaceae   *Woody Climber*
Evergreen

An interesting evergreen climber which requires a protected aspect in very favourable areas, but is well worth inclusion if the right conditions can be provided.

Origin From Japan and Korea.
Use As a self-twining climber for warm walls and fences or for growing in conservatories and large greenhouses.
Description *Flower* Male and female flowers each have between three and seven slender, white to violet tinged, fragrant petals. Flowers produced in short racemes in mid spring. *Foliage* Pinnate leaves with oval leaflets each up to 4 in (10 cm) long. Leathery texture. Light green to grey/green. Leaves presented in bunches of three to seven at each leaf joint. *Stem* Wiry, dark olive green, twining. Medium rate of growth. *Fruit* Egg-shaped, tinged with purple, up to 2 in (5 cm) long. Dark green, ageing to yellow. Fruit juice is sweet to taste. Only produces fruit in hot, dry summers.
Hardiness Tolerates a minimum winter temperature of 23°F (−5°C).
Soil requirements Does well on all soil conditions with no particular preference.
Sun/Shade aspect Requires a sunny, sheltered, warm wall in full sun to light shade.
Pruning Shorten back trailing tendrils in winter to induce new growth the following spring.
Training Allow to twine through wires on fences, walls, pillars and pergolas. Will also ramble through large shrubs or small trees.
Propagation and nursery production From semi-ripe cuttings taken in early to mid summer. Should always be purchased container grown; will have to be sought from specialist nurseries. Best planting height 1–3 ft (30–91 cm).

Stauntonia hexaphylla in flower

Problems Not entirely hardy and may be better in a large conservatory or greenhouse unless very mild, warm conditions can be guaranteed all year round.
Similar forms of interest None.
Average height and spread
Five years
6 × 6 ft (1.8 × 1.8 m)
Ten years
12 × 12 ft (3.7 × 3.7 m)
Twenty years
24 × 24 ft (7.3 × 7.3 m)
Protrudes up to 9 in (23 cm) from support.

SYRINGA MICROPHYLLA 'SUPERBA'

DAPHNE LILAC, LITTLELEAF LILAC

Oleaceae   *Wall Shrub*
Deciduous

A lilac giving two flowering displays, one in spring and one in autumn, adapting well as a fan-trained wall specimen.

Origin Originally from northern and western China, but the form 'Superba' is of garden origin.
Use As a fan-trained flowering shrub for walls, fences or pillars.
Description *Flower* Panicles 3 in (7.5 cm) long and 1½ in (4 cm) wide of fragrant, rosy pink

Syringa microphylla 'Superba' in flower

flowers in mid to late spring, often with some autumn display. *Foliage* Leaves small, ovate, pointed, up to 2 in (5 cm) long. *Stem* Thin, wispy, light brown to grey/brown, forming a widespreading fan shape. Medium to slow growth rate. *Fruit* Insignificant.
Hardiness Tolerates a minimum winter temperature of 4°F (−15°C).
Soil requirements Does well on all but severely alkaline soils.
Sun/Shade aspect Tolerates all aspects in full sun to light shade.
Pruning Fan-train but once the plant is more than three years old remove one third of its branches to ground level in spring every five years to induce regrowth.
Training Requires tying to wires or individual anchor points.
Propagation and nursery production From semi-ripe cuttings taken in early summer, or from budding or grafting on to *Ligustrum vulgaris*. Plant bare-rooted or container grown. Availability varies. Best planting height 1–2 ft (30–60 cm).
Problems Young plants often look small and insipid and require a year or more to develop.

Average height and spread
Five years
3 × 3 ft (91 × 91 cm)
Ten years
5 × 5 ft (1.5 × 1.5 m)
Twenty years
7 × 7 ft (2.1 × 2.1 m)
Protrudes up to 2 ft (60 cm) from support.

SYRINGA × PERSICA

PERSIAN LILAC

Oleaceae   *Wall Shrub*
Deciduous

A small-flowering, very fragrant lilac whose growth adapts well to fan-training.

Syringa × persica 'Alba' in flower

Origin From Iran to China.
Use As a fan-trained shrub or freestanding against walls or fences. Can also be pillar-trained.
Description *Flower* Fragrant panicles, 4 in (10 cm) long and 2 in (5 cm) wide, of mauve or off-white flowers produced in late spring/early summer. *Foliage* Leaves lanceolate, 1¼–2½ in (3.5–6 cm) long, dark green, giving some autumn colour. *Stem* Upright when young, becoming more spreading with age, forming a wide, fan-shaped shrub with training. Dark green tinged purple. Medium growth rate. *Fruit* Insignificant.
Hardiness Tolerates a minimum winter temperature of 4°F (−15°C).

Syringa × persica in flower

Soil requirements Most soils, although extremely alkaline types may cause chlorosis.
Sun/Shade aspect Tolerates all but the most severe of aspects. Full sun to very light shade.
Pruning None required.
Training Allow to stand free or secure to walls and fences by wires or individual anchor points.
Propagation and nursery production From budding, layers or semi-ripe cuttings taken in early summer. Purchase container grown; relatively easy to find. Best planting height 15 in–2½ ft (38–76 cm).
Problems Young plants may be shy to flower and can take two or three years to establish.
Similar forms of interest *S. × p.* 'Alba' A variety of off-white, scented flower panicles. Interesting but not showy. *S. × p.* 'Lanciniata' (syn. *S. × p. afghanica*) Very attractive, finely divided leaves unlike those of any other syringa, not more than 1¼ in (3.5 cm) long. Flowers slightly fragrant, lilac-pink but often sparsely produced. Benefits well from the protection of a wall or fence. Two thirds average height and spread.
Average height and spread
Five years
5 × 5 ft (1.5 × 1.5 m)
Ten years
7 × 7 ft (2.1 × 2.1 m)
Twenty years
9 × 9 ft (2.7 × 2.7 m)
Protrudes up to 3 ft (91 cm) from support if fan-trained, 10 ft (3 m) untrained.

SYRINGA × PRESTONIAE

CANADIAN LILAC

Oleaceae   **Wall Shrub**
Deciduous
An elegant, large-flowering shrub which can be fan-trained to good effect but needs a large space.

Origin A range of hybrids produced in Canada by crossing *S. reflexa* and *S. villosa*.
Use As a shrub for large walls and fences, either fan-trained or freestanding.
Description *Flower* Graceful, 6–12 in (15–30 cm) long and 3 in (7.5 m) wide panicles of scented pink to red/pink or purple/pink flowers, depending on the variety, produced in late spring/early summer. All varieties single-flowered. *Foliage* Leaves long, lanceolate, 2–6 in (5–15 cm) long and 2–3 in (5–7.5 cm) wide, dark green with prominent veins. *Stem* Upright when young, strong-growing, forming a narrow-based, wide-topped, large shrub or can be fan-trained. Grey/green to grey/brown. Fast growth rate when young, becoming slower with age. *Fruit* Grey/brown seedheads may be retained into winter.
Hardiness Tolerates a minimum winter temperature of 0°F (−18°C).
Soil requirements Does well on most but alkaline types may produce narrow, yellow,

chlorotic leaf margins. On very alkaline soils this may become acute and cause distress.
Sun/Shade aspect Tolerates all aspects in full sun to medium shade.
Pruning Remove one third of oldest flowering wood to ground level after flowering on established plants more than three years old to encourage rejuvenation from base, otherwise the shrub can become very large and woody and will produce fewer flowers.
Training Requires wires or individual anchor points if fan-trained.
Propagation and nursery production From semi-ripe cuttings taken in early summer, from budding, grafting or from layers. Purchase container grown for best results, but may also be planted bare-rooted or root-balled (balled-and-burlapped). Some varieties rather scarce. Best planting height 2–3 ft (60–91 cm).

Syringa × prestoniae 'Elinor' in flower

Problems Often underestimated for its overall size and in too small an area may become dominating.
Similar forms of interest *S. × p.* 'Audrey' Deep pink flowers, early summer. May not be easy to find. *S. × p.* 'Desdemona' Pink panicles of flowers, late spring. Not easy to find. *S. × p.* 'Elinor' Pale pink/lavender flowers purple/red in bud, borne in upright panicles, late spring, early summer. The most widely available variety. *S. × p.* 'Isabella' Red/pink flowers in erect panicles in late spring/early summer. May be hard to obtain.
Average height and spread
Five years
9 × 9 ft (2.7 × 2.7 m)
Ten years
15 × 15 ft (4.6 × 4.6 m)
Twenty years
20 × 20 ft (6 × 6 m)
Protrudes up to 4 ft (1.2 m) from support if fan-trained, 20 ft (6 m) untrained.

TEUCRIUM FRUTICANS

SHRUBBY GERMANDER

Labiatae   **Wall Shrub**
Evergreen
A useful silver grey/blue flowering shrub that benefits from winter protection from walls and fences.

Origin From southern Europe and North Africa.
Use As a fan-trained shrub or freestanding specimen in front of walls and fences. Can be trained up a pillar if required.
Description *Flower* Light blue flowers, ½ in (1 cm) long and wide, in 3 in (7.5 cm) long terminal racemes, throughout summer.

Syringa × prestoniae 'Isabella' in flower

Teucrium fruticans in flower

Foliage Leaves ovate, ½–1½ in (1–4 cm) long, light grey/green upper surfaces, white undersides. Some limited yellow autumn colour.
Stem Upright stems, becoming branching, forming a dome-shaped shrub if free-standing. Grey to silver-grey. Fast growth rate in spring, slowing with age. **Fruit** Insignificant.
Hardiness Tolerates a minimum winter temperature of 23°F (−5°C).
Soil requirements Well-drained soil, dislikes any waterlogging.
Sun/Shade aspect Requires a sheltered aspect in full sun.
Pruning Previous season's growth should be shortened by two thirds or three quarters in mid spring to encourage new foliage and flowering.
Training Requires wires or individual anchor points to fan-train.
Propagation and nursery production From semi-ripe cuttings. Always purchase container grown. Generally available in mild districts, less easy to find elsewhere. Best planting height 6–12 in (15–30 cm).
Problems Its susceptibility to cold and wet conditions is not always appreciated.
Similar forms of interest *T. chamaedrys* (Wall germander) Deep green foliage and dark, red/mauve flowers in mid to late summer. Upright habit, reaching only one quarter average height and spread.
Average height and spread
Five years
5 × 5 ft (1.5 × 1.5 m)
Ten years
7 × 7 ft (2.1 × 2.1 m)
Twenty years
9 × 9 ft (2.7 × 2.7 m)
Protrudes up to 2 ft (60 cm) from support if fan-trained, 7 ft (2.1 m) untrained.

Teucrium chamaedrys in flower

THUNBERGIA ALATA

BLACK-EYED SUSAN

Acanthaceae   *Annual Climber*
Deciduous

An extremely colourful, attractive annual climber, needing some attention to cultivation to achieve good results.

Origin From South Africa.
Use As an annual climber for walls, fences, archways and trelliswork, or to ramble through medium to large shrubs, brushwood or pea sticks. Ideal for container growing on patios or in conservatories and greenhouses and for hanging baskets.

Thunbergia alata in flower

Description *Flower* Bell-shaped tubes consisting of twelve calyxes opening to form a reflexed mouth 1 in (2.5 cm) across. Bright yellow with purple base and a distinct black centre. Mid summer to early autumn. *Foliage* Oval, up to 1½ in (4 cm) wide and 3 in (7.5 cm) long. Light to mid green with slight grey overtones. *Stem* Light to mid green. Upright. Not self-supporting except for limited twining. Fast rate of growth. *Fruit* No fruits of interest.
Hardiness Not winter hardy. Seeds do not survive in soil over winter.
Soil requirements Requires a well prepared, highly organic, moisture-retaining soil to encourage good growth. If grown in containers, use a soil-based potting compost and a large container.

Sun/Shade aspect Requires a sheltered aspect out of strong winds to prevent damage to foliage and flowers. Full sun to medium shade with light shade for preference.
Pruning Not required. Dies in winter.
Training Tie to individual anchor points and wires. Allow to ramble freely through medium-sized shrubs or over pea sticks or brushwood.
Propagation and nursery production From seed sown under protection with bottom heat in early to mid spring. Do not plant out until all danger of spring frosts has passed. Always purchase container grown; will have to be sought from specialist nurseries or garden centres, in particular those growing a wide range of bedding plants. Best size to purchase 3–15 in (7.5–38 cm).
Problems The need to produce this plant annually can be a drawback, but it is well worth the effort to achieve good summer colour.
Similar forms of interest *T. a.* 'Alba' Pure white flowers with black centres. Not readily available and will have to be sought from specialist nurseries. *T. a. lutea* Pale yellow with white centre. Scarce.
Seed will have to be sought from specialist seedsmen.
Average height and spread
One year
6 × 6 ft (1.8 × 1.8 m)
Protrudes up to 12 in (30 cm) from support.

TRACHELOSPERMUM ASIATICUM
(*T. divaricatum*, *T. crocostemon*)

KNOWN BY BOTANICAL NAME

Apocynaceae   *Woody Climber*

One of the most fragrant of all climbing plants, but requiring a little attention to its needs.

Origin From Japan and Korea.
Use As a close-growing evergreen climber for walls, fences and pillars or for conservatories and greenhouses.

Trachelospermum asiaticum in flower

Description *Flower* Open clusters up to 2½ in (6 cm) across at the ends of short shoots consisting of small, creamy-white, five-petalled flowers ¾ in (2 cm) wide. Flowers from mid to late summer. *Foliage* Leaves dark glossy green, narrowly ovate, pointed and up to 2 in (5 cm) long and ¾ in (2 cm) wide. *Stem* Dull, dark green, predominantly upright in close formation. Slow to medium growth rate. *Fruit* No fruit of interest.
Hardiness Tolerates a minimum winter temperature of 14°F (−10°C) although severe wind chill conditions may damage evergreen foliage and stems. Established plants will rejuvenate in spring, but young plants may be killed outright.

Soil requirements Moderately alkaline to acid. Resents drying out. If grown in a conservatory or greenhouse, the container must have a diameter of not less than 21 in (53 cm) and a good quality soil-based potting compost must be used.
Sun/Shade aspect Sheltered aspect. Full sun to light shade.
Pruning Normally requires no pruning.
Training Will require tying to wires, trellis or individual anchor points.
Propagation and nursery production From semi-ripe cuttings taken early to mid summer. Always purchase container grown; may have to be sought from specialist nurseries. Best planting height 6 in–3 ft (15–91 cm).
Problems Slow to establish. Young plants particularly susceptible to cold winds in early years. Can often become stunted and lacking in vigour; a liquid fertilizer given annually in mid summer normally corrects this.
Similar forms of interest None.
Average height and spread
Five years
3 × 3 ft (91 × 91 cm)
Ten years
6 × 6 ft (1.8 × 1.8 m)
Twenty years
12 × 12 ft (3.7 × 3.7 m)
Will continue to grow, probably reaching 20 × 20 ft (6 × 6 m) in 30 years. Protrudes up to 12 in (30 cm) from support.

TRACHELOSPERMUM JASMINOIDES

KNOWN BY BOTANICAL NAME

Apocynaceae *Woody Climber*
Evergreen

An attractive climber requiring a protected aspect in mild areas.

Origin From China.
Use As an evergreen climber for very sheltered, warm walls or for growing in conservatories or large greenhouses.
Description *Flower* White, five-petalled, fragrant, 1 in (2.5 cm) wide and carried in terminal racemes up to 4 in (10 cm) long. Flowers produced in mid summer. *Foliage* Ovate to lanceolate, up to 4½ in (11 cm) long and 1½ in (4 cm) wide. Grey/green, variegated forms with white marginal irregular variegation, turning pink towards winter and regaining full variegation in following spring. *Stem* Dull, dark green. Moderately close formation. Upright, becoming spreading with age. Slow to medium rate of growth. *Fruit* No fruit of interest.
Hardiness Tolerates a minimum winter temperature of 14°F (−10°C). Cannot be fully trusted except in the warmest areas unless grown under protection.

Trachelospermum jasminoides **in flower**

Trachelospermum jasminoides **'Variegatum' in autumn**

Soil requirements Moderately alkaline to acid. Dislikes extremely dry conditions.
Sun/Shade aspect Requires a very sheltered aspect. Full sun to light shade.
Pruning Not normally required, but can be restricted in size to a certain extent by cutting back shoots after flowering.
Training Will require tying to wires, trellis or individual anchor points.
Propagation and nursery production From semi-ripe cuttings taken in early to mid summer. Always purchase container grown; will have to be sought from specialist nurseries. Best planting height 6 in–3 ft (15–91 cm).
Problems Slow to establish, often dormant for two to three years after planting.
Similar forms of interest *T. j.* 'Variegatum' Variegated form, less hardy. Two-thirds average height and spread. Scarce.
Average height and spread
Five years
5 × 5 ft (1.5 × 1.5 m)
Ten years
10 × 10 ft (3 × 3 m)
Twenty years
15 × 15 ft (4.6 × 4.6 m)

Growth rate and size may well be exceeded under protection of conservatories and greenhouses. Protrudes up to 12 in (30 cm) from support.

TROPAEOLUM MAJUS

NASTURTIUM, INDIAN CREST

Tropaeolaceae *Annual Climber*
Deciduous

Some people may think nasturtiums mundane, but used in the right location they can make a very spectacular climber, particularly useful for infilling while other more permanent plantings establish.

Origin From Peru.
Use For walls, fences and pillars, to ramble through medium to large shrubs or over brushwood, pea sticks or pyramids of canes. Ideal for ground cover with or without support. Can be used in hanging baskets and tubs. Best out of doors but can be grown under cover as an early flowering plant if required.
Description *Flower* Various range of colours, including orange, red, pink, yellow. Up to 2 in (5 cm) across, consisting of either single or double, dependent on variety. Flowering from early to late summer, possibly into autumn. *Foliage* Up to 3–4 in (7.5–10 cm) across, light green with some variegated forms. Orb-like in shape with heart-type indentations at base. Yellow autumn colour. *Stem* Light green, trailing, not self-clinging. Medium annual growth rate. *Fruit* Small,

round fruits of limited interest other than for collecting for following season's plants.
Hardiness Not winter hardy. Plant killed by first frosts. Seeds can stay viable in soil throughout winter to regerminate in following spring. Plants raised under protection can be planted out from mid to late spring when danger of frost has passed.
Soil requirements Tolerates all types, including extremely poor. Will tolerate dry conditions as long as adequate moisture is provided for establishment.
Sun/Shade aspect Tolerates all aspects from full sun to medium shade, with light to medium shade for preference.
Pruning Not required, although can be cut back when young to encourage branching and to keep within bounds.
Training Allow to ramble over wires, trellis, brushwood or pea sticks, or through branches of medium to large shrubs.

Tropaeolum majus **'Alaska Mixed' in flower**

Propagation and nursery production From seed, either saved from previous season's crop or purchased from seed merchants or garden centres, all of which carry a good range of varieties. Young plants can be purchased from garden centres in spring. Best planting height 2–6 in (5–15 cm).
Problems Can suffer attacks of blackfly which are difficult to control. Can become invasive in ideal conditions. Seed naturally sown in autumn can sometimes become a nuisance in following year.
Similar forms of interest *T. m.* 'Alaska Mixed' A good range of colours. Flowers double to semi-double. Foliage very attractive, white and cream splashed variegation on pale green. Not vigorous, only reaching 50 per cent of average height and spread. *T. m.* 'Climbing Mixed' A general mixture. Single flowers

Tropaeolum majus 'Jewel Mixed'

basically yellow and red. Strong growing. *T. m.* **'Double Gleam Mixed'** Semi-trailing variety. Large double flowers. Reaches only 50 per cent of average height and spread. *T. m.* **'Dwarf Cherry Rose'** Semi-double, brilliant cerise-red flowers held well above foliage. Reaches only 20 per cent of average height and spread. *T. m.* **'Empress of India'** Very dark foliage. Crimson-scarlet flowers. Only reaches 20 per cent average height and spread. *T. m.* **'Fiery Festival'** Scented, deep scarlet flowers carried in good amounts. Reaches only 20 per cent of average height and spread. *T. m.* **'Golden Gleam'** All yellow, semi-double. Reaches 40 per cent of average height and spread. *T. m.* **'Jewel Mixed'** Semi-double. Very bright colours. Only reaching 20 per cent of average height and spread. *T. m.* **'Orange Gleam'** Deep orange/red flowers. Reaches 40 per cent of average height and spread. *T. m.* **'Peach Melba'** Light yellow with scarlet blotches. Only reaching 20 per cent of average height and spread. *T. m.* **'Red Roulette'** Semi-double. Fiery red blooms carried well above foliage. *T. m.* **'Scarlet Gleam'** Orange/scarlet, semi-double flowers. Only reaching 40 per cent of average height and spread. *T. m.* **'Whirlybird Mixed'** Semi-double. Good range of colours through cherry, rose, gold, mahogany, orange, tangerine and cream. Flowers face upwards. *T. lobbianum* **'Spitfire'** Deep yellow to orange and red blooms. Strong growing. Ideal as a climber.

Average height and spread
One year
5 × 5 ft (1.5 × 1.5 m)
Protrudes up to 2 ft (60 cm) from support.

TROPAEOLUM PEREGRINUM

CANARY CREEPER
Tropaeolaceae　　　*Perennial/Annual Climber*

Deciduous

Canary creeper does not produce its flowers until mid to late summer, but they do make an extremely attractive display.

Origin From Peru.
Use As a fast-growing perennial or annual climber for walls, fences and arches, or to cover brushwood or pea sticks. Ideal for trailing through medium to large shrubs and for intermingling amongst other climbers. Attractive when grown with a dark background, such as conifers.

Description *Flower* Three large, lower spade-shaped petals with two smaller upper petals with fringed edges; $\frac{1}{2}$–$\frac{3}{4}$ in (1–2 cm) across from mid to late summer and early autumn. Bright yellow. *Foliage* Five ovate, lobed leaflets make up a hand-shaped leaf, light to medium green with a grey sheen, 2–4 in (5–10 cm) across. Some yellow autumn colours. *Stem* Light green, becoming yellow/green. Twining, but not entirely self-supporting. Weak in constitution and easily broken during cultivation. Fast annual rate of growth. *Fruit* No fruit of any significance.
Hardiness Not winter hardy above ground but seeds may survive in soil over winter.

Tropaeolum peregrinum

Root stool will tolerate a minimum winter temperature of 14°F (−10°C), particularly if some additional mulch or covering of organic material is given to the area in which it is growing to act as insulation. Young spring-grown plants from seed should not be planted out until all danger of spring frost has passed.
Soil requirements Tolerates all soil. Does best in a moist, well fed type high in organic material where the roots can spread fast and produce good growth at the top.
Sun/Shade aspect Tolerates all aspects. Full sun to light shade, with full sun for preference, although roots should be in the shade.
Pruning Not required. Dies to ground level in winter.

Training Allow to ramble over wires, trellis, brushwood or pea sticks, or through medium to large shrubs.
Propagation and nursery production From seed sown in spring under protection. Always purchase container grown from 2–12 in (5–30 cm) tall. Not readily available and will have to be sought from specialist nurseries and garden centres. Seed will have to be sought from specialist seed merchants.
Problems Can often be forgotten, as is relatively late flowering, and is unobtrusive until the flowers burst into bloom.
Similar forms of interest None.
Average height and spread
One year
8 × 4 ft (2.4 × 1.1 m)
Protrudes up to 6 in (15 cm) from support.

TROPAEOLUM SPECIOSUM

FLAME NASTURTIUM, FLAME CREEPER
Tropaeolaceae　　　*Perennial Climber*
Deciduous

One of the most spectacular of all perennial climbers, but requiring specific cultivation to achieve results.

Origin From Chile.
Use As a perennial creeper, best used when grown over medium to large shrubs or against a background of *Taxus baccata* (English yew) or other evergreens.
Description *Flower* Five reflexed petals, the lower three larger, make up a flat flower, presented in small groups in mid to late summer. Flowers $\frac{1}{2}$–$\frac{3}{4}$ in (1–2 cm) across, carried on short shoots 1–1$\frac{1}{4}$ in (2.5–3.5 cm) long. *Foliage* Five, sometimes six, lobes make up a hand-shaped leaf, 1$\frac{1}{2}$ in (4 cm) across with a hairy covering. *Stem* Light green, trailing but not twining. Supported by intermingling. Medium growth rate. *Fruit* Round, turquoise/blue seeds often appear in attractive clusters with late flowers.
Hardiness Dies to ground level in winter. Roots are able to survive a temperature of 14°F (−10°C).
Soil requirements Alkaline to acid. Requires an extremely well prepared soil with over 50 per cent of organic material added to a depth of not less than 18 in (45 cm). Material such as sedge peat, spent mushroom compost, garden compost or very well rotted manure is ideal and 1 sq yd (1 sq m) should be prepared for any chance of good results.

Tropaeolum speciosum **in flower**

Tropaeolum speciosum in fruit

Sun/Shade aspect Flowers in full sun to light shade. Roots should be in shade.
Pruning Not required. Dies to ground level in winter.
Training Allow to ramble over medium to large shrubs, including shrub roses. If grown against a hedge of *Taxus baccata* (yew) or other conifer it often needs some additional support with canes.
Propagation and nursery production From root cuttings, selecting underground rhizomes and rooting into pots containing a soil-based potting compost. Propagation is difficult and it is therefore only obtainable at a high price from specialist nurseries. Best height is as clumps in pots before growth matures in spring or later with top growth of not more than 2–3 in (5–7.5 cm).
Problems Without adequate soil preparation rhizomes normally die. A number of attempts may be needed to establish. Grows better in wet, humid areas.
Similar forms of interest None.
Average height and spread
One year
6 × 4 ft (1.8 × 1.2 m)
Protrudes up to 12 in (30 cm) from support.

TROPAEOLUM TUBEROSUM

KNOWN BY BOTANICAL NAME
Tropaeolaceae   *Perennial Climber*
Deciduous
A climber which is rarely seen but deserves a wider planting.

Origin From Peru and Bolivia.
Use Grow over medium to large shrubs or against a background of *Taxus baccata* (English yew) or other evergreens.
Description *Flower* Extremely attractive red and yellow tubular flowers with a basal spur, carried on long, graceful stalks. Up to ¾ in (2 cm) long, produced in mid to late summer. *Foliage* Five-lobed leaves on long stalks. Light to mid green with some purplish hue, particularly towards autumn. Attractive white veining. *Stem* Light green to grey/green. Trailing, not truly self-clinging but intertwining. May need additional support. Medium growth rate. *Fruit* No fruits of interest.
Hardiness Root stool tolerates a minimum winter temperature of 14°F (−10°C) but will require a good surface mulch of not less than 3 in (7.5 cm) of organic material over at least 1 sq yd (1 sq m) to protect it in most locations.
Soil requirements Tolerates all soil types, but requires extremely good preparation with up to 50 per cent of organic material added to a depth of not less than 18 in (45 cm). Material such as sedge peat, spent mushroom compost, garden compost or very well rotted manure is ideal and 1 sq yd (1 sq m) should be prepared for good results. Tubers should be planted at least 6 in (15 cm) deep, and in light soils up to 8 in (20 cm) is not unacceptable.
Sun/Shade aspect Flowers should be in full sun to light shade and roots in shade.
Pruning Not required. Dies down in winter.
Training Allow to ramble over medium to large shrubs, including shrub roses. If grown against a hedge of *Taxus baccata* (English yew) or other evergreens, often needs additional support from canes.
Propagation and nursery production By removal of large root rhizomes and planting into individual pots containing a soil-based compost in late winter/early spring. Propagation generally reliable by this method. Purchase as root rhizomes or as pot-grown plants up to 2½ ft (76 cm) in height. Will have to be sought from specialist nurseries.
Problems Care must be taken with soil preparation and some winter protection given by mulching.
Similar forms of interest
T. t. 'Ken Aslet' Good-sized orange flowers in summer.
Average height and spread
One year
4 × 4 ft (1.2 × 1.2 m)
Protrudes up to 12 in (30 cm) from support.

VIBURNUM (Best Fruiting Forms)

KNOWN BY BOTANICAL NAME
Caprifoliaceae   *Wall Shrub*
Deciduous
Useful large shrubs that can adapt well to fan-training to show off their fruit to full effect.

Origin From China.
Use For growing freestanding against large walls or, for better results, fan-trained.
Description *Flower* Clusters of small, white flowers, 3 in (7.5 cm) wide, in mid spring to early summer. *Foliage* Leaves ovate, 2–4 in (5–10 cm) long, mid to dark green, often with good golden autumn colour. *Stem* Dark green or purple/green, upright, strong, becoming branching and spreading with age, forming a large, wide, narrow-based shrub if left untrained. Fast growth rate when young, slowing with age. *Fruit* In bunches, either red or black, depending on variety, produced profusely in autumn.
Hardiness Tolerates a minimum winter temperature of 4°F (−15°C).
Soil requirements Any soil.
Sun/Shade aspect Tolerates all but the most severe of aspects. Prefers light shade, tolerates full sun to medium shade.

Viburnum lantana

Pruning On established plants more than five years old, remove one third of oldest wood to ground level every two to three years to encourage new basal growth and keep the shrub healthy.
Training Requires wires or individual anchor points to achieve a fan-trained shape.
Propagation and nursery production From semi-ripe cuttings taken in early summer or from seed. Always purchase container grown, most forms will need to be obtained from specialist nurseries. Best planting height 1–3 ft (30–91 cm).
Problems Takes five years or more to reach maturity and produce good fruiting displays.
Forms of interest *V. betulifolium* Clusters of white flowers in early summer, set off by ovate to rhomboidal, coarsely toothed, dark to olive-green foliage. Red fruits hanging in large bunches from long, arching branches, maintained well into winter. It is often recommended that several shrubs should be planted nearby to encourage fertilization, but in fact single plants will fruit well at maturity. May have to be obtained from specialist nurseries. From central China. *V. hupehense* White clusters of flowers in late spring/early summer give way to interesting, egg-shaped, orange/yellow fruits in autumn, ageing to red in early winter. Ovate, coarsely toothed leaves, light to mid green, giving good autumn colour. Obtain from specialist

Tropaeolum tuberosum in flower

nurseries. From central China. *V. lantana* (Wayfaring tree) Creamy white clusters of flowers 3–4 in (7.5–10 cm) across in late spring/early summer, giving way to clusters of oblong fruits, red at first, ageing to black. Grey/green, felted, upright leaves, broad and ovate, 6 in (15 cm) long, velvety-textured on undersides, turning dark crimson in autumn. Fairly easy to find. Used as understock for all viburnums that are grafted. From central and southern Europe, spreading through northern Asia to Asia Minor and North Africa. *V. l.* **'Variegatum'** (syn. *V. l.* **'Auratum'**) Young foliage golden-yellow to yellow/green. Colour not retained well and turns light green in mid to late summer, although fruiting is very good. *V. lentago* (Sheepberry, nannyberry) Upright growth, strong in stature. Creamy white flowers produced in terminal clusters in late spring, early summer, giving way to clusters of blue/black, bloom-covered damson-shaped fruits. Ovate leaves, dark shiny green tinged purple or red. Good rich autumn colour. From eastern North America. *V. l.* **'Pink Beauty'** A variety with pink flowers, otherwise identical to its parent. *V. prunifolium* (Black haw) Upright stems with horizontal side branches. Clusters of white flowers give way to large blue/black, bloom-covered, edible fruits. Foliage bright green and shiny-textured, ovate to obovate, giving good autumn colour. Hard to find outside its native environment of eastern North America. *V. sargentii* White flowers with purple anthers in early summer give way to large clusters of translucent red fruits lasting well into winter. Strong, grey/green stems support maple-shaped leaves with good autumn colour. Stems develop a cork-like bark. From north-eastern Asia.

Average height and spread
Five years
5 × 5 ft (1.5 × 1.5 m)
Ten years
9 × 9 ft (2.7 × 2.7 m)
Twenty years
15 × 15 ft (4.6 × 4.6 m)
Protrudes up to 3 ft (91 cm) from support if fan-trained, 13 ft (4 m) untrained.

VIBURNUM
(Early Flowering Forms)

KNOWN BY BOTANICAL NAME

Caprifoliaceae   Wall Shrub
Deciduous

A group of plants not normally considered as wall shrubs but which have a lot to offer when used as such.

Origin Forms originating from China, many of garden origin.
Use As fan-trained or upright, freestanding shrubs in front of walls and fences.
Description *Flower* Clusters of pink or white, 1½ in (4 cm) wide, tubular, fragrant flowers produced on bare stems in early to mid spring. Also some intermittent flowering from late autumn through winter during periods of mild weather. *Foliage* Leaves lanceolate to ovate, ½–4 in (1–10 cm) long, dark green with red tinge, intensifying towards late summer/early autumn. Some autumn colour. *Stem* Forms an upright shrub of stout habit, or a widespreading, fan-trained shrub with training. Purple/green when young, becoming mahogany-brown with age. Medium growth rate. *Fruit* Insignificant.
Hardiness Tolerates a minimum winter temperature of 4°F (−15°C), but any flowers produced in winter may be damaged by sudden temperature changes.
Soil requirements Any soil, including alkaline.
Sun/Shade aspect Tolerates all aspects, although some protection will prolong the flowers in very severe winters. Full sun to medium shade.
Pruning Four or five years after planting, re-

Viburnum × bodnantense in flower

move one third of oldest flowering growth to ground level in early to mid spring, thereafter pruning every two to three years, depending on shrub's vigour.
Training Requires tying to wires or individual anchor points if fan-trained.
Propagation and nursery production From semi-ripe cuttings taken in early summer. Purchase container grown, bare-rooted or root-balled (balled-and-burlapped). Availability varies. Best planting height 2–3 ft (60–91 cm).
Problems Grows larger than is generally foreseen.
Forms of interest *V. × bodnantense* A cross between *V. farreri* and *V. grandiflorum*. Strong, upright habit, covered with clusters of scented, rose-tinted flowers from December to February. *V. × b.* **'Dawn'** An improved variety, with vigorous habit and larger foliage. Large, pink scented flowers. *V. × b.* **'Deben'** Flowers pink in bud, opening to white. Sweetly scented. Flowers may be damaged by severe frosts or excessive wetness. *V. farreri candidissimum* Slightly less freely flowering, producing terminal and lateral clusters of white, tubular, scented flowers. Foliage light green. *V. foetens* (syn. *V. koreana* Gaunt, stout stems, mahogany-brown tinged purple, forming large, goblet-shaped shrub. Clusters of good-sized, tubular, white, very fragrant flowers, susceptible to frost damage. Large, ovate, dark green leaves, tinged purple. Scarce, must be obtained from specialist nurseries. Very slow-growing, eventually reaching up to 6 ft (1.8 m) in height and spread.

Average height and spread
Five years
5 × 5 ft (1.5 × 1.5 m)
Ten years
9 × 9 ft (2.7 × 2.7 m)
Twenty years
15 × 15 ft (4.6 × 4.6 m)
Protrudes up to 3 ft (91 cm) from support if fan-trained, 13 ft (4 m) untrained.

VIBURNUM
(Large-leaved Forms)

KNOWN BY BOTANICAL NAME

Caprifoliaceae   Wall Shrub
Evergreen

Fan-training on large walls can often enhance the aristocratic appearance of these shrubs.

Origin From China.
Use As large fan-trained or freestanding shrubs for walls and fences.
Description *Flower* White to dull white clus-

ters up to 4–6 in (10–15 cm) across of short, tubular flowers produced mid spring through early summer, according to variety. *Foliage* Leaves ovate, 2–6 in (5–15 cm) long, dark to mid green upper surface. Some smooth, some glossy, others felted, often with grey undersides. *Stem* Normally strong, upright, becoming branching, forming a large, spreading fan-trained shrub or round-topped if untrained. Smooth or felty-textured, depending on variety. *Fruit* Blue or black clusters of round or oval fruits in autumn.
Hardiness Tolerates a minimum winter temperature of 4°F (−15°C).
Soil requirements Any soil.
Sun/Shade aspect Tolerates all aspects. Prefers light shade, tolerates full sun to medium shade.

Viburnum henryi in flower

Pruning May be left unpruned. Alternatively, remove one third of oldest wood on shrubs five years old or more to encourage rejuvenation.
Training Requires tying to wires or individual anchor points if fan-trained.
Propagation and nursery production From semi-ripe cuttings taken in early summer. Purchase container grown or root-balled (balled-and-burlapped). All forms fairly easy to find. Best planting height 1–3 ft (30–91 cm).
Problems Space must be allowed for eventual size of mature shrubs.
Forms of interest *V. buddleifolium* An almost evergreen shrub which occasionally defoliates in hard winters. White clusters of flowers up to 2¾ in (6.5 cm) across in early summer, fol-

lowed by clusters of red fruits which turn black. Oblong to lanceolate leaves, pale green, velvety-textured and with grey felted undersides. Two thirds average height and spread. From central China. *V. cinnamomifolium* Small clusters of dull white flowers up to 4–6 in (10–15 cm) across in early summer, dark, glossy, leathery-textured leaves. Clusters of egg-shaped, blue/black, shiny fruits in autumn. Good in light to medium shade. May be slightly less hardy and more difficult to find. Two thirds average height and spread. From China. *V. henryi* A variety of open, upright habit. Pyramid-shaped panicles of yellow/white flowers, early to late summer. Elliptic, glossy green, leathery-textured leaves on stiff, upright red/green branches. Bright red fruits, later turning black. Obtain from specialist nurseries. From central China. *V. × hillieri* (syn. *V. × hillieri* 'Winton') Semi-evergreen, depending on winter severity. Creamy white panicles of flowers in early summer, red fruits, later turning black. Foliage narrow, ovate, dark to mid green tinged copper, turning bronze/red in winter. From China. *V. japonicum* (Japanese viburnum) White fragrant flowers in rounded trusses produced in early summer, only on mature shrubs, followed by red fruits. Leathery-textured foliage, up to 6 in (15 cm) long and 4 in (10 cm) wide, glossy dark green with paler undersides. Stout, orange/green leaf stalks. Two thirds average height and spread. From Japan. *V.* 'Pragense' Clusters of pink buds opening to creamy white, produced at terminals of branches in late spring. Corrugated, elliptic leaves 2–3 in (5–7.5 in) long, dark green with white felted undersides. Extremely hardy. Obtain from specialist nurseries. Two thirds average height and spread. Raised in Prague, Czechoslovakia. *V. × rhytidophylloides* (Lantanaphyllum viburnum) Clusters of yellow/white flower buds produced in autumn and carried through winter before opening in late spring. Foliage elliptic to ovate or oblong to ovate, rough-textured, often hanging limp in cold weather, giving drooping, almost shabby effect. Some orange/brown autumn colour. Of garden origin. *V. rhytidophyllum* (Leatherleaf viburnum) A strong-growing variety, with clusters of creamy yellow flowers in late spring, formed in previous autumn and carried through winter as felted closed buds. Leaves large, up to 8 in (20 cm) long, elliptic or oblong, with corrugated surface, dark glossy green, undersides grey and covered with matted hairs. Oval red fruits, finally turning black, produced in autumn and maintained well into early winter. For good fruiting effect a number of shrubs should be planted fairly close together. Relatively easy to find. From central western China. *V. r.* 'Roseum' Flowers tinted rose-pink, otherwise identical to its parent. *V. r.* 'Variegatum' Rarely seen variety

with white-splashed leaves, otherwise identical to its parent. *V. utile* (Service viburnum) Clusters of white, scented flowers in late spring followed by blue/black fruits in autumn. Sparsely produced branches. Ovate to oblong, glossy dark green foliage with white undersides. Obtain from specialist nurseries. Two thirds average height and spread. From central China.

Average height and spread
Five years
7 × 7 ft (2.1 × 2.1 m)
Ten years
12 × 12 ft (3.7 × 3.7 m)
Twenty years
18 × 18 ft (5.5 × 5.5 m)
Protrudes up to 3 ft (91 cm) from
support if fan-trained, 16 ft (4.9 m) untrained.

VIBURNUM OPULUS

GUELDER ROSE, WATER ELDER, EUROPEAN CRANBERRY BUSH VIBURNUM

Caprifoliaceae   **Wall Shrub**
Deciduous

Fruiting shrubs with flat lacecap or snowball-shaped flowers and an attractive autumn display, adapting well to fan-training on walls and fences.

Origin From Europe, northern and western Asia and north Africa.
Use As fan-trained shrubs on walls or fences where they will afford an attractive display in autumn.

Viburnum opulus 'Notcutt's Variety' in flower

Description *Flower* Either white, flat, 4 in (10 cm) wide lacecap flowers with central small flowers surrounded by a ring of ray florets or a globular 3 in (7.5 cm) cluster of florets. The lacecap forms are fertile whereas the globular forms are not. *Foliage* Leaves light green, 2–5 in (5–12 cm) long, often with orange tinge or shading in late summer. Five-lobed, maple-shaped, giving good autumn colour. *Stem* Upright when young, becoming spreading and adapting well to fan-training. Grey to grey/green. *Fruit* Lacecap forms produce clusters of red and yellow round fruits in autumn, depending on variety. Globular varieties do not fruit.
Hardiness Tolerates a minimum winter temperature of 0°F (−18°C).
Soil requirements Any soil, tolerating alkalinity and acidity, dry and even boggy or waterlogged areas.
Sun/Shade aspect Tolerates all aspects. Prefers full sun, but will tolerate medium shade.
Pruning Can be fan-trained or alternatively, on shrubs more than five years old, remove one third of oldest wood to ground level in spring. Repeat every two to three years to induce new growth from ground level and to prevent shrub from becoming woody.
Training Requires tying to wires or individual anchor points.
Propagation and nursery production From semi-ripe cuttings taken in early summer or hardwood cuttings taken in winter. Purchase container grown, bare-rooted or root-balled (balled-and-burlapped). Most forms fairly easy to find. Best planting height 2–3 ft (60–91 cm).
Problems Can outgrow its desired area unless adequate space is allowed.
Similar forms of interest *V. o.* 'Aureum' White, lacecap flowers with some red fruits in autumn. New spring growth bright yellow, ageing to yellow/green. Unfortunately will scorch in full sun and therefore requires very light shade protection. Not readily available. One third average height and spread. *V. o.* 'Fructu-luteo' White, lacecap flowers in early summer. Lemon-yellow fruits, tinged pink and ageing to chrome yellow, retaining faint shadings of pink. Obtain from specialist nurseries. *V. o.* 'Notcutt's Variety' A very good form with large white lacecap flowers, followed by bunches of succulent red fruits in autumn. *V. o.* 'Xanthocarpum' White lacecap flowers, pure golden yellow fruit, becoming darker and attaining translucent appearance when ripe. *V. o.* 'Sterile' (syn. *V. o.* 'Roseum' (Snowball shrub)) Globular, creamy white, snowball-type flowerheads. Non-fruiting.
Average height and spread
Five years
7 × 7 ft (2.1 × 2.1 m)
Ten years
12 × 12 ft (3.7 × 3.7 m)
Twenty years
18 × 18 ft (5.5 × 5.5 m)
Protrudes up to 3 ft (91 cm) from support.

Viburnum rhytidophyllum 'Roseum' in flower

VIBURNUM PLICATUM

DOUBLEFILE VIBURNUM, JAPANESE
SNOWBALL, LACECAP VIBURNUM
Caprifoliaeceae   *Wall Shrub*
Deciduous
Of all the viburnums, the *plicatum* forms
adapt themselves best for use against walls
and fences.

Origin From Japan and China.
Use As a medium to large fan-trained or
freestanding shrub, depending on variety, for
growing against walls and fences.
Description *Flower* Either globular heads of
white florets, 4–5 in (10–12 cm) wide, or heads
of flat, lacecap flowers up to 6 in (15 cm)
across with central fertile small flowers, surrounded by white ray florets, ½ in (1 cm) wide.
Foliage Leaves 2–4 in (5–10 cm) long, ovate,
with pleated effect and pronounced channel-
ling along veins, light to mid green. Some
good autumn colour, deep orange to
orange/red, particularly after a dry, hot
summer. *Stem* Upright when young, quickly
becoming spreading, forming a dome-shape
if freestanding. Light green to grey/green.
The tiered effect which is seen on some varieties can be maintained when fan-trained.
Medium growth rate. *Fruit* Clusters of oval,
red to red/orange fruits in autumn on shrubs
more than five years old on relatively dry to
average soil. Fruiting can be erratic.
Hardiness Tolerates a minimum winter temperature of 4°F (−15°C).
Soil requirements Tolerates a wide range of
soils but care must be taken not to allow root
system to dry out or become waterlogged or
its fine-textured root system will be damaged.
Sun/Shade aspect Tolerates all aspects.
Prefers light shade but tolerates full sun to
medium shade.
Pruning None, other than that required for
training as and when necessary.
Training Tie to wires or individual anchor
points to achieve a fan-trained shape or allow
to grow freestanding.
Propagation and nursery production From
semi-ripe cuttings taken in early summer or
from layers. Purchase container grown or
root-balled (balled-and-burlapped); most
varieties fairly easy to find. Best planting
height 15 in–3 ft (38–91 cm).
Problems Very susceptible to root damage
from cultivation such as hoeing and from
drought or waterlogging. If roots are damaged a section of top growth will die back. In
severe cases this can be terminal.

Viburnum macrocephalum in flower

Similar forms of interest *V. p.* 'Cascade'
Large, white, flat, lacecap flowers. Fertile
inner small tufted florets, surrounded by a
ring of bold white ray florets. Red fruits after
hot summer. Large, ovate, pointed foliage,
giving good autumn colour, on branches
arching to give semi-weeping effect. Less
likely to die back than other varieties. Two
thirds average height and spread. *V. p.*
'Grandiflorum' (Japanese snowball) Sterile
flowerheads in spring, large, round to globular, attractive green, ageing to white, taking
on pink margin then flushing overall pink
before becoming purple and eventually
brown. Good autumn colour. Must have
good moist soil and light dappled shade to do
well. Resents full sun. Two thirds average
height and spread. *V. p.* 'Lanarth' White,
large, flat lacecap flowers produced in defined
tiers along horizontal branches. Large, ovate,
mid to dark green foliage, giving good
autumn colour. Sometimes listed as shorter
growing shrub; when this variety was first
catalogued it was confused with *V. p.* 'Mariesii', 'Lanarth' being described as the lower of
the two varieties, but the reverse is the case. *V.
p.* 'Mariesii' White lacecap flowers borne on
very horizontal, tiered branches. Good fruiting with fine autumn colour. Reaches half
average height and spread. *V. p.* 'Pink
Beauty' Ray florets of white lacecap flowers,

ageing to attractive pink. Small to medium,
ovate, dark to olive/green foliage. Good
autumn colour. Two thirds average height and
spread. *V. p.* 'Rowallane' White lacecap
flowers in late spring. Small, ovate, tooth-
edged foliage, mid to dark green, giving some
autumn tints. Closely tiered branch effect. Extremely reliable fruiting form. May be more
difficult to find than most. Two thirds average
height and spread. *V. p. tomentosum* Lacecap
flowers 2–4 in (5–10 cm) across, creamy white
and surrounded by white ray florets, giving
way to red, oval fruits, which age eventually
to black. Bright green, pleated, ovate foliage.
Good autumn colour. Not easy to find. From
Japan, China and Taiwan. *V. p.* 'Watanabe'
(syn. *V. semperflorens*) Very compact, producing good-sized white lacecap flowers in
early summer through to mid autumn. Some
orange/red fruits, late summer through to
autumn. Reaching only two thirds average
height and spread. *V. macrocephalum* Semi-
evergreen. White, round, large, globular
heads of sterile flowers, 4–6 in (5–10 cm) long.
across, late spring. Medium-sized, ovate foliage, light green, up to 2–4 in (5–10 cm) long.
Less hardy than most, requiring a favourable
sunny position where temperature does not
fall below 23°F (−5°C) Difficult to obtain.
Average height and spread
Five years
8 × 6 ft (2.4 × 1.8 m)
Ten years
12 × 10 ft (3.7 × 3 m)
Twenty years
16 × 16 ft (4.9 × 4.9 m)
Protrudes up to 4 ft (1.2 m) from support if
fan-trained, 16 ft (4.9 m) untrained.

Viburnum plicatum 'Pink Beauty' in flower

Viburnum plicatum 'Grandiflorum' in flower

VIBURNUM (Spring Flowering, Scented Forms)

KNOWN BY BOTANICAL NAME

Caprifoliaceae   **Wall Shrub**
Deciduous and semi-evergreen

Some of the most highly scented of all spring flowering shrubs, adapting extremely well to fan-training.

Origin Basic forms from Korea, with many garden hybrids.
Use As large, fan-trained shrubs for walls and fences.
Description *Flower* Round, dense clusters, 3–4 in (7.5–10 cm) across, consisting of many tubular, very fragrant flowers in varying shades of pink to white in early to late spring. *Foliage* Leaves ovate, medium-sized, 2–4 in (5–10 cm) long, grey/green, some yellow autumn display. *Stem* Upright but can be trained into a narrow fan-shape. Covered with grey scale when young. Medium growth rate. *Fruit* May produce blue/black fruits in autumn.

Viburnum carlesii in flower

Viburnum × burkwoodii in flower

Hardiness Tolerates a minimum winter temperature of 4°F (−15°C).
Soil requirements Most soils, disliking only very dry or very wet types.
Sun/Shade aspect Tolerates all aspects, but will benefit from some protection when in flower. Prefers light shade, accepts full sun to medium shade.
Pruning None, other than that required for

training which should be done in early spring, but remove any suckering growths appearing below graft or soil level.
Training Requires wires or individual anchor points to create a fan shape.
Propagation and nursery production Normally from grafting on to an understock of *V. lantana*. Some varieties from semi-ripe cuttings taken in early summer. Purchase container grown or root-balled (balled-and-burlapped); best planting height 2–3 ft (60–91 cm). Most varieties fairly easy to find, especially when in flower.
Problems All forms, particularly *V. carlesii* and its varieties, suffer from aphid attack. Root systems of all forms are very fibrous and surface-rooting and react badly, sometimes succumbing completely, to damage caused by cultivation, drought or waterlogging.
Forms of interest *V. bitchiuense* (Bitchiu viburnum) Clusters of pink, scented flowers, mid to late spring. Foliage ovate to elliptic, dark metallic green. Open habit. From Japan. *V. × burkwoodii* (Burkwood viburnum) Clusters of pink buds open into fragrant, white, tubular flowers, early to mid spring, followed by clusters of blue/black fruits. Semi-evergreen ovate foliage with dark green shiny surface. As leaves die off in autumn they turn scarlet, red and orange, contrasting with remaining dark green foliage. Reaches one third more than average height and spread. *V. × b.* **'Anne Russell'** Semi-evergreen. Large clusters of pale pink, fragrant flowers in mid spring, dark pink in bud. *V. × b.* **'Chenaultii'** Semi-evergreen. Flowers similar to parent, but does not reach same overall proportions.

Two thirds average height and spread. Not easy to find. *V. × b.* **'Fulbrook'** Large white flowers, pink in bud and sweetly scented. *V. × b.* **'Park Farm Hybrid'** A form with larger, more vigorous habit of growth. Flowers, mid spring, slightly larger than the form. Good glossy green foliage. *V. × carlcephalum* A deciduous hybrid producing large, white, tubular florets, pink in bud, very fragrant, borne in extremely attractive clusters 4–5 in (10–12 cm) across. Large, ovate to round, grey/green foliage, may produce good autumn colours. *V. carlesii* (Koreanspice viburnum) Clusters of highly fragrant, pure white, tubular flowers, opening from pink buds in mid to late spring. Ovate to round, downy, grey to grey/green leaves with grey felted undersides, producing good red/orange autumn colouring. Some forms of *V. carlesii* are weak in constitution and named varieties may be more successful. *V. c.* **'Aurora'** Red flower buds, opening to fragrant pink tubular flowers produced in clusters, mid to late spring. Good ovate grey/green foliage. Good constitution. *V. c.* **'Charis'** Good, vigorous growth. Flowers red in bud, opening to pink and finally fading to white. Very good scent. Foliage disease free and grey/green. May be difficult to find. *V. c.* **'Diana'** A good variety of compact habit. Flowers pink, red in bud. Good fragrance. May be difficult to find. *V. × juddii* (Judd viburnum) Clusters of scented, pink-tinted tubular flowers, produced at terminals of branching stems in mid to late spring. Grey/green ovate foliage with some autumn colour. Open in habit when young, becoming denser with age. Two thirds average height and spread.
Average height and spread
Five years
5 × 5 ft (1.5 × 1.5 m)
Ten years
8 × 8 ft (2.4 × 2.4 m)
Twenty years
12 × 12 ft (3.7 × 3.7 m).
Protrudes up to 3ft (91 cm) from support.

VIBURNUM TINUS

LAURUSTINUS

Caprifoliaceae   **Wall Shrub**
Evergreen

An attractive evergreen winter flowering shrub, benefiting from the protection of a wall or fence.

Origin From the Mediterranean regions of eastern Europe.
Use As a loose, fan-trained or freestanding shrub for planting in front of walls or fences.

Viburnum × carlcephalum in flower

Description *Flower* Small, 3 in (7.5 cm) wide clusters of white tubular flowers often pink in bud, in late autumn through until late spring, with peak performance in mild spells. Resistant to frost. *Foliage* Leaves broadly ovate, 1½–4 in (4–10 cm) long, evergreen, dark green with lighter silver undersides. *Stem* Upright when young, becoming spreading and branching. Can be loosely fan-trained or left to form a round-topped, broad-based shrub. Dark green to green/brown. Fast growth rates when young, slowing with age. *Fruit* Clusters of oval black fruits in autumn.
Hardiness Tolerates a minimum winter temperature of 14°F (−10°C).

Viburnum tinus in flower

Soil requirements Most soils. Tolerates both alkalinity and acidity but resents extremely dry or waterlogged conditions.
Sun/Shade aspect Requires a sheltered aspect. Prefers light shade, good from full sun to medium shade.
Pruning Can be reduced drastically and will rejuvenate quickly, flowering from early stage. Alternatively, on shrubs more than five years old, remove one third of oldest wood to ground level in early spring to encourage rejuvenation from base.
Training Allow to stand free or secure to wires or individual anchor points for fan-training.
Propagation and nursery production From semi-ripe cuttings taken in early summer. Purchase container grown; best planting height 12 in–2½ ft (30–76 cm). Easy to find in good garden centres and nurseries.
Problems Suffers from severe winter cold, especially wind chill. Can appear old and straggly if pruning is neglected.

Similar forms of interest *V. t.* **'Eve Price'** Flowers carmine-red in bud, opening to white with pink shading. Foliage smaller than parent. Two thirds average height and spread. *V. t.* **'French White'** A good, strong-growing variety, producing large white flowers. *V. t.* **'Gwenllian'** Flowers deep pink in bud, opening to white with pink tinge. Small leaves, compact habit, reaching only two thirds average height and spread. *V. t.* **lucidum** Flowers large, white, in early to late spring. Good, vigorous form with larger, glossier leaves than parent. Slightly tender and benefits from the protection of a wall or fence. *V. t.* **'Purpureum'** White flowers. New growth tinged purple, older foliage very dark green. Benefits from the protection of a wall or fence. Two thirds average height and spread. *V. t.* **'Variegatum'** White flowers. Attractive white to creamy white variegated foliage. Two thirds height and spread. Benefits from the protection of a wall or fence.
Average height and spread
Five years
3 × 3 ft (91 × 91 cm) freestanding
5 × 5 ft (1.5 × 1.5 m) fan-trained
Ten years
6 × 6 ft (1.8 × 1.8 m) freestanding
9 × 9 ft (2.7 × 2.7 m) fan-trained
Twenty years
12 × 12 ft (3.7 × 3.7 m) freestanding
15 × 15 ft (4.6 × 4.6 m) fan-trained
Protrudes up to 4 ft (1.2 m) from support if fan-trained, 10 ft (3 m) untrained.

VINCA MAJOR

GREATER PERIWINKLE, LARGE PERIWINKLE
Apocynaceae *Perennial Climber*
Evergreen
A creeping ground-cover plant rarely considered as a climbing specimen but can be adapted to such and, in its variegated form, extremely attractive when used in this manner.

Origin From Europe.
Use As a low climber for walls and fences or to creep through other established shrubs. Can also be used to cover a wall by cascading down from the top.
Description *Flower* Blue to purple/blue, five-petalled, 1 in (2.5 cm) wide, forming a single saucer-shaped flower in mid to late spring. *Foliage* Ovate, pointed, 1–1½ in (2.5–4 cm) long. Light green when young, quickly becoming glossy dark green. Some yellow autumn colour. *Stem* Light green, becoming

darker with age. Glossy texture, rambling habit. *Fruit* No fruit of interest.
Hardiness Tolerates a minimum winter temperature of 0°F (−18°C).
Soil requirements Tolerates all soil conditions with no particular preference, although for good climbing results adequate plant nutrient must be available.
Sun/Shade aspect Tolerates all aspects and deep shade but growth will be thicker and more lush in full sun to light shade.
Pruning Reduce all previous season's growth to ground level in early spring to encourage new annual formation of climbing structure.
Training Allow to ramble through other shrubs or wires.
Propagation From rooted tips, from layers or from semi-ripe cuttings. Can be purchased bare-rooted from late autumn to early spring or container grown as available. Normally stocked by most garden centres. Best planting height: root clumps to 18 in (45 cm).
Problems Plants often look insipid when young, quickly establishing once planted. Can become invasive in ideal situations.
Similar forms of interest *V. m.* **'Variegata'** Attractive white to yellow/white variegated foliage. *V. m.* **'Maculata'** A rarely seen variety with a central splash of green/yellow on each young leaf. Splash deteriorates as leaf ages and is produced only in open, sunny positions.
Average height and spread
One year
3 × 3 ft (91 × 91 cm)
Protrudes up to 12 in (30 cm) from support.

VITEX AGNUS-CASTUS

CHASTE TREE
Verbenaceae *Wall Shrub*
Deciduous
An attractive, uncommon shrub useful for its autumn flowers and benefiting from the protection of a large wall or fence.

Origin From the Mediterranean area and central Asia.
Use As a fan-trained shrub for walls and fences.

Vitex agnus-castus in flower

Description *Flower* Fragrant, violet, small tubular flowers in slender racemes, 3–7 in (7.5–18 cm) long and 3 in (7.5 cm) wide, produced at ends of current season's growth, early to mid autumn. *Foliage* Compound leaves consisting of five to seven ovate to lanceolate leaflets, 2–6 in (5–15 cm) long, on short stalks borne in pairs along stems and shoots. *Stem* Graceful, grey, downy shoots, when trained forming a rigid fan shape. Medium growth rate. *Fruit* Small grey/brown seedheads of little interest.
Hardiness Tolerates a minimum winter temperature of 14°F (−10°C).

Vinca major in flower

Soil requirements Well-drained soil, dislikes any degree of waterlogging.
Sun/Shade aspect Requires a sheltered aspect in full sun.
Pruning Once fan framework is formed shorten all previous season's growth back to two or three buds.
Training Tie to anchor points or to wires.
Propagation and nursery production From seed or semi-ripe cuttings taken in early summer. Purchase container grown from specialist nurseries. Best planting height 15 in–2 ft (38–60 cm).
Problems Likely to succumb in wet, cold winters, hardier in dry, cold conditions.
Average height and spread
Five years
5 × 5 ft (1.5 × 1.5 m)
Ten years
7 × 7 ft (2.1 × 2.1 m)
Twenty years
12 × 12 ft (3.7 × 3.7 m)
Protrudes up to 3 ft (91 cm) from support.

Vitis coignetiae in autumn

VITIS 'BRANT'
(*V. vinifera* 'Brandt' *V. v.* 'Brant')

ORNAMENTAL GRAPE VINE
Vitaceae   *Fruiting Vine*
Deciduous

Good covering foliage in summer but coming into its own in autumn with flame-orange foliage.

Origin From Asia Minor and the Caucasus.
Use To cover walls, fences, wires, ideal for growing through large shrubs and trees. Will cover buildings, pergolas and other similar structures.
Description *Flower* Small, creamy green clusters 3 in (7.5 cm) long of inconspicuous flowers, often hidden by foliage, are produced in early to mid summer. *Foliage* Five-fingered maple-shaped leaves, up to 5 in (12 cm) wide and long. Light green when young becoming slightly duller and yellower in summer, in autumn turning startling copper/orange/red, often in a defined pattern on the upper surface of the leaf. *Stem* Light grey/green when young, ageing to yellow/brown, finally grey/brown when mature. Vigorous, able to make in excess of 9 ft (2.7 m) of growth in one season. Clinging tendrils produced from leaf axils make it partially self-supporting. *Fruit* Small clusters up to 4–5 in (10–12 cm) long containing

numerous small grapes ¼–½ in (5 mm–1 cm) in diameter, purple blue with a silver bloom. Edible in early to late autumn.
Hardiness Tolerates a minimum winter temperature of 4°F (−15°C).
Soil requirements Does well on all soil types but requires adequate moisture to aid the production of the vigorous vine growth.
Sun/Shade aspect Tolerates all aspects in light shade to full sun.
Pruning Can be left to ramble or treated as a fruiting vine. All current season's shoots not required for covering can be removed in early to mid spring, cutting back flush with the main stem. This will lead to larger foliage and possibly increased fruit production.
Training Wires or some form of framework will be required. The vine is semi self-clinging by the use of leaf tendrils, although young and heavy branches may need tying in.
Propagation and nursery production Semi-ripe cuttings taken in early to mid summer. Always purchase container grown, best planting height 1½–3 ft (45–76 cm). Available from good garden centres and nurseries.
Problems Birds may take fruit. Autumn colour may be poor following wet summers.
Similar forms of interest None.
Average height and spread
Five years
10 × 10 ft (3 × 3 m)
Ten years
20 × 20 ft (6 × 6 m)
Twenty years
30 × 30 ft (9 × 9 m)
Protrudes up to 3 ft (91 cm) from support.

VITIS COIGNETIAE
(*V. kaempferi*)

JAPANESE CRIMSON GLORY VINE
Vitaceae   *Woody Climber*
Deciduous

A most attractive autumn foliage climber with particularly interesting leaves.

Origin From Japan.
Use As a fast-growing climber for walls, fences, trelliswork, pergolas, gazebos and small buildings. Attractive when grown up large conifers, large shrubs and other trees.
Description *Flower* Small clusters of round, light green flower buds of little overall attraction. *Foliage* Up to 12 in (30 cm) across, heart-shaped, coarsely toothed, with three to five lobes. Glabrous above with downy, orange underside. Particularly brilliant autumn colours of crimson and scarlet. *Stem* Light grey/green, becoming green/brown, finally grey/brown. Fast growing. *Fruit* Small, ½ in (1 cm) wide, black, grape fruits in short clusters. Not always reliable in their production and not normally edible.
Hardiness Tolerates a minimum winter temperature of 4°F (−15°C).
Soil requirements Tolerates all soil types, except extremely alkaline. On very wet soils autumn colour may be decreased.
Sun/Shade aspect Tolerates all aspects. Best in light shade but will tolerate full sun to medium shade.
Pruning Select and train a vine system of shoots with individual laterals no closer than 18 in (45 cm). Prune back all other laterals flush with main vine system in early spring. This will induce larger foliage display.
Training Allow to ramble through wires, trellis or the branches of large shrubs and trees. Not self-clinging, not twining, but normally interlaces itself giving support. May need tying to wires and individual anchor points when young but can be left free-growing without pruning.
Propagation and nursery production From semi-ripe cuttings taken in mid summer. Always purchase container grown, best planting height 1½–4 ft (45 cm–1.2 m). Readily available from garden centres and nurseries.
Problems Often slow to establish, taking up to two years to make any amount of growth, but, once established, very fast-growing and can outgrow the area allocated for it.
Similar forms of interest None.
Average height and spread
Five years
10 × 10 ft (3 × 3 m)
Ten years
20 × 20 ft (6 × 6 m)
Twenty years
40 × 40 ft (12 × 12 m)
Protrudes up to 3 ft (91 cm) from support.

Vitis '**Brant**' in fruit

VITIS VINIFERA
(Grape Vine Hybrids)

GRAPE VINE

Vitaceae   *Fruiting Vine*
Deciduous

Attractive climbers, displaying both pleasing foliage and edible fruits.

Origin Most hybrids of garden or nursery origin.

Use As a climber for walls and fences, to cover pergolas and similar structures. Can be used in the open garden on a post and wire framework or can be allowed to grow through trees. Many varieties are suitable for greenhouses and conservatories. Fruit can be eaten or used for making wine.

Description *Flower* Very small, soft green flowers of little interest, produced in mid to late spring. *Foliage* Three- or five-lobed, up to 6 in (15 cm) long and wide. Normally light green to grey/green. Good yellow autumn colour. *Stem* Light grey/green, quickly becoming grey/brown, finally grey. Not self-supporting. Attractive in winter. *Fruit* Hanging bunches up to 12 in (30 cm) long of round fruits, either purple or light green to soft yellow, with grey bloom. Edible, sweet flavoured. Some varieties suitable for wine-making.

Hardiness Tolerates a minimum winter temperature of 0°F (−18°C), except for those varieties marked for growing under protection.

Soil requirements Tolerates all soil conditions, except extremely dry and extremely wet. Varieties used for growing in greenhouses or conservatories should be planted outside and laid in through an appropriate opening to allow their roots adequate space.

Sun/Shade aspect Tolerates a wide range of aspects but the more sheltered and sunny the aspect, then the better the fruit. Some varieties must be grown under protection, not only to ripen fruit but to induce flowering.

Pruning Once established remove all annual side growth back as close to stem as possible in early spring to encourage fruiting.

Training Young plants should be cut to within 12 in (30 cm) of soil level in early spring. Train ensuing shoot or shoots upwards and horizontally. In second year again reduce vertical shoots to within 12 in (30 cm) of origin and reduce side shoots to one bud. Tie in ensuing growths vertically and horizontally and

Vitis vinifera 'Black Hamburg'

repeat this process until adequate height and area is covered. Tie to wires or individual anchor points.

Propagation and nursery production From vine eyes (buds) by taking one single bud and a small area of stem growth and inserting shallowly in a grit and sand rooting medium with assisted heat, or from hardwood cuttings approximately 4–6 in (10–15 cm) long taken in winter. Can also be layered by taking the tip of an existing plant and burying it in a sand/soil mixture. Once rooted, replant in final position. Purchase bare-rooted from mid autumn to early spring or container grown as available. Some varieties can be found in garden centres and good nurseries, others may have to be sought from specialist growers. Best planting height 10 in–4 ft (25 cm–1.2 m).

Problems The training requirements can be daunting. May suffer from mildew and vine weevils may attack. Proprietary controls will normally eradicate. Needs a large root run area to achieve good results.

Forms of interest
UK
OUTDOOR VARIETIES – WHITE 'Chardonnay' White fruit. A variety good for the cooler areas. A good wine grape. 'Nimrod' Seedless golden fruit for wine-making. Must have a sunny position. 'Madeleine Angevine 7972' Early autumn fruiting. Pale green fruit can be used for both dessert and for wine-making. Good in less favourable areas. 'Madeleine Sylvaner 2851' Good flavoured fruit used for both dessert or wine-making. Tolerates cool conditions. 'Mueller-Thurgau' Mid autumn fruiting. Possibly the best wine-making variety for the amateur. Golden brown fruits. Good in cool areas. 'Muscat de Saumur' A very old variety for wine-making with good muscat flavour. Must have a sunny position. 'Pinot Blanc' Very good wine-making grape which does well in cool English summers. 'Précoce de Malingre' Early fruiting. Good flavoured small grapes for dessert or wine-making. Must have a warm, sunny position. 'Seyval' Mid autumn fruiting. Large grapes with good flavour, best for wine-making. Prefers a warm, sheltered aspect. 'Seyve-Villard 5/276' Early fruiting. Golden fruit can be used for both dessert and wine-making. Good on alkaline soils. Must have a sheltered, warm position. 'Siegerrebe' Late fruiting. Good-flavoured, golden yellow fruit for dessert or wine-making. Heavy cropper. Dislikes severely alkaline soils. 'Traminer' Can be late fruiting. Rosy coloured grapes best for wine-making.

OUTDOOR VARIETIES – BLACK 'Baco 1' A wine-making variety. Strong growing, needs space. Heavy cropper. 'Black Hamburg' Often said to be best under protection but in the author's observation grows well outdoors in sheltered, sunny positions. For dessert and wine-making. 'Brant' Small fruits with a tart flavour for dessert and wine-making. Good ornamental foliage. 'Léon Millot' Good wine-making variety. Large crop. Strong growing, needs space. 'Marshall Joffre' Good wine-making variety. Strong growing, needs space. 'Millers Burgundy' ('Pinot Meunier') Small fruits, good for wine-making. Foliage attractive with a white woolly down when young. 'Pirovano 14' Good flavour. Can be used for both dessert or wine-making. Must have a sheltered, sunny position. 'Seibel 13053' Large crop. Vigorous, needs space. Good for red or rosé wine-making. Must have a sunny position. 'Schuyler' Good flavour for wine-making. Strong-growing. Must have a sunny, warm wall. 'Strawberry Grape' Small dessert fruit with musky flavour. Of medium crop and vigour. Must have a warm, sunny position. 'Triomphe d'Alsace' Strong growing. Must have a warm, sheltered position. Good for red wine production.

VARIETIES FOR GREENHOUSES – WHITE 'Buckland Sweetwater' Very popular variety for dessert and wine-making. Sweet, juicy, amber-coloured fruit in good numbers. Best in unheated greenhouses. 'Chasselas d'Or' Late fruiting. Good-flavoured, golden yellow fruit for both dessert or wine-making. Must have heated greenhouse for success. 'Foster's Seedling' Early to mid season. Large crop of amber-coloured fruits of good flavour, sweet and juicy. For dessert or wine-making. Can be grown in both cold or heated greenhouses. 'Lady Hutt' White, sweet, good-flavoured fruits, borne late. For wine-making. Medium to heavy cropper. Best in unheated greenhouses. 'Mireille' Early fruiting. Large white grapes with good muscat flavour for wine. Best in unheated greenhouse. 'Mrs Pearson' White/yellow grapes with good muscat flavour for wine. Vigorous. Needs heat to induce flowering and ripening. 'Muscat of Alexandria' Possibly the best white variety under glass. Amber-coloured fruits, sweet and good-flavoured, for dessert or wine. May need additional heat to ripen fruits in poor summers. 'Syrian' White grapes, borne late. For wine-making. Strong growing, needs space. Heat is required for ripening and to induce good flavour. 'Trebbiano' Late, large crop of white fruits, good for wine. Very

Vitis vinifera 'Mueller-Thurgau'

Vitis vinifera 'Muscat of Alexandria'

strong growing, needs space. Must have heat to induce flowering.

VARIETIES FOR GREENHOUSES - BLACK **'Alicante'** Becoming very popular for wine-making. Black fruits with good flavour, borne late. May be shy to flower without additional heat in spring. **'Black Hamburg'** Performs well in greenhouses, both heated and cool. May also succeed outdoors in favourable sunny positions. For dessert and wine-making. Early to mid season fruiting. **'Frontignan'** Good muscat-flavoured black fruits for wine-making. Must have heat in the greenhouse. **'Gros Colmar'** Late, large crop of black grapes for wine-making. Very strong growing. Must have heat to induce flowering. **'Lady Downe's Seedling'** Black grapes. An old wine-making variety of medium vigour. Must have heat to induce flowering. **'Mrs Pince'** Old muscat variety with black fruits of good flavour for wine-making. Strong growing. Must have heat for flowering and ripening. **'Muscat of Hamburg'** Late, heavy cropping. Red to purple, muscat-flavoured fruit for dessert or wine-making. Needs heat for flowering and ripening.

USA
These varieties are best in the areas shown but may be suitable for wider areas depending on their hardiness.

Grapes for the Northeast and Midwest
AMERICAN VARIETIES **'Buffalo'** Mid season ripening. Medium to large clusters of red/black grapes, good for wine or juice. Good also in the Pacific Northwest. From New York. **'Catawba'** A red grape, very popular commercially for wine or juice. Ripens over a long season. Also good in southerly areas. From North Carolina. **'Cayuga White'** White grapes in tight clusters. Good for dessert. From New York. **'Concord'** Dark blue grapes with a rich flavour which is retained in wine. Late fruiting. From Massachusetts. **'Delaware'** A green grape used for wine-making and juice but also good as a dessert. Vines subject to mildew. From New Jersey. **'Edelweiss'** Medium-sized grapes good for dessert use. Hardy. From Minnesota. **'Fredonia'** Black fruits of good flavour for wine-making. Hardy. May sometimes be difficult to pollinate. From New York. **'Nimrod'** White seedless grape for wine-making. Vines can be brittle and need careful handling. Moderately hardy. Good also for the Northern states. From New York. **'Interlaken Seedless'** Medium-sized clusters of small, sweet, seedless, green/white grapes for wine-making. Moderately hardy. Also ideal for the Pacific Northwest. From New York. **'New York**

Muscat' Red/black berries in medium clusters. Rich, fruity muscat scent. Good for wine and juice. Not entirely hardy. From New York. **'Niagara'** A very popular white grape for wine-making. Strong-growing and moderately hardy. From New York. **'Ontario'** White fruits in large open clusters. Good for wine. Strong-growing and moderately hardy. Does well on heavy soils. Also good for the Pacific Northwest. From Ontario, Canada. **'Schuyler'** Soft and juicy fruit with a tough skin. Good for wine. Moderately hardy. Good disease resistance. Ideal also for the Northwest. From New York. **'Seneca'** Somewhat small golden-skinned fruits which have a sweet, aromatic flavour. Good for wine. Hardy. Also good in the Pacific Northwest. From New York. **'Swenson Red'** Medium to large red fruits with good flavour for wine-making. Hardy. From Minnesota. **'Veesport'** Black fruits in medium-sized clusters. Good for wine and juice but also can be eaten as dessert. Strong-growing. From Ontario, Canada.

FRENCH HYBRIDS **'Aurore'** **('Seibel 5279')** Early fruiting soft white grape with a good flavour for wine. Strong-growing. Dislikes heavy soils. From France.

Grapes for the West **'Baco 1'** Black grapes for wine-making. Heavy cropper. Strong-growing, needs space. Good over a wide area. From France. **'Cabernet Sauvignon'** Black fruits. Used to make red Bordeaux wine in France. From France. **'Cardinal'** Medium-sized clusters of large, dark red dessert fruits with green flesh. Early ripening. Ideal for training purposes. Good in coastal and valley areas. From California. **'Chardonnay'** White fruits for wine-making. Good in cooler areas. From France. **'Chenin Blanc'** White, strong-growing, medium-sized fruits for wine-making. Ideal for coastal areas. From France. **'Delight'** Early-ripening green/yellow dessert fruits with good firm flesh and muscat flavour. Best in coastal valley conditions. From California. **'Emperor'** Late-ripening large red dessert fruits with firm, crisp flesh. Stores well. Origin unknown. **'Flame Seedless'** Red to light red, seedless, sweet dessert fruits with a crisp texture. Early-ripening, medium-sized, loose clusters. Requires heat to ripen but best colour is developed with cool nights. From California. **'French Colombard'** Medium-sized white fruits with high acid content for wine-making. Good in coastal valleys and also the Central Valley of California. From France. **'Muscat of Alexandria'** Amber-coloured dessert grapes, sweet and good-flavoured. Best in Southern states or under protection in the North. From

North Africa. **'Niabell'** Large black dessert fruit of good flavour. Performs well in coastal valleys but will tolerate hot inland areas. Mid season ripening. Strong-growing. Resistant to powdery mildew. From California. **'Pierce'** Black dessert fruit requiring a hot summer to ripen. Strong-growing. Best in central California. From New York. **'Pinot Noir'** Small black grapes, used to make the French Burgundy wines. From France. **'Ribier'** Large, jet black fruits. Use for dessert. Best in hot inland areas. Fruits do not store well. From France. **'Thompson Seedless'** Green, mild-flavoured dessert fruits in good-shaped clusters, ripening early mid season. Used for raisin production. Will only grow well in hot climates. From Asia Minor. **'Tokay'** Large clusters of large, firm, red grapes with limited flavour for wine or dessert. Ripens late mid season. Does well in cool valley climates. From Algeria. **'Zinfandel'** Used both for red and white wines. Very reliable and a good variety to start with. Origin unknown.

Grapes for the Southwest
MUSCADINE VARIETIES Attention must be given to providing pollinators for some of these varieties. **'Hunt'** Dull black fruits of good quality. Ideal for wine-making and juice. Strong-growing and very productive. Use any other variety as a pollinator. From Georgia. **'Jumbo'** As its name would imply, very large black fruits. Good for wine. Ideal for garden use. Vines disease resistant. Use any other variety as a pollinator. From southern USA. **'Magoon'** Red/purple berries of medium size with attractive aromatic flavour for wine-making. Vines vigorous and heavy-cropping. Self-fertile. From Mississippi. **'Scuppernong'** Green to red/bronze fruit, depending on the amount of sun. Late ripening, sweet, juicy aromatic flavour. Good for dessert or wine-making. Use any other variety as a pollinator. From North Carolina. **'Southland'** Very large, purple, dull-skinned fruits with good flavour and high sugar content. Good for wine. Moderately vigorous and productive. Good for the central and southern Gulf Coast states. Self-fertile. From Mississippi. **'Thomas'** Small to medium red/black, very sweet fruits for wine-making. Excellent for fresh juice. Use any other variety as a pollinator. From southern USA. **'Topsail'** Sweet, green fruit, splotched with bronze, for winemaking. Good muscadine flavour. Limited production of fruit. Not hardy but disease resistant. Use any other variety as a pollinator. From North Carolina. **'Yuga'** Sweet red/bronze fruits of good quality for wine. Late ripening but somewhat irregular. Ideal for gardens. From Georgia.

Average height and spread
Five years
9 × 9 ft (2.7 × 2.7 m)
Ten years
18 × 18 ft (5.5 × 5.5 m)
Twenty years
30 × 30 ft (9 × 9 m)
Protrudes up to 2 ft (60 cm)
from support prior to spring pruning.

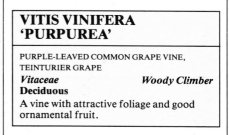

VITIS VINIFERA 'PURPUREA'

PURPLE-LEAVED COMMON GRAPE VINE, TEINTURIER GRAPE

Vitaceae   *Woody Climber*
Deciduous

A vine with attractive foliage and good ornamental fruit.

Origin From the Caucasus and Asia Minor.
Use As a rambling vine for walls, fences, pillars and pergolas and for covering roofs of gazebos and small buildings. Looks extremely fine when used in association with silver-leaved shrubs and trees.
Description *Flower* Small, oval, green, ageing to black, often with a blue bloom. *Foliage* Up to 6 in (15 cm) long and wide, hand-shaped, with three or five lobes. Claret red, downy

Vitis vinifera 'Purpurea' in leaf

upper surface, purple/blue undersides. Good purple autumn colour. *Stem* Purple becoming purple/green, eventually purple/brown. Loosely twining, medium to fast growing. *Fruit* Round grapes, ¼ in (5 mm) across, purple with blue bloom, carried in bunches.
Hardiness Tolerates a minimum winter temperature of 4°F (−15°C).
Soil requirements Tolerates all soil conditions with no particular preferences, only disliking extremely dry soils.
Sun/Shade aspect Tolerates all aspects, except extremely exposed. Best in full sun but will tolerate light shade.
Pruning Train into a vine system with each vine 15–18 in (38–45 cm) apart. Attempt to remove all other surplus vines in early spring. This will encourage better foliage, shape, size and colour. However, can be left free-growing without pruning.
Training Not self-clinging, but semi-twining and will climb by twisting around wires, trellis or other suitable thin supports. May need tying in if trained or when young.
Propagation and nursery production Semi-ripe cuttings taken in early summer. Always purchase container grown, best planting height 1½–3 ft (45–91 cm). Readily available from good garden centres and nurseries.
Problems Can suffer from a form of mildew which seems to be specific to this variety. Can be cured by a proprietary controlled fungicide and is not normally terminal or disfiguring.
Similar forms of interest None.
Average height and spread
Five years
10 × 10 ft (3 × 3 m)
Ten years
15 × 15 ft (4.6 × 4.6 m)
Twenty years
20 × 20 ft (6 × 6 m)
Protrudes up to 2 ft (60 cm) from support.

WATTAKA-KA SINENSIS (*Dregea sinensis*)

WATTAKAKA
Asclepiadaceae   *Tender Woody Climber*
Deciduous
An interesting climber but requiring a very sheltered growing location or the protection of a greenhouse or conservatory.

Origin From China.
Use As a small flowering climber for very sheltered, sunny walls.
Description *Flower* Up to 25 long-stalked, downy florets make up a flower 3 in (7.5 cm) across, with a central trumpet ½ in (1 cm) wide with five lobes, red with small white dots. Produced in mid summer. *Foliage* Ovate, broad, pointed leaves up to 4 in (10 cm) long

and 3 in (7.5 cm) wide, produced on stalks up to 1½ in (4 cm) long. Light grey/green, with downy, velvet undersides. Some yellow autumn colour. *Stem* Mid green, sparse, loosely twining. Medium growth rate. *Fruit* In extremely favourable conditions and under the protection of a greenhouse or conservatory may produce interesting incurving fruits, consisting of two parts, down-covered, up to 2 in (5 cm) long and ½ in (1 cm) wide and tapering in shape.
Hardiness Tolerates a minimum winter temperature of 25°F (−5°C).

Wattaka-ka sinensis in flower

Soil requirements Prefers a neutral to acid soil, but will tolerate a certain amount of alkalinity.
Sun/Shade aspect Requires a very sheltered aspect or the protection of a greenhouse or conservatory. Full sun to light shade.
Pruning Not normally required.
Training Allow to twine through wires or trellis.
Propagation and nursery production From seed grown under protection. Always purchase container grown; very scarce in commercial production and will have to be sought from specialist growers. Best planting height 6 in–2 ft (15–60 cm).
Problems Difficult to find and not fully hardy.
Similar forms of interest None.
Average height and spread
Five years
4 × 4 ft (1.2 × 1.2 m)
Ten years
8 × 8 ft (2.4 × 2.4 m)
Twenty years
12 × 12 ft (3.7 × 3.7 m)
Protrudes up to 2 ft (60 cm) from support.

WEIGELA

KNOWN BY BOTANICAL NAME
Caprifoliaceae   *Wall Shrub*
Deciduous
Early summer flowering shrubs adapting well to fan-training on walls and fences.

Origin Most forms from Japan, Korea, north China and Manchuria but many cultivars and hybrid varieties are of garden origin.
Use As a freestanding shrub grown in front of walls or fences, or can be fan-trained to good effect.
Description *Flower* Funnel-shaped, 1 in (2.5 cm) long and ½ in (1 cm) wide, in varying shades from yellow to white, pink and red. Flowers produced on wood two years old or more, late spring through early summer, possibly with intermittent flowering through late summer and early autumn. *Foliage* Leaves ovate, 1½–5 in (4–12 cm) long, dark to mid green with some light green varieties and golden and silver variegated. Yellow autumn colour. *Stem* Upright, becoming spreading with age. Grey/green to grey/brown. Medium growth rate.
Fruit Seedheads dark to mid brown, of some attraction in winter.
Hardiness Tolerates a minimum winter temperature of 0°F (−8°C).
Soil requirements Any soil.
Sun/Shade aspect Good in exposed situations. Prefers full sun, tolerates light to medium shade.
Pruning From two years after planting remove one third of old flowering wood annually to ground level, after flowering.
Training Allow to stand free or secure to the wall or fence by wires or by individual anchor points.
Propagation and nursery production From semi-ripe cuttings taken in early summer or hardwood cuttings in winter. Purchase container grown or bare-rooted. Most varieties easy to find but some may have to be obtained from specialist nurseries. Best planting height 15 in–2½ ft (38–76 cm).
Problems If unpruned can become too woody and flowers will diminish in size and number. Large, established shrubs can be cut to ground level and will regenerate, but will take two years to come into flower. *Weigela* was once classified with the closely related *Diervilla* but in recent years these shrubs have been classified separately.
Forms of interest *W.* 'Abel Carrière' Large trumpet-shaped, rose-carmine flowers with gold markings in throat, opening from purple/carmine buds. Good, bold, green foliage. *W.* 'Avalanche' A good, strong-growing, white flowering variety. May have to be obtained from specialist nurseries. *W.* 'Boskoop Glory' Large, trumpet-shaped

Weigela 'Abel Carrière' in flower

Weigela 'Aureovariegata' in leaf

flowers, rose pink ageing to salmon pink. A beautiful form. Two thirds average height and spread. *W.* **'Bristol Ruby'** Possibly the most popular of all flowering forms. Ruby red flowers profusely borne on upright, strong shrub in late spring/early summer. *W.* **'Candida'** Pure white flowers with slightly green shading. Light green foliage on arching stems. Two thirds average height and spread. *W.* **'Carnival'** Flowers pink and white on the same shrub. *W.* **'Eve Rathke'** Bright crimson-red flowers with yellow anthers, produced over a long period from late spring to late summer. *W. florida* **'Albovariegata'** Attractive creamy white edges to ovate leaves.

Weigela 'Boskoop Glory' in flower

Pale to mid pink flowers produced profusely on stems two or three years old. Two thirds average height and spread. *W. f.* **'Aureovariegata'** A variety with yellow variegation, often producing pink to red tinged leaves, particularly during autumn. Pink flowers profusely produced in late spring to early summer. *W.* **'Looymansii Aurea'** Flowers pale pink, contrasting with foliage which is light golden-yellow in spring, ageing to lime-yellow in autumn. Must be in light shade or it scorches. Obtain from specialist nurseries. Often looks weak when young. One third average height and spread. *W.* **'Lucifer'** Very large red flowers carried later than most. *W. middendorffiana* Arching branches with attractive grey/green winter wood. Flowers bell-shaped, sulphur yellow with dark orange markings on lower lobes, mid to late spring.

Ovate, light green foliage with some yellow autumn colour. Prefers light shade, although not fussy. An all-round attractive variety, reaching two thirds average height and spread. From Japan, northern China and Manchuria. *W.* **'Mont Blanc'** Fragrant white flowers, strong-growing. Obtain from specialist nurseries. *W.* **'Newport Red'** Good, dark red flowers. Two thirds average height and spread. *W. praecox* **'Variegata'** A variety with ovate to obovate, creamy white variegated foliage, rigid and deeply veined. Flowers honey-scented, rose pink with yellow markings in throat in late spring/early summer. Obtain from specialist nurseries. From Japan, Korea and Manchuria. *W.* **'Rubidor'** Golden yellow variegated foliage which may be susceptible to scorching in strong sunlight. Dark pink flowers. *W.* **'Stelzneri'** Good mid pink flowers borne in profusion. Interesting upright growth. Not widely available. *W.* **'Styriaca'** Carmine-red flowers produced in good quantities in late spring/early summer. Strong, old-fashioned variety.

Average height and spread
Five years
4 × 4 ft (1.2 × 1.2 m) freestanding
5 × 5 ft (1.5 × 1.5 m) fan-trained
Ten years
5½ × 5½ ft (1.6 × 1.6 m) freestanding
7 × 7 ft (2.1 × 2.1 m) fan-trained
Twenty years
7 × 7 ft (2.1 × 2.1 m) freestanding
9 × 9 ft (2.7 × 2.7 m) fan-trained
Protrudes up to 3 ft (91 cm) from support if fan-trained, 6 ft (1.8 m) untrained.

WISTERIA FLORIBUNDA
(*W. multijuga*)

JAPANESE WISTERIA
Leguminosae   Woody Climber
Deciduous
An attractive group of climbers not always receiving the attention they deserve.

Origin From Japan.
Use As a large climber for sunny walls, fences, pergolas or growing through large shrubs or trees. Can be trained into a small weeping standard.
Description *Flower* Racemes 10–12 in (25–30 cm) long of small pea-shaped flowers up to ½–¾ in (1–2 cm) long and wide. Violet/blue, pink or white, depending on variety. *Foliage* Light grey/green to olive green. Up to 15 in (38 cm) long, pinnate, consisting of up to 19 leaflets each 1 in (2.5 cm) wide and 3 in (7.5 cm) long. Oval in shape. Good yellow autumn colour. *Stem* Grey/green, twining,

Wisteria floribunda in flower

ageing to grey/brown. Fast growing. *Fruit* May produce, in warm summers, pods ½ in (1 cm) wide and 6 in (15 cm) long, velvety, grey/green in colour. Poisonous.
Hardiness Tolerates a minimum winter temperature of 14°F (−10°C).
Soil requirements Does well on all soil conditions, only disliking extremely alkaline types. Must have adequate root-run to allow it to spread and produce the maximum amount of top growth possible.

Wisteria floribunda 'Alba' in flower

Sun/Shade aspect Warm, sheltered aspect. Full sun to very light shade.
Pruning Prune tendrils in late summer and autumn to form a framework, then remove all current season's tendrils back to two buds from the point of origin.
Training Train to a vine system with one vine every 18 in (45 cm) laterally from a central upright stem.
Propagation and nursery production Grafted plants should always be chosen from a known parent source. Always purchased container grown, best planting height 2-4 ft (60 cm-1.2 m). May have to be sought from specialist nurseries.
Problems Often planted in areas where it cannot reach its full potential. Some varieties may be hard to find.
Similar forms of interest *W. f.* 'Alba' Attractive white flowers in racemes up to 2 ft (60 cm) long. *W. f.* 'Rosea' Pale rose-pink flowers. Scarce. *W. f.* 'Violacea Plena' Double, violet-purple flowers.
Average height and spread
Five years
10 × 10 ft (3 × 3 m)
Ten years
20 × 20 ft (6 × 6 m)
Twenty years
30 × 30 ft (9 × 9 m)
Protrudes up to 4 ft (1.2 m) from support.

WISTERIA FLORIBUNDA 'MACROBOTRYS'

JAPANESE WISTERIA

Leguminosae   *Woody Climber*
Deciduous

Possibly one of the most spectacular of all wisterias, with its flowers exceeding any other variety in length.

Origin From Japan.
Use As a free-growing climber for walls, fences, pergolas, through trees and over large shrubs. Can also be grown as a small weeping standard tree.
Description *Flower* Racemes of dark violet/purple, pea-shaped flowers up to 21 in (53 cm) long and 5 in (12 cm) wide. Racemes produced very uniformly along the branches and giving an effect of a waterfall. *Foliage* Pinnate leaves up to 18 in (45 cm) long and 8 in (20 cm) wide with each leaflet up to 4 in (10 cm) long. Light green, giving good yellow autumn colour. *Stem* Twining, smooth, light grey/green when young, ageing to yellow/brown and finally dark/grey brown. Fast growing. *Fruit* May produce inedible, green pea pods in very hot summers but not reliable or attractive.
Hardiness Tolerates a minimum winter temperature of 14°F (−10°C). In very cold wind chill conditions stems may be killed in winter but rejuvenation from the base normally occurs the following spring.

Wisteria floribunda **'Macrobotrys' in flower**

Wisteria sinensis **in flower**

Soil requirements Does well on all soil types but to achieve full potential, needs a root run of 50-64 ft (15-20 m). Very alkaline soils may induce chlorosis, identified by a yellowing of the leaves in mid summer. This will restrict flowering but normally will not kill the plant.
Sun/Shade aspect Must be in full sun to very light shade, otherwise will not flower.
Pruning Cut back all current season's growth to within two buds of point of origin in mid to late autumn. This pruning is carried out once the framework has been achieved. Over shrubs and large trees it is not normally possible to prune and the climber must mature before flowering to its full potential.
Training It is not a good policy to retain all of the season's growth. Only use tendrils produced in current season to form a framework of shoots, ideally one or two major upright shoots with side branches encouraged to grow 18 in (45 cm) apart. Use wires on walls and fences to achieve the framework training.
Propagation and nursery production Must always be grafted, will not come true from seed. Always purchase container-grown plants, may have to be sought from specialist nurseries. Best planting height 2-6 ft (60 cm-1.8 m).
Problems May be difficult to find. May be slow to establish, taking three years before major growth is forthcoming. Takes up to six or eight years to flower and then possibly another four years to come into full flowering potential but truly worth the wait.
Similar forms of interest None.
Average height and spread
Five years
18 × 18 ft (5.5 × 5.5 m)
Ten years
36 × 36 ft (11 × 11 m)
Twenty years
50 × 50 ft+ (15 × 15 m+)
Will continue to spread beyond this for up to 50 years. Protrudes up to 3 ft (91 cm) from support.

WISTERIA SINENSIS

CHINESE WISTERIA

Leguminosae   *Woody Climber*
Deciduous

Of all the climbing plants from China this surely must be one of the most spectacular with its long flowing racemes of blue flowers.

Origin From China.
Use As a fast-growing climber for sunny walls and fences, for growing over pergolas, buildings and through trees. Can be trained as a small weeping tree.

Description *Flower* Racemes of mid blue pea-like flowers, 6-9 in (15-23 cm) long and 3-4 in (8-10 cm) wide, are produced in profusion from mid to late spring. *Foliage* Pinnate leaves up to 12-18 in (30-45 cm) long and 4-6 in (10-15 cm) wide with seven to nine leaflets. Each leaflet 3 in (7.5 cm) long by ½ in (1 cm) wide. Light green with good yellow autumn colour. *Stem* Twining, smooth, light grey/green when young, ageing to yellow/brown and finally dark/grey brown. Fast growing. *Fruit* Long grey/green, bean-like pods, 6-8 in (15-20 cm) long, ¼-½ in (5 mm-1 cm) wide, produced in hot summers. Poisonous.

Wisteria sinensis **'Alba' in flower**

Hardiness Tolerates a minimum winter temperature of 14°F (−10°C). In very cold wind chill conditions stems may be killed in winter but rejuvenation from the base normally occurs the following spring.
Soil requirements Does well on all soil types but must have adequate root run - needs up to 20-30 ft (6-9 m) to perform to its full potential. On very alkaline soils may show signs of chlorosis in the form of a yellowing of the leaves in mid summer; although this will restrict flowering, it is not normally terminal.
Sun/Shade aspect Must be in full sun to very light shade, otherwise will not flower.
Pruning Cut back all current season's wood in mid to late autumn to within two buds from point of origin. This procedure is carried out once basic framework is achieved and the more that can be removed, the sooner it will flower. Over shrubs and large trees this

is not normally possible and the climber must mature to achieve full flowering.

Training Use the long tendrils produced in current season to form a frame-work of shoots, ideally with one to two upright shoots with side branches encouraged to grow 18 in (45 cm) apart. It is not a good policy to attempt to retain all of the season's growth. Wires will be required on walls and fences to achieve the framework system.

Propagation and nursery production Can be grown from seed but resulting plants may vary greatly in their final flowering performance, flowers being between a light grey to a good blue and racemes from 3–9 in (7.5–23 cm) long. Best results are obtained from plants grafted on to rootstocks of *W. sinensis* and the graft taken from a known, good source. Can be planted bare-rooted from mid autumn to mid spring or container grown any time except mid summer, with early summer for preference. Best planting height 2–6 ft (60 cm–1.8 m). Readily available from garden centres and nurseries.

Problems Its requirement for a sunny wall and the area that it covers are often underestimated. Because of its propagation method, can be expensive.

Similar forms of interest *W. s.* 'Alba' A white-flowering variety. *W. s.* 'Plena' Rare double blue flowering variety. *W. s.* 'Prematura' Flowers earlier in its life than its parent. Mauve blooms. *W. s.* 'Prematura Alba' An earlier, white-flowering variety. *W. s.* 'Variegata' Golden variegated foliage, violet blue flowers. Poor grower.

Average height and spread
Five years
18 × 18 ft (5.5 × 5.5 m)
Ten years
36 × 36 ft (11 × 11 m)
Twenty years
50 × 50 ft+ (15 × 15 m+)
Will continue to grow for up to 50 years. Protrudes up 4 ft (1.2 m) from support.

WISTERIA SINENSIS (Modern Hybrids)

HYBRID CHINESE WISTERIA

Leguminosae　　　　*Woody Climber*
Deciduous

A range of varieties with blooms of differing colours and all reliable for their flowering performance.

Origin Of nursery and garden origin.

Use As fast-growing climbers for walls, fences, pergolas, buildings and through trees and large shrubs. Can be trained as a small weeping standard.

Description *Flower* Racemes of pea-like flowers, 6–9 in (15–23 cm) long, 3–4 in (8–10 cm) wide are produced in profusion from mid to late spring. Colour will depend on variety, ranging through pink, white, purple and blue with some bi-colours. *Foliage* Light green pinnate leaves up to 12–18 in (30–45 cm) long, with seven to nine leaflets. Each leaflet 3 in (7.5 cm) long by ½ in (1 cm) wide. Good yellow autumn colour. *Stem* Twisting, smooth light grey/green when young, ageing to yellow/brown and finally dark grey/brown. Fast growing. *Fruit* In very hot summers may produce inedible, green bean pods but not reliable.

Hardiness Tolerates a minimum winter temperature of 14°F (−10°C). Stems may be killed by very cold wind chill conditions but rejuvenation normally occurs the following spring.

Soil requirements Does well on all soil types but requires root run of at least 16 ft (4.9 m). On very alkaline soils may show signs of chlorosis in the form of a yellowing of the leaves in mid summer.

Sun/Shade aspect Plant in a sheltered aspect in full sun to very light shade otherwise it will not flower.

Pruning Once the framework of climber is

Wisteria sinensis 'Pink Ice' in flower

established, cut back all current season's wood in mid to late autumn to within two buds of point of origin.

Training Use the long tendrils with, ideally, one or two major upright shoots and side branches encouraged to grow 18 in (45 cm) apart. Wires will be required on walls and fences to support the trained growth. Over shrubs and large trees training is not normally possible and the climber must mature to achieve full flowering.

Propagation and nursery production Will not come true from seed, must always be grafted. Always purchase container-grown, may have to be sought from specialist nurseries. Best planting height 2–6 ft (60 cm–1.8 m).

Problems May be in limited supply. Can take up to five to eight years to come into full flowering. May be expensive due to its method of propagation.

Forms of interest *W. s.* 'Black Dragon' Double, dark purple flower racemes up to 30 in (76 cm) long. *W. s.* 'Caerulea' White flowers. *W. s.* 'Caroline' Deep blue, scented flowers, free-flowering. *W. s.* 'Domino' (syn. *W. s.* 'Issai Fuji') Lilac blue flower racemes 20 in (50 cm) long well before the foliage. *W. s. formosa* 'Issai' Lilac blue flowers from an early age. *W. s.* 'Peaches and Cream' (syn. *W. s.* 'Kuchibeni') Rose pink in bud opening to off-white flowers in racemes 40 in (1 m) long. *W. s.* 'Pink Ice' (syn. *W. s.* 'Hond Beni') Rosy-pink flower racemes up to 40 in (1 m) long. *W. s.* 'Purple Patches' (syn. *W. s.* 'Murasaki Naga Fuji') Racemes of violet-purple flowers 30 in (76 cm) long. *W. s.* 'Snow Showers' (*W. s.* 'Shiro Naga Fuji') Racemes up to 50 in (1.3 m) long of pure white flowers.

Average height and spread
Five years
18 × 18 ft (5.5 × 5.5 m)
Ten years
36 × 36 ft (11.5 × 11.5 m)
Twenty years
50 × 50 ft+ (15 × 15 m+)
Will continue to grow for 50 years. Protrudes up to 4 ft (1.2 m) from support.

XANTHOCERAS SORBIFOLIUM

YELLOWHORN

Sapindaceae　　　　*Wall Shrub*
Deciduous

An interesting, rare, spring flowering shrub with attractive foliage, adapting well for planting against a tall wall or fence.

Origin From northern China.

Use As a tall, upright, trained wall specimen.

Description *Flower* White flowers with carmine eyes, over 1 in (2.5 cm) wide, presented in upright panicles 4 in (10 cm) wide and 5 in (12 cm) long on previous year's wood in late spring. *Foliage* Leaves pinnate, consisting of nine to 17 lanceolate, sharply toothed leaflets 8–10 in (20–25 cm) long, giving some yellow autumn colour. *Stem* Upright, can be trained flat against a wall to good effect. Grey/green. *Fruit* Shaped like a child's top, three-valved, walnut-like seed pods, containing large numbers of chestnut-like seeds.

Hardiness Tolerates a minimum winter temperature of 14°F (−10°C).

Soil requirements Tolerates most soils, including alkaline.

Xanthoceras sorbifolium in flower

Sun/Shade aspect Requires some protection in full sun to light shade.

Pruning None required except for training.

Training Tie to wires or individual anchor points to form an upright, rather than fan-trained, shape.

Propagation and nursery production From seed. Purchase container grown; very hard to find, must be sought from specialist nurseries. Best planting height 1–5 ft (30 cm–1.5 m).

Problems Slightly slow to develop and plants are usually small when purchased.

Average height and spread
Five years
5 × 7 ft (1.5 × 2.1 m)
Ten years
7 × 9 ft (2.1 × 2.7 m)
Twenty years
9 × 15 ft (2.7 × 4.6 m)
Protrudes up to 2 ft (60 cm) from support.

PLANTING CLIMBERS AND WALL SHRUBS

Successful establishment of a climber or wall shrub begins with the important stage of preparing a correctly sized planting hole. The planting process may seem somewhat laborious, but it is worth while providing the best conditions in which the plant can grow and thrive rather than merely survive. A climber or wall shrub may be a principal focal point of the garden and can give years of pleasure, so good preparation is rewarded.

Preparing the planting hole
Any perennial weed roots, such as couch grass, dock or thistles must be cleared from the site, otherwise they become almost impossible to remove once planting is established. If the planting area is grass-covered, turves should be removed before preparation of the planting hole. If the turves are free from perennial weeds they may be buried upside down at least 9 in (23 cm) deep in the planting hole and will conserve moisture.

The planting of climbers and wall shrubs raises a number of problems, the most important of which is that the plants will dry out if in close proximity to walls and fences. It is no less vital than with any other plant to prepare the soil thoroughly to an adequate depth to allow for good plant growth and to provide a hole of a diameter not less than 3 ft (91 cm).

It is often the case when planting climbers and wall shrubs that the planting hole is in close proximity to a path or other obstruction, so a diameter of 3 ft (91 cm) may not always be practicable. In such cases prepare the hole to the same overall volume but in a different shape – for example, an oblong of 4 × 2 ft (1.2 m × 60 cm). Occasionally even this is not possible and if the open surface area cannot be achieved then excavation under the surrounding obstruction must be considered.

Remove the top 9 in (23 cm) of topsoil and fork over the lower 9 in (23 cm). Add a good quantity of organic material to the latter and

at least 25 per cent by volume into the former. Organic material holds moisture and plant foods and allows for rapid root growth and, therefore, fast establishment of the climber or wall shrub.

Planting container grown climbers and wall shrubs
A container grown climber or wall shrub should be well watered before it is planted, ideally at least one hour beforehand.

Place the plant, still in its container, in the planting hole and adjust the depth so the rim of the container is just below the surrounding soil level. If the plant is in a rigid or flexible plastic container you can now remove this, taking care not to disturb the soil ball around the roots of the plant. Peat composition or treated paper pots can be left in place as the material is decomposable, but if the surrounding soil is dry or you are planting in mid summer it is best to remove them.

Never lift the plant by its stem, as this can damage the roots. Handle the whole rootball carefully and, once the container has been removed, take care that small exposed roots do not dry out. Replace the prepared topsoil around the rootball of the plant to the level of the soil around the planting hole. Tread the soil gently all around the plant to compress it evenly. Unless the soil is very wet, pour a bucket of water into the depressed area. Fill the area with more prepared topsoil, bringing the level up to just above that of the surrounding soil. Any surplus topsoil should be used elsewhere in the garden, not heaped around the newly planted climber or shrub.

Planting climbers to ramble through trees
Climbers that are intended to ramble through trees should have holes prepared as for those planted against walls. Dig the planting hole on the outer edges of the tree canopy and lead a string, chain or wire from ground level to a branch, taking care not to damage the latter. A black flexible tree strap around the branch will protect it. The climber can then be tied to the wire and left to climb up into the tree branches. This process is slow and it may often be several years before the full effect is achieved. It should also be borne in mind that the climber may eventually damage the tree.

Planting bare-rooted climbers and shrubs
The basic method is the same for bare-rooted

or root-balled (balled-and-burlapped) plants as for container grown, but it is even more important that the roots should not be allowed to dry out. When returning the top-soil to the hole, take care to work it well in around the roots of the plant, leaving no air pockets in the soil.

Planting position
Plant the climber or wall shrub at least 15–18 in (38–45 cm) away from its support, laid back towards it, using either the cane it was supplied with or providing one if not. Planting this distance away from the wall will ensure that the plant always has an adequate moisture supply.

Growing climbers in pots and tubs
As a general rule it is not advisable to attempt to grow climbers and wall shrubs in containers because the lack of soil will render the plant unable to make growth. Even with a large container filled with a good potting compost and given regular feeding, only 20–30 per cent of the potential growth of any climber or wall shrub will be achieved and this growth will always be at risk from drying out in summer thus causing damage, often of lasting effect.

Watering
The danger period for loss of any plant is in the spring and summer following planting. In dry conditions, water the climber or wall shrub well at least three times a week. Stems and foliage benefit from an all-over fine spray of water at the same time; if new leaves and wood become dehydrated the plant may die.

Feeding
If the climber or wall shrub is planted in the autumn apply one gloved handful of bone-meal per sq. yd (sq. m). If planting is carried out in spring or early summer a general fertilizer should be applied as recommended in the instructions. A general purpose liquid fertilizer can be applied annually in mid summer.

Planting times – Europe
Bare-rooted or root-balled climbers and wall shrubs can be planted at any time from late autumn to early spring, except in the harshest of winter conditions. Do not plant when the ground is frozen or waterlogged. Container grown climbers and wall shrubs can be planted at any time of year but with autumn and spring for preference, unless weather conditions are extreme. Do not plant when the ground is frozen, dried hard, or waterlogged.

Planting times – USA
The best time to plant bare-rooted climbers and wall shrubs is in late winter or early spring, just before bud-break. Bare-rooted plants lose most of their root surface – and water-absorbing capacity – during transplanting. New roots will not develop until spring, so if you plant in fall, there is the risk that buds and twigs will dry out over winter.

Fall is the best time to plant balled-and-burlapped and container grown climbers and wall shrubs, because it gives them a long season of cool air and warm soil for strong root growth. Roots put on most of their year's growth after leaf-fall. Climbers and wall shrubs planted as early as possible after their leaves have dropped will be able to establish a root system before the soil temperature drops, and will therefore require less watering in the following season.

Planting times – Australia and New Zealand
Bare-rooted or root-balled climbers or wall shrubs can be planted at any time from late autumn to early spring, unless the ground is frozen hard or waterlogged.

Container grown climbers and wall shrubs can be planted at almost any time of year unless weather conditions are extreme. Do not plant when the ground is frozen, dried hard or waterlogged. It is advisable to avoid planting in mid summer when conditions are extremely hot and dry.

PLANTING CLIMBING PLANTS

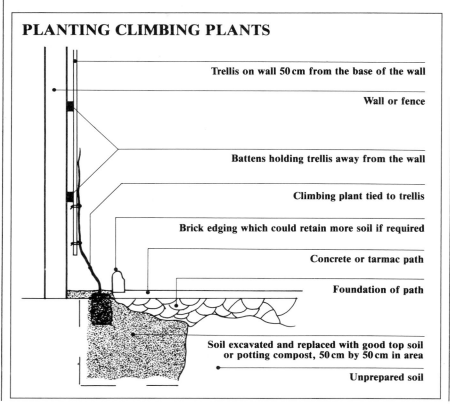

Trellis on wall 50 cm from the base of the wall

Wall or fence

Battens holding trellis away from the wall

Climbing plant tied to trellis

Brick edging which could retain more soil if required

Concrete or tarmac path

Foundation of path

Soil excavated and replaced with good top soil or potting compost, 50 cm by 50 cm in area

Unprepared soil

SUPPORTS FOR CLIMBERS AND WALL SHRUBS

Once you have chosen the climber or wall shrub you wish to plant you must consider what kind of support it will need to assist it in covering the required area.

The support can take a number of different forms but no matter what kind you use you must bear in mind the following points:
1 The support must be able to accommodate the weight of the fully developed plant – a weight which may be considerable, especially when the plant is subjected to rain, snow and wind.
2 The support should not be unsightly, especially in the years while the plant is attaining its full coverage.
3 A clear air space of at least 2 in (5 cm) must be left between the support and the fence or wall. This allows free passage of air, keeping attacks of fungus disease such as mildew to a minimum.

Individual anchor points
Many climbing plants and wall shrubs and trees in particular can be adequately supported by individual anchor points consisting of some type of DIY masonry nail. Adjustable tree straps, secured to the wall or fence by masonry nails, are worth considering, particularly for heavier, freestanding plants.

Vine eyes and wires
Vine eyes come in two forms, normally 4–6 in (10–15 cm) long. The first has a thread, so that it may be screwed into a rawlplug inserted into a pre-drilled hole in the mortar. The other kind is wedge-shaped, and again a pre-drilled hole is made in the mortar course and

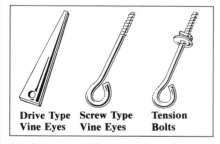

Drive Type Vine Eyes   Screw Type Vine Eyes   Tension Bolts

the vine eye carefully driven in, making sure that it is horizontal, with the holes facing latitudinally along the wall. On wooden fences, screw-thread vine eyes can be simply screwed into wooden support posts.

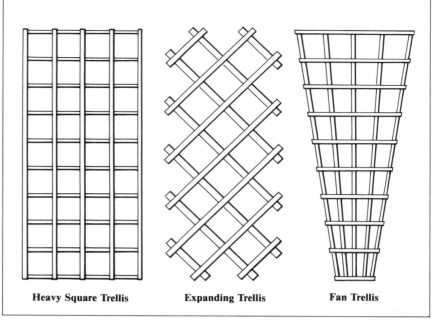

Heavy Square Trellis   Expanding Trellis   Fan Trellis

The spacing of vine eyes is important. Place them 6 ft (1.8 m) apart in width and at 18 in (45 cm) intervals up the wall from ground level to the total area required for covering. Stretch a strong wire, either galvanized or plastic coated, between the vine eyes. On a long stretch of wall a system of tension bolts may be necessary to form a secure climbing framework.

Plant the climber or shrub at the base of the support, with a 3–5 ft (91 cm–1.5 m) cane inserted near the base of the plant and tied to the first one or two wires. Encourage the plant to climb this cane until it reaches the wires, where it will probably grow up of its own accord, although it may require some help to climb to the next wire, simply by tying in once it is long enough.

This form of support is one of the simplest and, if done correctly and neatly, can be one of the tidiest. It has an additional advantage in that if the wall has to be remortared or the fence painted or creosoted, the wire can simply be cut and detached and the plant laid down away from the wall. New wires can then be supplied, the old wires cut out and the plant reinstated in its former climbing position.

Plastic or wire netting
Galvanized or plastic covered wire netting, with a minimum of 1 in (2.5 cm) wide mesh, can be secured to the face of the wall, either

by vine eyes or by screwing 2 in (5 cm) thick battens to the wall and then attaching the netting to them. Whichever method is used the fixing must be secure as it will take the full weight of the plant. Vine eyes and 2 in (5 cm) battens both allow air space between the plant and the wall. Extra netting can be added as required, although it is a good precaution to buy enough in the first instance to cover the entire surface and then store the surplus until it is needed as it is often difficult to find identical netting in subsequent years. Netting has the advantage of reducing the attention given to training as the plants find their own way between the relatively small squares in the wire mesh.

Extruded plastic netting is available in green, white and brown, providing a good match for the wall or fence. It is often sold in convenient lengths designed to accommodate average plant growth.

Timber trellis
A number of timber trellises are available with either a square or diamond pattern. Some are rigid, others work on a concertina basis, and they are supplied either in a natural wood colour or painted white. The trellis is attached to the wall on a 2 in (5 cm) thick support batten, which again allows for the free passage of air behind and supports the weight of the plant.

This is one of the most attractive forms of support but it has two disadvantages: the trellis will only last for 10–15 years and maintenance of the wall and support is more problematical.

Wires and posts in open garden
Fruit trees, climbers and wall shrubs (particularly roses) can make very good open garden divisions and screens. To support these, drive posts securely into the ground, leaving a height of 5–8 ft (1.5–2.4 m). The posts should not be more than 8 ft (2.4 m) apart and the end posts will require bracing to allow wires to be stretched tightly between them. Attach the wires to the posts by wire staples, with the first wire 18 in (45 cm) above the ground and the remaining wires every 18 in (45 cm) thereafter.

Securing climbing plants to supports
It is best to avoid all forms of wire, plastic (except adjustable types) or combinations of wire and paper; any tie that does not naturally decompose within 18 months is not advisable as severe restriction is caused to stems and branches and in many cases damage is terminal. Soft string or raffia is the best material to use.

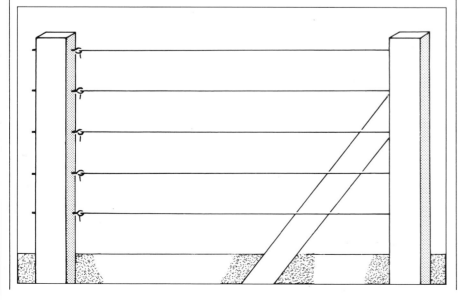

PRACTICAL GLOSSARY

Acid The term applied to soils with a pH of 6.5 or below, usually containing no free lime.

Alkaline The term applied to soils with a pH of 7.4 or above, commonly but not exclusively associated with chalk or limestone soils.

Annual climber A plant normally grown from seed under protection in the spring, producing its display in summer and autumn then dying completely in winter. Seeds are not viable when overwintered in the soil and have to be harvested, dried and stored until the following spring.

Annual/perennial climber There are a few plants that can be treated as either annual or perennial. Normally the local climate will dictate the best growth pattern to adopt.

Aphids The general term for a number of small sap-sucking insects which cause damage to leaves, stems and new plant tissues. See **Blackfly, Greenfly.**

Balled-and-burlapped The description of a plant which has been dug from the soil on which it was grown with a ball of soil surrounding the roots, kept intact by a wrapping of coarse cloth or net. This root ball should not be disturbed. Also called root-balled.

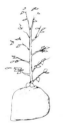

Bare-rooted The description of a plant which has been dug from the ground and is sold without soil around its roots; alternatively the roots may be contained in a polythene bag with a small amount of peat.

Blackfly A small suckering insect which attacks the young parts of plants, damaging the tissue.

Bottom heat Heat applied to rooting compost and rooting mediums to encourage the production of roots on cuttings.

Brushwood Small pieces of branching shoots used as support for certain climbers.

Budding A propagation method in which a single bud from a selected tree or shrub is grafted on to a rooted understock to produce a new specimen with the characteristcs of the selected parent.

Canker An airborne fungus disease which enters damaged stem tissues and gradually surrounds the stem. If left untreated it will cut off the growth system of the plant with fatal results.

Chlorosis Yellowing of the leaves of a plant caused by lack of iron and nitrogen, seen particularly in plants grown on alkaline soils such as chalk or limestone which lock up these necessary elements.

Collar rot Damage to bark and underlying growth tissue at the base of a tree or shrub, caused by excessive build-up of moisture in the affected area. This problem is commonly associated with heavy clay soils; good soil preparation and staking of the plant help to prevent it.

Conifer A cone-bearing tree which adapts well to fan-training and is normally hardy under all conditions.

Container grown The description of a plant grown in, or potted on into, a container of rigid or flexible plastic, treated paper, peat composition or earthenware.

Containerized The description of a plant permanently grown in a container, for example as a patio or conservatory plant.

Coral spot A fungus disease which first attacks dead wood and then spreads into healthy growth. It is visible as small coral pink spots.

Cordon Many wall shrubs, in particular fruiting forms, are trained as a single shoot and have all side growths reduced in late winter/early spring to within 2 in (5 cm) of the main shoot to encourage flowering. They are often planted at an angle of 35° for the same reason.

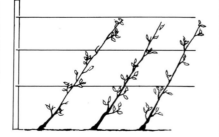

Cross pollination (As in fruit) The requirement of certain groups of fruiting plants to have pollen taken from one plant to another to achieve fertilization.

Deciduous (of a tree or shrub) Losing leaves seasonally, i.e. at the end of the growing season, to regenerate new foliage at the start of the following season.

Die-back The condition of a plant in which twigs, stems and sometimes whole branches dry out or become very brittle and turn dark brown or black. All damaged shoots must be cut back to healthy tissue and cuts of any size treated with pruning compound. Die-back usually occurs due to winter frost, summer drought, or mechanical root damage.

Division A method of propagating shrubs by digging up the root ball and dividing the clump at the roots to replant the section separately.

Double-digging Preparing ground for planting by digging out the soil to the depth of the spade then turning over the same depth within the planting area before returning the topsoil.

Ericaceous The description of plants belonging to the family Ericaceae which typically require acid soil conditions for successful growth.

Espalier See **Horizontal-trained.**

Evergreen (of a climber or wall shrub) Retaining foliage throughout the year, except for a small proportion which is unobtrusively shed.

Fan-training A method of training a tree, wall shrub or climber against a wall so the branches radiate from the base or trunk, forming a fan shape. Some form of support is required to train the growth.

Fire blight A fungus disease which becomes visible when a plant or section of a plant appears as if burned. It cannot be controlled and the plant must be destroyed. It is a notifiable disease and its occurrence should be reported to the relevant government agency.

Fruiting canes Annually produced canes which produce edible fruit and benefit from training as wall specimens.

Fruiting shrubs Shrubs (bushes) that produce edible fruit and adapt to training as wall shrubs.

Fruiting vines Vines which bear fruit and will train against walls, fences or other similar constructions, where they benefit from the protection or support given.

Garden or nursery origin Many plants originate in the wild but others are hybridized by nurserymen and gardeners and then grown on as individual varieties in their own right.

Gazebo A construction made out of metal, wood or stone in the shape of a building but with open lattice-work to the sky, over which various climbing plants can be grown.

Glabrous (of a leaf or stem) Smooth and hairless.

Glaucous (of a leaf or stem) Covered with a blue/white or blue/grey bloom.

Grafting A propagation method in which a section of wood from a selected plant is grafted on to a rooted understock and subsequently develops into a new plant with the characteristics of the selected parent.

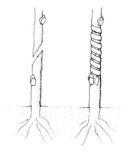

Greenfly A small sucking insect which attacks young parts of a plant, damaging the tissues.

Ground cover A closely spaced planting of low shrubs which spread to cover a particular area. Apart from creating a good display, this assists in soil retention and keeps down weeds.

Hardwood cutting A section of stem taken from hard wood of the previous season's growth, placed in soil to root and propagate a new plant.

Hardy The description of a tree or shrub able to withstand winter frost.

Heel A small fragment of previous season's wood left at the end of a cutting for propagation purposes.

Horizontal-trained (espalier) Many wall-trained trees, shrubs and climbers are trained into a horizontal tiered shape to show off their beauty to the full and also to aid ripening of fruit. Support is required to maintain this shaping.

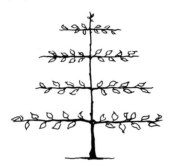

Hybrid A plant derived from a cross between two species to combine or improve upon the characteristics of the parent plants.

Internodal cutting A section of stem taken between leaf joints (nodes) for propagation.

Layering A method of propagating a new shrub from existing stock by making a small cut below a bud on one side of a healthy young shoot and bending the shoot downwards to bury the cut section in the soil. After one year the buried bud has produced roots and new shoots and can be detached from the parent plant.

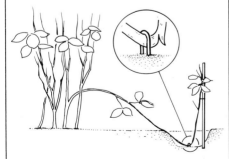

Leaf scorch Discoloration and shrivelling of foliage due to strong wind, excessive sun or severe frost.

Mildew An airborne fungus disease which produced a white, downy coating over leaves, stems and fruits. It is encouraged by high humidity and warmth and commonly appears in late summer or early autumn.

Mulch A dressing applied to the soil surface around a tree or shrub, consisting of decayed leaves, grass cuttings, manure, etc. which retains moisture in the soil, provides natural foods for the plant and keeps down weeds.

New wood A stem, branch or twig grown in the current growing season.

Old wood A stem, branch or twig grown in the previous year's growing season or earlier.

Organic material Rotted and decomposed organic vegetable material such as garden compost and farmyard manure which, when added to garden soil, forms moisture and nutrient-holding material. Also opens and lightens clay, heavy or difficult soil.

Peat Organic matter in a condition of partial decay, formed naturally in waterlogged areas and used to improve soil texture and supply plant nutrients.

Perennial climber A hardy plant normally dying to ground level during the winter and rejuvenating the following spring. May, under certain circumstances in mild areas, produce a permanent woody structure but this can often be to the detriment of future foliage and flower production.

Pergola A timber, metal or stone construction, built in such a way as to make an open or lattice-type roof over which plants can grow. Sometimes used to form tunnels and semi-enclosed walkways.

pH The measurement of acidity and alkalinity in the soil which in practical terms can be ascertained using a soil-testing kit. The numeric scale used defines soils with pH of 6.5 or under as acid, 6.6–7.3 neutral, 7.4 or over alkaline. A general rule is that chalk or limestone soils tend to be alkaline while lime-free soils tend to be acid, but the determining factor is not the actual soil composition but the origin of the water supply underlying the soil.

Pollinator A tree or shrub planted for the purpose of supplying pollen to another plant to help in formation of fruit.

Rejuvenate (of a tree or shrub) To generate new growth after severe pruning, damage or die-back.

Rich soil A soil high in organic material such as garden compost, leaf-mould or well-rotted farmyard manure, used to encourage root growth and subsequent stem and foliage production.

Root-balled See balled-and-burlapped.

Root cutting A method of propagation in which a section of fleshy root is cut from a plant and set in a tray or pot filled with a mixture of peat and sand. New roots and shoots are formed from the root section.

Root rot A fungus disease which attacks plants with fibrous root systems, visible when the plant's leaves wilt for no apparent reason. The plant eventually dies. Good soil preparation lessens the likelihood of this occurring.

Rust An airborne fungus producing a red, rust-like coating on the plant.

Scab An airborne fungus disease which produces grey/brown lesions on leaves and fruit, particularly seen in *Malus* varieties.

Scale A small leaf or bract; also a small flat growth on the surface of a flower, leaf or fruit.

Semi-evergreen (of a tree or shrub) Normally evergreen, but likely to shed some or all leaves in unusually cold conditions to which the plant is not acclimatized.

Semi-ripe cutting A section of stem taken from one-year-old wood in early or mid summer, placed in soil to root and propagate a new plant.

Shrub A woody plant with a growth pattern of stems branching from or near to the base rather than having a distinct single main stem or trunk.

Silver-leaf fungus A fungus disease apparent as a silver sheen on leaves in late spring or early summer, generally persisting until mid summer of the following year, when the foliage appears burned and drops, at which stage there is also some stem damage. There is no effective treatment and the tree should be destroyed.

Single planting, solo planting Planting of an individual climber or wall shrub in an area which will accommodate its full ultimate size and allow a distinctive display of its overall shape and special features.

Softwood cutting A section of soft stem taken from current season's growth in spring, placed in soil to root and propagate a new plant.

Specimen plant A plant grown singly for display in an area able to accommodate its full growth potential.

Sport A shoot occurring by chance that differs in some characteristic from the parent plant; propagated by cuttings, grafting etc. to maintain the distinctive characteristics.

Stool A permanent woody base from which annual growth is remade each year, formed by removing all current season's growth in spring back to within 2–3 in (5–7.5 cm) of its origin.

Subsoil The layer of soil directly below the uppermost layer (topsoil), generally having a poor composition and containing fewer nutrients.

Sucker New growth on a plant generally arising from an underground root, which may appear some distance from the parent. In some plants this is a natural method of spreading new growth, but suckers from understock of grafted plants are usually undesirable and should be ripped out to remove all dormant buds in the new growth.

Suckering The production of suckers.

Sun scorch Damage to leaves in the form of browning, mottling and shrivelling, caused by exposure to strong sunlight.

Tender greenhouse climber A climber maintaining a woody structure but unable to tolerate any winter frost and requiring a protected growing environment such as a greenhouse or conservatory except in very mild areas.

Tender tree A tree which is not fully hardy but under some conditions may be grown against walls and fences where it is afforded extra protection.

Tender wall shrub A shrub not normally considered fully hardy but adapting well to fan-training on walls and fences or growing freestanding in front of them, where it gains added protection. Also of use grown under the extra protection of greenhouses and conservatories.

Tender woody climber A climber not fully hardy under most winter conditions but benefiting from the protection of a wall, fence, greenhouse or conservatory and normally maintaining a woody structure.

Topsoil The uppermost layer of soil having a workable texture and containing a high proportion of plant nutrients.

Tree A woody plant typically producing a single stem (trunk) crowned by branches.

Understock A selected or specially grown young plant used as the rooted base for creating new plants by the propagation techniques of budding and grafting. The physical characteristics of the new plant are gained from the grafted material, not the understock, but this may dictate overall size and growth rate.

Vegetative propagation Methods of raising new plants from existing specimens, e.g. by budding, cuttings, division or grafting rather than from seed. These methods ensure that the new stock is identical to the parent.

Vine eyes Wedge-shaped metal supports which carry wires for training plants (see also p.169)

Wall shrub A hardy shrub which adapts well to training on walls or fences, normally in a fan-trained shape. Can also be planted untrained and will benefit from the protection of the wall or fence.

Weeping standard Some climbing plants will allow themselves to be trained with one or two single upright stems from which top growth emerges and forms a weeping habit. These plants are not normally sold in this form and have to be trained in the garden.

Wind scorch Damage to leaves caused by wind when water vapour is too rapidly lost from the leaves.

Woody climber Normally a hardy climber maintaining a rigid or semi-rigid structure of growth throughout the year. Can be either evergreen or deciduous depending on species or form.

Whitefly A small sap-sucking insect which hides on the undersides of leaves and causes leaf damage.

BOTANICAL GLOSSARY

Alternate (of leaves) Growing one above the other on a stem from separate leaf nodes; not opposite.

Anther The pollen-bearing part of the male organ of a flower.

Axil The angle between a stem and leaf stalk, or between two stems or branches.

Berry A succulent, normally several-seeded fruit which does not split or burst open.

Bipinnate (of leaves) Divided into segments which are themselves divided; doubly pinnate.

Bisexual (of a flower) Incorporating both male and female organs.

Bloom A fine, powder-like deposit, as on the surface of a fruit.

Bract A modified leaf at the base of a flower or flower cluster, sometimes very colourful and more prominent than the flowers.

Bud The early stage of a new shoot or flower. The term refers not only to an obvious growth bud but also to an incipient swelling.

Calyx The circlet or whorl of sepals which encloses the petals of a flower before it opens.

Capsule A dry seed pod of several cells.

Catkin A flower spike or spike-like raceme consisting of very small stemless flowers covered with scale-like bracts. The term is also applied to a similar arrangement of tiny fruits.

Clusters Flowers carried in moderately condensed groups.

Compound (of a leaf) Divided into several distinct parts (leaflets).

Corymb A flat-topped or domed flowerhead in which the flower stems grow straight up from the main stem and the outer flowers are first to open.

Cyme A flat-topped or domed flowerhead in which the flower stems arch outwards and the inner flowers are first to open.

Dioecious (of a plant species) Bearing either male or female flowers on a particular plant. See also **Monoecious.**

Dissected (of a leaf) Deeply cut into a number of narrow segments.

Double (of a flower) Having more than the usual number of petals, sometimes having petals in place of style and stamens.

Downy Lightly coated with hairs.

Elliptic (of a leaf) Narrowing at both ends, with the widest point at or near the middle of the leaf.

Embryo A rudimentary plant.

Fastigiate (of a tree or shrub) Having a growth habit in which branches and stems are dense and erect.

Fibrous (of roots) Thin but densely growing.

Floret A single, small flower in a flowerhead or clustered inflorescence.

Fruit buds Buds laid down in previous seasons as in apples, pears etc.

Hermaphrodite A bisexual flower, incorporating both male and female organs.

Inflorescence The flower-bearing part of a plant. See **Corymb, Cyme, Panicle, Raceme, Spike, Umbel.**

Lacerated (of a leaf) Irregularly cut at the margins.

Laciniate (of a leaf) Fringed, i.e. with the margin cut into narrow, pointed lobes.

Lanceolate (of a leaf) Spear-shaped, swelling above the base and tapering to a point.

Leaflet An individual section of a compound leaf.

Linear (of a leaf) Long and narrow, with almost parallel margins tapering briefly at the tip.

Lobe A protruding part of a leaf, distinct but not separated from the other segments.

Midrib The vein or rib along the centre of a leaf.

Monoecious (of a plant species) Bearing both male and female flowers on the same individual plant.

Monotypic (of a plant genus) Having only one species.

Node The point on a stem where the leaf is attached; the leaf joint.

Nut A hard, one-seeded fruit which does not split or open.

Oblong (of a leaf) Longer than it is wide, with long edges almost parallel.

Obovate (of a leaf) Broadening towards the tip; the reverse of ovate.

Opposite (of leaves) Borne from the same node and opposite each other on a stem.

Orbicular (of a leaf or petal) Disc-shaped, almost circular.

Ovate (of a leaf) Broadening from the base and tapering towards the tip.

Palmate (of a leaf) Lobed or divided, resembling fingers on a hand. A palmate leaf is usually five- or seven-lobed.

Panicle A flower spike or raceme with several small branches, themselves also branching.

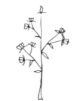

Pea-flower A flower having the typical shape of a sweet-pea blossom.

Pendulous Hanging or weeping.

Perennials (Herbaceous) Plants with root systems that become dormant or semi-dormant in winter with all top growth dying to ground level in winter and being regenerated in the following spring.

Petal A modified leaf, usually brightly coloured, which forms part of a flower.

Petiole A leaf stalk.

Pinnate (of leaves) Divided and composed of leaflets arranged on either side of a central stalk.

Propagation The act of increasing a particular plant under controlled conditions by softwood cutting, grafting etc.

Prostrate (of a stem or growth habit) Lying along the ground.

Raceme An elongated flowerhead composed of stalked flowers on a central stem.

Recurved Curving down or back.

Rhomboidal Diamond-shaped.

Self-clinging A plant which supports itself by stem, root or sucker pads, or by leaf tendrils or twining habit, and does not normally require further assistance.

Semi-double (of a flower) More than one layer of petals but not completely double.

Sepal Green shields that protect the petals before they open and in some cases provide added interest to the flower. In some plants, for example clematis, they replace the petals.

Serrated (of a leaf) Having saw-toothed edges, with the teeth pointing towards the leaf tip.

Single (of a flower) Having only one ring or layer of petals.

Spike An elongated flowerhead composed of stalkless flowers.

Stamen The male organ of a flower, consisting of a pollen-bearing anther supported by a filament.

Stigma The female organ of a flower; the part that receives pollen for reproduction.

Stolon A shoot running from a plant at or below ground level which gives rise to a new plant at its tip.

Style Part of the female organ of a flower, a stalk linking the stigma to the reproductive organ.

Tendril A fine modified stem or leaf which twines to provide support for a plant.

Trifoliate (of a leaf) Having three separate leaflets.

Twining (as in stems) Twisting in an anti-clockwise or clockwise motion around suitable supports, encouraging semi or full self-support.

Umbel A usually flat-topped flowerhead in which stalked flowers arise from a common point on the main flower stem.

Universal pollinator A variety of fruit tree that is able to pollinate itself and a wide range of other varieties. Some ornamental trees can also pollinate dessert or culinary fruits, e.g. *Malus* 'Golden Hornet', which is a universal pollinator for most apples.

Vine eyes A name given to the buds of *Vitis vinifera* (vine).

× Preceding a species or variety, indicates that this is a botanical hybrid cross.

CHOOSING THE RIGHT WALL SHRUB OR CLIMBER

There is a wide range of climbers and wall shrubs now available from garden centres and nurseries. The following selections have been made to guide the reader to the plants suitable for a particular purpose.

Once the initial selection has been made, the reader should refer to the various needs of the chosen plant, taking into account flowering time, hardiness, area covered in height, spread and forward protrusion, soil conditions and any particular maintenance that is required for its well-being. Only when all these criteria are fulfilled should the final selection be made.

FASTEST COVERING CLIMBERS AND WALL SHRUBS

ACACIA (Hardy Forms)

ACER *negundo*

ACTINIDIA *arguta*
    chinensis

AMPELOPSIS *brevipedunculata*

ARISTOLOCHIA *macrophylla*

AZARA *dentata*

BUDDLEIA *alternifolia*
    (Tender Forms)

CAMPSIS *grandiflora*
    radicans

CATALPA *bignonioides*

CEANOTHUS (Evergreen Forms)
    (Deciduous Forms)

CELASTRUS *orbiculatus*

CLEMATIS *alpina*
    armandii
    (Double and Semi-Double)
    flammula
    × *jouiniana praecox*
    (Large-flowered Hybrids)
    montana
    orientalis
    vitalba

Clematis 'Mrs Cholmondeley' in flower

174

CORYNABUTILON *vitifolium*

COTONEASTER × *hybridus pendulus*
    (Medium Height, Spreading Evergreen and Semi-Evergreen Forms for Walls)
    (Tall Deciduous Forms)
    (Tall Evergreen Forms)

CRATAEGUS (Autumn Foliage Forms)
    oxyacantha

CYDONIA *oblonga*

CYTISUS *battandieri*

ECCREMOCARPUS *scaber*

ELAEAGNUS × *ebbingei*

ESCALLONIA

EUCALYPTUS

× FATSHEDERA *lizei*

FATSIA *japonica*

FICUS *carica*

Ficus carica 'Brown Turkey' in fruit

FREMONTODENDRON *californica*

HEDERA *canariensis*
    colchica

HUMULUS *lupulus* 'Aureus'

JASMINUM *officinale*

KOLKWITZIA *amabilis*

LATHYRUS *latifolius*
    odoratus

LAVATERA *olbia*

LIGUSTRUM *ovalifolium*

LONICERA × *americana*
    caprifolium
    etrusca
    japonica 'Halliana'
    japonica henryii
    japonica repens
    periclymenum (Hybrids)
    tragophylla

MAGNOLIA *grandiflora*
    (Large-Growing, Star-Flowered Forms)
    × *soulangiana*
    (Summer Flowering Forms)

MAHONIA × 'Charity'

MALUS (Fruiting Forms)
    (Green-leaved Flowering Forms)
    (Purple-leaved Forms)

Passiflora caerulea 'Constance Elliott' in flower

PARTHENOCISSUS *henryana*
    quinquefolia
    tricuspidata 'Veitchii'

PASSIFLORA *caerulea*

PHASEOLUS *coccineus*

PHILADELPHUS (Tall-growing Forms)

PIPTANTHUS *laburnifolius*

PLUMBAGO *capensis*

POLYGONUM *baldschuanicum*

PYRACANTHA

PYRUS

ROBINIA (Pink-flowering Forms)
    pseudoacacia
    pseudoacacia 'Frisia'

ROSA (Climbing Musk Roses and Similar Forms)
    (Rambler Roses)

RUBUS *fruticosus* (Blackberry Hybrids)
    loganobaccus (Loganberry Hybrids)

SOLANUM *crispum*
    dulcamara 'Variegatum'

SORBUS *aria*

TROPAEOLUM *majus*

VIBURNUM *opulus*

VITIS 'Brant'
    coignetiae
    vinifera (Grape Vine Hybrids)

WEIGELA

WISTERIA *floribunda*
    floribunda 'Macrobotrys'
    sinensis

CLIMBERS AND WALL SHRUBS WITH LEAST PROTRUDING GROWTH WHEN FAN-TRAINED

ABELIOPHYLLUM *distichum*

ACTINIDIA *kolomikta*

AKEBIA *quinata*

AMPELOPSIS *brevipedunculata*
    brevipedunculata 'Elegans'

BERBERIDOPSIS *corallina*

BILLARDIER'A *longiflora*

BUPLEURUM *fruticosum*

CHAENOMELES

Clematis viticella 'Abundance' in flower

CLEMATIS *alpina*
  armandii
  campaniflora
  cirrhosa
  (Double and Semi-Double Forms)
  × *durandii*
  × *eriostemon*
  flammula
  florida 'Bicolor'
  × *jouiniana praecox*
  (Large-flowered Hybrids)
  macropetala
  rehderiana
  texensis
  viticella

COBAEA *scandens*

COTONEASTER *horizontalis*

DECUMARIA *barbara*

ECCREMOCARPUS *scaber*

EUONYMUS *fortunei*

HEDERA *canariensis*
  colchica
  helix
  helix angularis 'Aurea'
  helix 'Buttercup'
  helix 'Cristata'
  helix 'Glacier'
  helix 'Gold Heart'
  helix 'Luzii'
  helix sagittifolia

Hedera helix sagittifolia 'Variegata'

JASMINUM × *stephanense*

MAHONIA *fremontii*

PARTHENOCISSUS *henryana*
  quinquefolia
  tricuspidata 'Veitchii'

RIBES *laurifolium*
  speciosum

RUBUS *tricolor*

SCHIZOPHRAGMA *hydrangeoides*

THUNBERGIA *alata*

TROPAEOLUM *majus*
  peregrinum
  speciosum
  tuberosum

TRACHELOSPERMUM *asiaticum*
  jasminoides

WATTAKA-KA *sinensis*

EVERGREEN CLIMBERS AND WALL SHRUBS

ARBUTUS

AUCUBA *japonica*

AZARA *dentata*
  microphylla

BERBERIDOPSIS *corallina*

BUPLEURUM *fruticosum*

CALLISTEMON *citrinus*

CAMELLIA *japonica*

CARPENTERIA *californica*

CEANOTHUS (Evergreen Forms)

Ceanothus 'Topaz' in flower

CESTRUM *elegans*

CHOISYA *ternata*

CISTUS

CLEMATIS *armandii*
  cirrhosa

COROKIA *cotoneaster*
  × *virgata*

CORONILLA *glauca*

COTONEASTER × *hybridus pendulus*
  (Low-growing, Spreading
  Evergreen Forms for
  Walls)
  (Medium Height, Spreading
  Evergreen and Semi-
  Evergreen Forms for
  Walls)
  (Tall Evergreen Forms)

CRINODENDRON *hookerianum*

DESFONTAINEA *spinosa*

DRIMYS *winteri*

ELAEAGNUS × *ebbingei*
  pungens

ERIBOTRYA *japonica*

ESCALLONIA

EUCALYPTUS

EUONYMUS *fortunei*
  japonicus

FABIANA *imbricata*

× FATSHEDERA *lizei*

FATSIA *japonica*

FEIJOA *sellowiana*

FREMONTODENDRON *californicum*

GARRYA *elliptica*

HEDERA *canariensis*
  colchica
  helix
  helix angularis 'Aurea'
  helix 'Buttercup'
  helix 'Cristata'
  helix 'Glacier'
  helix 'Gold Heart'
  helix 'Luzii'
  helix sagittifolia
  (Shrubby Forms)

HOYA *carnosa*

ILEX × *altaclaerensis*
  aquifolium

ITEA *ilicifolia*

Itea ilicifolia in flower

JASMINUM *fruticans*
  humile 'Revolutum'

LAPAGERIA *rosea*

LAURUS *nobilis*

LIGUSTRUM *lucidum*
  ovalifolium

LOMATIA *myricoides*

LONICERA *japonica* 'Aureoreticulata'
  japonica 'Halliana'
  japonica henryii
  japonica repens
  nitida

MAGNOLIA *grandiflora*

MAHONIA × 'Charity'
  fremontii

MANDEVILLA *splendens*

MELIANTHUS *major*

MYRTUS *communis*

NERIUM *oleander*

OSMANTHUS

PHLOMIS *fruticosa*

PHOTINIA × *fraseri* 'Red Robin'
  stranvaesia

Photinia × *fraseri* **'Red Robin' (juvenile foliage)**

PILEOSTEGIA *viburnoides*

PIPTANTHUS *laburnifolius*

PITTOSPORUM

PYRACANTHA

RAPHIOLEPSIS *umbellata*

RHAMNUS *alaterna* 'Argenteo-Variegata'

RIBES *laurifolium*

ROSMARINUS

RUBUS *henryi bambusarum*

SOLANUM *crispum*
  jasminoides

SOLLYA *fusiformis*

SOPHORA *tetraptera*

STAUNTONIA *hexaphylla*

TEUCRIUM *fruticans*

TRACHELOSPERMUM *asiaticum*
  jasminoides

VIBURNUM (Large-leaved Forms)
  tinus

VINCA *major*

CLIMBERS AND WALL SHRUBS FOR DIFFICULT, EXPOSED POSITIONS

ACER *negundo*

AMPELOPSIS *brevipendunculata*

AUCUBA *japonica*

CARAGANA *arborescens* 'Lorbergii'

CELASTRUS *orbiculatus*

CHAENOMELES

CLEMATIS *montana*
  vitalba

COTINUS *coggygria*

COTONEASTER × *horizontalis*
  hybridus pendulus
  (Low-growing, spreading Evergreen Forms for Walls)
  (Medium Height, Spreading Evergreen and Semi-Evergreen Forms for Walls)
  (Tall Deciduous Forms)
  (Tall Evergreen Forms)

CRATAEGUS (Autumn Foliage Forms)
  oxyacantha

CYDONIA *oblonga*

ELAEAGNUS × *ebbingei*
  pungens

EUONYMUS *fortunei*

FORSYTHIA *suspensa*

GINKGO *biloba*

Kolkwitizia amabilis **in flower**

HEDERA *helix*
  helix angularis 'Aurea'
  helix 'Buttercup'
  helix 'Cristata'
  helix 'Glacier'
  helix 'GoldHeart'
  helix 'Luzii'
  helix sagittifolia

HYDRANGEA *petiolaris*

ILEX × *altaclaerensis*
  aquifolium

JASMINUM *nudiflorum*

KERRIA *japonica*

KOLKWITZIA *amabilis*

LABURNOCYTISUS × *adamii*

LABURNUM × *watereri* 'Vossii'

LIGUSTRUM *lucidum*
  ovalifolium
  quihoui
  sinense

LONICERA *japonica* 'Halliana'
  japonica repens
  nitida
  periclymenum (Hybrids)
  tatarica

LYCIUM *barbarum*

MAHONIA × 'Charity'

MALUS (Fruiting Forms)
  (Green-leaved Flowering Forms)
  (Purple-leaved Forms)

PARTHENOCISSUS *henryana*
  quinquefolia
  tricuspidata 'Veitchii'

PHILADELPHUS (Medium-sized Forms)
  (Tall-growing Forms)

Parthenocissus tricuspidata **'Veitchii' in autumn**

PHILLYREA

POLYGONUM *baldschuanicum*

PYRACANTHA

PYRUS

ROBINIA *pseudoacacia*

ROSA (Climbing Musk Roses and Similar Forms)
  (Modern Hybrid Climbing)
  The following varieties:
    Alchemist
    Aloha
    Compassion
    Dance du Feu
    Dreaming Spires
    Golden Showers
    Leverkusen
    Maigold
    Masquerade, Climbing
    Mme Edouard Herriot
    Mme Grégoire Staechelin
    Mme Henri Guillot
    Morning Jewel
    New Dawn, Climbing
    Paul's Scarlet
    Pink Perpetue
    Queen Elizabeth, Climbing
    Rosy Mantle
    (Rambler Roses)
    (Shrub and Species Roses for Fan-training)

RUBUS *phoenicolasius*
  tricolor
  ulmifolius 'Bellidiflorus'

SORBUS *aria*

VIBURNUM (Best Fruiting Forms)
  (Early-flowering Forms)
  (Large-leaved Forms)
  opulus
  plicatum
  (Spring Flowering, Scented Forms)

VINCA *major*

VITIS 'Brant'
  coignetiae

WEIGELA

CLIMBERS AND WALL SHRUBS WITH ORNAMENTAL FRUIT

ACTINIDIA *arguta*
   chinensis
   kolomikta

AKEBIA *quinata*

AMPELOPSIS *brevipendunculata*
   brevipendunculata 'Elegans'

ARBUTUS

AUCUBA *japonica*

BILLARDIER'A *longiflora*

BUPLEURUM *fruticosum*

CALLISTEMON *citrinus*

CELASTRUS *orbiculatus*

CLEMATIS *alpina* (seed heads)
   armandii (seed heads)
   campaniflora (seed heads)
   cirrhosa (seed heads)
   (Double and Semi-Double) (seed heads)
   flammula (seed heads)
   × *jouiniana praecox* (seed heads)
   (Large-flowered Hybrids) (some seed heads)
   macropetala (seed heads)
   orientalis (seed heads)
   vitalba (seed heads)
   viticella (some seed heads)

COTINUS *coggygria*

Cotoneaster simonsii in fruit

COTONEASTER × *horizontalis*
   hybridus pendulus
   (Low-growing, Spreading Evergreen Forms for Walls)
   (Medium Height, Spreading Evergreen and Semi-Evergreen Forms for Walls)
   (Tall Deciduous Forms)
   (Tall Evergreen Forms)

CRATAEGUS (Autumn Foliage Forms)

DECAISNEA *fargesii*

EUONYMUS *fortunei*

× FATSHEDERA *lizei*

FATSIA *japonica*

FEIJOA *sellowiana*

HEDERA *canariensis*
   colchica
   helix (all forms)
   (Shrubby Forms)

HUMULUS *lupulus* 'Aureus'

HYDRANGEA *aspera* (sterile bracts)
   paniculata (sterile bracts)
   petiolaris (sterile bracts)
   quercifolia (sterile bracts)
   villosa (sterile bracts)

ILEX × *altaclaerensis*
   aquifolium

LIGUSTRUM *lucidum*
   ovalifolium
   quihoui
   sinense

LONICERA × *americana*
   × *brownii*
   caprifolium
   etrusca
   fragrantissima
   × *heckrottii*
   japonica 'Aureoreticulata'
   japonica 'Halliana'
   japonica henryii
   japonica repens
   nitida
   periclymenum (Hybrids)
   splendida
   tatarica
   × *tellmanniana*
   tragophylla

LYCIUM *barbarum*

MALUS (Fruiting Forms)
   (Green-leaved Flowering Forms)
   (Purple-leaved Forms)

MORUS *alba*

MYRTUS *communis*

PASSIFLORA *caerulea* (following hot summers)

PHASEOLUS *coccineus*

PHOTINIA *stranvaesia*

PIPTANTHUS *laburnifolius*

PITTOSPORUM (following hot summers)

PONCIRUS *trifoliata*

PYRACANTHA

PYRUS

RAPHIOLEPIS *umbellata*

RHAMNUS *alaterna* 'Argenteo-Variegata'

ROSA (Climbing Musk Roses) (many varieties)
   (Climbing Species Roses) (many varieties)
   (Modern Hybrid Climbing) (many varieties)
   (Old Climbing Roses Prior to 1920) (many varieties)
   (Rambler Roses) (many varieties)
   (Shrub and Species Roses for Fan-training) (many varieties)

Rosa 'Superstar, Climbing'

Sorbus aria 'Lutescens' in leaf

RUBUS *tricolor*

SCHISANDRA *grandiflora rubrifolia*

SOLANUM *crispum*
   dulcamara 'Variegatum'

SORBUS *aria*

STAPHYLEA *colchica*

STAUNTONIA *hexaphylla*

SYMPLOCOS *paniculata*

TROPAEOLUM *speciosum*

VIBURNUM (Best Fruiting Forms)
   (Large-leaved Forms)
   opulus (most forms)
   plicatum (some forms)
   tinus

VITIS 'Brant' (edible)
   vinifera 'Purpurea' (edible)

WATTAKA-KA *sinensis*

XANTHOCERAS *sorbifolium*

CLIMBERS AND WALL SHRUBS WITH SCENTED FLOWERS

ABELIOPHYLLUM *distichum*

AZARA *dentata*
   microphylla

CHIMONANTHUS *praecox*

CHOISYA *ternata*

CLEMATIS *montana* (some forms)

COLLETIA *cruciata*

CYDONIA *oblonga*

CYTISUS *battandieri*

DRIMYS *winteri*

ELAEAGNUS *commutata*
   × *ebbingei*
   pungens

HAMAMELIS (some forms)

HOHERIA

HOYA *carnosa*

ITEA *ilicifolia*

JASMINUM *officinale*
        officinale (Variegated Forms)
        polyanthum
        × *stephanense*

LATHYRUS *latifolius*
        odoratus

LIGUSTRUM *lucidum*
        ovalifolium

LOMATIA *myricoides*

LONICERA × *brownii*
      caprifolium
      etrusca
      fragrantissima
      japonica 'Aureoreticulata'
      japonica 'Halliana'
      japonica henryii
      japonica repens
      nitida
      periclymenum (Hybrids)
      tragophylla

MAGNOLIA *grandiflora*
      stellata
      (Summer Flowering Forms)

MANDEVILLA *splendens*

OSMANTHUS

PASSIFLORA *caerulea*

PHILADELPHUS (Medium-sized Forms)
       (Tall-growing Forms)

Pyracantha 'Orange Charmer' in fruit

PHILLYREA

PONCIRUS *trifoliata*

PYRACANTHA

RAPHIOLEPSIS *umbellata*

ROSA (Climbing Musk Roses and Similar
      Forms)
      (Climbing and Species Roses)
      (Modern Hybrid Climbing)
      (Old Climbing Roses Prior to 1920)
      (Rambler Roses)
      (Shrub and Species Roses for Fan-
        training)

SOLANUM *jasminoides*

STAUNTONIA *hexaphylla*

SYRINGA *microphylla* 'Superba'
      × *persica*
      × *prestoniae*

TRACHELOSPERMUM *asiaticum*
          jasminoides

VIBURNUM (Early Flowering Forms)
      (Spring Flowering Scented Forms)

VITEX *agnus-castus*

178

CLIMBERS AND WALL SHRUBS WITH GOOD AUTUMN COLOUR

ACER *negundo*

ACTINIDIA *arguta*
      chinensis
      kolomikta

AKEBIA *quinata*

AMPELOPSIS *brevipendunculata*

ARISTOLOCHIA *macrophylla*

BIGNONIA *capreolata*

BUDDLEIA *alternifolia*

CAMPSIS *grandiflora*
      radicans

CARAGANA *arborescens* 'Lorbergii'

CATALPA *bignonioides*

CEANOTHUS (Deciduous Forms)

CELASTRUS *orbiculatus*

CERCIS *siliquastrum*

CHAENOMELES

CHIMONANTHUS *praecox*

CLEMATIS *alpina*
      flammula
      macropetala
      orientalis

CORNUS *florida*
      kousa

COROKIA *cotoneaster*

CORONILLA *glauca*

CORYNABUTILON *vitifolium*

COTINUS *coggygria*

COTONEASTER *horizontalis*
        (Tall Deciduous Forms)

CRATAEGUS (Autumn Foliage Forms)
      oxyacantha

CYDONIA *oblonga*

DECAISNEA *fargesii*

DECUMARIA *barbara*

ERYTHRINA *crista-galli*

EXOCHORDA × *macrantha* 'The Bride'

Exochorda × *macrantha* 'The Bride' in flower

Bignonia capreolata in flower

FICUS *carica*

FORSYTHIA *suspensa*

GINKGO *biloba*

GLEDITSIA *triacanthos* 'Sunburst'

HALESIA

HAMAMELIS

HEDYSARUM *multijugum*

HOHERIA

HYDRANGEA *paniculata*
      petiolaris
      quercifolia
      villosa

INDIGOFERA *heterantha*

JASMINUM *fruticans*
      officinale

KERRIA *japonica*

KOLKWITZIA *amabilis*

LABURNOCYTISUS × *adamii*

LAGERSTROEMIA *indica*

LONICERA *fragrantissima*
      tragophylla

LYCIUM *barbarum*

MAGNOLIA (Large-growing Star-flowered
      Forms)
      × *soulangiana*
      stellata

MALUS (Green-leaved Flowering Forms)
      pumila (Apple Hybrids)

MORUS

PALIURUS *spina-christi*

PARTHENOCISSUS *henryana*
         quinquefolia
         tricuspidata 'Veitchii'

PASSIFLORA *caerulea*

PHASEOLUS *coccineus*

PHILADELPHUS (Medium-sized Forms)
       (Tall-growing Forms)

PHYGELIUS

PIPTANTHUS *laburnifolius*

PLUMBAGO *capensis*

POLYGONUM *baldschuanicum*

PONCIRUS *trifoliata*

PRUNUS *armeniaca* (Apricot Hybrids)
    avium, P. cerasus, P. mahaleb
      (Fruiting Cherry Hybrids)
    domestica (Damson, Gage and Plum
      Hybrids)
    persica (Nectarine and Peach
      Hybrids)

PYRUS *communis* (Pear Hybrids)
    glossularia (Gooseberry Hybrids)

RIBUS *sativum* (Red and White Currant
      Hybrids)
    speciosum

ROBINIA (Pink-flowering Forms)
    pseudoacacia
    pseudoacacia 'Frisia'

ROSA (Climbing Musk Roses and Similar
      Forms)
    (Modern Hybrid Climbing)
    (Old Climbing Roses Prior to 1920)
    (Rambler Roses)
    (Shrub and Species Roses for Fan-
      training)

RUBUS *fruticosus* (Blackberry Hybrids)
    loganobaccus (Loganberry Hybrids)
    phoenicolasius

Rubus fruticosus 'Himalayan Giant'

SOLANUM *crispum*

SORBUS *aria*

STACHYURUS *praecox*

STAPHYLLEA *colchica*

SYMPLOCOS *paniculata*

TEUCRIUM *fruticans*

TROPAEOLUM *majus*
    peregrinum
    tuberosum

VIBURNUM (Best Fruiting Forms)
    (Early Flowering Forms)
    opulus
    plicatum
    (Spring Flowering Scented Forms)

VINCA *major*

VITIS 'Brant'
    coignetiae
    vinifera (Grape Vine Hybrids)
    vinifera 'Purpurea'

WATTAKA-KA *sinensis*

WEIGELA

WISTERIA *floribunda*
    floribunda 'Macrobotrys'
    sinensis
    sinensis (Modern Hybrids)

XANTHOCERAS *sorbifolium*

CLIMBERS AND WALL SHRUBS WITH INTERESTING WINTER BARK

Abelia chinensis in flower

ABELIA *grandiflora*

ACER *negundo*

ACTINIDIA *arguta*
    chinensis
    kolomikta

ARBUTUS

COLLETIA *armata*
    cruciata

COROKIA *cotoneaster*
    × *virgata*

COTONEASTER *horizontalis*

DECAISNEA *fargesii*

ELAEAGNUS *commutata*

FICUS *carica*

FORSYTHIA *suspensa*

GINKGO *biloba*

HYDRANGEA (Large-leaved Forms)
    petiolaris
    villosa

JASMINUM *fruticans*
    mesnyi
    nudiflorum
    officinale
    officinale (Variegated Forms)
    × *stephanense*

KERRIA *japonica*

LABURNUM × *watereri* 'Vossii'

LIPPIA *citriodora*

LONICERA *fragrantissima*

PONCIRUS *trifoliata*

RUBUS *phoenicolasius*

SCHISANDRA *grandiflora rubrifolia*

SCHIZOPHRAGMA *hydrangeoides*

SOLANUM *crispum*
    jasminoides

SORBUS *aria*

VIBURNUM *opulus*

VITIS 'Brant'
    coignetiae
    vinifera 'Purpurea'

CLIMBERS AND WALL SHRUBS WITH WINTER AND EARLY SPRING FLOWERS

ABELIOPHYLLUM *distichum*

AZARA *microphylla*

CHAENOMELES

CHIMONANTHUS *praecox*

CLEMATIS *cirrhosa*

ELAEAGNUS × *ebbingei*

× FATSHEDERA *lizei*

FATSIA *japonica*

FORSYTHIA *suspensa*

GARRYA *elliptica*

HAMAMELIS

HEDERA *canariensis*
    colchica
    helix (all forms)

JASMINUM *nudiflorum*

LONICERA *fragrantissima*
    japonica 'Halliana'

MAHONIA × 'Charity'
    fremontii

RIBES *laurifolium*

VIBURNUM (Early Flowering Forms)
    tinus

CLIMBERS AND WALL SHRUBS WITH INTERESTING SUMMER COLOUR OR SHAPE OF FOLIAGE

ACACIA (Hardy Forms)

ACER *negundo* (variegated forms)

ACTINIDIA *chinensis*
    kolomikta

AKEBIA *quinata*

Akebia quinata in flower

ALBIZA *julibrissin*

AMPELOPSIS *brevipendunculata* 'Elegans'

ARISTOLOCHIA *macrophylla*

AUCUBA *japonica*

179

AZARA *microphylla*

CATALPA *bignonioides*

CHOISYA *ternata*

CISTUS (grey-leaved forms)

CLEYERA *fortunei*

CORYNABUTILON *vitifolium*

COTINUS *coggygria* (purple-leaved forms)

COTONEASTER *horizontalis* (variegated forms)

CYTISUS *battandieri*

DECAISNEA *fargesii*

DECUMARIA *barbara*

DESFONTAINEA *spinosa*

DRIMYS *winteri*

ELAEAGNUS *commutata*
　　　×*ebbingei*
　　　pungens

ERIOBOTRYA *japonica*

EUONYMUS *fortunei* (variegated forms)
　　　japonicus (variegated forms)

×FATSHEDERA *lizei*

FATSIA *japonica*

FEIJOA *sellowiana*

FICUS *carica*

Desfontainea spinosa in flower

FREMONTODENDRON *californicum*

GARRYA *elliptica*

GINKGO *biloba*

GLEDITSIA *triacanthos* 'Sunburst'

HEDERA *canariensis* (variegated forms)
　　　colchica (variegated forms)
　　　helix (all forms)

HEDYSARUM *multijugum*

HUMULUS *lupulus* 'Aureus'

HYDRANGEA *aspera*
　　　quercifolia
　　　villosa

ILEX × *altaclaerensis* (variegated forms)
　　　aquifolium (variegated forms)

JASMINUM *officinale*
　　　officinale (Variegated Forms)

180

LIGUSTRUM *lucidum* (variegated forms)
　　　ovalifolium (variegated forms)
　　　sinense (variegated forms)

LONICERA *japonica* 'Aureoreticulata'
　　　japonica repens
　　　splendida

MAGNOLIA *grandiflora*

MAHONIA × 'Charity'
　　　fremontii

MALUS (Purple-leaved Forms)

MELIANTHUS *major*

MYRTUS *communis*

PARTHENOCISSUS *henryana*
　　　quinquefolia
　　　tricuspidata
　　　tricuspidata 'Veitchii'

PHILADELPHUS

PHLOMIS *fruticosa*

PHOTINIA × *fraseri* 'Red Robin'
　　　stranvaesia

PILEOSTEGIA *viburnoides*

PIPTANTHUS *laburnifolius*

PITTOSPORUM

PYRACANTHA (variegated forms)

PYRUS (silver-leaved forms)

RHAMNUS *alaterna* 'Argenteovariegata'

ROBINIA *pseudoacacia* 'Frisia'

RUBUS *henryi bambusarum*

SCHIZOPHRAGMA *hydrangeoides*

SOLANUM *dulcamara* 'Variegatum'

SOPHORA *tetraptera*

SORBUS *aria*

STAUNTONIA *hexaphylla*

TEUCRIUM *fruticans*

TRACHELOSPERMUM *jasminoides* 'Variegatum'

VIBURNUM (Large-leaved Forms)
　　　tinus (purple and variegated forms)

VINCA *major* (variegated forms)

VITIS 'Brant'
　　　coignetiae
　　　vinifera 'Purpurea'

XANTHOCERAS *sorbifolium*

Vitis 'Brant' in fruit

ACTINIDIA *chinensis*

CYDONIA *oblonga*

FEIJOA *sellowiana*

FICUS *carica*

MALUS (Fruiting Forms)
　　　pumila (Apple Hybrids)

MORUS

PASSIFLORA *caerulea*

PHASEOLUS *coccineus*

Prunus persica 'Lord Napier'

PRUNUS *armeniaca* (Apricot Hybrids)
　　　avium, P. cerasus, P. mahaleb
　　　(Fruiting Cherry Hybrids)
　　　domestica (Damson, Gage and Plum
　　　Hybrids)
　　　persica (Nectarine and Peach Hybrids

PYRUS *communis* (Pear Hybrids)

RIBES *grossularia* (Gooseberry Hybrids)
　　　sativum (Red and White Currant
　　　Hybrids)

RUBUS *fruticosus* (Blackberry Hybrids)
　　　(Hybrid Forms)
　　　loganobaccus (Loganberry Hybrids)
　　　phoenicolasius

VITIS 'Brant'
　　　vinifera (Grape Vine Hybrids)

CLIMBERS AND WALL SHRUBS NEEDING OR RESPONDING WELL TO CONSERVATORY OR GREENHOUSE

ABUTILON *megapotamicum*
　　　megapotamicum (Large-leaved and
　　　Flowering Forms)

ACACIA (Hardy Forms)

ALBIZIA *julibrissin*

AMPELOPSIS *brevipendunculata* 'Elegans'

AZARA *dentata*

BERBERIDOPSIS *corallina*

Bougainvillea spectabilis in flower

BIGNONIA *capreolata*

BILLADIER'A *longiflora*

BOUGAINVILLEA *spectabilis*

BUDDLEIA (Tender Forms)

CALLISTEMON *citrinus*

CAMELLIA *japonica*

CEANOTHUS (Evergreen Forms)

CESTRUM *elegans*

CLEMATIS *florida* 'Bicolor'

CLIANTHUS *puniceus*

COROKIA × *virgata*

CORONILLA *glauca*

DECUMARIA *barbara*

DRIMYS *winteri*

ECCREMOCARPUS *scaber*

ERIOBOTRYA *japonica*

× FATSHEDERA *lizei*

FATSIA *japonica*

FEIJOA *sellowiana*

HOYA *carnosa*

IPOMOEA *hederacea*

JASMINUM *mesnyi*
　　　　officinale (Variegated Forms)
　　　　polyanthum

LAGERSTROEMIA *indica*

LAPAGERIA *rosea*

LOMATIA *myricoides*

LONICERA *splendida*

MANDEVILLA *splendens*

MELIANTHUS *major*

MYRTUS *communis*

PASSIFLORA *caerulea*

PITTOSPORUM

PLUMBAGO *capensis*

RHODOCHITON *atrosanguineum*

SOLANUM *jasminoides*

SOLLYA *fusiformis*

SOPHORA *tetraptera*

STAUNTONIA *hexaphylla*

TEUCRIUM *fruticans*

THUNBERGIA *alata*

TRACHELOSPERMUM *asiaticum*
　　　　jasminoides

WATTAKA-KA *sinensis*

CLIMBERS AND WALL SHRUBS FOR LARGE POTS AND CONTAINERS

ABUTILON *megapotamicum* (Large-leaved and Flowering Forms)

ACACIA (Hardy Forms)

ACER *negundo*

ALBIZIA *julibrissin*

AMPELOPSIS *brevipendunculata* 'Elegans'

AZARA *dentata*
　　　　microphylla

BOUGAINVILLEA *spectabilis*

CALLISTEMON *citrinus*

CAMELLIA *japonica*

CARAGANA *arborescens* 'Lorbergii'

CESTRUM *elegans*

CHOISYA *ternata*

CLEMATIS (Double and Semi-Double)
　　　　flammula
　　　　(Large-flowered Hybrids)
　　　　montana
　　　　orientalis

Clematis montana in flower

CLEYERA *fortunei*

COROKIA *cotoneaster*
　　　　× *virgata*

CORONILLA *glauca*

DESFONTAINEA *spinosa*

DRIMYS *winteri*

EUONYMUS *fortunei*
　　　　japonicus

FABIANA *imbricata*

× FATSHEDERA *lizei*

FATSIA *japonica*

Feijoa sellowiana

FEIJOA *sellowiana*

HEDERA *canariensis*
　　　　colchica
　　　　helix (all forms)

HOYA *carnosa*

HYDRANGEA *petiolaris*
　　　　quercifolia

ILEX × *altaclaerensis*
　　　　aquifolium

JASMINUM *humile* 'Revolutum'

LAGERSTROEMIA *indica*

LAURUS *nobilis*

LIGUSTRUM *lucidum*
　　　　ovalifolium
　　　　quihoui
　　　　sinense

LIPPIA *citriodora*

LONICERA *fragrantissima*

MELIANTHUS *major*

MYRTUS *communis*

OSMANTHUS

PELARGONIUM

PHOTINIA × *fraseri* 'Red Robin'
　　　　stranvaesia

PITTOSPORUM

PLUMBAGO *capensis*

PONCIRUS *trifoliata*

PYRACANTHA

RAPHIOLEPIS *umbellata*

RHAMNUS *alaterna* 'Argenteo-Variegata'

ROSMARINUS

SOPHORA *tetraptera*

Many other climbers and wall shrubs may perform well with this type of cultivation but those listed are the most reliable.

In all cases the container should be no less than 18 in (45 cm) in depth and 21 in (53 cm) in diameter. The larger the container the more success will be achieved with growth, flower and fruit.

The container should have a drainage hole or holes in its base and also have adequate drainage material. It should be filled with a good quality potting compost and be regularly watered through spring, summer and autumn. Feed at least once a week with a liquid fertilizer through late spring and early and mid summer.

181

INDEX OF COMMON NAMES

INDEX OF LATIN NAMES